Flesh Embodied

Sufferborn Book 3

J.C. HARTCARVER

Dorwik Publishing

Flesh Embodied

Copyright 2023 Jesslyn Carver

This is a work of fiction. Names, characters, businesses, places, events, locales, and incidents are either the products of the author's imagination or used in a fictitious manner. Any resemblance to actual persons, living or dead, or actual events is purely coincidental.

Cover art "A Deity Comes" oil on linen, and all interior illustrations by Jesslyn Carver. The back cover image is a digital artwork made by Jesslyn Carver.

Fan mail can be sent to J.C. Hartcarver via the "contact" page on her website: www.jchartcarver.com.

ISBN: 979-8-9874210-0-0 (paperback)
979-8-9874210-2-4 (hardback)
979-8-9874210-1-7 (ebook)

Library of Congress Control Number: 2023902057

Dorwik Publishing
Greenbrier, TN

Table of Contents

In loving memory of
Meme
and Uncle Jan.

FLESH EMBODIED

Prologue

Crack!

Daghahen's nose bone snapped. The sudden impact filled his vision with haze, and burning sunlight beamed through, shimmering. All feeling disappeared for the moment, and sound became an everlasting whine overlapping a deep roar.

The tight fist reared back and sprang again, spreading another tremor through his head. Warmth spread over his lips and down his chin. Daghahen's limp body fell against the large tree, and his brother's muscle power pressed him down. His other fist kept hold of Daghahen's collar. A throbbing ache began in his face, and shapes solidified in his vision.

"You don't need her, you fool! And neither do I!"

The voice rattled Daghahen's aching head. His throat tightened up, and his lip quivered under the blood. He wanted to look to his right, but Lambelhen shook him by his collar, nearly strangling him, and swatted his head. His fierce, yellow eyes centered on Daghahen, and his frowning lips curled into a snarl.

Blood and bile mixed in Daghahen's mouth, and he opened it to release a wail, but the sound caught in his throat. Choking on it, he tried a second time, despite his burning chest. If he couldn't scream, he'd die.

"*M-m-maaaaaah!*" he managed between fitful sobs.

The frown on Lambelhen's adolescent face deepened. "Idiot! Look here." He leaned over to douse his free hand in their mother's blood and slathered it across Daghahen's face. "It's only flesh!"

The smell rushed up Daghahen's nostrils. The blood cooled immediately and sat heavy on his skin. Lambelhen leaned back, and Daghahen took in the sight of her lifeless body, her head caked with a moist, red muck.

"You don't need her. I will take care of you now!" His brother's speech came as a blend of Norrian and Lightlandic, two cultures they'd juggled for their whole lives. "Our adulthood begins today," Lambelhen announced and released him. He stood, glaring down at Daghahen. "You'll follow me if you're wise."

Daghahen shook all over now, teeth chattering, whimpering. His face throbbed with pain. He hugged his knees while staring at the one person he'd hoped to protect forever. "W-wh-why did you do it?" he whined.

"It was an accident." Pausing to sneer at Daghahen's pathetic posture, Lambelhen roared, "No more dreaming now!" He lurched forward and slapped his face away from the body. "Wake up!"

Daghahen's eyes shot open. He sucked in air as a rush of wind roared through the grass in its passage over the rolling Darklandic hills.

Voices erupted behind the loud gust. "Hold that down, Brother Egan!"

Lying in the grass, Daghahen ignored the chatter. With a shaking hand, he touched his nose. Crooked as always. It had been broken many times throughout his life, especially recently when he'd wandered around dressed as a mercyman. But that original break... He left it buried in his memories, and only his nightmares brought it out to remind him now and again.

As he rolled over to curl up on the soft earth and dead vegetation, under which any manner of insect and rodent lived, the grass parted behind him and someone called the name he commonly offered to strangers.

"Brother Ibex. We could use your help!"

Daghahen yawned and dragged his sore bones upright. Might as well get to it. Sleep always posed the threat of bringing unfavorable memories back, and Daghahen liked doing it about as much as he liked stargazing. The man called his name because the small canopy they erected at night was waving raucously in the wind. Daghahen took a rope and lent whatever measly ounce of strength he could spare.

"Just a little more! Good!" one of the elder mercymen shouted.

With their success and the calmed breeze, Brother Egan motioned for him to sit under the canopy. "Cuppa tea, Brother Ibex?"

Daghahen took a licorice chew stick out of his pocket and stuck it between his teeth. "I'll take my tea in the mornin', thanks."

For now, the canopy helped to shield him from the stars behind the parting clouds. The other mercymen moved about, doing this and that. Some collected dead grass to feed the dying fire under the kettle, while others spread their hands to pray and thank the Creator for the calmed wind.

Daghahen rolled his eyes to watch them. He hadn't prayed since... since he'd visited that hospital several weeks ago, not that it mattered. All he had now was what might lie in front of him. Behind him, he had nothing.

"What is that in your mouth, Brother Ibex?"

His attention drifted to the old man pointing at his licorice. "You've never seen this?" He took another out of his pocket, broke it in half, and gave the man a sample. He smiled at the sour face the man made. "Cleans your teeth at the very least," he offered.

Nodding at his words, the man held the stick between his lips and mimicked Daghahen's casual stance.

Daghahen had met these people earlier today, a modest group of kindly old mercymen, one of them a bit on the young side. They'd found him out here in the grassy hills wearing his "mercy hood." He couldn't fathom why they weren't as shocked to find him as he was them. He had assumed mercymen only assembled in the Lightlands.

Apparently, the Darklands kept a few jokes even Daghahen could fall for. Like these men, who were a short-lived joke with a dark emphasis on "short-lived." So many sorcery factions roamed around as these fools did. So many vipers waited to strike down this group of pacifists and take their petty valuables. They had showed him kindness from the start, though: they never questioned his authenticity as a mercyman and easily welcomed him into their group, fed him from their rations, and kept him as warm as a soul needed with a little fire and a little tea.

"So, you say you're headed north, Brother Ibex?" Brother Elfric said, coming up beside him. Elfric's name made Daghahen smile whenever he heard it. The bald man looked nothing like an elf with that round face and puppy-dog eyes of his. Then again, Daghahen didn't look much like an elf these days either.

"Yeah," he answered Elfric around the licorice in his teeth.

"How far north?"

Daghahen had no reason not to tell the truth. If they threw him out of the group, so be it. They'd probably fare better without the foul luck he carried. "As far as Ilbith," Daghahen said.

The round little man scrunched his face, but his eyes retained the bright warmth of kindness. "That desolate land of heathens?"

"That's the one." Daghahen turned slightly away.

"But its greatness is gone—long gone, smashed by the dark, iron hand of Wikshen." Daghahen winced at the thought. "It's just ruins now. Nothing but an empty shell infested with things worse than venomous insects."

Oh God, please stop talking, you fool! Daghahen's teeth crunched down on his licorice. He didn't want to hear that name which started with W, much less such a pointed metaphor of what had become of his son's body!

Nonetheless, he swallowed his bile and replied, "You're right there too. But I have to go… I think my wife might be alive there."

"Your wife still lives?"

Elfric referred, of course, to Daghahen's own elderly appearance. What this man would never guess was that Orinleah happened to be centuries younger than him: thirty-seven in elf years, which wasn't much different from seventeen in human years. In normal elven society, a thirty-seven-year-old *faerhain* could still be weighing her marriage options. Orinleah had been a mere nineteen years when Daghahen met her and when they... He sighed. When they conceived Dorhen. So young, but Daghahen had picked her out. Lonely and desperate, he lusted for her, loved her, and proved himself no better a person than his brother.

Daghahen nodded to Elfric's question. "I'm hoping she's alive," he whispered. She'd be all he had left, and that possibility would be thanks solely to Dorhen, her son. How would he ever explain his reasoning to her for releasing Wik on their son? He would have to find a way.

Off to the side, the youngest mercyman bickered with the second youngest about the stars. "No, no, and no! The Dancing Maiden dances toward the east, always toward the east! It's one thing you can count on in the constellations!"

The other mercyman growled and scrubbed his greasy hair in response. Daghahen turned his eyes down to the grass, resisting the stars' lure as it caught everyone else's attention.

A bystander pointed up. "Then what is she dancing *with* right there? I don't recognize those three stars at all."

Daghahen's heart sped up. He tucked his hands under his arms, sitting forward.

"Yes!" the youngest said. "You make the point I mean to make. What are those three stars?"

Daghahen's voice barked out before he could decide to keep quiet. "Those three stars are new and won't last long." He closed his eyes, keeping his face pointed downward.

Elfric put a hand on his shoulder. "Brother Ibex, if you know, won't you settle their argument once and for all?"

Daghahen huffed out a sigh that hurt his lungs. He pointed his gnarled finger at the sky without needing to look. "They spin as the hours pass."

The mercymen murmured to each other at his statement. "How do they do that?" someone asked.

"Same way the Maiden dances toward the east, I suppose." He surveyed his companions as they ogled the sky. One of them sketched tonight's star patterns. "This constellation is temporary," Daghahen explained. "It comes and goes every few years. Doesn't stick around long."

"Brother Ibex, where did you learn of this? What does it mean?"

"I don't know what it means. But look..." He finally observed with everyone else. "The Pointing Young Man is showing it to us while the

Maiden dances past it every night. And it spins, so you'll see the long end pointing some other direction tomorrow night. If, of course, the clouds stay away."

The man who sketched the star formations paused his charcoal and asked Daghahen, "Do you know what it's called?"

Daghahen nodded. "I do." He took a deep breath. "It's called Sufferborn."

Chapter 1
A Shadow Opens

Y ou think you can fool me, Dorhen?" Kalea closed her eyes at the end of her question, disbelieving her own insanity. She'd just called him "Dorhen"—Wikshen of all people! She couldn't decide if the boiling sensation in her gut was hope that she'd found him or absolute dread.

Wikshen studied her with a hard shadow over his eye. He still hadn't turned to face her squarely. She could only note one of his eyes and his profile. He had a strong face with a large, handsome nose and high cheekbones, not to mention the pointed ears of elven heritage. If Wikshen were human, at least then she would have no doubt of their differences and wouldn't be quite so curious about him.

His deep voice rumbled out. "Why are you here?"

Kalea sucked in a breath and held it. Why *was* she here? To find Mhina. To find her novice sisters. To find… No; impossible. Dorhen lay dead, and Wikshen had admitted responsibility. Now Wikshen sounded completely different. Why weren't they picking up their conversation from the Alkeer temple? Or from Hathrohskog, when he fought Bowaen, Gaije, and Del? Kalea had hit him over the head with her washing bat back there. Did he not have any complaints for her?

"Why do you think I'm here?"

His mouth cracked with a slight glint of his teeth and a huff of something like sarcastic laughter. He started to turn away.

She snapped out the next word. "Dorhen!"

He halted and twisted to regard her.

She gasped and covered her mouth with both hands. *It is him!* "Dorhen, where've you been?"

Now he frowned and shook his head. "You better get inside. Who knows how many more of those monsters are creeping around?" He pointed to the tiny, glittery pebbles on the ground which used to make up the sanguinesent's eyes.

Tears collected in her own eyes. "What's wrong with you? Do you have nothing to say to me?"

"Besides 'get inside'?" He pointed to Dyii, whom he'd knocked out a moment ago and now lay sprawled on the ground against the mossy stone wall. "I don't know what he's about, but he could wake up any moment." The more he talked, the more he sounded like Dorhen, only lacking the warmth and life Kalea remembered.

"No!" she said, and stepped forward. "You and I have to talk."

He backed away from her pursuit. When she reached for him, he dodged. Putting her slight illness aside, she followed him all the way to the end of the alley, where the misty, chilly rain fell.

"Wait," she ordered, but he didn't listen. At the edge of the awning, she grabbed his arm. "I said wait!"

Growling, he twisted around. She fell on a misplaced step, and he caught her. They met eye-to-eye. The size of his body towering over her—much larger than it used to be—made her feel so small. Now under the strong light beam of a glowing hearth through the kitchen window, his face could be seen easier.

"Oh, dear Creator," Kalea murmured. "It really is you." He resembled the Dorhen she expected, only stronger and more mature. He could be Dorhen's older brother if nothing else.

At her words, his mouth firmed. His turquoise eyes showed that familiar reflective glow and twinge of sadness. The tears running down her cheeks mixed with the rain, but she didn't notice in her astonishment.

"You want to talk? Come with me."

She kept the gap between them slim when he took a step back, afraid he'd leave her out in this cold, wet night.

She followed close on his heels into another nearby alley—a darker alley. He chose a decayed door at its dead end.

Kalea shivered. This was no time to make herself afraid, but a flea-sized sliver of doubt entered her thoughts. What if this wasn't actually Dorhen? She could be in serious trouble. No, it *had* to be him.

He opened the door. The old hinge whined. He motioned for her to enter first. No way out once she stepped into the shadow. In the dense new blackness, his presence raised chills at her back, somehow hot despite the distance between them.

"I can't see a thing." Her voice shook.

"Hold a minute," he replied.

Clack, clack, clack! A flicker accompanied each sound until a flame erupted on a candlewick. Wikshen...*Dorhen* held a striker similar to the one Del used to light his pipe. The single candle revealed the shadowy shapes of crates and sacks, most of them rotted in this neglected storage room. The back half of the floor stood higher, at knee level, probably for the sake of storage compartments underneath.

"I often come here to be alone," Dorhen said, kneeling beside the crate and candle.

"Oh, Dorhen." She went to him.

He shot to his feet. "Don't touch me!"

His sudden, booming command made her freeze. He moved to the steep step in the floor and sat with one foot on the higher level, his other braced on the lower level. The black drapery about his hips flowed down to the floor in ripples.

"Now why don't you sit there and tell me what the *fuck* you're doing here, of all places?"

Kalea tensed up even more. Despite his burning stare, she found her bravery somewhere in all her nerves and said, "Hello to you too, *Dorhen*. I came here to ask you that same question!"

"I'm existing, that's what I'm doing," he said.

"Well, I'm surviving." Pouting, she perused the dank, cobweb-riddled space. She took a seat on the splintery box he'd referred to. "What did you expect me to do after those sorcerers took you and all my sisters away?"

"I expected you to go to your parents' house and live the rest of your life in safety, if not continue on as a vestal."

"A vestal?" She shrieked the word.

"Lower your voice."

She ignored his stern order. "Why would I want to live in that convent any longer after what happened there?"

"Which's why I assumed you'd most likely go to your parents in Taulmoil instead."

"Tch. I don't want to live with them. They dumped me at the convent when I was ten. They gave up on me, but you didn't! I made a promise to you, and when the sorcerers took you from me—"

"They could've taken you too, and you wouldn't have liked it at all."

"*When* they took you from me," she said again, "I could entertain no other option than to find you. I made it my determination."

He rubbed the bridge of his nose with a sigh. "Well, here you are."

"Indeed. Here I am."

A long moment of silence. She studied him in the weak lighting, attempting to puzzle out his demeanor, but all she could see was his blue hair shimmering along the edge of his head where the candle shone. His limbs had grown longer in his absence and his muscles twined magnificently over his frame. Whatever had happened to him, his appearance alone carried a bewitching aura, and she couldn't yet tell if it had the power to snag her as it did the shamans and witches. He avoided her eyes and kept his gaze averted from the candle.

Kalea pulled herself out of her stare and broke the awkward silence.

"As you'd expect…I want to know how you got this way."

Another unhappy smile stretched his mouth. "Even if I could figure out how to explain it, you would never be able to imagine—to understand. I don't understand it myself."

"I'll try to understand if you can try to explain it. Start with the night of the convent raid."

He took a deep breath and shook his head. "That creator-goddess you worship is a cruel, cruel—"

She cut him off. "Did you just say 'goddess?' What are you talking about?"

He finally looked at her again and his brow narrowed. "Your religion? The goddess who created everything?"

Kalea stood up. "There is no goddess!" she shrieked.

He scowled. "In my blind desire for you, I never realized how dumb you can be."

Kalea reared back and blinked at him. "Dumb?" she repeated. "Dorhen, the One Creator is male. He's like our unearthly father."

"That's stupid," Dorhen said. His words boiled her heart. "Who would want to worship a good-for-nothing father figure?"

She clenched her fists. "Why are you talking to me like that? The One Creator is an ideal and marvelous being, someone we couldn't hope to be as good as."

"And He's a lie, because I can easily tell you—"

"Stop it!" She stormed across the room and stood over him.

Something about her action or her shout made him flinch to alertness. His wide eyes glowed in the light. His posture grew more tense, his left arm trembling as his right wandered over to touch it. He huffed out a breath and said in a calmer tone, "Don't talk so loud."

"You and I have a lot of talking to do tonight, so you'd better—"

His eyelids fluttered shut. "You better shut up… And…don't stand so close."

Kalea didn't listen. "Why were you saying such things about my God? What's all this about a goddess?" she demanded, yelling down at him.

"Shhhh." He was shaking. He whispered, "Go sit down and I'll tell you… The goddess is a—"

"Why are you being so mean to me? Didn't you miss me?"

On her last word, his left arm sprang out and grabbed her wrist. He stood up, alarm on his face. He grabbed his own wrist, which held hers. A short moment of silence passed as they stared at each other in surprise. His hand tightened on her wrist.

"Why are you squeezing me?" she asked.

"I'm not," he replied.

The pressure increased. "Yes, you are!" She attempted to pull away, but he wouldn't let go. He squeezed tighter. "Stop it!"

"*Don't* yell." He sucked in a breath and repeated softly, "Don't yell."

"It's starting to hurt!"

"Shhh."

The circulation in her wrist slowed. In her increasing panic and pain, she hardly noticed the candlelight dimming. He held his own wrist firmly now, licked his lips, and concentrated on his hands, but the grip only tightened more.

"Owww!"

"Shut up!" Dorhen's calm washed away, as did hers.

She whimpered. "You're hurting me!"

"I don't want to!"

She screamed and tried to pull away, but he held solid. No escape. She screamed louder.

"Stop yelling!" Now he yelled too. She kept on. "Shut up!"

His grip squeezed. Her hand grew numb, red, and swollen.

Tighter. Her screaming turned to panicky weeping.

Tighter. He would squeeze her hand right off if this continued! He raised his voice to combat her volume. Her struggling didn't help either; it only intensified the horror in both of them. He began to pull her toward himself. His other hand fought the progression. "Your yelling makes me want—" He gasped.

Her wits flew away. When his grip reached a level she couldn't begin to gauge, her screaming beyond hysterical, her vision darkening, he lurched forward and bit his own forearm.

Kalea fell free to the floor.

Run.

But how could she run in this darkness? Somehow the candle had gone out, or maybe that was just her eyes. Her hand was numb. Her heart raced. Somewhere nearby, Dorhen panted hard.

The candlelight reappeared amidst a haze of mist swirling about the room, like a cloud of airborne soot. Painful tingles surged into her hand. She decided not to dart out the door and dash back to her bed in the main tower's basement. Rain pattered softly on the roof. Dorhen kept panting. Her adjusted vision revealed him lying on his back on the raised floor, ribs pumping up and down. His arm lay beside him in a bloody mess. More than bloody, he'd…torn it up. He'd ripped out his own tendons—the only reason he managed to let her go.

"Get out of here," he whispered when his breathing slowed. His blood dripped down to the lower level.

She pointed. "Your arm. I have to go get someone to help you, or you may bleed to death!"

"Don't bother! Just go!"

She stood up but didn't do as he told her. The hanging threads of tendons, sprawled in the pooling blood, suddenly slithered back into his arm! His arm repaired itself! His fingers twitched and flexed as the tendons secured back into place. A look of relief washed over his face as the healing neared completion.

"I don't need help," he grumbled, rubbing his fingers over the newly sealed skin on his forearm.

Kalea gawked at the phenomenon, clueless as to what she'd just witnessed. A surge of strange feelings whirled around inside of her. Illness, fear, waning panic, and...

Tingles in her stomach that traveled southward.

"Uh-oh," she muttered.

Dorhen turned his head to observe her. Her fear and illness receded quickly under the growing delight of the darkness coiling around her. Her breathing deepened.

"What's the matter?" Dorhen asked, forgetting about his arm.

It was a dark ecstasy, but she couldn't let it take over! She held her ground, trembling. "What's going on?" she demanded of him. Dorhen breathed heavily, but more at her change in mood than what he'd just done to himself. He didn't even seem surprised at how his arm had laced itself back together.

"D-Dorhen," she said in a sigh. He stared at her intensely. "I told you I want answers."

"But what's wrong with you?" His voice became breathy to match hers. Apparently, he didn't know about the ecstasies.

"Never mind that. Tell me why you look so different! Why did you attack me? Why did you bite your arm?"

He sucked the air deep into his lungs and closed his eyes as if he too felt her ecstasy. Could he? Hadn't Knilma told her that an ecstasy was Wikshen's way of choosing girls he liked? He breathed her name. "Kalea."

She considered asking him what he felt or if he knew about the ecstasies, but resisted. There were more important things to talk about, but her head grew cloudy.

He stood up, totally restored of his brutal self-inflicted injury, and his towering form with its wide shoulders and cascading hair was the most irresistible sight she'd ever beheld. Her knees gave way, and she collapsed to the old dirt floor. He lurched at her fall but made a visible effort to stop himself.

"Tell me," she demanded from her new position, "what happened after the raid on my convent?" Instead of trying to get up, she kept her seat, squeezed her legs together, and moaned. The dark, oily mist swirled around her.

Dorhen's breathing sped up even though he only stood there. He held his hands as rock-hard fists at his sides. His rough-edged breaths tickled her senses. He was the most gorgeous thing she'd ever seen, at least in her current state of mind, a state of mind which was becoming increasingly hard to fight.

"Dorhen," she whispered. "Will you kiss me?"

His lips peeled back to show his clenched teeth. He must be tense all over, not only in his fists. He took a step forward, and a thrill washed over her. Another step caused a rippling effect.

Murmuring outside the door made him pause. His dark, moody countenance vanished. He watched the door, eyes alert.

"The shamans are coming," he whispered, and leaped backward onto the raised platform.

In the same instant the door creaked open, Dorhen rushed to the darker side of the space, into hiding.

"Well, I can't imagine who in this place would've attacked Dyii like that—" Kilka's voice began.

Kalea moaned loudly. Her frustration easily gave way to weakness in the face of her ecstasy, and her tears flooded out.

"Oh, my! What've we here?" Two of the shamans knelt beside her.

"It's you!" Kilka said to Kalea. "Are you having another ecstasy? I was told how intensely you've experienced them in the past." She said to her accompanying shaman, "Let's get her inside and away from any prying warlocks, although we'll need a man to carry her."

Kalea stuttered, trying to tell them that Wikshen was in the room and pointing to the dark shadow he had leaped into. He didn't emerge from his hiding place. He didn't seem to be in the storage room at all anymore.

"Bring a sheet," Kilka ordered a younger witch who had accompanied them. "It's a damn good thing this girl escaped Dyii during this most sacred hour. We'll wrap her in a sheet and tell the warlock who carries her that she's merely ill. We'll need some more men to carry Dyii to the dungeon before he can awaken and pose any resistance."

Now in full swing, Kalea's ecstasy didn't let up. She fought them all the way as they bound her up tight in the sheet and covered her face with its corner, but she was too weak to stop them.

Before the warlock arrived to help them, Kilka told her, "You're a very lucky girl, you hear? Not only for escaping Dyii's advances. Your unmerciful ecstasies are clear proof that the Mastaren wants you most of all."

Chapter 2
Negative Space

He couldn't let the shamans find him with Kalea! Dorhen lunged into the shadowed corner of the storage house before the door swung open. There would be too much to sort out later. He had never intended for Kalea to wind up in this place and see his current...problem. It was strange enough that she recognized him at all!

He never could've guessed merely hiding in a corner could cause an issue, though, but at the other end of the room, the shadow swallowed him up before he knew it. Like a thick glob of jelly, the darkness covered him. He fought his way through, dragging his limbs with all of the strength of his new body.

On the other side, he found another place where shadows moved all around with violent energy. Out of nowhere, a huge, hulking form swiped an enormous arm at him. He dodged and checked behind himself to find more gelatinous shadow. Kalea and the storage shed had vanished. No going back. Before him stretched a massive new world with hardly any color beyond black and blue shadows with hot streaks of light zipping to and fro. It dizzied and disoriented him. Nothing to do here but dodge.

Run, fool! Wik's voice chimed in his head.

Where am I? Dorhen asked him as he did so.

The usual sandy laughter mocked him. *You've shadow traveled by accident.* More laughter. *This is a place located between the mortal plane and Kullixaxuss. A great ability if you can master it.* Wikshen *certainly has. We will use it to travel to other locations quickly.*

I can't even see, Dorhen said. *What are all these shapes?*

They're demons trapped in here. A common thing that can happen when sorcerers botch their own summoning spells.

As Dorhen listened, the ground—if it could be called ground—rose up like a wave and spilled him over. He rolled upon landing. A great wind like a demon's hateful breath caused the turbulence and it swooped at him for an attack.

Run! Wik reminded.

In his frantic haste, Dorhen didn't bother to differentiate his mind speech from his physical voice. "How do I get out of here?"

The best I can tell you is to look for another flash of light and dive into it.

You could end up virtually anywhere. Eventually, you'll learn how to navigate this place.

Several different roaring sounds arose and gave chase.

The demons want to take you over. They want to use you to get out of here.

"I don't understand!" Dorhen pumped his legs and panted.

Nothing to understand except "run."

He did. Though the creatures and environment whirled and crackled around him as if nothing were tangible, Dorhen focused on the setting as a whole. Chaotic blobs of black and blue shapes moved, swayed, and turned upside-down while occasional slits or blooms of light flashed by too fast for him to catch.

A giant paw with claws swiped at his feet and tripped him. Dorhen yelled. He rolled and rolled again, feeling the dark rise of one of the shapes chasing him, like a cloud with a mind of its own. With the sharpest show of agility he'd managed in his new body, he worked to his feet and darted to the side. By sheer luck, one of the slits of light opened up beside him, and he fell into it…

Into a calm forest. All the noise and moving shapes of madness vanished in a blink, replaced by a nighttime setting with elder and oak trees. With his Wikshen eyes, he could see his surroundings perfectly well, doused in blue rather than the various colors of daytime. His heart pounded from the thrilling—yes, thrilling—and terrifying run through the shadow realm. He landed sprawled on the ground with his head spinning in delirium. Above him loomed a stone shrine to Wikshen, currently bare of incense and without the offerings he was used to seeing at Wikhaihli. Its sacred shroud waved on the light breeze.

A strange energy rushed through him; he couldn't help but jump to his feet in the sense of excitement that lingered. He laughed out loud, barking, and sprinted among the trees. Feeling light, he danced. The wind stirred his hair, and he loved it. He was strong and full of vigor, and the night was cool and nothing could stop him! Now to find Kalea…

He paused, still smiling, and looked around at the forest. It wasn't Hathrohskog. It could be any forest. The confusion couldn't suppress his mood for long. He laughed again and bent over to catch his breath before realizing he didn't need to do that. He still had tons of energy. He almost wished to go back into that shadowy space and take on its legions of demons for fun.

"Wik," he finally said, "where's Kalea? I feel great!" He followed the statement up with more delirious laughter.

You have every reason in the world to feel such a way. You're Wikshen. No one can challenge you. And those who do, die.

"Why do I feel so good? It was scary in there."

This is how it feels to use Kraft magic…and to be Wikshen.

Dorhen stepped over the twigs and brambles to lean against a tree and close his eyes. It didn't make sense, but he also didn't want to question a good thing. He flexed his hands and watched them move. He had control of both, unlike a few minutes ago when he'd lost the use of his left one and it had taken it upon itself to try to grab Kalea.

"I like it," he whispered, savoring the pleasure while it lasted.

Of course you do.

"I don't feel like a prisoner in my own body right now. Why?"

Why question it? You can do anything you want. You only need to want it. So, what would you like to do next?

"See Kalea." His smile remained constant. He sang her name a few times. "Ka-leee-ahhh!"

He wouldn't find her by standing still, so he traversed the forest until a foot-beaten path appeared, which led him to a short wall around clusters of buildings.

Stop, Wik warned with an ominous tone that dispelled a bit of his bliss. *Don't be stupid. Look above.*

Dorhen did. A red flag waved on a hewn branch above the buildings. He could tell its color by its tint under the blue haze of his supernatural vision. A red flag announced Ilbith's control over the village. They wanted to capture him.

Better leave this village unravaged until you've gathered more strength. Wik's raspy laughter followed.

Dorhen regained enough presence of mind to speak telepathically. *You said I was unstoppable.*

You will be, Wik corrected. *Don't be rash yet, but do use Kraft.*

Where am I anyway? Dorhen asked. His thought process halted at the sound of footsteps shuffling along the grassy path headed toward the village.

He leaped off the path and pressed his back against a tree. He held his breath and assured himself an average person wouldn't see him in this dense shadow. In fact, the darkness increased with the rising of the miasma which tended to follow him around. It had filled the entire storage shed while he was with Kalea.

He held his breath when the person trod closer, following the path to the buildings. A girl. Dorhen watched her as she went, waiting for his chance to move again without being detected.

She slowed when the path brought her closest to him, lifted her delicate chin, and observed the canopy with a quizzical expression. A tall, lithe figure with a slender neck, she frowned and hugged herself with a shiver, pulling her shawl tight.

Dorhen closed his eyes and breathed again slowly. The dark miasma now swirled around her. He could…feel her through it like he had felt Kalea earlier, the contours of her body under her heavy layers. At first it happened by accident, but once instigated, he easily took control of it with his mind, feeling her all over. Like his first taste of stolen candy, he couldn't stop himself from continuing. He fell back against the tree and lived for the moment in the strange medley of good emotions and urges.

The girl put a hand to her chest and bowed her head with a heavy pant. Her long hair hung around her shoulders like a silken capelet. With a hand extended, she weakly made her way to a tree and leaned against it.

The night chased away the sunset, filling the sky with ribbons of elaborate blues and inky blacks and purples that Dorhen had never seen with his old body's eyes. Everything about this moment was beautiful, except it lacked one thing: Kalea.

The girl gasped and arched backward. She moaned, and the sound reignited Dorhen's arousal but also edged him closer to lucidity. He could tell through the miasma's touch that this wasn't Kalea. Knowing by intuition how to do so, he pulled the cloud back, releasing the stranger from its pleasurable embrace, and she found her balance and staggered away. The farther away she got, the better for both of them.

Fool, Wik said. *What will I do with you? You passed up a glorious opportunity to show this specimen what a real deity can do. Maybe you can catch her if you make a running snatch before the gatekeeper sees you.*

Just tell me how to shadow travel back to Wikhaihli! Dorhen's high state of mind was withering, leaving bare the sexual frustration and confusion his mischief had caused.

Fine. Better you return anyway. It's too dangerous here.

"What was that?" Primora huffed as she staggered on back home. First, she'd heard some crazy man laughing in the woods near Wikshen's forest altar, and then the night took on the strangest denseness she'd ever seen, and finally that feeling set in…like the mist had hands, dragging its fingertips up and down her sides, around her legs, and…over other places too. She shivered. An eerie feeling, yet strangely she yearned for more. She shook it off and hurried on, pulling her shawl tighter around her shoulders.

She ducked her head upon meeting the Ilbith guard keeping watch at the town gate. She and her family didn't want the sorcerers to know anything about them. Their religion didn't blend well with the sorcerers' harsh rules, and these men had also proven dangerous to the women of the village. Primora and her cousin did all they could to avoid their interest.

"What have we here?" the sorcerer asked. "You look spooked to Kullixaxuss."

"I got lost. The fog and shadows took a strange shift." It wasn't a lie, even though one wanted to share as little with these folk as possible.

"Well, you almost missed curfew. What were you doing out there?"

Her shivers intensified. She couldn't tell him she was gathering sticks or picking berries; she had no evidence to present for it.

At her stuttering, he said, "Hmm? What was that?" He reached out to grab her shawl, but she dodged and put a wide step through the open gate.

"I was bathing in the lake. Sorry I'm late!"

She sprinted through. That was an awful lie because her hair wasn't even wet. She couldn't tell anyone where she'd been, especially her mother. Primora would be sacrificed on Wikshen's altar if her family found out she had been cuddling the woodcutter's handsome son beyond prying eyes. That Jonaril put special feelings in her. Lasting feelings. Her knees shook as she ran. Twisting around to see if the sorcerer pursued, she saw that no one was there, and slowed. Butterflies kept her stomach dancing. She'd never felt this way before.

Taking a deep breath, she opened the door to her house, to murmuring voices. It sounded like Mother and Aunt Falli were discussing the village's poor state again.

"Welcome home, child," Mother said.

Primora gave her a weak smile. Her cousin, Cygnet, was in here too, stacking twigs beside the fire.

"But that's what I'm worried about," Falli said, continuing their prior conversation. "It was a damn good thing I buried my altarpieces because the sorcerers came right into my house yesterday. It's dangerous!"

"But they didn't see your altar?"

"No. I had already disassembled it. We should move your altar out to the woods. Tonight! We'll use its components to expand the forest altar."

"I don't know," Mother replied. "I can't upset Wikshen by disrespecting the altar I've kept for thirty years. He'll be here soon. The sorcerers said so themselves."

Primora rolled her eyes as she went to the teapot over the fire. Wikshen *wasn't* coming back. He didn't exist. The sorcerers had only come here warning of Wikshen's threat to scare them. It had achieved the opposite effect on her family members, but the rest of the village fell for the sorcerers' trick, and now here they were. They used to have a nice, thriving village, but the sorcerers had already depleted their resources and made everyone constantly afraid. Last night, Mother and Falli had tallied up a few missing girls. Aunt Falli was right, though. The sorcerers kept a hostile attitude about Wikshonites, or any other religion for that matter, and would punish them badly if they ever found her mother's elaborate basement altar.

"They're talking about moving the altars again?" Primora asked her young cousin by the fire.

"Yeah. But this time my ma has a good reason—you heard her."

"I agree with her," Primora said. "I don't want to be skinned by those scaly sorcerers. To worship Wikshen, all we need is a dark room."

Sitting on the rush mat on the floor, Cygnet hugged her knees. "I don't like it. There's a bright, empty spot on the wall where our shroud used to hang. It made me feel safe. Now it's gone."

"You'll get it back someday," Primora offered.

"I wish the sorcerers would leave already. I hope Wikshen comes and kills them soon."

Primora shrugged. "Keep faithful."

The empty words she dispensed felt odd on her tongue, but they made Cygnet smile. Primora had been alive for twenty-one years and had seen or heard nothing of Wikshen's return until the sorcerers had decided they wanted to share in her community's riches. He hadn't been around for over six hundred years, or so people said. If he hadn't come in all that time, why would he now? Because he didn't exist. He was a myth, but she couldn't say that aloud in front of her family.

A sudden bang on the door shut everyone up. "Is the midwife in there?" a gruff male voice thundered.

Falli shot to her feet, and Mother followed. Cygnet and Primora threw blankets over themselves to keep low-key in front of the sorcerers. Wikshonism specified that they had to remain pure, and the dirty sorcerers had already proven themselves wolves in the community.

"Yes!" Mother answered as she ran to the door and attempted to crack it open. The sorcerer on the other side shoved the door wide and stepped past her. "Sir, why so forceful? We are only defenseless women in here."

Falli met them at the center of the room. "I'm Falli. What do you need?"

"Dammit, woman, we broke your own door down because you weren't answering it!"

"I apologize," Falli said, her voice now irked. Stern men in red cloaks filed into the house, carrying one of their own, who hissed and grunted. "I'm often found here at my sister's house," she explained. "What can I do for you, good sirs?"

"It's Corul. He stepped on a rusty nail, and now he's got black streaks crawling up his leg. Help him!"

Falli used a sympathetic voice Primora knew to be fake. "Oh, dear. Bring him in and make him comfortable. This isn't good at all."

"Can you heal it?"

"I can certainly try," she said.

The sorcerer in charge of the group narrowed his eyebrows. "What were you bitches talking about in here, anyway?"

Falli spread her hands. "The garden. Pottery. The usual sort of thing."

"Your voices sounded a bit heated to be talking about gardening and pottery, old woman." He took a moment to eyeball her.

"My garden is very important to me and will soon prove very important to your comrade. Now, no more talking," Falli said. "This is a very serious infection! Cygnet, bring my tools and poultices."

Primora stayed curled up tight in the corner, enduring the unwelcome men and their loud voices in her home all night.

Chapter 3
A Memory Returns

After a more direct and well-executed "shadow travel" under Wik's instruction, Dorhen crept back into Wikhaihli from the dark, rolling hills and checked the storage room to find Kalea gone.

Up in the tower, even as he opened his mouth to ask Knilma about her, the old woman took his hand with a bewildered look on her face. "Mastaren…" Dorhen waited for her words. "There's a girl we found in a moldy old storage shed…"

Kalea. It suddenly struck him: should he let them all know of his relationship to her? If he did, what would ensue? The strong-willed shamans often invented wild ideas. Maybe he didn't need them putting any more pressure and stress on Kalea than the black maid duties she already bore. Especially since she was so religious already, she wouldn't want to partake in all this Wikshonism. Dorhen chose to show no impression on his face.

"This girl is what I would consider a sacred item, most worthy of your attention. We found her hiding in the storage, in full dark ecstasy."

Dark ecstasy? Those words were new. "What does that mean?"

"You don't know, sweet Mastaren?" Knilma's wrinkly face scrunched. "She fell into a feverish need…for you."

Suddenly, his heart sped and the virile feelings caused by all that shadow travel and Kalea's screams peaked. "Feverish need" sounded very close to what he felt right now.

"Is she all right?" he pressed. "Where is she now?"

"I won't lie, Mastaren, she'd lost her mind in place of longing. We almost put her in your room tonight, but in her exhaustion, she fell asleep too quickly. She's in her own bed in the black maids' quarters now."

Dorhen stood stiffly, doing his best to bottle up his excitement. Shadow traveling felt so good. And so did Kalea's loud sounds. Had she not been in distress when she was yelling at him? And even now, she yearned for him?

At his silence, Knilma bowed her head as far as her old frame allowed. "Your chamber is freshened up and ready for you, with a feast of steaming dinner."

She had barely made it through her statement when Dorhen left her and headed the opposite direction from his chamber. He marched down the stairs and through the corridors, startling shamans around corners all the way. Each one dropped into a bow at his passing. This was probably the first time he'd wandered around the tower on his own without a ceremonious entourage of shamans.

He bypassed the entrance to the bathing area where the concubines spent their afternoons, as well as the nave and the practice rooms, going all the way down to the musty basement. He could almost smell Kalea's sweet scent laced with one of those strong herbal oils the shamans put on the prettier girls.

He met an atmosphere of warm, glowing candles under a cold, vaulted ceiling. Before him awaited a field of beds arranged in neat rows over the hard stone floor. Kalea slept on the floor? He scanned the room for her, somewhere among the other young maids moving about in preparation for bed. They had all shed their aprons and hung them neatly on hooks secured into the wall. Several sat upon their bedspreads combing their hair. One washed her face in a bucket. Others bent over in prayer, invoking the name of Wikshen, which Dorhen could easily hear. Tingles ran down his spine at each syllable. Even the candle glow couldn't dull his excitement.

Where is she? He scrunched his face. Some girls were already asleep, and she must be one of them. *Hold on.* He concentrated from his place under the arched entrance to the tunnel. Against his better judgment, he allowed his keen Wikshen senses to take over. There were many different vibrations going on in here, but if he really listened, he'd pick out Kalea's.

There! She was a sleeping one, the most exhausted, curled up at the center of the beds. He easily recognized the rhythm of her breathing.

"It's the Mastaren!" a girl shrieked in high pitch at his next step forward.

He froze in surprise.

"It is!"

Suddenly, he had every eye on him and the whole room flew into a frenzy. Hairbrushes were dropped. The bucket got kicked over. Every person present, except Kalea, swarmed him. The noise didn't interrupt her oblivious slumber.

"He came to us!"

"He came!"

"He did!"

"I love you!"

"He's so beautiful!"

"I can't believe it!"

Before he knew it, he was bombarded. They threw their hands all over him. Having allowed himself to be receptive to the vibrations, he now dealt with a torrent of hundreds of different sensations, some good, some bad, but all of them at once was too much.

The first row of girls fell to their knees in worship. One hugged his leg while others grabbed and kissed his battleshift. Somewhere in the mess, slobbery lips touched his bare feet. Their stooping allowed the second row behind them to eagerly reach forward, throwing their hands to his waist, chest, and arms. He found himself covered in girls! More than one hand dipped its fingers down the top of his battleshift.

All the rows behind the second desperately pushed forward, crushing their fellow maids and squeezing Dorhen into a tight hold. He didn't know how to push them away without hurting them. The spiking, agitated screams of some of the girls on the floor, now desperate for air or getting their hands stepped on, renewed his sexual excitement.

Kalea's sleeping form was the only one left back in the bigger part of the room until the housekeeper emerged from an adjoining space, her face long in inspection of the commotion. Her shock showed clear when she saw why her subordinates frenzied at the entrance.

"Stop it!" she ordered, rushing forward. "Show the Mastaren respect! What's wrong with you?"

So many maids had stormed him, the housekeeper couldn't get close. She pulled one girl away from the group by her braid, slapped her face, and then did the same to the next one.

Dorhen worked his way backward, peeling their hands off his arms and plucking others out of his battleshift. They hadn't seen much of him until now, he realized, especially in regular lighting. The shamans kept him sealed away and escorted him from room to room swiftly through dark corridors. His most active time occurred after the maids retired, and he occupied the throne for only one or two hours during the day. Tonight, he'd foolishly strolled straight into their dorm without all the usual pageantry.

In the next few seconds, with the housekeeper's help, the maids calmed down and corrected themselves, assuming proper prayer positions.

"M-mastaren," the housekeeper began, obviously sharing in her maids' excitement to a degree. Ignoring her speech, Dorhen ran back the way he came the second he broke free.

He was shaking by the time he made it to his room, and also laughing about the incident in some humiliated sort of shock. He turned the key in his door, half-afraid a raving girl would follow him and barge in. He dropped into the chair at his private dining table. Covered dishes still waited for him, dishes he'd forgotten about in his lust for Kalea.

This room was a temporary accommodation. Currently, the shamans oversaw the construction of a grand chamber on a higher floor. Wikhaihli had been a rat-riddled slum in decay before his arrival. These days, the number of staff members grew—like those maids—as well as the worshippers, and they all worked hard to raise money to tidy and restore the place.

For now, he occupied this cozy little room with a fireplace, mostly kept cold, and a bed softer than anyone else's in the whole complex. At the thought of bed quality, Kalea reentered his thoughts. She didn't have a soft bed...yet.

Dorhen left the delicious-smelling platters on the table covered. His persistent erection made it damn hard to concentrate—even on being hungry.

He went to the large mirror and removed the black sheet from it. The shamans kept the mirror covered all day long to prevent it from reflecting sunlight from the window, which they also kept shuttered. One of those maids had said he was beautiful. For the first time ever, he examined himself in full-length. He'd only seen his altered face in small, hazy reflections as of yet, but this mirror gave him the chance to see the whole picture.

He didn't know about "beautiful," but everything about him was certainly...impressive. His height. His muscles. Muscles now bulged on his stomach and sides—they'd never done so before. His face had become harder, sharper, and handsome. His hair flowed so much longer, and it was blue.

He hardly found the chance to wear a shirt lately. All he seemed to need was the battleshift wrapped around his hips. He smiled to see what his smile looked like. The effort didn't come too difficultly tonight. He increased the smile to show his teeth. That one tooth still hung overgrown on the left side, a remnant of the old Dorhen. He flicked his tongue across it. This new person was what everyone saw. The maids went crazy for this face and body. Even before tonight, the concubine candidates would sigh and stare when they saw him in any lighting.

He let his smile drop. The image was surreal. Good, but surreal. His battleshift hung to the floor, though it never got under his feet. He opened the slit and put a leg out: muscled and powerful, as expected. Did Kalea also like him like this? Why wouldn't she?

A twinge of foolishness and hesitance failed to stop his hand from raising the battleshift higher. It might be important to observe how his lower body had changed too. He let his penis out, standing stiff and strong. Longer. He'd known about that, though. It also hung longer while asleep. It was thicker too, to go along with his other limbs.

He looked his reflection in the eye as one would challenge another fierce male. This was him now. His heart pounded. His erection throbbed, holding back the battleshift on its own. When he flexed his arm to see the huge bulge of his new bicep, he couldn't contain his amusement and pride. He laughed. He couldn't wait to see Kalea again.

Kalea.

Throwing the sheet back over the mirror, he turned to the bed. His dinner could wait a few minutes. He extinguished the Kraft flame on the table to enjoy a more comfortable darkness and slipped under the sheet, into the soft embrace of his feather bed. He slept in the battleshift every night because he couldn't take it off. Moving the battleshift out of the way, he took his cock in hand and rubbed it slowly up and down. The touch instantly soothed and would quickly deliver relief.

He let *her* into his fantasies. Maybe he'd been stupid for leaving her alone in the storage house. He had thought he'd scared her to death with his untrustworthy arm, but apparently, he'd aroused her. He was stupid even now, for opting to jerk it off rather than march back down to the basement and crawl into her bed. Maybe he should let all the other black maids watch. Watch how much he favored Kalea over everyone else.

Exploring those ideas egged him on until something better occurred to him: Kalea in the bathtub at her convent, as he watched through the window.

Kalea raised her arms for the attending girl to rove her hands over her perky young breasts with the fragrant soap. A fragrance he remembered exactly.

He increased his speed.

He had pondered all night long after that incident what it would've felt like if those hands were his.

Kalea.

He panted.

A graceful deer, that girl.

Kalea.

She stood up in the bath, rivulets of water running softly over her contours. Her soft little bottom when she turned around. Her graceful frame under supple flesh. Her breasts colliding as she bent and climbed out of the tub.

Dorhen hardly noticed the grunts he made. Each strangling up-draw built pressure in his ever-thickening member. Closer. Closer. Closer.

He gripped the pillow under his head with his other hand, lying on his side, gnashing his teeth. He growled. His hips began to pump instinctively—the way he actually wished he could get off tonight.

Rather than shame himself with might-have-beens, he went back to Kalea in her beauty and lack of care. A little novice in a convent. So innocent. So soft and smooth.

And out in the open.

Vulnerable.

Wet…

Dorhen gasped and panted hard as the final pulses erupted, making a mess on his bedsheet. He held the squeeze until it was well over.

Relief. Comfort. He caught his breath and rested. He turned to lie on his back, never minding the puddle he'd made on the bed. His vision spaced, staring at the dark ceiling. Thinking of Kalea. His pounding heart gradually slowed.

He didn't care to rise again to move to the table. He closed his eyes and thought of her some more. The same magnificent images he'd spied through the convent window lulled him to sleep.

Chapter 4
Wayfaring Desteer

Lehomis dipped his head into a bow for the third time to the grieving widow sitting on her ox, standard ritual proceedings for seeing off the funeral party headed to *Laugaulentrei*, the huge tree where the elves laid their dead to rest.

"And please return at peace," he followed up to finish the rite.

Because he was Elder of a clan that had survived such a violent calamity, performing this ritual had become his biweekly routine. The poor widow was a younger *faerhain*, now without her new husband. He hadn't even survived long enough for the two to produce a child. Her mother and mother-in-law both accompanied her, so Lehomis had organized an extra-large entourage of *saehgahn* to escort them.

The next step in his duty was to inspect them all to make sure they were sharpened and ready for the task. A party this big usually required a few horse riders, but they no longer had that luxury, so the *saehgahn* all stood at attention, ready to set out.

Lehomis pulled one's dagger out of its sheath and inspected the blade. "Mm-hm." He slapped each of them hard on the shoulder to show his approval. He checked all of their bowstrings, daggers, and stances. If one slouched, he knocked him in the shoulder to set him straight. He continued down the line, putting his pipe firmly between his teeth.

Thank the Bright One this was the last funeral party! When they returned, maybe Clan Lockheirhen could heal and take its first steps toward a flourishing new future—that is, if they could get some new life blooming. They needed much more than young, fresh horses.

He came to a very young *saehgahn* standing in the stiffest pose possible and smirked around his pipe stem. "I smell mischief. What are you doing here, young one?" He was barely a *saehgahn*, named so only two nights ago.

"M-my father said that I would shine in this job, Elder," he said, keeping his jaw as stiff as his spine.

Lehomis took his pipe out of his mouth and eyed him, then looked down the line of better, more experienced *saehgahn*. The young one was an extra, so he hadn't replaced any of the original *saehgahn* Lehomis had allocated. He checked his dagger, bowstring, bracers, stance, boots, and even the tightness of his side braids. Obviously, his mother wanted him to make this trip to prove himself too.

Lehomis feigned turning away but quickly knocked him in the shoulder to throw him off-balance, and the lad held firm enough to impress even him. He laughed and nodded at the lad. "This doesn't replace your *caunsaehgahn*, ya know."

The lad bowed his head. "I am aware, Elder."

Nodding again, Lehomis moved to the *saehgahn* beside him, slapped him on the shoulder, and said, "Look after the babe."

"Yes, Elder."

Lehomis made quick work of the rest of the line, as if releasing them to their task would get them home any faster. He faltered in his step at the painted face at the end of the line. "A Desteer maiden?" He blinked stupidly at her.

"That's right, Elder," she said in a hard, matter-of-fact voice.

Their clan maidens usually didn't go on these journeys. Instead, the grieving widow visited other clans' Desteer along the way. He stepped back and observed the line again, mostly the trio of females. The widow kept quiet on the ox with her head hanging low, and her mother and mother-in-law offered Lehomis a shrug each.

"It's not their idea, Elder," the maiden said. "I have a duty to attend to in another clan. These *saehgahn* will take me to the clan I need and then continue on their way."

He squinted to try to see beyond her ghostly face paint. "You're one of the younger ones, aren't you?"

"My age is no business of yours."

Lehomis waved his hands, one holding his pipe. "Relax. I was just thinking how much sense it makes to send one of the younger maidens. Sometimes treks through Norr are hard."

"What makes you think I don't know that, Elder?"

Lehomis huffed. "So, this isn't your first time leaving the village?"

"Of course not."

"What's yer name?"

"Kennaha."

"Fine." Lehomis stepped back and raised his right arm to signal the whole company. "Return safely, Kennaha. Take care of the widow for however long you'll be with her."

"I'm only going two clans over."

After his gesture, the travel party moved forward, a long parade winding through the trees. In truth, he couldn't care less what the Desteer did. And if he never saw that great tree again, he'd consider his life good.

"And now, how's my little girl? Ready to talk?" Lamrhath asked, taking a seat in the chair in the corner.

Mhina, the little elf-girl from Norr, remained silent at the room's center. All the other children were cleared out so he could have his one-on-one time with the most important of them, something he'd worked into his daily schedule. The protective young elf-boy, Bairhen, had been relocated to separate living quarters altogether. Mhina's nanny remained in the room and kept to the opposite side.

"Forgive her, my lord," the nanny said. "She still doesn't speak much. She knows a little of the common tongue, but we're not yet sure how much. The other children claim she speaks well."

Lamrhath gave the little one a smile, a thing which came easy when he was around her. He could sit comfortably, his pain briefly forgotten in her presence.

"No worries," he said, relaxing back in the chair. "We have all the time in the world to get to know each other."

A long silence passed. The little girl didn't move from her spot at the center of the round carpet. The wind whistled through the cracks in the roof, but the window revealed a lovely day with a blue sky and clouds sailing slowly by, above and below their level. He usually reserved this hour for thinking about what to say to the girl and then failing to get anything out before the visit expired. He enjoyed this peaceful time nonetheless. Eventually, he'd get a conversation going. For now, he looked at her. Her shimmery honey hair. Her pale lavender eyes. A radiant and perfect little creature.

Often, he came in here with an offering of flowers from the garden. He took a certain level of joy in pondering what sort of gifts he'd bring during the winter months. It would have to be trinkets instead, or sweets. This silent hour proved also to be the best for those thoughts. The rest of his day bulged to bursting with business and stress and pain. This hour was good.

"You don't have to stand there," Lamrhath finally said. He waved his hand from the window to the little chest full of dolls and wooden swords the children all shared. "Be at ease."

She raised her chin and made eye contact. "No."

"Why not?"

"This is not my home. Those are not my toys."

"So, you *can* speak the common tongue." Lamrhath relaxed in his chair despite the nanny's uncomfortable shift. Resting his elbows, he put his fingers into steeples. He didn't know much etiquette for dealing with children. Normally, one might ask a child about her home and family, but the law of Ilbith forbade talk of times and places that might be better. She lived in Ilbith now, and Lamrhath was her family.

"Was Tumas kind to you?" he asked. "When you traveled here?"

"I don't know who that is."

"Didn't he…escort you from your original location?"

"I just wanted to help Dorhen."

Lamrhath sat forward and stared. "What did you say?"

"I said I wanted to help Dorhen. He was hurting."

Lamrhath squeezed the chair's arms, bracing himself on them. "What does that mean? How do you know the name 'Dorhen?'"

Mhina pouted and shrugged. "I don't know."

When Lamrhath checked himself again, half his ass hung off the chair with his legs ready to lunge across the space to shake the girl. "How do you know that name?"

Her pout increased. She shrugged again. "I don't know."

"Then how was he hurt?"

"He cried out…in my head."

Lamrhath blew a breath through his cheeks. He managed to keep his seat and twist his mouth into a fake smile for her benefit. "This is good," he said, unable to keep his voice from shaking or his brow from moistening. "Sounds like you have telepathic abilities. You are very talented." He swallowed. "Now, can you give me more detail? How do you know Dorhen?"

"He rode on one of our horses. He was trapped."

"Trapped on a horse…"

She turned half away from him.

"Look at me, please."

She did so with outward reluctance.

"What happened between you two?"

Mhina threw up her arms. "Whoosh!" Lamrhath kept his gaze fixed on her as she stood with her arms in the air. "I flew."

"How?"

"He picked me up."

"Dorhen did?"

"It wasn't Dorhen," Mhina dropped her arms and pouted. "But I could still hear him."

Lamrhath guessed, "It was Wikshen. He rode a horse and picked you up."

She nodded.

Lamrhath sat back again and breathed, shifting his eyes as he tried to make sense of what he had heard. So *Wikshen* was the one who took her, and Tumas lied about the story for a reward. By the time Tumas and his crew had reached Norr and found Mhina, Dorhen was already Wikshen and traveling with them. From what the child described, she heard Dorhen's voice, "hurt" and "crying" in her mind, while simultaneously, his body rode a horse and snatched her up. In Dorhen's pixtagen state, she could detect his soul "trapped" within his body. *There* was a detail about Wikshen the history books couldn't have known.

He whispered, "Fascinating."

Mhina met his eyes again, as if gauging his expression. How much of his own thoughts could she hear? Or see? Before his ponderings could go any further, he crossed the room in a few long strides.

"Thank you, Mhina. I'm happy to have you with me. You are a delight and a talented *farhah*." He was out the door a mere second after finishing the statement.

Several nights ago…

Damos endured the long, chaotic journey of being dragged through the mud and brush. Away from the warmth of Kalea's arms. Away from the campfire's safety. She screamed after him in his helplessness to stop the sudden, stunning turbulence. An angry being dragged him along by his arm. A hateful spirit. Under the sound of snapping dry brush, calling voices, and his own yelling, the hateful one cursed him.

After that, all he knew was that he couldn't dig himself out of a mud pit, no matter how hard he squirmed and kicked. A force deep underneath the earth's surface dragged him down deeper and deeper, smothering his face and cutting off his air.

And then for a long while, nothing.

The world suddenly returned to him after an unknown length of time. He found himself trapped in an enveloping compression.

A voice shrieked, but with a song-like quality. It possessed a millennia of power, which…moved the earth around him. The soil became like an upward jet of water pushing him higher, toward the surface. His head emerged first, followed by his shoulder, arms, and the rest. A breath, new, involuntary, and desperate, rushed into his lungs. Helpless to move, he lay in the open air, gasping. Starving. Burning.

The song ceased, and a figure moved over him. A gnarled hand brushed his hair aside. Unbearable stinging pain arose in the fingers' wake. The figure stood back and waved an arm for darker figures with metal faces to scoop him up and carry him over the rising and falling muddy terrain.

Damos opened his eyes again, though they registered only bleary lights and shapes. An earthy smell dominated the space, as well as the heavy aroma of urine and dirty bodies. Dulled voices hummed in the background.

A shadowy figure blocked the light—the same figure as before. It held a roll of cloth. A woman—that was all he could tell due to his damaged vision. The woman began wrapping the cloth around his head, over a heavy coating of ointment on his blistered face. It made the application of the cloth less painful, as did the bandages already applied to his chest and arms.

He tried to focus and look around the room as the woman worked. Fuzzy shapes of other people occupied many beds. He also sat in a bed. His hearing sharpened over time, and the sounds...

Moaning. Crying. The other people rolled and writhed in agony. He couldn't blame them.

The woman tied off his bandage after covering his entire head, leaving his mouth and eyes free. Some of his hair dangled out of the bandage and over his view. He squinted, eager to see the goings-on in the room better. The many heavy shadows and highlighted shapes were difficult to separate.

The woman stood back and surveyed her work. From a large pocket in her black robes, she drew out a dark metal object and extended it toward him. He shrank back against his bedding but had nowhere to escape to before she fastened the cup-shaped thing over his face: a metal mask which covered his mouth and nose. He didn't recognize the type of metal; it was dark, with spots of blooming iridescence flashing in the light.

The woman paced around the room, perusing the other patients. She paused at a girl tied to a bed; Damos knew it was a girl by her shaky voice. The girl wriggled and whined when the woman reached toward her.

The girl screamed, begging, "Please, no!" and followed up with stuttering slurs.

Numb to her pleas and emotion, the woman reached out and put her hands on the girl's face. A shrill piercing wail of agony and despair rattled Damos. He tried to rise, to lift his hand and call for the woman to stop harming the girl. His hand wouldn't budge. Both of his hands were tied to his bed! He lay fastened down like the girl—like everyone in this little underground infirmary!

As the girl screamed, the woman shuddered, holding her hands firmly on the girl's face. A slight rumbling in the earthen walls arose around them, responding to the powerful connection between the two.

When the woman finally released her, the girl fell back to her pillow in exhaustion. By now, Damos's vision was sharpening like his hearing. The woman rose to a taller stature, a new show of strength in her posture. She'd done something to the younger woman to steal her energy and replace her own.

He could only stare with his mouth agape, praying to the One Creator that their host wouldn't turn back his way.

Chapter 5
A Stain Sets

Up before the sun. Each miserable day dragged Bowaen out of his musty bed with the burlap blanket and hauled his ass down the narrow trail on the steep bluff to the muddy beach, where he was tasked with digging up hideous clams that looked like pissing cocks. Geoducks. Later that evening, they would eat the same ugly creatures in a horribly salty recipe he'd nicknamed "sweat stew."

He'd nearly lost track of the days they'd spent at Wikhaihli due to exhaustion. They weren't prisoners, as they'd knocked on the gate several days ago asking to be let in to worship Wikshen, but the situation felt no different. Each day that went by without seeing Kalea built his anxiety higher, but all of Del's reports assured him of her well-being. The two shared a sort of rendezvous spot at the window of a garderobe where they'd exchange updates.

Kalea's latest message told of a sickening and hardly believable surprise: Wikshen risen from the dead. Impossible. He couldn't have survived being stabbed with Hathrohjilh! Bowaen had held the damned sword personally, experiencing for himself the force of Wikshen's weight slamming into him—the impact and sound of the blade ripping into the freak's stomach, punching all the way through his back. They'd left that bastard dead and bleeding a flood over the muddy ground of Hathrohskog. How in hell could anyone come back after being impaled so brutally? But Kalea had seen it happen with her own eyes, so...

Bowaen stopped to take a breath, muddied up to his armpits. The thigh-high leather boots the warlocks let them wear for wading didn't help much. He usually left the beach with his beard soiled up. Plunging his arms so deep put a strain on his emotions too. Just the other night, he'd tried to fish Damos out of a bog similar to the way he searched for geoducks now.

Not too far away, Del and Gaije chatted as they did most mornings. Sometimes they bickered instead. Bowaen and those two kept a rhythm of gradually making their way away from the other clam diggers. It was nice to be able to talk amongst themselves. They'd developed a code word system for when around others. Any time Bowaen could slip the phrase "fish in a bucket" into a conversation meant an order to check on Kalea as soon as Del could manage. Making up curse words with nonsense about "talking fish" usually cued Del to tell him what Kalea had said. In order to hear the news, they needed a private place to converse, so "take a piss" usually worked for the purpose of speaking in private.

They couldn't stay here forever. The day was soon approaching when they'd have to get Kalea and hightail it out of there if Mhina wasn't in the complex. An escape from this place was sorely needed. The jackass warlocks didn't even give a care for Del's broken wrist; they still had him down here running buckets. Hopefully, their code system should help them get all their plans together.

Bowaen checked Gaije over his shoulder. Day by day, the elf got more tense and irritable, but right now, he hung onto every word Del relinquished. He was talking about sex, of course. Del was twenty-four years old and very interested in the subject, especially since he hadn't experienced much along the lines of relationships so far. From what Bowaen caught in their chatter, Gaije wasn't far from Del's age and knew practically nothing about it—probably didn't even know what his cock was truly for.

Bowaen whistled at Del. "Shut up, will ya? They'll hear you." Though they'd moved a nice distance away from the other workers and warlock-overseers, they couldn't ever be far enough away. Much like Gaije's home culture dictated, Wikshonite men couldn't have sex or fall in love with women, so they'd get a severe beating if caught talking like this.

Ignoring Bowaen's warning, Del brightened up and told Gaije, "You should pursue Kalea."

Gaije scrunched his nose. "Kalea?"

"Yeah, why not, man? She's short one elf anyway. It would comfort her and give you some valuable experience for your marriage rites."

Gaije had explained the elven marriage process to him earlier—not that he knew much about it himself. Apparently, elves were so private and secretive about such things, male elves didn't really know what to expect of the process of getting married. They knew the females proposed to them, and then a nighttime ritual followed—which was what Gaije fretted over, naturally.

"That's so…wrong," Gaije replied to Del's suggestion.

"Nah, it's not!" Del's smile spread wide. "A human woman wouldn't mind. They do it out of wedlock all the time."

Gaije shook his head, having paused in his work at Del's idea. "That wouldn't work," he reiterated.

"What won't work?"

"Me and Kalea. The feeling she gives me."

"She gives you feelings?" Del's teeth glinted in the faint light of dawn. The ocean crashed and roared in the distance behind him.

Bowaen also waited for his explanation.

Gaije shrugged, keeping his gaze on the churned-up, knee-deep mud. "She gives me the same kind of feeling my sister gives me. She's like a second sister to me."

Bowaen smiled and returned to his work.

"Bowaen?" An old woman's voice. "Are you he?"

Bowaen looked up through a squint. A decrepit old hag rode on a little sedan chair held by two warlocks with half-shaven heads. "Yeah!" he answered across the distance.

"Come here now."

Annoyed at having to wade back through the difficult mud to the grassy bank, Bowaen stifled his swear words and pushed on anyway.

When he finally arrived, the old woman lounging in her seat asked, "Are you the one who arrived with Kalea?"

Bowaen's face drained. A slight hesitation and an urge to glance back at his companions struck him. He resisted. "Yeah."

"Are you her father?"

"No, ma'am."

"What are you to her?"

"I'm her..." Good Creator, what should he tell this woman? They hadn't discussed how they might answer such questions. Did his acquaintance with Kalea matter? "I'm just her escort. We...met up and pilgrimaged here together. She needed protection, ya know?"

The old woman nodded her head. "So you don't know her personally?"

"Not much."

"What do you know, then?"

Bowaen cursed on the inside. What did she hope to learn? "Ma'am, you might have to be more specific," he tried. Hopefully, a logical question to clear up confusion shouldn't offend her.

"Have you..." The old woman paused and searched for her words now. "Are you aware of her ecstasies?"

Bowaen squinted as he mouthed the word. "I hardly know what an ecstasy is, ma'am. I'm a simple peasant."

"Perhaps." She eyeballed Bowaen for a few seconds. "Has Kalea ever acted strange in your company?"

Hell yes. Bowaen chose words different from his initial thought. "She's a good girl," he said, completely ignorant as to what kind of answer this old bag was looking for.

"Of course, I see her as good too. Exceptionally good, which is why

I came all the way down here to find you." The old woman tapped her gnarled finger on her sunken cheek. "I'll try once more: has Kalea showed signs of wanting a man, especially at night?"

All the time! Especially if his name's Dorhen. Bowaen once again rejected his first answer. "No, ma'am. She's a good religious woman and…" He caught himself about to spill details about her faith in the Creator and twisted his statement into something else. "She lives only for Wikshen. No one else. She's a model Wikshonite."

The old woman drew in a long breath through her nose. "Very well. Thank you for your cooperation." At her signal, the men in black turned the sedan and began the treacherous journey back up the cliff. Bowaen stared at her until the overseer yelled at him to get back to work.

Back in the mud, Bowaen dug his arms in again to feel around for the phallically shaped clams. Why did the old witch harbor so much interest in Kalea? Wasn't she a maid, sweeping floors and shaking out mattresses? Del had reported she spent all day cleaning the jakes and couldn't get quite deep enough into the tower because of her station.

Hardly thinking about geoducks anymore, Bowaen turned his gaze upward, to the hint of a black roof on the high cliff. What was going on in that place?

Dorhen snapped awake at the sound of his door tapping closed. Sometime during his sleep, he'd rolled over on his stomach. From over his crossed arms, he scanned the room with one eye. The sun was poised to break the horizon, and a soft grey light pierced through the cracks around the shutters.

The scent of his daily breakfast feast teased his nose and quickly awoke his empty stomach. The sound of the door closing must've been the usual shaman delivering the food. He'd never gotten around to eating last night, but that didn't matter.

He stirred to a sitting position easily after enjoying the best sleep he'd known in years. All his usual tensions were gone, including those of his mind. Kalea slept downstairs. He knew where she was, he realized. Her recent appearance had originally alarmed him. He hadn't wanted her to see him this way and, more importantly, he feared losing control of his body in her presence. But today, he'd woken up with a sense of peace in his new body for the first time.

Yawning and stretching, he smiled to think of her. Today, he'd talk to Knilma about getting her a comfortable room of her own—close to his, of course… Unless Kalea preferred to sleep in his room, to which he'd never object.

Stomach roaring, he sat at the table and uncovered a few of the dishes. The shamans fed him like this every day at breakfast and supper. The cook must've worked through the night to prepare it all. Biscuits and butter, flatcakes with sugared apples, a mushroom and cheese omelet, fish, berries, pudding, and pastries with cherries in the center.

Before digging into the flatcakes, Dorhen paused and thought again of Kalea. His smile brightened. Putting a biscuit between his teeth, he rose and covered all the dishes back up. He looked around and noted the bed. Stuffing the biscuit into his mouth and finishing it off, he dragged his blankets apart and took the topmost one to the floor.

When the sheets were separated from the rumpled mess, he noticed a big white stain on the black linen. He'd almost forgotten what he'd done. Shrugging the semen-stained sheet away, he proceeded to spread the blanket on the floor and stack the hot, covered dishes on it. He finished by tying the corners over them and then lifted the sack of clanking dishes over his shoulder to transport them out.

All the black maids had risen and gone off to do their work for the day, leaving their beds folded up neat and small in perfect rows. Kalea remained in her bed at the room's center, snoozing well past sunrise.

Checking to make sure no other maids remained, Dorhen braved the strengthening sunbeams through the high windows and made long strides over to her. She slept curled up in her blankets like last night, her face peaceful and relaxed. She breathed deeply.

As quietly as he could, he placed the sack of dishes on the floor, opened the knot, and laid them out neatly for her to find. This should make her happy. Dorhen couldn't hold down his smile. Part of him wanted to sit on the floor and watch until she woke up, but he also wanted her to be surprised. Let her see it and know he'd left it. She'd know he loved her.

Starting to feel intoxicated again by her residual perfume and unable to control his excitement, Dorhen stood up and flipped the blanket over his shoulder. Before hurrying away, he stopped. He couldn't resist reaching down to touch her hair. Just one slight touch of the back of his finger sliding over the curve of her head and her soft brown locks. Besides her lovely breasts, her hair was his favorite part. Strangely, it made him feel…safe. When she stirred at his touch, he rushed to the dark corridor leading to the stairs.

Along the trip back to his bedroom, Dorhen perused some of the house's vacant rooms. Which one would suit Kalea best? He wanted her to be close to him, but he would also demand the utmost comfort for her.

She needed a fireplace…a big bright window…and a bookshelf!

His perusing turned into a full-blown exploration of the tower. From what he'd been told—and struggled to grasp fully—he ruled this house. A strange role he'd fallen into. With Kalea here, his interest in being the master of the house piqued. She could inspire him to make a lot of changes to this place. He'd ask her what she wanted and act accordingly.

Bah, too small. And there's no window, he criticized, closing the door to one room, which was already owned by some old shaman. He turned a few heads as he moved down the hall. The maids acted more reserved this morning; they must've earned quite a scolding after their behavior last night.

Knilma's voice rang behind him as he stared into one of the empty chambers, daydreaming about Kalea. "Mastaren? What are you doing?"

He whipped around, ready to dispense the announcement that Kalea would get her own room. "Knilma, I…" He paused to stare at the trio of black maids scurrying past behind her.

Knilma turned around to see what he stared at. "Your wandering is making it hard for the maids to concentrate on their tasks. Do any of them please you, Mastaren?" Knilma was always trying to put a woman in Dorhen's bed, and he'd yet to approve of any of them.

"No," he said quickly, "but I want to talk to you."

"About what, dear Mastaren?"

About finally agreeing to take a woman to his bed might've been a decent answer, but not in this lively corridor. "Come see me in my room in a few minutes."

Knilma bowed her head stiffly and set off at her best pace, considering her age. Later, he'd also have to track down Kalea—hopefully, after she washed off the perfume that made him shake all over. They had some catching up to do, but he didn't want to recount the horrors of the past.

The future: he'd speak of that. He might be Wikshen now, a living deity and lord of this grand house, but they should be able to work things out. He was in charge now, no longer barred from what he wanted by the constraints of her society, her convent, his rugged forest life, or Arius Medallus. Wikhaihli offered the perfect situation for them to live happily together. He could already feel how calm she made him. More than calm, she made him feel good. She made him feel strong and in control, as long as she didn't scream. He'd shelter her in his domain. Keeping her safe was all he'd wanted from the beginning, after all. But she'd have to get used to his being a deity, because he couldn't let her leave. The Darklands were too dangerous.

Dorhen reentered his room to find a black-clad maid inside, taking his bedding apart for cleaning. This one wasn't Kalea, to his disappointment, and though she should be working, she sat idly by the bed frame instead. Dorhen scrunched his nose. "What are you doing?"

She jumped at the sudden sound of his voice and yanked a corner of his blanket from her mouth.

From her mouth? Dorhen looked again. The sheet, after falling from her hand, showed a stressed wet spot, as if she had pushed it deep into her mouth and wet it with her saliva.

"What the hell's going on?" Dorhen yelled in disgust. He lunged and jerked the sheet away from her.

She yelped, jumped to the side, and huddled in fear. "Forgive me, Mastaren! I was only... I did not expect you to return so soon!"

Examining what she'd done to his sheet, he sneered. "What's wrong with you?"

She shrieked and huddled tighter until he whipped the sheet at her. "Get out! Get out!"

Crying and darting for the door with her head covered, she clipped the stone wall before dashing into the hallway.

Behind her, Dorhen stuck his head out and roared, "Knilmaaahhh!"

It took Knilma all of two seconds to emerge from a room two doors down. "Mastaren, I can't tell you how good it feels to hear you shout my name," she said on her way over.

Dorhen couldn't match her pleasant mood right now. He shoved the dampened sheet at Knilma and yelled, "That maid was licking my sheet! Why?"

Knilma frowned for the moment, looking at the sheet and then at his angry face.

"I think I want to puke," he added at her hesitance.

"She was...licking your sheet?"

He spread his hands and huffed. "I caught her sucking on it. Is there something I should know? Something about the religion saying we have to suck on sheets?"

"'Suck on sheets?'" she mimicked, and suddenly burst into laughter.

Dorhen crossed his arms. "It's not funny." Her laughter helped nothing.

"It's maniacally droll!" She laughed on.

"Care to explain the joke to me?"

Knilma made a visible effort to calm herself, clearing her throat. "No, Mastaren. It's not a custom to lick sheets here. Are you sure that's what you saw her doing?"

"Don't you see her spit on it?"

Knilma's quizzical frown returned as she looked it over again. "Was there anything on the sheet to be licked? Perhaps some jam from your breakfast? Did you eat in bed?"

Dorhen's stomach dropped to the floor at a revelation. The maid's spit stain mingled with the dried semen stain he'd left there. The idea gagged him. Stress built higher.

"Because if so," Knilma continued, "we can have her beaten for trying to share your meal."

"It wasn't jam." A little beading of sweat appeared on his upper lip as soon as he said it.

"What could it be then, Mastaren?"

"Um…" He slicked a hand over his hair and turned away from her. "Last night I…came on the bed."

"You came to what on the bed?"

He growled and spun his hand around to try to find the words, and also to keep her eyes off his reddening face. "Last night, I felt an urge…"

She clapped her hands together. "Oh, Mastaren! You did? Which girl did you choose?"

"Not a girl. I was alone…when I got the urge. I took care of the urge…by myself…with my hand."

Knilma's smile melted. "Why would you do that, Mastaren? Are the girls of Wikhaihli not pretty enough? Kilka and I work so hard everywhere we go to pick out the most glorious beauties of the Darklands. What are you hoping for in a—"

"Nothing! It wasn't like that." He wanted to bury his face in his hands. Instead, he kept his chin high. "I didn't feel like I needed a girl in that moment. I just needed to take care of it quickly."

When he finally chanced a peek down, he found Knilma squinting at him. "I think I understand."

They stood in silence for far too long.

"So," Dorhen said to create some noise at least, "that's what was on the sheet. A stain."

Knilma studied the linen in her arms again. "A white stain on a black sheet. I suppose it stood out well when the maid tended to your bedding."

He nodded.

More silence.

"I want to know," he said slowly and softly. "Why did she lick the semen stain?"

The old woman stared at him, the sheet forgotten in her hands. "Mastaren," she said, "you don't know why a maid—why a *woman*—would want to eat your semen stain?"

Feeling as frustrated as ever, Dorhen threw his arms out to the sides. "No!"

"Mastaren… Your greatest, most magnificent…"

"What? Hurry and tell me!"

Knilma hobbled to the doorway where shamans and maids alike had silently packed in to listen. She shooed the maids away and sent one of the shamans for a book called *Kraft la Ungearth*. Then she tossed the sheet toward the rest of his disheveled bedding and motioned for him to sit at the little table.

When the book arrived, Knilma closed the door and locked it before sitting across from him and resting her elbows firmly on the book's cover.

"Mastaren," she said with an air of seriousness he'd not yet heard from her, "I'm going to explain it all to you, as I know you've forgotten much. I understand it's normal for each generation of Wikshen to forget and have to relearn things from his past. It's an honor for me to teach you this one thing at least, the greatest feat of a Wikshen. Now, I don't know if you remember your life before becoming Wikshen—I'm talking about your host body person…"

Of course, he remembered. He was *Dorhen*. He was Dorhen now. The one Wik often referred to as "true Wikshen" hadn't suppressed his consciousness yet.

"But when you were a mere elf, your healthy body could make children with female elves."

Dorhen waited for her point.

"Your body no longer does such a thing."

He lowered his eyebrows.

"Your body has changed into something greater than it was or ever would've been."

His gaze trailed to the covered mirror he'd used last night to inspect the very thing she talked about. His body *had* changed. Dramatically. Only a slight hint of *Dorhen* remained in his features.

"So why was she licking my sheets?" he asked again.

Knilma's smile returned a gentle warmth to her demeanor. "Every woman within our faith desires your semen. It could easily be professed the reason you are a deity." She regarded him a little longer with her warm eyes.

The statement brought back the images of hysterical maids crowding around him, throwing their hands onto his waist and hips. *He came to us!* The voice echoed fresh in his ears.

"Mastaren," Knilma said, "when you *bless* women, they transform."

The old book's spine creaked as she opened it. She flipped straight to the page she needed. Turning the book, she showed him an ink drawing of a past Wikshen crouched over a peasant girl, her legs emerging under his arms to each of his sides. The drawing next to it showed the girl changed into a creature with horns and glowing eyes.

"When you have sex with women," Knilma said, "you grant them great powers. Their appearance changes, sort of like yours did. They gain mastery in Kraft magic, although they can't use morkblades like you can."

She turned the page to show Wikshen mounting another woman with a line of others waiting behind her. The line stretched over the horizon of the scene. "As a deity, it's your main task to have sex with women again and again." She turned the page to show more of the same thing. "And again."

The last drawing showed demonic women of many shapes and sizes standing beside Wikshen as they conquered the Darklands together. Knilma continued her speech as Dorhen stared at the hideous pictures. "They transform into the superior beings widely known as dreadwitches."

Dreadwitches, he repeated in his head.

"Now, I don't exactly know why," she went on, "but traditionally, the first woman to earn Wikshen's blessing is special. We call her 'First Sister,' as in the firstborn among many sisters. She is a woman who catches Wikshen's adoring eye. When he blesses her first, that communicates to all who he favors most."

Who he favored most? He'd used nearly the same words last night when fantasizing about taking Kalea with the other maids watching, all the while masturbating his enthusiastic cock. If he had lived out that fantasy, the scene would've looked exactly like the one in the book.

"Are you all right, Mastaren?"

He suddenly realized he was rubbing his face hard over the pages. He had believed he was in a good place last night. He'd assumed his thoughts were his own, but he couldn't be so sure about that anymore.

Knilma continued, "First Sister is second in command to Wikshen himself, almost a goddess to his followers. *Almost*. Do you have any questions for me?"

He preferred to run into the garderobe and vomit. Nonetheless, he thumped his finger on the page once. "Why are they all so ugly?"

"Ugly?" Knilma smiled slyly. "Is that what they are? We don't notice. We only notice that they have been blessed. It's a sign of power."

"Power," he repeated.

"Yes, Mastaren. Dreadwitches have great powers. They can live for hundreds of years beyond their human lifetimes. They sometimes fly. Or screech loud enough to deafen an army. Or make chasms in the earth to swallow up your enemies."

"Like the shamans can do with drums?"

"Better than the shamans. Even a dreadwitch who isn't capable of the greater feats can rip armored men to shreds with her claws."

He sat back in his chair, enduring his ill feelings. He wanted to slam the book closed. "This... This is why you want me to take women to bed?"

"Yes, Mastaren. We are all waiting with bated breath for you to make your first choice. Your First Sister shall be your ally."

Good goddess! Last night, he could've turned Kalea into a monster! He would've if the maids hadn't blocked him.

Knilma turned the page again. "Look at this one. They are not all monstrous. Some of them are unearthly beauties whose dangerous traits are invisible." She pointed to a drawing of a voluptuous woman with long, flowing hair. Her lips had been drawn plump, along with her breasts and soft, curvaceous hips. She wore little clothing, of course. Wikshen stood behind her with his arms in a god-like pose, gazing down on her head in lust and intrigue.

"H—" He struggled to get his voice out anymore. "How can my... *body* do this to women?"

"It's the blessing of your sacred phallus, my sweet Mastaren. A sacred nectar."

Sacred nectar. The words sounded so strange, yet so familiar.

"They can take your nectar in any way you please, Mastaren: into their vaginas, naturally; or into their mouths—anywhere, so long as it enters their bodies. It's a magic potion with transformative abilities."

"And that's what the maid tried to do? Eat the 'magic potion' off my sheet?"

Knilma nodded deeply. "She desires your blessing and the power it bestows. Sadly for her, she'll be beaten and demoted for trying to steal your blessing. The choice must be yours. Luckily, the semen had dried up overnight and will have no effect on her."

"What if I don't do it? What if I don't want to do this?"

Knilma cooed and gave him a grandmotherly pout that made him feel like a child. "Now why would you say that? It's good for you to give in to the deeds that feel good. Practicing Kraft makes you sharper, absorbing minerals makes you harder, eating makes you faster, and appeasing your lust fortifies your kingdom. All Wikshens must make dreadwitches, and to do that, all Wikshens must enjoy what gives them pleasure. It's a win-win."

Dorhen looked around his small chamber and noticed very little about it. Last night, he *had* practiced Kraft—and it felt good. He had traveled through shadow and used the miasma to grope that random woman without a smidgen of thought for the shame in it. And then the orgasm he'd given himself. It was the best. It felt one hundred times better than it used to before he became Wikshen. He swore it gave him a boost of extra energy for today. But last night's fun would end it. He now knew he couldn't have sex—with anyone. Especially Kalea. He couldn't spill anymore semen on his sheets either. The tension he'd whisked away last night crept back into his muscles to think such a sad thought.

"This is why you've paraded women around me, showing me so many naked bodies," he said.

"Have you not liked any you've seen yet?"

None were Kalea. He wanted Kalea. So bad. Even as he sat here in illness and dread, she aroused him with all the senses of memory and fantasy.

"Why do you look so troubled, Mastaren?"

No. Maybe it wasn't true. It might be a myth all these people believed, but it couldn't be true. Surely he wouldn't turn Kalea into a monster when they made love. But could he take that chance?

If everything else far-fetched turned out to be real—his transformation, his morkblades, his healing ability—then his "blessing" could also have a real effect. He couldn't do it. He'd have to limit his interactions with Kalea and *never* give in to her, Wikshen's, or his own lust.

The sounds of distant seagulls through the open basement windows registered first.

Whispering.

Kalea didn't want to open her eyes. Last night, sleep had claimed her unwillingly. So many events cluttered and confused her brain. Dyii. Running through the rain. Maybe a sanguinesent. Its eerie call… Wikshen. She remembered getting an ecstasy and calling Dorhen's name, but seeing Wikshen standing there. Had he not taken advantage of her weakness? None of it made sense. Her muscles ached all over, and reluctance to open her eyes delayed her morning routine.

But she wasn't alone. She dragged her eyelids open to find maids kneeling around her—with shamans. Kilka stood among them. The smell of food. Against her tearing neck muscles, she raised her head and tried to puzzle out the assembly of people staring at her. Covered dishes stood stacked on the floor beside her bed.

"Glad you're finally awake, maid," Kilka said without an ounce of friendliness in her voice. "Care to explain why you've stolen the Mastaren's breakfast?"

Kalea groaned and fought to sit upright. "What?"

"The housekeeper approached to wake you up because you were sleeping in, and she found these dishes. They are the Mastaren's breakfast. Only the Mastaren may eat this food, you understand? Why did you steal it?"

Kalea rubbed her face. Her head might as well have been stuffed with cotton; her muscles felt like tendrils of dried leather. She couldn't fathom what the woman was talking about.

She mustered up the voice to say, "That's not right. I've been sleeping." Wasn't it obvious?

The group's glare hardened as Kilka's words sharpened. "Everyone knows not to try to eat the Mastaren's breakfast! You didn't just sneak a roll away, you got his entire spread! How in Kullixaxuss did you manage to steal all of this?"

"I didn't."

"Don't lie!"

She opened her mouth but had nothing to say to this bizarre accusation. She wanted to ask how she could steal all of this after last night's ecstasy, but too many people were listening. She couldn't tell how many of them knew about her ecstasies.

"This meal is no less than a sacred offering," Kilka said. "It's for him alone to consume. *No one* is permitted to share his meal."

Sitting up straighter, Kalea spread her hands, devoid of useful words.

"You'll be beaten and sent out to slop the hogs and muck the stables with the common workers."

"No!" Kalea burst out. She couldn't lose her status and access to the tower—she needed to find evidence of Mhina! "Please, I…didn't do it."

"Prove it."

"I've been asleep. Maybe someone put this here to get me in trouble."

Kilka nodded to the shaman next to her and then said to the small group of black maids, "Take Wikshen's food back to the kitchen and tell the cook to prepare a new hot spread." She turned to Kalea. "And you, girl, come outside and strip."

When Kalea hesitated, the shamans took her by both arms and dragged her through the corridors to the back courtyard. The closer they drew, the harder she fought and argued and begged.

"I didn't do it!" she pleaded. "I was asleep! I was with Wikshen before that. He was with me! He…"

"Stop lying!" Kilka shouted over her. "Take her clothes off. She doesn't deserve the uniform of a black maid."

Panicking, Kalea's eyes roved around the setting. Everyone who happened to be in the area froze to watch the spectacle. She scanned for Wikshen. Would he vouch for her, reveal that he'd blessed her and left her too exhausted to steal even a pebble off the floor? She'd hoped she'd left atonement beatings behind in her old convent, but she absolutely couldn't lose her status as a black maid. It would be impossible for her to explore deeper into the tower if she were kicked out. Kalea whined and begged and called for Wikshen.

"You've no right to call on our Mastaren!" Kilka followed up her statement with a slap to Kalea's face.

A horrid sting spread across her head. She finally shut up, groggy, aching, and now dizzy. Maybe Wikshen was asleep. He was a creature of the night, so maybe he always slept during daylight hours.

Kilka didn't reach for the chimes hanging off her belt to deliver the mere feeling of a lash, she ordered an actual whip brought out to cut into Kalea's back.

Now tied to the post in the courtyard and naked except for her little black braies, Kalea decided to remain quiet. She firmed her jaw. She'd been lashed many times before; she could take it. She wouldn't give this woman the satisfaction of a scream, although she couldn't guess how many lashes she'd receive.

Complete silence washed over the entire courtyard. Kalea clenched her fists and waited.

The whip cut through the air as Kilka reared it back.

Whack!

Every muscle in Kalea's body tensed at the first strike. She kept her jaw locked tight. Her eyes watered. A searing pain traveled to every finger and toe.

Kilka reared the whip back again.

"Kilka?" an elderly voice rang. "What are you doing?"

Knilma hobbled over the compacted earth of the courtyard. With her tired muscles barely mobile and now throbbing in pain, Kalea did her best to twist around. She couldn't see well through her watery vision, but the funny old woman's shape and hunched walk painted the picture well enough.

Kilka pointed the whip at Kalea. "This little harlot stole Wikshen's breakfast."

Knilma's jaw hung open at the scene. She squinted hard at Kalea. Did she recognize her?

"Kilka," Knilma said, "this girl, last night…" Her voice lowered to a whisper. "She is *his chosen*."

"Are you senile?" Kilka hissed. "Didn't you hear what I just told you?"

Knilma turned to the crowd and ordered them all to go about their business. She snatched the whip out of Kilka's hand. "Did you even ask around for witnesses?"

"What was there to witness?" Kilka asked. "This girl had every one of Wikshen's dishes at her bedside."

Kalea whimpered in her residual pain. Knilma's interception caused a level of relief and emotion that added more tears to her eyes. "M-maybe h-he gave it to me." She let out a sob at the end of her ridiculous suggestion.

Knilma studied her. She turned her gaze to Kilka. "Her case is worth questioning."

"And I did question it!"

"I had a long chat with the Mastaren earlier this morning, Kilka. Indeed, no dishes were on his table. He didn't mention anything about it to me, and I didn't think to ask. Other concerns kept his mind busy. Why don't we take the girl to him and ask the Mastaren himself if he minded her having his breakfast—and more importantly, *if* she should lose her status as a black maid?" Knilma paused to make sure everyone left the courtyard before adding, "Because you and I know how intensely this girl experiences ecstasies. You saw for yourself last night!"

Kalea shivered in the cold morning air as they bickered, crossing her arms over her chest. Without many more words, both shamans clamped a hand on each of Kalea's arms and dragged her, nearly-naked, back into the tower and through the complex toward the grand throne room.

The shamans had paid extra care to make the nave as dark as possible today. Additional black coverings stood in front of the tall, tarred windows, and the incense smoke proved especially dense today.

Like most every day, a long line of pilgrims stood on their bleeding knees on the harsh stretch of black carpet leading to Wikshen's throne. New drapes hung around it to further darken the space around him. Wikshen. Today, he actually occupied the throne and listened to the pleas and praises of his pledges.

Numb from all the shock of the bizarre day she'd awakened to, she found it difficult to be embarrassed of her nudity in front of all these people. Folk of both sexes stood waiting. The shamans hauled her all the way to the front of the line, where a special incense put off black smoke to dance and distort the image of the deity on the throne. Only a soft little Kraft flame lit the area, making it easy for him to see them and not vice versa. Kalea couldn't keep her nerves calm as she approached the spectacle. This was Alkeer all over again—except she wore less clothing this time.

Behind her, the people in line murmured and pointed until Kilka sent them a stern gesture of silence. She pushed down on Kalea's head to make her bow. "Stay down in this pose, slut," she growled above her.

Regardless, Kalea chanced a peek to try to see past all the shadow and swirling smoke. A big, pale foot rested at the edge of his throne platform.

Kilka and Knilma both bowed and recited a prayer to Wikshen in unison before presenting their case. As Kalea waited, a trail of blood trickled down her spine and into her braies from the throbbing gash across her back.

"Mastaren," Knilma began calmly.

Kilka stole the floor. "We found your breakfast at the foot of this girl's ragged floor mat. She seems to have stolen from you."

Wikshen held silent after her claim, so silent that Kalea chanced another peek at his foot.

Knilma attempted to speak again, "We don't yet know if she stole it, Mastaren. It could've been a rival maid. Nonetheless, Kilka wanted to strip her of her status before we decided to bring her to your judgment."

Wikshen finally moved, by the sound of his fabric rustling. When he stepped down from the platform, Kalea struggled to make out his face behind all the dark smoke, but his pale, shapely torso showed clearer above the kilt wrapped around his hips.

"Put her clothes back on her."

His deep voice echoed softly through the hall and struck Kalea's core. Dorhen's voice! She must not have dreamed their conversation. Her lip quivered, and her eyes watered once again. *Dorhen.* She stared up at him, looking for the comfort of his eyes until Kilka pushed her head down again.

At his order, Knilma snapped at an attending maid to send her running back for Kalea's uniform. His voice beat on, and Kalea's heart fluttered. "She didn't steal my breakfast," he said. "Leave her in her station. It's where I want her."

Kalea's mind jumped into racing. *He gave me his food, of course! It's what he does. This must mean he still loves me, even though we argued. Maybe he meant it as an offering of apology.*

But why was he being so cold and formal now? Though she wished to say his real name and ask him one hundred questions, she held her tongue. Dorhen stood there, acting like a god. There must be a good reason he held back from welcoming her in front of everyone.

"Mastaren," Knilma said, "she claims you came to her last night. Did you?"

A short moment of silence. "I did. I also gave her my breakfast, so send her back to work after tending her wound. Leave her alone." He reclaimed his seat.

A chorus of whispers echoed his statement through the nave. "He gave her his breakfast?"

Kalea dwelled on a different line. *Send me back to work?* Going back to work wasn't a bad idea right now; she needed to process what was happening. For now, her tears ran freely into her cupped hands. She hated how he acted coldly and didn't rush to comfort her for some reason of Wikshonite propriety, but it didn't matter. From his seat of power, he'd saved her. Why in Kaihals was he even in that seat?

Lounging on his throne again, he ordered, "Next," prompting Kilka and Knilma to lead Kalea away.

With her back soothed and cleaned, Kalea squatted before the fountain shrine as she did every morning, taking an extra-long drink of the soft, cool stream that trickled down into the little drainage hole at the bottom. The incense smoke danced up her body, delivering a religious sort of cleanse. Fresh water straight from the minerals of the earth. Her eyes were closed, and she lost track of the minutes she'd been doing this. The revelation that Dorhen had somehow become Wikshen changed everything. All of a sudden, drinking the shrine water didn't feel so shameful.

"Come on now." The attending shaman pulled her to standing. "There are others waiting."

Her head went light and deliriously cheerful, as always after performing the fountain ritual. Now it was time to warm herself in a nice, hot bath.

Obviously, all the concubine candidates had heard about the breakfast fiasco on the witches' whispering network throughout the tower. A little war ensued as soon as she entered the bathing room. Her fellow black maids wanted her to converse with them, but the concubine candidates wouldn't have it.

In the end, the concubines won, and she walked with Metta hand in hand to their side of the pool. She couldn't produce any answers for all of their prodding, but intended to keep them in the dark about her ecstasies and leave them to their speculations. Metta seemed awfully quiet about all the news.

"No, really!" Kalea threw back at the shrieking, antsy girls in the bath. "Nothing happened between me and Wikshen! I'm telling the truth."

"Then tell us how he 'came to you!'" Brielle demanded.

"A warlock attacked me last night and Wikshen stopped him. He didn't want his…woman to be defiled by a warlock, that's all. Maybe he gave me his breakfast out of sympathy."

"Well, do you know yet which black maid got the massive ecstasy?" Velle pressed.

"No, I don't. I'm sorry!"

The whole naked lot of them erupted into a storm of grumbling except for Metta, who remained silent beside Kalea throughout the confrontation.

"I'm going to finish my bath now, if you don't mind." Kalea went straight back to her washing at the edge of the pool.

The rest of the day felt no less bizarre than the morning. Kalea kept her eyes wandering around in search of *him*—more so than yesterday, before she knew she'd found Dorhen. Thoughts of him kept her maddeningly distracted. What should she tell Bowaen and the others when she saw them? What would Dorhen do if he saw her in ecstasy again? Apparently, he hadn't "blessed" her as she'd assumed. Would things be different if they met under similar circumstances next time?

Throughout the day, it became increasingly obvious how hard it would be to get his attention. He didn't spend very long on his throne before he rushed off to somewhere else. To where, she couldn't guess, nor could she ask. Her station was too low to ask for his whereabouts, much less request to speak with him. Wikshen must've been busy in his routine as a "deity." Tracking him down became an all-day quest disguised under her cleaning and scurrying about at any shaman's order.

Knilma forbade her to go outside the tower anymore. Her ecstasies were too frequent and too extreme to take a chance out there. After Wikshen's kindness, she'd become some kind of untouchable knick-knack, and yet more of a prisoner here than before.

Chapter 6
Miraculous Doctor

"She heard Dorhen's voice telepathically, even as Wikshen rode by and snatched her up in her home village," Lamrhath explained what Mhina had told him to Talekas in the man's cozy little office.

Talekas sorted whisper stones and pressed his signet ring into puddles of wax as he listened. "So Dorhen remains in attendance within the body," he said.

Lamrhath dipped his head in a nod. "Yes." He'd told the whole story with both his hands flat on Talekas's desk, half-annoyed the man hadn't held total eye contact.

Talekas finally looked up from his work. "But this story is off somehow. I thought Tumas acquired Mhina as a gift for you."

Lamrhath shook his head. "He lied."

"How do you know?"

"Because Mhina is an elf, and elves *don't* lie. It's part of their culture. Besides, her point wasn't about who took her, it was about hearing Dorhen's voice in her head."

"Sounds like the magic of elven religion."

"The Desteer," Lamrhath confirmed with a nod. "This girl seems to be one."

"She grows rarer and more valuable by the day, doesn't she, my lord?"

"None of us have any idea," Lamrhath said through grinning teeth as he glanced at the door. "And Wikshen... We have to get him back."

Talekas raised a finger. "My lord, our conversation about rarities reminds me: this morning we got a special delivery."

"Of what?"

"Over here, if you please?" He moved to the corner and slid a large crate to the middle of the floor.

"From Wikhaihli?"

Talekas's eyes flared. "Better." He lifted the already-loosened lid to reveal several bundles of paper nestled in straw.

"More sweaty elven scalps from the grasslands?"

"Oh, ho ho, my lord needs patience. Look." He unfurled one bundle to release a long braid of shiny black hair, the most exquisite strands Lamrhath had ever seen, perfectly combed and kept.

Lamrhath held his breath at the initial shock. His mouth quirked. "They *actually* did it." He let his lips curl into a full smile to share with Talekas before letting it drop. He couldn't help but reach out and run a finger along the shiny cascade. It tingled upon contact, not from any magical effect, but because this touch was so damned forbidden! "It's a *faerhain*'s."

Talekas smiled fiercely. "It is. And look at these." He put the first lock aside to unfurl another one. A brown one. That color reminded Lamrhath of Orinleah, causing him to swallow at the sight of it. "We have all colors, my lord, so you can take your pick. Red, blonde, some with a hint of cherry. I've never seen such beauty in my life!"

"You've never been to Norr."

"We also have the recipe for the yarn we ordered." Talekas tapped on the stack of letters on his desk. "We'll try some of the more complex weaves soon."

"Don't practice with this hair."

"Wouldn't dream of it," Talekas said with a deep bow. "That's what those sweaty, scabby *saehgahn* scalps are for. We're getting new spinning wheels too, by the way, for faster production."

"I want to see what you've made so far."

"As you wish." Talekas packed the hair back up and closed the crate. "Care to accompany me to the conference?"

He shook his head. "I'll meet you there. But do start without me. I trust your judgment in looking at their ideas. I have to do my usual constitution."

A few hours later, sitting at the long conference table, Lamrhath rubbed his lower abdomen in an attempt to stave the blooming pain off. He had work to do now. Even though he'd opted to do his constitution before coming here, the pain crept back in quickly. The stress of his work didn't help his ailment at all, but he couldn't let it slow the progress of Ilbith's fast ascent to greatness.

Upper-level sorcerers vied for his attention as they each presented something they'd found in the Darklands or their sketched schematics for contraptions to imprison Wikshen. In his pain, Lamrhath sat, looked, and listened. He didn't have the strength to keep order. The next sorcerer shoved the previous one's plans aside and laid his own down.

"My lord! With some good lamp oil, we can create a pipe system." He pointed to the rough charcoal drawing for visual aid. Lamrhath found hardly any interest in most of what he'd seen. A meager few good ideas were harvested out of many bad ones. "This pipe system would be installed in a stone cell. Through this system, imagine great pillars of fire shooting out through vent holes!" He traced his pointing finger to the illustration of the effect he described. "A blazing cage of fire to hold Wikshen in."

Lamrhath scoffed. "Just to hold him? For indefinite amounts of time? 'Twould be far too expensive. Get out of my face!"

The sorcerer skulked away, leaving his drawing on the table to be thrown aside by the next eager man who presented a drawing of shining spheres. "My lord! I've recently returned from an expedition in the northwest. My group discovered a brand new mine of gleaming schileezen!"

Lamrhath's eyebrows shot up, his pain finally vanishing for an instant. Schileezen was a valuable stone they could use to harness energy. It worked better than gold.

"We'll mine it," the man continued, "cut and polish spheres of different sizes—huge ones, if you please. The deposit is rich. Imagine what we could do with this new resource!"

Lamrhath pointed to him. "See me later."

The sorcerer bowed low. "Yes, my lord!"

After him, a handful of other sorcerers filed in with bad ideas, either too expensive or utterly asinine, though all beamed with enthusiastic inspiration. The challenges Wikshen brought hadn't dulled their zeal for sorcery; it had piqued it instead. Some of their ideas required the help of powerful pixies or at least enslaved sprotts, and others were designs of clever engineering.

With his eyes glazing over, Lamrhath sat back and tried to breathe slowly. They'd formulate something soon. Maybe he wouldn't have to get too involved. Everything around him ran smoothly. They even boasted a friendly shaman in communication with Lamrhath to keep Wikshen under close watch. Her latest report stated several odd deficiencies that Wikshen exhibited. He wasn't doing what Wikshens throughout history had done, particularly showing interest in women; the shaman had reminded Lamrhath that Wikshen should carry a keen sexual fervor. Lamrhath couldn't stop wondering whether Wikshen's new host was to blame: Dorhen.

"I've seen enough," Lamrhath said to the room, and everyone hushed to listen. He leaned forward, curling over the pain. "Go and improve your plans and designs." He did his best to keep his voice sounding strong despite the agony. "We'll assemble here again tomorrow. And don't forget to explore methods to relocate the sword, Hathrohjilh."

He kept his seat, waiting for everyone to leave so they wouldn't see his discomfort as he made his way back to his room—a miserable distance away. Talekas moseyed over to sit next to him at the long table.

"I'll organize a great system to mine that schileezen, my lord," he said. When Lamrhath didn't answer, Talekas cocked his head. "It appears… your ailment is getting worse."

"Because it is," Lamrhath hissed. He propped his elbow on the table to rest his head. "The next expedition should be to find a cure for this misery."

Talekas leaned his head in closer. "Come to think of it… I too have a pitch for you."

"Tell me quickly. I have to get to Silva—now."

"We occupied a village a few weeks ago, and this one has a great doctor to boast."

"What has he cured so far?"

"*She*, my lord. This doctor is a midwife and also a sort of witch-woman who knows much about medicine. When I heard of this, I ordered more information on her." He owned Lamrhath's attention now. "She also boasts great knowledge about the human body."

"I'm not human, stupid," Lamrhath reminded him.

"I understand, my lord, but how different can elf and human bodies be? I mean, really? This doctor is a rare gem. She may've only treated humans, but she's one of a kind, the best we've ever found. Recently, our people witnessed her skill in action when she cured a bad bout of blood poisoning in one of them." Talekas's eyes flicked downward. "We can bring her here to have a look at you. She may actually heal your ailment. What say you?"

Lamrhath clenched a clump of his own hair in his fist. "I say yes. I'll try anything at this point. Bring her."

Chapter 7
A Maid Wanders

K alea opened her eyes to a dark dorm at the tail end of night. Twenty or so black maids slept soundly around her. Exhausted from the previous day's events, she lay in a state of blankness. A figure stood at the front of the room. A tall, dark figure.

"Wikshen," she whispered at the risk of waking the other maids.

The figure shifted, and the soft lighting through the window lit up a set of turquoise eyes.

She shot to a sitting position, prompting him to turn and retreat. "Dorhen!" she yelled, finally managing to disturb the other maids.

"Shut up, already," one groaned, and a few others sighed and turned.

She ran after him down the aisle of arranged bedding, bare feet slapping the floor.

The other black maids cursed and groaned louder. "What's wrong with you?"

Kalea paid them no mind. Dorhen wouldn't wait for her. He disappeared into the shadowy corridor.

The next morning, she found he'd left a cloth-covered pastry with cherries in its center—something fancy enough to appear in Wikshen's breakfasts. The smell of it riled her empty stomach. Before anyone could catch her with the incriminating item, she scarfed it down.

There she was. As soon as the maids rose to start their day, Dorhen jumped to tracking her down. It wasn't enough just to check up on her while she slept; he could stalk her all day. The complex was large, both on the ground level and underground, so it took some time and effort to find her. He also had to take precautions not to be seen in the busier sections, lest another episode happen like the other night. But now he had found Kalea at the underground fountain shrine for her mid-morning devotional hour.

After acting so mad when he had insulted her One Creator, she still fulfilled her Wikshonite devotions so easily—and without a high-ranking person there to force her? She actually enjoyed drinking the water trickling from the little stone nozzle.

Dorhen liked it too. He *felt* her devotion somehow, like a tickle in his core. As of late, he could feel many of his followers' devotional prayers and acts. Casting Kraft must have something to do with it. But none of that mattered now.

He chose not to disturb her, but instead traced his eyes along the curving outlines of her naked form, glistening in the balmy air of the cave. Falling against the wall, he sighed. This was close enough to that bathing scene he'd revisited in his head over and over. How could he interrupt such beauty? He'd watch a little longer and maybe retreat to his room again, whatever it took to keep himself satisfied and away from Kalea.

Oddly enough, though, like the first time he had spied on her, she wore a cruel mark across her back. That idiot Kilka had marred her again, as if Kalea didn't have enough scars to remind him that she'd suffered outside of his ability to protect her. He reached an arm over his shoulder to touch his own back. As usual, the sympathy pains stung. Maybe he'd punish Kilka later.

Nonetheless, Kalea was admirably tough. Soon she'd be off to clean more floors and make more beds in the sunlight.

The sound of a foot scuff on the ground put a stop to his enjoyment. Behind him stood Knilma, with her cane and a knowing smile on her face. Dorhen pushed off the wall and resumed a casual but stern stance. He offered her no explanation before walking away.

The presence radiating behind Kalea caused her to twist around, pulling her lash wound wrong, and she winced. Knilma had been standing there watching her.

"As you were, girl," Knilma said and proceeded around the corner, leaving Kalea with questions and a reawakened humility.

So Dorhen is Wikshen. Kalea went over her hazy memories of their encounter, followed by his appearing to give her a pastry this morning. *But how? How!*

That was a question only he could answer, if she could ever find another moment to talk to him. She had other mysteries to solve here, though. Like where was Mhina, and had Dorhen actually kidnapped her? Maybe Gaije was mistaken about that. Dorhen would never harm a child. He couldn't harm anyone unless they meant to do harm, she knew that much about him. But then another hazy memory replayed of him in Alkeer, talking very coldly. He hadn't sounded like *Dorhen* then, and Kalea didn't like that concept at all.

She entered the bath house to the usual question of who to bathe with today, the maids or the concubines. She slipped into the middle section of the large, steaming pool, choosing neither or maybe both at once. Let them fight over her for all she cared. She could pick out each side's conversation. The usual stuff about the mysterious maid with the ecstasies passed around both groups, as well as the breakfast dilemma— and everyone knew he'd given his food to Kalea. Many eyes poked through her thin bubble of relaxation. Those concubines would probably stake her to the ground and question her raw if they could. And the maids... By now, they might be deducing amongst themselves that Kalea was the one with ecstasies. She was the only one not openly talking about it.

"Well, last time the Mastaren didn't even show up. Maybe he didn't want to sit next to you," a concubine said to another, pulling Kalea's ear to their side of the bath.

"He wouldn't have known where I sat, stupid, not when he wasn't even there!"

Kalea waded over, half-swimming in the elbow-deep water to hear more. Knowing Wikshen was Dorhen changed everything they said about him for Kalea. That was *her* elf they were all fighting over!

Nan used the whiniest voice in today's argument. "It's just not fair! I won the last round, so why should we do it all over again for the upcoming banquet?"

Banquet? Kalea remembered that one well. She had been slotted to be the head maid for refilling Wikshen's drink, but he hadn't appeared. He apparently hid instead of eating dinner with all these girls in a dark, incense-filled dining room. Everything made a lot more sense now that she knew his true identity. But what was going on today?

"It is too fair. At least we all get a chance," Brielle shot back at Nan. The girls erupted in bickering, all speaking at once. Few of them sided with Nan's complaint.

"What's going on?" Kalea asked Metta. At least she had the sense to stand back a bit and observe, throwing in only a few words where necessary and only to try to douse the fire. Kalea liked Metta for her kindness and patience, but...it stabbed her heart to remember what she had said about Wikshen: *Kalea, I desire*, she'd said, *to make love to him. How beautiful it would be...*

"Oh, Kalea," Brielle drawled, "how did the Mastaren's breakfast taste today?"

Kalea's face heated. It had tasted good, of course. He left her a portion because he was Dorhen and he loved *her*. "Don't be silly," Kalea replied in a voice matching Brielle's pettiness.

"Psh!" Brielle waved her hand as if Kalea were a fly. "Anyway"—she looked back at her fellow concubines—"you harlots better shape up if you want to get ahead of me. I've been practicing my poses and dances on my own time. This next banquet, *I'm* sitting next to the Mastaren."

Beside her, Nan's whole naked body flared red with anger, and Kalea probably matched her. She couldn't get near him—*her* Dorhen—but all these stupid girls were going to have a banquet with him! Who knew what other time they were getting to spend with him? After all, they were concubine candidates.

Concubines! She knew from her convent's history texts that concubines were pampered women whom the old emperors of Kaihals used to sleep with before the construction of Hanhelin's Gate had divided the whole continent. And here Kalea was, just a maid. This situation was a nightmare—one from Kullixaxuss—and Kalea had no idea how to wake up from or cope with it. A meeting with Bowaen might be in order, but first, she needed to offer him a good update on Mhina.

Time to get serious. Kalea marched straight back to the basement and hurried to her folded bed, where she extracted Del's roll of lockpicking tools from its folds. Dropping it into her apron's patch pocket, she strode out into the corridors and sprinted up the stairs to the shamans' quarters, where she had attempted lockpicking before. Up here was also the room where she'd spied Wikshen rising from the dead—which made such little sense now, considering! All the more reason to try to contact him. She was on the hunt for more than documents and glimpses of imprisoned elf-children today.

Hours later, Kalea sighed in her scrubbing work, feigning her duties while she waited for a giddy group of shamans to go by so she could resume her sneaking. They were excited about Wikshen. He was apparently a new Wikshen and gave them much hope for the future. Kalea didn't understand how. What did they want with her elf? Thinking of and worrying about him did distract her quite a bit. She'd failed to unlock a lot of doors today, probably because of that. Also, the halls were too busy, more so than last time.

From what she'd eavesdropped so far, there would be a formal worship session later, while now he occupied the throne—which was why Kalea abandoned her bucket of cleaning implements, tucked her lockpicking tools deep into her pocket, flexed her spine after so much stooping, and headed downstairs to get in line with the pledges.

The black smoke swirled again, and the line of people stretched half the length of the nave, twice as long as usual. It could take any amount of time for her to get her chance. Wikshen never promised to see all of the pilgrims in one day. People often waited overnight.

Regardless, the line moved at a good pace. Her knees were bruised and scraped up by the time she made it close to Wikshen's throne, looming high in all of its dark glory. She set her determination on getting all the way to the front. She couldn't speak to him plainly, of course, especially with Knilma standing in attendance beside him. She'd have to somehow weave a message into a spiel of religious drivel, a message pleading for him to meet her in private. He could answer all of her questions if only he would try.

The line got her so close, his bare foot came into view, resting at the edge of his platform. His sacred shroud spilled down the throne and under the rope between him and the crowd. The pledges bowed their faces to the floor, said whatever words of reverence they wanted to say, and kissed the shroud's edge.

"Kalea?" the housekeeper shrieked. "What are you doing there?"

Kalea jumped at the voice and met the woman's eyes with alarm.

"Maids are not allowed to join the line. Get back to work!"

All of the pledges paused and turned to eye the spectacle. At this point, Dorhen should also be alerted to her. Knilma craned her neck to watch curiously.

The housekeeper yanked Kalea's arm. She stumbled to stand up. "And look what you've done to yourself!" She pointed to Kalea's burning, bloody knees.

She'd nearly forgotten about keeping herself pretty for Wikshen. Did it matter anymore, after Kilka's hasty lash to her back? Another scar to add to her collection.

"Go back to the infirmary and get yourself bandaged up."

Kalea did as instructed and emerged from the medicine room with her knees coated with ointment and fresh linen to cover them. She wasn't finished, though. Speaking to Wikshen on his throne wouldn't work, so she'd catch him somewhere else, somewhere he spent the majority of his time.

The tower livened up with worshippers right before midnight; the staff kept the house up through the daylight hours. Now was a good time for Kalea to really open her eyes and perk up her ears. If a worship session happened soon, there was a chance she might see Dorhen in the halls and pass him a message. She knew he couldn't read, so she didn't bother trying to inscribe the message on anything. Somehow, she'd send him gestures instead.

Opposite the corridor to the basement was another hallway that led to some stairs to the underground catacombs. She ventured that way. If the Wikshonites were hiding anything, they were probably hiding it underground anyway.

The concubines cut off her progress to the wing in question, jarring her to a freeze, heart racing. Hopefully, they didn't suspect she was headed to the same doorway. Like always, they ignored her as they floated along in their line, cloaks drifting on the gentle breeze they created, too damn important to pay any mind to their friend Kalea the maid. Tomorrow morning, they'd twist her arm for an update on the mysterious "ecstasy maid." What would they do if they found out the maid who outranked them in Wikshen's graces was her? The mere thought of it made her smirk as she stood aside with her rag in hand. Even Metta offered not a word to her as she brought up the rear.

Kalea tailed the concubines down the stairs and soon lost sight of them. She followed the essence of pennyroyal they left trailing in the air. Following her nose took her back to the old book about the adventures of Lehomis when he would track animals or bandits, using his keen senses to guide him. Gaije—apparently Lehomis's descendant—had also used his nose a lot when they were searching for sorcerers. Kalea smiled to have those terrifying episodes as memories now.

She'd developed her own keen way to navigate the dark corridors of Wikhaihli, though, partially thanks to the initiation ritual when the shamans made her walk blindly through a tight, dark tunnel. All those uncomfortable experiences seemed to have made her stronger. Tolerating the dark was easy these days.

The tunnel stretched on and the maids had disappeared long ago, leaving her to navigate the complex alone. It grew more confusing the deeper she ventured. Once in a while, a small Kraft flame lit the way. In some areas with forked paths, a brighter glow from a glass lens in the ceiling offered greater illumination. At the first one she found, Kalea had to look up and gawk in wonder. She could see nothing behind it but other lenses to intensify the light. The blue tint hinted that a Kraft flame was burning behind the lenses.

Kalea was on a mission, though, so she shrugged off the ingenious wonder and took a step toward a tunnel that smelled more powerfully of pennyroyal. She'd have to run so the concubines didn't get too far away. But she stopped again at a voice—a male voice.

"No," it said. "I told you already."

"Dorhen?" she whispered in hopeful surprise. It was him! She crouched down in the shadow and waited. He walked by with purpose, a shaman nagging at his heels.

"But Mastaren, getting outside could do you some good." Kilka's voice. She was the last shaman Kalea wanted to get caught by. "It's fresh air. Fresh night air is a wonderful thing for one such as you."

"Don't you have drums to beat?" Dorhen asked blandly. His rumble put a spark in Kalea's stomach. She resisted jumping up and revealing herself. He slowed as he passed by and smelled the air.

Kilka whined on. "Wikshens are supposed to go on campaigns, Mastaren, and you seem to have completed none since your arrival. If you go out on the road, you'll come to a crossroads. Each direction will send you to a fine village full of resources and eligible girls for the taking. I implore you, walk out to the crossroads. You'll see what I mean."

He paid no mind to Kilka's nagging. His glowing eyes passed over Kalea, and her urge to reveal herself leaped. She didn't, and before she could work up the nerve, he strode on down the tunnel, ignoring Kilka.

Kalea stared down the tunnel after them. Was he avoiding her? Or did he not want to speak to her in front of Kilka?

Kalea dropped the cleaning rag she'd been absentmindedly kneading in her hand and followed in that direction. No sign of him around the corner; his long strides got him pretty far ahead. She explored deeper. Down here, the walls became rough, more cave-like. She passed a little nook at a junction with a fountain shrine nestled into it and another magnified light overhead. Like the one she normally used, two sacred shrouds hung on either side of the shrine. She randomly picked a path at the junction, the scent trail now fainter than ever. Several minutes escaped as she continued on.

"Dorhen," she called softly, and decided not to try again. Shaman voices echoed from somewhere. Drums began. Must be tonight's worship ritual. Padding on numb feet along the smoothed stone floor, she followed the drumming to a complex of doors. The booming rhythm beat on behind one of them slowly, though it increased in speed the longer she spent listening.

Soft, chanting voices became apparent too. Beautiful voices. Women's voices. Kalea found which door hid the drums and all the people. A blue light glowed under the crack. Kalea listened. It churned her stomach to think of Dorhen in there among a bunch of women, participating in a heathen ritual.

A hand grasped her shoulder, and Kalea shrieked and spun around. "Shhh."

"Dor—!" Kalea stopped her voice short of uttering his name. Dorhen was not the one standing behind her. Knilma was.

"It's not safe to scream at this hour," the old shaman warned. She raised an eyebrow. "What are you doing down here?"

Kalea had no good lie for her question.

"Looking for *him*?"

Of course she was.

Knilma tugged Kalea's sleeve. "Come this way."

"Am I in trouble?"

"Should you be?"

"No, ma'am," Kalea said.

Knilma gave a soft cackle. "I don't care. Matter of fact, we gotta talk about something, girl."

"Like what?"

"Psh." She erupted again in laughter. "What do you think?"

Kalea didn't bother to guess. Her nerves were at their ends—she'd been caught somewhere she wasn't supposed to be—listening in on a ritual—and Dorhen was in there! As of yet, she didn't know what to expect.

Knilma made her wait until she'd half-dragged her back to the fountain shrine with the magnified light and started untying Kalea's wrapped dress.

"What are you doing, ma'am?"

"Take your arm out of your sleeve." She looked it over, similar to Kilka's initial inspection. "Had any more ecstasies?"

Kalea shook her head.

"Take your top down."

Kalea sighed, left without a choice. At least Dorhen was the only male allowed in this tower and cave complex. She peeled down the loosened section of her dress and let it hang over her tied waist strings.

"Mm-hmm." Knilma acknowledged her breasts, level with her face due to her humble stature. She gave one a brief grope. "Small, which I knew. It's surprising considering the Mastaren's interest in you, though. I'm learning an ocean of new things about him these days. My old Wikshen wanted all the jiggliest bodies we could find in the Darklands. I couldn't have foreseen this new Wikshen enjoying the opposite."

New Wikshen. Those words resonated. What did it mean, though? Kalea would rip her hair out if she couldn't uncover this bizarre mystery. "Opposite how?"

"Wiry. Flexible. Swan-like." She guided Kalea by the arm to turn around, and then unwound the bandage wrapped around her waist to inspect her back lash. "It should heal well. Although our Mastaren of today doesn't seem to mind your scars."

Kalea sighed again, through her nose.

"What're you about?" Knilma asked.

Dorhen loved her as a person, but she couldn't tell the shaman that. She covered by saying, "I'm very self-conscious about my scars and I wish not to hear any more about them."

Knilma snorted. "You'll always be ridiculed about them by the other concubines."

Kalea whirled around to meet her eyes intensely, whether she was still inspecting the wound or not. "*Other* concubines?"

Knilma's wrinkly faced bunched into a grandmotherly smile. "It's my job and Kilka's to pick out and stock the Mastaren's harem with all the best, just like I did for the last Wikshen. Kilka thinks Wikshen likes little blondes with forked tongues, and though Wikshens of the past have chosen such a personality type, this Wikshen has proven to be different in every possible way.

"Before you came along, I placed my bet on Tamas, that sturdy brunette from the grasslands. I erred, to say the least, but he does seem to favor brunettes. Quiet ones. Taller ones. Thoughtful ones. Independent ones. Girls like you." Knilma turned her enigmatic grin on Kalea again. "But you particularly…" She squeezed Kalea's bare shoulder. "You've set him on fire. Trust me."

"I-I have?"

Knilma raised her hands as if in defense. "Don't ask me how I know this—please!" She burst out a laugh again, leaving Kalea in the dark about some kind of joke. "So listen to me now."

Kalea concentrated hard on what she'd say.

"You're going to eat a good breakfast from now on. I'll do my best to get those knees and your lash wound healed. You'll wake up *extra* early tomorrow."

"Why?" Kalea asked.

Knilma nodded with her eyes closed again. "I know Wikshen said yesterday that he wanted you as a black maid, and once one is slotted into a station here, she can't be promoted except by Wikshen's blessing." Knilma leaned in closer and changed her volume to a whisper. "Early in the morning, every morning, before your chores begin, you'll meet me in a special place. I'm going to train you in concubine talents."

Chapter 8
Low Resources

Well, what do you expect?" Lehomis shouted in the trader's face. "We took a bit o' damage from a rabble of maddened, stray Sharzians naught but a few months ago!"

He ended his outburst, pinching his nose bridge as if to stop his own words by force. The poor horses he needed to trade were trying to back away against their taut reins, eyes wide at his volume.

"Apologies, Lockheirhen—may the Bright One shine on you again soon—but Clan Kellah asked for fifteen of your prime horses, and you're offering me eight and asking for the same amount of grain as you do every year. I can only trade you as much as your eight horses are worth."

Good Bright One. Lehomis had faced some difficult trials in his clan's early days, but he'd never been forced back into foraging like in hardships past. For the first time, Lockheirhen had suffered a true raid. They'd lost almost an entire generation's worth of young horses ready to go off to their new homes, and the annual Tinharri traders hadn't shown yet. These were the common traders, who traveled around Norr picking up and dropping off items between all the clans.

The trademaster waited for Lehomis's decision while his associates sat on the wagon or leaned against it, yawning. Lehomis motioned to his own lads holding the horses' reins, and the swap was made: eight horses left over from the raid, one an old nag, for six sacks of grain. Not nearly enough to distribute throughout the clan.

Hang the Tinharris! Lehomis scoffed to think of them. They'd taken away six Lockheirhen *faerhain.* They would get no horses this year! Lehomis would have to meditate a bit on how to supplement the clan's supplies for the winter.

While his lads loaded their wagon with the goods, Lehomis caught the trademaster's arm. "One more thing." He produced a rolled parchment from his lapel. "Give this word only to the clans on the east side, and some to the south."

"A tournament?" the trademaster said, skimming over the text.

"After all that's happened, I'd say it's in order," Lehomis said.

"I would agree, Lockheirhen. My home clan lost fourteen *faerhain* to the Tinharris this year."

Lehomis hissed at the number. "Then you'll share the invitation with your elder too?"

"I have no choice, do I? It's the elder's decision. Makes my teeth long to imagine losing an additional *faerhain* to the tournament, though."

"That's a gamble we all make, don't we?" Lehomis gave him the unsmiling, bared-teeth courtesy all males displayed in hellos and goodbyes. The trader bared his teeth in return before packing up and rolling away.

"Gamble" made a good word for what the tournament was. In his letter, Lehomis invited the clans to assemble for three days of music, games, and lots of peacockery. The peacockery would be the true event, as all the eligible clan males would use the opportunity to show themselves off in every conceivable way. Any eligible *faerhain* could pick a husband out and bring him home, but in order to entice fierce competition among the *saehgahn*, each clan put a participating *faerhain* into the "pot." The champion *saehgahn* won the right to pick one out, not too unlike what the Tinharri had done, except in this case, the *faerhain* chosen was obligated to marry whoever selected her.

This type of tournament was very illegal, and would have to happen under both the Tinharris' and the Desteer's noses. If one Lockheirhen male could find this as a way to get married, even if he left the clan to be with his new wife, Lehomis would smile. If one of his lads could come out as the champion and bring a new *faerhain* into the clan, that would be everything.

In most cases for tournaments, a great rotation of males and females could happen between the clans. More often than not, the prize *faerhain* would insist on bringing her widowed mother, sister, or young daughter—if she was a widow herself—to her new clan. More *faerhain* for the clan. Widows with young sons added more strong arms and good future studs to entice the females of the new clan. Such a rotation of people freshened things up and kept bloodlines strong and primed for the future.

Every twenty years, the palace held nationwide tournaments for the health and growth of all the clans, the difference being that the official tournaments did not feature the *faerhain* prize. In official tournaments, the Tinharri clan also participated, and Lehomis wouldn't have that.

Another day done. Lehomis threw his boots off and entered the sitting room for a long evening by the fire. "Anonhet!" he called. The house hadn't been so noiseless since he and Anonhet had inhabited it by themselves. A sad twinge touched his mind. He missed his little granddaughter, Mhina. He'd tried not to think about her too much...

"Yes?" Anonhet called back.

"I'm home," he said. "When's supper?"

"Just a minute please."

He opened the chest along the back wall of the sitting area and perused the old relics inside, looking for his pennywhistle. This junk hadn't been disturbed in a century or more. An unworn cloak of Sharzian silk he'd bought ages ago, still wrapped in paper with herbs to keep the moths away, sat nestled tightly between an old drinking horn and a flattened velvet hat. He found a belt pouch made from a wooly Norrian ox on the other side of the trunk—a smart-looking accessory. The pennywhistle in question gleamed in the corner, but Lehomis kept browsing, finding things he'd long forgotten about. Things that might be worth a little money.

Tirnah watched Lehomis rummage through his old chest until Anonhet crept up on her and made her jump. She turned on the lass with her hand over her mouth. "Don't make me scream," she hissed. She went back to spying on Lehomis as he gave up his exploration and retired to the cushions to lie on his back and play a little tune with the instrument he'd found.

"Would you like to help set up?" Anonhet asked.

Tirnah didn't answer. She watched Lehomis, wringing her hands until Anonhet took one of them and held it.

"You're thinking of telling him, aren't you?"

Blinking her eyes, Tirnah turned away from the scene. "I can't."

"Well, you can't delay either," Anonhet argued under the music's cover. "His wife gave birth to twelve children. You think he won't be able tell by your looks and mannerisms when you're a little farther along? Do you want to drive him crazy with wondering, or spare him such by telling him about the ba—"

Tirnah hissed to shut her up. "But he's been under so much stress," she said. "Look at him."

Lehomis missed a note, and the pennywhistle squealed. He cursed in Lightlandic. Remaining on his back, he started the song over.

Anonhet put her hands on her hips. "Tell him right now or help me with dinner. He'll be happy to hear it."

Tirnah hurried out to the kitchen.

"But where are you taking me? I don't want to go!" Mhina shouted as

Lamrhath led her by the hand away from the nursery she'd been living in.

"You're all right," he said back with a hard edge he didn't want to use with her. Her nanny accompanied them, so he didn't see why she should be so alarmed.

Losing the patience he normally mustered up just for her, he yanked her forward, and she stumbled along the carpet. Her echoing squeals of protest drew more stares from the passing servants, and even some red-robed sorcerers joined them. Their silhouettes froze in front of the big, bright windows on one side of the hall.

"That hurts!" Mhina went on. "This *saehgahn* is evil! Stop him!" she shouted to anyone who might listen. Regardless of her chosen words, none would dare thwart the kingsorcerer in this place.

"Well, I wouldn't hold so tightly if you'd walk like a good child!" he barked back.

She answered his statement with a defiant pout.

He took a deep breath into his nose and exhaled through his mouth. "I'm not trying to hurt you," he said. "Trust me, and come like a good *farhah*. I have something to show you."

He stopped by a door nearly as grand as the one to his bedroom and drew a heavy ring of keys from his belt.

"This is where you'll live from now on, my dear." He made an effort to shift his voice back to his practiced, honeyed tones. He pushed the door open and allowed her to enter first.

The candles in the room had already been lit for effect. A pale grey light from the window added cool shadows to mingle with the warm. It was a grand bedroom decorated in pale purple, finally complete and not a second wasted in moving in its new permanent resident.

A grand canopy bed draped heavily in fine silks of purple and gold stood to the side. Thin drapes hung loosely from the carved wooden frame while heavier drapes were tied back with colorful ribbons. Among the numerous plush pillows, fine new dolls of both cotton and porcelain loaded the bed. Two regular windows were on each side of a massive stained glass one. The room was complete with a vanity, dresser, two wardrobes, a huge ornate divider screen, feminine wall tapestries, a large fireplace, and a private garderobe. A table and chairs with a silver tea set sat nestled in a rounded corner of the room.

Lamrhath waited in the doorframe for several moments, allowing her to take in the sight and watching for her impression. So far, she surveyed the space with a blank stare.

"What is this all about?" she asked.

"This is your new home. It's for you," he said, trying to sound kind after all the irritation she'd caused him.

Her next word baffled him. "Why?"

"You don't want to sleep any longer in that filthy nursery, do you?"

She took one more look around the bedroom before turning back to him with a twisted mouth. "I hate purple."

Bile rose in his stomach as Lamrhath's immediate thoughts dispersed in favor of the familiar, blank-minded anger that, according to onlookers, made his eyes flare with their own fiery inner light. He clenched his fists, focusing the tension into them to show less anger on his face. His heat rose and his vision darkened. The nanny. He could hit her to disperse his anger.

No! he told himself. Better not let Mhina see him act violently. In anyone else's presence, he would've already struck. He took a deep breath and concentrated hard until his vision lost its tunnel frame. He forced a smile.

"It's fine, we'll change it," he said, and opened one of the wardrobes. "I want you to put on a lovely dress. You have exquisite new ones in here. Tonight, you'll eat supper with me…as you will do every night from now on."

Mhina's expressionless façade withered, and she put out a stammer. She lowered her brow. "Do you mean to make yourself my father?"

"If you wish me to be." He turned to leave.

"I do not!" Her stare grew cold. "My father is dead, but he is still a far better father than you could ever hope to be."

Lamrhath gave her his best nonchalant shrug. "My condolences, but I never said I wanted to be your father." He left her at that.

Chapter 9
A Chime Burns

Knilma stood over Kalea as she awakened, holding a candle in the night darkness. "Are you ready to learn how to serve your Mastaren?"

With great difficulty and reluctance, Kalea dragged her body out of bed and followed the old woman through the corridors to a small chamber deep in the complex of caves under the tower. She closed the rough-cut door behind them. The floor beneath her bare feet wasn't as smooth as the more heavily-trod common spaces below Wikhaihli, and the walls were rougher too. Nothing much could be found in this room besides the heavy wooden trunk Knilma approached.

"Now," the old woman began. She tossed Kalea a black rug after a little rummaging. "Spread that on the floor. You've so much to catch up on."

She next handed her a folded black outfit consisting of a pair of long socks with open toes and a similar pair of long, fingerless gloves to match. The rest of the outfit consisted of a top and bottom piece that barely covered anything.

Kalea couldn't imagine what she'd need a rug for. Knilma bid her to stand on it with a spread stance. "Widen your feet," she ordered. "Wider."

Kalea wobbled as she spread her feet again and again until Knilma nodded. By then, each foot was planted at opposite ends of the rug.

"Raise your arms and bend. Bend, I said! Form your arms like this." Knilma's arms were too old and stiff to demonstrate her point well.

Patiently, Kalea adjusted her pose until she found what the shaman described. It finally hit her that she was doing "Kraft Positions," those poses Wikshonites performed as a daily devotion to their religion. For now, Knilma had put her up to a fairly easy one.

"Hold it there," Knilma said, and sat on the trunk.

A few moments passed in silence.

"Why am I doing this?"

The old woman shushed her. "For meditation." A few more seconds went by. "Although this may also be my chance to get some lecturing out of the way." Knilma sighed. "Your knees are shaking already. You've got some toning up to do. Bend at your hips some more."

When Kalea obliged, her inner thigh muscles pulled to their limits and her old scratch wound flared; she used to think it was completely healed. Soon, the rest of her body shook pathetically.

"You have a good frame," Knilma said. "Limbs like a swan. My Mastaren chose well."

"Am I going to be a concubine?" Kalea asked after a few silent minutes.

Knilma frowned and squinted at her as she usually did. "You can't. You have to continue being a black maid. However, I'm going to make sure you're prepared for when he calls you. *When*, girl, not *if*. He will call you, and when that happens, you're going to give him the greatest moment of his life."

Kalea flushed all over; her face burned, but the warmth showed up in other places too. By now, she shook so badly from exhaustion, she'd lost the precision of her pose.

Knilma stood up. "Take a rest."

No sooner had the words escaped through Knilma's lips than Kalea's arms fell and she collapsed to the rug.

Knilma opened the trunk again and rummaged around. "Every morning, we'll do exercises, a pose or two, and this…" She revealed a few scrolls in her fist. "A lecture."

Kalea rested on her knees upon the rug. "A lecture about religion?"

"Sometimes," Knilma said. "What's most important for you to learn is your worship technique."

"Which is…" Kalea lost all her words when Knilma unrolled one of the scrolls. She resisted covering her eyes.

"What do you know about sex, my girl?"

Cringing at the pictures on the scroll, Kalea said, "It's something you do when you are married…and then a baby comes."

"Wrong." Knilma cackled. "Not terribly wrong, but wrong in the case of where you are now." She laid the scroll out on the floor with smooth stones to hold down the corners, and then went for another one to add to the layout.

The drawings were similar to those in Vivene's love manual, but less romantic and more informative.

Knilma held up one finger. "And…" She rummaged again. "Where did I stash it? I spent all day yesterday getting these things together without anyone noticing. Ah!" She held up a bundled cloth and unwound it. "Let me tell you, girl, how long it took me to find this."

"A turnip?" Kalea asked. "Don't you have a lot of turnips?" They appeared in the geoduck stew every day.

Knilma unwound the rest of the turnip. "This one has a special shape. Use your imagination."

The turnip had grown into an elongated formation that looked similar to the drawings… Kalea gasped and caused Knilma to laugh again.

Knilma held the vegetable out to her. "See how far you can put this down your throat without gagging."

After Knilma's educational hour, Kalea was long past ready to take her bath and wash all of the…education away.

Before dismissing her, Knilma answered a tap at the door. She opened it a crack and received a tray of food from the person on the other side, taking care not to let them see inside the room. She placed the tray before Kalea. It was a rich breakfast, complete with eggs and milk and a pastry. These items were close to what they served Wikshen, except not so fancy in presentation.

"Eat it before you go," Knilma said. "It'll put some meat on your bones. A few weeks of eating this paired with our exercises, and you'll be beautiful beyond recognition."

Kalea ate it greedily and blessed Knilma's name. A whole day's worth of maid duties awaited, and the breakfast provided much-appreciated energy.

Despite Knilma's fatty breakfast, Kalea could hardly think straight by midday due to her exhaustion. She'd been used to waking up earlier than most people in her convent life, and staying up later too, but today she'd woken up even earlier!

"Look at me, I'm washing clothes like old times," she said to herself with a chuckle as she sat in the courtyard with her arms plunged into a tub of warm water, back aching. This place echoed feelings of the convent all over, except their deity walked around here in the flesh, and the women inside were expected to do sexual acts when "called" instead of denying the notion of sex altogether.

She swirled the little black garments around in the soapy water. Her eyes glazed over as she watched the light dancing on the water's surface. She used to see a face in the effect—Arius Medallus's face. Did he still watch over her? Did he watch over Dorhen?

She agitated the garments against themselves to scrub the dirt from the fibers. A nice escape. "My Cre-a-tor, my Cre-ator," she sang as she worked. "Ohhh-oh-oh-oh-ohhhhhhhh." She fished for a garment and wrung it out over the ground. Her legs didn't stay dry through this chore. "La-la-la-lo-lahhhhhhhh." She hummed until the melody brought her to the next verse. "One day as I waaaaaaaaalked along my lonely paaaaaaath—"

"Is someone singing out here?"

Kalea paused to regard the shaman who'd entered the courtyard. A drove of other shamans and witches accompanied her. Some popped their heads out of windows.

"Um…Yes," Kalea answered.

The shaman stormed her. "Come here!" She grabbed Kalea's hair. "Wikshonites don't sing, you understand? It's not allowed here!"

"Why?" Her foolish response sprang out too fast. Kalea attempted to grab her hair back, and the shaman slapped her hand.

"Only drum song is allowed here, besides bells! Didn't you know?" The woman jerked Kalea by her hair. "Kneel down!"

Kalea did, and when her head bowed, a chime rang, announcing one of those shredding stings across her back. It was only a sensation, but she swore it surpassed the ache of the physical lash she received the other day.

Kalea pleaded, "I didn't know! I'm sorry!"

The sound chimed again.

"I won't sing anymore!"

The woman appeared to not care as she continued her chiming, sending ripples of pain across Kalea's back. Goosebumps popped up all over her limbs.

She looked up in search of Knilma or someone who might help. Someone better stood in a window on the second floor—Dorhen! His eyes were bright and his mouth locked in a firm frown.

She called his name and reached toward the window. "Dorhen!"

She made a piercing scream at the next intangible strike of pain. He clenched his teeth and covered his ears, and then quickly disappeared from view.

Good, she thought, *he's coming down to stop them! He saved me once, so he'll be there for me today.*

Kalea waited for him, enduring several more sensational lashings.

She waited.

Ding!

"Ahhhh!"

She watched the door.

Ding!

Kalea screamed again.

How long should it take to walk down one flight of stairs to put a stop to her punishment?

Ding!

Kalea's body shook. She fell to her hands and knees. Soon she'd fall flat. She kept her eyes on the door. *Where are you, elf?*

Ding!

Kalea collapsed and lay on the ground. Other black maids gawked in the corners of her vision. Her cheek rested on the dirt.

Ding!

The pain covered all of her senses. The maids in her peripheral vision blurred. She waited for the next chime. It didn't ring.

The shaman stood over her, fastening her chime bowl back to her belt. Her voice boomed hard and flat. "Don't ever sing again."

Kalea forced her weak neck muscles to move, to raise her head. Had Dorhen appeared yet? No. He wasn't there. Did he even care?

Chapter 10
Cruel Queen

Vivene gingerly closed the door to the servants' closet, enclosing her in the darkness with as many ex-novices as she had managed to wrangle.

"How have you all been?" she asked, turning her gaze around the circular formation in which they stood. Sabina had brought the single candle by which they saw each other. No more daylight was left to supply them through the tiny window between the wooden shelves.

The shaking of Maggy's teary-eyed head drew her attention first. "I can't do it anymore, Vivene, I—" She finished with a sob, grabbing at Vivene's clothes.

"Maggy, calm down." She used her best effort to be patient with her. They'd been in Ilbith for a few weeks, and Vivene was already used to it. The other girls standing in the circle managed to keep their faces dry. "Be strong," she told her.

It was useless advice, but all she had. They were residents of Ilbith now. Vivene had long managed to numb herself to the foul treatment. She'd even learned to enjoy the daily sex the sorcerers demanded of the servants. She knew her friends all had various levels of tolerance for it, of which, Maggy displayed the least.

Vivene squinted at the lot of them. Someone was missing. "Where's Rose?"

Millie grunted. "You know she can't follow directions."

Vivene shrugged, gently pushing Maggy to stand on her own. "But otherwise, she's okay? How about the others?"

Opal piped up. "I saw Vera the other day. She complained of stomach cramps."

"Could that be why she's not here now?"

"Probably."

"How about the children?"

Cornelia raised her hand. "I was curious about them too. One of the sorcerers gave me a favor token for the way I...um." She dabbed her forehead with a handkerchief, her blush apparent in the candlelight. "I'm just trying to say, I'm working to get closer to them. Trying to let the sorcerers know I'm good with kids. If I can get a position in the nursery,

I'll be able to keep an eye on them."

Vivene nodded. "Good work."

Opal's foot tapping filled the next moment of silence. "Are we done here?" she asked. "Baromond'll be going to the dining hall soon. I want to be there to fill his drink."

Vivene reared back to give her a sour eye. "And what's going on with *you*, Opal?"

She smirked. "Baromond's really good. He's the best! And I think he likes me. So, if you'll get outta my way…"

The candle flickered in Sabina's hand as Opal passed. "You slut," she grumbled under her breath.

Millie gave her a light shove. "Shut up. We're all sluts now, aren't we?"

"N-n-not me," Maggy said through her tears.

Vivene pinched her nose bridge at the foolish girls. Most of them were coping, which was good. Not so much for Maggy. And Rose. Rose was innocent…no matter what happened to her. "Watch out for those sorcerers," she said to Opal as the girl pushed her way through the tight space to the door. Millie followed her.

"Yeah," Millie said to Vivene. "Give Bargo my regards."

"Shut up."

The next morning, Vivene's quick pace carried her through the halls of Ilbith to her next phase of chores before someone found her lagging and ordered a beating. Going up a few flights of stairs and through the servant's entrance to the Chimera Tower, she bumped shoulders with several other servants and yapped out a "sorry" before hurrying on. A few paces from the door, Vivene stopped at the sound of a harsh voice within.

"What's wrong with you, girl?" A man's voice.

The snap of leather whipping dully across fabric came next. Vivene winced at the sound. She wanted nothing more than to spin on her heel and walk briskly away, but she needed to get in there and retrieve her tools, or she'd be in that other servant's place later.

Stiffening her spine, Vivene tiptoed toward the closet to get her things. It spanned large enough for a servant to be reprimanded. She moseyed around to peruse the shelves full of folded rags, buckets, brushes, wax scrapers, and other items to keep the Chimera Tower tidy.

Turning back to the door, Vivene paused again when she saw the person being beaten. "Rose," she whispered. She hadn't seen her in several days. How many beatings had the girl endured already? Probably many, not that Vivene could tell by looking at her face, which was dry as beached wood. She squinted her eyes throughout the ordeal, though, and kept her mouth tight as she clung to the frame of one wooden shelving unit. Rose seemed to take it better than anyone else. Regardless, Vivene couldn't stand to see someone like her go through such ill treatment.

Without giving it any thought, Vivene ventured closer to the spectacle. A sorcerer in red delivered the beating. If it had been this wing's housekeeper, she would have let them be, but the sorcerers were a world harsher.

Reaching out a hand, Vivene said, "My lord, please have mercy on her."

The sorcerer turned his glare on Vivene for her audacity. "What did you say?"

Vivene bowed and gave a quick curtsy. "Forgive me, but I know this girl. She came from the convent like I did. She's not right in the head. She...she doesn't know things."

The sorcerer snorted and spat on the floor. "You don't lie. She's stupid as a dunce. She doesn't follow orders. She wanders and gets distracted."

Vivene nodded rapidly. "I know, my lord. That's how she is."

The man lowered his eyebrows. "It's how she is?" Sneering, he reached for the dagger fastened to his belt. "If she can't function like a normal person..." He ran his eyes down and up Rose's form. "She hardly looks normal. I'll have to put an end to her. If she can't work, we'll waste no more food on her." He drew the dagger.

Vivene lunged forward. "No!"

He paused and turned his vicious mien to Vivene. "What right do you have to tell me 'no?'"

Vivene held her arms stiffly at her sides. He could easily decide to slit her throat along with Rose's. "None, sir."

As if of its own will, her hand shot to her apron pocket, fished out her single favor token, and held it out to the sorcerer in one motion. She'd been saving it for a rainy day—to get some form of comfort for herself. A pity she'd gone to such trouble to get it, degrading herself at the whim of a particularly vile sorcerer.

She mustered up the words, "I'd like to trade in this token...f-for Rose's life, at least on this one occasion. L-let her mistake be forgotten, p-please." Vivene's hand shook, but she held it extended with the coin shining on her palm.

The sorcerer raised an eyebrow at her coin and exhaled through his nose. "There are many better things to trade that token for, little girl."

Vivene nodded. "I understand. I promise Rose won't do it again."

He snorted and snatched the token off her palm. "You said it yourself: that's how she is. You've wasted this valuable trinket."

He pocketed the favor token and exited the room, leaving Vivene to collect herself. Rose stared blankly after him, her head scarf crooked and her bodice laced up all wrong. Simply looking at her made Vivene feel more tired than usual. She crossed the room to straighten Rose's headwear and fix up her other disarrays.

"Vivene," the girl said.

"What is it, Rose?"

"Where's Joy?"

Vivene stopped to observe her. "Are you kidding?"

She wasn't. Her innocent eyes made it obvious. How could she forget about Joy's death? She had been there when the ceiling caved in.

"Joy's not here," Vivene said. "She can't look after you anymore, so you'd better get your mind straight and learn how to look after yourself." Vivene wanted to be annoyed. On any normal day—in the convent—she probably would've been. Rose's situation made her lip quiver aside from the exhaustion.

"Why do you cry?" Rose asked.

"Why don't you?"

Rose shrugged.

Vivene went back to straightening her hair and headwear, blowing a breath out. Maybe she should've let the sorcerer kill the girl. A simple person like Rose shouldn't be in a place like this. Vivene might've saved her life today, but tomorrow, when she returned to bumbling around in her duties, any one of those sorcerers could come to the same conclusion as the one Vivene had bargained with. Back at the convent, Rose's "duties" had been more like games to occupy her throughout the day, like feeding the chickens and having her run to fetch things, leaving everyone else to tackle the real work.

Vivene took Rose by her soft, round chin. "Now listen to me. I don't have any more favor tokens to save you with, and I can't chaperone you all day—the sorcerers wouldn't allow it. You listen to what they tell you and do as you're told. You might keep yourself out of trouble. Understand?"

"Vivene?"

Vivene sighed. "What?"

"When's Kalea getting here?"

A cold shock hit Vivene. She narrowed her eyes as Rose waited for her answer. "Never. Kalea escaped."

Rose shook her head. "But when is she getting here?"

Vivene released her chin. "You must've been dreaming or something. No one's coming, especially not Kalea. What good could Kalea do us if she *was* coming?"

"She has a shadow with her."

Vivene wrinkled her nose. Her exhaustion increased by a degree. "Everyone has a shadow, you dummy. Next time you have a dream, ignore it." She put her hands on the girl's shoulders and shook her. "We're stuck in here. Now go back to your chores and don't make any more mistakes!"

She gave Rose a shove toward the door, and the girl stumbled on her way. Rubbing her face, Vivene shook her head. "That stupid kid." Her innocent and unreasonable questioning made everything worse. Vivene wanted to keep up with her convent sisters to make sure they were all doing okay here, but they often reminded her of how stuck she was, especially Rose.

Two masked men stood over Damos's bed when he opened his eyes, one poised with a gnarled club.

"Don't struggle," the one to his right warned.

There wasn't much Damos could accomplish with his hands tied to the iron rigging that was affixed to the wall behind him. He'd spent several days on this ammonia-rich mattress. In the first few days, he wouldn't have dreamed of trying to move; it hurt his sore skin too much. He'd been spoon-fed and cared for all this time, his bandages changed every few days, and today he wished for nothing more than to stand up and work his joints. He couldn't be sure these men were here with any good intentions, though.

The man with the club raised his weapon. "One squirm, and I'll bash yer skull."

Damos kept his lips tight, still wearing the bandages around his head that obscured his expressions. He waited for what they'd do.

The man on his right unsheathed a dagger. Damos tensed up. He leaned over him, leaving Damos no choice but to watch as they now both wielded weapons. He considered his magic. A good lightning bolt could latch on to that dagger and extinguish the man's life. The club-wielder might follow, considering his metal mask. But there was one problem: Damos's ring was missing! They must've taken it off of him when he was drawn out of the mud.

His stomach pitched. The ring was crucial for using the spell, and most others. If he attempted the spell without it at his skill level, the lightning could branch all over the place and catch him up in its deadly trap, metal mask or not.

The man with the dagger cut his bonds. His muscles burned as his arms finally dropped into a more natural position. He couldn't move them at first because of their initial numbness. A rush of painful tingles changed that.

"You must do exactly as you're told," the dagger-wielder said. "You're a drone now. The queen needs your service."

"The queen?" Damos echoed. Images of his mother flashed. Oh God, he missed her. But they weren't talking about his mother; she'd died years ago. Was their queen that witchy woman who had drunk the energy out of the teenage girl? From his bed, Damos had had the misfortune of watching the old woman return to suck her life away several times until the girl was left as a dead body, withered and dry.

"Follow us."

At least these two were understanding enough to wait patiently as Damos reclaimed the use of his limbs. He hadn't even stood up in days and couldn't guess how long he had dwelled in the burning mud pit. Pissing into a pitcher in bed with one hand remaining tied had grown terribly old. Regaining normal, everyday function would be a great step toward escaping this place.

After a good amount of stretching and flexing, he attempted to walk on his own, following them on his wobbly legs across the now-empty room. He was the last of his group to graduate from this smelly cave. Half of the others walked out like he now did, while the other half were dragged in sacks. He could finally see what lay on the other side of the door.

Tunnels. Hand-carved tunnels. Some with doors on hinges, others with arched windows showing nothing but a damp night beyond. The other two "drones" carried a blue light in a lantern.

"This is what's under Hathrohskog?" he murmured to himself.

"Quiet! No talking. The queen needs you obedient."

Damos flinched, half-afraid of getting a blow from the club-wielder at the boomed command. He received mercy for now and kept his thoughts inside. He had to wonder how many of these drones had fallen straight through the mud and wound up here in servitude.

His answer came around the next corner when another set of drones dragged a screaming girl inside a net. She had no blistered skin, and had yet to be fitted with a mask or any other indication of having been here long. Maybe the drones were trapping people up above and bringing them down here to be used and integrated into the population. As their two groups passed each other, he clenched his hands helplessly, devoid of resources for helping her right now. He would need to learn more about this place. If only he could get his ring back.

Kalea's well-being also dawned on him. Had she been captured too? By that terrifying shadow man? He shivered.

Every turn, every door, every path they traversed, Damos kept track of in mental notes. Some paths were narrower than others. Rough walls enclosed a few corridors, and roots riddled many other areas. The drones kept a nursery of glowing mushrooms in one of the darkest caverns, which made a good landmark.

Their escort became a tour when they reached the areas where Damos would be working. In a finer setting with smoother walls and carved steps in the sloped flooring, many drones scurried by, bearing pillows and large folds of black cloth.

Once they reached the section where several men hung such swathes of fabric as if decorating for a party, Damos couldn't help but ask, "Why the decorations?"

"The queen is expecting a visit from her god. He's going to bless her," his escort explained. "She ordered these corridors to be made beautiful and comfortable for his stay."

Damos had no idea what any of that meant and couldn't find the courage to ask. They took him farther, into what could only be a loot-sorting area. Everything from clothing to riches sat in piles. He knew by the sight of his boots thrown in a corner among other mud-caked apparel that it all must've been gathered from the victims of Hathrohskog. When one of the attendants moved their blue flame light, something better glimmered at him from the smaller pile of jewelry: his ring!

Damos covered his gasp and tried to act casual. He needed to get it back, especially before it could be stashed away in some locked vault. But he couldn't make a run for it from this distance. His legs were still shaky, his muscles too stiff.

"Never you mind this area. You're needed elsewhere." The drone behind him gave him a shove, forcing him to bypass his best defense along the way to the corridor across the space.

They finally stopped in an enormous cavern with plants growing from dark corners and vines riddling the walls, where little feathery seeds often broke off to drift in the air. The many drones in here were sure to catch rogue seeds in linen nets on long poles. Some seeds drifted too high and were closely watched by the net-wielders. Alongside the gardeners, other drones broke rocks and harvested minerals from the walls, shiny black minerals that must be what all of their masks were made of.

A strong hand against his sore, unready shoulder pushed Damos onto a stool. He reflexively tucked his shoulder to his ear and hissed.

"Here's your work," his drone escort announced. He pointed to a dark, gooey-looking substance in a barrel. Next to it stood an empty barrel. Before Damos could make any new inquiries, the man tossed him a stiff, smelly apron and a pair of leather gloves. "Yer gonna want to wear this."

Damos hid his hands in his armpits. "What is it?"

"Seeds." The man lifted what he could only imagine was a very wet and meaty peach pit, still wearing lots of fruit around it. But these were not peach pits. They smelled of rotten flesh.

The man proceeded to stick his knife into the gooey substance. "They all have a slit, if you look hard enough. Pry them open." He demonstrated and revealed the true seed within the shell. He dropped the seed into the empty barrel and threw the messy shell onto a garbage pile. His hands came away red from handling it, and he wiped them on Damos's apron.

"That looks like blood," Damos said.

"It is blood, my friend."

Damos dropped the apron in horror.

The man pointed to it. His voice came laced with utter seriousness. "Pick it up, or your clothes will look the same."

"Why is there blood on the seeds?"

"Because these plants you see all around us grow from human bodies."

Chapter 11
Jaded Wikshonite

"Of course I love you," Primora said, batting her eyelashes against Jonaril's cheek.

"So what's the problem?"

Primora gazed into his eyes. Such a handsome man, despite his being two years younger than she. Jonaril. He made her laugh, sigh, sing… She couldn't lie: she loved this man, but…

"You know about my religion."

Jonaril sighed and turned his eyes to the ground.

They sat holding each other behind the old barn as they did any time they could get away. Lively voices in the distance carried on, farmers talking as they wrapped up the day's work, a middle-aged wife calling the cows. Those voices had become strained in the last few weeks since the sorcerers arrived. Life in the village had grown exceedingly complicated with the new tax system, the snide Ilbith representatives glaring over everyone's shoulders, missing girls, and whispers of attack. Primora escaped it all whenever she joined Jonaril back here in his embrace, a secret realm where peace and their love reigned supreme—if not but for a few minutes.

Jonaril ran his fingers through her long brown hair, and then placed his forehead on her shoulder. "Why do you torture me like this if you also swear by your religion?"

She sighed too. "I don't know…"

"I don't see why we can't get married, though. For so long, your religion has kept you from experiencing life. You're twenty-one! Almost a crone."

Primora reared back, causing him to take his head off her shoulder and meet her eyes. "We've only been together three months, for starters. You're younger than me. If I had married earlier, it wouldn't have been you."

"True. But does our blossoming love matter? Does it have to wither before we can finally join?"

"Yes, it does matter. And also because…"

"Tell me."

"I'm not ready yet."

"Ready to marry or ready to renounce your Wikshonism?"

Primora frowned. "Please don't say it out loud. The red cloaks are all around, and even you shouldn't know about it. Please try to understand, I was born into this way of life. It's all I know."

"So you believe a wild man with dark powers will return to the Darklands. What has he to do with us marrying?"

"It means…" Primora spoke breathily. She knew as well as he did how far-fetched the mythical scenario was. Even the sorcerers couldn't convince her of Wikshen's existence. Greed motivated them to spread these rumors, and thanks to those red cloaks, everyone in town was on high-alert about "dangerous Wikshonites." At least Jonaril hadn't fallen into that frenzy. "It means I have to remain celibate and wait for him."

"Hold on," Jonaril said. "You also mentioned that your mother and your aunt were Wikshonite witches."

"Yeah."

He snorted. "Obviously *they* didn't stay celibate. They each have a daughter."

Primora avoided his eyes. "They weren't supposed to, though."

"But they did."

"Yes."

Jonaril gave her the signature snarky face he always did when he felt he'd caught someone off guard.

"These things happen," Primora said. "Life is messy."

He took her chin in his fingers and pressed his lips to hers. Lightly. Sweetly. "So it is."

She relinquished her kiss to him and said against his mouth, "I can't marry you."

"That's fine," he replied spiritedly. "Your mother and aunt never married anyone…but look what they did anyway. We can do the same."

Primora shivered as he traced his fingers up the back of her neck. They kissed for several long minutes. Open mouths, tongues mingling. She arched her back against his wandering hand. His other hand traced her leg into the slit of her wrapped skirt. She stopped his hand before it ventured too high.

"Not yet," she whispered.

He hissed and scrubbed his fingers through his hair. "You drive me crazy," he said, and stood up from their seat on the hay bale. "I guess Wikshen wins again tonight, huh?"

She stood with him. "Just give me time. It's getting dark anyway, and it's a long walk home. Care to walk me?"

He snorted a laugh. "I thought you Wikshonites loved the dark forest."

They did. But she hadn't enjoyed the trail since that night of the eerie feelings and the laughing man. She gave Jonaril a playful shove on the shoulder, though she didn't feel any mirth.

"Same hour tomorrow?" he asked.

"Yeah," she said. "Promise."

They leaned in for one more peck on the lips before parting, and then Primora headed toward the forest across the small grazing field. She had a lot to ponder along the way.

Thankfully, her trek home was uneventful this time, and the man at the gate didn't bother her. Her luck ended when her mother met her on the carpet as soon as she walked through the door and threw a spray of water in her face from a slotted shaker used for religious rites. The water mixture was cold and laced with potent herbs. She didn't appreciate the surprise.

Her mother erupted into hums and words of prayer in the dark room. Primora checked behind her while she carried on, paranoid the sorcerers would hear this impromptu ritual. Her mother paid no mind, either to the door or to Primora's hesitance. This wasn't an abnormal thing in their house, but also not routine.

"What's going on?" Primora ventured to whisper while her mother wrapped up her resonant humming.

She patted Primora's shoulders and head with a small bundle of fresh pennyroyal. "My daughter," she whispered back, taking her face between her hands. "I gave birth to you *for* Wikshen."

Primora nodded.

"We will draw him to us. It's time for you to carry out the task you were born to do."

"Draw Wikshen to us?"

Her mother hummed some more and pulled open Primora's lapel to smear a smelly cream across her clavicle. From birth, she had been taught all of this. Wikshen liked certain strong smells, and he liked women. He also liked vibrations.

"Are you crazy? We can't be banging any drums or metal plates."

Her mother put a finger to her lips. "We won't. Your job is to obey. It has begun."

The "it" she spoke of was Primora's born duty. Her mother had dedicated her to Wikshen inside the womb and anointed her halfway out at birth. Ever since, she'd been groomed and nurtured like a prized flower to lure and seduce Wikshen.

"This is the worst time to attempt the spell," Primora said. "The sorcerers will hear it, and we haven't even moved the altar."

Her mother shushed her. "Wikshen will come and destroy the sorcerers...after he blesses you. This is the best time to call him."

Primora bit her lip. Wikshen *wouldn't* come, and their rituals would only draw the sorcerers into their house—to kill them! It was too risky!

Her mother motioned to a small wooden tub in the corner, steaming with fresh, herb-strewn water. "Take your clothes off. Tonight will be the cleansing ritual."

Primora swallowed at that. These rituals, particularly the one meant to summon Wikshen, were in-depth and time-consuming. It might be a long while before she saw Jonaril again.

Chapter 12
A Deity Speaks

It must've been the hot presence radiating in the otherwise drafty chill of the basement dorm which woke Kalea up. A groggy groan crept out of her. The struggling dawn light through the small windows high on the wall helped her to see in the dark atmosphere. Faster than her senses could return, the hot presence flew away and the chilly air rushed in to replace it.

"Dorhen." His name formed in her next sleepy groan. Yesterday's trauma had shaken her to exhaustion. Her radical shifts in emotion hastened her daily fatigue.

A shadow loomed by the exit corridor like before, and his eyes flashed in the morning glow. The fragrance of fresh baking registered. He had brought her another pastry from his breakfast. As soon as she moved to rise, he disappeared in a blink.

Knilma would expect her soon. Letting him go, she rubbed her eyes and turned to the pastry he'd left. She didn't mind all the extra food she'd been receiving from both Dorhen and Knilma lately. As she ate the berry pastry, she noticed something else he'd left. Scarfing the rest down, she unfolded the white cloth that accompanied it.

A chemise similar to the one she used to wear at the convent. He had found and given this to her? She hadn't seen anyone wearing anything similar, and by now knew better than to take the chance of wearing it. If it wasn't a black maid uniform, she'd get another chime beating, so she hurried to cover it with her blanket and made the bed as usual.

"You're late, girl." Knilma frowned with her arms crossed as Kalea gingerly nudged the door open and entered the room the old woman had claimed for Kalea's concubine lessons.

"Sorry," she offered.

A slight grin cracked on Knilma's face. "I hear you're still earning beatings."

Kalea shrugged.

"Apparently, I'll have to fill you in on the rules of this religion too." On a table to the side, covered dishes waited. "Hurry now," she said, "go down on your knees and assume the pose I taught you yesterday."

Kalea's sore muscles weren't used to this new activity yet. When she complained about the difficult pose, Knilma made a *bah!* sound and waved her hand.

"Your body will get used to it," she said. "The key is to have discipline and do your poses and exercises every day."

So as Kalea endured, Knilma talked briefly of each basic rule the Wikshonites kept. Rule number one was, "No sex, except with Wikshen." Kalea knew that much, but it held so much importance that Knilma listed it first. Kalea didn't know what to think of that rule. Making love to Dorhen was something she actually wanted to do, but she did *not* approve of him coupling with all of her peers. To avoid having to deal with unnecessary stress and anxiety, she chose not to dwell on that part right now.

"And as you found out yesterday," Knilma went on, "music and singing is outlawed here."

"Why?" Kalea ventured to ask.

Knilma spread her hands over the cane she rested them on. "A Wikshen long in the past forbade it. The most important factor to know about Kraft, my dear, is that it's an earth magic and that our bodies are catalysts for it, just as vibrations move through the earth."

Kalea cocked her head, and Knilma asked, "How does the earth behave?"

Kalea couldn't guess what answer she truly wanted but tried anyway. "Rockslides happen. Earthquakes. Sinkholes." She paused there, and Knilma nodded her old head.

"Precisely. It moves slower and more subtly than water and air, but it does move. It holds its formation, strong and sturdy, unlike water, which only takes the shape of its container. But it's also treacherous, as you've put in, and earthquakes and rockslides can catch us unprepared and do great damage. Kraft draws its energy from the vibrations of the earth, you see. It's not the sounds so much as the deeper vibrations which can have an effect on Wikshen. The deeper part he can *feel*."

"He can feel them? Can't we all?"

"Through his patron element of earth, Wikshen can feel more vibration than we can, and with such sensitivity that he can tell them apart by their infinitesimal characteristics: rhythm, pitch, and whatnot. Vibration is like a whole other voice he receives through his surroundings.

"Long ago, the shamans discovered this. Not only could they contact him by beating certain drums or gongs, but they found they could alter him too. With more and more research and practice, they developed the magic style of Kraft into what we use today—from the old primitive discipline, of course. A discipline that can control the earth."

Alter him? Dorhen had already been "altered," and in such an extreme way.

"In fact," Knilma went on, "we used Kraft to sculpt many of these very tunnels under Wikhaihli, because vibrations are what move the earth."

Kalea shook her head. "If vibrations are so important, why is singing outlawed?"

Knilma spread her hands. "I'm not sure, girl, but you must also know that certain vibrations bring negative effects. Some can drive him into a rampaging madness. It's safer for us all to stick to the approved vibrations."

"But what was the singing I heard from the worship room?"

Knilma closed one baggy eye and pointed the other accusingly at her. "Should I ask why you were listening in on the worship session?"

Kalea bit her tongue.

"We chant, we don't sing," Knilma explained, letting the accusation go. "Our chanting is monotone. The vibrations speak to Wikshen's soul. Singing, apparently, has a different effect." She extended three fingers. "Drums, bells, and chanting. Those are the sounds we use to praise Wikshen. Now, let's try a new pose."

Knilma next introduced not quite a pose but a motion that challenged Kalea's back and stomach muscles to their limits.

"You must build strength," she declared, "to move in ways that will pleasure your Mastaren. You need lots of stamina to perform such moves for long periods of time. When you find yourself finally in his chamber, you'll be well equipped to deliver whatever he orders of you."

Kalea found her body in tangles that made her feel downright gross at first. Although it hurt her already-sore muscles and worked new ones to agony, she could also feel the sensuality in them. She made graceful, repetitive motions that seemed senseless on the surface of her thinking, but in all honesty, they excited a deeper, darker side of her mind. Knilma promised the exercises would make her beautiful as well. Kalea wouldn't mind that outcome.

When Knilma finally found her mercy and allowed Kalea to drop to the rug and rest, she set the platter of covered dishes on the floor before her. "And this'll complete the image," she said with a grandmotherly smile as Kalea welcomed the best part of concubine training.

Kalea was already mentally drained by midday. Knilma's lessons rolled through her head again and again, each round more confusing than the last. Knilma thought Wikshen liked her well enough to "call" her, but where had he gone after he saw her getting beaten? Even on the day when he had saved her from a beating, he barely lifted a finger to do so! Where was he now, if she was so special to him? She would have expected him to acknowledge her a little more now that they'd reconnected.

Kalea's back muscles roared as she scrubbed the bench of the jakes where people sat to relieve themselves. She mumbled to herself absentmindedly about her frustrations and her aches and pains, not caring who might hear. A tap at the window made her pause.

"What in Kaihals…?" She reached up to open one side of the shutter. A familiar face stared at her from the other side.

"There you are!" the young man said, trying to keep his voice down.

"Del?" She almost asked what he was up to, but he always contacted her through this window. She should've expected him. He wore a bandage on his wrist from when Wikshen—or Dorhen—had broken it.

"What's going on in there?" he demanded. "I've been waiting outside this window for the past two days, and you haven't shown. You know how dangerous it is for me to get this close to the tower?"

"Sorry…" Kalea rubbed her temple. "I forgot, I guess. How's…how's Bowaen and Gaije?"

"They're itching to leave. You got anything to share about Gaije's sister? Is she in there? Gaije is losing his mind, and he's getting more worried every day."

"I went looking for her a day or so ago."

A strange grogginess clouded Kalea's head, especially for the time of day. Her routine was so tight these days, full of so many duties, so many punishments she'd endured. For her sanity, she looked forward to visiting the soothing water fountain shrine, the steamy baths, and even the meditative practice sessions with Knilma. A new lust for Dorhen had come upon her since those sessions began, one that trumped whatever fondness she'd developed before for the innocent brown-haired boy, and her visits to the water shrine intensified it.

Then it hit her. *Dorhen!*

She leaned out the window to get closer to Del. "Listen," she told him. "I'm on the cusp of getting some good answers. I need a bit longer."

Del shook his head. "Tell me what you got right now, and I'll relay it to Bowaen and Gaije."

"Nothing," she replied.

He frowned. "Nothing? It's been almost two weeks now, and you've found nothing yet?"

"No, but I told you I'm close! A little patience, please!"

"What are you up to? Maybe I can help," he said. "We're dying to get

out of this place. You know how hard they work us down on the beach?"
He caressed his bandaged wrist absentmindedly.

"Give me more time," she urged.

"How much?"

She closed the shutter.

"Dammit, woman!"

She shushed him and left the garderobe.

Kalea spied Wikshen's throne from around the corner. Like every day, a long line of newly arrived pledges waited to kiss his shroud and proclaim their allegiance. Like most days, Dorhen lounged in his dark space, listening to their speeches. Kalea couldn't get in line with them to try to send him a message. She'd already tried and failed once. She couldn't see him through all the draping black linens enshrouding his throne and the curling streamers of black smoke, but she also couldn't help staring until her mouth dried.

When she finally tore herself away from the spectacle, she forced herself to think again. That incense was so…potent. Being wrapped up in Wikshen's world made it difficult to think, but she tried…

The only other place she'd ever caught him was in her own dorm, before all the maids awakened.

Lying in bed, Kalea couldn't tell how long sunrise had to go, but maybe it didn't matter. She had stowed some extra blankets under a stone bench built into the wall, and now she rose from her bed and tiptoed between the rows of sleeping maids to their hiding place.

She carried the large bundle back to her bed, freezing in horror when one of the maids groaned and turned over beside her. The girl didn't speak; she was still asleep. Kalea softened her steps the rest of the way back to her own bed and peeled back the top cover to pile the extras where she'd normally lie. Fluffing and patting, she formed them to look like a human figure. Proud of the illusion she'd pulled off, she left the sculpture to do its work and tiptoed to her predesignated hiding spot in an alcove by the entrance, where she crouched and waited.

She might've nodded off once or twice. The sound of a door whining open perked her out of one possible snooze. She clamped her mouth shut. It could be anyone: the housekeeper, Knilma here to wake her up for her lesson, or it could be…

Softly padding feet registered in the little corridor to the stairs. Slow footsteps. Bare feet. Everyone went around barefoot in this place.

A presence drew closer; Kalea could feel it. Closer. She held her breath, her eyes wide in their attempt to see in the dark.

A tall figure.

It's him! Kalea stiffened. *What should I do now?*

His long hair shrouding his head like a hood and hanging down his back, he—Dorhen—paused his slow walk toward the group of young women sleeping in their bedrolls on the floor—right beside Kalea's hiding spot. Her bed, with its dummy figure, lay at the center of the other beds. Dorhen appeared to study the room. His left hand clutched a tied handkerchief with a fragrant, fruity pastry inside. His wide shoulders held square, his hands motionless at his sides...until they weren't.

He spun around and lunged, hooking his free hand around Kalea's arm. She gasped but managed not to scream.

"What are you up to?" he whispered in his deep, stern voice.

She didn't need him to fall for her trick; getting his attention was her aim. She turned the sternness back on him, his negligence to save her from the chime whip fresh in her mind. "We need to talk."

He held an angry demeanor for someone who was kind enough to drop by and leave an offering of his own food every morning. "Not a good idea." He spat the words as if angry about her request.

"Not a good idea? What's not good about giving me a second of your time after I've walked so f—"

He shushed her with a firm shake of her arm.

"Ow!"

"Fine," he said. "We'll talk in the storage shed like before. Meet me there this afternoon. And if anything happens to you because of it, I won't be... Never mind."

He released her and stepped back, dropped the bundled food on the floor, and sprinted back into the corridor. She considered chasing him but wouldn't be able to keep up with his impressive speed. She also puzzled over his canceled warning. What in the world could happen to her if they set up a meeting?

Nonetheless, she recited the directions, *The storage shed this afternoon*, in her head. She trusted he'd keep his word—for now. His warning must've been about running into bad warlocks or getting another ecstasy in the wrong place. Going outside the tower was indeed a risk. Kalea's ecstasies happened so intensely and so frequently that Knilma had banned her from going to the common areas where the warlocks moved about, but she'd find a way.

All morning long, Kalea kept her eye on possible exit routes. Whenever she passed an untarred window, she looked out to see how busy Wikhaihli's large cloister was. The warlocks going about their business outside didn't bother her, although she did have to wonder what had become of Dyii after the night Dorhen had punched him out for assaulting her. From what she'd experienced, her ecstasies only hit in the dark of night. High noon should be a safe time to go outside. Instead, she worried about the shamans who might catch her trying to leave the tower. Maybe they were the reason Dorhen preferred to speak his mind outside. Not to mention the housekeeper would punish her if she were caught not doing her chores.

Kalea put the chemise Dorhen gave her on under her maid's kirtle; the two garments made a smart ensemble. Taking her ratty blanket from her bed, she fashioned a cloak from it. With her head held low, she did her best to blend in with the common peasants who wandered about in the nave, visiting the shrines or filing into line. Wikshen was in, so he wouldn't be waiting for her when she arrived at the storage house, but his presence kept the shamans focused as they fussed at the pledges on either side of his throne, allowing her to sneak by with ease. As usual, she couldn't see through his veils of smoke and shadow.

Outside the main door, Kalea shrugged away from the group of chatty witches who made their way toward the nave. After living in Wikhaihli for two weeks, this new world grew small. Many of the faces she recognized, and they could easily recognize her too. She ducked into the first shadow available, under the gallery that wrapped around the cloister, and hurried along, eyeballing alleys all the way. Now to remember which alley hid Dorhen's storage shed…

She couldn't keep her eyes from shifting left and right. Where *was* Dyii? He must've earned a bad punishment after their little incident, especially with Dorhen as this place's leader. A shiver ran through her. So odd to consider that revelation. *Her* Dorhen—the elf who couldn't find his place in the Lightlands, in Norr, or in Kalea's religious institution, now sat as the deity lavished and adored by this community. She wouldn't let him leave the storage house until he'd spilled all she wanted to know.

Bowaen nudged Del and nodded to the alley across the cloister. "Hey. There she goes."

"What's she up to, you think?" the younger man asked.

Kalea disappeared around the corner, into the shadows. Bowaen grunted as he watched her. "She really didn't have any news to share?"

"Yeah, but I don't like it. I don't trust that girl at all. She's hiding something," Del said.

"Where's Gaije?"

"Tool shed, putting up his rake. Why?"

Bowaen drew his hood down tight. "Because we're about to have a little trouble. Look." He pointed to Wikshen, strutting toward the same alley Kalea had gone into. His black cloak couldn't do much to hide his tall stature and the streamers of blue hair catching the breeze.

"Oh, God—"

Bowaen cut off Del's curse with another nudge. "Go get Gaije. We're about to get into it if that freak means Kalea any harm."

The storage house still bore dark, dried bloodstains in jagged rivulets on the wooden platform from when Dorhen had…torn his own arm open with his teeth. Kalea shivered continuously in this place. Something disturbing plagued her elf.

She sat quietly on the platform beside the bloodstains for some amount of time. She couldn't guess how long and forgot to try counting. The door creaked open. Her heart stopped. She tensed up. It could be Dorhen, but it could also be anyone else in the world.

His figure darkened the doorframe. His pointed ears stuck out to each side of his silhouette. He stepped in, carefully closed the door behind him, and went straight to the candle on the crate.

Kalea wanted to speak, but her head went blank. Her belly flared with all sorts of excitement.

Click. Click. Click. Sharp little sparks of light illuminated him for split seconds as he worked the striker. The flame erupted on the wick, and he winced away from it before standing up in the soft lighting. His face was somber. He didn't look at her. He moved to the opposite side of the room and sat on the ground, leaving plenty of space between him and the flame, and also between the two of them.

"Dorhen," she finally said.

"My name's Wikshen now," he said quickly.

Silence.

"I disagree," she replied. "Nonetheless…" She stood up and slowly approached him. His eyes roved over her, perhaps seeing the gown he'd given her, before turning away again and avoiding her eye contact. "Please tell me," she said. "Tell me what happened to you."

He closed his eyes and leaned his head against the wall, resting his arms on his knees. "So that's it," he said. "You really want to know."

"Of course."

"It's in the past."

"Yes, but Dorhen, you must understand my confusion. What's going on? Please tell me, I beg you!"

He closed his eyes against her raised voice, waved a hand, and said, "I saw the girls from your convent."

Kalea covered her mouth with both hands. She dropped to her knees beside him, careful not to miss a word. When he didn't say any more, she asked, "Where were they? Are they okay? What about Rose? What happened in the convent with all of you?"

The muscles around his mouth firmed even more and continued until they twitched. He stared hard at the wall to his side. "They…" He paused to close his eyes and draw in a breath. "They were swaying on their feet." He huffed out the breath he'd taken in.

"What does that mean?"

"They didn't look good. They stood in line for…" He leaned forward and made a choking sound.

"Dorhen." She put her hands on his shoulder, over the strands of his shimmering blue hair. His shoulder… He felt different, harder and bigger than she remembered from when they had embraced at the forest wishing well. Her heart hammered in her chest, hitting against her ribs.

"Lamrhath," Dorhen added.

I know that name. Where had she heard it, though?

When he finally met her eyes, only turning far enough to show one of his, it was reddened. "Lamrhath has them," he clarified.

She echoed the name. "Where are they?"

"I don't know." He dropped his knees to cross his legs and buried his face in his hands. Slowly, his fingers curled into fists, squeezing his hair.

Reactively, Kalea rubbed his shoulder. She expected him to pull away, but he'd yet to do so. "Dorhen," she said his name in a breath, "tell me what happened to you. Why are you like this?"

He shrugged away. "Don't."

"Don't what?"

His body tensed up harder. "Don't make me revisit…" Something resembling a sob came out next. "Look, it's done, okay?"

"What's done? You have to try to explain it. Please." Her heart breaking for him, Kalea fell against him and planted her lips on his shoulder. She wrapped her arm around to his opposite shoulder. "I want to help you." She nuzzled his neck, burying her face in his hair.

"You can't," he growled.

She stroked the back of his hair and took his wrist in attempt to pull his hand away from his face. "Look at me," she whispered.

Finally, he did. He let her take his hand and he dropped the other one.

"What happened to you?" she asked again.

"Kalea." His eyes misted over, his whisper weak. The candlelight ignited the blue-green flash in his eyes. "Forget about your sisters."

Kalea's mouth dropped open, but she refused to make a sound or challenge his statement.

"They're gone." The sad, empty light in his eyes was too much. Her lip quivered. She couldn't help but believe him. Her own emotions and determination would drive her disagreement, but for now, she needed to hear every little word he offered.

"Start with the night of the attack on my convent. What happened after I ran away?"

Fighting to keep his composure, Dorhen stared at the wall and shook his head. "They took us away to another place—through a magic door. I have no idea where we wound up."

Kalea nodded slowly. "Okay, and then…"

"And then everything gets hazy for me… They made me breathe smoke. It smelled like flowers. And I lost the ability to think clearly." He swallowed. "And I did something you wouldn't like."

"What?"

A gust of wind whistled through the small holes in the building. Kalea shivered, but not from cold.

"I didn't mean to… I was confused. I thought you were with me for a moment. I swore it was your voice…"

A thick knot tightened in Kalea's throat. "And what about my sisters?"

Dorhen paused to look at her. Kalea shook her head. His lips held open, poised to speak again. She didn't want him to. "I lay down and let some woman I didn't know touch me."

Exactly what Kalea didn't want to hear. Her equanimity faded and cracked. Her eyes watered. She covered her mouth with both hands again, half-fearful she'd throw up.

His voice dragged lifelessly. "I thought you'd want to know. It's my confession."

A sob escaped her throat as Kalea bowed her head. "Dorhen-you-don't-have-to-confess-anymore—" she said within another sob. She clamped her mouth shut. Now she couldn't keep calm, and Dorhen had gone blank.

"I'm sorry," he whispered.

When she looked at him again, glistening wetness covered his cheeks. Tears dripped off his chin. Kalea couldn't deal with this right now. She'd found Dorhen, yet he couldn't seem to fill her loneliness as she'd hoped he would. A bizarre feeling. A nightmarish feeling. She couldn't speak yet, so they sat in silence.

She attempted another look at him, a difficult effort. He was no longer the sweet and innocent elf she left behind. More than his appearance had changed. He'd accumulated a world more experiences in such a narrow timeframe. Then again, so had she.

Her voice scratched as she said, "You didn't tell me how you got this way. Why is your hair blue? Why do you look so different?"

He took a long breath through his nose. "That memory is murkier than the other I told you." He thought for a moment. "My father was there."

"Your father?" Kalea repeated without actually registering the words. He'd said when he met her that he had no family. His father had murdered his mother by setting their house on fire.

Dorhen nodded. "He was in the place where I went. He wore a red robe like the sorcerers there. He's a sorcerer too."

"Dear Creator," Kalea murmured.

Dorhen put his hand out and posed his crooked fingers wide as if he held an apple. "My father had this…black ball, and he…" He frowned and waved his hand back and forth. "He juggled it or something. And he threw it wide. It was made of glass. It shattered next to me. I don't remember much after that. Now there's a voice in my head that calls me a fool all the time."

"A voice in your head." Kalea's stomach dropped.

"Yes," he said. "Its name is Wik. It tells me I'm a god."

"Dorhen…" Kalea's voice died on the end of his name. In a breath, she squeezed out, "You're possessed." She knew all about demonic possessions from her religion's lore. Demons were a deadly business.

She gasped when she realized what she'd been doing in this place. On the first day, a shaman had shoved her head down to bow three times: once for the pixie, again for the host who lent his body, and a third for Wikshen. Finally, it all made sense! Dorhen was the host body! He was possessed by a pixie—the worst type of possession! No one survived this condition!

Kalea shook her head, once again without words. She wouldn't believe it—she couldn't!

"The voice tells me I deserve the world," Dorhen continued, paying no mind to Kalea's external show of emotion. "It tells me to take anything I want and to enjoy myself." He turned to face her. "To do as I wish."

He reached out and took her numb hand. "This place is mine," he said to her, his expression hardening. His eyes turned intense. "I used to fight against the pixie, and it paid off, because now I mostly have control."

"Mostly?"

He went on, "Things are much better lately. I have great skills now. These people follow me. And now you're here."

"Dorhen, you have to—"

He cut her off. "I realized after you showed up that I can and will take care of you just like I wanted to do before."

She stared at his serious expression.

He spoke again before she could. "You have to keep being a maid, though, and stop angering the shamans. I don't like it when they punish you." He put his hand on the back of her head. He pulled her closer to him, but stopped before they could reach kissing distance. He stroked her hair. "I'm going to take care of you," he said again, his voice low, resonating, and ragged.

She still couldn't find her own opinion in her numbness, much less share it. She couldn't even feel the tears rolling down her cheeks.

"Back in the Lightlands, I couldn't get close enough to keep you safe. I held no power. It's different here," he said. "I've realized lately how much better we have it in my tower. We can live in it together." He combed his fingers through her hair, and then traced one along her cheek to her chin. "I won't let any man touch you ever again, because now I'm strong."

Dorhen's hand trailed from her cheek, his fingers barely grazing her skin, down her neck and farther...

The door slammed open, and both of them jumped.

"Get away from her!"

"Bowaen?" Kalea stood up, shocked. He brandished Hathrohjilh— and Gaije held his bow taut with a magical green-flame arrow at the ready.

Kalea put her arms out and jumped in front of Dorhen. "No! Put your weapons down!"

Dorhen whipped in front of her, and Kalea fought him for the foreground.

"Get back, Kalea!" Bowaen ordered.

"Listen to me!" she shot back, darted to Gaije, and wrestled the bow to make him lower it.

Dorhen stepped in to stop her, and the situation heightened in confusion and panic. They became a large tangle of arms and shouting until Kalea's closeness forced Bowaen to lower his sword and Gaije to let his bowstring slacken. Del stood off to the side with his pipe poised.

Now locked in a cage of aggressive masculine arms, Kalea took the first quiet moment to say, "Bowaen. This is Dorhen."

Bowaen took a moment to process her words before his rugged face scrunched. "Dorhen? What are you talking about? Dorhen's dead."

The new confusion offered a better silence for her to speak. "No, he's not," she panted. Alarm and adrenaline replaced her earlier dread. "This is Dorhen. Dorhen became Wikshen. They are one and the same."

"Kalea, who are they?" Dorhen asked, his demeanor menacingly calm. He loomed over the lot of them, watching the exchange. One of his hands gripped her shoulder, ready to pull her away if any violence erupted.

She turned to him. "These men are my friends. They won't hurt me." She turned back to Bowaen. "Dorhen means no harm—he won't hurt me, so let's relax and talk."

Bowaen did pull back to create a little space between them all, but he scoffed and barked, "You're crazy! That can't be him, he's nothing like you described! Besides, we already killed him once!"

Kalea cringed, standing between them all, making sure to have equal space between her and the others at each side. "They traveled with me all the way from the Lightlands when I searched for you," she said to Dorhen. "They really are friends, and because they're my friends, they're your friends."

Dorhen's eyes centered on Gaije, whose face showed the reddest anger she'd ever seen. His hands fidgeted on his bow and arrow. It hit her: Gaije had witnessed Dorhen kidnap Mhina.

She whirled to face Dorhen. "Do you remember kidnapping a little elf-girl?"

Dorhen's eyes widened and his facial muscles slackened. "That wasn't me."

Gaije exploded, drawing his bow. The ethereal green flame erupted on the arrowhead again. "You lie!"

Kalea reached to stop Gaije.

Dorhen lunged to put himself between her and the arrow.

Bowaen shouted.

Del shouted.

Someone's elbow knocked Kalea to the side, and she hit the dirt floor. Bowaen and Gaije both pinned Dorhen to the ground with their weapons pointed at his head.

Kalea shrieked, "Stop!" She scrambled to her feet, and Del held her back with his forearm across her clavicle.

"Sorry," he said to her. "Bowaen told me to keep you out of the way."

She ignored Del. "Stop," she said again, and tried her best to explain. "He really is Dorhen." Her tears fell through the rest of her speech. "Don't you see? Every time you move, he only moves to protect me. He loves me. Dorhen's possessed. That's why he did bad things in the past.

He said it wasn't him—his demon acted for him, moving his body. That's what happens in a possession."

Bowaen and Gaije half-turned to listen to her.

"If we can all calm down," she continued, "Dorhen might tell us where to find Mhina."

Gaije pulled his bow tighter. "So tell us."

Dorhen's nostrils flared as he lay on the floor under their weapons. His chest rose and fell heavily. "The sorcerers," he said.

"We know that much," Bowaen growled down at him. "Be more specific."

"A faction called Ilbith," he said.

"You mean you don't have her as a prisoner here?" Bowaen asked. Better that he did the talking because he could keep a cooler head than Gaije.

"The *sorcerers* have her. I'm not a sorcerer. They took her away from me soon after I…grabbed her." His language tightened Gaije's bowstring even more. The tension had leaked from Dorhen's body, and he now lay limply with his arms on the ground. He closed his eyes and breathed for a moment. "If I can remember right, the voice in my head planned to give the girl to Lamrhath."

"You hear that?" Kalea said to the group. "Mhina and the novices are held by a person named Lamrhath in the Ilbith sorcery faction." She jerked out of Del's hold.

Bowaen and Gaije turned their stares back to Dorhen.

"All right, so where—"

Dorhen kicked Gaije in the leg with his heel and simultaneously tipped his bow, causing him to misfire. With a coordinated thrash of his arms and legs, Dorhen cleared the other men from his space, tripping Bowaen and leaping to his feet. During his movement, his arm grazed Bowaen's blade and a cascade of blood spilled down. Gaije's arrow flew into a stack of crates, and an eager flame ignited to engulf the dry wood. Another panic of arms and shouting followed.

Kalea stood gaping. It all happened too fast. One of the men swept her up. Her feet left the ground and she found herself upside down, draped over a strong shoulder. With such strength and speed, it couldn't have been anyone else but Dorhen. He carried her out, put her feet on the ground, and dragged her roughly through the alley as the fire raged behind them.

She planted her feet in a wide stance. "What about my friends?" She tried to pull away, but he held her with impossible strength. With his teeth clenched, he jerked her forward.

Bowaen, Del, and Gaije's voices rang in the open air behind her. Yelping against Dorhen's rough treatment, she twisted around in time to see them stagger out of the fiery building, all three of them coughing.

"Wait!" she demanded of Dorhen, pulling backward against his hold. "I need to... Bow!"

Pausing at the mouth of the alley with smoke filling the space behind them, Bowaen was pointing at her and Dorhen while saying something to the others. Meanwhile, Del was rubbing his eyes, and Gaije had dropped into a squat to continue coughing. Otherwise, they appeared all right.

Sighing her relief, Kalea gave up her fight against Dorhen, who didn't seem to care if her friends survived at all. He hauled her onward, looking paler than she'd ever seen him, with a glisten of moisture around his edges, especially on his lip. His face remained hard as he dragged her all the way back to the tower, giving her not a fraction of a minute to breathe, much less attempt to run back to her friends.

A walking cloud had moved over the complex, preventing all but a few people outside from seeing them. The sight of Wikshen yanking a woman through the streets stirred a huge interest in the bystanders who did.

Dorhen opened the grand door to the nave so roughly a crack sounded in the wood at one of its hinges. If they had made much of a spectacle out in the mist, they certainly did in the nave where all the pledges and shamans went about their business.

"Mastaren?" Knilma said when she managed to hobble close enough with her cane. Otherwise, the whole place fell silent. Her eyes skimmed to his arm, where blood ran down and dripped off his fingers.

"Don't ask," he said with a rough edge to his voice that sent a spark through Kalea's abdomen. Some of the concubine candidates were present to share in her feeling with outward shivers of their own. He shoved Kalea forward. "I found this maid outside, but don't punish her. It wasn't her fault."

"Whose fault was it?"

He walked toward the back corridors with long, fierce strides. "Forget it." He paused and turned around. "But there's a fire in an alley. Put it out."

He turned and walked on, leaving Kalea with the gawking crowd. Knilma turned her scrutinizing gaze to her. Kalea didn't want to have to stand there and make up some kind of story that would protect her friends but match Dorhen's statement, so she curtsied awkwardly and ran to the maid's dorm. She couldn't help but notice that Dorhen didn't order the arrest of her three friends.

Chapter 13
Short Hair

Lehomis turned the little spool of fishing line over in his hand, his cold pipe held between his teeth. One of his clan's *saehgahn*, a husband in his mature years, waited with crossed arms. He'd made the fishing line carefully from silkworm gland. With this, Lehomis could catch fish to supplement meals for his household during the upcoming lean months. Satisfied with the product, Lehomis reached into his pocket for one of the old treasures he'd found in his storage trunk, a shiny hairpin from the Darklands.

"How's this?" he asked the *saehgahn*, holding the trinket out on an open palm.

As the *saehgahn* looked at the thing, his face flared red.

At his expression, Lehomis shrugged. "Sorry it's not anything more useful. Should make your wife happy if you gift it to her." His mouth spread wide mischievously. "Maybe you'll get another child after giving her this."

"That's just it, Elder," the *saehgahn* said. "The other day, my wife returned from the Desteer hall with her hair cut short."

Lehomis's mouth slackened around his pipe; his hand relaxed and curled over the hairpin. "Cut short," he mimicked.

"Yes." The *saehgahn* nodded with rapid tension. "I'm upset about this—to me, her hair was…" His words stopped, but he put his hands out helplessly.

"You mean to say you liked her hair?" Lehomis offered. He made sure to choose his words and gestures carefully, because if he indicated that he himself thought this other *saehgahn*'s wife's hair was lovely, he could be lawfully, albeit brutally, attacked on the spot by her husband and have to fight for his life. All he wanted right now was some fishing line.

The other *saehgahn*'s hands dropped. "Yes, I did."

Of course, he did! Long, lustrous hair was the main feature female elves could flaunt in their culture besides their pretty faces and warm smiles. Looking at the back of a *faerhain*'s head in public, at her silky hair, was every young *saehgahn*'s secret pleasure. Married *saehgahn* enjoyed the privilege of running their fingers through it.

Lehomis shook his head, making a show of sympathy for his

fellow clansman. He'd already caught whispers on the wind about the new protocol and had eavesdropped on *faerhain* arguing with Desteer members about the new haircutting ritual. Seemed like every year the Desteer thought up a horrid new rule to keep *saehgahn* and *faerhain* from enjoying each other's company. Now they were stepping in between married couples and had robbed this poor fellow of his reposeful right to run his fingers through his wife's hair on cozy, private nights.

Shoving the hairpin back into his pocket, Lehomis slapped the other *saehgahn*'s shoulder. "I might have something else for you, then," he said, and sifted through a different pocket on his long, green tabard.

He took out a little drawstring bag full of brass buttons—something virtually unheard of in Norr. They tied all their clothes together with string instead. Maybe if things had fallen out differently a few hundred years ago, if the chain of wars between Sharr and Norr hadn't happened, they might've traded a lot more and elves might all be using buttons today. Good for Lehomis they didn't, though.

He presented the shiny things, recently polished before he had taken them out of the house, and explained how they worked. Despite his gloomy mood, the *saehgahn* took the deal, and Lehomis walked away with his fishing line. Now to find someone who would trade for some hooks.

Along his journey through the bustle in the village square, Lehomis saw what they'd been talking about. Not one or two but *three faerhain* sported short hair shaped around the curve of their heads, no longer than the jaw, which easily showed off their ears. The sight stunned him, and not in a good way. Several young *saehgahn* stopped with him to stare in shock. The fact that the short-haired *faerhain* wore the bright colors of the unmarried put a twinge of sadness in his heart. A shame, but Lehomis couldn't imagine it causing any *saehgahn* to turn down their marriage proposals. The *saehgahn* longed to marry regardless.

"Do you like the fish?" Lehomis leaned over his plate later that evening to ask Tirnah. He'd managed to catch two small trout out of the river and cook them up himself for his household females.

Tirnah finally stirred out of the odd silence in which she'd been nibbling at her food. "Oh, Grandfather, sorry. My thoughts distracted me. What was your question?"

Anonhet sat next to Tirnah, looking at her with a caring gaze.

"Are you not hungry?" Lehomis asked her. He'd given Tirnah the biggest piece of fish…at Anonhet's recommendation.

"Actually, I'm starving, Grandfather. Thank you for catching this fish for us." She bowed her head deeply over her steaming plate.

For the moment, Lehomis forgot about his own plate. They sat on the skin rug, eating under the pavilion of the outdoor kitchen. Anonhet had lit the candle lanterns dangling at each corner for extra light. Crickets sang all around them under the distant sound of a neighbor practicing a wind instrument. A soft *too tii! too tii!* kept the silence away. The breeze of the new summer wafted crisp and fresh.

Lehomis leaned over on his hand, searching Tirnah for whatever could be bothering her right now. Maybe she missed Trisdahen, in which case, Lehomis didn't want to pry. Beside Tirnah, Anonhet displayed her own tension.

"I went to town for fishing implements," Lehomis said to both of them, "and one of the *saehgahn* told me his wife now has short hair. I also saw other *faerhain* in town with short hair. Do either of you know what that's about?"

Anonhet opened her mouth, but Tirnah beat her to the punch. "The Desteer have been asking us to partake in a new haircutting ritual at Faerhain Devotion, Grandfather."

Once again, this was not quite news to him. "Do you know why?"

Tirnah nodded with a quick blink of her eyes. "They don't want the *saehgahn* to"—she lowered her voice— "*er* over *faerhain*, married or unmarried."

"The humans have a word called 'lust,'" Lehomis explained. "You can say that instead of you-know-what."

"Lust," Tirnah parroted. "That's the reason for haircutting."

Lehomis gestured to both of them. "Have the Desteer pressured either of you to cut your hair?"

Tirnah and Anonhet both nodded faintly.

"At the last Faerhain Devotion," Anonhet said, "they were asking all the *faerhain* to partake. When they started walking toward Tirnah and me, we hastily slipped out as if important chores awaited."

"Good," Lehomis said. All *faerhain* attended Faerhain Devotion in Norr, a weekly ritual to keep them close to the Bright One. It also gave them a chance to ask the Desteer for advice on what might be bothering them during any given week. When Lehomis was a young *saeghar*, he had once overheard *faerhain* whispering about one meeting. He gleaned from the whispers, to his great curiosity, that the Desteer were handing out advice on how to "soothe their husbands." Apparently, things had changed. Now the females were learning how to push their husbands away and make them disinterested in their hair.

"You did the right thing." Lehomis left it at that.

They all continued eating. When his food was almost gone, Lehomis announced, "I'm going to Theddir soon."

The two females' heads popped up to stare at him.

"Only for a week or so," he added. "I didn't have enough horses to send with the traders, so I'm going down there to sell some of my trinkets for money, which I will use to buy the clan some flour and dried goods and such."

Tirnah closed her mouth and spread her lips, not quite smiling. "Whatever we must do, Grandfather," she said, and bowed her head again. "Anonhet and I will forage all summer and dry some mushrooms for our pantry, won't we, lass?"

"Of course," Anonhet responded.

Lehomis nodded to them in return. "We'll be fine and comfortable this winter."

Chapter 14
Dark Pits

Of all the dark, unfriendly corridors and shafts she'd seen in the Ilbith tower so far, nothing turned Vivene's stomach or crept into her nightmares quite so often as the Grave. The man pushing the wheelbarrow chatted beside her on the way to Ilbith's lowest level, clearly not as anxious as she. The smell became apparent two floors before they reached this cavernous level. Instead of stairs, a spiraling slope through the tower's center led down for wheeled vessels to access it from any floor.

"Oh, dear Creator," Vivene groaned with a lurch of her stomach. She buried her nose in the cleaning rag she carried.

"Creator?" the man said. He shook his head and shot her a wary glare. "Don't be sayin' that, girl. I'd hate to see you get thrown down there too." Hands clamped firmly on the wheelbarrow's handles, he shuddered and hunched his shoulders. He served the upper class too. As a general rule, the servants regarded each other as family.

The man continued, his ragged beard flopping limply under his chin, "We are only allowed to say things like 'blessed kingsorcerer,' or 'dear Naerezek.'" His eyes shifted to her again. "If they hear you invoking the name of deities they don't favor, you'll get beat pretty bad, and they won't care if it kills ya."

As hard as Vivene clamped her nose inside the rag, he spoke despite the noxious open air. The dead body in the wheelbarrow didn't seem to bother him either. She'd helped him load it up and cover it over with a tarp. Just another poor servant who'd died from an illness currently circulating in the south wing's lower levels. Vivene didn't like going there either, but she and some other servants had to make their rounds to feed the sick ones and see if anyone had died the night before.

As the Grave's cavernous space opened up far and deep below the tower, her stomach churned and sank lower.

"I see ye going pale," her companion said. "Have you been here before?"

"I have."

"Good," he said. "I'll need your help tipping 'im over the edge, but don't get dizzy on me. Can't risk you falling in."

At the edge of the enormous pit, her companion finally put his bandanna over his nose. The servants' noses must be dulled after breathing all the bad smells of Ilbith for years, including each other's body odor. This was where they dumped all of Ilbith's garbage, including the dead. Expired sorcerers too, although she'd also heard of sorcerers' bodies being kept cold for long periods before being offered up to evil spirits to feast upon. That thought made her shiver harder.

The uneven, rocky path sloped downward, as if the Grave wanted to suck them in. One could easily slip and roll down or become dizzy and lose their footing thanks to the putrid air, which was so foul it stung her nose and scratched her throat. Not to mention she always heaved up mouthfuls of bile. Her companion waited for her to compose herself, watching her over his covered nose.

"You all right?"

She put up her finger and spat.

"We're almost done. C'mon, take the other handle." He removed the stained tarp to reveal the dead old man curled and kinked in the wheelbarrow's narrow space. He'd already stiffened, and his face had turned a pale yellow.

"Oh, dear Creator," Vivene said again by sheer force of habit and turned away—which did no good, because the only other thing to look at was the Grave itself, the lowest point in Ilbith, the center of all filth and stench.

The Grave's chasm didn't span as wide as it was deep, and she couldn't see much of what lay beyond the shadows, thank goodness. The light points shooting through the cave walls from the outside could almost reveal a glimpse, but she didn't venture to look down long enough to find out.

It took a lot of muscle for her to help the man dump the cadaver without also losing the wheelbarrow, but they managed. Vivene kept her spine bent backward to resist stumbling forward on the steep slope that ended in the cliff-like edge, balancing to stay safe. She prayed to the One Creator to keep her tattered suede shoes firmly gripping the stone floor. The worn soles proved slick on many of the tower's various floor surfaces.

The dead man slid off and spent a few seconds in silent freefall before the final echoing *smack!* of his heavy body and knobby bones coming to an abrupt stop. Vivene winced at the sound, and a sharp shiver followed. She wouldn't recover from the residual feeling until she got several stories back up into the tower.

Her companion's arm came around her shoulders. "Come on now," he said. "No sense wasting another second in this hellish place."

They didn't share any words on the long walk back up, but they walked together nonetheless. All the servants, they stood together.

Back in the big kitchen in the lower levels of Ilbith, Vivene hurried straight to the waiting bucket of water to splash her face, followed by a second and third time. She stood over the rippling water and breathed. The phantom scent of the Grave burned on, along with the dead stare of the old man in the wheelbarrow.

She closed her eyes and breathed some more; water dripped off her chin. In the kitchen, people moved around her with the dreaded haste of poor souls who didn't like the severe punishment that came with serving the sorcerers their dinner a minute too late. At least she had a better appointment after this, one to help her ease the horror of Ilbith.

The sugared glaze covering the top of the warm, baked roll made Vivene's jaws tingle with pleasure when she bit into it. She hadn't eaten treats like this in years, not since she was a small child at her father's house. She let the rapturous feeling take her over, and for one sweet moment, she let herself forget where she was, where she'd been, and what she'd do after. She chewed the soft, sticky bread slowly and let it glide down her throat to settle in her starving stomach.

"Mmm," she hummed.

The hands that hooked around her body brought her back down to earth, but she ignored them. Another bite let her spirit float to the ceiling and swim around in delight.

"I thought you'd like that, my little dumpling," the raspy voice from a throat that smoked too much whispered in her ear from behind.

Vivene gave the next bite her full attention, attempting to ignore him further.

The hands began pulling the laces slowly out of her bodice. With no choice in the matter, she let them. This middle-aged sorcerer gave her treats in exchange for spending a little extra time in his room. By now, she knew he enjoyed watching her eat as much as he enjoyed groping her soft body. An upper-level sorcerer, he had access to the elite kitchen. He didn't even order her to turn in a favor token in exchange for the treats.

Vivene couldn't deny that she didn't mind spending the evening with him either. His alcohol breath wafted from the direction of his greasy, swarthy face, but at least he wasn't the worst company she'd shared, and he offered the benefit of the delectable desserts she'd otherwise never expect to enjoy.

Standing hotly behind her, he dipped his finger in a bowl of custard and offered it to her mouth. This, Vivene didn't care for, but it was part of the game. From there, it escalated and advanced through the usual process.

Then Vivene stepped out of his door to resume her duties in the musty, unfriendly Ilbith halls. She took a moment to lean against the wall and collect herself, satisfied in more ways than hunger. All morning long, she'd looked forward to visiting this chamber. She harbored no love for the sorcerer within. Bargo was his name, and he stank, looked like a boiled ham, and harbored a little too much interest in Vivene's rounded curves. The way he watched and groped her as she ate was…creepy. The food, however, banished the hunger she'd been used to since the convent's troubles started—a miracle!

And the sex… She liked it. Which was wrong. Her feeling of satisfaction defied everything she'd been brought up to believe as a religious woman, as well as a normal, respectable woman with pride and standards. If this wasn't a sin worthy of the worst of penances, she didn't know what was. She could hear Kalea's disapproving voice in her head, urging her to confess. She'd seen the lavender scars crisscrossing that girl's back at bath time. Vivene never wanted those scars; she couldn't stand pain and didn't confess a crumb's worth compared to the amount Kalea did. All the novices confessed weekly, and Vivene had always offered petty little incidents like being jealous of another girl's pretty hair or telling a frivolous lie. She never whispered in the confessional about the book she'd found in a vestal's room, and how tingly it made her feel, and how it inspired her to perform little experiments on herself deep into the night as everyone else slept.

Nevertheless, if she could confess and go back to being a silly girl in a convent, she would. At the same time, she anticipated tomorrow's session with Bargo.

Primora collapsed onto the altar after spending all night tied to a trellis. Her mother wrung the black ribbons that were used to bind Primora's wrists in place, on the edge of tears.

"It doesn't make sense!"

Ignoring her mother's incessant lamentations, she curled into a ball and shivered, surrounded by freshly cut herbs and cold dishes of food Wikshen had failed to come and eat. Her arms and legs tingled from being tied down so long in a decorative pose as yet another offering to their Mastaren. She too wanted to cry, but not for the same reason. She'd spent far too many hours in the dark silence by herself.

Though she'd been trained for this very thing, all the years of holding Kraft Positions and sitting in the dark basement hardly helped her keep her sanity. Those dishes of wasted food, the nuts and berries, the cold cup of tea they'd fixed for him… Primora was one of them. Nothing but an offering to be devoured by a dark entity—if he did exist. He didn't, and somehow that made her feel worse. This was what her mother thought of her: a piece of meat to offer to a false deity.

Primora dragged herself off of the platform, eager to act and be treated like a human again. She aimed her stance at the ladder leading to the outside world, where the living went on with their lives. The sun was rising. Another day approached, bringing new hope—and a visit with Jonaril. But there sat her poor mother, wrenching the ribbons between her fists in defeat.

Primora patted her back. "We'll be fine," she offered. She couldn't promise it, but those words were all she could offer.

"Why didn't he come?" the old woman asked, looking more haggard today than yesterday.

Maybe he doesn't exist. "Maybe he wanted a different meal."

Her mother nodded. "I'll make salmon with walnuts and dill next time."

Primora stifled her sigh. Of course, she wouldn't give up. Primora would find herself tied up again in no time. Hopefully not tomorrow.

"Or maybe…" Before reaching the ladder, Primora turned around to hear her. "Maybe my daughter didn't say her chants right. Did you remember your mantras?"

"Of course." Primora couldn't keep the wobble out of her voice. She hadn't been reciting her lines, she'd been pondering her sad existence instead.

The older woman stood up to face her. "Don't lie to me, girl. Did you even keep your pose? Legs open, bosom forward as he likes it?"

She swallowed. "You found me posing in the right form, didn't you? It's not like I could change positions on my own."

Her mother gave a heavy sigh. "You're right." She stroked Primora's arm. "How could I question my daughter, the finest Wikshonite this land will ever see? The sacrifice that'll save us all. Possibly even First Sister if he hasn't claimed her yet."

That's what Primora was in her family's religious dynamic: not a witch or a shaman but a *sacrifice*. Her whole existence rested on being beautiful and smelling good, and sitting her rump right on his altar as one of his offerings, waiting for him to come and force himself on her. It made her shudder to think of it. If she wasn't ready to make love to Jonaril, why would she want to do it with a monstrous "wild man" deity? She could imagine Wikshen's red glowing eyes and horns curling out from his skull like a goat, rancid breath steaming from behind razor-sharp teeth.

The conversation had gone on long enough, so Primora turned back to the ladder, but her mother caught her arm.

"I have a better idea."

"What?"

"Maybe we don't to need call him to us."

Primora's head sprang into rapid nods.

Her mother followed up, "Maybe we'll go to Wikshen."

"Go to Wikshen? You mean to go to Wikhaihli?"

"I do."

Primora stuttered. "B-but it must be on the other side of the world. How can two women—?"

"Falli and Cygnet will come too."

"How can four women, two of them with creaky knees, make such a long pilgrimage?"

"Would you rather stay here until the sorcerers decide they like you?"

She'd rather marry Jonaril. "I can't do th—"

"What?" Her mother's face tightened fiercely in the expression that usually preceded a beating. Being in training for Wikshen's sacrifice hadn't been the easiest life Primora could imagine. In the tense split second of that stare, Primora's armpits dampened, and her lower back followed suit. Her sacrifice garb, which displayed her bare breasts despite its itchy feathers and strings of beads, wasn't the best outfit for a nervous sweat.

Primora twisted her comment into something else fast. "I can't think of a better destiny than to embrace Wikshen on such holy ground, possibly in his own bed. It makes my loins hunger for his sacred phallus already."

Success. Her mother's tense expression transitioned into a smile. "Of course, my dear. You're the most beautiful woman in this village. The women at Wikhaihli will be hard-pressed to take him in before you."

On her way out of the basement to visit Jonaril after donning real clothing, Primora's mind raced. Her life was about to change. At least Wikshen wasn't actually here. An even more religious life awaited her at Wikhaihli, and she'd have to leave Jonaril—but at least the sorcerers would be left behind! So many points to weigh. But suddenly her pace quickened as a new option entered her mind.

In the privacy of the forest, after the initial, desperate kisses of two lovers who hadn't seen each other in more than a day, Primora told him everything.

"If you come with us, I promise, Jonaril, I promise we'll marry. Secretly. No one has to know."

"But we'll have to live in the hive of witches?"

That part of her idea had twisted his face as soon as it left her mouth, making her feel instantly foolish. His question about the "witches" didn't sound good. Even though she'd tried to soften the idea of the Wikshonites to him before, it was still difficult for him to grasp the notion that it wasn't dangerous. He'd told her before that he and his father believed in wood fairies which helped their career as woodcutters. The wood fairies kept the trees growing strong, or so they believed. In addition to that, Jonaril had heard from a passing peddler of the "Great Sea," a water god who sounded amazing. So Jonaril also harbored an interest in seeing the ocean someday.

"It won't be a bad life, I promise."

"I don't know." Jonaril had done nothing but shake his head since she brought this up. "I don't consider hiding a marriage to the woman I love a good life."

"Well, what if it's the only life option we have? Besides, you said last time that we don't even have to be married because my mother and aunt never were."

He eyed her up and down. Her heart sped. Was he sizing her up, weighing his love for her? "I thought you wanted to marry me."

She wanted a life with Jonaril over the life of a celibate, naked altarpiece any day. In her desperation, she raised her shirt and showed him her breasts in the crisp breeze and radiant morning sun. It was what he wanted! He wanted to make love to her, so she said, "Here, I'm yours! Marry me now, right here, and consummate it! But come with us! I know you don't want to deal with the sorcerers anymore either."

His gaze dropped to what she showed him. She bit her lip, heart thundering now. She resisted looking down at herself in hesitance or self-consciousness. Better to keep up her confidence—or rather, her feigned confidence. She was the most beautiful woman in the village— she'd heard it many times. Jonaril himself had told her so, which meant he should like this! He'd always wanted to see her naked. Why wouldn't he?

He frowned. Gauging his reaction, Primora's frown followed. She lowered her shirt halfway, heart pounding.

"I thought you were better than...this!" He waved his hand at her body, and she dropped her shirt the rest of the way, her dignity used up. "You call that a marriage?"

"I thought you loved me!" Primora burst into tears at the end of her statement.

Still scoffing, he dropped to sit on a fallen log, shaking his head. "Thanks for the peek, but I always thought a marriage should be proper. Not secret, in a hive of witches."

Primora swallowed and wiped her eyes on her sleeve. "Don't you think a secret marriage is better than none at all, if two people love each other?"

"I don't know, Primora." He stood up. "I don't know. What I do know is that I don't want to go to Wikhaihli. Even if we had a casual arrangement, it would work out better here than at the center of your stern religion. Show me your breasts again if you change your mind about going."

He left her standing there.

Chapter 15
A God Resists

A horrible screaming led Kalea deeper into the basement. A man's scream. She bypassed the beggars and sick elderly asking her for a bowl of porridge. Before attempting to find a solution to their starvation, she had to find out who was screaming and what was wrong. The sound drew her all the way down to the morgue, where the hospital put the recently dead until a grave could be dug for them. She walked down the rows of bodies laid out on the floor, covered by sheets.

"Aaaaaahhhhh!"

Some man was suffering down here. She supposed he was having a gangrenous limb amputated or some such...but then she heard the voice of Father Rayum say, "Tie his hands to the post."

"Yes, Father," a younger priest answered.

Kalea nudged the door open a crack. "Father?" she asked, but he didn't answer in his deep concentration. He erupted in a string of prayers to the One Creator. It was an exorcism going on in the basement of the hospital. Kalea shivered in fear. She hadn't stumbled upon very many of these, maybe just one during her earlier trips to volunteer at the hospital.

The man in question screamed louder at the prayer. This one was bad, worse than what she'd seen before! She nudged the door open a tad farther, revealing more of the candlelit room and the foot of the bed. A large bare foot came into view, its ankle secured to the bedpost with rope.

How awful!

"How awful!" The younger priest echoed her inner voice.

At the end of his prayer, Father Rayum barked at the man to keep working. "Get more candles! This demon can't stand light. It's a pixie, so the body will need to be torched to dust to get rid of it."

"Yes, Father!" The younger priest flung the door open wide, startling Kalea, and flew past her, paying no mind to her intrusion.

Kalea's jaw dropped. "No!" she shrieked. The man tied to the bed was Wikshen, his blue hair stringy and hanging over his face. He was screaming in pain, yet at the same time smiling eerily. He regarded Kalea and suddenly laughed.

Kalea stepped back, shaking her head. This wasn't right. That wasn't who she had thought it was in the bed. She remembered something and looked behind her at all the dead shapes lying under yellow-stained sheets, some with old bloodstains.

"I remember now," she said to herself. "Dorhen's hiding under one of those. He followed me down here to play a prank or something. That silly boy."

She left Wikshen and Father Rayum to fight against each other's spiritual powers. "I'll find Dorhen and get out of here." She remembered which one he was too, and went right to him. "Get up now," she said. "It's not safe. We're going to the woods, remember?"

She peeled down his sheet to find him. Dead. Pale eyes staring at her. Skin grey and withering. Lips turning black. Kalea jumped in horror…

And woke herself up. Shaking. Covered in cold sweat. It was only a dream, though. She was back at Wikhaihli with the other sleeping maids. Only a dream. Dorhen was fine; he wasn't dead, he was…Wikshen.

He was possessed.

Kalea couldn't concentrate very well during Knilma's secret training, nor could she focus on coming up with good answers to the old woman's questions about what she had been doing in the storage shed when it went up in flames. Kalea gave flimsy answers, hoping her tone would sound nonchalant instead. Wikshen had sent her outside on an errand. She had an accident with the candle she used to see in the dark. Who cared about a forgotten storage house when Dorhen was possessed and they were all worshiping him? He was possessed by the worst type of spirit. He wouldn't survive this ordeal—she knew that from all of her religion's lore!

Another trip to the fountain shrine followed. Kalea finally found a short moment's respite from the visions of her nightmare when she breathed the incense wafting up from the fountain's base. She drank the water heartily and welcomed its mystical invigoration. It really worked to unwind her nerves a little.

How could she possibly help Dorhen now, knowing he was possessed? She could think about it a little later. She preferred to clear her mind for now and savor the tingles roving across her every limb.

Another dunk in the hot pool with the other girls who wanted to lie with Wikshen. They chatted and bickered and talked dreamily of him, of traits they loved about him. Apparently, they'd seen him in lighting that accentuated the rippling muscles down his torso. He'd had good muscles when he stripped for her as Dorhen; those muscles were bigger and more pronounced now.

They talked of his "sacred phallus" too, and made it known that he was no shyer now than when Kalea met him. Velle spoke in humming tones about the time she got a view of it during worship, and how well it stood for their impeccable performance. How honored she was to know that, even though he didn't use it. Kalea wanted to be angry about how they talked of his body. Instead, she felt something else…

"Have you ever caught him smiling?" Myrtle asked, and a mere few of the other concubines nodded. She hugged herself. "I love it, it's warm and special. I wish he'd smile for me."

Kalea had seen him smile—as Dorhen. She knew that smile very well. Their deity possessed some traits he'd taken on after his possession but retained many of the traits he used to have as a normal elf. She couldn't deny she also liked some of his new traits.

Her usual maid duties followed. Daily chores here were as peaceful and meditative as in the convent. She used them to keep herself calm. Contemplating Dorhen's problem seemed a good idea at this time too. Instead, images of Wikshen rolled through her head.

Sitting on her knees, she pushed the rag up and down on the floor. Up and down. Up. Down. Up. Down. Knilma made her practice similar motions every morning. Her thighs and buttocks had gained a measure of strength because of it. Her breaths came steadily and rhythmically, similar to another of Knilma's lessons.

The shaman had told her all of these combined practices could potentially soothe Wikshen's "sacred phallus," to put a blessing inside of her and make her into his adored partner, First Sister. She'd told Kalea to imagine herself perched on top of him, making up and down motions, remembering to breathe to keep the motion going longer. Wikshen wouldn't be touching her back in an official rite, but she'd be caressing him with her body lovingly, and her work would ignite a passion within him that would erupt as the most sacred and coveted token of their whole religion, which would be passed into her.

Kalea gasped out loud and had to stop her thought process. She clamped her mouth shut and looked around her. The idea of being with Wikshen was too exciting.

"Dorhen, I mean!" she hissed to herself. "Not Wikshen. Dorhen!"

She quieted herself at the chatter and footsteps approaching, and snatched her rag back up to look busy. Shamans and witches passed her in the corridor as she worked. When the prayer bell tolled outside, everyone dropped to their knees and bowed their heads, Kalea among them. She didn't recite the prayer to Wikshen in dread of an ecstasy ensuing, but doing this routine calmed her like all the others. She'd come to expect and rely on that religious calm.

As she got back to work on the old wooden floor, glazing a sheen of wetness over its dark surface, a shaman hurried past. The old woman kept her hood pulled low and muttered "Excuse me" in an odd voice. Kalea knew almost all of the shamans here, but this one's voice didn't register. She also lacked the aloofness of most shamans. Kalea raised her head, pausing in her mopping motion to eyeball the shaman, but when she quickly disappeared around the corner, Kalea shrugged off the oddness and continued her business.

In the usual garderobe where Kalea spoke to Del almost daily, a knock on the shutter caught her attention.

There he was.

When Kalea opened the window, she started at the hard, dirt-smudged faces of Bowaen and Gaije, and her surprise morphed quickly into a sigh of relief. "Are you all okay? Where's Del?" she asked.

"Never mind him," Bowaen grunted. "You want to hurry and explain to us what's going on with you and Wikshen?"

"I already told you. He's Dorhen."

Bowaen exchanged glances with Gaije.

"How did you know to find me in that storage place?"

"We saw you hurrying through the mist in the cloister," he said. "We kept back long enough to see Wikshen go down the same alley you did, so we knew you'd need our protection." Before Kalea could respond, he cut her off. "He's dangerous. Listen, girl, right now we're hatching a plan to get you out of there. We're also stowing away a good lot of supplies—"

"No."

Bowaen scrunched his face at her refusal. Gaije kept stern and silent beside him as always. "What do you mean, 'No?'"

"I'm not leaving. Dorhen needs my help," she said. "Besides, if I can talk to him again, he may reveal more information about Mhina."

Bowaen crossed his arms. "We already know who has her."

"Sure, but we don't know where."

"Maybe so," he shot back, "but as long as we ask around about Ilbith and the kingsorcerer, we should be able to scrape up some answers— especially if we go back to Alkeer. Lots of folk in that city might know somethin'—"

"I said no!" Kalea snapped.

Bowaen stared at her with his mouth agape. Gaije's expression also took on a worried or confused light.

"Kalea," Bowaen said, "I meant to explain this to you slowly once we got back on the road, but…"

Kalea waited, breathing hard through her nose. A firm frown tweaked her mouth.

"Wikshen's lyin' to you," he said, prompting the eruption of Kalea's anger. "He must have some kind of charm spell on you, because that creature…" Bowaen pointed toward the bigger side of the tower. "He can't be Dorhen. Your little brown-haired lover boy couldn't have changed into that…large, blue-haired thing you were cuddling in the storage house!"

"You don't know!" Kalea said.

"It's impossible," he added.

Reaching out the window, she pointed her finger at Bowaen's face. "You don't know anything… I know Dorhen. I know him very well."

"Didn't you say you talked to him for no more than a week after you met him?"

"Two weeks!"

Bowaen snorted, but no mirth touched his face. "Kalea… Wikshen is lying to you," he said again, enunciating his words.

Kalea slammed the shutter closed. Muffled swear words followed as she marched away. She would leave this place with Dorhen or not at all.

Living in Wikhaihli as Wikshen had its ups and downs. Dorhen had come into a new sense of being, one that felt fresh and alive. One that could use the darkness as a tool, hear the prayers of his followers, and fight to defend the woman he loved like never before. He'd become used to the comforts that came with it. He knew where Kalea was, and when she was safe and asleep. He even knew where she bathed…but tried hard not to wander that way.

He had come to question such progress, though. Why hadn't he needed to fight for control of his body lately? In fact, where was Wik's voice? He hadn't heard it in days.

I'm still here, fool.

He pursed his lips. *Of course you are.* He took care not to speak to Wik aloud with anyone nearby. Currently, Knilma walked beside him, droning on and on in the underground halls of Wikhaihli.

Wik, he said quickly before going back to blissfully ignoring the obnoxious spirit, *why've you been so quiet? Why haven't you tried to dominate my hand?*

Wik gave him its signature sandy laughter. *You don't need me so long as you're practicing your Kraft.*

What did that mean? Dorhen asked that question, and Wik chose not to answer. The spirit could never be counted on, which had been an annoyance in the past when Dorhen had gotten lost shadow traveling. Nonetheless, if using Kraft kept Wik quiet, opened up his freedom to control his own body unhindered, and made him strong enough to protect Kalea, he couldn't disagree with it too much.

"Are you listening, Mastaren?" Knilma asked, then went back into her speech. "I said, the girl claimed an ecstasy caught her in the cloister and she ran to the storage house."

Knilma was still on that subject. The shamans had been hounding Kalea for answers about yesterday's events. He supposed he couldn't blame their curiosity, but he really preferred they leave her alone. He nodded firmly and avoided all eye contact.

"She lit a candle," Knilma went on, "and it tipped over."

"Everything she told you is correct," he said, walking with his eyes set forward.

"What's funny, though," Knilma began, and stumbled slightly. "Mastaren, could you slow down please?"

He finally realized how fast he was walking, as if trying to outwalk the conversation. He didn't like Knilma's treatment of Kalea, and kept away from her to spare her from the attention of the shamans. Such hesitance had kept him from putting a stop to her chime lashings, and he mentally lashed himself for allowing her such pain—not to mention that her screams' vibration through the window glass had jolted his cock to full awareness as a bonus to his whirling emotions in that moment. Kalea didn't need all of their overbearing nonsense. She needed peace, and obviously his tactic wasn't working. Dorhen needed to find a way to make her life better here without outwardly showing favor for her, because if Knilma found out how much he wanted Kalea, the harassment would be so much worse.

"It's strange, though," Knilma continued despite his disinterest in this false story, "how it happened at midday. She couldn't have been in ecstasy. Not that I doubt that your shadowy essence can move around outside in the daylight, but I've yet to see it happen."

"I just told you," he said, finally stopping to regard her.

"Mastaren, how do you feel about this girl?"

He had known she'd ask that sooner or later. *I don't have to answer,* he reminded himself. Since living as Wikshen, Dorhen had found no obligation to answer questions he didn't want to. *Kalea doesn't need all the attention they'll shovel on her.*

Before making the decision to talk or walk, the strong stench of body odor wafted to his keen nose. His sense of smell had sharpened since his transformation.

"Do you smell that?" he asked.

Knilma sniffed the air. "Smell what?"

"It's awful!"

He scanned the area. They'd reached the central underground plaza where foot traffic flowed throughout the day. Little prayer shrines filled the corner voids, and the witches liked to display their Kraft poses here. Lots of black hoods bobbed around under his tall point of view. Shamans, witches, and devout young pledges wearing little clothing moved around him, leaving a wide space of reverence where he stood.

"It smells like a damned man!" he roared, and stepped forward in search of the unwanted person. Thinking about it, he had to wonder why he was so offended about a man in this place, but the rage was so intense, he didn't care right now.

Everyone in the area stopped to stare at him. Knilma gasped when he lunged and grabbed one of the hunched people under a black hood, the only person who didn't stare up at him. He ripped the hood off the person's head, and screams ensued. A man, as he expected. Dorhen took hold of the man's ponytail and twisted his head around to sneer at his face. He let the undeniable anger and offense guide his actions.

"How dare you—?" He stopped and squinted at the young man's shocked face, recognizing one of Kalea's friends who had burst into the storage house and interrupted his moment with her. Dorhen kept his mouth clamped about that, though this fool wouldn't get away with sneaking down here into this realm of solitude he was beginning to feel at home in.

In exertion of his barely manageable anger, Dorhen jerked the intruder's ponytail to make him stumble.

"Ahhh!" he hissed, favoring a bandaged hand, but didn't offer to speak.

Knilma reacted to the discovery with a long face of shock. "What in Kaihals? How did you get in here?"

"Isn't it obvious?" Dorhen asked her, and proceeded to rip the shaman-style cowl and poncho over his head. Underneath all of it, his pockets bulged with the coins and jewelry typically collected from the daily pledges.

"A thief!" Knilma declared.

Dorhen let him go as a rush of angry shamans moved in with chime bells to hurt and subdue the young man.

"Get him out of here!" Dorhen ordered. Under his breath, he followed up, "This is *my* house."

No one had lost interest in the mysterious black maid. Kalea stood stewing in the hot bath water among the concubine candidates with her elbows braced on the edge of the pool. Didn't they ever get tired of this conversation? They certainly considered the maid in question a threat. Each concubine hoped to get "First Sister" status, which, as Kalea had learned from Knilma's lectures, was the first woman Wikshen would bless at the start of his campaign. It could've happened to Kalea a few nights ago during her ecstasy in front of him! What would these silly girls have said if it had? But she had to ask herself the same question in a different way: what would it have been like if Kalea had made love to him—possessed?

"You seem quite content these days," Metta said, smiling, and swam over to drape an arm around Kalea. Her breast smashed against the side of Kalea's.

"Really?" she asked, and Metta nodded. Kalea didn't feel any better. She felt worse. The possession problem might as well be tossed on top of the heap of worries she carried, like knowing that if she and Dorhen remained here after he made love to her, Dorhen would go on to…do the same to the concubines. She couldn't shake the feeling that he was slipping through her fingers.

"So have you been asking around?"

Kalea blinked out of her thoughts and regarded Metta, who'd hooked her other arm around Kalea's collarbones in a loose embrace. "About what?"

"About the maid, of course! Did she get any more ecstasies?"

"Not that I've heard," she lied. "What exactly will you do when you find out who this maid is?"

Metta shrugged her naked shoulders. "Be jealous, I guess." She followed up with a giggle. "Nothing we can do, especially if she has the Mastaren's favor. We're just really curious, and it drives us mad!"

Kalea forced a smile and nodded. "I understand. I feel the same way."

Metta squeezed her in a tight, naked hug, and she didn't cringe. How long had she been here, doing this routine? About two weeks maybe? The sight of naked women no longer put her off, and Knilma's sex talks were becoming normal conversation too. Not only had Kalea learned words like "clitoris" and "perineum," but she could now repeat them casually.

And these concubine girls—she rarely saw them after the daily bath, so she only really recognized them by their nude bodies. Back home at the convent, nudity wasn't special like it was here, and the novices had covered themselves up with a towel straight from the bathtub. Here, the girls casually lounged around chatting in full nude view before dressing and going out to their practice and worship routines.

Their bodies, which they groomed and prized so much, were practically their identity, each one shaped and colored uniquely. Tamas had her bronze skin and dark hair and eyes. Brielle was blonde and all pale with pink points. Metta emitted a luminous ivory glow. Hetael wore faint patterns of freckles in the places the sun usually touched, and her black hair ignited with an amazing red flare under the sunbeams. Thinking of all the girls like this somehow obscured their humanity. It bizarrely started to feel like looking at a room full of cats instead, as cats were generally identified by their coloring.

Shrugging out of Metta's arms, Kalea ascended the little steps to exit the pool. On the tiled clay wall straight in front of her, a mirror reminded her of her own nakedness—her willowy limbs, not so bony anymore. Her hair was brown and her eyes green. Her posture deflated to have to look at herself as the others: a naked plaything trained to please Wikshen. An animal judged and sorted by her structure and coloring.

Knilma stopped Kalea on her way back to the maids' quarters to retrieve her cleaning implements. "You," she said, "as well as the other maids, gather together to primp yourselves."

"Why?" Kalea asked.

The old woman stood crooked, huffing and puffing. "Remember when we set up a feast for him to eat with the concubine candidates, but he didn't show?"

Kalea didn't have to ask for elaboration on "he." She nodded.

"We're trying it again," she explained. Kalea recalled hearing something like that the other day. "Remember your pennyroyal perfume. And don't wear your undergarments."

Kalea placed a tray of oysters arranged in a fancy pattern on the long table with sixteen settings. The most prominent one at the end consisted of an extra-soft seat cushion on a raised platform resembling the throne downstairs. Just like last time, her heart pounded. However, now her heart pounded with a blend of anxiety brought on by the notion of *Dorhen* eating with a load of girls who wanted to sleep with him. Kalea would have to wait out in the hallway while they reveled all night.

She sneered at the oyster platter. Back in the Lightlands, oysters were considered to be an aphrodisiac. Apparently, they believed the same thing here. More than oysters though, this whole setup…

Kalea shifted her eyes from the table to the pennyroyal incense cones, the large collection of floor cushions at the back of the room, and back to the table. The craftspeople here had found more imaginative ways to serve Wikshen's dinner than the usual pottery and porcelain. Suggestive-looking seashells were used as serving vessels.

Stepping back and looking at the completed arrangement, Kalea shook her head. She felt ill, and the incense wasn't yet lit. Before she finished scoffing, Kilka rushed into the room dinging a chime bowl to supplement the lack of light with a little Kraft flame. Since it was late afternoon, heavy black drapes kept the room as dark as possible. Kalea could barely find her way out in the blue flame's struggling glow.

After ordering the attending maids to move their position down the wall, Knilma pointed to the free spot by the door and ordered Kalea to kneel. She put the black glass pitcher into her hands once again.

The drums began. *Dtoom…dtoom…dtoom…*

Kalea's heart raced. These Wikshonites really knew how to put on a show of pageantry. The concubine candidates filed in, mostly hidden under hooded black cloaks.

As Kalea listened to them find their seats and settle in, Kilka spoke to them in a hushed tone. "Remember to bow your heads until he is seated. Say the prayer in unison afterward. Once he starts eating, you may also eat. You have permission to murmur amongst yourselves too, but do not speak to him until he speaks to you first."

Many other rules followed, and Kalea would've listened, but Knilma asked her to stand up so she could look her over. She straightened Kalea's skirt and smoothed it with a hand.

"Perfect, my dear."

When the drums suddenly changed rhythm, Knilma hissed at her to resume her kneeling pose. Another shaman at the end of the corridor threw the drape over the last window, and they waited in the dense darkness.

The door to his room clicked open. The drums stopped. Everyone went silent. His bare feet padded along the stone floor toward her.

Kalea raised her head to look at him. Too dark. Nonetheless, a little stirred air indicated he passed right beside her to enter the dining room. Kalea listened hard in the long moment of silence.

A bell rang once, prompting a chorus of young female voices in prayer. "Father of the darkness… Your beautiful majesty… Your fists righteous… We await your blessing…" and so on.

Kalea caught herself praying along and paused, hissing out her next breath rather than uttering another blasphemous word. She should slap herself, but if she dropped her pose, she'd earn another punishment! She'd heard this and prayers like it so often over the past two weeks. In some cases, she had recited it to please her superiors, but this time it flowed naturally. If only she could get some fresh air; this place was becoming a little too comfortable.

She kept her head bowed and listened to the rest of the prayer. A few seconds after its end, the concubines began their casual murmuring. Dorhen must've taken his first bite. Kalea wondered what he chose: an oyster? A lick of posset from the conch shell? The thought of his tongue dipping into that dish caused her body to shake all over, and her mouth dried fast. This atmosphere was too much.

She returned to listening for his voice, assuming that if he spoke, all the concubines would shut up. The minutes dragged on. Metta piped up, asking another girl to pass the dumplings—another dish sporting a suggestive shape. Certain things Kalea didn't recall setting on the table were geoducks, sausages and other heavy meats, or even carrots or turnips.

Time passed, so much her muscles began to hurt as she kept up her servant's posture. Those Kraft Positions were nothing compared to this.

An owl hooted distantly outside the window, announcing nightfall. Still, she knelt by the door, holding the full pitcher in her tired hands. Dorhen hadn't yet asked for his drink to be refilled.

The concubines murmured on in the same soft tone, without Dorhen's participation. The pennyroyal incense wafted from the room. She imagined it billowing out the door as a huge plume of smoke in a room with light. Dishes clanked. Some of the girls' voices sighed and commented on the delicious meal. No one had emerged from the dining room yet. Most of the shamans waited in the hall with the maids. A few attended in the dining room, including Knilma and Kilka.

As if by a psychic prompt, Knilma came shuffling through the door and stopped by Kalea. She bent over to whisper in her ear, "He finished his punch an hour ago and hasn't asked for a refill. Go on in and fill it anyway."

Kalea pointed to herself.

"Of course, you. Stand up now."

Kalea forced her stiff legs to move. At least she could work out her kinks for a few seconds before stumbling through the dark to accomplish a feat much easier done in the light. She sucked in a deep breath, threw back her shoulders, and propped her pitcher on her hand.

She entered Wikshen's dining room.

At the long table, low to the floor, fifteen concubines sat comfortably on cushions and Dorhen sat at the head in the heavy shadow. She couldn't see him from here with only the one little Kraft flame. The incense filled the room with its strong, herbal musk, minty and dry.

Kalea paused in shock when she beheld the concubines. They had shed their cloaks, and now wore little beyond narrow strips of black cloth where necessary across their pale flesh, which glowed in the blue light. They held precise sitting poses with their busts jutting forward and one knee up high. The ones who noticed Kalea's entry stopped to smirk. Metta, sitting farther up the table, gave her a vacant smile before sipping from her cup.

How did Dorhen handle being in the company of curvaceous young women? At the far end of the table, his throne-like seat had a tall back with sides, like a three-sided box. He also sat with his knees up, but more casually than the girls. He leaned against the side wall of his seat.

Kalea squinted to see him better in her slow approach. If she tripped in the dark, all these girls would laugh at her.

He sat reserved. He hadn't spoken, and apparently, he wasn't looking at them either. His plates were cleaned. The conch shell sat empty. Brielle, at his immediate left—she must've won the contest for who would sit next to Wikshen—shot Kalea a hateful stare.

Dorhen didn't move, but he breathed heavily. He cupped his forehead in his hand as he rested against the side of his wooden chair. His other hand touched his lower abdomen. She wanted to say his name but kept it inside. She assumed these girls didn't know his real name.

Kalea leaned over the table, against Brielle's obvious annoyance. She began the pour and took the chance to study him closer. His whole body shook noticeably.

Are you all right? She couldn't say it aloud, so she asked Brielle, "Is he all right?"

"Of course," the girl growled back. "He's always like this when we hold ceremonies."

Dorhen opened his mouth and panted as if he'd been holding his breath. He locked eyes with Kalea, but his stare showed vacant. His clammy skin glistened in the pale light. He gnashed his teeth, rubbed his stomach, and turned away from her.

"What's wrong with him?" Kalea dared to ask. She, too, trembled to see him like this.

Brielle waved her hand and made a smug smile. "It's the atmosphere. Our impeccable worship, the incense—all of these elements have proven to work. He's very horny, but he doesn't like any of us enough to use us." Brielle finished by draining the rest of her glass.

Kalea found herself staring at him again. "He's…" She bit her lip to keep from repeating Brielle's words.

He returned his face to the palm of his hand and breathed raggedly. Little groans creaked out every so often. All around him, the concubines chatted like nothing was unusual.

"What the hell are you doing, maid?" Brielle asked, twisting around to see her lingering and gawking at Wikshen in his…state. "Aren't you finished here? Get out and only come back when we call you."

That's when Kalea felt it. The darkness. The darkness crept up her dress and spread itself across her skin. In Wikshen's state of arousal, it filled this room and nearly swallowed the Kraft flame. Kalea considered what Brielle said about him always acting this way. It must mean they always sat inside the black miasma. They taunted and tempted Dorhen like this in their regular ceremonies? With the incense and the oysters? Poor Dorhen!

Kalea couldn't think about it any further, because a shock of pleasurable need ignited her belly. At Brielle's order to leave, Kalea bent over her pitcher and hurried out, stifling her involuntary gasp at her sudden bodily change. She moved as fast as she could with her legs flaring up in tingles. The miasma followed her, petting her all over—face, arms, and body beneath her dress.

Right before she exited, Dorhen moaned, drawing everyone's attention to him. Kalea put the pitcher on the floor before her trembling fingers could drop it.

"Kalea?" Knilma asked carefully.

She couldn't answer, much less reclaim her place by the door. She bent over, eased herself to the floor, and rolled onto her side. She bit her lip to keep from crying out, put her hands between her legs, and squeezed her thighs. She clenched her teeth, and all she could think about was Dorhen feeling the same way.

"Uhhhhng," she erupted, unable to pin up her feelings with the miasmic hands touching all over her. Another moan from Dorhen in the dining room seemed to answer her.

This must be her most intense ecstasy yet. All the other maids fell out of formation to gape at her. The concubines poured out of the room.

"Kalea?" she heard Metta shriek.

The chorus of whispering ensued.

"It was you all along!" Brielle growled.

Kalea couldn't bother to care about their eyes and judgments. She arched her back. Her lapel was already loose, although she didn't remember tugging it open. Her body roared. She screamed. The darkness thickened even though the shamans lit candles and opened the drape to allow in the moonlight.

Knilma's wrinkled hand patted Kalea's face, but she didn't feel it. She saw it instead. Her lower body stole all of her attention, throbbing and tingling and aching. She arched again and moaned in fast, consecutive breaths, already feeling pleasure from the coitus that was yet to happen.

Though many candles now illuminated the space, the darkness kept the light down. It touched her between the legs. Ethereal fingers slid up and down her sides. The shamans ordered all the maids and concubines to be quiet, and they fell to staring at Kalea in her desperate hour while the shamans bickered.

"It's the best we can do!" Knilma hissed at Kilka. She leaned down into the group of shamans who bent over Kalea and put a dab of oil on her forehead. She recited a short prayer to Wikshen.

"Clear the table," Knilma ordered.

"What if Wikshen doesn't—" one shaman attempted to talk back.

"Now!"

The shamans hastily untied Kalea's dress and laid her bare for all to see.

"Blessings on you, girl." Knilma finished her prayer, rubbing her hands down Kalea's face in several strokes.

Her ecstasy didn't let up, so she barely registered any of it. All the heat in her body concentrated in her nether region. A cold sweat doused her forehead.

"Go with bravery," Knilma said. "Go with heart. Wikshen's blessing awaits you. Go now." She motioned to the other shamans. "Go," she repeated.

Two of the younger shamans carried Kalea into the dining room. Silence replaced all the chaos, except for Kalea's own rhythmic moans of sexual misery. They placed her on the table and ceremoniously spread her legs before Wikshen. One of the shamans ran her fingers lightly over Kalea's face, as if to give her one more blessing.

Wikshen sat in his seat in the same pose as before. They wouldn't be alone for this; the shamans entered and lined the walls of the room and bowed over. The maids and concubines remained in the hall, poking their heads through the doorframe.

Kalea couldn't slow her rapid breathing. Her rib cage pumped up and down, raising her breasts into the darkness-thickened air. Up and down. Up and down. Her legs trembled. She kept them up and spread her knees, the most natural position in the world right now.

She'd quieted her moaning in favor of the heavy breathing. Wikshen's breath beat out to complement hers. Kalea waited, listening to him. What was taking him so long? When she chanced a look, bending her spine to see him, he was leaning forward in his seat, drawing in long breaths. He didn't touch her, but the darkness continued to do it for him. Could his senses be tied to it somehow?

This waiting might kill her! She groaned and squeezed her thighs together again; they'd become wet and slippery from her own bodily fluid. She could pick out her own scent of arousal from all the incense and food lingering on the table, and she didn't have to guess whether he could too.

Wikshen stood up and loomed over her. Kalea reached for him. He planted his foot on the table beside her. He leaned over her, smelling the air. His eyes still showed vacant and sleepy. He closed them. After one more long inhale through his nose, he groaned raggedly on the exhale.

She reached for him with both arms. He slid his hands underneath her, scooped her up. He lifted her high; the motion dizzied her. She put her arms around his neck and hung on.

"Where are we going?" she groaned.

He didn't answer.

From their crouched positions, the shamans watched him in study as he carried her out. Dorhen shook all the way, panting and rasping over her face. He took her past all the other girls, through the corridor to his bedroom. Weak but desperate for his attention, she reached up and licked his neck, which was as salty and as sweaty as she. He gasped at her touch and fell against the wall. After a moment, he regained his own balance and entered the room, kicking the door closed behind them.

Dorhen placed her on the bed. She arched her back and put her lips on his neck again, earning a loud groan from his gaping mouth. His knees collapsed beside the bed, and for a second, she had him in her embrace, increasing the pressure to a suck, and then on to a bite, along his neck.

With shaky arms, he pushed out of her captivity and staggered to the fireplace, where he threw open the firewood storage box. He stacked all of the logs on the hearth, and all the kindling. All of it?

Kalea waited for him, spreading her legs and thrusting her bosom up into the darkness. She wanted to call his name, but moaning came easier.

He worked to get the fire going, often stopping to groan and pant. His hands shook more violently each time he reached out with the flint striker to put sparks on the kindling.

Click, click...click, click...

When no more clicks ensued, Kalea looked up to see what was

happening. The moonlight through the window showed him lying on the floor, panting. The darkness wouldn't leave her alone, yet Dorhen wasn't touching her enough, so she rolled to get off the bed and crawled toward him. She put her hands on his chest, and her lips followed with haste.

He moaned in response. His fingers touched the back of her hair and fell into a caress. She ventured her lips to his bellybutton and swirled her tongue around it. His fingers tightened around her locks, adding a painful tension to her scalp that she hardly noticed.

He arched his back and whispered, "Fuck," between panting.

Indeed, she thought, without the strength to say it aloud. Feeling a little stronger and more capable than before but no less aroused, Kalea snuck her hand to the region below his navel. *It* pushed up against the fabric of his kilt like a thick, hard tent pole. It radiated more heat than the rest of him.

Dorhen moaned louder. He snatched her hand before she could grab it or snake her hand under his garment, and sat up. His growling, ragged breathing made a new, strong wave of tingles wash over Kalea, and she keeled over. He caught her before she could crack her head on the stone hearth.

He carried her back to the bed. She lost the strength she'd been using a second ago, and could only arch her back and cry for him again. Leaving her on the bed, he trailed his hand over her naked breast as he dragged it away. Stepping away from the bed, he stumbled and caught himself on the hearth.

"Shit!" he hissed, and then groaned another sexual sound, running hot through his deep voice.

Click…click…click… He attempted to light the fire again. Kalea herself wanted to curse now—at *him* for leaving her in misery! A fire flared up, and Dorhen winced away from it. He paused to swallow and got straight to fanning the young flame.

With a good flame ignited, Dorhen staggered to the little table and chugged water from the waiting pitcher. The fire grew, raising heat and light in the room. He braced his arms on the table weakly and watched her as she watched him.

The fire rose hotter and brighter by the second, eating at the many logs he'd stacked. The miasma receded. Kalea fell limp. She could only lie there now, helpless and naked. A few awkward steps carried Dorhen back to the bed. She raised her arms in invitation.

"Please," she could finally utter. The fire helped bring her back to her senses.

He reached across her to grab the extra folded blanket on the bed, unfurled it, and spread it across her.

"Oh, please!" she cried again when he turned his back. What was wrong with him? How could he not indulge with her when they were so perfectly together right now?

Ignoring her sounds of need and frustration, Dorhen rubbed his face with both hands. He too appeared steadier in the light. His large, muscly curves made a delightful silhouette against the fire. Kalea wept softly. Though he twisted around to check on her, he didn't give in to her beckoning.

Exhaustion set in, which usually followed an ecstasy. Her eyelids drooped. She let them close.

When she opened them again for a brief second, Dorhen was standing by the fireplace. She didn't want to fall asleep; she wanted to speak to him at least. Sleep barreled in on her anyway. Her wits scrambled as it won the battle.

Dorhen started breathing fast again on the other side of her eyelids. A rapid, wet sound accompanied his ragged breaths. She tried again to open her eyes, and managed in time to see him bracing one hand on the fireplace mantle while the other whipped up and flung something into the fire.

Whoosh! The flames flared at his motion.

Afterward, he stumbled to the table, fell into a chair, and dropped his head and one arm on the tabletop. He fell asleep as fast as Kalea.

Chapter 16
Red Cloaks

Lamrhath spread his lips into the brightest smile he could display for Mhina. The little girl held her pout firm, watching emptily as he knelt down before her and opened a flat wooden box containing a glittering necklace. So far the most exquisite piece he'd come by, its gold had been shaped into delicate little branches with sparkling pink diamond flowers and deep green emerald leaves. After days of agonizing over whether this gift should go to Orinleah or his new little *farhah*, he had decided on the latter. Its light colors and delicate arrangement would suit Mhina's lustrous blonde hair with its halo of fiery radiance better than Orinleah's dark haired, forest-like coloring. Orinleah dazzled better in maroons, greens, and blues.

Mhina puzzled over the necklace, and he extended it closer to her. "Why don't you try it on?"

She lifted it out of the box and held it above her head to see it shimmer in the morning light. A feeling of genuine, smug pleasure lit every corner of Lamrhath's being to see her receive it. Holding it in her hand, Mhina stepped backward, turned, and went toward the door to the garderobe.

Lamrhath's smile went limp as he watched the unfolding event. She stepped inside, lifted the lid off the jakes, and dangled the pendant above its mouth. He kept silent but took a jerky step forward, reacting too late.

She dropped the pendant. Below the floor of the garderobe was a long pipe. The pendant fell down through it for many stories until it landed atop a heap of putrid compost in the Grave.

Lamrhath's stomach boiled. He tightened his fists at his sides, having dropped the pendant's box absentmindedly.

Now Mhina smiled.

Lamrhath worked his tense jaw for a bit before saying, "Oh, dear." He laced his best somber acting into his tone, and it must've worked because her expression shifted. "This isn't good."

"What isn't good?"

"I just feel sorry for those poor children."

"My friends? What about Bairhen?" she demanded.

"Him especially. Because every time you do something naughty, like throw such a valuable bauble down the jakes, Bairhen and all of your other friends get beaten."

Mhina's hands shot to her mouth.

Lamrhath shrugged. "They were assigned a mean new nanny, you see, who is magically linked to my sadness. When you make me sad, she gets angry, and when she gets angry, she takes it out on children."

Mhina didn't say anything, but her face paled.

Lamrhath held down his smile. "I'm sure they'll survive this time, though. I look forward to eating dinner together tonight." He turned on his heel and walked out.

Putting Mhina out of his mind, Lamrhath stepped into one of the biggest rooms the sorcerers occupied in Ilbith. All around him, voices buzzed and spells crackled. Many injuries were acquired here, so a team of skilled medicine men stood by. Burn wounds were the most common injury since the majority of their spell-casting shenanigans had to do with fire, so the smell of burnt flesh or hair tended to stink up the atmosphere of the practice hall, but not today.

"My lord, you made it!" The spritely voice of Haerdar piped up at his entrance. He hurried toward Lamrhath with one of his assistants on his heels, arms spread, one hand clutching a book of scribbles. "We're making headway today," he said. "Please come this way; don't mind the mess."

Not many sorcerers were practicing spell-craft today, at least not the fire sort. For the most part, the sorcerers were standing around one area, murmuring and poising themselves for a shot at one focal target, a dummy body made from tightly packed straw and twine over a clay base. The dummy wore one scrap of fabric across the chest, a narrow strip of woven hair.

"We just got this in from the spinning room, my lord." Haerdar presented a similar piece to Lamrhath.

"Woven from the ratty hair of dead *saehgahn*," Lamrhath guessed.

"Indeed, it is." Haerdar drifted to a nearby table full of weapons and magical implements and lifted another, half-burned sample. "It can't hold up against our fire spells—not surprising. But the weaving is no less magnificent than we'd imagined. It does hold up against frost spells."

"No getting frozen wearing this, I suppose," Lamrhath mused.

"And goblin humors don't dissolve it, we've found, which is excellent news."

Lamrhath let his gaze drift over the other sorcerers, sharing in the excitement of their spokesman. "Trips through Goblin Country, then. What about the soil of Hathrohskog?"

Haerdar's face twisted into curling glee. "Indeed, my lord." He motioned to the nearby crate of soil collected from that very place. "I was thinking we could use this shorter, scrappier *saehgahn* hair to make boots for that terrain."

Lamrhath nodded his approval. "This is good news, all of it." Even his pain lifted from his abdomen slightly as he took in all of these exciting new developments.

Haerdar brought his attention to the various knives laid out on the table. "We've several types of metal here, iron, steel, and whatnot, but none of them can cut through the elven-hair fabric, not even the obsidian stone. See for yourself."

Lamrhath picked up the black dagger of deadly, sharpened stone and attempted to cut the remaining side of the half-burned fabric sample. Nothing. He couldn't get through it, no matter how hard he sawed the blade across the weave. "Amazing. How will we cut it, then?"

"Our metalsmiths are working with the recipe now. We'll have our first set of shears soon."

"Yet the hair is easily cut when in its original form," Lamrhath said. He knew that firsthand, of course. He had his own hair trimmed every few months to keep it beautiful and healthy.

"Blending it with these other fibers is amazing, my lord," Haerdar confirmed. "I've never seen anything like it in my life."

Lamrhath rubbed his thumb over his bottom lip, staring at the piece of magical cloth on the dummy. "If only we hadn't lost Wikshen," he said. "What I really want to know is, can a morkblade cut it? I assume it can."

"That's what we intend to find out today, my lord," Haerdar said. He motioned to a certain man standing amongst the sorcerers. "Let's try it now, while our lord is here to witness the result with us. Everyone, step back."

They did so as the man began a spell, murmuring many syllables Lamrhath knew well.

"He's conjuring a specter sword?"

Haerdar nodded. "A Haxikhrah sword, to be precise. We've deduced that this specter sword could be close to a morkblade, the closest we can get without delving into Kraft."

When the man finished the chant, he raised his hand and caught the sword as it swirled into existence, as if particles of dust from the air were joining together to create the object. It looked similar to the illustrations of morkblades in books. A black handle appeared first, which Haerdar's man snatched while he could; he was well practiced in this. The blade came next, flaunting a highly polished bronze color with an iridescent sheen and black-tipped barbs all over.

The man wasted no time once he got the specter sword in hand. Yelling fiercely as if this were a battlefield, he put his all into striking the dummy where it wore the elven-hair fabric.

The sharp sound of the blade running along each hair strand pierced Lamrhath's ears and made his teeth clench. That must've been the sound of the fabric cutting, meaning that a morkblade would surely also cut it. He couldn't have everything, he guessed.

After that one strike, the blade went up in a puff of glittery red smoke. The spell was meant to deliver one deadly strike to destroy an opponent—if its wielder could deliver the hit before it expired.

The clearing smoke revealed that the fabric remained intact. The sorcerers clapped in applause as a group. Stunned, Lamrhath approached to inspect the fabric. He ran his hand along the weaving. Not a hair broken. Behind him, Haerdar and his men beamed.

"Gentlemen, you've done it," Lamrhath said.

"No, *you've* done it, my lord. Praise Kingsorcerer Lamrhath!"

The other sorcerers echoed Haerdar three times.

"You all deserve a reward," Lamrhath said, still caressing the fabric even though the hair of this one had come off of a sweaty male running around in the grasslands. "I think we have found a great tool, not only against Wikshen, but perhaps against any other sorcerous faction who might try to defy us."

In the secret spot behind the barn where Primora usually shared her kisses with Jonaril, she sat with her cousin Cygnet instead. Cygnet's sleeve showed a damp spot after all of Primora's crying on it.

"I wish you or someone could understand," Primora groaned under the whistling wind. The old barn's side door whined on its rusty hinges, nudged by the wind.

"Well, I'm trying to understand," her cousin said.

Primora brushed at the wet spot on the girl's sleeve.

"If you hadn't been dallying with that boy, you wouldn't be upset right now."

She'd told the whole story to Cygnet, from her secret meetings with Jonaril all the way to now. Cygnet rubbed her back while Primora hiccupped, staring at the forest across the field. "I'm thinking of running away with him."

Cygnet's hand paused in its soothing motion. "Are you crazy?"

Primora shrugged. "I guess I am."

"You can't, Primora, no!"

"Well, what am I supposed to do?" she shot back. "All this stuff is nonsense! I just want to live like an average woman!"

"Your dedication to Wikshen is a blessing!"

"How?"

Cygnet paused. "I've always envied you."

"Why?"

"Because... You're so beautiful, and when Wikshen comes back, he's going to bless you."

Primora shook her head with an ironic smile. A new set of tears rolled down her cheeks.

Cygnet went on, "You've been pampered all these years, and it'll only increase when we get to Wikhaihli."

"Yeah, it'll mean I get to sit half-naked on an altar in a musty Wikhaihli chapel with more people than my mother forcing me. It's painful!"

"But your chores are lighter, and you're eating rich foods now."

"Maybe I like doing work, and all that food makes me ill," Primora said.

"You might get to be a concubine."

"Whose concubine?" Primora asked. "Wikshen doesn't exist."

Cygnet didn't have to say anything due to the bristling energy radiating from her. "Take your blasphemy back," she finally hissed.

Primora waved her hand. "Show me proof of his existence."

"The sorcerers saw him."

"And you believe them?"

Cygnet stuttered for a response. "But—it's just—Wikshen, he..."

Primora stood up, finally done with the conversation. She could usually talk to Cygnet about anything, but her cousin's warm, friendly support ended where doubts about Wikshen began.

Around the corner, a string of red-cloaked sorcerers were filing through the door of her mother's little cabin.

Primora ran all the way over, and wedged herself into the house full of smelly men.

"She's off foraging!" Primora's mother said to the men.

They sought out Aunt Falli again? Primora scanned the group of red cloaks for an injured one. No one favored any apparent injury. Nonetheless, they could be here to take medicine for something else, particularly a disease of the genitals. Aunt Falli excelled at making medicine for those kinds of illnesses. Primora's mind hovered on the word "take," which was exactly what they would do. The sorcerers didn't buy or trade for anything. They exploited and wrang the good, honest people dry.

Primora made her way over to clasp hands with her mother. Cygnet stepped through the doorway next.

"Ah!" the leader of the red-cloaked group said. "I know this girl." He grabbed Cygnet's arm, and she squealed. "This is Falli's daughter."

Cygnet pulled and whimpered as he retained his hold on her.

"Please don't hurt her, sir!" Mother shouted across the group. "Her mother will be in soon."

"She will, because this little goose is going to stay with us in the meantime," he said.

"Don't hurt her now!" Primora's mother pleaded as Cygnet's whimpering continued.

The man's eyes clung to the girl. "She's a fetching little goose, isn't she?" he said. "Is she a virgin?"

Primora and her mother exchanged looks of dread.

"She was named for a young swan, sir, and we don't speak about such information. Please be careful with her, she's just a child."

Another man stepped up to the one holding Cygnet. "Hold on now, hold on." He observed Cygnet's face from an uncomfortably close distance. "She's a little too pretty, wouldn't you say? I never noticed before."

The other man shared a silent stare with him. "Yeah…I guess she is." His lips spread into a bright smile. He turned back to her. "My little lady, you are welcome to accompany your mother back to Ilbith."

Primora gasped.

Mother yelled, "What?"

"Hey!" a man by the door barked. "Here she comes across the field!" He stuck his head out the door and whistled to Cygnet's mother.

"Start the portal."

At the command, two men revealed golden rods from under their cloaks. Primora's face went cold and damp at the developing events. The two rod-bearers chanted and tapped their instruments on the wooden floor at certain beats. Two other men hummed deep, long notes. Eerie notes, unlike those heard in song. Sparks began to pop and crawl up the rods. A static charge prickled the floorboards under her bare feet.

The red-cloaked men prompted Aunt Falli to run straight into their trap. A dark hole appeared between the two poles as dancing wires of lightning wrapped around each and arced overhead. They meant to take Falli and Cygnet away to Ilbith, and they weren't going to give anyone a choice!

Aunt Falli arrived at the door, panting. "What's wrong?" she asked.

They grabbed her and started passing her down the line of men crammed into the house. They did the same to Cygnet. Acting fast, Primora grabbed the broomstick from the corner and whacked the sorcerer next to her.

"Primora, no!" Mother shouted.

Too late. Primora headed toward the men with the poles to ruin their spell. Many hands grabbed at her, locking onto her dress.

A choking sound erupted behind her. Her mother had slit the throat of one who would've caught her. Primora couldn't spare a blink to wonder at her mother's quick thinking. She charged forward and swung her broom at one of the pole-bearers. She aimed for his head, but instead got his shoulder.

He didn't budge. He blinked, but continued his chant as if nothing had happened. An image bloomed inside the black hole between the golden rods: a stone wall. Other people stood waiting there.

A nearby sorcerer lunged to stop Primora, and her mother jumped to her side to slash her knife at him. All the sorcerers went after the woman with the most dangerous weapon.

Despite the confusion, Cygnet and Falli were dragged all the way to the magic portal. Primora saw the split second when they pushed Cygnet into the space; elbows and heads blocked her view after that.

A storm of men swiped at Primora. One hand clipped her face and put a dizzying pain on her senses. Behind the stars streaking around in her vision, a plume of dust arose in the house.

"Cover your mouth, girl!" Her mother held the powders they had stored for this very purpose: self-defense. Wikshonites weren't always treated fairly, after all. She uncorked the bottle of sleeping powder and flung it into the air. It hit a ceiling rafter and shattered, and the powder clotted up the air.

Primora raised her skirt to bury her mouth and nose. The sorcerers, for the most part, didn't think to try that with their cloaks quickly enough.

Thump—thump—thump! Heavy male bodies fell. With the room half-cleared, Primora found both Cygnet and Falli missing. The portal expired as one of the pole-bearers dropped in the plume of smoke. The rest of the sorcerers elbowed their way out the door.

Her mother grabbed her hand and yanked her toward the back window. Primora could hardly feel anything in her panic, eliminating the issue of the splintery windowsill and the bruises collecting on her shins as she scrambled out. Her black skirt tore. Next came her mother, and

Primora pulled her through without a care for her heavy old body. The pumping adrenaline helped.

On the other side of the house, they made a fast decision about which direction to run before the sorcerers stormed around the corner. Her mother yanked her arm, and they ran to the nearest alley.

The best way to reach the forest was to sneak through the village to the other side. Otherwise, it would be a long run across a field. Good thing most of the village's sorcerers had assembled at their house to collect Falli and Cygnet—this gave Primora and her mother the opportunity to sprint right across, keeping mostly to dark alleys so less people would see them. If word got out, the villagers would easily give them away to the sorcerers. The fools favored their fear of the sorcerers over their friendship with the two women.

They reached the shady trees at the other side of the village, and Primora couldn't guess if anyone saw them. When they finally stopped running, her mother bent over to wheeze and pant. She was too old for such a chase. She plopped to the ground to rest, and Primora put her hand on her back for comfort, staring lifelessly into the trees. They were outlawed now, and stranded without supplies.

"We'll keep wary," her mother said. "We'll watch the house, see how long it takes the sorcerers to clear out of it. Maybe we can sneak back in to get some things later, if they don't loot it to hell."

"What will we eat out here?" she asked.

Her mother plucked a fistful of grass and threw it. "You know which mushrooms are good."

Primora fell silent.

"We've lost our only family and are now on our own. Can't live in the village anymore," the older woman said. She shrugged her shoulders, draped in her black shawl. "Time to go to Wikhaihli."

Primora bit her lip. Her voice peeped out, "It's so far away."

"It's all we have in the world."

Damos's hands ached from the many days he'd spent prying open shells covered in rotten human remains. These seeds would take someone else's life later.

Another drone came with a wheelbarrow full of more bloodied pits. This man, Girgen, was kinder than the first bunch he'd met, just another trapped victim like him.

"You might want to try working faster," Girgen told Damos as he shoveled the foul-smelling muck from his wheelbarrow into Damos's barrel.

"When will I be done?"

"Not long now," he answered. "The forlustweed reproduces in spring and into the summer. The seeds stop coming by fall, and then the plant's fertilizer will dry up. The whole plant dies, and we do it again in January."

Damos shuddered. By "fertilizer," the man meant human bodies. "Where do you find the bodies to farm these plants?"

The other man looked around, his expression unreadable beneath his dark muzzle. "They're not hard to find."

Before he pushed his empty vessel away, Damos shot to his feet and grabbed the man's sleeve. "Girgen." They locked eyes. A hunch told Damos the man knew what he'd ask. He asked nonetheless. "Have you ever thought about hatching a plan to escape these caves?"

A long silence preceded his rough voice ringing his metal mask. "I have."

At that, Damos dropped back to his stool and hastily opened more shells. Girgen pretended to tidy the floor around him, tossing debris onto the garbage pile behind Damos.

"Listen hard," Damos said. "I'm a mage, and I saw my ring on a pile of jewelry spoils in the sorting room. I can use it to cast spells and fight our way out. Can you get it for me?"

"Perhaps. I have a friend, Derndig, who would also be in. Describe the ring."

Damos did. It had a big blue stone which should be hard to miss, but he went on to tell Girgen about how its setting twisted and curled around it. They went so far as to set up a meeting place, an escape route, and even how Girgen would set Derndig to collecting food for the road.

"It's worth a try," Damos concluded.

Girgen nodded.

Damos awoke the next morning to the prodding of some other drone whose name he didn't yet know. "The queen is asking for you."

Damos's stomach sank. Why did she want to see him? Was he in trouble? Did she know about his plot with Girgen?

He had no choice but to follow. He couldn't attempt his escape now. Not so haphazardly and without his ring. So down he went, through the corridors into a very deep section of the caves. The air grew cooler and smelled like water. Water flowed somewhere nearby, but he never saw any. A tight, upsloping corridor took them to the biggest cavern he'd seen yet. A long, wide path zigzagged between gaping holes from which cold air blasted up. Maybe the water lay below this chamber. Numerous other drones appeared along his way, and the queen's throne room became apparent after he passed an enormous black curtain spilling from the ceiling.

Glowing mushrooms of blues and greens that resembled the tiny ones he'd seen in the nursery grew to the size of mansions here. Many other vined plants tangled up the back wall among them—not forlustweed, thankfully. In front of that impressive display of horticulture, the drones worked vigorously to erect a canopy of more of the same black linens. Stacks of pillows like those he'd seen before waited for arrangement, probably in anticipation of the god-figure the queen was waiting for. Hopefully, Girgen could pass the ring to Damos before that ever unfolded.

Damos left his thoughts at that and resisted asking about what he beheld. All around him, the drones went to and fro, carrying decorative items or tools. A dozen of them tirelessly went over the stone floor with rags and brooms, not just cleaning but shining it up to as high a degree as possible. But he didn't see anyone who could be the queen yet.

"Are you he? Damos?"

Damos spun around. A woman in several ragged veils approached. Four drones accompanied her. Damos nodded.

"Bow to the queen, fool!" one of her drones barked, his voice muffled under his mask.

This was her? No wonder he'd failed to spot her. She looked more like one of the old beggars littering the streets of Beldamin, a neighboring city to Sharr's capital.

She extended her hand, and her drones' lantern light revealed a skeletal talon with drooping, milky skin over it. Damos stared at it, half in disgust, half in confusion. He couldn't kiss her hand with this mask locked around his head. In fact, he and the others only ate mushy gruel, practically liquid because it was easily sucked through a straw stuck into the mask's slits.

The drone who had brought him here elbowed him. "Take her hand and touch your forehead to it."

Damos scrambled to perform that gesture, not even liking touching her corpse-like hand to his hair. She quickly snatched the locks that sprouted from between his bandages.

"You are an exotic type."

"I'm from Sharr."

She hummed. Despite her appearance, her voice was high and youthful, if a bit like a whiny violin. Any time he chanced a look up at her face, all he saw was a chin with thin lips struggling to cover a set of teeth, as if her…flesh was withering away. She could manage to sound her O's with a great effort to pull her lips together. The rest of her face was hidden under the shadow of her veils.

"I am glad," she replied, pulling that fiddle bow tight across her vocal cords. "I suspected as I tended you that you were a fair one." She held out her hand to the drone on her right. "Remove some of his bandages so I can see how his healing is coming along."

Damos winced as he endured the stinging peel of the linen strip rising off his face. As she watched, the queen opened a little purse and took out an oddly-shaped thing. A mushroom? It was brown and wavy like a mushroom, one he'd never try to eat if out in the wilderness, for it looked poisonous. Apparently, it wasn't, because she placed it on her tongue and gingerly worked her teeth over it. Her purplish lips struggled to hide her mastication.

"What is that?" Damos asked without thinking, and then shrank at what he'd done.

"Do not move, Damos," the queen recommended after finishing her snack. "I so dearly want to see your face. Let the man unwrap you." She motioned to her purse, which was as tattered as the rest of her ensemble. "I assume your brother drones have informed you of the impending arrival of our god, the Mastaren."

Damos swallowed. She took another mushroom out and held it for him to see better. He'd never seen its type before. Metallic scales flashed along its cap.

"These mushrooms serve a special purpose for me. I must make myself hospitable when he comes." She ended by popping it into her mouth and replaying the hideous show again.

When half of Damos's bandages were down off his face, she leaned forward to inspect him with another whiny hum. She smelled…stale.

"I'm afraid for your eyebrows," she reported. "Let's hope they grow back." She reached her gnarled hand to pat his head. "At least your hair seemed fine when I tended you. No worries there. But truly, I will not mind if your eyebrows don't grow in. We can draw new ones, can't we?"

"Draw eyebrows?" He couldn't even hear his voice over his pounding heart. "Madame, may I ask why my looks are so important?"

At that, she reared back and gave a giggle behind her hand, like the pretty girls of Damos's past. He couldn't see her eyelids, but he imagined them also batting. If she had eyelids.

"My dear boy, it's not important. It really isn't." She dragged her voice seductively. "Only a luxury, that's all."

He officially shut his brain off. Damos did not want to know why she considered his looks a luxury. A luxury?

She shared more regardless. "Though I hear you've done a good job in the garden, I have a better position in store for you later. As soon as you're healed and groomed, you'll be moved to my chamber. The boys in my chamber help me to be beautiful as well as prepare me for the Mastaren's arrival."

Damos nodded slowly. So…he'd put slippers on her feet and help her in and out of the bath? He'd be the equivalent of a handmaiden. As degrading as that sounded, it seemed better than prying open seeds covered in dank human flesh.

"I'm glad you agree, my child." She tickled under his chin with her bony finger. On second thought, he really didn't care to see any more of her than what he saw now. "Truly, you'll have the most important job in the palace."

She considered this cave a palace?

She pointed to her mouth with its dry, receding lips around her teeth and gums. "When the Mastaren comes, I must be ready. You see what I mean? *Ready.* The rest of me isn't doing much better than my poor lips, so I take great pains and require daily upkeep to massage and stimulate the place I need him to visit. After he comes, I'll be a shining new girl. You understand?"

He didn't. Damos nodded slowly, knowing his act wouldn't convince. He just wanted her to go away so he could get back to planning his escape.

The queen ordered her man to rewrap Damos's face, and she watched while greedily stuffing one mushroom after another between her teeth. When the other drone stepped away from him, the queen ordered, "Show me your tongue."

The drone took his mask off of him after unlocking the straps with a little key. Unable to guess why, and not wanting to explore the idea, Damos pushed his tongue out through his lips and the bandages. This was the first break from the mask he'd received since his arrival.

"Very good, Damos. You'll make a fine chamber boy."

At her signal, the drone started putting his mask back on him. It took all of his willpower not to fight it.

Just get on your way, he told himself. *Get out of her eyesight.*

By the Creator's grace, she did move on. And because his face was still so raw, he had time before having to go work in her chamber.

As Damos left the throne room, Girgen emerged from the tunnel of his destination. His face brightened to see Damos. They walked calmly to meet each other. Maybe Girgen had some news. When he was within one hundred paces of Damos, he reached into his pocket and flashed something shiny.

My ring! He's done it already!

Girgen kept calm and continued his casual stride, probably planning to slip it into Damos's hand in passing.

Two men ran through the opening behind Girgen and pointed to his back. Girgen's bright smile shifted to panic. He faked a stumble, throwing the ring toward Damos. It slid across the floor, but the man's aim was off. Damos tried his best not to lurch, but changed his direction to wherever the ring might land. The men caught up to Girgen.

"What were you doing back there?" one demanded, and proceeded to turn his pockets inside out.

"I doubt you were given permission to enter the sorting room!" the other reproached.

Damos feigned nonchalance, tracking the ring's progress, but it had too much momentum. It skidded far and fast, and disappeared into the shadowy side of the cavern. He stifled his panic and continued that way, hoping to find it among the pebbles. His foot nearly slid into a hole where cold air rushed up from below.

No. Please, Creator, no! The ring had slid well into an area with a complex of holes hanging above a huge body of water below. In all likelihood, it had fallen through one, into the Creator knew where. He'd lost it. Damos was doomed.

Chapter 17
A Whisper Travels

A bright sunbeam beat down on her eyelids. Stern voices thumped at her ears. Kalea's eyelids fluttered.

"Wake up!" snapped a middle-aged woman. It sounded like Kilka.

"Give her a moment," the more patient voice of Knilma hummed.

Kalea lay limply over soft, fluffy padding. A real bed, for once. It made waking up harder than ever. The brightness on the other side of her eyelids was unusual; the basement didn't let in so much light. Cracking her eyelids open by a needle's width, she found herself not in the black maids' dorm but a smaller, cozier room. A big window stood to the side, its shutters wide open, letting in the brisk and damp morning air. A soft tumble of mist spilled in from a walking cloud and evaporated near the warm fireplace. A set of nice furniture accompanied the bed: a table, two chairs, and something in the corner with a black cloth draped over it. A mirror, perhaps?

"She doesn't look any different," some unfamiliar shaman said. Kalea had an entire audience!

Kilka resumed her impatient patting of Kalea's face when she didn't open her eyes wide enough. "Wake up now!"

Kalea made an effort to rise, and struggled.

"Care to tell us where Wikshen is and why you're still a virgin?" the woman said.

"Still a virgin?" she echoed.

Kilka held up her index finger. "We checked you. Last night you failed somehow!"

Kalea dropped her head to the pillow and tried to make sense of the swirling memories of shadows, flames, and Dorhen's hot, masculine body against hers. Really? Through all that, she had managed not to lose her virginity? Good thing!

"I don't know," she said, confused but also relieved. In her extreme ecstasies, she wouldn't have the head to ponder the consequences of making love to a possessed man.

Before Kilka's expression morphed into something angrier, Knilma put her hand on her shoulder.

"Kilka," she said, "you remember how much lucidity this girl lost during her ecstasy. I don't think we can put too much responsibility on her for anything that did or didn't happen. You saw Wikshen carry her in here himself. We were all certain he'd do the deed." She turned to Kalea. "But any detail you might remember and share, share it."

Kalea propped herself on an elbow. "Um…" She tried hard to process all of it. "I remember him building a fire."

The numerous shamans in the room twisted to observe the dim embers.

"Why would he do that?" Kilka demanded.

Kalea shrugged her bare shoulders, completely naked under the blanket. That's right, the shamans had taken her clothing last night.

"Maybe I was cold," she offered.

All the shamans' faces fell long, and they turned to regard each other.

Knilma eyeballed Kalea. "He started a *fire?* For your comfort?" she asked.

Kilka flexed her hands rapidly. Knilma drew her wrinkly lips tight. Maybe she was puzzling over everything concerning Kalea and Wikshen as a whole, all the favoritism he'd shown her. How could Kalea explain to them that she had known Wikshen before he was a deity? *Should* she try to explain it?

"Kilka…" Knilma said. "I think a meeting is in order soon…to talk about Wikshen…and this girl…"

Kilka squinted at Kalea as she listened. "Indeed," she said. "In the meantime, get out of Wikshen's bed."

Kilka produced her neatly folded maid's uniform and seared Kalea with her stare the whole time she dressed. Meanwhile, Knilma threw the top blanket off the bed and inspected the black linen sheets closely. Strangely closely.

Whether she told them or not, if Kalea continued to live here, she might not be able to hide much anymore. Kalea sighed through her nose at the tricky situation. A lot of it wouldn't work. If she had to watch him only from afar, see him in a state of extreme arousal and eating and interacting with those concubines, bear his feigned disinterest in her, and fill his glass but not be allowed to eat or talk with him…she wouldn't make it. Eventually, something would have to change. She might need to find some way to research pixie-possession, but first she had to get him out of this place. It couldn't be helpful that he now lived immersed in this wicked culture that worshiped *him!*

A bizarre idea passed through her mind: what if she seduced him? Obtained his "blessing"? She'd gain more privilege if she did, status, and a sort of seniority over the other girls. She would achieve a permanent closeness to him. She'd have his ear, a seat next to him at dinner, not to mention his love. Maybe with some added power and privilege, she could change his mind about things and get him to leave this place with her. Despite the scary notion of making love to a possessed Wikshen, the idea was worth considering. The notion that burned her heart was the reality that if she didn't achieve this fast, some other girl would beat her to it.

All the shamans filed out of the room, grumbling about clean sheets and Kalea's "failure," but Knilma hung around. Kalea looked up and found the old woman's baggy eyes squinting at her.

"Too late for a lesson today, my dear. Get on with cleaning the floors." Kalea nodded.

Before Knilma turned to leave, she said, "By the way…"

"Yes?"

"Dyii informed us you came to this place with two men and an elf."

Kalea's heart skipped. She'd forgotten about her friends. Despite the entire night she'd spent with Dorhen, she had yet to siphon any information they could use to find Mhina. "Yes," she confirmed.

"Well, one of them is in the dungeon."

"What did he do?" she asked, trying to keep her voice from shrieking.

"Something bad, dear. He trespassed in Wikshen's domain and stole money from our coffers."

Del! Leave it to him to ruin everything!

"Wikshen is the only male allowed in the tower and in the catacombs, you understand? Everything in here belongs to him—everything from the riches in our coffers to the bodies of the females."

Kalea nodded once. "I can't imagine what got into him," she said, lacing a cold, honest thread into her tone. "I'm very disappointed."

"What is he to you?"

She shrugged, finishing tying off her dress strap. "Just a friend I met on the road."

Knilma dipped her head and dragged it back up with effort. "I see. You've come a long way since you arrived." She reached out and pinched the flesh on Kalea's arm to test its softness. "Don't be late for tomorrow's lesson. We'll have a lot to talk about after what happened last night."

Down in one of the main corridors of Wikshen's tower, Kalea pressed against the wall to wait for her chance. She'd left her bucket and rag stashed behind a row of hanging cloaks in a closet. Two shamans were talking and blocking her path; at least one of them had been in Wikshen's room when she woke up earlier. They spoke of her incident, blaming Kalea for failing to inspire Wikshen to "produce a blessing."

Kalea rolled her eyes. Last night, sleeping had been the last thing she wanted to do. She remembered crawling toward him as he lay on the floor and putting her hand on his... Her face turned hot fast, finally feeling ashamed of her bold behavior.

She could only wait and hope neither of them walked past her when they parted. They'd recognize her, as Kalea was becoming the most famous black maid in Wikhaihli's history. That, too, was pointed out in the gossip she overheard all morning. Apparently, no black maid had ever been elevated to First Sister before.

Normally, she wouldn't care to hear such tales, but today shamans and witches were sharing stories about black maids past Wikshens had "blessed." From what she gathered, he'd never granted any sort of kindness or favor to one. In fact, he tended to be rough on women in her league, Kalea's begrudging ears picked up. Something about their stooped working poses riled up his desire and also his sense of humor. He had liked to catch them unaware and "punish" them quite erotically when they dropped their guard. He found that funny?

By the time the shamans closed their discussion, Kalea was more than ready to give story time a rest, and their footsteps finally padded away. Except one pair of footsteps came toward her.

No, please don't come this way! Kalea squeezed her eyes shut and held her breath. She pushed against the stone wall, trying to flatten herself as if part of it, and pressed the back of her head hard. *Shadow, hide me!*

Immediately, Kalea realized what she'd done. The shaman strolled past her and through the corridor, a little jingle bell bouncing on a string from her belt.

Kalea let her breath out. Her heart raced—at herself, not at the close call! She lowered her gaze and beheld her dirty, sore feet. She'd just prayed to the damned shadow! They really had made her into a Wikshonite!

"Dear Creator," she whispered. It had been too long since she'd prayed to the Creator, and a dreadful guilt welled up inside her to try it now. She shook her head. Her chores and duties called; she couldn't ponder about everything she'd done wrong lately.

Now clear of anyone who might question her actions, Kalea sprinted down the hall to exit the tower at the alley where the compost wheelbarrows waited to be hauled away. She couldn't guess where the dungeon might be. She also hadn't had enough forethought to try to get a disguise so her uniform wouldn't stand out. She wasn't supposed to leave the tower...especially after last night.

Actually, she didn't truly know what "last night" would mean for her future. It didn't take a lot of imagination to predict that each new encounter with Wikshen would only tighten their leash on her. Maybe soon, they would order her to spend more time with him, which might help her plans. She'd think hard about sleeping with him to put her claim on him before the other girls could.

Kalea bopped the side of her head with the heel of her hand. She was going crazy. Del was in dire trouble, and all she could think about was Wikshen!

Focus, stupid girl!

From the alley, the ocean made itself known through its salty, moist air and distant background roar. How long did her friends spend on the beach every day? As far as she could tell, the sun had reached high noon. Who knew where Bowaen and Gaije would be at this moment? No matter. She needed to find the dungeon.

She stopped at the end of the alley and peered across the wide space of the cloister, a sort of courtyard with compacted dirt and patches of grass where many bare feet tread. The witches' dorm, where the concubine candidates lived, lay straight across from her position.

On her visits to the bathhouse, she'd caught wind that the candidates would move into the tower soon. Several parts of Wikhaihli were undergoing heavy construction these days, and continuous noises of hammering, shouting, and clinking of chisel against stone complemented the busy new goings-on. She understood the concubine candidates would move into one such new addition.

Scaffolding crawled up the side of the tower like morning glory to enable work on higher floors and repair the place's leaky roof. Wikhaihli's grounds had livened up since Kalea's arrival. A large flock of chickens clucked about instead of one or two, and a pen with wooly goats now filled the far corner—and over there by the workshop, a carpenter assembled a new spinning wheel.

Kalea marveled at it all for a bit. All of this was paid for with riches brought from pledges who wanted to show Wikshen their devotion. The odd, wandering elf who had, once upon a time, decided he needed her to show him the way, now stood as the axel of all this activity and fanaticism.

Scanning the complex from the cover of the awning, Kalea recognized certain buildings. She stood one building down from the kitchen. The center of the area displayed the big bell tower. A little door stood at its base with a smaller bell dangling over it. That was where Dyii had spooked her and she'd run from him. Kalea shivered to revisit that strange night, from Dyii's behavior to the sanguinesent's arrival...and Dorhen. She hadn't thought of Dyii lately either, or seen him among the many men in warlock black going about, cursing and ordering the lowly workers around.

Kalea squinted. The walking cloud currently moved through, but it lightened up by the minute, allowing the sun to shine down. Where would the dungeon be? She wouldn't have thought this place had a dungeon. On the other hand, she'd seen its underground complex of prayer halls, bathing pools, shrines, and catacombs, so why not a dungeon?

One worker, a short, round man with a bald head, walked past her alley with a long board on his shoulder. She reached out and tugged his sleeve. The little man stopped to eyeball her, and his brows shot up when he beheld her uniform.

"Hello," she said in a hushed tone.

"Why are you whispering?" he replied in his own whisper.

"Do you know where the dungeon is located?"

Frowning, he pointed to a general corner of the complex.

"Is it well guarded?"

"It's a dungeon," he said.

Kalea sighed and dropped her whisper. "Thank you." She clenched her fists when she realized she should probably give him a coin for his help, but he moved on before she could say anything else.

Feeling a bit naked in her wrapped dress with bare arms, she carried on. She should've borrowed a cloak from the closet where she hid her bucket, but her wooly head, stuffed with thoughts of Dorhen and last night, couldn't manage to think that far. Being out in the warm sunlight and crisp air seemed to help her mind. Last night's fireplace setting had helped her out of her ecstasy too, she realized. Something inside the dark halls of the tower, maybe the darkness itself, maybe all the meditation and Wikshonite talk, or maybe the shrine water…did something to her. Her lusty disposition dried up under the sunshine too. Otherwise, a few times each day, she'd get caught up in thoughts about sex and feel odd sensations in her body.

Along her hasty path around the cloister toward the building at the corner, Kalea jumped and ducked under a window at Kilka's voice. She'd reached the witches' dorm, and Kilka and other familiar voices conversed in a practice room. The shutter stood open a crack. Kalea didn't have to worry about being seen through the space, but she could hear their conversation well enough.

"That's what the other shamans and I are trying to figure out," Kilka said.

Brielle piped up. "But she's so plain and bony. I don't see why the Mastaren is so interested in her."

"No sense questioning the Mastaren," Kilka told her. "He knows what he wants."

"Well, what about my ecstasy?" she replied.

Kilka huffed. "Your ecstasy was nowhere near as important as hers. Damned fools—you'd better shape up, or that silly maid will outrank you!"

Brielle's next words grumbled out, barely audible. "My ecstasy proved that at least some small part of the Mastaren wanted me too."

Kalea moved on with a shudder, ducking past the window. She couldn't listen to those sneaky girls plot against her to steal Dorhen. Dorhen loved *her*!

Kalea reached the door she guessed the worker had pointed to. She opened it to the same musty, old smell all the buildings put off, although this one also smelled like sewage and sweat.

Immediately inside the door, a warlock sat at a desk with a big book and writing implements. He sported long, black hair on only one side. The other side was freshly shaved, a hairstyle reserved for high-ranking warlocks.

The man's eyes grazed up her form to settle on hers. "You lost?"

"Is this the dungeon?"

He leaned back in his chair and crossed his arms. "Yeah."

"Then no." Kalea had forgotten to form some kind of plan for once she was inside the dungeon. "Wikshen sent me."

He smirked at her. "Wikshen sent a maid? To do what?"

"See the prisoners."

"A *maid*?"

"Yes."

The warlock guard leaned forward and glared at her. "When Wikshen wants a status update on the prisoners, he usually sends a shaman, or maybe a witch. Shouldn't you be in the tower, scrubbing his chamber pot?"

Kalea froze for a response until something burst out. "I'm his favorite."

The warlock leaned back again and lowered his eyebrows. "You... *her*? The illustrious maid?" A smile cracked his mouth at the end of his question.

Kalea put her fists on her hips and nodded. "I am."

The warlock's teeth glinted between his parted, smiling lips. "I can see it." He nodded as he ogled her again. "So, what's going on between you? Been groping and snogging a lot? When will he fu—"

"Stop now," she demanded without meaning to. Redirecting the conversation back to the prisoners would be much better.

"You know, all the warlocks have some wild ideas about you two.

Not much around here is as fun as picturing a little maid with her fanny peaking from under her short skirt as she's bending over to clean floors and such, vulnerable to the moment when Wikshen sneaks up on her and—"

The warlock animated his hands in his excited banter, and Kalea had to shout to make him stop. "The prisoners!" She took a breath. "Yes, I'm his favorite maid," she confirmed before he could say more about the embarrassing subject. The gossip about her and Wikshen really had spread to all corners of Wikhaihli. "And Wikshen has given me permission to visit the newest one, whom I know personally."

The warlock stood up and loosened a ring of keys from his belt. He unlocked the door at the back of the room and held it for her. "This way, *maid*."

Kalea entered, and he followed behind her. A long, down-sloping corridor curved around and turned into stairs. In the enclosed space, the two stayed quiet, only their feet crunching along the dirt-covered stones. An iron gate sectioned off the floor beyond the base of the stairs. He unlocked it too.

"So, what have you two done so far?" the warlock asked, eyeing her sharply as she passed through the open gate. "Has he slipped you the tongue?"

Kalea's stomach lurched in horror and embarrassment. She averted her eyes and kept walking.

"How 'bout the finger?" After falling behind her brisk pace, he jogged to beat her to the next locked gate secured into the stone walls. A second warlock manned this gate, and as Kalea walked through, she could feel the first warlock gesture at her.

"That's the maid," he whispered to the second guard, whose face lit up.

Immediately ahead, a complex of cells made up the underground space. Kalea ignored them. Her face radiated heat and a trickle of sweat itched her back. "May I please have a moment of peace?"

The two idiot warlocks smiled and stepped back. Kalea moved forward and perused the cells, most of them empty. The first one displayed a hapless worker who must've done something wrong out of ignorance. Real Wikshonites stood out quite a lot from ordinary pledges. While observing this community's growth, she had guessed that lots of ordinary people would be attracted to the prospect of joining the cult for security and prosperity, not only because they feared Wikshen's wrath. The stipulation that came with this new home was having to learn the religion and its rules quickly.

The next person in a cell made her start. "Dyii?" she burst out without thinking.

His head popped up from his huddled position, and then he sprang to his feet and legged to the front of the cell. Kalea stepped back in case he tried to grab her. At least the two warlock guards watched from the gate entrance. Surely, they wouldn't let "Wikshen's illustrious maid" come to any harm.

"Kalea," he hissed and, two cells over, Del rushed forward at the sound of her name.

Leaving Dyii there, she ran to Del's cage. "Are you all right?" she asked. "What in Kaihals were you doing in the tower?"

"You can probably guess," he said with a sigh. His face was sooty and his clothes daubed with beach mud. He didn't have his headband anymore, but he'd used a piece of twine to tie back his messy hair.

"Are you mad?" Kalea hissed the words.

He dropped his voice to a whisper. "I was on a mission. We're leaving this place soon… Well, we were going to leave."

"I've already told Bowaen I'm not leaving," she replied.

He took the moment to study her.

"I've found Dorhen."

Del shook his head. "He's dead."

"No, he's not."

"What the hell are you talking about?" Del stopped himself and shook his head. "It doesn't matter because I'll be dead soon too."

Kalea's mouth fell open. "No."

"They've already said it. I stepped into Wikshen's 'realm' or whatever, and stole some valuables. They're going to chop my head off and make a public spectacle to"—he huffed—"to inspire fear of 'the Mastaren.'"

Kalea's whole body went cold, and the sweat she wore made her shiver. "We'll get you out of here."

"I'm not holdin' my breath." He shook his head as if the words came with difficulty. "I don't think Bowaen knows yet."

She reached her hands through the bars. Del stood back looking at them, fingering the dingy bandage around his injured wrist instead. His hand appeared to have a bit more mobility today. "I'm trying to comfort you," she explained. She could feel the warlocks' eyes on her. If touching the prisoners would get her in trouble, she'd take it in stride. Nonetheless, Del didn't take her hands. He'd never been very warm with her. Even Gaije didn't mind her friendly contact, or holding her hand over difficult terrain. Del had never offered to help her with things like that.

"I don't want you to be afraid," she tried to explain further. "What's your problem? You've never seemed to like me much. What have I ever done to you?"

He shook his head, and she might've seen a tear run down his cheek, but the lighting was too dim.

"I hate vestals," he said.

Kalea frowned and slackened her reach. She rested her hands on the crossbars. "You...hate vestals," she parroted.

He shrugged and turned to pace in a circle. "They're nothin' but a bunch of crabby old bitches who want to keep everyone from having fun."

"What?"

Del stopped pacing. He avoided her eyes and stood there, scratching at his head. "When I was orphaned, my home burned down—my whole damned village burned down. At the next town over, a constable found me in the street and dragged me to the local orphanage, where, as you should know, vestals ran the place."

He shook his head and rolled his eyes. "I hated it. I hated the vestals there. They'd hit me with a switch if I fidgeted during their long lectures. I memorized long, boring passages from the Creator's Word because they made me. I missed my ma." Del made a visible effort to swallow, turned his head, and spat to cover it. "I just hate vestals," he said with a shrug. "And you're one of them. So, what do you expect?"

Kalea spread her hands, resting them on the bars. "I'm not a vestal anymore. I thought you knew that." She tilted her head and laid it lightly against one of the vertical bars. "If you were in an orphanage, how did you meet Bowaen?"

"I met him as soon as I got to the new town, actually. He gave me some water and a piece of bread. After that, I spent my days in and out of his shop. Got caught, sent to the orphanage. And then I snuck out one night and ran back to Bowaen's shop. He let me stay with him after that."

Kalea nodded as she listened. "I'll try to find Bowaen to tell him about you. Maybe he and Gaije can..."

She paused to turn her eyes to the warlocks, who whispered to each other—probably about her and Wikshen, making up all kinds of rubbish theories they'd spread to the others, which would morph into horrid new rumors. At the thought of Wikshen, she turned back to the prisoner.

"Del," she said with new life in her hushed voice, "I'm going to help you. Be patient. Hold firm. Pray." She mentioned the last one despite the fact that he probably wouldn't want to hear it. Days like this were when many people decided to give the Creator a chance.

She turned to leave and, as if automatically, she stopped beside Dyii's cell. He moped around in there as heavily as Del. "How about you?" she asked him. "Are you also slotted to die?"

He stepped forward and shrugged. "Kalea," he said, and reached his hand through the bars. She stayed back, not so eager to hold this one's hand.

Behind her, the guard yelled, "Touch the maid and get yer arms knocked off with a hammer!"

Dyii withdrew his hand. In attacking a woman who was the property of Wikshen, he had committed a crime as bad as Del's, if not worse, she realized. Strangely, he didn't display nearly as much anxiety as Del. Dyii lowered his chin and gazed at her with his glowing red eyes through his eyelashes. His jagged bangs fell low, framing his face. One cheek and jaw still showed signs of Dorhen's angry fists, although the bruises had shifted to shades of yellow by now.

"Kalea," he whispered again. "Has he touched you?"

"Why does everyone ask me that?" she grumbled. Every time someone brought it up, it made her want to vomit. Her and Dorhen's private interactions were no one else's business!

"It's important," he said. "Especially to me."

"Why is it so important to you, though?" Images of her frightful night in Valltalhiss flashed in her head. Red-eyed people. King Kerlin cuddling her in his ratty bed, proclaiming her a goddess. Proclaiming he'd…mate with her.

Kalea hugged herself and stepped farther away from Dyii's cell. According to ancient lore, something magical or instinctive drew the Thaccilian people to Luschians. Kerlin had explained how when they mated, the Thaccilians turned human. She imagined Kerlin would've lost the red hue in his eyes, his ability to hear her heartbeat, and the need to eat hearts if he had had his way with her. Did Dyii want the same thing? Kalea didn't have time to puzzle over it, or to ask if he knew anything about the legend.

"He hasn't touched me."

Holding her stare, Dyii nodded.

"But you should forget about me," she followed up. "I'm not interested in Thaccilians."

She didn't bother to observe his deflating body language at her statement. With one more glance to Del, who paced nervously in his cell, she hurried away.

Chapter 18
Elusive Cure

No sooner had Lamrhath walked into the room to meet his new doctor than she stormed him with desperate questions about her daughter. It was probably a good thing his men had brought the girl along.

"Relax," Lamrhath said to her as she stood tied up in the sorcerers' hold. "Your daughter's fine. She will be fed a fine meal tonight, and you can see her as soon as you've carried out my instructions."

When the woman appeared to calm down, they let her stand by herself. "What do you need me to do?"

One of her escorts poised to slap her for asking a question. Lamrhath lurched forward to stop the man's hand at the expense of his ever-aching abdomen. "Hold!" he ordered.

The sorcerer shrugged away, and the doctor twisted to frown at him.

"Do not ask questions here," Lamrhath told her, trying to keep patience in his voice. "First thing tomorrow morning, I need you to heal an illness that plagues me. You'll create a cure, or at least tell me what we need to gather to make one, and then I'll reunite you with your lovely daughter... Her name is Cygnet, am I right?"

The so-called miracle doctor nodded her head nervously.

Lamrhath twisted his mouth into what should look like a smile, a gesture he rarely felt like making anymore, even when it was genuine. "And your name is..."

"Falli," she told him.

"Falli," he recited.

"My lord," she said, "I should like to know what is wrong with you so I can prepare your treatment."

The sorcerer shot Lamrhath a look, and he put his hand up to prevent any punishment from befalling the doctor.

Shifting her eyes between the two, Falli said, "My lord, it would be difficult to keep from asking questions. Asking questions is exactly what medicine women like me have to do in order to be useful. It's not too far from solving a mystery. The main method for solving mysteries is asking questions."

Lamrhath inclined his head slightly to make a show of graciousness.

"Did everyone hear?" he said to his group. "Doctor Falli is allowed to ask questions, especially if the purpose is to cure my ailment." He turned back to her. "I'm told you've inspected men's genitalia and cured problems like impotence, correct?"

Falli nodded.

"I have a similar malady, except the opposite."

"The opposite of impotence..." she said thoughtfully with squinted eyes.

Lamrhath studied her briefly. "You don't look so confident now."

She shook out of her quizzical body language. "Forgive me, but I've never heard of such a problem. In my village, we would consider this a blessing because it brings many children."

"For me, it's a problem. Can you not help me?" By the end of his question, he spoke through his teeth. Anger simmered in his gut.

She waved a hand. "Please don't be discouraged by my confusion, my lord. It doesn't mean I can't listen to your complaints and cure your 'ailment,' it only means I'll have a bit of a journey in learning about your special case to create a...cure. To be honest, a mystery is an invigorating thing for me. Medicine is my passion. The inquiry I'll have to undertake is exciting—and this is all good for you. I'm highly successful, my lord, and I thank Wiksh—*the gods*—I thank the gods for my gift of passion."

"I'm glad to hear that," Lamrhath said, raising an eyebrow at her stutter.

"There may be many facets to my inquiry," she continued. "Do you have a wife?"

"I have two."

Falli shrugged. "Which one are you closest to?"

It would take a while to get used to this woman's questioning. Only his highest-ranking sorcerers were allowed to ask questions of him, as the pattern of questioning in Ilbith took a down-ranking motion. Each rank only asked questions amongst themselves and of lower ranks. The servants and slaves could ask questions of no one except their own; their purpose was only to take orders. Falli, as a rare and valuable person—a doctor with keen knowledge and skill—could possibly forge a new league of people with the privilege to ask questions. Right now, in her tattered black garments and with messy hair swirled into a bun behind her head, she looked like any old servant of Ilbith.

Answering her question proved hard too. Which wife was he closest to? He got along much better with Silva—so much better that he'd slept in her bed all coiled together with her last night and the night before. Something about her...

Before he opened his mouth to give his answer, Talekas, who'd been fixated on every detail of this meeting, taking notes as he did in most situations, leaned in to whisper in his ear, "My lord, might I suggest you consider Orinleah? She is an elf like you. The most…natural mate you keep."

Nodding at the advice, Lamrhath answered, "I've had an elven wife for sixteen years."

"Perfect," Falli said. "Bring her to the examination because I'll have many questions for her."

Lamrhath reared his head back and considered asking why. What did Orinleah have to do with his ailment? Instead, he let it go, then gave Falli a respectful nod, turned on his heel, and exited the room. It would take a bit of work to survive the rest of the day with his ailment aside from his regular study and spell preparation, but then tomorrow his examination would take place and it would all be over. Lamrhath would finally know peace.

Orinleah entered the small chamber they'd set up to meet the new doctor with a sniffing naerscouel on each arm—strong men with heads like jackals. Lamrhath used this beastly order of guard for his own personal purposes, mostly as a show of intimidation to all who lived below his status. His sorcerers had stocked the room with various herbs spread on a table for the doctor to use, a mortar and pestle, and a comfortable chair for him. A sense of anxiety wreaked havoc in his core, blending a thrill for his impending cure and dread about having to speak of his intimate business with a strange old woman.

The naerscouels shoved Orinleah in and closed the door. Her lovely lips pouted and her brow narrowed as she ogled the odd setup. She hadn't been briefed on today's inquiry, and Lamrhath hadn't seen her in several days because he'd been enjoying an unexpected serenity in Silva's embrace.

Seeing Orinleah now, though, with her silky, brown hair cascading to her narrow waist, excited him to an extreme level of ruthless *saehgahn* virility. No one, not even Silva, made Lamrhath feel more masculine than Orinleah did. When her eyes settled on him, sitting comfortably in his chair and hiding his raging bodily feelings, she folded her arms over her midsection.

"You may stand here next to me," he said.

She crossed the room and planted herself on the spot he indicated.

"I've called you here for a great cause," he said, doing her the courtesy of answering the question she wasn't allowed to ask. "We're going to talk to a wonderful medicine woman I've found. She's going to cure my ailment."

At her continued silence, he looked up to see how heavily she breathed. "I know how much you hate me," he said, "but this is good." He paused to sigh with the twinge of pain in his gut brought on by the sight of her slim dress hugging her curves. "It means I won't suffer anymore. We can forge a more normal relationship. A romance."

He decided to turn his eyes away from her to try to slow his burgeoning pain. Bracing his elbow on the chair's arm, he combed his fingers into his hair and closed his eyes. "You don't know how hard I try…" he continued. "How badly I dream of your love. How cautiously I try to plan our evenings together. To no avail."

He was panting by now. "After today, I'd like us to start over. I'll court you the way the best of men court women. I'll earn you instead of take you."

When he chanced a peek at her, she was staring down at her clasped hands. "The doctor wishes to speak to you. Please help me today."

A few more long moments passed, and he said, "I see you're wearing the necklace I gave you. Do you wear it every day like I asked?"

She absentmindedly ran her fingers along its rubies and nodded once. "I wear it so much, sometimes I forget to take it off."

"Good." He looked forward again. "It makes you so much more beautiful, complementing your hair and dark eyes."

Orinleah wrung her hands when the door opened and Falli stepped in with her naerscouel escorts and Talekas.

"Will you need anything else, my lord?" Talekas asked.

"No," Lamrhath said. He didn't bother to rise from his seat. "Leave someone outside the door until we're all finished in here."

Talekas bowed. "Good luck, my lord." He closed the door and left the three together in the awkward air of the tight room.

Falli rubbed her hands together and perused the table of herbs. "Well, I see they got all the herbs I asked for. Thank you, my lord."

"Forget the niceties," Lamrhath snapped. "I'm beginning to feel pain already. Hurry and cure me."

"Forgive me," Falli said, "but I must repeat myself that your…problem is new to me. I'm about to begin a study here, not a quick fix."

Lamrhath sighed through his teeth.

"Why don't we begin by you explaining what your problem is?" She turned to Orinleah. "And you are?"

"Her name's Orinleah," he answered for her.

Falli put her hands out and took Orinleah's warmly. "Pleasure to meet you, my dear." She turned to Lamrhath. "You didn't tell me your wife was such a radiant flower."

"I'm not his wife."

Falli frowned.

Lamrhath clenched his jaw and glared at her. "Don't start your rubbish now."

Falli looked to Lamrhath. "But you said that for sixteen years…"

"I'm married to his brother."

"Who's dead," Lamrhath corrected. "And I told you the truth. She and I have been together—in a sexual relationship—for sixteen years. Now if you'll both shut up, I'll tell you my problem!"

Falli darted her wide eyes between the two of them, chose Lamrhath's attention, and bowed low. "Yes, my lord, let's get down to business. Tell me what is wrong."

The tension in the room escalated his pain to its highest peak. "When I don't have sex, I get immense pain and nausea in my abdomen."

Falli squinted and nodded. "And how long has this been happening?"

"I'm not sure. Ever since I was thirteen, I've enjoyed sex. I did it as often as I could, like eating, I suppose."

"Like eating," she echoed. "So, for you, sex became a need as important as eating. Have you felt this pain—similar to hunger—ever since age thirteen?"

He shook his head and dabbed the sweat from his brow. "No, I didn't have the pain. I just liked the deed. I got very ambitious in my conquests."

When he chanced another look at Orinleah, she was frowning deeply. Her hands kept still. She didn't know these things about him, nor about his ailment. In her solitude, she had no way of knowing about all his concubines, Silva, the fetching servant girls he sometimes spotted in the halls, the brothels he'd visit when out on the road, and the dark, succubus-like spirits he honored for certain sorcery rituals. As soon as he entered Orinleah's room, he threw himself at her, and that was as much as she knew.

"I see," Falli responded. "Can you remember when your first bout of pain struck?"

"No," he grumbled, and took a moment to think. "But it happened in my young years."

"How young?"

He buried his face in his hand. He'd never thought about this. He had his regular routine, almost nightly. The memories he'd long forgotten rushed before his eyes, smothering the image of Falli's round, inquisitive face.

He and Daghahen. They had gone to the Darklands, free from all connection and responsibility—two wild, young *saehgahn*. Getting laid. Getting rich. Meeting up with hapless bands of sorcerers. Stealing from them, but not before syphoning a sorcerous trick or two.

Lamrhath had indulged in far more fornication than Daghahen. Daghahen started to question him on it, to which he'd strike his twin on the head and say, "Well, why don't you?" or "What—are you limp?" Lamrhath took pride in his libido. He craved sex. After a while, if he didn't get his orgasm, he'd get upset. Tense. Cranky. And sometimes when he found himself in inconvenient situations, he felt little twinges of pain in his stomach. When he finally ejaculated, it seemed to flush out all the tension and discomfort.

Sex. It was his everything.

"Twenty-five years old maybe, I don't know!" he said to the woman.

"I'm going to have to do an examination next," Falli said.

Lamrhath put his hands out. "Isn't that what we're doing?"

"I'm sorry, my lord, but there's more to an examination than talking. I'm going to have to…look at it."

Lamrhath glared at her in disgust. Orinleah stood with her eyes bulging. She hadn't appeared so scared since their first night together as a couple.

"Why in Kullixaxuss would you have to look at it?"

Falli put her hands out. "Let's be calm now; being on edge won't make it any easier. Now, I must explain…" She cleared her throat. "Sometimes, when one experiences pains that are connected to one's genitals or intercourse, it means he or she has a disease of that region. The disease is caused by fornications with many people. It's a matter of uncleanliness."

He half-rose from his seat. "Are you implying I'm *dirty*?"

"No, my lord, I explained a simple cause-and-effect truth. Now if you will please"—she sighed— "take your pants down. And answer me this question: does it hurt when you pass urine?"

"No," he grumbled as he worked the strings of his codpiece. Orinleah stared in shock at the unfolding events.

"You are erect?" Falli said.

He flared his eyebrows and scowled down at her. "Yes. That's the problem! I'm always erect! And if I don't service it, I hurt! Now fix it!"

The woman winced and leaned over to have a close look at his penis.

"It looks…fine," she said. "I see no disease."

Lamrhath huffed.

"Now there's more we must do," Falli said, and rubbed her hands together rapidly before breathing on them. She reached her hand toward his cock, and he tensed up. She paused. "Are you okay with this, my lord?"

"I guess I'll have to be," he replied, arching his neck backward and pointing his face toward the ceiling.

"I would think so…You don't seem to be the type of person who'd mind a stranger touching you."

He clenched his teeth to keep from swearing or thumping her on the head or *something*. Her words rang true, though.

Another glance at Orinleah showed how stiffly she stood, staring at the door. Maybe her presence made the situation strange. He kept his relationship with Orinleah private; his other intimate relationships…not so much.

"It looks healthy. Everything about it," Falli said after a few very uncomfortable seconds.

"Of course it does," he said. "I know what you're talking about when you describe the diseases. I don't get those diseases. Elves don't get the same diseases humans do. Didn't you know?"

"Forgive me," Falli said. "I've never treated an elf before, especially for this type of problem. For humans, I can do everything from deliver babies to treat impotency."

Lamrhath neared the edge of his patience. If she didn't do something helpful in the next instant, he'd walk out. "I already told you, I'm the opposite of impotent—!"

"With all due respect, my lord," she said over his rage, "please calm down. I'm beginning to sense that your 'ailment' is somehow connected to your mental and emotional state, but I'll have to make sure. Please take a breath and try to relax."

She turned to the table and selected a long glass flask like the ones they used in their alchemy practices. "I'll look at your urine now…if you don't mind…"

Falli held up his flask of piss by the light of a candle since this room lacked windows. He dared to check his side again as the doctor did her study and found Orinleah in the corner, resting her forehead against the wall like a child who'd been naughty. Falli had yet to ask her any questions. Mortified by all this, Lamrhath regretted calling Orinleah in here. It would've been easier with Silva.

Falli placed the flask down on the table with a notable show of care and rubbed her nose bridge. "Nope," she said. "It all seems fine. Even the smell." She glanced up at Lamrhath with a nervous new light, and then shifted her attention to Orinleah. "Do you two have any children?"

Lamrhath frowned at the same moment that Orinleah lifted her head and snapped a quick, "No."

"Then I may have to examine her as well to see which one of you has the fertility issue. If you've been married for sixteen years, something should've happened by now."

"I have a son," Orinleah said.

Falli studied them both hard. "By your..." She nodded to Lamrhath. "By her...*other* husband?"

Lamrhath put out a gruff, "Yes," and averted his eyes.

"In that case, I shall have to inspect you, my lord, to see if you have a fertility issue. It may be connected to your ailment."

Behind him, Orinleah exhaled loudly through her nose. "He has the Overseas Taint."

The room fell silent.

"What is the Overseas Taint?"

At her question, Orinleah shrugged her petite shoulders with a flourish of her willowy arms. "It's the reason I shouldn't be married to him. My husband has the taint too. I wasn't supposed to marry either of them, but I loved my husband. I loved him more than myself. And by the light of the Bright One, I was blessed with a son."

Lamrhath butted into Orinleah's rudeness with a growl in his voice. "The taint is a stupid superstition the Norr elves have."

"I know nothing about this," Falli said, "but from what I've learned from the conversation so far, your...brother—her original husband—successfully sired a son, even with the Overseas Taint. Therefore, I don't see any reason why you shouldn't be able to as well, my lord."

Lamrhath nodded. He'd noticed over the years how difficult it seemed for Orinleah to conceive for him. He had long ago decided to put it out of his mind because the thought hurt him too much. The Norr elves hoarded many other superstitions, including one that females wouldn't conceive for males they hated. If that belief was rubbish, if this problem could be remedied by curing his ailment... He wouldn't know what to think right away. Maybe it would bring him joy.

Falli handed him another glass vessel from the table, this one smaller. "I'll need to inspect another humor, my lord." Her eyes fell to his lower body and returned to his face.

"You're joking," he replied.

Holding out the glass dish, she shrugged. "I'm not, my lord. I can tell easily by looking at a man's semen if he has a negative quality that affects his fertility."

Lamrhath snatched it from her hand. He actually didn't begrudge this test as much; it would mean he could get some relief, which would help him get through the rest of the inquisition. He took one look at Orinleah and Falli before sticking his head out the door and ordering the attending sorcerer to retrieve his best concubine. He made Falli and Orinleah wait outside as he produced the next humor sample, and then sent the concubine away.

Holding the white sample up to the light, Falli swished it from side to side as if the way it slid around the little glass jar meant something to her. He grimaced when she brought it up to her nose and inhaled deeply. However, Lamrhath could now stand slack and casual, leaning against the wall beside Orinleah, his pain gone for the next hour or so. His eyes shifted to her while he waited, and they shared a short, silent exchange of gazes before she pulled hers away.

Falli put the jar down and huffed, bracing her arms on the table— not a good sign from what Lamrhath had seen. She turned and strode across the room to regard Orinleah squarely. The *faerhain* shrank under her stare. "My lady," Falli began. "How often does my lord come to you?"

Orinleah glanced at Lamrhath. "About once per week. Sometimes more."

"Once per week would be accurate," Lamrhath confirmed.

Orinleah began to toy with the ruby necklace he'd asked her to wear every day.

"Is his stamina the same for every visit? Does it waver?"

Orinleah's mouth dropped open, and she sent Lamrhath a silent plea for something… Permission? Or perhaps a pardon from this questioning?

He nodded to her.

She shrugged at Falli. "He can never resist touching me for long. I can tell when he enters my room, every time, that he wishes to talk, but he can never talk for long. He leaves abruptly afterward, before seeming to get enough words out to satisfy him."

"And he has good stamina? He never misses an ejaculation, or fails to keep rigid?"

"Um…" Orinleah swallowed. Her voice shook. She checked Lamrhath for permission again. "He's the same every time. His enthusiasm never wavers."

Falli turned to Lamrhath. "How old are you?"

He clenched his teeth and bared them at her. "I'm nearly nine hundred and eighty years old."

Orinleah gasped and turned to him. Falli's reaction showed a quieter incredulity.

He gave her a joyless grin. "Which means your darling Daghahen is also that old."

Falli mouthed the words in repetition of his age. "And how long do elves usually live?"

"Four hundred at best," he said. "Longevity seems to be one of my Bright One endowments."

"'Bright One endowments?'"

Orinleah answered before he could. "In Norr, we worship a god called the Bright One. He is the light we follow through the forest, leading us to safety and prosperity. Some elves are born with abilities considered magical. We credit the Bright One for such abilities." She flicked her eyes to Lamrhath and back. "However...the Overseas Taint can bring special abilities too."

Lamrhath bristled once again, and the slight jerk in her stance showed her fear.

Falli watched both of them. Already, she'd gotten away with far more prying than he'd allow anyone else to do and remain alive. She spread her hands, her eyes wide and her mouth poised open, possibly running out of questions. "My lord, how many rounds of sex have you had in one day—on the most extreme of days?"

"I don't know..." He rolled his eyes and scanned the room, which shrank and lost its air by the minute. "Twenty-three? Or four?"

Falli bowed her head to wipe her moist face on a handkerchief. "I see." She retreated to the table, where she absently arranged the glass containers and sprigs of herbs. She turned back around. "My lord, may I take a walk? To think deeply about this?"

He put his arm out. "If it will help you hurry up and decide how to cure me. However, you'll walk under supervision." He added under his breath, "Just because you've inhaled my piss doesn't mean I trust you yet."

He opened the door and said to the sorcerer standing guard, "Take Falli to the garden. She wants to walk. Bring her back in five minutes."

Falli could hardly scamper out before he closed the door on her.

Alone with Orinleah again, he noticed she was shaking. "My lord, I'm sorry," she said, and bowed her head.

"You did what you were asked," he replied. A long moment passed. "Thank you for trying to help."

Another silent moment.

"Orinleah." Her name slid through his teeth. "Why haven't you reappeared in my dreams in all these years?"

She turned her head and narrowed her eyes at him.

"I used to have these dreams about you. I call them 'healing dreams' because that's exactly what they did. They worked better than anything I've tried." He sniffed. "Your Bright One endowment. Dreamwalking."

Her breathy voice lacked any of the conviction she'd shown when answering Falli's questions. "I've no idea what you're talking about."

"They were beautiful dreams," he whispered, staring into the emptiness of the room. His loneliness. Standing solemnly beside him, she listened. "I didn't bring you here out of malice, you know."

His words drew her eyes, but he didn't meet them. "It was the dreams..." Lamrhath continued. "Daghahen left me...on my own in this tower. One day, a striking dream about a *faerhain* hit. You came to me. I woke up to find it was a wet dream, and my stomach no longer hurt. A wonderful and bizarre moment."

He shrugged. "And then later, I found Daghahen. I went only to check up on him. I didn't know he'd be married or have a child... But I saw you there. It was...*you*! How would you expect me to feel?"

She opened her mouth and worked it for a bit. "How...how did you feel?"

He regarded her squarely to show her his sincerity. "I felt you were mine." He preferred to show a casual smile, but his mouth twisted into a difficult frown. "A foreign feeling. You...were..." He chose his words carefully. "Already mine. There's no other way to express the sensation. My natural instincts raged."

He made a tight fist at his gut. "I wanted to murder Daghahen on the spot. I thought about it as he stood by the hearth, holding a cup of tea he'd poured for me. I resisted. I didn't know how to deal with my confusion. It took time to sort out. I couldn't murder my brother in that moment. My flesh."

Orinleah shook her head.

"What?" he probed.

"I belonged to Daghahen first." Her face flared red, and she clenched her teeth at the onset of tears. "The dreams started after I met Daghahen. Do you understand?"

"You were only dreaming about *him*?"

"I dreamed of him," she confirmed. "Not you." She covered her mouth, and the tears fell generously.

"Maybe you met him first but made love to me first—in that original dream."

She shook her head, still covering her mouth. "Daghahen convinced me to lie down for him by the end of our second meeting. I was so young, I..."

Lamrhath's stomach dropped.

"He was very..."

Lamrhath raised his hand to stop her. He didn't want to hear about what she had done with his brother. "Persuasive," he finished for her.

Orinleah wept. "I knew nothing about dreamwalking, and somehow I—I seduced you. I didn't mean to."

Lamrhath reached out to touch her hair. If he did, it would ignite his passion again and the pain would return, so he stopped his hand short. He crossed his arms and stared ahead at the door as they awaited Falli's return. His voice ran hard. "It's not your fault."

Her tears stopped bizarrely quickly. "I suppose I'm here by my own fault." Her voice hardened; the emotion drained out. "I seduced you in your dreams but thought you were Daghahen."

She shot him a sharp look, but the door whined open before he could pose a question about it. Wrapped up in his trance of memories and visions, Lamrhath didn't look up.

"My lord," Falli said. "I've taken my walk, and have reached a conclusion."

That piqued his attention. He waited. He probably lost his usual stern countenance in favor of wide eyes and a pursed mouth, waiting for the defining moment this doctor, this expert of the body, would tell him how to banish his pain forever.

"There is no medicinal cure for what you have."

Lamrhath held still. He heard the words but waited for more, for better words.

Falli shrugged. "Your special case is out of my league, I'm afraid, though I do know what's wrong with you."

Still numb for the moment, he asked lifelessly, "What is wrong with me?"

Falli's chest swelled. Her hands clasped together in front of her, as if she prepared to sing an aria. "My lord," she said, "this problem is not in your body. It's in your mind. I'm afraid there is no cure, so to speak, for your unique problem. I do not believe hope is lost for you, though."

He shook his head, his emotions returning, his nerves flaring in every digit. "Wait. Did you just say there is no cure for my ailment?"

"Yes." She huffed; walking around the garden patio shouldn't have put her this much out of breath. "Your body has no illness. It's your mind that wants to experience intercourse so often. I believe the pain is due to your personal stresses and bodily tensions, so you cannot cure your stomach pains and need to copulate by taking any medicines I might create."

Orinleah piped up. "What about castration?"

Sneering, Lamrhath's rage flared hotter than his desire. He shot his hand out and grabbed Orinleah's hair. She yelped.

Falli lurched forward and waved her hands. "My lord, please! Do not hurt her, she has only asked a question."

Lamrhath let her hair go, and Orinleah retreated to the corner.

"Your wife asks an intelligent question which may be worth a hypothetical look at least: would castration cure your ailment? Though I'm sure you don't like the idea, the real question is: what would you pay to end your suffering, my lord?"

Lamrhath's mind plunged into a slew of what-ifs. That's what the doctor wanted to know. Was he willing to do whatever it took to stop the pain? He thought about it for a moment. A long moment.

Under his empty stare, Falli shrank. "My lord," she said, "you may be relieved to hear that I believe castration is *not* the answer. It may put an end to your erections, but it would not end your stomach pain and nausea, not to mention, your mind would still yearn for intercourse. Your pain is a phantom pain."

The numbness returned to Lamrhath's head. A phantom pain. No cure. It only existed in his mind?

A hand touched him from behind. He turned to find that it was Orinleah's. She wore a sad veil. Normally, her touch would flare his need, but for now he remained numb.

He started walking. He crossed the room, passing Falli as the petite woman pivoted to make way. He walked out the door.

Chapter 19
A Maid Pleads

Where is Wikshen?" Kalea demanded of Knilma the second the old woman hobbled through the door for their morning meeting.

Knilma frowned and squinted an eye to study Kalea through her better one. "Who are you to ask, 'Where's Wikshen?'"

Kalea didn't back down at her criticizing glare. She'd looked for Dorhen all day yesterday after seeing Del in his dungeon cell. She'd watched for Dorhen this morning too. He hadn't shown up to give her a piece of his breakfast.

Balling her hands into fists hidden at her sides, Kalea said, "I *must* speak to the Mastaren. Where can I find him today?"

Knilma clicked her tongue. "You'll find him wherever he pleases, my dear." She went to the chest of practice implements and took out the rolled practice mat. "Here," she said. "Take position."

After her early morning chores, Kalea hesitated to enter the bath house. She hadn't faced the concubine candidates since they saw her ecstasy. She took a few deep breaths to work up the nerve to walk in there, exhaling slowly similar to her Kraft Position exercises.

Everyone froze at the sight of her.

After she stripped off her clothes, a tug at her hand announced one of the black maids. "Kalea, you must bathe with us," the girl said with a glow in her eyes. The other black maids watched her with similarly captivated expressions. "Kalea," she said again. Her eyes burned. "Please..." She lowered her voice to a whisper. "Do you know how important you are?"

An image hit Kalea at her question, of Dorhen bowing down to her and weeping, pleading for her to let him stay near her. The fact that she was holed up in a convent where he couldn't go used to bother him. He'd been so smitten by her, and she was nothing but bad to him back then. Thinking of her past treatment of him stung, but he remained a mystery to her, a mystery which had intensified since his change.

Kalea twisted around to regard the concubines as the girl retained her hand. The concubines all watched her. She nodded and allowed the girl to lead her to the black maids' side of the pool. Metta's face hung quite long. Kalea gave her a little wave to reassure her of their friendship, and

Metta didn't respond.

As soon as Kalea settled into the soothing water, the barrage of questions ensued. She answered them as shallowly as she would've answered the concubines' inquiry.

All day long, Kalea listened for talk of Wikshen, where he might be, or what he would be doing that day. Instead, she collected more and more tales and rumors about herself—the mysterious maid the Mastaren desired. If he wanted her, why was he avoiding her?

He didn't even show up to sit on his throne at the normal time to hear pledges. The people, a load of grimy peasants with a few well-dressed lords and ladies sprinkled in, all waited in line, some sitting. They could be there for days before getting their chance to see Wikshen. If he failed to show after long enough, the shamans would put a sacred shroud on the throne and let the pledges kiss and worship it in his stead. Kalea's stomach sank to think of it. Dorhen hadn't left Wikhaihli, right?

She refused to give up. Kalea poked around, pretending to clean, and strayed into some of the deepest parts of Wikhaihli she'd yet seen. She found many doors locked. Some parts of the catacombs were sectioned off with locked iron gates fixed to the stone walls like those in the dungeon. She sighed when she encountered the fifth one. He could be anywhere in the places she couldn't go…but she could approach the underground worship chapel. This deep underground, she couldn't tell how late it was, but worship time should be drawing close.

Several chapels riddled Wikhaihli, some for shamans, at least one for pledges, and one located outside the main mansion for the warlocks, but Kalea needed the one for the concubines—one of the most deeply carved chapels. Finding it might prove a challenge. She chose from a few forked paths, thinking and hoping that they were familiar.

She certainly recognized the fountain shrine at the juncture, with its soft, constant stream flowing out of a sculpted nozzle and into a hole at the base. Beyond the hole's opening, a faraway, echoing trickle hinted at how deep the hole plunged. Kalea stopped to drink from it, as well as to take position and meditate to calm her nerves. When she stood up again, she felt light and giggly. She didn't laugh, but the water's good feeling made its presence known in her core and branched outward, like a cool breeze on every limb.

A little farther down, Kraft flames appeared in nooks on the cave walls. As she'd hoped, drums echoed distantly through the stones. Exhilaration surged through her, mingling with the cool water's caress. A pleasant heat blossomed deep in her abdomen too.

The drumming grew louder, similar to the other night. He must be down here. Maybe he hadn't left Wikhaihli. Other facets of her being awakened: physical, spiritual...sexual—but she couldn't forget her mission. Del's life hung in the balance. She steeled herself to ignore those feelings, focusing instead on the lightness the water had delivered.

She could see easily enough in the lighting of the sparse Kraft flames. They flickered with a measured distance from one to the next. She trailed her hand along the smoothed rock wall in such areas, but otherwise tried to keep her speed up.

Dtoom, dtoom, dtoom-dtoom-dtoom. Dtoom, dtoom, dtoom-dtoom-dtoom. The vigorous rhythm kept steady and grew louder the farther she ventured.

Her heart flew. *He's in there. I'm going to see him!* She needed to see him. She ached to see him. She loved him! Wikshen!

The door became visible around the bend. A blue Kraft flame flickered on a sconce above it. Kalea threw the door open, never stopping to wonder if it would be locked or if the shamans would be angry about her intrusion.

She exhaled a hard and fast breath at the scene within. The shamans inside held their drums, and they fell out of rhythm when Kalea barged in. The concubines all crouched in a crescent formation before an altar decorated with a tall, black shroud and huge bouquets of the usual herbs. Pennyroyal, lavender, evergreen branches. Several plates of tasty, hot food—delicacies—*masteries* of culinary skill—stood arranged on tiered platters beside the altar.

And him. Wikshen.

He sat upon the altar on a thick cushion, a living idol for all to adore and worship. His shrine was huge, taking up the whole wall, with a tall, wide platform decorated with many other cushions and heavy black drapes. A comfortable setup, amply big enough for more than one person.

For now, he sat on it alone, much like the way she had seen him at the banquet, with his knees up and head bowed in a sleepy daze. Seeing it all reminded her of the heaviness of his condition. Dorhen was no longer himself. Being possessed would ultimately kill him, so he still needed rescuing as urgently as if the sorcerers had shackled him.

She ran to him, leaping past the line of huddled concubines, who were partially naked. Kalea didn't pause to be appalled at them. She went straight to Wikshen, shouting his real name. He perked up at her disturbance, shaking all over as before.

Kalea fell to her knees before him. "Dorhen! Dorhen, listen, please!" She grabbed his ankle.

He made an effort to observe her from his perch, breathing through his mouth, chest rising and falling deeply. Was he lucid enough to receive her plea?

Behind her, the concubines stirred out of whatever trance they'd achieved, and the shamans spouted angry words as they lowered their drums. Their voices grew louder and closer.

Kalea spoke fast to try to get her words in before they could catch her. "Dorhen, listen, you must pardon Del! Please don't let them kill him, please! He's my friend. Dorhen! Do you understand? Dorhen?"

Dorhen swayed in his struggle to fight his own trance. The miasma around her tickled, attempting once again to seduce her. She bit her lip hard and focused on his eyes. Whatever happened, she needed to get him to grant the pardon first!

The shamans shouted behind her, half at her and half at each other. The concubines also rose with questions and scoldings.

Kalea grabbed Dorhen's kilt to pull herself closer to his face. His trembling body touched hers. His erotic energy proved contagious. He slid a leg off the altar to place his foot on the floor. Kalea met him halfway. She put her hands on his sides, and he shuddered and sighed, arching his neck back. When he met her eyes again, a small amount of sense had sharpened his gaze, but his breathing remained deep and rhythmic. His lust burned against her and set her body on fire.

"Don't let them kill Del! Please," she tried again. She wrapped her arms around his waist as he now stood on the floor, leaning against the altar. His erection stabbed into her gut through his kilt. Her clinging made him hiss and sigh. He put his hands on her arms. "Will you spare Del's life?" she asked.

He opened his mouth, and his hot breath beat against her forehead. "Yeah." The answer was nearly lost within his sigh.

Behind her, the shamans fell silent.

Dorhen's shaky hands trailed to her back, where her low-cut dress allowed her shoulder blades to show. His fingers traced them until she shivered. Relaxing a bit, he folded his big arms around her, welcoming her into a hot embrace. No space was left between them, only her maid's dress and his long, heavy kilt.

She didn't want to relax yet. "Dorhen," she said, her voice weakening in a blossoming dark ecstasy, "tell them to spare Del's life. Tell them right now."

When a cool wave of air passed over her head, she could tell he had raised his face away from it. "Knilma," he said in a voice deep and loud but lacking the strength of an everyday state of mind. "Don't kill the intruder."

"Mastaren," she said behind Kalea's back, "the young man has committed a dire offense. His foul feet trod sacred ground."

Dorhen took one hand off Kalea's back and outstretched it to stop the shamans from coming closer. "I demand this. Put ten lashes on his ass if that'll satisfy you, but don't kill him."

Kalea squeezed Dorhen's middle. "Oh, thank you."

Knilma, apparently, still disagreed. "Mastaren, you aren't thinking clearly. You must consider his crime in the morning when you can discern—"

Dorhen's stomach muscles tensed under Kalea. "Are you saying your Mastaren doesn't have a clear head?" he yelled.

"I was merely saying that—"

He cut the shaman off again. "Listen to me!"

A new thrill passed through Kalea at his shout. No matter how angry he sounded, his erection held firm, perhaps firmer than ever before. It poked her to the point of pain, pushing up against the bottom of her rib cage.

"Tonight's worship is over." One of his hands slid into Kalea's hair as he spoke. "It will resume tomorrow night, *after* the intruder receives his punishment. If he lives through it, I will make my choice." He drew his hand out of her hair and glided his fingertips along her jaw to her chin. "I will bless my favorite."

Everyone else in the room burst into gasps of shock and murmurs of wonder. Kalea shivered with a tingly thrill, wrapped comfortably in his arms. She stood with his support, melted into him. He went back to caressing her scapulae and wandered his fingers down the curve of her back, over her thin dress. His wandering hands made his own breathing increase until he decided to loosen his hold. Harsh, cold air washed around her when their contact broke, waking her up unpleasantly to the goings-on around her.

"Tomorrow," Dorhen said again. He took Kalea's wrist and guided her to the door. "Make sure she returns safely to her quarters."

The shamans hurried to Kalea's side at his order.

"Until you carry out my will, I'm finished here." Dorhen also exited the chapel, leaving all the whining concubines behind him. To Kalea's dismay, he took a different tunnel away from the area.

The whole scenario happened too fast before Kalea found herself being whisked through the dark corridors up the sloping paths back to the main tower, a shaman tugging each arm.

What just happened? Something was about to change. Did he actually intend to do what he'd told the shamans?

Knilma kept up with her two younger cohorts as they led Kalea on. "Well done, my girl! Who knew it would take a little negotiation to finally get the Mastaren to endow the first miracle of his reign? Bless your young friend for being such an idiot."

"Indeed," Kalea muttered.

"Why, I can't even be angry at you for interrupting our worship," Knilma continued, and turned her attention to her sister shamans. "I knew we should've let her into our sessions all along."

A shaman at Kalea's side piped up. "But she's a maid, marm."

"And she shouldn't be, you understand?" Knilma replied breathily as they trekked along through the deep corridors. "Kilka judged her wrong—I *knew* this Wikshen would like the willowy brunettes. I read his personality by divination of his face." She sniffed. "No matter. This little mink won't be a maid for long. Tomorrow night, she'll be First Sister."

Numb in her shock, Kalea replayed those words through her head more than once to make sure she'd really heard them. She and Dorhen would finally make love. Her face heated up. Her body too. But…what about his possession?

Knilma drew her out of her thoughts. "Blast it, where is Kilka anyway?"

One of the other shamans hummed. "You're right, she wasn't with us at the ritual."

"She missed it—she missed a miraculous scene!" Knilma said, and clicked her tongue. "It doesn't matter. Now listen, dear, we have much to do before tomorrow night. No one can dictate how the choice is made except Wikshen. Sometimes he chooses his first on a whim without any plan or communication with his shamans, and sometimes he makes an announcement and an official worship ritual is carried out, complete with choreographed bonding moves. This occasion shall be the latter."

Twisting around to look Knilma in the eye as they walked, Kalea mouthed the words "choreographed bonding moves" to try to understand them.

"Nothing you haven't learned about in our little talks already. These will be carried out in a proper, practiced way. It is the most holy type of worship we offer to Wikshen. It's called Wikshen Adornka."

Kalea hesitated to ask questions. She didn't want to ruin anything. She'd succeeded in saving Del's life for now. Until everything fell into place, she'd go with the flow. When they made it to the main hub of the tower, the shamans sent word to the dungeon to get everything ready. The sun made its way down; it was earlier in the day than Kalea had guessed. Nightfall approached.

"Light the cloister with torches," Knilma told a younger shaman, "and set up all implements for a lashing. We'll carry out Wikshen's order tonight and take all day tomorrow to prepare for his most supreme worship ritual: Wikshen Adornka. He is going to bless First Sister."

At that, the other shamans went running. Knilma took Kalea's arm. "Go to bed," she told her. "You'll be waking up very early tomorrow."

"May I see the punishment?" Kalea asked.

"No," Knilma snapped. "The Mastaren has spoken. Your friend *will* be lashed and released to resume his duties. Don't worry about him. Now go to bed!"

Kalea nodded and took off in the direction of the lower corridors. Her stomach fluttered. She didn't like Del having to get any lashings, but what could she do? Dorhen was obligated to dispense punishment. It would look too odd if he let him get away with something they considered a horrible crime.

What she'd be doing tomorrow posed another concern. What would she have to do when she woke up? And Knilma had called it a "supreme worship ritual." She didn't know what to expect, but it sounded like her intimate moment with Dorhen would be made into some sort of display with drumming and prayers and an audience. She'd be forced to consummate her relationship without a chance to change her mind. And what *about* his possession? Was she about to step into a dangerous arrangement?

Kalea didn't go to bed quite yet. The dining room would be filling up with all manner of Wikhaihli residents around this time, most notably the concubine candidates. Maybe Bowaen too. She quickly donned the puffy-sleeved chemise Dorhen had given her under her maid's dress, borrowed a cloak from the linen closet, and hurried to the dining hall.

No sign of Bowaen inside. Maybe he and Gaije would show soon. She decided to have a bowl of stew to fill and settle her stomach before bed.

Mimara, the witch who served the stew, handed her steaming bowl back, and Kalea turned around as Metta entered the dining hall. Kalea froze with the hot clay vessel in her hands. Metta was another one she wanted to speak to, but looking at the girl's stiff shoulders and blank face now, Kalea couldn't tell if she would want to talk. Was Metta jealous about the turn of events?

Kalea didn't have the option to bolt and escape Metta's notice; their eyes locked before she could take a step, and Metta would be heading to the big pot of stew anyway. Kalea decided not to miss a beat. She put on her best smile and trotted to meet her.

"Metta," she sang as if nothing had happened and they were still the best of friends. "Just the woman I wanted to see."

"Hello, Kalea." Metta avoided her eye contact as she continued her way toward Mimara and the cauldron. She also wore different clothes for dinner instead of the skimpy worship costume.

"Can I sit with you?" Kalea asked. "I have...a troubled mind."

Metta finally met her eyes with a raised brow as she took her place in line to be served. "Why would your mind be troubled?"

Kalea winced. "I have issues... Maybe that's the wrong word. I don't know what's going on. I mean, I'm happy the Mastaren obliged my plea and my friend will live, but..."

"But what?"

Kalea lowered her chin. "I don't know what he was talking about afterward," she half-lied. "What is 'Wikshen Adornka?'"

Metta shot her a smile that didn't reach her eyes. "The greatest worship ritual we have."

"What will I have to do?"

"You'll have to use your best wiles to arouse the Mastaren. You'll use the beat of the shaman drums to carry the ritual to the end. Ultimately, you'll earn his blessing and become First Sister."

Kalea swallowed. Metta's words, though vaguely expressed, made her feel funny. "Is it hard?"

Metta shrugged. "How should I know? I've never seen it happen before. We concubine candidates all spend our days working our bodies to their limits to gain strength and stamina, as well as to sculpt them to perfection." A little smirk graced her face along with the one raised eyebrow. "I assume the ritual takes several grueling hours and lots of difficult bodily feats we *concubines* practice hard for." Metta's smirk shifted to an empty smile with curled lips. "You may not have too much trouble, though, as Wikshen seems easily aroused...by you."

Kalea bit her lip.

As irked as Metta appeared, she allowed Kalea to take the seat next to her when they sat down. Kalea woofed down the stew, more nervous than before talking to Metta.

"I'm sorry," Kalea said out of nowhere after swallowing another large bite.

Metta cocked her head. "Why?"

Kalea shrugged. "You seem to...love Wikshen. A lot."

Metta nodded. "We all belong to him. My turn with him will come soon... For a glorious few moments, I will own him."

Kalea winced, but let it roll off her back. On any other day she might've strangled Metta across the table for saying that, but tonight Metta had been scorned. It wasn't hard to imagine all the other concubine girls cursing Kalea's name when back together in private. Kalea hummed her next phrase through her teeth, as if she might somehow soothe Metta's pain. "There's something you don't understand, though."

"Like what?" Metta didn't look at her, but took a bite and darted her eyes about the dining hall.

Kalea struggled to breathe in the awkward air between them. *That I knew Wikshen before he was Wikshen. He's really just a lost elf who decided he loves me.*

Kalea danced on the edge of sharing those statements. Would it comfort Metta or make things worse? And if she did, how could she go on to explain to this Wikshonite that she didn't fancy the idea of consummating her relationship with her elven lover in front of a bunch of shamans with drums?

Kalea chose different words. "I'm still worried about my friend, Del." Faint drums beat outside as they prepared the public spectacle of Del's lashings. "He must be terrified right now."

"Well, it's like my old ma says: beating a child doesn't fix his brain, but it might fix the brains of the other children."

Kalea cocked her head at the thought of Metta's mother. "Is she still alive?"

"Oh, yes," Metta sighed.

"That's right," Kalea said. "Didn't you tell me your mother isn't a Wikshonite like you are?"

"It's true."

"What does she think of it?" Kalea could imagine her parents if they found out she'd joined the Wikshonites. They'd disown her immediately.

"I see her every once in a while. For the most part, I've moved on from her. A seedling has to grow and blossom, ya know?"

Kalea frowned. "Sure, I guess."

Metta pursed her lips to have to speak of this subject. It was the opposite kind of spectacle as seeing her talk about Wikshen. "Her type of witchcraft is more of the domestic kind: brewing herbal teas to cure illnesses, weaving magic cloth, that sort of thing. She didn't like it too much when I told her about my new religion. She says I have to be 'self-sufficient' and that joining a 'cult' will warp my mind and make me a weak person. But she doesn't know! She has no idea how strong Wikshen is. She hasn't even seen him yet."

Metta's speech only deepened Kalea's frown. She had joined Wikshonism too, though perhaps less eagerly than Metta had. In her discomfort, she directed the conversation back to her friend's harrowing situation. "I just wish that I could at least go and reassure Del that he won't be executed."

Metta hummed. "I don't think you have enough time. The shamans were quite direct when I last saw them. They intend to whip him tonight. Possibly in a few minutes." She shrugged. "We can go out and watch it happen."

Kalea cringed. Regardless of her own past lashings, including the ones that had happened at this place, she dreaded standing idly by while someone else suffered it, especially one of her friends. She certainly wouldn't be able to go to bed and sleep while he endured it though.

Despite Knilma's order, Kalea agreed to Metta's idea, and they spooned the rest of their stew into their mouths. The drumming outside made it hard to relax. The shamans were making such pageantry out of Del's punishment, the dining room was mostly empty. Everyone must have chosen to watch the spectacle before eating.

The two of them took their empty bowls out to the back alley, where two buckets of fresh water were set out for each individual to take care of their own dishes.

Metta squatted at the soapy bucket first and made quick work of her bowl. "I'll meet you out there," she said to Kalea as she set her bowl carefully on the drying rack after rinsing it in the clean water.

"Okay."

Metta flew back through the door. On the other side of the large building, Kalea could hear the drumming rhythm grow more elaborate. She hastily dipped her bowl in the cold, soapy water and reached for the rag.

A hand clamped over her mouth and another locked over her collarbone, wrenching her up and away from the bucket. The clay bowl cracked against the ground when it slipped from her wet hand. A large, sweaty palm muffled Kalea's squeal.

More than one voice murmured behind her. The second person took her hands and bound them behind her back.

"Shhh!" A harsh, masculine hiss blasted her hair beside her ear.

Kalea couldn't move; her bonds were too tight. She didn't know who, but someone had caught her.

Chapter 20
A Tide Rises

A cold sweat of terror doused Kalea. She shivered against the hard body of a man. Immediately after tying her hands together, he and his accomplice wrapped a cloth around her mouth and threw a burlap sack over her head.

When she whimpered through the gag and wriggled in the tight hold, the man shushed her again. Kalea quieted down. The sound he made…

He lifted her over his shoulder with a rush of upward motion, and then he walked carefully. The two whispered to each other as they carried her through a dark, secluded alley running along the city wall. Kalea stayed quiet, listening hard to their voices.

It's them? No chance, I can't believe it! she thought. She couldn't ask any questions because of her gag. *Why would they do this to me?*

"Through here," the one with an older, raspy voice said, a voice she knew too well.

The younger one carried her on his shoulder. With her wrists tied behind her back, she couldn't balance well, and his hands remained respectful, keeping to her legs and off her hindquarters. The position quickly pained her midsection, however, and she moaned.

"Sorry about this," the younger one said.

Kalea growled in annoyance. "Gaiye, hoot ne nyown!" she demanded despite the gag.

The one who carried her flinched. "Sorry!" he said again, and stopped to obey her command.

"Gaije, what the hell?" Bowaen said, dropping his whisper.

The hood whipped off her head, revealing Gaije kneeling before her, his eyes wide with concern. Bowaen stood bristling over him.

"Sorry!" This time Gaije directed his apology at Bowaen. "I just don't like this."

"We have to get her out of this place first!" Bowaen said. He turned and scrubbed his hair with his nails.

"Tell me what stupidity you're up to!" Kalea said as soon as the gag came off.

Gaije's eyebrows turned down. "Don't you want to get out of here so we can find your sisters and Mhina?"

"I told you both, we have to get Dorhen to—"

Bowaen swooped in to bow over her. "He ain't Dorhen! Shit, lady!" He spat a wad of saliva to the side.

Tightening her jaw, Kalea released a long exhale to pen up her anger. "Will you untie my wrists, please?"

Gaije moved to do so, but Bowaen barred him with an outstretched arm. "No," he said. "Do you know where Del is?"

"Yes, I do." She cleared her throat. "Del got himself caught trespassing and stealing from Wikshen. They were going to kill him, but *Dorhen*—the elf I've been looking for, who's still alive—used his authority to lighten Del's sentence to a few lashings. They're setting it all up right now in the cloister."

Bowaen gawked at her for a few seconds before hissing, "Shhhhit."

"I think Del will be fine. His behind will be sore, though," she said.

"We gotta get him outta there."

"Don't you dare!" Kalea said. "If you interfere, you'll only make it worse. He's only going to be lashed. He can handle it. And you'd better let me go, because I have to uphold my end of the deal if he's to get off with only a few slaps."

Bowaen squinted. "What's your end of the deal?"

Kalea cleared her throat and turned her eyes away. "It has to do with Dorhen... Dorhen made a promise to the shamans to get them to comply."

"No. No way in hell. We'll go and get Del, and tonight we're leavin'."

Kalea started yelling so loud, Gaije covered her mouth. All the while, Bowaen grunted and mumbled about how they'd ever convince her Wikshen was nothing more than a liar and a killer.

He leaned down to point in Kalea's face. "Show us the way to Del."

Gaije removed his hand so Kalea could speak. "Won't you untie me?"

Leaning back, Bowaen crossed his arms. "No. You got a cloak on, so you'll walk with your hands tied. You gotta leave here with us."

"You've no right to—"

Bowaen cut her off. "I'll let you walk without a gag. If you betray us to the Wikshonites, our blood'll be on your hands. Got it?"

Gaije said softly beside her as he clamped her mouth, "Please, Kalea. You entered this place to help us—to help your sisters. We've lost so much time already."

Kalea sighed through her nose. At her new calm, he removed his hand. "I'll show you where the dungeon is. I've wanted to tell Del not to worry anyway. He's probably scared to death with those drums beating outside."

Bowaen nodded.

"I'll help you," Kalea said, "and I won't betray you, but I'm *not* leaving Dorhen!"

"Let's talk about it after we get Del outta jail."

With her hands tied behind her back, Gaije helped her to stand while Bowaen straightened her cloak. "Follow me." She walked through the alley toward the constant drums with Bowaen and Gaije on her heels.

She strode with purpose, as if alone. Her panicked sweat returned when a shaman noticed her, followed by another. Knilma had ordered her to go to bed. She couldn't resist scanning for Dorhen in the crowd clogging up the cloister. Wikshonites of all ranks bustled in to see the criminal who'd dared to cross Wikshen.

One warlock leaned in close to another as Kalea passed. "Do you think Wikshen'll cut him down with his morkblades?"

"If he does, it'll be many slow cuts," the other replied.

So the crowd hadn't been told what they were about to witness. She stretched her neck, casually drifting toward the corner building that housed the dungeon. The clearing where Del would be tied up and whipped was apparent, but she didn't see any sign that Dorhen would attend. No altar or temporary throne complemented the setup.

"This way," Kalea murmured to her friends, and drifted as gracefully as possible with her bound wrists hidden under her cloak.

"There you are!" Metta's voice rang out. Kalea whirled in surprise. "What held you up? I've been waiting for you."

"Metta," Kalea sang with a false smile. Her restraints felt ten times more awkward than before. "I ran into my traveling companions. You might've seen them around. This is Bowaen and Gaije."

Metta shot them a look, but neither of them bothered to exchange niceties.

Kalea cleared her throat in the air of awkwardness. "Bowaen is Del's best friend, and he insisted on seeing him before the lashing, so we're going to the dungeon."

"I see," Metta said. She looked Kalea over. "Are you all right?"

"Yes, of course. Why do you ask?"

Metta shrugged. "You're standing a little stiffly."

"I'm worried about Del. I know how much pain he'll be in."

"You got lashed too the other day. Was it that bad?"

Bowaen and Gaije's eyes shot to Kalea. She avoided their gazes. "Yes, of course. Bless the Mastaren for saving me from it."

Metta's face soured. She pursed her lips, and her eyebrows floated higher. "Indeed."

Kalea winced, realizing she'd reminded Metta that Wikshen favored her. Kalea started slowly walking away, becoming increasingly self-conscious about her inability to move her arms. "We should hurry along now," she said.

Metta crossed her arms and turned back to the focal point where Del would receive his punishment. Kalea hastened her pace, praying no one else would try to talk to her. She ducked and darted at the sight of any shaman, and her companions weaved around people in their struggle to keep up.

When she nodded to the door, Bowaen opened it for her. She entered first. Inside, the same warlock occupied the desk.

"Well, hello." His voice leaped in recognition of her.

"How's the prisoner named Del?"

"I expect he's shitting his pants." When the warlock roared with laughter at his own joke, Bowaen's countenance darkened.

"I'd like to see him again," Kalea said. "These are my other friends. We'd like to give him some words of comfort." There was no telling whether or not this warlock knew Del would only get a lashing instead of the death sentence.

"Yes, my pretty maid." He rose and unlocked the door behind him.

"'My pretty maid'?" Bowaen grunted at the back of Kalea's head.

"I'll tell you later," she whispered, and led the way through the door the warlock held open. She wouldn't tell the warlock herself of Wikshen's decree. Let him find out through the great whisper network.

Inside the dungeon area, the second warlock wasn't present. The original one manned the complex alone today. Beyond the next locked gate, the first cell was empty. The worker who'd been arrested must've been set free.

She passed the next empty cell and nearly forgot about Dyii again. On second look, he wasn't in either. Kalea frowned. Surely they hadn't let him go. Had they executed him? No one outside had talked about it.

Kalea blew a breath through her cheeks and moved on to see Del. The warlock guard stopped to inspect Dyii's cell.

Del lay asleep, and Bowaen barked his name and rattled his door to make some noise. "Wake up, boy!"

Del slept quite deeply, considering the atmosphere and circumstances. The warlock stepped over to look at him, frowning.

"Del!" Bowaen said again. When the warlock approached his door with his jingling keys, Bowaen asked, "What have you people done to him?"

"Nothing…" the warlock said, focusing on getting his cell open.

Kalea stood back awkwardly with her hands tied as the warlock and Bowaen shoved into Del's cell. Bowaen patted the young man's face, and he finally began to stir.

"Enough with the termites!" Del moaned in his sleepy confusion.

"Termites?" Bowaen said, "You're dreaming. Wake up now!"

The warlock guard reached over and ran his fingertip down Del's cheek. He sniffed his finger. Stepping to look closer, Kalea finally noticed that Del wore a dusting of light powder all over his face.

"Del was drugged," the warlock said, keeping his voice down regardless of his disturbed tone. He stretched his neck to regard Dyii's cell again. "And Dyii is missing." He sprang to a stand.

Bowaen patted Del's face again. "What happened to you, boy?"

The warlock bent over Del. "Did you see how Dyii got out?"

Del rubbed his eyes, and then lifted his shirt to wipe his face, all muddled and drowsy. "I dunno," he said.

"Who hit you with this powder?" the warlock pressed.

"An older lady wearing black."

The warlock leaned back with his lips pulled tight. Older ladies in black abounded in Wikhaihli. "Did she release Dyii from his cell?"

Del shrugged. "I don't know. All I remember is her calling me to the front of my cell. Dyii was there at that point, watching us."

When they turned back to the warlock for his opinion, he was squinting. "I never let anyone in tonight—until you all." He paced to the entrance gate and back. "How did she get in here?"

Bowaen watched him hard. As soon as the warlock turned again, Bowaen lunged and hit him on the back of the head with Del's heavy smoking pipe. He'd been hiding it under his tabard. The warlock's knees buckled, and he dropped.

"C'mon, Gaije!" Bowaen ordered. Together, they dragged the warlock into Del's cell, took his keys, and snapped the padlock in place. He turned to Kalea, who watched the whole thing with her mouth agape.

"I told you not to mess things up!" she said. "Dorhen made a deal with—"

"Stuff Wikshen's deal!" Bowaen spat. "No sense in waiting around for Del to take a punishment when we're all leaving anyway." He took Kalea by the arm and pulled her to walk with them. "Let's go now. We got our weapons, bags, and everything we need waiting outside the wall."

"No," Kalea said weakly. She couldn't try to fight him and wouldn't betray them to the Wikshonites, but she didn't know how to escape without doing so. Sheer panic wracked her. Del stumbled up the sloping corridor toward the front entrance, struggling to recover from his daze. Kalea knew exactly how he felt.

When they arrived at the entrance, voices murmured on the outside of the door. Bowaen cussed, spun around, and fumbled the keys to unlock the entrance to the dungeon again.

Kalea trembled under her cloak, helpless to do anything. Bowaen pulled her cloak, and they all darted back to the dungeon.

"Was that a good idea?" she asked.

"Shit!" Bowaen said. "I don't want to get into a fight. There are a lot of people stirred up, and now we're trapped."

Nonetheless, they continued in that direction. As Bowaen struggled with unlocking the next door protecting the dungeon area, voices echoed behind them. The shamans were coming to retrieve Del for his punishment.

Del slurred in his sleepy daze, "There's gotta be a secret way out. How else did the old lady in black get in without the guard knowing?"

Bowaen flung the door open with a rusty whine. "And you didn't see how she got in?" he asked.

"I only remember turning around and seeing her walking from the corner of the room."

"Which corner? Show us," Bowaen urged him, and Del staggered to a dark area next to a little Wikshen altar with a hanging shroud.

Bowaen brushed the shroud aside to inspect the wall for any openings. "Nothin'," he reported. He moved the little wooden box with the cold incense sticks and bowls of fragrant plant fragments and found nothing behind or under it.

Kalea regarded the shadowy corner beside the altar, seeing only black. She walked toward it.

"What'cha doing, Kalea?" Bowaen asked.

"There's something different here."

The shadow seemed…alive, similar to the black miasma she'd been so friendly with in her ecstasies. Kalea walked into the shadow. It crackled and radiated around her, enveloping her. Behind her, Bowaen and the others drew their weapons to take on the approaching shamans and warlocks. Kalea put her foot forward to the wall. It smooshed into the stone like pudding.

She gasped and twisted around. "It's a spell. Hurry, before it wears off! And hold your breath!" She stepped forward, breasts first, hands bound behind her, and pushed into the wall the same way the woman and Dyii must have escaped the warlock's notice. Someone had cast a Kraft spell to soften the stone.

Kalea took another step, then another, pushing herself through the thickness. The spell was growing old and wearing off. The thick feeling increased as she worked her way through. She could only hope her friends would follow and all get through before someone got a limb fused inside the stone. No time to explain it all to them because of the approaching shamans either.

She wouldn't know what she'd find on the other side, whether it was Dyii and the woman or something else treacherous, until she arrived. The darkness went on before her. The wall wasn't very wide, perhaps two feet's width. A hand met her shoulder as soon as she pulled herself out and found stale, open air. Gaije. Her friends had paid attention after all. She waited as the rest of them fought their way through the wall to meet her in the dark cave on the other side. Every sound they made echoed.

"Is everyone okay?" Kalea asked.

"Yes," Gaije said, followed by Bowaen and Del.

"Good."

"What's wrong with the wall?" Gaije asked.

"Whoever helped Dyii escape softened the stone using Kraft," Kalea offered. "Their magic discipline has much to do with the vibrations of earth, Knilma told me. She said the shamans used it to shape the underground shrines, probably the dungeon too."

Bowaen's voice echoed next. "Where are we now?"

"I don't know," she said. "We'll have to feel this place out. Grab my cloak. I have experience walking around in dark caves."

"What does that mean?" Bowaen asked, but she didn't answer.

Instead, she said, "It would be nice if you'd untie my wrists. We've made it this far anyway."

"I agree," Gaije said, swiping her cloak aside to cut her wrist bonds.

Kalea flexed her arms in relief. "You retrieved your belongings from our hiding place?" Before entering Wikhaihli, they'd stashed all their things, particularly their weapons, under a hedge out in the hills.

"Yeah," Bowaen said. He and the others linked hands behind Gaije, who took Kalea's cloak. "But we didn't bring everything with us, just what we thought we'd need to get you out of here."

Kalea scoffed at their plan for her as she proceeded forward, tracing her hand along the rock wall.

"Hathrohjilh is still out there," he continued. "It woulda attracted too much notice."

"And also Leho's Bow," Gaije said.

"Where do you think we are?" Del asked.

"I don't know," Kalea answered softly. "There is a large complex of caves like this under the tower. I never would've guessed it might lie under other parts of Wikhaihli. Makes sense, though." The path under her bare feet sloped upward, potentially a good sign.

"One of us should lead the way," Bowaen said. "In case someone bad meets us at the end of this."

Kalea shushed him. "Let's keep quiet, and maybe they won't detect us."

The tunnel curved and bent, sloped up higher, and then down again. Kalea frowned. She wanted to get outside, not go deeper underground.

Shadow, show me the way, Kalea prayed, and caught herself in the act again. Maybe she really had spent too long in Wikhaihli. She could tell by her friends' nervous whispering and short breaths how uncomfortable they were in this darkness. She didn't feel such discomfort. Pondering it all, she realized she should feel anxious and relieved to leave all the darkness behind. How could she have gotten so used to it?

A constant whisper echoing through the tunnel became apparent as they moved forward. Squinting as she puzzled over the sound, she forgot to keep vigilant about the path she couldn't see. She dropped.

An arm hooked around her upper body and cut off her yelp. She didn't fall. Her toes met a landing beneath the ledge she'd unknowingly stepped off of.

"I'm okay, Gaije," she said. He'd slowed her fall and saved her from a broken bone or sprained ankle at least. "There's a steep step here," she told the lot of them. "Make your way carefully."

Behind her, her friends' bare feet slapped against the lower level one by one.

As they ventured farther on, the whispering sound's volume increased.

"Do you hear it?" Gaije asked. "It's the ocean. We may find the way out of here."

Aligning with what Gaije said, the sound sharpened into raucous, nighttime ocean waves. The air became cooler and saltier, fresh compared to the stagnant version they had breathed since walking through the wall.

No light brightened up the space as they drew closer to the cave's exit. Another foggy night in the Darklands. Kalea didn't like the water's extreme volume under that blinding effect.

"The tide must be comin' in," Bowaen said at the same moment of Kalea's thought.

Gaije pushed ahead, and Bowaen snatched her arm. He still didn't trust her not to run away and go back to Wikhaihli. Strangely, Kalea couldn't decide if she wanted to break away from them or not. She didn't want to abandon her friends, especially Gaije with his sister and the plight of the novices, but… Dorhen. Allowing Bowaen's hold on her, Kalea bit her lip.

A salty blast of wind roared into the cave. Gaije's vague form appeared as he leaned against the wall with his knife drawn. He checked outside both ways and abandoned his caution when a freezing flow of water surged in up to their ankles. Kalea gasped at the shock.

"Damn!" Bowaen said. "Go on, Gaije, let's get out of here."

Gaije hauled Kalea forward by her hand.

"So, this is the beach where you collect geoducks," Kalea said over the roaring waves. She'd found herself on a beach for the first time ever and still couldn't see the ocean.

"Yeah, be glad you're not a man," Del replied.

Bowaen hissed at him.

"Be quiet," Gaije said to the group.

No sooner had he finished speaking than a low but forceful wave rolled in and swept Kalea off her feet. Gaije's grip tightened, and she held his hand with both of hers as she regained her footing on the soft, muddy ground. They sank in. Gaije also had to pull his knees high to get around, but he was more adept at it than she.

Bowaen panted at her back, and she could easily imagine that he held on to Del because of his daze. "I wonder if the trail going up is close," Bowaen said.

Kalea attempted to look up the cliff toward Wikhaihli.

"We got all our stuff waiting up there." Bowaen pointed.

She couldn't see the top of the cliff in the dark, but it was a long climb, and the water rose higher with each crashing wave. It already covered her knees. When Bowaen's hand landed on her shoulder, his body moving closer, her fear escalated.

Another big wave. Gaije and Bowaen locked her in. Del hung onto Bowaen's arm as the current swept his legs up. They moved as one tight group toward the rocky base of the cliff face.

"There it is! I see it!" Bowaen pointed past Kalea to the slight hint of steps carved into the bluff. They wouldn't have seen it if the clouds hadn't parted a slit to let a little moonlight through.

Now practically floating, Kalea didn't have to do much to move along. Gaije and Bowaen pulled her through the water. Gaije went up the steps first, and Bowaen pushed her next. She still couldn't see the top, and the journey up the cliff quickly became a vertical procession. She'd been through a lot already, and her energy waned. Her wet dress weighed her down, dripping like a fountain shrine. She sure could use some of that fountain water right now.

"Keep going," Bowaen urged from behind her. Her effort to climb up the steep path quickly turned into a painful fight for her muscles to see the task through.

Dorhen stalked his way through the corridors under Wikhaihli, relying on his new ability to will the shadow to obscure him in the scarce lighting whenever a shaman rushed by, calling his name. It was such a useful and easy ability to recede into the darkness. The shadow was like a friendly spirit which wanted to interact with him. A mere shift of his thoughts, and willingness caused it to spring into action for him, more than ready to do whatever he wanted. This included using it to feel the atmosphere around him like an extra pair of hands.

Why had he been so stubbornly against trying to use this ability before? It was easier than pulling a magic hood over his head to disappear from sight—which had been an imperfect spell to begin with. The failure of his magic hood had led to his meeting Kalea, though. But now he had the shadow, a force he was discovering he could bend to his will, and he couldn't deny it suited him better, especially for protecting Kalea.

His heart picked up speed the farther he ventured toward her basement dorm. That was where she had been ordered to go, and hopefully there wouldn't be many other maids with her at this time.

"Mastaren, where've you gone?" Knilma hobbled by as he flattened himself against the wall, holding in his mischievous laughter. Her voice echoed down the hall after she passed. "We have to talk about your promise!"

He'd made a promise all right, a big one, and it excited him to his core. He suppressed his glee. This was exactly why he needed to speak to Kalea privately. The whole complex had flown into a tizzy at one little thing he'd said: *I will bless my favorite.* He'd done it this time. Now everyone knew Kalea was his favorite. He'd said it under the effects of the worship they were performing. Those words had felt so good coming out of his mouth. It also made a great bargaining chip for getting Kalea's friend off the chopping block. Now her life was about to change, and to a greater extent than he could imagine. He needed to warn her—about the shamans, about the balance of power in this place…about what he was going to do to her.

He entered a dark, hollow basement. No voices. No maids moved around down here yet, as they were still finishing up their chores on the floors above. Now free to walk in the open, he strode through the entrance corridor and across the big floor where the maids slept, cringing at the harsh sleeping arrangement as always. At least Kalea wouldn't suffer this discomfort for long.

Something was amiss. She hadn't come down here yet. He ran to the far corner to look down the adjoining corridor which led to the housekeeper's room. No one in there. His heart picked up even faster from its amorous rhythm. There wasn't any need to panic yet, but he didn't like not finding her where he expected her to be. He took off out of the maids' dorm to find her elsewhere, no longer bothering with the concealment spell.

Dyii stopped fast, grabbed Kilka's collar, and yanked her to the window. He pointed out.

"Damn you, stupid boy! How dare you jerk me around?"

He shushed her. "Out there, he goes."

Kilka shut up and blinked, straining to see what he pointed at in the night. Dyii couldn't see either, but he could hear the heart of Wikshen, which Kilka had instructed him to find.

"He went outside?" she asked. "Where's he going?"

"How the hell should Dyii know? You say you want Mastaren. There he goes. There goes his heart."

"So where's he—?"

He shushed her again. Subordinates, especially warlocks, weren't supposed to be so disrespectful of the shamans around here, but Dyii was different. He'd just spent too many days in that damned dungeon, and he had such a pain in his gut right now that he didn't care about much. "He's upset about something," Dyii offered. "And his heartbeats get fainter and fainter. I think he's leaving."

"Leaving!" Kilka shrieked.

"You are stupid for shaman, to speak so loud," Dyii said with an eyebrow raised.

"Where's he going?"

He firmed his jaw and held out his hand. "First, you owe me. Dyii is starving. You get him heart, and then he tell you more about Wikshen's heartbeat." He should've gotten his meal two nights ago. Part of their deal about him coming here was that Kilka would feed him the hearts of those who were executed, but the worker imprisoned next to him had earned his release since his crime had not been all that bad anyway, and the one called Del had been somehow given a lighter sentence.

Now, Kilka summoned the nerve to jostle him toward the door of the little room in Wikhaihli's west building where they were hiding. He had planned to hide here until everything calmed down.

"It doesn't matter where he's going," Kilka said, "because you're gonna follow him. I couldn't convince him to go out on campaign, so maybe you can somehow trap him at the crossroads."

Dyii allowed her to push him all the way to the door. Before opening it, he gave her a questioning look with a quirked frown. "How do you expect me to trap a Wikshen?"

"He's really leaving the complex?"

Dyii concentrated again, sorting through the many tremors in his head of heartbeats within his radius. Wikshen's lusty and irked rhythm had vanished from the mess of others. "He's leaving," Dyii confirmed.

She slapped his shoulder. "Then go. Watch where he goes. You've lived here long enough to know what our deity likes. Bait him if you can." She handed him a tiny leather pouch with a hard shape within, a whisper stone. "Alert your master that he's on the move. Tell him everything Wikshen does and says. They might find the perfect chance this way. And tell him my debt is paid."

Dyii nodded. "And my meal?"

Kilka blew a loud trill through her lips. "Why should I care who you kill when out in the grasslands? Go get a heart—but outside Wikhaihli! We don't need any more missing persons besides you."

Before he left, she grabbed his arm again. "And Dyii."

He raised an eyebrow.

"If I see you back here again, we'll both be on the chopping block."

And then Dyii found himself out in the busy Wikhaihli cloister, inside a hurricane of thundering heartbeats that intensified his craving by every half-second. Better to get out fast, especially before he lost track of Wikshen's heart.

He pulled his hood low and tucked his chin. Blending in and keeping one's eyes hidden was the way for all Thaccilians. Their red irises were the main trait that marked them as inhuman. The elves with their pointed ears, pretty faces, and shiny hair, never bothered to hide their species; in fact, they flaunted it as "culture" before the other citizens of Alkeer. The Thaccilians were different. They weren't a proud, cultured species. They were predators. Humans wanted to remain at the top of the food chain, and thought they were. Laughable.

Climbing up on the wall around the complex brought Wikshen's heartbeat faintly back to his ears—and a few others too. Kalea's was out there. That heartbeat, he could never stop. He wouldn't.

His stomach growled, and a new heartbeat drew his attention away from it. Somewhere in the distance between him and Wikshen—another woman's. It could be a witch or shaman or servant from Wikhaihli, someone else out there who wanted to follow Wikshen. It seemed Kilka would have far more than one missing person, but that wasn't Dyii's problem. Once he was outside of Wikhaihli, he'd consider anyone he encountered fair game.

"How much farther?" Kalea asked. Each step up the steep stairs looming over the raucous ocean tide put a deeper ache in her legs.

"A bit more," Bowaen assured her.

"Hold onto my belt if you need," Gaije offered. He grasped the steps with both hands, as Kalea did, and she didn't want to burden him with any extra weight.

Eventually, they made it. The ocean roared on below them. Kalea collapsed to her stomach on the grass at the top. Her leg muscles burned. It didn't seem to matter how much she'd worked them during Knilma's concubine training.

"I can't believe you three climb up and down that every day."

"More than once." Bowaen leaned down to nudge her. "Get up. We can't dawdle."

Kalea groaned again and pushed herself up. She wobbled on her legs. He took her by the arm as they started off, once again treating her like he didn't trust her.

Wikhaihli's huge wall loomed in the distance. "Let me sneak back in for a few minutes," she said. "I'll tell Dorhen we have to leave."

Bowaen squeezed her arm. "No." His hard voice reverberated in her head. He'd never sounded so serious before.

"Bowaen," Kalea said, feeling like a prisoner, as if he'd march her back to the dungeon and throw her in a cell, "why are you being like this?"

He didn't answer.

A ways off from the wall, a donkey waited, hitched to a cart with a small stack of goods loaded up. The donkey brayed when it noticed them. Bowaen manhandled Kalea all the way to the cart, trying to retie her hands.

"Is this necessary?"

"Yes," he said. "You just asked to reenter Wikhaihli, so what's to reassure me you won't jump out and run away?"

"What if I *want* to stay in Wikhaihli?"

Bowaen growled. "See? You're acting crazy! You're saying Wikshen is Dorhen, you're mumbling about shadows—"

Kalea pouted and attempted to argue, "I wasn't mumbling about shadows."

Del piped up. "Yes, you were."

"And you don't even seem to realize it!" Bowaen said. She winced, knowing the truth. "On top of that, you're trying to abandon your novice sisters!"

He took a moment to scoff. Kalea watched him with her mouth hanging open. "I mean, I can't tell you what to do—rescuing a bunch of innocent, kidnapped victims isn't something you can force someone to do," he said. He wiped his hand over his mustache, mouth, and beard. "But after all of your claims about being determined to rescue your friends… Now you want to live in Wikhaihli because you think Wikshen is Dorhen…" He shook his head. "The whole thing makes me sick to my stomach."

Kalea waited for him to say more, but he didn't. His words resonated. With her hands now tied in front of her, she moved to the back of the cart and climbed into the bed to settle in beside the supplies they'd stolen from Wikhaihli. There was her basket and shoes, even her washing bat. Kalea moped quietly as the others carried on with their preparations to leave, pulling their boots on and taking the reins.

Bowaen lifted Hathrohjilh out of the cart and fastened it to his belt. Del sat in the driver's seat, his lucidity returned after that long, treacherous trek, and Bowaen rode next to him. Gaije walked beside the cart with his bow ready and a quiver full of fresh arrows. At his whistle, the cart lurched forward and rolled. Frowning, Kalea watched Wikhaihli and its glowing windows drift away to disappear into the mist and darkness.

What am I doing? she thought. *I can't leave Dorhen! Again!*

She stood up, stumbling on the moving surface, and lunged to the side to leap over. She stopped fast when Bowaen reached back to snag her dress.

He half-stood in his seat to hold her. "You wanna broken leg, girl, making foolhardy leaps from the wagon? Great! Now I gotta tie you to the cart! Del."

Kalea made a heavy sigh, pouting, and sat back down as the cart slowed. She lowered her eyes to her bound hands. "Don't tie me to the cart, please."

Bowaen complained back, "Yer not giving me too much choi—"

The wagon lurched again with a wild clatter. The donkey brayed in fright. The turbulence knocked Kalea over, and she struggled to get back into position.

"What the hell?" Bowaen yelled. He and Del twisted around to inspect the area behind them.

Kalea pushed herself up and twisted to look at a hand hooked onto the tailgate. Wikshen's scowling face hovered above it. His hair shaded his face under the faint moonlight, but his reflective eyes glared.

"Where do you think you're going?"

Chapter 21
Sticky Gruel

Damos hadn't seen Girgen since the fool threw his ring down the hole and got himself caught after doing something he wasn't supposed to be doing. When he saw Girgen's friend Derndig, the man reported that Girgen wouldn't be any good to continue with their escape plan. Derndig proceeded to propose a new plan for the two of them. After Girgen's sloppiness, Damos didn't want anything to do with either of them. He did ask Derndig what lay beneath the throne room, though.

"Big lake," Derndig answered. "Do you think you could smuggle away some…"

Damos raised a bloody, gloved hand to silence him. "I'll hear no more. Your ideas are terrible."

If he was to escape, it would have to happen alone—and before his face healed. Damos poked his own cheek to check his healing progress. Still sore, but much less so. It wouldn't be long now before the "queen" reallocated him to whatever horrific new position she had in mind.

Damos stood up and stretched his back. Shelling seeds was all he did for now. It had grown dreadfully boring—mind-numbingly so after the first day. From his standing vantage, he spotted Girgen working over a few rows of stalagmites, hauling a cart like a mule.

"Girgen!" he called. He'd really thought the man had been killed as punishment for his slip-up, so seeing him up and moving gave Damos a wash of relief—hope, even.

"Girgen!" he tried again when he didn't receive an answer. He made his way over, weaving around stalagmites, heaps of dross, and other carts full of the prized black rocks found in this cave.

"Girgen, can't you hear me?" he asked as he approached. The man trudged past him, staring forward. "Did you get punished? Are you all right?"

Waving a hand before his face didn't make him blink. A close inspection of his eyes made Damos gasp and stagger back. They had dulled, the pupils dilated, and what he could only guess was fungus crusted in the corners and trailed down his friend's nose bridge. Girgen didn't turn his eyes in any direction; they were…dead. How could he tell where he was going?

Damos placed a hand on his arm, and he still didn't react. "Girgen?"

Girgen trudged on, pulling the cart by a harness strapped around his body. Damos had seen several people acting this way, but had never tried to speak to them. His thin, straggly hair started below the crown of his head and sat behind his ear. That's where Damos noticed the strangest thing of all. A little piece of grass stuck out from it. He squinted and reached for it. It was actually a tiny vine. It zipped back into the ear, disappearing from sight as if to dodge Damos's fingers.

Damos gasped and stepped back as Girgen continued his work mindlessly. Girgen was no longer the spirited character Damos had come to know. He had been robbed of his mind, and his body might as well lie dead.

Vivene made her way to the Chimera Tower, a place she didn't like going. Although beautiful and polished and far away from the Grave, it was where the kingsorcerer and all of his most soulless, poison-tipped, high-level sorcerers lived. The door frames gleamed with gold leaf, beautiful reliefs of naked women were sculpted into some of the walls, and the jakes all came with a convenient flushing system, but the air in this wing hung thick and moody, as if the spirits of the dead or evil demons clogged the spaces, unseen but certainly felt.

Just as she shook off this place's dreadful sensation, stressed voices drifted around a bend in the corridor ahead of a group of sorcerers.

"The kingsorcerer has spoken," one sorcerer said to a man who wore rich red garments but also bindings around his wrists.

Two growling naerscouels, with the fur on the backs of their dog-like necks raised, hauled the prisoner along. Vivene shuddered to see them again. They were mostly used as guards in the Chimera Tower. She pressed against the wall and lowered her eyes to let the group by.

"But I'm the kingsorcerer's best friend!" the prisoner shouted. "I only meant well by introducing him to the doctor. How was I to know she'd fail him? It was merely worth a try!"

"Tell the kingsorcerer that in a letter from your cell," the other sorcerer told him.

The naerscouels, creatures trapped in a life of man and dog, yipped and bared their teeth through all the excitement. Their human bodies acted as human bodies would, holding the prisoner and walking calmly independent of their beastly heads. Vivene clenched her eyes shut until they passed.

She owed her thanks to Bargo for being here. A while back, he'd picked her out in the lower levels with a hungry fancy for her. He lived just outside of this wing but wielded enough authority to eat in its general dining room and get Vivene a new position as a servant in these higher levels.

She entered the maids' closet where the Chimera Tower's cleaning implements were located, and took her assignment from the housekeeper: scraping candle wax off of various surfaces with a sharp spatula. Later tonight, the sorcerers would replace the puddles of dried wax with new layers.

She sighed, going through the mundane motions of work. This job hurt her arms so much. She arched backward to alleviate the strain on her back and worked her shoulders.

Something caught her ear as she followed the wall to the next fixture with a still waterfall of wax. Singing. A singing voice echoed faintly through a metal pipe that allowed air to move through the Chimera Tower, which kept the place breezy and fresh unlike the lower levels where Vivene lived.

She put her ear to the little vent on the wall and listened to the beautiful voice ringing through. Vivene couldn't understand the words, possibly due to the distance and vibration, but she did understand the sadness. She'd never heard such beauty before, much less here in Ilbith. She knelt there listening until the song ended and silence followed.

Whoever stood on the other side of the door tapped again. Lamrhath stayed in bed, curling up tighter.

"My lord? Are you alive in there?"

Good question, but now he had to answer lest they start plotting to take his throne away and give it to some piss-poor lackey Lamrhath had probably already spat on.

"Come in," he said flatly, staying in bed but at least making an effort to sit up.

Bargo opened the door and stood in the frame. "Couple o' bad days, my lord?"

"What do you want?" Lamrhath rested his forehead in his palm as the man approached.

"Just checking in. They're wanting to know if we're still doing it: the big summoning."

Lamrhath sighed. He hadn't thought of it. He hadn't thought of much since Falli's diagnosis. Life would go on, but he'd still be in pain. "Of course, we're still doing it. Chandran accomplished it once, but we won't let him show us up, will we?"

"It might make it easy for us to capture Wikshen."

"We'll summon more than one," Lamrhath said, "and get more than just Wikshen."

"Like who, my lord, or what? I'll put it into the plans. How many demons will we need?"

"I don't know. More than one to capture Wikshen, I assume. But there's also Hathrohjilh. We need to find out if they can locate it. Maybe they have some special sense we don't yet know about." Brainstorming his sorcerous plans helped to dull his depression, Lamrhath had to admit. "I want Daghahen in custody. And there's a woman out there I may need, a Luschian. One good sanguinesent should be able to handle her."

Bargo produced a fold of paper and a piece of charcoal from his belt pouch and jotted something down. "Tell you what, my lord—"

Lamrhath grunted. "Could you back up? Or your alcohol breath will make me vomit."

He stumbled backward a bit and stood more stiffly. "I figure three sanguinesents to go after Wikshen," he said. "One for the sword, one for Dag, one for the Luschian. That makes six."

"Six, then."

"Before I go, my lord, I have some dreadful news."

Lamrhath gave him a hard stare. Throughout their conversation, he hadn't shared much eye contact until now.

"Alec, who delivers your wife's dinners, has fallen ill with the plague. He's now residing in the quarantine wing."

Lamrhath dropped his head onto the pile of pillows behind him. "What now? I trusted Alec. Can you find someone else?"

Bargo nodded. "Indeed, my lord. I'll get on it."

"Good."

"My lord."

"What?"

"My apologies for extending my visit, but will you be attending tonight's conference? We'll discuss the summoning, and you can share your wisdom on the matters of Hathrohjilh and the Luschian."

Lamrhath sat up again. Maybe he had spent too many days in bed. Probably better to get up and back to work. Working added stress, and stress added pain to his core, but he'd learned in the last few days that lying in added no less. "I'm coming," Lamrhath told him.

Bathed and dressed pristinely again, Lamrhath stepped out of his bedroom to find a homely maid staring at him over a platter of steaming gruel. It was brazen, how long she dared to keep contact with his gaze.

"What?" he demanded.

The girl blinked her beady, almond-shaped eyes, her round face frozen in awe with her mouth hanging open. In his bafflement, he checked to make sure this was the Chimera Tower. Of course, it was!

"Why's a servant so ugly scurrying around up here?"

She didn't answer right away, and instead she asked, "Are you Lambelhen?"

Half his face pinched in a combined squint and sneer. "How would you know that name? And why are you daring to ask *me* a question?"

The girl held her stupid expression.

"You're that dumb girl, aren't you? Dumb and ugly. You're not supposed to be in this wing."

"The Creator says you don't have many chances left."

Lamrhath halted his slow venture toward her. No matter how tall he made himself, or how much he sharpened his gaze, her demeanor didn't shift any closer to fear. "What sort of shit are you talking now?" he asked.

The girl swallowed, showing wonder rather than fear. "Why do you keep disappointing the Creator?"

He clenched his teeth. "Why do you keep asking me questions?"

He raised a hand and stormed forward. His hand didn't spring. She kept still and calm, looking up at him with the most sincere display of innocence and stupidity he'd ever seen. He lowered his hand slowly, towering over her, his intimidation efforts failing. Her eyes were like two beady, black nuts. She looked more like an overstuffed cloth doll than a person.

Lamrhath opened his mouth to speak again, to ask another question, but before he could get it out, a mouse darted along the wall beside them. The girl shrieked at the rodent and threw up her hands, releasing her tray in the air.

The bowl of mushy milk and oats flew and landed with a wide splash across Lamrhath's vest, running down to his leggings and all the way into his shoes. The upper flare of the splash splattered his chin with its hot points, including his lips, where he tasted the disgusting slop that had never been meant for his own dining table. The wooden tray bounced off the wall with a loud *blonk!* and spun to the floor with more noise. The bowl settled somewhere behind him, rolling a few rounds on its rim.

So many options ran through his head as the bowl's clatter resonated back to silence. His dagger itched at his side, an extension of his body when he used it—an extension of his anger. He also had nice, hard fists.

He balled one of them. Instead of letting her have its best, he extended one finger and pointed to the door opposite his own, the office of a high-ranking sorcerer. "Go in there and tell the man what you've done here."

The girl didn't change her expression, much less curtsy or mutter an apology.

Lamrhath opened the door for her. "Go," he ordered. Inside the office, the sorcerer raised his neck from the desk and widened his eyes at the mess Lamrhath had been made into.

Chapter 22
New Guardian

Battling the ever-present morning illness, Tirnah emerged from her room at the same time as Anonhet when Lehomis called. He still didn't know she was pregnant, and she kept her back straight and pleasant façade on to make sure he didn't take on the unneeded extra stress. Today, he prepared to leave for Theddir, to her dismay, but it was all necessary.

When they entered the house's central sitting area, or the *wyrrem* in Norrian, a younger *saehgahn* stood with Lehomis. Looming two heads taller than he, their guest's dark hair hung as long as his shoulder blades with the side braided back in the typical warrior *saehgahn* fashion.

"This is Tihen," Lehomis said in formal presentation, using a strong *saehgahn* voice for Tihen's honor.

Tirnah vaguely recognized Tihen from the village as a former *saeghar* who used to run around with Gaije. He had been gone on his *caunsaehgahn* for quite a long time between then and now.

Conquering her discomfort, Tirnah drifted forward with her hand extended. "I welcome you, Tihen, to our home." Anonhet followed her lead.

Tihen gave the formal bow, and then took Tirnah's hand between his. "*Harrenhenni,*" he said. As expected, his voice hummed much deeper than Lehomis's, matching his stature. He went through those same gestures for Anonhet.

As soon as he stepped back again, Lehomis slapped Tihen hard on the arm. "He'll be your house-guardian while I'm away." Lehomis turned his eyes to Anonhet to shoot her his signature smile of mischief. "Tihen is the biggest *saehgahn* in my rabble and also the best in the practice yard. He's been back from his *caunsaehgahn* for a year and a half now. He's the pride of Lockheirhen. Look at him, he's even built like a horse!"

Tirnah waved her hand in an arc, the practiced gesture of hospitable house matrons to their guests. "Then I am pleased to have him in our house, Grandfather." She said to Anonhet, "Lass, why don't you show Tihen to the guest room, and afterward fix him the tea of welcome?"

"*Awl, lem ba daan*—I will do that," Anonhet said formally, using words taken from the most archaic version of Norrian. All the lines they exchanged were formalities meant to initiate a guest into the family for however long they'd be present…except for Lehomis's showcasing of Tihen to the unwed *faerhain* in the household. That was just his characteristic shamelessness.

When Anonhet and Tihen retreated into the deeper side of Lehomis's cave-home, Tirnah took Lehomis's arm.

"What's the matter?" he asked, his face fading from mischief to concern.

"I've been dreading today."

Lehomis gave her a warm smile and put his hand on her shoulder. "You hid it well, but please don't worry, lass."

Tirnah pulled her lips in, fighting back some tears as she rubbed her hand over her midsection and hid the action under her house robe.

Lehomis took both her shoulders to look at her squarely. "How long did I say it took a *saehgahn* to walk from this spot to Theddir?"

"No more than a day and a half."

"Which isn't so bad, is it?"

Tirnah shook her head, looking at the floor.

"And if necessary, I could run home from there without stopping and get back in half the time."

Tirnah wouldn't believe that until she saw it, although *saehgahn* didn't lie, so there must be some sort of examined truth to his claim.

Lehomis reached up and patted her head as if she were still *farhah*; her height, which exceeded his by a thumb or two, didn't matter. "Be good to Tihen," he said. "You can rely on him. I made sure to test everyone out and pick the best of the best as house-guardian for my females." He looked her up and down and smiled.

"What?" she asked.

He opened his mouth and paused. "Nothin'." He finished with a breathy laugh.

Out of sheer compulsion, she seized him in a tight hug. *Don't go*, she wanted to plead but didn't. She couldn't. Her tears started falling instead. Though she knew how she wished he'd stay, she didn't know why she needed to hug him or cry about it. Pregnancy was always so emotional for her.

No longer laughing, Lehomis kept his arms out for a few seconds until he hesitantly returned her embrace, placing his hands carefully at the backs of her shoulders. "Don't be frightened," he whispered.

When she pulled back, she hid her mouth behind her sleeve. "I'm sorry, Grandfather. I don't know why I did that."

He shrugged and moved to lift a heavy leather bag off the floor, and then slung it over his shoulder. "No worries. I think I understand. You're in a fragile state."

She gasped at his response. "*What?*"

"I get it," he continued, and picked up a smaller bag to add to his burden. "You've only been apart from Trisdahen for a few weeks. It's going to take a long while to get used to being a widow. Take it from me."

"Right," she murmured.

Leaning over, he opened a box by the hearth and took out a long sprig of Norrian clove to stick between his teeth. He took it out again to say, "It's bad of me to leave you in such a state, though, and I'm sorry for that, but I have to try something to alleviate the hard times ahead. Selling off my collected junk will do wonders, you'll see."

Tirnah breathed. He still didn't know.

He raised a finger before moving on in his chores. "There's something funny, though," he said.

She waited, sweaty hands clasped.

"What I was tempted to say was that several weeks ago, I had convinced myself you were with child. Isn't that stupid?"

Tirnah felt her face heat up. She burst out a fake laugh. *I am! Please don't go, Lehomis,* she thought, but chose to stay quiet. Their clan and household depended on this trip. Telling him the news now would be a terrible idea. She just had to get over the fleeting insecurities of her state. There would be plenty of time for it later.

Instead, she asked, "What made you think that, Grandfather?"

He shook his head, smiling. "The Desteer gave me one of their silly offhand forecasts just because Trisdahen had come home." He put the clove stem in his mouth again and said around it, "I well believed in that lad's spirited virility, but sometimes I think those Desteer just have their minds in the pig pen." He chuckled again. "Probably comes from never being married."

He stepped closer to her, taking the herb out of his mouth. "But listen…" He gave her a new deep gaze with his pale-blue eyes. "Keep an eye on Tihen. If he sits too close to Anonhet or looks at her for more than two seconds, you tell me." Regardless of her sinking feeling and her flushed, tearful face, Tirnah burst out another laugh, this one genuine. "Grandfather, you paraded him before her."

Lehomis dipped his head and put a hand up. "I know, I know. He has to behave himself, though. I'm afraid he may have too much spirited virility, being the pride of Lockheirhen and all. Now I suggest you get in there and play chaperone."

She laughed again and shoved him with two palms to his shoulder.

***

Tirnah, Anonhet, and Tihen stood in a row, watching Lehomis drive his cart away, loaded with all sorts of trinkets and clothing Tirnah had helped him dig out and dust off for selling. Some of the clothing consisted of ancient silks once worn by Kristhanhea, his long-passed wife. Whenever Tirnah asked him about his decision to sell such things, he sniffed and said, "Gotta move on sometime, lass," or "Kristhanhea's gone, but you and Anonhet are here." At least he hadn't packed up all of Kristhanhea's belongings.

Off he rode, and Tirnah couldn't hold back her tears.

Anonhet patted her back. "You didn't tell him, did you?"

She shushed the lass and marched back to the foyer, wiping her eyes. She took three baskets and handed one each to Anonhet and Tihen. "Come and guard us," she said to him. "We're going to the forest to forage." She nodded to Anonhet. "We have a lot of hard work ahead of us."

Chapter 23
A Song Calls

Kalea stared disbelieving at the glowing turquoise eyes piercing Bowaen all the way to his seat at the wagon's front. The moment suspended in time. Gaije, stationed to follow the cart on foot, pointed an arrow at Dorhen's head. The donkey continued to whine in annoyance at the cart's rough handling.

"Dorhen," Kalea uttered, staying as cool as she could, "be calm. Everyone be calm."

Grasping the wagon's tailgate with one hand, Dorhen shook the entire structure. Kalea braced her hands on the floor. Her friends shouted. Dorhen's bared teeth glistened in the green flame of Gaije's arrow. Gaije tightened his bowstring, but Dorhen paid him no mind.

"Where are you going?" Dorhen asked Kalea in a cold, hard rumble.

Her attention was plastered to Gaije instead. "Please don't shoot him." She turned back to Dorhen. "I have to find the novices."

Behind her, Bowaen and Del seemed frozen to their seats.

"I told you to forget them," Dorhen growled.

Kalea blinked rapidly and pouted. "You should come too. Maybe…" she attempted, and tried again. "Maybe you can help us find Mhina and the novices."

Dorhen squinted. "You should stay in Wikhaihli so I can take care of you."

Kalea nodded eagerly. "You can take care of me out here too. Come with us and help us find the Ilbith sorcerers."

His twisting scowl hinted at what he'd say. Before he could refuse, she crawled forward on her knees, bracing herself awkwardly on her bound hands.

His eyes moved to her bindings. "They tied you up?" He regarded Gaije with a bright show of his teeth. Gaije kept the arrow trained on him with utmost concentration.

"They'll untie me now," she said, trying to put as much optimism into her voice as possible. She had to alleviate the tension somehow.

"Kalea," Bowaen whispered behind her as she edged closer to Dorhen at the back of the wagon.

She ignored him. At the tailgate, she reached to Dorhen.

"Kalea!" Gaije hissed.

She ignored him too and slipped her bound arms around Dorhen's head and pulled him to her chest. She shushed him in a soothing way, as one would calm a baby. He exhaled against her bosom, steaming hot, and the tension in his neck relaxed. She put her lips upon his hair and made more cooing noises meant just for him.

At Dorhen's sudden calmness, Gaije let his bowstring slacken. He stared at them in confusion now.

"Dorhen," she whispered into his hair.

He sucked in a deep breath. "You're wearing that perfume again."

"Knilma makes me wear it every day." She let out her own breath of relief at the change in atmosphere. "Get in the cart. You can protect me."

He released another steaming breath between her breasts and pulled away. She raised her arms to let him out.

Bowaen grumbled those words, "Get in the cart? Kalea, are you cr—?"

She shushed him. "He's the best chance we have to track down Mhina."

Eyes straining from person to person, Bowaen pointed his finger with his mouth open.

"I agree," Gaije said. "He took Mhina. He should know how to find her. And if he betrays us—"

"He won't," Kalea said. "I know him."

With a foot planted between the side panels, Dorhen vaulted over the edge to join her in the wagon bed. Before settling down, he untied her wrists and flung the twine into the grass. Kalea took a seat cozily close beside him. She nodded to Bowaen, who kept up that same unsure expression, and then he elbowed Del to drive the cart, which took off with a lurch. Bowaen sat backward in his seat to keep a close eye on Dorhen's every gesture.

As expected, the following moments stretched long in the silence, save for the sound of the cart rattling over the lumpy terrain and the crickets of night singing away. Gaije walked with his arrow nocked.

"How did you find me?" Kalea asked Dorhen when she'd decided the tense silence had gone on long enough.

"I went to your bed and didn't find you there," he said, his voice low. "When I came out to the courtyard, everyone was running around in a tizzy, looking for the missing criminal. Two criminals."

"Dyii," Kalea said.

"It didn't take a lot of thinking to come out to the fields. I heard your donkey braying in the night."

"You went to my bed," Kalea said. "Why?"

He shrugged. Sitting nestled under his arm, she couldn't deny the perfection of this outcome. Dorhen had come out of Wikhaihli. "I need to talk to you."

"About?"

"I don't know." He turned his face away. "I made a big statement to the shamans. There's"—he sighed—"an issue."

"What's the issue?"

He shrugged and shook his head, flicking his attention to Bowaen's piercing eyes. "Nothing I want to talk about in front of other people."

Kalea's cheeks heated up. She left it at that. They'd have plenty of time to talk about their intimate business later—not that she assumed her friends would allow her a moment alone with "Wikshen."

Dorhen leaned over and stuck his hand down one of the folds in his kilt, causing Bowaen to edge closer and Gaije's bowstring to tighten. He brought out a handkerchief folded over something and extended it to her.

"Here." Kalea took the bundle and unwrapped it to find a sort of biscuit within. "The shamans call it a cookie," he said. "It's one of my favorite things."

Kalea released a loud, delighted giggle and hoped it would ease her friends' tension. Gaije kept his stare firmly on them. They needed to learn that Wikshen wasn't made of pure evil. She leaned into Dorhen until he supported her completely and laid her head against him. She didn't care how uncomfortable it made the others. She nibbled the sweet treat in tiny bites to savor it as long as possible and periodically raised it up for him to take a bite.

"I understand your wanting me to stay in Wikhaihli," she said after a while, well aware how closely the others listened. "The shamans know how to make you comfortable. It's not too different from the convent I grew up in, except for the religion."

His voice rumbled over her head. "You have to go back with me."

She twisted to meet his eyes. "I will, but Dorhen… My sisters—and Gaije's sister—they must be suffering. Won't you help us find them?"

He made no attempt to answer that.

"I understand you don't know where they all are exactly," she continued, "but we're going to find out. You'll help us, won't you?"

Dorhen exhaled through his nose. "You don't know what you're getting into," he finally said.

"I think I have a good idea." She kept inside her the description of the Carridax cathedral's nightmarish underbelly—and Chandran. She wouldn't tell Dorhen about any of it. He didn't need to know how close to danger she'd already been. It would probably make him put his foot down about allowing her to search for the sorcerers.

She reached up and caressed the side of his face. He closed his eyes at her touch, showing her what an impact on him her touch had. She hadn't fully noticed before. "We'll also find out what the sorcerers did to you and how to reverse it."

That's when he took her hand away. "You can't reverse it."

"How do you know?"

"It's what I've been told. This is who I am now. Reversing it would kill me."

Bowaen coughed and grumbled on the end of it, "Whatever's gotta happen."

Kalea shot him a hard look. "I'll find a way," she said to the lot of them, keeping her serious eyes on Dorhen. "I know about demon possession, and I'll make it my determination to save you. Yes, it's not a very good situation to be in. You may die from it—but that's what I'm going to prevent. The demon is using you for its own pleasure. With the help of the One Creator, I'll figure out how to—"

He shifted to meet her square in the eyes. "I want to tell you that I'm fine."

She squeezed her brows together. "Fine?" She looked him over, taking in his striking new appearance. Beautiful, but also eerie and off. This wasn't what *Dorhen* looked like.

He nodded. "I have it under control," he said, and smiled for her, a faint smile.

"How do you have it under control?"

He shrugged, holding a cool expression of confidence she didn't wholly want to accept. "Ever since I started using Kraft, I've had a grasp on my possession. Wik has left me alone. Maybe being at Wikhaihli did me some good," he said. "I'm stronger. I can control it."

"'It' being the demon?"

"*Pixie*," he corrected. "And yes. I have control again." He flexed his right hand, reminding Kalea of the night his other hand had grabbed her and he had struggled with it. Struggled with it to the point of ripping his own arm apart with his teeth. She swallowed a hard lump.

Watching her unsure digestion of his claim, he tightened his lips and reiterated, "I know what I'm doing."

"So that means…" She pointed her finger toward his core. "Will the demon not attack me and my friends?"

He kept silent for a long moment. Too long for her comfort. "I won't attack you."

Kalea repeated her slow nod. "You hear that, Bowaen?" And she said to Dorhen, "That's good. Keep making progress with it. It's better that you're with us, regardless."

He ran his fingers through his hair and observed the dark landscape of wide, rolling hills, all black shapes under the stars. "Where are we going?"

Bowaen said over his shoulder, "That's what we're waiting on from you. Tell us where to find the sorcerers."

Dorhen's face hardened at that, and Kalea figured it would take a few more tender touches to soften it again. "I don't know."

"Then we're going to Alkeer," Bowaen replied, "Word must be floating around there of the Ilbith sorcerers' location." He whistled to Gaije. "Hey, elf, keep an eye on the monster!"

"Bowaen!" Kalea scolded.

Bow in hand, Gaije nodded firmly at his order, striding beside the cart untiringly.

Dorhen put a hand over his face.

"What's the matter?" Kalea asked him under her breath.

"It's you," he said. Kalea cocked her head. "You're making me confused."

"How?"

He shook his head, still hiding his face in his palm, and sucked in a long pull of air. The fragrance of pennyroyal stirred deep in all her fabrics and her hair, releasing itself with all of her movements. Was he being...*affected* by it right now? Did she allure him, and that's why he was compliant in riding along with them tonight? Why else wasn't he trying to carry her back to Wikhaihli? She formulated her own answer when he tightened his arm around her, pulling her closer until they sat like a cozy pair of doves. His warmth made her eyelids heavy. A groggy ache had long crept into her head.

"Dorhen. I like you being out here with me. Back there, I could barely find you. Let's stay out here for a while." She lowered her head to his muscular leg beneath his long kilt. "Dorhen," she said again.

"What?"

"What is this thing you wear?"

"It's called a 'battleshift.' It belongs to Wik."

Now her eyes did droop. She allowed them to close, barely registering his answer.

"Stop this thing!"

The rattling, abrupt stop of their vessel shook Kalea awake. The donkey brayed again. Dorhen stirred until Kalea lifted her head, and then he leaped out. Nighttime was ending. She could see better with the hint of light piercing the horizon.

"Dorhen," she said in alarm.

He headed to a tall mass of jagged-looking trees, easily recognizable as Hathrohskog. They'd rolled all the way there while she slept.

Kalea climbed out of the wagon and sprinted after him. "Where are you going?"

Her friends called her name behind her, but she paid no mind, fearing to the utmost that she'd be separated from Dorhen again. Her logic told her otherwise. Maybe he needed to answer a call of nature—although, if that were the case, he'd tell her. She called his name again, and he ignored her.

He stopped under the canopy in the dense fog that always seemed to live in this forbidding region. "Do you hear it?"

She listened for whatever he referred to. "Just crickets in the grass." Crickets were the only thing she'd heard all night besides the murmuring of Bowaen and Del under the rattling of the wagon.

Despite his question, Dorhen didn't acknowledge her answer. When she wrapped her arms around his huge one, he looked down at her. A little smile crooked his mouth. "I can still smell it on you. It makes me shake."

"It's just pennyroyal," she said. "Is it that strong?"

He leaned against the nearest tree and watched her. She moved in to wrap her arms around his middle. "Dorhen," she cooed. "You've no idea how bad…"

She checked over her shoulder to see the silhouettes of her friends coming toward them in the fog, backlit by the rising sun. They were far off yet. Suddenly feeling desperate to establish some deeper connection, to receive more of his attention than she'd gotten in two weeks, she pressed her lips to his abdomen. He sighed. She pecked another kiss below the first, and the third even lower. She looked up to see his serene face with his eyes closed.

"Dorhen," she said again. She loved saying his name! "Knilma taught me some things… Did you know?"

Her friends drew ever closer. She might have to ask them to give her a moment of privacy. She needed privacy with him for once, to speak honestly, to reunite, to learn more about his problems…to discuss… them. In the next few minutes, Knilma's humiliating "turnip exercises" might pay off. Thinking such thoughts, Kalea's whole body passed from its sleepy haze to a flare of excitement. She sighed too.

"But don't you hear it?" he asked with a shiver against her. "It's a song.

It's for me." He smiled.

"I hear nothing."

She moved to place another kiss along the descending progression, having to peel down his battleshift a smidge to do so, but he stepped away from the tree—and from her.

"That sound…" He sighed again. After a few seconds, he turned back to her, and his serenity faded. His face turned pale before her eyes in the blooming sunlight. He didn't like the light?

"Oh, no…" he said, and moved farther into the shady woods with a stagger.

"Where're you going?"

He paused to bend over and hug his stomach. His other hand clamped over his mouth. He heaved.

"Are you sick?"

He took off.

"Dorhen!" She ran after him.

Despite his outwardly visible illness, he weaved through the trees toward the deeper shadows Hathrohskog offered. Kalea followed, desperately hanging onto glimpses of his motion. Her friends shouted behind her. Dorhen gained so much distance that her view of him became sparser. Rarer. Until she saw him no more.

After stumbling over rocks and remembering to dodge the muddy patches, she stopped to catch her breath, no longer hearing his footsteps through the leaves.

Sucking in a deep pull of air, she cupped her hands around her mouth and called, "Dor-heeen!"

Her voice echoed. Silence. Only the sounds of her friends approaching behind her could be heard.

"Where'd he go?" Bowaen asked. Gaije darted around with his bow drawn. Del waited ready with his pipe in hand, cursing.

Kalea showed Bowaen her empty, helpless palms. "I don't know," she said. "I was with him, and he heard something I couldn't. He seemed to get sick suddenly, and then he ran! I don't…" She put her hand over her mouth. Her eyes watered. "He left me."

"The bastard couldn't have gotten far. He could be hidin'. Gaije! Del! Search this area! We can't let him get away!"

As he'd ordered, they searched behind every tree and fallen log in a large radius. They found Dorhen nowhere. It reminded Kalea of their night in the storage shed when Dorhen had heard the shamans' approach and darted to the back of the room and disappeared.

When the group met back up, no one had any words to offer. "This just kills it," Bowaen said. He hissed and shook his head. "I'm outta ideas."

Kalea wept softly. "He left me."

Ignoring her, Bowaen waved his hand. "Let's get back to the cart and collect our stuff." He worked his boots out of the horribly acidic mud he was standing in. "You realize where we are yet?"

Gaije's face turned ashy and long. Del kept silent, holding his weapon-pipe in hand, and Kalea sucked in a breath and released it slowly. She knew.

"We'll set the donkey free and do the rest on foot. The wagon's wheels won't be able to stay aboveground in this hellhole of roots, thorns, and killer mud anyway. We'll cut through and go back to Alkeer to get information on the Ilbith sorcerers. C'mon."

Chapter 24
Sweet Cakes

Hardly afraid of being caught anymore, Vivene placed her ear directly on the vent's mouth to hear that beautiful, faint melody again. She'd thought about it nonstop since her first discovery of it, a mystery to occupy her mind as she endured each grueling day.

Closing her eyes, she focused hard. For the past three days, she'd studied the song. It lasted only a few short minutes, but it started at the exact same hour each day. There weren't enough women walking around in the Chimera Tower to compare the voice to. Any woman she did hear couldn't match the loveliness that drifted through the vent.

The last note rang long and gentle until fading out, leaving only a sweet resonance in Vivene's ear. She missed the convent. Singing every Sunday. She missed the safety it provided, and even the day-by-day monotony of her old routine. She wiped her tears as she stood up.

Footsteps tapped around the bend, and she hurried to look busy. For the rest of her rounds, as usual, she searched for the singer, for new nooks and rooms, and for sorcerers who could catch her nosiness and punish her. She found no clue.

Today, Vivene treated Bargo extra nice to get him more enthusiastic about their ritual than usual. From her place in bed, she leaned over to pour another brimming mug of wine that spilled on her along its trip to him.

"You naughty, filthy woman!" he said, taking the mug and chugging it as heartily as ever. His whiskery face smiled when he lowered it. He handed her the mug so she could take a drink, and she topped it off again.

"Nu-uh," he said, putting his hand up. "If I have to drink, you have to eat another slice of cake."

"*That's* your deal?" she replied with a pithy laugh, and reached over to grab a slice and cram it into her mouth with the carelessness he liked. The cake went everywhere, smearing sugary icing all over her face.

He shivered. "Oh, you are a dangerous vixen, aren't you?"

Large bubbles of bile and food from tonight's overeating crawled up Vivene's throat. Handing him the mug again, she fought against her heaving stomach.

"Together," he said, and then they pressed their cheeks so he could pour the wine into both their mouths. By now, his bedding was a food-stained disaster, which Vivene would have to wash later, but he might be just drunk enough to suit her needs.

The wine erupted from Vivene's throat when she coughed against its flow. Bargo laughed and relaxed to lie back against the rumpled blankets. She stroked his hair to deliver further relaxation.

"Have you ever heard a song coming through those pipes in the walls in the Chimera Tower?" she dared to ask him against Ilbith's dreadful law.

In his drunken stupor, he snorted. "Oh, yes. It's something we're used to."

"Who's doing the singing?"

He twirled his hand, and then it fell limp in its propped position. Eyes closed, he gave a little snore. Vivene nudged him back awake. "I said, she's the kingsorcerer's wife."

"You mean the woman from the grasslands?"

He shook his head, eyes still closed. "Holy Naerezek, no. Lamrhath has two wives. One of them, we're not supposed to acknowledge."

Vivene's mouth dropped open. She wanted to press for more answers but didn't want Bargo to notice that she was asking questions, drunk or not.

"She's a bit of a legend here," Bargo went on. "I heard she came out of her room the other day as a rare occasion to attend a special meeting with the kingsorcerer."

"Is she a prisoner in there?"

"Eh." Bargo waved his hand again and licked his fingers when he noticed them wearing the sugary glaze. "I guess she is, but to be honest..." He snored again, and she poked him. "Being an elf, the kingsorcerer has a special kinda jealousy reserved for her. He's secretive about his relationship with her. I guess it aligns with their species. Otherwise, the lord doesn't care who sees him boff who, but not that first wife of his, no..."

So Lamrhath's first wife lived locked up somewhere and sang the same song every day, all cooped up, alone, and having to be married to *him*.

"Species?" she said. "She's also an elf?"

"Oh, yeah. It's a real funny situation," Bargo continued after Vivene assumed he'd fallen asleep again. "He built quite a home for her on the south side of the Chimera Tower."

"South side," Vivene whispered.

"It's like an escape-proof cage, but also made so no man can get access to her. Got more than one door barring folk from getting in. A hole in the last door allows them to pass her dinners to her in a box." He barked out a laugh, but Vivene suddenly felt sadder for the beautiful singer.

"Where exactly is her room located on the south side?"

Growing drowsier by the second, Bargo turned his head and groaned. "It's not hard to find."

Vivene left it at that. She'd spent a little too much time in here already. Some chores awaited her before retiring to bed, but when she stood up, she found what a mess he'd made her into. Even her hair wore cake crumbs. Eating so much would probably make her throw up before the night's end.

Now she had something to look forward to tomorrow, though: catching that beautiful song echoing through the wall. Maybe she could sneak upstairs and see the singer's room. The elf-woman being cooped up and ill-treated was sad enough for Vivene to think about. Though she liked the cakes Bargo gave her—and the sex—she liked the song more. It made her day not quite so horrible. If she could pass a word of kindness to the singer, it would make Vivene feel good.

Chapter 25
A Bird Mourns

What'd you expect from that monster?" Bowaen asked Kalea as they trudged through Hathrohskog, having returned to it too soon for anyone's comfort.

"He's not a monster!" she snapped. "He has a demon. I've told you this."

"The only thing to regret is that now he won't help us find the sorcerers he rode with."

"He said he doesn't know where they are. He must've escaped from them," Kalea said. "What I have to do now is help him."

Bowaen grunted. "I still don't get why you think he's Dorhen. People don't change like that. Hair doesn't just turn blue."

"I think its blue color is proof of his change," she said. "On what other kind of person have you seen blue hair?"

"No one," Bowaen grumbled. Gaije walked always with his bow ready. He hadn't shared any words at all since Dorhen had come and gone. Bowaen pointed his finger at her. "Your revelation that he's Dorhen doesn't change the fact that he's killed so many people, attacked us—attacked *you*—and kidnapped Mhina."

Kalea waved her hands. "And now we're going around in circles again, Bowaen. I told you, Dorhen has a *demon*."

The Darkland mist roved over them, sometimes lighter, sometimes as heavy as rain. By now, they were all soaked through their cloaks. The setting under the canopy of Hathrohskog was no less horrible than Kalea remembered. They walked across as many stones as they could find to prevent their feet from sinking into the damaging mud. The mud which had killed Damos. The gloom rode on Kalea's shoulders, and she knew it wouldn't let up until they found the other side of the forest. At least plenty of daylight hours remained to help them navigate. Bowaen ordered them to walk nonstop and find the other side before nightfall. It seemed possible, considering what they'd accomplished last time, and on so little sleep.

Before long, they found the spot where they'd battled Wikshen… where they'd battled Dorhen under the influence of his demon possession. It made her wonder if she could trust him around her friends. The rainfall of a few nights ago had softened all the scuffs and deep footprints they'd left in the mud. All the horrible memories flashed before her eyes, worse now that she knew Wikshen's true identity. They'd stabbed him—Dorhen—and left him lying on the ground, bleeding out.

Kyuuuuuurp! Kyuuuuuurp!

Kalea started at the sharp sound. They all did. Azrielle, Damos's pet parrot. It sat high in the branches, calling solemnly. Kalea's hands shot to her mouth and her eyes watered. Her group paused to look up at the sad sight.

"Poor Damos," she moaned. "Do you think we could take his bird out of here?"

Bowaen shrugged beside her. "I wouldn't know how to catch a bird, besides asking Gaije to shoot it. Leave it alone. It'll follow us if it wishes."

Kyuuuuuurp! Azrielle called again. *Kyuuuuuurp!* As if it called for its master.

Holding her hands over her mouth, Kalea turned her attention back to the task of traversing across the harsh, acidic ground. She stoppered up her emotion as well as she could. "How horrible."

She moaned again at the reminder of how Damos had died. It was her fault. She'd lured him into the shadow, away from the campfire's sanctuary, and…seduced him. Like a harlot. And then Wikshen caught him, or something controlled by Wikshen's power. Why had Wikshen not dragged Kalea away too? Could Dorhen have had anything to do with the incident? Was he jealous? The incident with Damos made more sense, yet it increased her confusion now that she knew Wikshen's true identity. Damos's death really was her fault.

She shook her head in argument with herself. *Not a chance!* The demon inside of him acted in its own irrational way because it was an entity of chaos and violence. It shouldn't have any care for Kalea. Why would it?

Kalea dismissed the whole thing and focused on placing her feet gingerly from stone to stone, or from grass clump to moss patch. One foot after the other would get her out of this little pocket of hell called Hathrohskog, a hole in the world that stirred up deep emotions, guilt, and agony that should otherwise be forgotten or forgiven.

The day dragged on and its light faded. The mist rolled in like a thick wall. A "walking cloud," they called it: an air mass that rolled over the land, engulfing everything and then moving on to dampen someone else's day.

A long rope bridge appeared on the trail; the cloud obscured the size of the chasm below it. Bowaen opted to have everyone go straight across, hoping not to delay their trek any longer by attempting to skirt around the cliff. The mist filling the chasm below helped Kalea to suppress her fear, as if she walked comfortably over a misty floor and not over a deadly drop. She did have to take a moment to wonder over the structure, still strong and firm under her feet. Who kept up this bridge? The Wikshonites?

When she reached solid ground on the other side of the long, swaying suspension, an odd feeling clenched her heart, accompanied by a rustle behind her, or maybe a twig snapping. Kalea rubbed her chest and looked around, seeing no one out there.

"Did you hear something?" she asked her friends. "It was like a footstep."

"Must've been an animal," Bowaen offered. Gaije didn't appear on any extra alert.

"I feel like I'm being watched… It's giving me a dreadful feeling in my chest."

"Stay close to me," Bowaen murmured. "Don't stop walkin' either. The more we walk, the sooner we'll get out of here."

So far, they hadn't seen another soul, but the dimmer the sky grew, the tighter her paranoia wound. The eyes of a lurker held her. It wasn't Wikshen's miasma, nor did it give her the sensation of safety like Dorhen had whenever he wore his magic hood.

By the time the early moon peeked through the random openings in the mist, Kalea could walk no farther. "Wait!" she called. She'd fallen behind. Her body simply refused to walk anymore. "Let me rest for only a minute. Please."

This would be their first stop all day. She plopped down on the mossy ground, a delightful change from the rocky earth and stinging mud pits they'd endured so far. She leaned back and breathed for a while before rubbing her numb legs and sore ankles.

Her friends built a campfire, and then passed around dried ration pieces. Del lit his pipe, adding a pleasantly familiar scent to the air, one which Wikhaihli had replaced with the essence of pennyroyal and other exotic incenses. Del's ordinary tobacco somehow whisked Kalea closer to home.

She finished gnawing on her piece of dried goat's meat, and then forced her body to stand.

"Where you going?" Bowaen made sure to ask as she turned away.

"Where do you think?" The eerie similarity of the situation hit. No strange feelings of irritation and unexplainable arousal bothered her tonight, though.

"Do I have to tell you not to go far?" Apparently, he felt the déjà vu too.

Now a little irritation touched her. "Oh, don't worry. By now, I've already lost my last shred of personal dignity." She didn't speak all sarcasm tonight, not after two weeks at Wikhaihli—the place where every woman got judged like a piece of meat, prodded in their most private places, and then laid out on a platter for the deity. Relieving herself right next to her male companions was no longer the most indecent thing she could think of.

She picked the thickest of the trees close to their resting area and grabbed her skirt to lift it. A voice caught her attention from the opposite direction of her friends. A frantic female voice in a struggle.

Kalea dropped her skirt and jerked upright in alarm. "Bowaen?"

He and the others heard it too. A shrill scream confirmed it for all. Over a few rows of tangled bushes, a figure in black emerged, waving its arms and stumbling over the terrain. "Help!"

Kalea called Bowaen's name again on instinct and launched forward without another thought.

"Kalea!" the woman called.

"M-Metta?" she called back. "What are you doing—"

A second figure appeared behind Metta from the tangle of dead vegetation. Metta was in trouble! Kalea fumbled for her washing bat but feared the worst. A silver blade glinted in the patch of white moonlight through the mist, followed by a set of red eyes.

"Look out!" Kalea called, pointing as she worked her way slowly over and around the bushes.

Dyii was chasing Metta. He raised his knife high.

"Kalea, get down!"

Kalea trusted Gaije's warning. She dropped, and he released an arrow with a green flame that roared over her head. No sound of pain followed. When Kalea looked up, a dead tree had caught fire. The arrow had narrowly missed Dyii, but served to distract him. Metta gained more distance. Kalea lunged to meet her.

"Thank the Mastaren I found you all," Metta cried.

Kalea opened her mouth to respond, but the ground dropped open beneath her. She fell fast into a dark hole, leaving her echoing scream behind with all the confused voices above.

Chapter 26
A Witch Sings

Millions of tiny water droplets kissed Wikshen's face. His eyelids fluttered open. Dark time. Time to wake up.

"Knilma," he groaned.

No answer. The mist suggested he was outside. His eyes easily registered his dark surroundings. The ethereal light in his vision lit up every airborne droplet like floating crystal beads.

There were trees. Somehow, he'd made his way home to Hathrohskog. Above him hung a black, draped canopy across the center of a ring of trees, and a few hanging walls loomed around. He lay in a bed. Covered platters of food stood arranged on a table beside him, with accompanying incense and a small Kraft flame. The mist couldn't snuff out a Kraft flame.

This was a forest temple, a temporary yet comfortable setup. There should be a witch or a shaman close by. Apparently, his host person had been in control until now, but his current awakening must be a good sign. It wouldn't be long at this point until the fool gave up his fight.

He slid a leg out of the blanket and placed it on the ground, finding a rug. So little minerals remained in his store at the moment, walking around on the soil would do him some good. Then he noticed it gone…

Moving the blanket revealed his naked body. The battleshift wasn't there. A slight frown of concern replaced his smirk. He darted his eyes around to see if it had been folded or hung somewhere close by.

Nowhere! A twinge of panic set off his nerves.

From the mist materialized a body coming toward him. Staying in bed with one bare leg hanging out, Wikshen squinted.

A woman. She wore a black cloak with the hood up and not much else. Her pale body glowed amid the twinkling mist in his night vision. The edges of the cloak lay neatly over her nipples, giving Wikshen a linear view of the center line running between her breasts to her jeweled navel and on to her soft, shaven pubis. Pale blonde hair, about the same color as her flesh, streamed from her hood on either side of her face. A string of black jewels ran across her forehead, and a neat arrangement of them, embedded into her skin, drew a perfect line down the center of her chest, torso, and beyond.

She stopped when her bare feet met the rug. Her full lips parted.

"Mastaren." She dropped her cloak to reveal her whole body, wearing nothing but those embedded gems.

Wikshen squinted harder. "Where's my battleshift?" he asked.

Without her cloak, she swept forward and bowed her face to his foot, raising her heart-shaped backside high. The embedded jewels apparently went all the way down and emerged at the line between her buttocks, stopping at her lower back. She touched her lips to the top of his foot and slowly trailed kisses up his shin to his knee. When she moved to go higher, he planted his palm over her face to prevent the next one.

"Where's my battleshift?" he asked again, adding a gruff edge to his voice.

When he took his hand away, she pouted. Her face showed a flawless complexion with curving lines along her cheekbones. Her eyes were a deep maroon, as far as he could tell in his night vision. As exquisite as her presentation appeared, his concern for the battleshift stifled any sexual feelings she might've caused. Even the pennyroyal mixed into the smoldering herbs had no effect on him.

"Don't fear, my sweet Mastaren. It's in a safe place."

"Who gave you permission to take it off of me?"

"You never minded before."

He took a moment to study her. She knew something he didn't. Holes stamped his memory, and apparently this person had fallen into one. "Who are you?"

Her curved eyebrow rose, along with one side of her mouth. "You don't remember me? I'm the other half of you, Mastaren. Your greatest companion. As one, we wield power beyond reckoning. It's me, Grella… Your First Sister.

A muscle in Wikshen's temple pinched, and he clenched his eyes shut to rub it. *Grella…* Grella? No, he couldn't remember her. He opened his eyes again to take in her sweet smile, alluring eyes, and the large breasts colliding together between her arms. She squatted there patiently in a frog-like pose.

"Oh dear, you don't remember," she said. Her voice chimed like a bell. "It's no matter. Losing your memory is normal. We'll realign and forge new ones, sweet Mastaren." Boldly, she placed her hands on his knee and perched her chin atop them. "I only need you to do one thing for me."

She didn't have to tell him. He knew exactly what she wanted: the same thing they all wanted.

"I've been waiting for your return for over six hundred and fifty years," she said. "I'll die soon if I do not drink of your bounty."

He sighed and let his shoulders slacken. "Whatever," he said. Taking his knee from her, he replaced his feet on the bed and whipped the black sheet aside with an annoyed snap, baring his body to her. He lay down and waved his hand before settling it over his head.

Smiling brightly, she rose to her knees and put her hand around his limp penis. She leaned toward his face.

He pushed her face back again. "Don't kiss me. Just do it. Quickly. Give me my battleshift as soon as you're done."

"Yes, Mastaren."

His coarseness did nothing to wilt the joy in her expression. She caressed him with her graceful fingers, but it failed to inspire his desire, so she went deeper with her prodding, using her mouth instead. Her effort soothed but couldn't entice.

Lying there with his eyes closed and arm over his head, Wikshen breathed slowly. Relaxing took a bit of effort. He wanted his battleshift back, and so far, he neither remembered this woman nor wanted to do this with her. But he loved releasing his seed, so he would try to enjoy this while it lasted.

Grella worked her tongue expertly, but still couldn't awaken his base instinct. Judging by her technique, she was a fine-tuned sexual instrument, long past the days of her innocence, but she'd apparently met her match tonight.

He concentrated as he lay there, filling his head with whatever dirty thought took his fancy. He didn't have many inspiring images to dream up or memories to go by, and her appearance apparently lacked. He did a practiced breathing exercise known to his Kraft, a discipline which should help produce the result she desired—which he quickly became determined to achieve because his limpness was too baffling and, in all honesty, annoying!

In fact, her futile, repetitive moves began to annoy him too. How could she be First Sister anyway? He cared nothing for her pale hair. A more earthy hair color might go a long way. Something comforting. Blonde reminded him of the golden sun and other unpleasant symbols. Where were the brunettes?

No one else moved about to tend the shrine besides Grella. If she had a companion or two with her, they might have a better touch than she. Her manicured nails grazing faintly up and down his inner thigh did nothing for him. His cock remained soft and unwilling in her mouth. Her other hand traced around his bellybutton—also nonsense.

"Enough." He pushed his palm against her forehead to make her cough up his long appendage.

"What's wrong, my Mastaren? Do you feel well?"

"I feel fine," he said, and used the bedsheet to wipe the slobber off his pecker. "But something's not right about you. You don't please me. Where's my battleshift?"

Now frowning, she stood back. Her body jewels shimmered in the soft lighting. "It's in a safe place."

She'd said that before. He squinted at her. A cold or sharp feeling crept over him. He couldn't place it. "Give it to me."

Kneeling beside the bed, she watched him, delaying her response. Nowhere on her face did he see any intention to hand it over without getting his blessing. He knew it. She knew it.

"Give. It. To. Me." He laced his voice with a hard warning signal. Images of red flashed before his eyes. Red over her face. His anger. In the past. He...

Bowing his head, he grunted and grabbed his own hair. A headache. Trying to remember this person too hard hurt. He did his best to breathe and ward the pain away as Grella rose to stand over him. She knew something he didn't.

"Might we try again, Mastaren?"

An itch erupted in his hand. His wrist twitched. His instincts were trying to tell him something. Morkblades. He should cast one into her gut right now before she could strike in whatever manner she plotted, but he didn't have enough energy for it.

He slowly rose to his feet, keeping eye contact with her. He towered over her, but she put off no indication of intimidation. He couldn't intimidate her, and both of them knew it.

"Get on your knees," he ordered in his hardest voice.

Her face muscles flicked to amusement. Slow and graceful, she lowered into the pose he demanded. When she was halfway down, as soon as her eyes parted from his, he snatched at her neck. She lurched backward, and he only managed half a hold on her throat. Opening her mouth wide, she flexed her neck muscles, and the vibration running through her cords touched his nerves before the sound of her shrill ring. A Kraft Song.

The song didn't only make him shudder, it rumbled the earth beneath his feet. The fall happened too fast to remember, yet slow enough to catch every detail on the way down. He clutched her, intent on not letting her get away alive, and they rode the destructive cave-in deep into the underground. Holding her as tightly as he could, he planned to bite her throat out as soon as they settled.

Rocks.

Dust.

Noise.

Pain.

Disorientation.

Wikshen roared. His limbs flailed to find a hold, to stop his fall. He crashed into the darkness. Soil fell on top of him. Grella's magic song ceased.

After the abrupt stop, he lay under a mess of rocks and soggy dirt. He'd lost her somewhere in the chaos. The Kraft Fire died, leaving him with only his night vision. The incense mingled with the airborne dust and falling mist.

He reached with one hand. Just because he'd endured the fall didn't mean he'd let Grella live another second. He groped, but only found air and more rocks. A warm trickle of blood registered on his face. Her mischief was all the more reason to kill her. A servant of Wikshen should do as she was told, not demand a blessing, keep his battleshift away, and then attack her Mastaren with his own magic style.

"Bitch," he growled, and received no response.

He dug himself out and looked around. No scrap of her body showed anywhere in the rubble. It would take more than a fall and a few rocks to break Wikshen's bones. Throwing big stones aside and digging in the smaller gravel revealed nothing.

"Where are you, bitch?" His voice echoed off the hollow cave walls.

Taking a moment to study a palm-sized rock, he noticed one important issue: it was brittle and full of holes. It didn't have the minerals he needed to restore his energy. He didn't have the battleshift to help him either. Without it, he couldn't cast his greater spells. He couldn't sing the earth to his will with his deep voice like she could. His particular voice and skill could contact trolls, but there wouldn't be any in this region.

Scowling, he crumbled the rock to bits in his hand too easily. Hathrohskog's soil was long depleted of its best minerals. What had happened to his forest sanctuary?

In anger as much as to send Grella a warning, Wikshen roared. As a master of Kraft Song, she should feel his voice's vibration.

At the tail end of his shout, a whisper answered back, running through the ground and straight to his ears. *Come to my chamber to restore me, and I'll relinquish your battleshift, thus restoring your godhood.*

Chapter 27
A Beast Strikes

A fast, slippery tumble into the earth overcame Kalea. Her unkind landing turned into a glide across Hathrohskog's slick, stinging mud down a tunnel of unfathomable distance. Helpless to stop herself, she could only ride the descent until the tunnel opened up and dropped her.

Her sudden stop knocked her breath away. She lay there, eyes closed and head spinning. She flexed her hands and felt around. She'd landed on a stale cushion that crunched under her ear when she moved her head. Her neck hadn't broken, at least.

Distant, echoing voices sounded above, her friends' and many extra ones. They shouted frantically. Gaije's arrow had set a tree on fire, but the voices shouted in opposition to other hostile male voices. The extra ones sounded muffled and metallic. Dyii's exotic accent shouted among them, though too drowned in all the chaos to understand. She groaned, not quite ready to move or speak yet, but they needed to know she'd survived.

When the mud on her arms began to burn, she jumped to a sitting position and swiped at herself in a useless effort to remove it. Now moaning in pain at the irritation, she stumbled in the darkness toward the echoing voices and yelled, "Hey!"

She reached for her chest to take out her moonstone in hopes of making it light the space... It wasn't there. In panic, she pawed at her chest before realizing she'd left it at Wikhaihli! It still lay beneath the flagstones under her bed in the maids' dorm.

She yelled to her friends, "I'm here!" but they were busy in a struggle against Dyii and several other attackers. Hopefully, Metta would be able to avoid the danger.

A new terror in the form of scuffing sounds stopped her thoughts. Frozen in place, eyes wide and desperate to see anything, she could only wait.

A glow seeped into her little cave chamber. An old mattress, filthy and discolored, had been placed on the floor as if someone down here anticipated people falling into the trap as she had. She'd soon meet the people responsible. The little chamber didn't offer any real hiding places, not that there was any time to try.

Two men stepped into the chamber, both wearing strange metal masks. One held a lantern with a blue Kraft flame and the other carried a noose. The man holding the lantern hummed dully through his mask. "We have one. A woman."

Kalea pressed her back against the wall, waiting for her chance to lunge past them. They anticipated such a move and stood side by side with their feet planted wide. As soon as Kalea moved, the one with the noose sprang and wrestled her against the wall. She screamed hysterically, hoping to alert her friends of her distress.

The noose tightened around her neck and squeezed, shutting off her voice. She couldn't breathe! All the noises settled down; the masked men didn't offer to speak beyond necessity. In her struggle to fill her lungs, her head became light and her knees gave way.

She might've heard Gaije's voice and the scraping sound of another body sliding down the same muddy shaft she'd taken, but she couldn't be sure. In her weakened state, the men dragged her away, partly by the noose around her neck and partly with their arms hooked under hers. She blacked out.

So many of those men in black masks had swarmed their camp that Bowaen and his companions couldn't count them. All he knew now was that he found himself underground. Del and Gaije hadn't fared any better as far as he'd seen. Who knew about Kalea and Metta, though? He'd lost track of Kalea at the start of it, while Metta seemed to slip away from the violence.

Now he sat tied up, heart racing, face throbbing. They'd nailed him good. Couldn't guess how and when he'd lost Hathrohjilh. Light flooded the earthen chamber at the whine of door hinges. Masked men entered, three of them. Bowaen clamped his lips shut. They'd get nothing out of him.

"This is the one who fought with the sword," one metal-voiced man told the others.

"He'll do, then," the second said, and nodded to the third.

The third man produced a mask just like theirs from his bag.

"Where's the other man and the elf?" Bowaen demanded as the stranger extended the thing to his face, leather straps poised.

"Never you mind," the first man answered. "From now on, you'll serve our gracious queen."

Bowaen spat as he strained his head to the left and right to dodge the uncomfortable-looking muzzle. "Like hell I will!"

Despite his efforts, the three men overcame him, forcing the mask over his face. It smelled like iron and vomit. Very little air could enter through the slits once it sat secured to his face. They snapped a small padlock closed in the back. His breath steamed inside, quickly filling the small space with a constant humidity.

The three men stepped back and observed their work. "This one is a perfect candidate for the scouel," Man Number One announced. The other two nodded.

"What's that?" Bowaen asked from behind his new prison. "A torture implement? Better just kill me instead, 'cause the minute I get out of it…"

A blade sliding against leather announced the dagger. Man Number Two stepped forward. Tied to his chair, Bowaen couldn't do much beyond squirm and protest as he lashed out and slashed his arm. Just a flesh wound.

Man Number One drew his fingers across the gash and smeared it over the front of Bowaen's mask. He hummed a few long words as he did, some kind of spell.

"Go to hell," Bowaen growled. He thought of spitting again, but quickly remembered his new mask.

Sound vibrated through Kalea's ears. Her eyelids fluttered; opening them proved difficult. A rough hand rattled her face.

"Get up," a low, humming voice ordered from behind a mask. "It's been hours, and we thought you were dead. The mistress needs you alive."

Kalea moaned. Her spinning head couldn't process his words yet. They had let the noose slacken, but she still wore it. Her head throbbed.

"Wait 'til Dorhen hears—" She attempted the threat, but the men spared no patience for it. They jerked her arm until she complied and stood up. She'd rather walk than be strangled and dragged anyway. Her washing bat tapped against her leg with each step. They hadn't thought to take it from her?

Their blue-flame lantern illuminated the rugged walls. Thick beams of wood reinforced the muddy, moldy tunnel. Though they dwelled beneath Wikshen's forest, these people didn't seem as much like Wikshonites as she might expect, since the similarities ended with the Kraft flame they carried. Who knew if her phony Wikshonism would change their attitude toward her?

With the noose around her neck, they led her like an animal on a leash. She held off the questions she wished to ask out of sheer concern for her safety. Her skin burned and itched where the soil caked, and her clothes weighed heavier than they should.

The man with the lantern halted, extending his arm to bar the one pulling her leash. "Do you hear that?"

They all listened. An ordinary dripping sound filled the silence, but not much else.

"I hear nothing," the other man replied. With open caution, they walked on, tugging Kalea's noose to make her follow.

A shiver ran up her spine, followed by a flash of hotness, and she hesitated. Something lurked behind her. She paused and glanced back, rubbing her upper arms.

The man with the rope grunted and tugged it unkindly. Kalea yelped and stumbled forward, grabbing the noose around her throat to loosen it.

"What do you think you're—" the lantern-bearer said, storming back with his arm poised to slap her.

A force knocked Kalea to the side as the strong arm of someone new lurched from behind her to grab the rope and rip it away from the masked man.

Kalea found herself against the muddy wall and shrieked at its contact with her skin. The two masked men struggled against a newcome figure, tall and full of vigor.

Kalea lit up, forgetting about the pain of the mud's bite. "Dorhen!" Joy laced her voice.

Paying no attention, he tore the mask off one man's face to expose his chewed, red skin beneath. Patches of his hair were missing too. Dorhen spared no sympathy for him or an instant of surprise. He took him by his patchy hair and knocked his face against one of the wall's support beams.

The other man stepped backward, staring, his jaw working. "You're— you're—you're—!"

Dorhen bared his teeth in a half-smiling, half-snarling show of menace. Their enamel glistened in the pale light of the fallen lantern. He stepped slowly toward him with his shoulders flexed and square. The man stopped stuttering and instead attempted to gain distance. Dorhen widened his steps to keep up.

The man clutched his mask tighter around his face and spat out the word "*zar-scouel-eha*," something foreign to Kalea's ears. The mask's outlines flared to thin lines of glowing red light as the accessory tightened over his head, fusing to it. The man's shoulders hunched and his head dropped as his whole shape morphed into something beast-like. His moaning human voice shifted into the hoarse howl of a sort of canine creature. Feathers grew out of his neck and flared like a rooster. He was changing into a creature that blended dog- and bird-like qualities.

Dorhen roared and lurched, spun, and slammed his heel into the person's face before he could finish the transformation. He hit the wall fast and hard before sliding limply to the floor. Kalea gawked for a long minute and then remembered to remove the noose from her neck.

Dorhen stared at her now with the lantern behind him, giving her a view of his huge silhouette. "Do you know the way out?" he asked in a hard voice, keeping the bristling air he'd used to deal with the masked men.

"Um... No."

He turned and walked away.

"Dorhen!" she called, and ran after him, picking up the lantern.

He didn't hesitate at her call. She put her hand on his arm, and, too quick for her to sort it all out, he reacted. She suddenly found herself locked in his hold; he held her wrists high and solid. She'd dropped the lantern and struggled to look at his face in the light's odd angle. His eyes glowed coldly.

"Did I say you could touch me?"

Realizing her mouth hung open, she forced it closed and struggled to swallow. His grip slowed the circulation to her hands. The glow of his eyes narrowed as he squinted. She asked, "What are you looking at?"

"I recognize you... You were a pledge. Do you answer to Grella now?"

"Dorhen," she whispered, "it's me... Kalea."

Holding his piercing eyes on her, he drew in a long breath through his nose. "Why do you call me that?"

"You mean your name? Dorhen?" His grip tightened, and she whined. "That hurts. Let me go."

His teeth caught the light when the side of his mouth twisted and stretched into a grin. Dorhen didn't recognize her. It was as if he'd become... someone else.

"Wikshen," she said in an exhale. She didn't mean to say it out loud; it happened with her shock at the revelation. She'd been bound to come face-to-face with the dark entity she had met in the Alkeer temple sooner or later.

His smile continued its spread into fullness. He released her wrists, and she dropped her arms to let the expected tingles course through. She wouldn't run, not when she'd found Dorhen—or at least part of him. Besides, he was all she had down here in this cave full of enemies.

"I do recognize you." He reached to her hair and picked up a lock from her shoulder. She froze at his motion. His smile lingered strong on his wide mouth. "It's brown," he said.

"Of—of course, it is," she replied, pouting. She rubbed her hands against her hips to get the blood back into her fingers.

He leaned in to smell her hair. "Pennyroyal." His voice hummed warmly against her ear. "It's better on you than back there."

"Back where?"

He ignored her question and put his hands along both of her shoulders to take her in visually. His eyes roved down her front. Kalea began to shake. He slid his fingers across her clavicle, undid her cloak, and let it fall. He untied and pulled open her chemise collar to look at her flesh, keeping very intent. Standing board-stiff, she let him wander without any idea of how to react or ask him not to. Over her chemise, she wore her black maid's dress, wrapped and overlapped snugly around her curves. Wikshen pulled loose one side of the front and slid his hand in to squeeze her breast, which was when Kalea batted his hand and wiggled away.

His grin turned downward. "What are you doing?" he asked.

"What am *I* doing?" she shot back, pulling her lapel back over.

He snatched her wrist again, faster than a snake. "Be good, little witch!"

"Little witch?" She fought against his hold, but her struggle only tightened his grip. She stopped herself against all the instincts urging her to fight or flee.

He wrestled her with ease until she found herself pressed against a wide support beam, like the one he had slammed the masked man's head against. Wikshen pressed his body hard against hers. Her breathing and heart sped up. Panic replaced her alarm. Her whimpers escalated to fearful moans, nearly screams.

He closed his eyes and turned an ear to her mouth. When her sounds died down, he whispered, "Do it again."

"Do what again?"

"Make sounds." When she didn't, too confused by his change in manner, he pushed harder against her, squeezing her air out. Her panic returned in full. She screamed, and he answered with a moan and put his nose into her hair, probably to breathe in her pennyroyal perfume.

Kalea's tears streamed out. His hand found her breast again and his pelvis ground against hers. His trembling grew raucous, similar to that night when she was in ecstasy and they had egged on each other's arousal, except for one important detail: she couldn't feel his erection poking her like last time.

He didn't have on his battleshift for some reason. Instead, he wore a little sarong-like thing tied around his waist, salvaged from torn black linen. If his erection could be felt through anything, shouldn't it be that?

Once again, her confusion quieted her hysteria, so he grabbed her hair and shook her a bit. She gave him what he wanted and shouted loud in his ear. He moaned some more and took her down to the floor.

She lay mere inches away from one of the dead bodies, but Wikshen didn't care. He half-mounted her and treated her to a wet kiss, covering her mouth with his. Their tongues collided, a soft and interesting feeling. Most bizarre of all was the taste of his sweet saliva. It gave her the odd sense that she was eating honey. She swallowed it first by accident, and then on purpose.

Reopening her eyes wide, Kalea blinked at the occurrence as a whole. What was happening? Her heart pounded. Everything Knilma had taught her rolled through her head. She knew exactly what was going on, but it was progressing so fast!

He ripped open her dress again and tore her chemise to put at least one of her breasts out into the open air of the stale cave. She wriggled in protest, but his weight pressed her down so hard, she couldn't accomplish anything besides lying stiffly with Wikshen in complete control. A tingly feeling sparked in her gut, and she gasped at it.

He took his mouth away from hers. "You're not making sounds," he growled over her face, and then pinched her exposed nipple between two fingers. Her piercing squeal traveled long through the halls and made him shiver.

A wave of anger snuffed her blooming tingles and helped her to think more clearly. To keep him from pinching her again, she made loud sounds on purpose and hummed phony sounds of helplessness whenever his tongue wiggled down her throat.

Contrary to his moaning, trembling, and deep, hungry kisses, he grunted a sound of anger and shifted his lower body. Keeping her occupied with his mouth and hand, he seemed to be busy doing something else with his other hand.

He breathed fast. Frantic. He leaned up and turned his head away, intent on something else going on. Still faking loud sounds of distress, Kalea rose up on an elbow and boldly put her arm over his naked shoulder. She peered around him, and her fake screams halted.

"What are you doing?"

"Shut up and scream again!" Rapidly, he slicked his hand up and down his penis as it lay limp in his palm. He stopped suddenly and leaned back against her, grabbed his own hair, and hissed, "Shit!"

"What's the matter?" she asked. Her head spun. She'd just been manhandled by someone she trusted, forced to the ground, yelled at, pinched, put in a rough sexual situation—which had caused a confusing desire to bloom in her—and now it all fizzled away.

"The matter is I'm impotent!" he roared, and sat forward with his back to her. He braced his elbows on his knees and cupped his face.

Kalea didn't know what that meant. The Kraft flame flickered smaller and dimmer, but she could still see the two dead men. Beyond them, a few tunnel openings waited, tempting her to dart down one of them. She looked back at Wikshen in his simmering annoyance and knew the answer right away: she wouldn't get far. Instead, she did her best to collect herself. Straightening her clothes and smoothing her hair, she assumed a more dignified pose on the ground. "What was that?" she asked aloud. The question echoed long through her thoughts. Trembling with excitement, the darker side of her whispered disappointment that he'd abandoned his course, but when she thought about it with her logical brain, she couldn't get past the notion of him being so rough with her. In some cruel, ironic twist, Wikshen had used Dorhen's body to press her against the wall, something Dorhen would never do. *Wikshen* literally wanted her to be in distress.

Still clutching his hair over his forehead, he twisted his neck to eye her. "I'm getting out of here."

He rose and offered his hand, practically naked in his skimpy covering. Her body flared again when her gaze trailed up the muscles of his long legs. Ignoring it, she took his hand and let him pull her to a stand.

"I can't leave without my battleshift, though," he said.

Kalea tied her chemise collar back together, and then noticed him stepping into the blood pooling under one of the dead men and kneeling to place his hands in it. Her question burst out. "What are you doing?"

He shushed her. "There's iron in the blood," he said softly, now seeming to want to keep things quiet. "I need all the minerals I can find since I don't have the battleshift."

He wiped his hands on the man's cloak when he finished the strange act. He located both of their metal masks and held them until the things crumbled in his hands. He dusted them off and rose back to his full, towering height. When he turned to leave, Kalea picked up the lantern and considered the tunnel openings again.

"You should follow me if you want to get out," he said, prompting her to spin around.

She couldn't tell how much longer the lantern's Kraft flame would last; she only hoped he could relight it after it expired. If not, she might need him to lead her through the dark. Without another word, he swept away through the tunnel closest to him, and she scrambled to keep up.

"Dorhen," she said after a few minutes of walking. "Where are we?"

"You keep calling me 'Dorhen.'" He sighed.

"It's your name. And mine's Kalea." A twinge of foolishness hit as soon as the words left her mouth, but in the next beat, he tried her name out on his breath.

"Do you serve under Grella?"

Her smile dropped. "You really don't know me?"

"I know you're a pledge. I recall telling you I had killed your 'Dorhen.'"

"And that was a lie," she said, shedding her hesitance and curiosity for now. "You *are* Dorhen. You should know me." She tried to keep her voice calm. "We knew each other before…um…*this* happened to you."

"Before what happened to me?" Kalea couldn't figure out if his question was serious or sarcastic. "You're saying you knew my host person," he clarified.

Her "yes" came as a breath. "I'm not a pledge—or a witch. I don't know if that matters to you. To answer your question, I have no idea who this Grella person is you're talking about."

"It doesn't matter to me what you are," he said. "Nor does it matter who I used to be…who you think I should be. And Grella is a blasphemer who's going to die soon."

Kalea's mouth dropped open and her heart burned at his words. This really wasn't Dorhen. Dorhen probably wouldn't know what the word "blasphemer" meant, although he'd seemed settled in pretty cozily at the Wikhaihli tower, so he might or might not have picked the word up. The whole situation churned her stomach.

"Are we still in Hathrohskog?" she asked.

"Yes."

"So, do you know the way out of this cave?"

"I asked *you* how to get out a few minutes ago."

"Oh…right."

He inhaled long and slow. "I'm compromised right now." Probably another word choice Dorhen wouldn't naturally make, but Kalea resolved to call him by his real name anyway. "Grella wants my blessing," he said.

Kalea grunted and said under her breath, "Of course…" Every woman who touched a foot to Wikhaihli's soil seemed to want that very thing, sometimes including Kalea.

Wikshen continued, "She took my battleshift away, demanded my blessing despite my disinterest in her, and then she sang me violently into a hole." He turned his head to regard the area they'd left behind. "Now I see she has minions down here. Male ones."

Kalea's brow tensed. "She *sang* you into a hole..."

Ignoring her confusion, Wikshen said, "I'm reduced to helplessness down here. All this acidic soil and spongy rock don't have the minerals I need to perform my transitional magic. No battleshift, no shadow travel, no morkblades. To make it worse, I... I can't do what she wants me to do."

His eyes perused Kalea in the ensuing quiet. He didn't seem to care if she noticed. "You suit me better, but not even when you..." He didn't have to finish his statement. His wild tumbling with her had turned to him touching himself in frustration.

When she met his eyes, she found them boring into her. He smoothed the back of his hand against her hair. "You please me."

Bristling at his bold touch, she asked, "Why were you making me scream?"

"Your vibrations," he said. "I need them if I can't get the minerals this forest is devoid of. I have no idea what happened here in my absence."

Knilma had told her that Wikshen could feel vibrations, unlike any common human. Come to think of it, when she had first met "Wikshen" at his temple in Alkeer, he provoked her to make loud sounds then too. He had acted as if they were caressing him.

Regardless of how openly he stared at her, Kalea couldn't meet his gaze. "So why didn't you..." she began. "Why couldn't you...bless me just now?"

He turned his stare forward, and his face soured. "I'd like to know why too."

A few more minutes of silence passed, and Wikshen's aura shifted to a wariness Kalea could feel. It didn't grant her any confidence in their situation.

"I used to know things..." he said out of nowhere. He shot a glance at her from his forward focus. The Kraft flame barely put off light anymore, and she would soon walk blindly.

"What do you mean?" she responded after a few more seconds of silence.

"I've recently...*awakened*. There's much I can't remember." He blew out a breath. "I can't sense exactly where we are under Hathrohskog, but I should know how to find an exit. I can't sense anything." His voice hardened the more he spoke. "This forest has become a dead shell, devoid of the valuable minerals I need."

"'Dead shell' is a good word for it," she replied.

"Well, there are vibrations in the earth. Lots of activity, but I can't hear it today, and I feel lost because of it."

Kalea ventured to twine her arm around his. "We're together. That's all we need."

She felt his eyes again. "You confuse me," he said.

"Why?"

He shrugged in her hold. She could feel him more than see him at this point. "You're not like a witch."

"I told you, I'm not one," she said.

"Doesn't make sense. You give me different feelings."

"Different how?"

A puff of air exited his nose. "I don't know. And you're touching me again."

"Yes, I am."

The cave tunnel stretched on a long distance, and his pace quickened. The Kraft flame winked out, and Kalea kept the lantern to perhaps use it later. She stumbled in the dark, holding onto his arm. A faint, cool light from somewhere barely lit the edges of his form; otherwise, she saw nothing.

"Slow down, I can't see a thing," she whined.

He shushed her and stopped abruptly, causing her to bump into him. A crumbling sound broke the heavy silence. "We're not alone," he whispered, and shook her off his arm. He stepped away, leaving her in the darkness.

"Dorhen," she uttered, reaching her hands to find him again. He'd exhibited a bad habit of running off on her several times already. She found a smidge of comfort when he shushed her. Afterward, he fell silent, and she could only wait for his word.

The air hung so quietly, with only the sound of his bare feet touching down on the stone path now and again. When she took a step, her leather shoe scuffed across the floor.

Wikshen exhaled as if in annoyance at her sound, but quickly barked, "Get down!"

She couldn't react fast enough to his order. His hair swept across her face, his body heat moved in close, and his hand pushed her head down, throwing her off balance. She screamed in surprise and fell the rest of the way. At the same instant, an object whipped the back of her head.

Wikshen roared as a strange man's yell morphed into a beast-like growl. Two glowing dots of light winked into existence with the growl and grew bigger, reflecting more light as their size increased.

Wikshen's presence flew away, replacing the space around her with the tunnel's cool breeze. He grunted and cursed, and charged at the big glowing eyes.

A guttural groan challenged him like an angry dog, and Wikshen didn't back down. Picking up enough momentum that his hair flew behind him, he charged. Kalea caught his big, arching arm gestures in the limited lighting.

He struck, and the beastly snarl opposing his angry sounds suddenly squeaked and went silent right before a loud, metallic *clank* echoed off the walls. The glowing eyes blinked once or twice, and then their light winked out.

Wikshen hissed through his teeth and exhaled a few consecutive huffs.

"Are you hurt? What happened?" Kalea worked to her feet and staggered until her hands landed on him. Her touch met a warm, slippery mess on his arm. Blood. "You're hurt."

"Doesn't matter," he said. "Grella is using a form of witchcraft other than Kraft in conjunction with those minions of hers to antagonize me. Two heavy offenses against Wikshen."

"What happened?"

"Another masked man. He threw something at us and tried to transform."

"Transform into what?"

Wikshen didn't answer. Kalea ran her hand along the back of her head. Whatever sharp projectile the man had thrown might've cut a lock of hair off. Wikshen's hand joined hers, smoothing along her head.

"He almost hurt you," he said.

His concern warmed her. She batted her eyes. "What about your arm?" she asked.

"It'll close up soon." He left her standing on her own again. "This adds to the list of her already numerous offenses. I'm going to make her pay."

He took Kalea's chin in his hand. "Listen to me," he said. "You'll do as I say, or you'll die." She suddenly forgot all her alarm, dizziness, achy old leg wound, and any other momentary discomforts. "Don't stray from me, and don't look into any holes. Don't open doors either. I'll open the doors."

Wrapped in the darkness, she stared toward the sound of his voice and nodded. She felt...safe.

Chapter 28
Red Flower

Vivene was running behind today and might miss hearing Lamrhath's first wife's song, which had quickly become the center of every day for her. Of course, she knew how silly she was being. She could get in trouble for pausing in her duties to listen, but this was Ilbith. Taking in the beautiful song for one sweet moment per day made all the difference. Otherwise, she could only look forward to the next romp with a not-so-bad sorcerer...or Bargo's desserts.

She approached the vent—the one through which the voice echoed best. A sound indeed resonated through it. Vivene frowned. It wasn't singing, it was weeping. Her heart dropped. No song lived inside the poor elf-woman today. What could be wrong? Vivene regarded her surroundings. Did anyone actually need a reason to cry in this place?

The sound proved infectious. Vivene patted her chest and swallowed to hold back her own emotion. While the song usually helped her to forget the sorrows of her life for a minute, the woman's weeping exacerbated the dread of Vivene's cruel reality. She could listen no more. Shaking her head, Vivene rose to a stand and trudged on before she could be caught lollygagging. Maybe tomorrow would be a better day.

A long afternoon of dumping chamber pots and changing bed linens in the Chimera Tower took Vivene to the highest section of the whole complex. She stretched her neck, looking around and taking in as much as possible. How far was Lamrhath's first wife's chamber from here? The higher she climbed, the more gilded and frescoed the walls became—ugly, demonic frescoes, but magnificent in skill level. The little wall murals in her convent weren't nearly as good.

Vivene ducked her head and lowered her eyes whenever a sorcerer walked through the area. A lowly servant such as her couldn't take the time to gawk. One mistake would demote her to slopping the hogs in the cavernous bowels of Ilbith. She only had Bargo and his sick kinks to thank for working in this tower in the first place.

Carrying a basket half-full of bed linens, Vivene wandered a little farther. Gigantic arches adorned the grand hallways—gilded, of course. Sconces with oil lanterns lined the windowless halls, some of which boasted red glass, a treasured thing back home. In this desolate land, Vivene imagined red glass held exponentially more value.

Her footsteps echoed as she traversed one such lit hallway. Not a soul hung around at this moment. She'd found quite an exclusive wing of the Chimera Tower. Possibly too exclusive. Her nerves danced as she pondered turning around and hurrying back to a more common area. Instead, she lingered and listened hard.

Click, boom! An enormous door opened and closed. Vivene jumped and fell to a kneeling position. She bowed her head, but couldn't resist peeking.

The kingsorcerer emerged from the large double doors up ahead, not as grandly dressed as she was used to seeing. He wore only a pair of red leggings, simple pointed shoes, and a long, black robe trimmed in red that left his chest bare beneath.

To Vivene's panic, he walked briskly down the hall toward her. Her heart thundered; she went lightheaded. She might be killed for being found here, off her regular duties! Too late now; all she could do was wait and feign innocence.

The kingsorcerer breathed through an open mouth. His oily, disarrayed hair framed his face without the usual crown or fancy circlet to hold it back. He crossed the hallway in front of her and stopped at the nearest door. Vivene might easily die in this moment—from her own fear if nothing else.

The kingsorcerer put his hand on the doorknob. He paused. A faint groan emerged through his heavy breathing. Another peek revealed how he leaned his head against the door. His other hand held a golden key poised, hesitating to put it into the slot.

When he moved again, Vivene darted her eyes back to the floor. She shivered in fear. Sweat dripped down her sides under her linen layers. The kingsorcerer's breathing shifted to something slower as he moved away from the door. Had he decided not to go in?

A nudge at her shoulder made Vivene jump and squeal.

"Shut up and listen!" a gruff male voice growled over her. The kingsorcerer had nudged her with his foot and now glared down at her with his creepy yellow eyes. One hand clutched the key in his fist and the other hand held his robe over his midsection in an equally tight, white-knuckled grip. "Go get Silva," he said, and paused to breathe. "Send her to my room."

And then he strode away, but not as confidently as she'd seen on other days. He stepped carefully, as if in pain, until he disappeared back into his own set of double doors and slammed them.

Before rising, Vivene glanced once more at the door he'd considered opening. Then she realized she didn't know where Silva lived or where she might be at this time of day! Vivene stepped in place. Which direction to try? She walked cautiously forward, hissing curse words to herself. If she couldn't figure out how to find Silva fast enough, the kingsorcerer would certainly slit her throat!

A touch of relief came when footsteps tapped through the hall behind her. It crossed her mind that if she approached a sorcerer and asked him where Silva lived, she'd be punished. The matter belonged to the kingsorcerer, though; no one could get mad at her when he was the one in need. She could simply report the kingsorcerer's order to discover how to find Silva.

When Vivene turned around, an even greater relief washed over her at the sight of a servant coming with a tray. He was the most well-dressed servant she'd ever seen, but still recognizable as lower class. The man didn't stop at her approach. Balancing the tray on one hand, he fumbled a key out of his pocket and aimed his walk at the door the kingsorcerer had been interested in.

"The kingsorcerer needs Silva," Vivene said with a twinge of urgency in her voice. "Where is she?"

The servant pointed his golden key down the hall. "All the way to the end, down a flight of stairs, and it'll be the first door on the right."

Vivene nodded to him. She couldn't help but wait to see what lay behind the special locked door: a tiny foyer with a second door. Before entering, the other servant eyed Vivene. "Whatcha looking at?"

"Nothing!" The word popped out of Vivene's mouth, and she hurried along, farther down the corridor. There was no way to be sure, but she might've found the chamber of the beautiful elven singer.

Vivene kept her eyes open for Rose the next day, but didn't see her. She could have easily earned a swift execution and been disposed of under Vivene's notice. She asked after Rose to the next fellow ex-novice she happened upon.

"I haven't seen her in a while," Opal informed her. That was exactly what Vivene had been afraid to hear. Opal shook her head and waved her hands, hardly interested in discussing the strange and troublesome Rose.

"Then what of the others? Have you seen anyone lately?"

"Just a few," Opal said. "Millie got promoted, I hear. She serves the higher-up sorcerers. Sabina's in the kitchen now. Maggy had a breakdown in the west wing the other day; they put her away for a while, I think. And Cornelia got the position as nanny over the kidnapped children. One of them is a little hellion of an elf-boy."

"And how are the kids?" Vivene pressed. "Are they all still alive?"

"How should I know? Viv, I can't stall any longer. Gotta get to Baromond's room, if you get my meaning." Opal shot her a smirk and hurried away.

Vivene's chest tightened at the lack of news about Rose. That girl was settling in Vivene's mind as some sort of living relic of the convent. A twinge of disturbance hit her about Opal, who seemed to be moving on in her new existence. Apparently, Vivene wasn't the only one of them who couldn't help but admit that she liked a little of the debauchery.

At least Opal had better things to say about Baromond than Vivene could share about Bargo. Bargo possessed a sick interest in watching Vivene gorge herself. Unlike Vivene's guilty enjoyment of her relationship, Opal didn't seem to harbor any similar confusing guilt for her own. For some reason, hearing of such things from any of the other girls turned her stomach. The novices were supposed to be pure. Rose, for one, hung onto her innocence, and if Vivene could help to preserve it…

Stretching her neck for a glimpse of Rose wherever she went, Vivene made her way to a room full of fabrics and looms and sewing tools. Opening the door released a potent, invisible cloud of herbal and chemical smells—some concoction used on the fabric to ward away moths. An elite group of seamstresses worked tirelessly in here. Vivene had never given a spit about sewing back at the convent.

In this workshop, the red fabrics hung and flowed, draped over tables and knees or laid out on the big rug for pattern cutting. Vivene stepped over one such spread to get to the first window for cleaning. The seamstresses never looked up from their work, nor did they talk to each other. Instead, the rhythm of the loom's wooden parts provided music to the space. The seamstresses' hands worked up and down with bone needles and red thread, faithfully bonding pieces together to make up the various articles of clothing the sorcerers wore. A specialized handful of the seamstresses worked on garments for the kingsorcerer's wardrobe; they occupied an adjoining section of the room, with their heads held down even lower.

Fighting the sleepy feeling the fabrics' preservative chemicals always gave her, Vivene went around and wiped every small pane of every window. She climbed a ladder on wheels, constantly going up and down to reach the windows' high ends. Her overseer had stressed the importance of light for the seamstresses, so she wiped vigorously in circular motions until her arm ached.

She took a minute's break to stretch and bend her back. She might be heavier these days because of her visits to Bargo, and it did no good for her cleaning routine. Sighing at her exhaustion, she turned back to the window and paused halfway at a scrap of red fabric on the floor. She cocked her head at the shape of its cut—a bit like the Creator's Flower symbol found everywhere in her old convent. Though the formation was obviously random, it happened to be so near perfection that she wanted to take it as some sort of sign.

Vivene snorted to herself and turned to the window with her rag poised, but returned her stare to the scrap. Her smile of irony dropped. Vivene shifted her eyes across the room to see if anyone was watching. They stayed busy on the demanding sorcerers' garment orders. As quick and casually as she could, Vivene dipped to swipe the scrap up and stuffed it into her cleavage. She continued her task.

Back in the kitchen, Vivene paused at Bargo's thundering voice. She ventured around the curving wall to see him among the servants and a few other sorcerers, his beer belly jutting out as he towered over their heads.

"Well, how was I to know the fool would take a wrong step and get himself killed? Now someone has to replace him, obviously!" he said.

"Alec had the kingsorcerer's favor. How will we find someone as competent as he to replace the man who replaced him?" a fellow sorcerer asked. "I think an audition should be held to find Alec's replacement this time." He wiped both hands over his face. "The kingsorcerer needs someone competent enough not to fall down the stairs serving his wife's dinners."

Vivene stood gawking. The man she had seen taking the elven woman's food tray up to the Chimera Tower had died?

Bargo's eyes landed on Vivene during the tense moment, and he whistled to her. "Come here, little muffin."

Vivene stepped carefully toward the group. The servants present frowned and kept their mouths shut. They must've endured quite an interrogation about Alec and his successor today.

When she arrived, Bargo took the back of her hair and puppeteered her head to show all its angles. "Argey, there's no need for an audition. Let me introduce Vivene, the best new servant we have!" he said. His naturally loud voice always neared shouting.

Another sorcerer scrunched his face. "That fat girl?"

Bargo shook his finger. "She's lovely to me. What does it matter when she's so hard-working and obedient? And"—his hand wandered down to her rump and squeezed—"she's healthy as a horse."

"Or a cow," the sorcerer named Argey said, crossing his arms. "The kingsorcerer only wants beautiful servants manning the Chimera Tower. This girl has crooked teeth and…"

"So slap some soot around her eyes and rouge on her lips, and she'll keep her mouth closed."

Argey stuttered for a response, and the others glanced at each other.

"Excuse me," Vivene peeped with a raised hand. Bargo retained his hold on her bottom. The others narrowed their eyes at her, and she couldn't figure out if she had permission to speak or not. She did anyway. "I was in the Chimera Tower the other day, and…" They all frowned. "The kingsorcerer saw me up there… He didn't get mad about my being there. In fact, he ordered me to fetch his human wife for him."

The sorcerers' eyes sprang wide at that. They mumbled amongst themselves. "He didn't scold her."

"She was up there…"

"She even sent Silva to his room?"

Vivene and Bargo waited for them to finish their exchange of words. She could feel Bargo smiling high above her.

"All right!" Argey shouted to silence them all. "Something has to be done before his first wife's food gets any cooler! As we know, none of us petty red-robes are allowed to pass even through her first door. The kingsorcerer doesn't want us anywhere near her. He trusted Alec, but Alec may not live; Alec's successor certainly didn't. So here's what we'll do…"

With his mouth shaped as a downward crescent, Argey pointed to Vivene. "For today only, *you* are going to deliver her food." He surveyed his fellow sorcerers. "And simultaneously, we're going to hand an official document over to Talekas's substitute, since he himself is in the hole right now. The document will state the problem and why we believe Vivene is the ideal stand-in. He will apply his seal, and then the document will make its way over to the kingsorcerer."

"Sounds like a plan," Bargo said, and squeezed his arm around Vivene's shoulders.

Her heart pounded; she couldn't believe what was unfolding.

"Unlock the first door, close yourself in, and relock it. Deliver the food quickly and proceed to let yourself out." Argey handed her the golden key.

She numbly received it, and then he lifted the tray of covered dishes to hand it to her. She tried to stop herself from shaking as she stood holding the thing until he gave her the order to move. She started briskly off, walking more stiffly than she'd ever walked before. She barely registered Bargo's flirting coo and reminder of tonight's appointment in his chamber as she passed him by.

A long walk separated the kitchen from the Chimera Tower. Not until after the assembly with the sorcerers did she realize what an onus she'd inherited. The key, forged from gold, said it best: the elven woman herself was a treasure. The kingsorcerer's personal treasure. In the face of this duty, no mistakes could be made.

Halfway up the Ilbith tower, Vivene stopped to catch her breath. She kept her hands firmly around the tray's handles, white-knuckled and without feeling. She'd paused in a hall where younger sorcerers lived and studied. The walls were tiled neatly with slate, all dusty and marked up with the young men's perverted graffiti. Places where the drawings had been wiped with a wet cloth and long dried showed easily in the oil sconce's light. One new image remained—a stupid phallic-shaped scribble—but had been hastily abandoned; the dropped piece of chalk lay on the floor below it.

Heart pounding again, Vivene too felt a bit of mischief come over her, just like it used to in the convent. She put the tray down and took up the chalk. Instead of adding to the crude wall mural, she fished through her bodice for the red fabric scrap shaped like the Creator's Flower. Spreading it neatly on the floor, she used the chalk to write, "Don't cry," on the scrap. She returned the chalk to the floor, put the scrap with its new message under one of the dishes, and lifted the tray to hurry forward.

She'd walked the Chimera Tower's halls several rounds before, of course, but this time her elite—though unofficial—duty added a new wariness to her nerves. The farther up she ventured, the quieter, stiffer, and warier she became. She checked left and right, forward and backward, when she finally reached the enormous, gilded yet dark corridor where the kingsorcerer and his wives lived.

She remembered exactly which door she needed. She balanced the tray across her forearm and reached into her pocket, trying to breathe calmly. The woman within could be a fairy queen for all she knew. She'd never met an elf before—although Kalea had—and this one's voice was so otherworldly and beautiful, it made Vivene's throat dry to think she might actually get to meet her. And when she had cried...that voice became a spirit of infectious gloom.

Vivene cracked open the first door and entered the little foyer. Her feet scuffed across the tiles. The second door had a little carved window with a flat surface for the tray and a shutter on her side of the door. So far, she heard nothing on the other side. Utter silence. Vivene unlatched and slowly slid the shutter open…

Daylight lit the room inside. She saw no elf-woman from this vantage point. Instead, she saw the floor, a corner of the stone room, and the edge of a bed. Yesterday's tray of dishes waited on the inside of the board.

Vivene peeked through the little slot. The opening and the covered ceramic dishes on the tray complemented each other perfectly. She pulled the old tray toward herself and rested her own on the landing. She waited. Should she say something?

Miss, your meal is here.

Miss, please enjoy your meal.

Miss, I'm Vivene, and I like your singing.

No. Vivene sighed and slid the tray forward. No one appeared to take it. The landing board was long enough on the inside for the tray to go all the way through so she could slide the shutter closed and leave quickly. She knelt at the door for a few more seconds, waiting for the woman to at least take the tray, but it didn't happen.

Vivene gave up. She carefully closed the shutter to avoid making any annoying sounds, latched it, and then unlocked the first door to let herself out.

Though the experience had turned out to be uneventful, her special new task replayed in Vivene's head for the rest of the day.

"You did quite good earlier," Bargo cooed softly as they lay together in his bed. He exhibited a mellower mood today and hadn't urged Vivene to overeat any extra cakes—not to say she wasn't full of sugary sweets, though.

Vivene lounged quietly. She didn't offer to respond.

Bargo turned on his side to face her. "Would you like to deliver the tray again tomorrow?"

"I'll do whatever I'm asked," she said, feigning nonchalance when in reality she urgently wanted to.

"Good," Bargo said. "You can get the key from Argey again. He'll be in the kitchen to meet you every day."

Every day? A flutter arose in Vivene's stomach.

Bargo continued, "Our meeting with the kingsorcerer's man went off like proud trumpets. When we told him about you, he too liked the idea. Though the kingsorcerer trusted Alec, a strong-handed young woman like you may be the one for the job."

She took his words with a little skepticism. Vivene spent her days poking around throughout her chores, listening for secrets, and sneaking over to the best air vent where she could hear the elven woman's song loudest. She was as mischievous a person as she'd ever known. These busy sorcerers, having to function without much guidance from their preoccupied kingsorcerer, just wanted a quick fix to a petty problem.

"This is good," Bargo hummed as he settled onto his back and closed his eyes. "One little issue resolved." His sentence ended in a gentle snore.

Lingering beside him an extra second, Vivene smirked. With the help of a pixie's enchantment, the sorcerers used daily sex to avoid sleeping, yet Bargo always fell asleep after their sessions. Must be all the desserts and beer he brought in.

The next morning, Vivene hurried up to the vent to listen to the elven woman as usual. Would she be singing or crying? Had she found Vivene's message? If not, she'd put it in plain sight on today's food tray.

When she arrived, she put her ear straight to the molded iron grate and waited. No exceptional sound. She could be early. By the look of the sun through the window, she couldn't be late. The sun always shone brightly at this elevated floor in the tower, leaving the dreary Darklandic mists sulking around below.

She waited, hearing only the grainy whistle of air moving through the pipes. At the scuff of oncoming footsteps, Vivene leaped to her feet and lunged across the walkway with her rag to wipe the window. She couldn't imagine most sorcerers caring which servant cleaned which window on any given day. Only a few overseers would be concerned with such details.

The sorcerers moved along behind her as she circled her rag over a glass pane. When they disappeared around the bend, she returned to the vent to wait for the song.

It never came.

A long day of aching legs, screaming arms, and reddened hands got Vivene, finally, to suppertime. During the afternoon, she had unluckily been stopped in one dark hall to satisfy a younger, very aggressive, sorcerer. The bulk of the sorcerers usually showed no interest in Vivene's chubby presentation, but something fierce had gotten into that young man, so she also nursed a few bruises from his handling in the stone corridor.

She left all of it behind her when she made her way to the kitchen to get the golden key and the hot tray of food for the elven woman. "My lord," Vivene said to Argey when he handed her the tray. "I noticed we serve the woman food once a day…"

Argey sneered and poised his hand as if he'd hit her. "Are you about to ask a question of me?"

Vivene winced. "No, sir!" She tucked her chin and darted her eyes. "I just... It's..."

He grunted. "You wonder if the kingsorcerer's first wife is starving in there."

She shrugged.

"I don't know, to be honest. We only follow the protocol as we're told. If it means anything to your concern, we often get the tray back with half the food uneaten. So what am I to care if she's getting any nourishment?"

Vivene's "oh" happened as a disappointed breath. She dipped into a curtsy and hurried away before he could decide to punish her for attempting to ask a question.

It was bad enough that the sound of weeping had echoed through the vent, followed by silence today. Vivene didn't want to have to wonder if the elven woman had died of starvation. How fast would it take someone to find out that she had perished if Vivene only delivered a tray once a day?

She found the big corridor in the Chimera Tower as empty as yesterday and got straight to shoving the gold key into the gold slot. She locked the door behind her as protocol dictated, and was glad for it. With the door locked behind her, no one could catch her trying to talk to the elven woman...except for the kingsorcerer.

Vivene approached the second door with careful, silent steps. She knelt down and clicked open the latch securing the shutter. The old tray waited on the other side, just as she had left it. Once again, she pondered the possibility that maybe the elf hadn't touched it at all. She could be dead in that silent room, lying on the floor malnourished, or maybe from suicide.

Blowing out a breath, Vivene reached for the old tray. The instant her hand passed to the other side of the door, another hand snatched it. Vivene yelped at the sudden, firm grip.

"You're not Alec." A dull, feminine voice resonated.

"No," Vivene began. She bobbed her head to try to see the other person. No luck; the elf kept out of sight. She pulled Vivene's hand farther into the slot and turned it over as if to inspect it.

"You're a woman."

"Yes," Vivene confirmed breathily. "I..." She couldn't decide how to finish the sentence.

The elf released her hand, and Vivene waited, watching through the opening. The old tray flew away from her view as the elf took it, and suddenly her face appeared in the space. The top of her head and her chin were cropped off by the narrow opening, but she was as beautiful as

Vivene had imagined…with all the glittery "fairy queen" aspects removed. A woman in the flesh gazed back at her, with high cheekbones, amazing purple eyes, and heavy, silken hair—brown hair, but a magnificent brown. It reflected light in ways normal brown human hair couldn't.

Vivene stuttered to her straight, frowning face, "Alec caught an illness, so now I'm bringing your food."

"What is this?" She held up the note written on the flower-shaped red cloth.

"I wrote it for you," Vivene answered quickly. "I heard you crying, and I just couldn't…"

The stern face staring back at her dashed all the rest of the expected delicate, ethereal loveliness. "You heard me crying?"

Now sweat formed on Vivene's temples. "It's more than that. I've been hearing you singing through vents in the walls. I tried to listen to it every day. One day you were crying instead. I guess I wanted to cheer you up."

The elf hummed with her lips pulled tight.

"I wanted to know if you were all right in there," Vivene went on. "I really love your singing."

Her beautiful eyes perused Vivene's token again. She pointed to it. "What is this marking you've made on it?"

Vivene's cheeks flushed. She'd written her a note, and maybe the woman couldn't even understand the written form of Lightlandic!

The elf traced her finger lightly along each looping letter. "This white substance…"

"Oh, you mean the chalk!"

"Chalk is what you call it? In my language, we call it *kwrerr*."

Vivene nodded rapidly, unsure what to say in reply.

"Will you bring me some 'chalk' tomorrow?"

In utter relief at the turn of the conversation, Vivene melted into a smile. "Of course."

"What is your name?" This elf's accent stiffened her speech more than the kingsorcerer's. He must've spent far more time speaking Lightlandic than she.

Vivene reached her hand through the food slot. "I'm Vivene. It's nice to meet you. Since I heard your singing, I have been eager to try to talk to you. I guess it's thanks to the One Creator that I got this position."

The elf took her hand. "Vivene," she recited. "I am Orinleah."

Vivene's lips rounded at the sound of her name. "Orinleah, I will pray for your well-being."

"Thank you." No matter what words they exchanged, Orinleah put off the same flat tone. Lifeless.

"I'll get you some chalk tomorrow."

Orinleah nodded once and replaced her old food tray on the board for Vivene to take away.

"Please enjoy your meal, miss," Vivene said.

Chapter 29
A Body Fails

"I think my friends are in trouble above," Kalea told Wikshen as she walked beside him through the caves below Hathrohskog, locked arm in arm with their bodies in almost constant contact. "I fell down here at the worst time. I knew that person, Dyii, was bad. I hope he didn't hurt Metta."

Wikshen responded with a lifeless hum, more intent on what was in front of them.

"If only we could get back up there. Would you help my friends fight the attackers—and Dyii?"

He didn't answer.

"Are you listening to me? Dorhen?"

"This Metta person you spoke of," he finally said. "Is she a witch too?"

"She's a Wikshonite," Kalea said, stifling her annoyance that he kept disregarding her denial that she was a witch.

"Is she also a brunette?" he asked without missing a beat.

Kalea cleared her throat and tightened her teeth together.

"Well?" he pressed.

"Yes! Why must you know?"

He shrugged. "Let's hope she survived then." The lightness of his voice implied that he smiled.

Kalea sucked in air, lining up choice words in response to what he implied, but suddenly he paused mid-step.

"Look," he whispered. He didn't have to point out the sliver of a glow ricocheting off the edge of the curved stone wall. Kraft Fire. Keeping her behind him, he proceeded forward, one step after the other.

A wooden door secured to the stone became visible around the curve. "There *are* doors down here—" she said, and he shushed her. Being in such a raw cave, she struggled to imagine what he'd meant when he told her not to open any doors.

Nudging her away, he proceeded forward. At least she could now see whatever transpired in this dark place. Making long, quiet strides toward the light source, Wikshen's pale skin glistened in the balmy air, and his long hair cascaded to the side as he hunched over to peek through the door. The blue strands shimmered.

When a considerable distance stretched between them, he checked back and waved his hand. "Don't get far from me," he warned. He stood up straight and pushed the door open. Its hinges whined.

Kalea rejoined his side and entered second. A huge feast spread across a long table waited within, with little Kraft flames to light the space. Kalea hurried forward, stomach roaring. Surely, he wouldn't mind if she ate of his offerings—it was easy to assume that's what this was. She took up the first thing within reach: a sugared date sitting atop a mound of others.

Wikshen snatched her wrist and shook it until she dropped the treat. "No!" he scolded, making Kalea feel suddenly and unfairly like a child.

"Can't I have one?" she whined, unwittingly completing the debasement.

"They're meant for me."

She leaned back to sharpen her eyes at him. "Oh, really? So now I'm not worthy of sharing your food? You hand-delivered parts of your breakfast to me for days."

He scrunched his face. "What?"

"You don't remember?" Of course he didn't; he had been "Dorhen" back then. "Wikshen" now controlled the body. Somewhere deep inside, however, "Dorhen" still existed. With patience and firm persistence, she'd dig him out. "You shared your food with me, *Dorhen*."

He motioned to the table heaping with steaming hot food. "Doesn't matter, because you shouldn't eat this. It's poisoned just for me."

She gasped when he picked up one of the dates and popped it into his wide mouth. "What are you doing? You said it was poisoned!"

Smiling, he shook his head. "I can smell it all over this food. It's all cooked with ingredients that are aphrodisiacs. I don't know what effect it would have on you. Could be bad." He reached over and took a greasy goose leg to tear it apart with his teeth.

She couldn't help gawking as he cleaned the meat off the bone in a few big bites and moved on to another item, despite what he'd told her about the food.

"This may help me," Wikshen added between sweet cakes. "If Grella wants a blessing, she'll get it."

Something about the tone in his voice and the way his eyes narrowed made Kalea puzzle, doubt, and reevaluate what she thought he'd said.

"Who is Grella?" Kalea asked, this time adding a sharp edge to her own tone.

After wiping his mouth across the back of his hand, Wikshen took a moment to close his eyes in some kind of meditative gesture. His fingers slid across his navel. He cupped his temple with the other hand. "I'm trying to figure that out," he finally answered. "She said she's First Sister."

Kalea reared back. "*First Sister*! As in—in…?"

He finished for her. "As in she who flaunts Wikshen's favor. There's something wrong with her claim, though, and basically everything I've seen her do has been blasphemy."

"But did you—did you and she…?"

He waved his hand. "Shush!" He picked up another sweet treat from the table and nibbled it, continuing to slide his fingers across his abdomen. "I'm going to figure it out. Needless to say, she doesn't please me." His face tensing in contemplation, he took a slow bite. "Or maybe…"

Kalea held her breath, waiting for what he'd say. He'd better produce an explanation soon!

"Nothing…" he said.

Kalea balled her hands into fists at her sides. Apparently, a woman he knew dwelled down here.

He took a deep breath. "I think I'm ready. I can try, at least…"

"Try to *what*?"

He took her hand, ignoring her bristled body language. "Come on."

Before exiting the room, Kalea took one of the dishes bearing a Kraft flame and placed it in her lantern. Wikshen trailed his fingers along the soft, muddy wall as they proceeded through the cave.

"So where are we going?" Kalea asked, unable to shake her turbulent gut feelings.

"If you want out of here, you'll have to trust me. Do you trust me?"

No. "Yes," Kalea said, overriding her thought. All she knew was she couldn't get out of this place fast enough—*with* Dorhen in tow.

He stopped at a fork in the tunnel. "Stay quiet," he reminded her, and paced to the wall. He put his ear and both palms to it.

After a few long seconds, his lips peeled back and his teeth glistened in her lantern light. "Shit," he hissed. "This empty, brittle earth is so starved of the minerals it's supposed to have, it doesn't carry the vibrations well." Stepping away from the wall, he sniffed and considered the two options. "I feel…maybe that one." He pointed to the path on the right.

He held her hand again as they proceeded, even though she had a new light to help her get by. "The good thing about it," he said, "is maybe it doesn't mean my ability to feel vibrations has gone dead."

He let his eyes scan her again. A little smile quirked on his lips. She could guess what he thought about. His hand tightened around hers, and her bodily chemistry simmered.

Kalea's puzzlement about her relationship with Dorhen twisted into an unfathomable thing now that she shared his company in Wikshen's persona. She knew she couldn't—and *shouldn't*—trust this person, but… even without the effect of a dark ecstasy, she faced a hidden nagging for him. The prospect of not knowing what he'd do next put a tickle in her belly, which she did her best to ignore.

"You and I are going to have a long talk when we get out of here," she told him.

His smirk increased. "Only if you promise to raise your voice."

A smile spread on her own face, and it widened. She laughed.

His smile shifted to a frown. "What's so funny?"

"You. Don't you like my laugh?"

His initial silence killed her mirth. "Not as much as the sounds you made before. However…" He rubbed his index finger up and down his temple. "A part of me finds it amusing. I'm not sure why."

That must be Dorhen! Dorhen is in there. I wonder if he can hear our conversation. The idea gave her hope, but her laughter vanished. Wikshen didn't like hearing her laugh? Instead, he preferred her screaming and helpless whimpering?

Before she could ask him further questions, he sped up his pace. "Hear that?"

Kalea listened when they paused. "No," she whispered.

"I think we've arrived." He pulled her by the hand down a branching path that wound to the right and dipped downward. It steepened into steps carved into the rock ground. A tension in Wikshen's hand complemented a visible tightness in his jaw, his lips pressed firmly. "Around there. I can smell her smoldering pennyroyal."

"Pennyroyal," Kalea echoed.

Wikshen pulled it deep into his lungs through his nose. "Listen," he said, "I'm going in there." He huffed the aroma again. "I want you to stay quiet, so go ahead and hit me."

Kalea's mouth dropped open. "You want me to do what?"

He took her by the shoulders and shook her, as if trying to rile her up like before. "You shouldn't yell at me here, so hit me instead." He turned his face to offer his cheek. "Right there. Hard as you can."

"Why in Kaihals…?"

He leaned in closer and squeezed her shoulders. "Remember what I said about vibrations?"

Kalea nodded with her mouth hanging open.

"A slap is a vibration too; it'll accomplish a similar effect."

"Which is…"

"My arousal. So hurry up." He guided her hand up and placed it along his face.

She yanked her hand away and hid it under her other arm. "No, I'm not going to"—she lowered her voice—"*arouse* you."

His brow hardened over a deadly stare, beautiful and equally intimidating. "You said you trusted me."

"Why do you want to be aroused?" she countered. "Are we talking about the kind of arousal I'm assuming?"

"Probably. So hurry."

"No!"

He fought to catch her hand again, and she resisted, dodging and batting at him until he pushed her down to the steps they'd recently descended and pinned her between his legs, practically sitting on her.

Kalea grunted and squealed, and at her sounds he closed his eyes and breathed slow. He didn't give her a moment to relax, though. He grabbed for her hands, and as a result, she thrashed them as he wanted her to do.

"I'm gonna hurt you!" he said, showing her his teeth in a mischievous grin.

Under his weight, Kalea's breathing grew thin and her lungs hungered for air. She growled back at him, and he relished the sound. As Kalea approached panic under the chaotic treatment, her eyes watered.

She screamed, and he moaned and breathed in rhythm. He must've forgotten his order for her not to scream in this part of the cave. She let him have all of it, plus the slaps he wanted. Her arms flailed haphazardly—at this point, she didn't care if she poked his eye out. Her voice echoed far through the cave.

Wikshen moaned and panted, arching backward as her flailing hands slapped his chest. Her nails scraped him. She just needed him to get off of her. Desperation fueled her final, long shout, and he shuddered, leaning farther, catching himself on his hand and reclining along the floor.

Kalea could breathe freely once again. Her hands stung with the same physical vibrations he had referred to.

Still leaning his head back, Wikshen hissed. His hand grazed along his crotch. "That's it," he said on one of his drawn-out breaths. "You did it." Smiling, he dragged himself to a kneeling position. He took her hand, not to manhandle her again, but to help her up. His face showed drunken pleasure. "I knew you could."

He grasped her face in one hand, pressing his fingers into her cheeks, and put his forehead to hers. He sighed against her mouth. Kalea braced herself. Images of him kissing her earlier flashed in her memory and her head went light; however, the anger over all his antics kept her gut stirred.

She slapped his shoulder, and he hissed with a laugh for the added pleasure. His fingers pressed deeper. He peeled them off her and shook his head. "Not too much," he said, "or you might actually get hurt."

"What's wrong with you?" she yelled.

He shook his head again and put a trembling finger to his lips. "I'm sure she can hear us."

He waved for Kalea to follow him, but she lingered on the stairs. "Come," his resonant voice beckoned with its distinctive sensual purr. She stood on wobbly legs and carefully moved forward. After several more feet, he stopped her.

"Her chamber door is around that corner," he said. "Wait here."

His hand still shook as he put it on her shoulder. Any touch he laid on her delivered a strange spark of sensual energy, a sensation that he seemed to share with her from his own body.

"Wait for me. Don't move from this spot. And take my advice..." He made an effort to focus his eyes on her through their relaxed glaze. "Whatever noises you hear, ignore them. I'll be back soon."

He released her shoulder and stepped back. A pinch in his eyes didn't get past her. He stepped backward a few paces, sending her a certain stare she couldn't read before turning around.

Kalea's heart pounded. She could only stare at him in overwhelming perplexity until the moment he disappeared around the wall's curve.

Leaving Kalea gawking behind him, Wikshen approached a door affixed to the cave wall, grander than the one with the banquet table. After checking to make sure the brown-haired girl wasn't following him, he nudged the door open.

Ding. Just as he'd thought, a Wikshonite prayer bell tolled softly, and with several minutes in between. He could have sworn it had registered through the weak stone a ways back, but he hadn't been sure. Inside, Grella must be doing some ritual prayers and using the bell to call him to her. Bells were meant to call him, for the most part. Everyone wanted a visit from Wikshen.

The bell was tuned expertly to make a specific note that aroused his lower body. Although the sound of it pleased his mind, his body still wasn't functioning the way it should. He reached under his covering to give himself a rub. Kalea's screams and slaps had perked his cock, but he couldn't carry a lot of confidence for how long it would last. He let his thoughts linger on her to try to maintain the state of mind he'd achieved.

A great billow of incense smoke flooded through the open door. A dark, comfortable atmosphere greeted him within. Grella knew how to work him. Every little detail—the smoke, the bell—stirred memories of his past lives. Things the Wikshonites used to communicate with and arouse him, like that bell chime, had been refined over the centuries.

Very small Kraft flames flickered around the room, meant for her use rather than his. The room appeared as he would expect, not richly constructed or decorated, but tidy and arranged with the loving hand of someone who lived in it. A small table stood by with more of the aphrodisiac food spread out, wardrobes for general storage stood against two of the walls, and there was a fireplace—left cold for now.

The center dais with its black sheer draperies made for the most extraordinary aspect of the room. The front-most curtains were tied back, all around the dais lay dried herbs known to relax him. She posed at the center among a load of furs and cushions, bent over in the prayer position, naked as usual. Her blonde hair was decorated with arrangements of small purple flowers and long thorns above her ears. He still didn't recognize her from any of his past lives.

"I'm here," he said, having to force the sexy purr in his voice he'd more easily used with Kalea. Stepping over the bundled herbs, he ascended the little steps to the platform.

From her crouch, Grella's soot-painted eyes trailed up him. Within the painted black rings, her garnet irises flashed a pale secondary color that made her appear like some unearthly dead creature. Her mouth corners curled at his entrance to the veiled platform.

"Now, where's my battleshift?" Did he really have to ask?

"You'll get it, Mastaren," Grella answered.

At the sound of her voice, what little bit of sexual feeling he'd been trying to keep went cold. Why did he feel he hated her so much? He considered asking her about their past relationship, but questions would only prolong his battleshift's absence: the thing that held him firmly to the earth and allowed him to direct his power with the greatest of ease. He could learn the details later. For now, he knew she'd told the truth about being First Sister. A sense of familiarity intertwined with his disdain, and everything he could vaguely sense about her aura pointed to her being a dreadwitch—someone he'd joined with in a past life.

"After we do this and you hand over what is mine," he said, "you're going to answer some questions for me."

Her smile deepened, and she batted her eyes. "It would be my sweetest pleasure, Mastaren."

She bowed her head and touched her lips to the rug before his toes. From there, with a graceful flourish of her arms, she arched backward and settled upon the spread cushions. With an equally graceful show, she raised her knees high and let her vulva bloom red, displaying more moisture than would be needed. The little stones embedded in her soft, pearlescent skin twinkled when she moved, and now he saw another one affixed to her swollen clitoris.

A wave of bile flooded his throat instead of what he should be feeling. He shook his head. "I don't want to look at your face. Turn over."

"Yes, Mastaren." Regardless of his insult, she used the same practiced grace to resituate herself, assuming a position on her knees, raising her rear end high.

This prospect helped no more to entice him, but he couldn't think of any other way to make his task easier. His cock hung flaccid. Moving his loincloth aside, he took position on his knees behind her and pressed against her backside.

He closed his eyes and let Kalea skip and dance in his imagination. He imagined the sound of her screaming and moaning in his ear. Planting his hands on the floor on either side of Grella, he rubbed against her the way cats mated, picturing the little brown-haired sweetheart beneath him instead, the one who waited not one hundred feet away. The one he actually wanted.

Concentrating hard, Wikshen reached under to cup her breast, and it reminded him again that this wasn't Kalea. He hissed in frustration. This woman—this dreadwitch—had already tried and failed to get his blessing with her mouth. If he couldn't release it now, he'd have to try to beat her power with what he had, which wasn't much.

Up, down; up, down. Keeping the motion going and his eyes closed, he asked, "Do you have any shamans here? We may need to conduct a formal ritual."

"No, Mastaren, it's only me down here."

"Don't lie, bitch. I killed three men who wore masks over their mouths. I know they're your slaves. What made you think you could take on any male servants?"

Grella kept faithful in her difficult pose as he rubbed his body against her. This position was common practice for his concubines—and that thought zapped his memory. He clenched his eyes in a need to remember more, but right now dirty thoughts claimed the most importance.

He added to his question, "Do your slaves keep you well-filled in my absence?"

"Not at all, Mastaren. Only you can satisfy my needs," she said. "Being alone down here has proven difficult over those six hundred and fifty years, though. When I started saving poor souls who found themselves trapped under the bog, I also found ways to enlist their help. I couldn't have built this grand underground home without them."

"Ruining my forest in the process," he put in. "It should be rich with life and minerals. Now the rocks are no better than sawdust. What've you done to it?"

She cooed her response. "Please, Mastaren, let's talk about this later."

He grunted, getting tired of the fruitless motions. "Are there no other witches down here?" Although Kalea wasn't one, he might need to employ her help in getting out some semen for Grella to swallow, but he immediately hated the idea. Grella would probably hate the idea too, as First Sisters usually strutted around full of pride, flaunting their Mastaren's favor and always expecting his priority. Also, he preferred to grant his blessing to Kalea: someone he now knew he'd actually chosen. He had known she was the one the moment she entered his Alkeer temple. Though his cock wore a generous coating of Grella's bodily fluid, it hung dead and cold. Maybe his body was trying to tell him something important…

Holding her hair away from her ear, Kalea stood by the door, listening to figure out what exactly went on in there. Soft murmurs were the best she could receive, since Wikshen's voice was breathy. She caught the word "bitch" erupt from his mouth, and soft speeches followed. His voice also carried a strange sort of rhythm, not quite the cool ups and downs of an average conversation.

Leaning against the cave wall, Kalea patted her chest to calm her heart. She couldn't let her imagination run wild. Why would they speak so often if they were up to any sort of intimate shenanigans? But then… long bouts of silence.

More silence.

She could hear Wikshen breathing in those long silences. Kalea couldn't quite control her own breathing anymore. Shaking her head, she began to step in place. He'd told her to ignore whatever she heard. Impossible. The lack of sounds only made her feel worse. She inched closer to the doorframe.

No, I can't. She shook her head again. She could trust him, right? Of course! Look at all the favoritism he'd shown her so far—and in Wikshen's persona!

Unable to stand the mystery any longer. Kalea turned the corner and stepped inside the door Wikshen had left open. Would it be so bad if she walked in on their conversation? That's all it was, a quiet conversation—or so she told herself.

Beyond the door lay a room barely lit by a few Kraft flames. Her eyes adjusted to the lighting change and beheld a tent-like thing at the center of the room, similar to his dwelling in Alkeer.

Wikshen's breathing grew louder as she paced closer to the tent. Closer. The black curtains prevented her from seeing inside. A sudden burst of desperate feminine moaning sped her steps. Kalea lunged over the fragrant herbs cluttered around the dais and, with a hand shaking beyond her control, she pulled the curtain slightly open.

Wikshen was hunched over someone who lay facedown as he ground his pelvis along her backside.

Kalea's heart paused.

The person beneath him—a woman—arched backward and let out a torrent of loud squeals. Kalea squinted to see better. Beneath her Dorhen lay a darkened, shriveled mummy with receding lips and wispy white hair.

Chapter 30
A Seed Sprouts

Wikshen's eyes turned to Kalea at the sound of her throat squeaking involuntarily. They widened and his lips parted. Before his partner could twist around and see her, Wikshen shoved her face down by the back of her head. "Did I say you could come before me, witch?"

Whipping his face back to Kalea, he swiped a hand at her to back away. A look of confusion twisted his eyebrows. He observed his partner once more and sprang off of her, making a sound of disgust. "What happened to you?"

He hadn't noticed he was fornicating with a dead-looking creature? Kalea gawked, wanting to run, but unable to.

Re-covering himself with the cloth scrap, Wikshen leaned to the back curtain as his partner righted her gnarled body with its bark-like dry skin and bony features. How could she be alive?

Wikshen winced when the *witch* noticed Kalea standing there. Her wrinkled lips twisted. "Is this why you're so distracted, Mastaren? You have a young tart following you around?" Her reddish eyes squinted at Kalea. "You haven't blessed her either?"

Wikshen let out a breath instead of any word.

"Do you even have the ability to bless?"

He still didn't answer.

The witch roved her eyes over him. "Oh, dear," she continued. "This isn't good. Didn't you eat anything from my feast table?"

"Yes," he growled. "Where's my battleshift?"

"Safe," she said, and arched her naked body backward with nearly as much agility as an average young person to dodge Wikshen's lunge forward. He poised his hands to throttle her neck. The witch pulled a rope hanging from a bell at the corner post of the tent.

Clang!

Wikshen froze, his teeth gritted. Though loud and piercing, the sound didn't bother Kalea nearly as much. The witch took the opportunity to roll away and spring to her feet. The doors to the wardrobes banged open, and out stepped men wearing black muzzles like the ones Wikshen had fought before. It seemed the wardrobes hid more tunnels.

Kalea stood gaping at the unexpected progression of events, and the witch struck her across her collarbone in her hesitance. The tearing feeling in her skin followed a second after. The hag reared back, brandishing a thorn in her fist which matched the one remaining in her hair.

Kalea yelped and shot her hand to the stinging wound. Her finger pads picked up a minor trace of blood. The damage was no deeper than a cat's scratch. Kalea lurched away from the witch, but the old creature moved on, receding into the shadows as Wikshen took on the drone-like men in masks.

From the shadow, the witch hissed out a loud command in a foreign language, which the men repeated in spirited, immediate shouts, as if reflexively. "*Zar-scouel-eha!*"

On cue, the muzzled men hunched and twisted. The Kraft flames didn't deliver enough light for Kalea to make sense of it all. They thrashed and moved about the room. Wikshen inched closer to Kalea bit by bit.

Within seconds, one of the men lashed forward with a beastly roar, flashing a face no longer a man's but a gaping maw full of razor teeth glistening in the blue light. His hunched stance became the natural shape of his body, now with a thick neck covered in black feathers. Huge wings stretched to the ceiling above his horizontal back. Together, the men-turned-animals filled the room with their enormous wings.

One darted to Wikshen, the other to Kalea. Wikshen ignored his own attacker and lurched to haul Kalea out of the creature's path.

"Grella!" Wikshen roared while holding Kalea behind him, his hand locked around her wrist like iron. "You're making a big mistake! Give me my battleshift!"

Grella lurked out of sight. Her lilting laughter was the only human response in a dark room full of snarling creatures.

"Dammit!" Wikshen barked under his breath as he turned to face the two stalking winged beasts which used to be men. He took an instant to shove Kalea backward. "Get out of here!"

He applied a bit too much strength, and Kalea tumbled and landed on her backside, elbows scraping the ground.

Getting up proved more difficult than it should've, but she climbed to her feet and opted to stay in the room to see what happened.

I'm not leaving Dorhen again! A situation like this had separated them in the first place. She wouldn't stand for it to happen a second time.

Wikshen widened his stance and flourished his arms in graceful arcs. He breathed in a deep, steady rhythm, building to an exhale as he pushed out with his palms forward as if to shove an invisible wall before him. All around his concentration, the creatures made raking growls and tapped their claws against the floor with each skulking step.

He repeated the motion a few times, adding speed each round. The two monsters hung their jaws and salivated long strings of drool as they appeared to wait for Wikshen to make his move. The sour smell of their breath turned Kalea's stomach.

Appearing to lose its patience, one beast leaped forward. Sucking in one more deep breath, Wikshen exhaled hard and shoved one arm forward, the second stopped halfway.

"Ha!" His powerful voice resonated loud and long, raking through the stone walls around and behind Kalea, vibrating under her feet and all the way up her legs. Her knees wobbled, and she fell.

It all happened at once: Wikshen made his move, and the monster collided with him. They fell into a tangle. It didn't look good.

Kalea screamed and fought to rise to her feet again despite the sluggishness creeping into her muscles. "Dorhen!" she cried.

The beast worked its front legs, clawing him, snapping its jaws. Roaring in anguish, Kalea rushed forward, taking up her washing bat from her belt. He rumbled—alive—from under the violent beast's body.

A new, beastly thunder beside her reminded that two more creatures prowled in the dark. Kalea dodged the next one's charge. On its four legs, the thing stood at the height of a horse. The second creature put itself between her and Wikshen as he struggled to fight beneath the first one.

Sheer adrenaline kept Kalea on her feet instead of huddling on the floor in fear. She couldn't stand to take on this monster like Wikshen, but tried swinging her bat at it. It sidestepped and sprang, aiming its jaws at her middle. Kalea went down, losing all the air in her lungs with a punching ache.

When she reopened her eyes, she found Wikshen with his hands at the corners of the creature's jaw, holding back its bite. If not for his strength and speed, the beast would've ripped her gut open.

Wikshen held his teeth clenched; his arm and shoulder muscles bunched. Growling to match the ferocity of the beasts, he hauled the creature backward by its head, his fingers hooked into its cheeks. Kalea took that instant to wiggle backward and climb to her feet.

The other creature mauled Wikshen, freeing its companion. The beast's teeth sank into his shoulder. He went down again.

Hardly considering a plan, Kalea grabbed the nearest dish with a Kraft flame and, with her bat poised in the other hand, searched the dark corner of the room where the witch, Grella, had retreated before this fight erupted. If Kalea could…hurt or capture the witch, she might help win Wikshen's battle.

The corner revealed nothing. No Grella. Kalea moved farther, checking the darker corners beside and also inside the wardrobes, where gaping holes led to more tunnels. Grella must've used one to slip away.

Behind her, Wikshen growled and grunted on as he struggled with the two enormous, winged beasts. "Kalea!"

She whirled around, but he was already upon her. Wikshen swept her up and shot for the door, jostling and bouncing her all the way. She dropped the flame but retained her bat.

Out in the corridor, she could see nothing in the dark—but Wikshen could. He rushed to keep distance between them and the monsters. Growls rang and claws tapped the floor in pursuit behind them.

Wikshen took sudden turns Kalea couldn't anticipate in her blindness. With his effort, the creatures' sounds grew fainter. Kalea's body was numb by the time he slowed down, otherwise she'd be whining about the discomforts of riding draped over his arm. He'd grown so much bigger than the Dorhen she used to know that he could easily carry her wherever he pleased.

He let her down gently, but Kalea couldn't stay on her feet for long; she stumbled and collapsed. Wikshen paused to observe her. He'd brought her to a place where the sun shone through little gaps in the ceiling, a cavern close to the surface.

"What's wrong with you?" he asked, kneeling to study her further.

"Nothing," she answered. "I'm in shock, I think. I need a few moments to rest."

Squatting at her level, he reached out and put his hand on her chest, but not to grope her again. He slid his fingers across the sticky scratch Grella had made on her collarbone. "I don't like this."

She shrugged. "It's just a scratch."

"Does it burn?"

"Yeah. It's throbbing."

His mouth firmed into a downward crescent at her answer.

"It hurts as expected, but I'm fine," she said. "Dorhen…"

He narrowed his eyes at her. He didn't identify with that name, but she resolved to call him by his true name anyway.

"What were you doing with her?" Kalea pouted and blinked her eyes at the end of her question. This conversation should wait, but she couldn't help asking.

"Failing is what."

"What does that mean?"

He dropped his head, and his hair fell forward in a silky cascade. "Grella is—apparently—First Sister. She wants my seed to renew her life because she's ancient at this point and wants to make sure she continues living. She's hiding my battleshift somewhere and demands a blessing in return for it. I can't leave without it."

"I don't understand what you're talking about."

He narrowed his eyebrows at her. "She wants my *blessing*. What's not to understand?"

"Your...blessing will help her live longer?"

"Among other things." He stood up, and she attempted to follow, but wobbled in a hopeless, dizzy mess. He put his hands on her to steady her. "She poisoned you."

Kalea's stomach soured. "Did she?"

"What did she scratch you with? Her nails?"

"A big thorn, I think."

He huffed, turned, and put his face in one hand. "That's even worse."

"Well," Kalea said, "it's not my first poisoning."

He turned back around and grabbed her upper arm with his big hand to keep her steady. "This is a spelled poison, not a humor-type poison. If we don't get her to cancel your spell, you'll die. I'm not sure how quickly."

Kalea stared up at him as he returned her gaze. She didn't feel near death yet, but the weight of his words washed her with dread.

He tightened his grip around her arm. "I don't want you to die."

Kalea's lip quivered, but she resisted panicking in the face of impending death for now. She forced a smile despite her inner turmoil. "Well, thank you very much."

She turned away, and he let her arm go. Before attempting to walk, she faced him again. "What about your shoulder? I saw the monster bite you."

He brushed his blood-matted hair aside and showed his entire arm and half of his torso painted red. The sight worsened Kalea's wooziness. "Don't worry about me. I can heal quickly," he said.

Kalea nodded despite her illness.

"The real problem I face is impotence. If I can't kill her without my battleshift, and I can't give her the blessing she wants..." His face pinched. "For some reason, it fills me with emotion to think of you dying. I don't know why."

"It's because you love me, Dorhen." Her voice rang weakly, and she wasn't sure if her illness caused it or not. "And because of that, I don't want you to"—she sighed—"'bless' her." Replacing a sexual word with "bless" felt so wrong. In her religion, "blessing" was something the One Creator did for His children whom He loved.

Wikshen took her arm again. "Walk," he ordered. "If we don't move, we won't get anywhere, and you'll die on this spot. The least we can do is try."

"Can't you promise me you won't bless her?" she asked.

"Tch. You're poisoned right now, and all you can worry about is whether or not I boff a witch?"

"Yes." She gave the most genuine answer she'd ever expressed.

"To me, intercourse is meaningless—it's a token I give, no more valuable than a pocketful of acorns. Why should it bother you if I do it?"

"It does." She sniffed. "Putting it like that makes it even sadder."

"Then what if I do it to save your life?"

"It's the same," she said. "I just don't want you to do that with any woman, especially Grella."

"Shut up and walk."

She did. Their conversation didn't help her condition at all. It might have if he would just promise not to betray her in that way, but he'd flatly refused—even to offer a comforting lie. He might as well directly promise to "boff" another woman.

They walked in silence a long way through the roughly carved tunnels. As harshly as he'd recently spoken to her, his gestures in helping her traverse the path expressed the opposite. Dorhen was definitely still alive somewhere in his transformed body.

"How do you think Grella managed to create this big tunnel complex?" Kalea asked as he guided her through a darker section. He held her hand as she took one careful, blind step after another.

"There's a short step down right here," he warned before answering her question. "Aside from using her voice with Kraft, I assume she has many more men in muzzles doing all sorts of work for her down here. The problem there is that they aren't warlocks, and Wikshonite women aren't permitted to ally themselves with men. Usually, they'd form a coven for surviving in places like this, but Grella... She's going far beyond the life of a Wikshonite. She's formed her own domain down here, under my forest of all places, and depleted its lifeforce to do so."

He paused, and Kalea bumped face-first into his sweaty back on her next step. "Listen," he whispered.

She could hear it too: faint booming sounds at sporadic intervals. "What is it?"

He shushed her and listened some more. "What I suspected. I hear tools scraping the stone." He guided her onward, choosing paths leading closer to the noises.

"Look at this," he said, and they paused again in another tunnel with faint light. He ran his hand along the wall, where decayed roots stretched along, embedded in the stinging soil. "All the trees above are dead. They've no more life to give."

"I could have told you that," Kalea said.

"It's worse than I thought," he went on. "I'm guessing Grella sucked their life away to keep herself alive."

"You can tell by looking at the roots?"

"I can tell it by looking at her. Dreadwitches can live for a long time, but not forever." He reclaimed her hand. "Let's see what else she's done to my forest. The tunneling is more expansive than it should be, so I can imagine the huge, impending cave-in if she doesn't stop."

Kalea didn't like those words, not while she ventured around underground. As if to complement his claim, their little tunnel ended at a massive open cavern ringing with the sounds of pickaxes and men's voices. The ground was carved into a network of winding paths that sometimes tunneled through large stalagmites. The voices kept hushed, more strained than Kalea would expect from any normal worksite.

Dirty, hunched men trudged this way and that, pushing wheelbarrows and hauling large baskets. They were harvesting some type of moss off the walls, as well as digging pieces of earth—some form of mineral—out of the rocks. Other men sprinkled water over strange underground plants with stems as thick as a human leg, vines like arms, and enormous pods sitting at the center of each.

As she gawked at it all, Kalea finally noticed it wasn't moss they harvested—it was seeds, which also flew apart from the strange plants on the moist breeze, many escaping through daylit cracks in the cave.

"Dorhen?" she said. "What are they doing down here?"

Though he'd shared his insight plenty of times before, now he stood at a loss, staring with her at the intricate network of underground workers.

"Kalea?" someone other than Wikshen responded to her.

They both turned at the sound of her name. One of the worker men, a ragged one with a lithe body and a young voice, stood across the path from them. His face was bound up in soiled rags. He and all the other men had a large section of their faces covered over the ears in addition to the black metal masks covering their mouths and noses. This one's black mask helped the wrappings to conceal his entire face.

Kalea squinted, trying to place his voice despite it being muffled. It couldn't be Del's or Gaije's. It certainly didn't belong to Bowaen.

A slight stutter came out of him next. "K-Kalea, it *is* you!"

Kalea's mouth dropped open, and she covered it. *Nonsense, I'm dreaming!*

The young man stepped forward. "Kalea," he said again, and it was all she needed.

"Damos?"

He nodded. She couldn't tell his expression behind all the bandages and the muzzle over his mouth, but his gestures and cautious steps hit her uncannily.

"Yes," he said. His voice grew more hopeful with each word. "It's me."

Kalea's eyes watered. She stepped forward as well, closing the gap between them. His steps quickened, as did hers. "I thought you were dead!"

She didn't know whether to burst into tears or laugh and praise the One Creator. When he opened his arms for a joyful, relieved hug of reunion and welcome, Kalea widened her arms to receive him. This was her friend whose death she'd carried such guilt over. Seeing him alive took it all away. A tearful laugh of absolute joy and wonder escaped her throat.

And then a shadow stepped between them, bent Damos over on a hard fist to his gut, and followed through with a careless shove to his forehead to drop him to the floor. Damos's relief withered to a cry of pain as he curled on the ground.

Kalea froze in shock, which quickly shifted to confusion and progressed on to an anger that made her poisoned wound flare in pain. "Dorhen!"

Men all around stopped working. Her fast heartbeats made her nauseous as the poison was carried farther through her body. She swayed on her feet.

Wikshen pushed her backward with a careless hand to her breast and hovered over Damos's helpless form. He pointed a stern finger down and said, "Don't touch her!"

Kalea grabbed Wikshen's arm and attempted to pull him away from Damos. "What's the matter with you?"

Try as she might, she couldn't break his solid stance. Wikshen half-turned to eye her. "What do you mean, 'What's the matter?' He wanted to touch you!"

Kalea spread her hands and opened her mouth to her absence of words.

"No one can touch you but me," Wikshen growled, his eyes sending a warning to her and Damos alike.

Kalea's friend, who'd returned from the dead, sat chastised and injured on the floor as Wikshen stood bristling, his arm muscles bunching, veins popping. She wanted to argue with him, but it would accomplish nothing right now. Damos also fell silent, as if no longer in the mood to talk.

Instead, Wikshen crossed his arms and spoke to him. "What's going on down here?"

Damos flicked his face up and back down, reluctant to look at either of them now. A lump rose in Kalea's throat. Damos remained sitting on the floor in silence until Wikshen seized him with one hand to his face.

Kalea jumped in fright with a short scream, and then stood petrified to see what he'd do next. The other drones in masks paused briefly at her sound and went back to their tasks. Holding Damos by his metal mask, one huge hand across its structure, Wikshen turned his head to regard Kalea's sound. She couldn't predict his thoughts through his hard expression.

Wikshen merely took his hand away, and Damos's mask crumbled. He'd absorbed its best metal elements and left behind brittle chips that fell over Damos's lap. His mouth was now free through a slit in his face bandages. He must be wearing the bandage because his skin had been severely damaged by the flesh-eating soil of Hathrohskog.

Still staring at her, Wikshen said, "You arouse me again, but this isn't the time or place."

He dropped his hand, stepped away from Damos, and then worked his fingers as if about to play a musical instrument. He widened his stance and took up a pose similar to the one he'd used to face the winged beast. He thrust one arm forward and pushed out practiced breaths, speeding up the motion until his arms were pumping fast and hard.

"What are you doing now?" Kalea uttered. Damos also watched from the ground.

"Dammit!" Wikshen hissed. "This isn't good. None of this is good." He'd been saying that a lot.

"What isn't?" she pressed.

"I can't cast Morkblades without my battleshift. We're as good as dead down here."

Kalea's hand shot to the poisoned scratch line going across her clavicle. Her voice emerged breathily. "Don't say such things."

Wikshen breathed through his teeth, flexed his muscly shoulders, and worked his arms in frustration. "I'm only telling the truth! With it, I could throw the lightest version of Morkblades without having to absorb minerals. I would've killed those scouels back there!"

"Scouels?"

"Those big winged creatures," he said. "Grella has found a way to channel them from Kullixaxuss through the use of human bodies."

Kalea's stare shot to Damos. Wikshen's statement sounded like the method Damos used to change his pet parrot into a ravian. Damos kept his somber seat on the floor, as if he'd given up. Her heart melted for him.

She carefully stepped closer and reached out her hands, needing to make sure he was all right, but Wikshen snatched her wrist and yanked her away with an angry force.

"Ow!" she shouted. "Stop it."

"What did I say?" he yelled in her face.

She scowled at him in defiance. "I have to check on him. He seems in a lot of pain."

Wikshen shook her. "No!"

She shot back, matching his volume, "You're going to have to stop doing that!"

During their stare-off, Wikshen's lips spread to show his teeth. The long one on his left revealed its own proof that this really was Dorhen's body. His eyes narrowed to complete the sleazy grin. "I can play with you as easily as I can play with him. The difference is, I won't let you die… until I'm ready."

She narrowed her eyes and tightened her frown. "I'm not afraid of you."

His smile widened the rest of the way. "My little witch," he said in a lower voice meant only for her.

"Don't call me what I am not."

He shoved his face closer to her, enough so their breaths mingled. She could feel Damos staring at them from his helpless place on the floor. "Would you like to join Grella's underground kingdom of madness like all these hardworking drones?"

Kalea worked up all the nerve she had left to give him a smirk. "You won't leave me down here, *Dorhen*. I know you."

He closed his lips over his grinning teeth and tousled her hair. "Right," he said. "Because you're mine now. You're not going anywhere."

A chill traveled through her limbs at his amused, matter-of-fact words. He let her go, and she stood on her own, poisoned, weakened, and rubbing the circulation back into her wrists. She couldn't keep the pout off her face.

"And you…" Wikshen turned back to Damos, grabbed his soiled shirt, and hauled him to his feet. "I asked you a question. What's going on down here?"

"There's a witch who's making us work," Damos answered. The light caught his eyes as they shifted to Kalea more than once. "She makes the men do work, and she uses the women to keep herself alive. She drains their lives away so she can look pretty for a few minutes."

Wikshen glanced at Kalea in the next instant, then back to Damos. "So what is all this?" Wikshen swirled his finger at their surroundings with all the drones who faithfully pushed handcarts and swung nets. "What are these unnerving plants?"

Damos's eyes widened as he said to Kalea, "That reminds me. Kalea, cover your face, especially your ears."

"Hey!" Wikshen snapped. He gave Damos a firm slap to his face and turned his chin back to attention. "I asked you a question."

Damos began with a stutter. "She calls these plants 'forlustweed.'" His shoulders shook in the next beat as he took an uncomfortable breath. He put his face in his hands. "We have to leave. Kalea…"

She waited.

"We just have to go."

Wikshen growled and raised a fist. "That's exactly why I'm letting you live. You'll help us get out of here."

"But, Damos," Kalea said, having to keep her distance with Wikshen standing stiffly between them, "what's forlustweed?"

"Come with me," Damos said with a somber light in his eyes.

He chose the narrower, less-used paths that led into a deeper, darker area of caves. Wikshen stayed silent, holding Kalea's arm as if paranoid she'd get too close to Damos.

The poison slowly making its way through her system must've caused the ill state Kalea walked in, but she knew that was only half true. It was the multifaceted situation she'd come into. Damos was alive. She didn't have to see his face; she knew him well enough. At the least, his beautiful blue eyes offered the truth, now dulled to lifeless depression in the twist of fate he'd found.

Another facet caused her deeper discomfort: Wikshen was the one who had "killed" him in the first place. Mere weeks ago, Kalea had been with Damos aboveground in Hathrohskog, shedding clothing in some wild and confusing urge to establish an intimate relationship. That was when two arms—Wikshen's arms—reached through the darkness to drag Damos away from her. The image stayed forever burned in her memory. The shapes of the big arms… They were definitely Wikshen's.

Now, the three of them walked together in the most awkward alliance Kalea could think of. All by her own hand.

"It's around here. Be quiet," Damos said, and waved them along.

Walking in closer proximity than before, they tiptoed into a chamber carved smoothly with a door fixed to the opening. An infirmary of sorts lay behind it, with a bed blotched all over with huge brown stains—old bloodstains. Clay jars holding the-Creator-knew-what cluttered up shelves affixed to one wall, and a few wardrobes stood along another wall. The back of the room offered a door leading onward, which Damos opened slowly to prevent the hinges from whining too much. The next room was longer and fitted with many wooden cages...containing humans.

Kalea gasped and ran to the first one. "Dear Creator!" She put her hands on the wooden crossbars and locked eyes with a half-dead girl who appeared to be no older than she and starving to death.

Wikshen lunged to pull her away, and Damos shushed her again. Women occupied all the cages, young ones. Strangely, they kept silent, even with the intruders' presence.

Gaping in horror, Kalea rounded her lips, looking for the right word to start her question, but couldn't find it.

Damos beat her with an answer. "The witch keeps these girls in stock. She uses them to..."

As Damos trailed off in a huff, Wikshen finished for him, "To temporarily turn herself into a supple, naked beauty with shiny hair and a pierced pussy."

Kalea's jaw dropped open, but Wikshen paid no mind.

"She lied about not having other women here with her," he added.

Across the way, Damos nodded. Through his bandages, his throat could be seen trying to swallow. "Witchcraft," he mumbled.

Wikshen stepped forward to observe the dying girl in the cage. Her overall coloring had faded like old cloth: her skin now showed a sickly yellow mingling with grey. Hunched over in the little cage, she shivered. Rags covered her body but didn't conceal the bony formation of her shoulder.

Observing her with less emotion than Kalea, Wikshen said, "Grella's using the lifeblood of others." He turned his attention back to the door with the infirmary and bloodstained bed. "She puts a glamour on herself, which she used to try to seduce me. This isn't Kraft. She's long since passed from my favor...whoever she is."

Beside them, Damos began with another stutter, "S-so you're that... the...'Mastaren' she's been talking about?" Wikshen didn't answer him, so he continued, "She's been getting us all ready for your arrival."

Wikshen turned to Damos. "How?"

Damos spread his hands. "She didn't want you to see all this down here. We've been hiding away our greatest secrets and putting up walls and partitions and places for your comfort."

Wikshen grunted. "That much is obvious. She knows what goes against my laws."

When Wikshen took a step back toward the door, Kalea jumped in front of him. "Dorhen, no, wait! We have to let them out."

He met her with bland eyes. Kalea put her hand on the wooden cage again. "We have to…" She would've merely repeated herself, but couldn't. Her tears threatened to flow. She'd throw herself at his feet and beg him if he didn't act right away.

Wikshen shook his head. "Not much we can do for these little morsels of witch-food."

Kalea's eyes pinched. Her hot tears streamed down her cheeks.

"However…" He put his hand on the cage's padlock and held it until the metal crumbled. He did the same to the hinges, and the door fell off. He proceeded down the line, absorbing the rest of the metal from the cages.

Hanging back, Kalea motioned to the girl within, who swayed weakly. "Come out," she said. "Free yourself."

The girl didn't. When Kalea stepped forward, a hand took her arm. She was surprised to find that it belonged to Damos and not Wikshen, who kept busy taking padlocks and hinges off cages.

"No, Kalea," he whispered. "You can't help them."

Kalea pulled her arm away for his own sake before Wikshen could catch them in contact. "Why not?"

"They're too far gone, and we can't carry them." He sighed. "You'll have to follow me, and I'll show you."

None of the young women in the cages bothered to move after Wikshen dropped their doors.

"Let's get out of here." Damos flagged them back to the entrance. Wikshen took Kalea's hand and pulled her when she hesitated in concern for the defenseless young girls who sat lethargically in the cages.

They backtracked through the infirmary, where they continued through the corridors, and within several paces, Damos pointed out their next destination. Once again, he reminded them to be quiet.

"People are in and out of these rooms all day, and this one is probably in use, so we must sneak to get a close look." The room Damos opened held stacks of crates. "These hold the seeds we harvest." He lifted one's lid by a sliver. "Be on your guard."

Wikshen half-stepped in front of Kalea, making her stretch her neck to see what Damos was showing them. Damos took a rag out of his pocket and used it to pluck one of the seeds out of the crate. Holding it carefully with the rag, he closed the lid and showed them the odd little seed. The thing made hasty efforts to sprout thin spiderweb-like threads and tiny green stems. The webs moved as if they belonged to an animal instead of a plant.

"This is an awakened forlustweed seed. Some of the other drones call it 'reaper vine.'" He pointed at the tiny feather-like formations beside its threads. "It uses these wings to drift on the wind like a dandelion seed, and the threads can latch onto surfaces and creatures."

Wikshen stepped a little farther in front of Kalea's view, and she put her hand on his arm to peer around him. "Put it back in the box," he ordered, and Damos obeyed, sealing it tight to prevent any of the others from flying out.

"Damos," Kalea said. "Why are you all collecting these seeds?"

"That's what I'll show you next."

The room beside this one was divided by wooden bars similar to those which made up the cages holding girls in the other room. Damos put his finger to his lips and motioned for them to duck behind a stack of more crates holding thousands of forlustweed seeds. Little slithering noises sounded within.

"These seeds are more mature," Damos whispered. "They're crawling around"—he shuddered—"looking for a host."

Kalea's eyes drifted to Wikshen as he squatted beside her at the boxes. "Looking for a host" echoed in her head. She put her hand on his shoulder, and he twisted backward to regard her.

"What?" he said.

She shook her head. "Nothing."

Damos gestured for them to stay quiet at the same second that Wikshen closed his eyes and put his palm flat on the stone floor. "Someone's coming," he said.

The three of them huddled down close to the creepy boxes of moving seedlings. Footsteps as well as the sounds of a struggle scraped through the hall and into the space on the other side of a wall made of wooden slats. Two men in black muzzles hauled a dirtier one. The two men were dressed in black clothing and appeared more prominent than the one they held, as if they were Grella's guards and he a drone who'd been digging and harvesting seeds.

Damos hissed through clenched teeth. His eyes pinched in sympathy as if he knew the man in trouble. The guards tied the dirty man down to a bed and used a key to unlock and remove his mask. His unmuffled cries escalated, but once he lay secure, he simmered down to panting instead.

Wikshen's hand slid around Kalea's upper arm again. When she checked him, he stared at the scene intently, absentmindedly tugging her closer to him. He was so protective of her despite the offensive things he'd said during their earlier argument.

The man's screaming drew Kalea's attention back. His captors opened a crate. Wikshen's hand tightened. One of the guards reached into the crate with a pair of tongs as the other shoved the lid back in place as soon as he brought out what they needed: a palm-sized, wriggling plant with longer green stems and much longer spiderweb threads.

The forlustweed seed used its stems to feel around, searching for something to hold, and when they found the iron tongs, the threads followed, grasping the tool in an effort to free itself. The man in control of the tongs kept utmost concentration as he hovered the seed over the tied man's head.

This made the captive scream and writhe in his bonds, shaking his head to resist the inevitable. When the seed's stems found the side of the man's head, it abandoned its hold on the tongs and immediately slithered its threads to grasp and stick to his face with a thrilling urgency. The screaming turned to weeping as he—and everyone else—knew the scene would end in the next few moments.

When the seed showed more interest in the tied man than anything else in the room, the guard loosened the tongs from around it. The tiny plant-creature used its slithering threads to drag itself into the man's ear and disappear altogether.

The man cried louder, now in pain, and Kalea cringed. She found her own hand squeezing Wikshen's arm in return.

The screaming stopped. The man's eyes ceased all of their shifting and blinking and swiftly dilated. He lay motionless. His mouth dropped open. His breathing continued, though.

The two guards took this as their cue to untie him, and he didn't offer to move with all his limbs unrestrained. A guard reached down behind the crates and wooden slats and brought out a rope, which he tied into a loop and placed around the now-catatonic man's neck.

Kalea stifled her gasp behind two hands. This scene seemed familiar to her. As she expected, the guard used the rope leash to guide the catatonic man off the bed to stand solemnly, no longer possessing the ability to fight or even form an opinion. When the guard dropped the rope end and let it hang off his neck, the catatonic man waited, swaying slightly in his new submissive state, until the guard led him away by his rope like a horse in a bridle.

Kalea had seen this exact same thing before, in the Carridax Cathedral where the sorcerers who occupied the holy building led around similar people. The sorcerers called these people "dunces."

When the two muzzled guards and their new dunce exited through a branching corridor, the trio relaxed and inched away from the crates full of wicked seedlings. Wikshen eyeballed their wooden surfaces through narrowed lids and a furrowed brow.

Damos shook his head. "I knew that man," he said, confirming Kalea's guess. "Derndig. He'd been whispering about escaping this place. I had already tried to cooperate with his friend and failed. Derndig's plan had too many holes to even consider." He shook his head throughout the speech. "He's been caught already." Damos motioned back to the room behind the bars. "That's what happens to people who betray Grella."

Damos stopped talking as his eyes landed on Kalea, who was absentmindedly clinging to Wikshen's arm. He cleared his throat and stood up. "If we're caught now, the same will happen to us."

"Not me," Wikshen replied in his deep, resonant voice. "I'm going to destroy her." He pulled Kalea to stand also, and then guided her away from the eerily noisy crates.

"But she has your battleshift," Kalea said. "How will you get it back?"

Wikshen turned to Damos. "You know your way around here."

Damos raised his hands, palms out. "Not as well as you might think. I've only been here a few days...at least since I woke up from..." He shifted his eyes to Wikshen, and then back to the ground. He chanced a quick glance at Kalea in the next awkward moment.

Wikshen made a throaty grunt. "If Grella wasn't a concubine, she wouldn't have the ability to take the battleshift off of me. It's unnerving to think how such a creature could stay alive so long."

Kalea cocked her head. "What do you mean, concubine?"

"She's an ancient one from my last life."

"What do you mean by 'the power to take it off?'"

Wikshen spread his lips to show his teeth again, but this time not in a smile. "Concubines are connected to me by a spiritual power. Only they can remove my battleshift—"

His speech stopped abruptly as he bent over to cup his forehead. "Hrrrrrrr!" he roared.

Kalea's eyes sprang wide, and so did Damos's. Damos shushed him, but Wikshen didn't stop his sounds of pain. He clawed at his own hair, pressing against his temples as if he suffered an excruciating headache.

"Dorhen?" Kalea said, also losing the forethought to keep quiet.

Wikshen dropped to one knee, and his pain drove him to more growling.

Kalea put her hands on his bare back. "What's the matter? Dorhen?" she said.

His roaring turned to moans of pain. "Damn her!"

"Who?"

Letting go of his head with one hand, he regarded Kalea with vicious, glowing eyes. Murderous eyes. "I'm going to kill her!"

"You mean Grella?"

His lips widened around his clenched teeth. "I remember who she is now."

Chapter 31
White Chalk

The elf woman—Orinleah—took the chalk from Vivene's hand through the food slot in the door and unwound it from the cloth. She turned the lump of soft stone around in the light, and it left white residue on her finger pads.

Vivene pushed her face close to the hole. "Now, I won't get in trouble for bringing this to you, will I?" Orinleah raised her eyebrows, fixated on the chalk as she listened. "Especially if you go marking up the walls in there?"

The elf shook her head and spread her lips into some sort of smile. "No," she said. "I have an idea."

Vivene blinked. "What's your idea?"

"Can you bring me other things?"

"Like what?"

She didn't answer right away. "I'll give it some thought and tell you next time."

"O-okay," Vivene said. She remained in a squat for a few seconds more, waiting for the elf to speak again. "Miss," she finally said. "How long have you been in here?"

Orinleah tore her eyes off the chalk and rewrapped it in the handkerchief. "I stopped counting long ago. But I can tell you that my son is twenty-two years, four months, and one day old now…" She sighed. "Lambelhen can tell you we've been married for sixteen years, though."

"Who's Lambelhen—?" Vivene stopped herself. "Oh. Right. That must be his name… The kingsorcerer." She couldn't deny Orinleah's tone when the conversation turned. "You don't like being married to him?" Vivene bit her tongue for having asked such a stupid question.

"I'm not married to him," she said.

"Of course."

"I'm his sister-in-law. None of this should be. None of it."

Vivene stuttered for a response. The elf's story sounded long and tangled, and she wasn't sure if she'd be welcome to ask after the details. "I'm sorry," she got out.

Orinleah could no longer be seen through the narrow vantage of the food slot, but she apparently sat inches to the side of it. "I just want my son back."

Yet another line to make Vivene's heart bleed. Vivene paused in her thought path and turned it slightly. "It's a lullaby, isn't it?"

"Hm?"

She inched closer to the slot to try to see her new elf-friend. "That song you sing is a lullaby. You sang it to your son, didn't you?"

"You are well-versed."

Vivene smirked. "Actually, no. It was foreign to my ears, different from our lullabies. It took me a while to figure out. Hey, you haven't sung for the past few days. How come?"

A sniff on the other side of the door. "I don't know…"

Vivene waited for more, angling her ear to the slot.

"Weeks ago, he told me he found my son. I don't want to believe him…but what if he's telling the truth?"

Vivene shrugged despite knowing the elf didn't see her. "I haven't seen any other elves around here besides you and the kingsorcerer." The image of Kalea's lover-elf with his wrists tied flashed in her head. She also remembered the blue-haired one—Wikshen—being hauled out of the basement of the hideout. Vivene shook the visions away. "I'll look around here and see if I find anyone."

"You'd do that for me?"

"I got you the chalk, didn't I? The young kids hide it so they can make graffiti. Snatching a piece became a palm-sweating maneuver, but I'd do it again."

Orinleah reached her hand through the slot. "Then I must thank you."

Vivene squeezed her hand. "You're welcome."

"You should go, Vivene. Lambelhen is coming to my room today…or rather, he is supposed to. He missed his visit last week."

Vivene knew that. She had watched him approach the door and decide against going in. "Damn," she replied. Just because he missed one appointment didn't mean he'd miss them all. He was the last person she'd want to run into in this tiny foyer. "Talk to you tomorrow. I'll be looking for elves until then."

The following silence made Vivene imagine the woman sitting alone on the floor by the door with her fine red dress pooling around her. She must be dreading her upcoming meeting with the kingsorcerer. Vivene sure would. She took yesterday's tray and made a hasty exit.

Lamrhath took a few deep breaths before sticking his golden key into the slot. After all the preparation he'd done for this visit, it still wracked his nerves. This would be the first time he'd seen Orinleah since his embarrassing episode with the "great" doctor. From that day on, her voice had haunted his memory: *There is no medicinal cure for what you have.*

Hope no longer stood proudly on the horizon for him, ushering him toward the future. No end to the pain. This news came after he'd promised Orinleah things would change for the better. Things would not change for the better. He'd probably die from his pain, and he couldn't fathom how long and how intense the agony would grow until then. He sighed when the lock clicked. She would hear it, knowing he approached.

He entered to find Orinleah sitting at her little table, eating her dinner. A bit late, he'd say. "Why haven't you finished eating?" he asked her. "Have your meals been delivered late? Is it cold?"

She sat with her back to him, staring at the empty space above the extra chair. Strangely, the chair stood pulled out as if someone sat in it.

"Nonsense," Orinleah said after a few seconds. "I'm actually slow to start eating. I gave many prayers to the Bright One."

Lamrhath smirked, thankful for the icebreaker. "Don't mind me."

He strolled across the room with his boot heels tapping and sat on her bed. He didn't sprawl out yet. The act of sitting on this particular piece of furniture only made him think of what was coming next, and... and it didn't feel good. It hurt. He stared forward at the window in the awkward silence. Orinleah's utensils scraped and tapped the porcelain. Lamrhath crossed his arms.

"You skipped the last visit."

Lamrhath closed his eyes at the sound of her voice. It didn't help his condition any more than her other traits. "I was busy."

Her utensils clinked again. "My lord," she said. He couldn't predict what she'd say, and waited for it with bated breath even though he wasn't looking at her. So few times throughout their history had she spoken to him so softly. "I would like some chalk."

He turned to regard her. "You're asking something of me?"

She fed another pea-sized bite into her mouth, keeping her gaze down on her plate.

"Chalk," he mimicked. "Why would you want that?"

She shrugged her shoulders. "These walls are empty. I thought I might draw on them."

"You've never asked to draw before." She hadn't asked for anything in later years because of the question prohibition she'd quickly learned about when she came here.

"I used to do creative activities when I was...when I lived in Norr. I did a number of ornamental things for the house."

At his smirk, she put her utensils down and placed her hands in her lap. She kept her eyes on her half-empty plate. Long, combed locks of her hair cascaded down in perfect proportions over her shoulders. She sat alone at the table, where the waning daylight left her in a cool shadow.

"In Norr…" She swallowed. "The *faerhain* ask their husbands to bring them things. They can also ask it of potential husband choices. This custom challenges the *saehgahn*'s ability, resourcefulness, and obedience."

Lamrhath snorted. "Chalk is an easy one."

Orinleah bowed her head, keeping her eyes averted. How relieving it was to enter her room and get a request instead of her usual coldness and insults.

She stood up. "I am finished eating." She waited, and they both knew what for. Although his stomach pained him and his erection pulsed, trapped in its confined space, he hesitated. A strange sort of peace settled in here. Sitting on the bed, he watched the clouds drifting beyond the window.

"I…" He huffed and lowered his eyes. "I haven't been well."

Silence.

Orinleah's garments rustled. She took a few slow steps toward him. Her voice ran cool and smooth. "What is wrong, my lord?"

Why was she being so nice? He didn't care. He knew he'd come into a vulnerable phase, and her treatment right now felt too good. "You know all about me now, don't you? After the doctor's examination."

The slightest sound of her breath hissed.

"Are you disgusted with me?"

"I'm sad for you."

He raised his head to look at her. She'd crossed the room halfway, her hands clasped meekly before her.

"I didn't realize you were hurting," she said.

"Maybe I should've told you about it sooner."

"And that unfair thing I did to you in your dreams," she continued, shaking her head. "I committed a crime against you. If I know anything about *saehgahn*, it's that they can't be teased… They make themselves appear so strong and hard on the outside, but they are tender within."

Despite how intently he stared at her, his thoughts blurred, and he missed how close she drew.

"Our recent conversation has opened my eyes," she continued, "and you claim my husband is dead. In my culture, that makes me free to choose another."

Her hand landed on his shoulder, and a thrilling shiver traveled out from it in all directions. "What are you telling me?" he asked.

"Lambelhen," she whispered his real name. It filled his cock to bursting. "If you are willing…I would like to be wed to you. I don't have a marriage token to make this official."

He tensed up at those words. "Official?"

She nodded. "All these years, we've been missing something." She took both his hands, and he melted inside. Her face held solemn and warm. "I formally apologize for my crime."

He blinked, disbelieving what he was hearing.

"We've been missing honesty, for one," she said.

At her stare with a looming smile on her lips, his breath picked up heavily. "Yes," he said in a sigh. He lurched forward, *desperate* for contact. To bond. To release. She'd never said such sincere words to him. Ever. He wanted more. He needed it.

She stepped away from him and snatched his face between her hands. "Focus, *saehgahn*."

He loved it when she called him *saehgahn*! It validated him as a member of her own species. He'd never felt such union with other elves, Daghahen included. Both of them lived outside of their culture. Not that he needed to, but to have a *faerhain* accept him as an elf, as a husband, as her own—that was everything. More—he needed more!

"What would you have me do? Say it. Whatever you want!" he urged.

"Just a simple rite of tradition," she said. "There are a few things we need. Once you've brought them to me, we can carry out the Norrian marriage ritual." He shivered at the touch of her fingers sliding into his hair. "We'll make love, as it's worded in the common tongue. I will give myself to you. Will you do this with me?"

A calm passed over Lamrhath unlike anything he'd experienced in ages. A slow sort of pleasure awaited him. He couldn't describe it. She'd proposed a gift that would gradually unwrap itself the further along they went. He'd bring her the gifts she'd ask for, and then they would… come together in beautiful harmony. Both sides willing. It would be an arrangement they had never made before—one he hadn't carried out with anyone, in truth. She was inviting him to the most sacred, secret, delightful initiation—ritual—coming-into-being—of a *saehgahn*'s life. She had all but said she would choose him! She was asking of him something all male elves burned to be asked.

He met her deep, amorous eyes. A holy doe's eyes, innocent yet wise. Her mouth kept straight—she played no games here. Under her sincerity, something happened to him that he never thought would happen…

His pain vanished.

His eyebrows leaped. He looked down at himself in surprise, reluctant to look away from her; when he did, a twinge of tension returned to his core. He wasn't healed quite yet, but something would change soon. He could be healed after all. Orinleah possessed the power to do it.

Lamrhath did something he normally wouldn't dream of: he dropped to his knees. He took her hand and pressed his face to the back of it. "I will do this," he whispered against her skin. He kissed it.

He rose to his feet to look her in the eyes squarely, *saehgahn* to *faerhain*. He took her face and pressed his lower body to hers, moving in for a kiss.

She pulled away. Her action put another twinge back into his body, and with it, his annoyance. She placed her gentle fingers along his face as it withered back to its normal angry countenance. "Keep calm," she said. For some reason, her words comforted him. He wanted to believe and obey everything she told him. "I asked you for chalk. It will be your first gift." He nodded, listening harder than he'd ever listened. Her smile warmed him. "We must do this right."

"We will," he said. His voice carried the energy he had trumpeted at age sixteen and full of all sorts of virile humors.

Her lips spread into a confident smile. "I will request a number of things, and the last item will be a white ox pelt. Once you've brought it to me, we will come together upon it, and I will treat you as a fine *saehgahn* ought to be treated."

He closed his eyes and sighed in pleasure. He shook all over! How he resisted forcing himself on her now went beyond his reckoning. A fresh form of excitement enveloped his being, taking him back once again to the days of his youth.

"Will you…" He had to pause to swallow. "Will you be on top?"

Her smile widened deep into her glowing cheeks. She patted the side of his face with a sensual light in her eyes he'd never seen before. "It will be an all-night bonding ceremony. One you will never forget."

He smiled. He really smiled. He took her hand off his face only so he could leave the room faster to retrieve her first gift.

That damned doctor was wrong. Lamrhath would be cured.

Chapter 32
A Bone Snaps

What do you think Grella does with all those evil seedlings?" Kalea asked as she walked through the cave tunnel beside Wikshen with Damos trailing behind.

For a long moment, no one answered, until Damos mumbled, "She exports them."

"She does? To whom?"

"I don't know," Damos said after a lifeless shrug.

"Sorcerers." The word popped out of Kalea's mouth, unpreceded by any thought. She knew it for a fact if that was really how the dunces were created.

Wikshen eyed her as they walked. "Sorcerers, huh?"

Kalea nodded. "I think the sorcerers use those dazed people to carry out mundane activities, especially to fill out a battlefield. Gaije described something like them when he told me about the sorcerers who attacked his homeland."

Listening to her speech, he squinted ahead. "Grella is dealing with lowly sorcerers," he grumbled. "Another reason why she deserves to die."

Damos groaned behind them. "She has too large an operation down here. Best to sneak out and escape."

"Did I ask you?" Wikshen barked, twisting around to give Damos the full effect of his intimidation.

Damos didn't recoil, nor did he reply. Kalea put her hand on Wikshen's arm in effort to calm him down.

"I've been dead way too long," Wikshen said, his softened voice grating. He fell into silence before making a solitary sharp breath.

"What's the matter?" Kalea asked.

"You don't see that?"

"No."

"It pierces my eyes!" He ran forward, leaving her to stumble in the dark. A beam of light suddenly shot from the wall at Wikshen's prodding. Apparently, he'd found a soft wall and scraped at the soil to make the hole bigger.

"You found the outside!" Kalea said, hurrying to join him. She took up her washing bat and helped him dig at the crumbling wall. Damos stood back and watched, ever frowning.

A bright, lush oasis appeared through the opening they made. Daytime already? They'd been underground for so many hours. Outside loomed tall walls standing around a grassy field—the bottom floor of a chasm where the sun shone down to nurture all the plants below. They hadn't found freedom on the surface world after all. A familiar rope bridge stretched across the vast opening above, most likely the one she had crossed when the area was engulfed in mist.

Kalea raised her knee to take one big step over the muddy threshold, but Wikshen stopped her with a hold on the back of her dress.

"No," he said with that same old sternness lacing his deep voice.

"Why?"

"It's not safe." He pointed at the high, rocky walls surrounding the little garden. Greyish-black shapes perched all over the sides like gargoyles. "More of those scouels, not to mention more of the brain-eating plants."

Indeed, forlustweed grew in the shaded corners with their limbs still. No airborne seeds drifted around out there, thankfully. Otherwise, a few trees bearing huge red pears grew about, and Grella's drones kept a vegetable garden at the center of the space where the sun shone brightest.

Wikshen was tugging her back away from the opening when Damos lunged past them to point across the wide, green field.

"But look," he hissed. A big door stood in the stone at the other side. "I'm sure that door leads to the exit."

"How sure?" Wikshen asked.

"Sure enough. I've been through there at least once. We're getting somewhere, finally."

"So you propose we cross that enclosed field, dodging those enormous, swooping scouels all the way?"

Damos shrugged. "How fast would you like to get out of here?"

Wikshen squinted across the distance; even from here, the sunlight appeared to pain his eyes more than Kalea's or Damos's. "I do see lots of iron reinforcing the door." He flexed his hands. "Maybe if we're careful…"

Instead of finishing the statement, he stepped over the crumbly threshold, having to bend low to get his head through, and motioned to Kalea behind his back. "Stay close behind me. And you, boy, stay close behind her…so the scouels'll get you instead."

Damos didn't bother with a response.

Kalea stepped carefully over the obstacle, keeping her hand on Wikshen's arm for the feeling of security if nothing else. Wikshen paused to survey the landscape.

"The shadowy corners are too sparse to walk all the way across." He finished by blowing a breath out. One more step put him in the sunlight. He huffed as he kept on. "Shouldn't be this sunny in Hathrohskog," he said.

"Is there a problem?" Kalea asked him.

He took another step. His next one happened more cautiously. Slowly. He sidestepped, as if catching himself in a sway.

"Are you all right?" Kalea grasped his arm to support him instead of herself.

Wikshen groaned. "The light." He pushed on, each step more dizzy and unsure than the last.

"The light hurts you?"

"Yeah." He sighed sleepily. "It drains me."

Kalea observed the sky above them. It *was* sunnier than any other day she'd spent in this forest. It didn't help that the chasm spanned so wide, and the leafless surface trees couldn't hope to cover the field.

Hugging Wikshen's arm, she asked, "Can you get to that tree over there?" Maybe if he could walk from tree to tree, resting for a few minutes under the shade, they could make it to the other side.

He didn't answer, but took another step and stumbled.

"Dorhen," she said as he faded fast. His hair shone beautifully in the bright light in its various values of blue, with darker tones in the lower layers and highlights at the top of his head. Streamers of it waved in the light breeze. "Come on," she urged, putting her hands on his waist in a vain effort to keep him on his feet. His arms dangled and his head bobbed. "Get to the shade. Just a few more paces. Dorhen!"

He collapsed to his knees and flopped over with a groan. Kalea fell with him, experiencing a bit of her own dizziness thanks to Grella's poison. She crawled to his head and checked his face, which was smashed against the ground with his mouth open.

"My battleshif…" he groaned. "Without it, I can't withst…the light." His slurred speech transitioned into steady breathing. He'd fallen asleep?

She shook him. "Dorhen? You can't sleep now!"

Kalea barely registered the footsteps rustling the grass behind her. "Now's our chance!" Damos said, and yanked her along behind him toward a shady side of the chasm.

"What are you doing?" She jerked against his hold, but he held firm.

"I'm saving you." He marched forward, dragging her along. Her weakness prevented her from successfully yanking her arm free.

"Why?"

Damos twisted around to meet her gaze and echoed, "Why?" His eyes darted back to the sight of Wikshen lying facedown in the grass. "You're asking me why?"

He dragged her all the way to the nearest side wall, dangerously close to one of the parasitic plants, and took out a bundle of extra bandages to hand her. "Put this around your head. Cover your ears. Your mouth too."

Kalea hesitated, studying his bandaged face, trying to see the Damos she remembered. He did have a good reason to try to "save" her from Wikshen. "Damos," she said.

He nodded to the bandages in her hand. "Hurry and cover up. All it takes is a nudge to loose those seeds onto the breeze."

"I'm not leaving him," she said.

His eyes narrowed at her. If he didn't have most of his face covered, she'd be able to read him better.

"Remember when I told you about my elven lover?"

He nodded.

Kalea pointed to Wikshen, motionless in the grass. "That's him. He's Dorhen."

Damos stared at her for a long minute before blinking. He took her wrist and started to rise. "Let's go, Kalea."

She held back. "Did you hear me?"

"And what did you just claim again? That that...*thing* is the sweetheart you said had died?" She dipped her head at his tone. "No, no, no," he corrected, "you actually said that thing *murdered* your sweetheart!"

"Are you angry?"

"Angry?"

She blinked at him in the tension. Dingy bandages covered his whole body, some with lasting bloodstains from the night Wikshen had dragged him into the dangerous soil where he must have nearly suffocated besides taking on severe injury to his skin. She observed them both, finding nothing to say to comfort Damos about this. He'd been through nothing but hell since the night of his attack, and now she'd told him that the monster who attacked him was Dorhen. Of course, he wouldn't believe her.

She sighed. "Damos…"

A piercing call stopped her speech. One of the scouels perched on the wall above them stirred, stretching its wings wide. Its clawed feet easily gripped the stone and it walked along, sniffing at the air.

Damos took Kalea's arms and manhandled her to a stand. "Our voices disturb those monsters." He hauled her toward the door on the far side of the field.

Another horrible shriek announced the scouel again. It noticed their movement and launched off the wall to glide toward them. Kalea and Damos dove separate ways to avoid its talons.

"Kalea!" Damos shouted when she took off in the opposite direction toward Wikshen. A burst of adrenaline set her off, but after a few yards, she stumbled in dizziness from her poison. Staggering the rest of the way, she knelt by his head and patted his cheek.

"Get up!" She shook him. A weak groan was the best he could offer. She persisted, shaking him harder and slapping his face. She screamed in his ear, recalling how much he'd enjoyed it earlier. He flinched! Her screams really did help to rile him up.

Damos grabbed her again, and she screamed, mostly at Wikshen, as he forced her to follow him toward the door. Wikshen twitched in the grass at her louder, more frantic sounds.

"Damos!" she protested. "You don't understand, we need him!"

"No, we don't. I know the way out!"

"I need him! He's *Dorhen*!"

"No, he's not! What's gotten into you?"

Kalea was getting sick of people not believing her revelation about Wikshen's true identity. They tromped across the little vegetable patch in the center of the field. No drones were out to protect it or catch Damos at this time.

When they reached the big, iron-reinforced door, Kalea couldn't help but notice that the scouel hadn't tried to attack them since the first attempt. Instead, it circled around Wikshen! She gasped and lunged backward, only to be stopped by Damos's firm hold on her wrist. She fought him.

"Let go!"

He wouldn't. Damos tried the door handle. "Locked!" he spat.

Checking on Wikshen again, Kalea yelled when she found that the scouel had landed on the ground. The others on the wall sniffed the wind with their canine noses and watched their companion's activity. The scene resembled a vulture approaching a carcass.

"Dorhen!" she screamed. She finally tore out of Damos's sweaty grip and sprinted back across the field.

Damos growled and followed her. "We'll have to go back through the hole anyway," he said.

Ignoring him, she headed straight for Wikshen, who had regained a bit of his alertness and propped himself on an arm to see the salivating scouel stalking near him.

At full height on its four legs, the scouel stood taller than Kalea, and its wings reached higher than a house. It flexed them as if for simple intimidation. Hardly thinking anymore, Kalea lunged at the creature and roared, hoping to scare it as she would an ordinary wild animal.

Wikshen groaned behind her. He reached out with little energy to spare and grabbed her ankle.

"Don't trip me!" she said, bending backward, but that was his intent exactly; he yanked her leg, and she went down in time for the charging beast's jaws to miss her. He rolled her over, creating a tangle of sweaty bodies to get between her and the scouel.

In the background, Damos cursed, looking for his moment to step in and take Kalea out of the line of danger.

Panting, Wikshen worked his way to his feet. His bare legs, soiled with dirt and bits of grass, shook in his weakness. Had the sunlight drained his energy this much? If he couldn't run back to the cave, the scouel would get him. It might get her too, because she wouldn't leave him.

His arms also trembled as he attempted to spread them into a ready position, elbows bent, hands open. The creature lunged. Kalea screamed. Her eyes reflexively closed. The force of a sweaty body jostled her to the side. Steaming, roaring breath burned against her face.

She cracked her eyes open, chancing a peek, and found Wikshen's forearm in the huge canine's jaws, its slobbering teeth crunching down on it. Blood rolled out. Wikshen roared, keeping focused with his teeth gritted.

"Get outta here!" he ordered, and threw his other arm around the scouel's head to wrestle it and keep its mouth busy so Kalea could try to scuttle away.

Damos inched closer to the struggle. He hissed her name and reached to grab her arms. He pulled her, but Wikshen's heavy form pinned down one of her legs and part of her skirt—until the scouel reared up and Wikshen went with it, thrashing around. He clung to its head throughout. Damos hauled Kalea back toward the opening through which they'd entered.

"No," Kalea begged, feeling weaker than ever now as her heart pumped the poison through her body.

Damos didn't listen. He supported half her weight with her arm around his neck. She cried Dorhen's name, twisting to try to see how he fared.

"That's not Dorhen!" Damos reminded her, to her annoyance. She couldn't spare the energy to argue with him. Was it not enough for Damos to see how Wikshen defended her from the scouel?

The two of them jumped when a form emerged from the entrance as they approached. A person in black—a woman—and someone Kalea recognized.

"Stand aside!" Damos warned.

The woman's eyes perused the field behind them. She dropped the black hood from her head, revealing shiny black hair with cropped bangs.

"Metta?" Kalea said. "How're my friends? Are you all right?"

Metta jumped and observed her. "Kalea? Oh, dear!" She reached her hand out from a bundle of fabric she'd been hugging, and Damos walked them backward to avoid it.

"It's okay, Damos. I know her," Kalea said.

Metta remained fixed on Wikshen's struggle with the beast. He flew off the thing's monstrous head and rolled across the ground for several yards.

Metta's hand shot to her mouth as she witnessed it too. "He needs his battleshift!" She darted past them.

Damos started for the cave again, but Kalea resisted. "No!" she said, and followed Metta, but had to stop halfway to rest.

By now, the other scouels had launched off the rock walls and circled above the struggle. Metta ran toward the danger, unfurling the long, black fabric in her arm. It waved wildly on the breeze kicked up by the many wings beating inside the tubular chasm. Kalea gawked at the unfolding spectacle.

"Mastaren!" Metta called over the shrill cackling of the swirling monsters. For now, Wikshen only dealt with the original one, but two others dipped lower and prepared to join the brawl on the ground.

At Metta's call, Wikshen's expression flared into a show of feral excitement, flashing his teeth. He pulled open the sarong's knot at his hip. Metta reared back with the big sheet of black linen, twisted, and flung it. The roaring wind picked it up easily.

Wikshen threw the sarong aside, leaving himself completely naked for an instant before catching the big sheet of fabric Metta threw at him. Metta had somehow found the battleshift and delivered it to him.

The battleshift caught Wikshen rather than the other way around. It slid around him as if alive. He didn't have to do anything to complete the dressing process. The fabric, slithering like a wide, flat snake, settled around him as Kalea had always seen him wear it. Its strings crossed and tightened at his hip, leaving an open slit at the front. Simultaneously, armbands, fingerless gloves, and toeless socks appeared on his limbs in brief, grainy clouds. The black outfit showed off his muscles and pale skin contrasting against the dark fabric.

With the added battleshift and supplementary garments, Wikshen's strength returned in full. He stood against the accelerating wind with his blue hair waving. His eyes sharpened, his jaw firmed, and his fists tightened. With a wide stance, he stood ready to take on the scouel and all of its companions. Before doing so, he took off toward the big door at the opposite side. His waving battleshift stayed out of the way of his long, lunging legs.

Damos jerked beside Kalea as if unsure which direction to take. They needed that door, but now Wikshen led the scouels to it and away from them, leaving them a chance to escape the same way they had entered. Metta also stood idly a ways into the field, as if unsure what to expect.

Wikshen put his hands on the door and waited. Before their eyes, the wrought iron fixtures thinned and crumbled as he took all of the metal's best ingredients into his body. When he moved his hands away, the door exhibited nothing beyond a few withered flakes and pale outlines where its iron used to be. He stepped aside to let it fall forward uselessly.

With the opening available, he waved the rest of them over. Metta twisted around and waved to Kalea as if she were too dim to receive the signal from Wikshen. They now faced crossing the wide, dangerous field. Damos grasped Kalea's arm, pressing all of his fingers into her skin.

"Ow!"

He ignored her whine and pointed upward at the little flying seeds Kalea would've written off otherwise. The seeds from the forlustweed! The scouels' whirlwind had pulled them off the plants to fly rapidly about.

Damos frantically motioned for Kalea to cover her face. She fumbled the bandages he'd given her out of her belt, and he helped wrap one around her head to block her ears and another over her mouth and nose. The new accessory hindered her breathing. Metta mimicked Kalea's head wrappings with a black scarf she had handy.

They turned to make a mad dash across the field, but by now most of the scouels circled low, like hungry hawks in a cage. Far across the way, Wikshen made it his new task to clear their path to the door.

Three scouels landed and approached him with teeth bared and wings spread. The first leaped at him, and he dove to the side. Scrambling back to his feet, he worked his shoulders and put his hands up, keeping a close eye on the movement of his opponents.

Kalea took Damos's arm. "Do something! Cast magic to help him!"

Damos kept his mouth clamped as he watched. He bore no intention to help Wikshen.

Wikshen flexed his arms and swirled them the way he'd practiced before. Taking a sturdy stance, he waited poised, eyes fixed on the next scouel to attempt an attack. After the first scouel's lunge, it took to the air again, and the next two jumped at him with roaring ferocity.

Wikshen dove headfirst to dodge one. He landed gracefully on one hand and followed through with a roll that brought him effortlessly back to his feet. He whirled his arms at the other scouel in the same dance and pushed his palm at the beast, making his own roar to compete with the creature. Every muscle and tendon in his body tensed. Blood streaks from the bite he'd endured earlier painted him, but he acted as if it had never happened.

The scouel's face met his hand. Kalea's toes curled within her shoes to watch; her fingers tightened into her palms. Wikshen's hand…slid through the scouel's skull.

The creature's legs locked, and its momentum slowed. Its beastly voice turned to a weak groan. An instant later, she realized that a big black blade had emerged from Wikshen's hand and cut the beast down the middle, from its head all the way through its back leg.

The thing fell apart in two steaming, bloody pieces, settling on either side of Wikshen, who stood tall between them. The blade continued, shooting far to the other side of the chasm before it hit the wall and disappeared, leaving only a dusty signature in the air. A flying scouel shrieked in pain, crippled, as the projectile had apparently injured its back leg along the way.

Wikshen howled in delight, pumped a fist, and took off with a hurdle over the scouel's steaming carcass. He showed off with a one-handed cartwheel, and Kalea didn't miss Metta's coo of awe at his antics. Kalea caught herself staring as soon as she noticed Damos watching her.

Wikshen stopped showing off and swooped his arms again, swaying his weight from one leg to the other and searching for his next flying victim. The scouels called to each other in some form of sharp, barking communication. They all knew now what he could do to them.

He shot off another blade, which spun high to cut through a scouel flying near the top of the chasm. Its two heavy, bloody halves plummeted and bounced off the ground with loud *thu-thumps*. Wikshen shot another one, then another. Soon, many black feathers joined the floating deadly seeds in the vortex whirling around him.

The scouels' voices intensified in their communication. One landed nearby and turned in the direction of Kalea, Damos, and Metta. They tightened as a group. From this angle, Wikshen couldn't throw a blade at the beast without hitting one of them, so he ran toward them.

"If only Azrielle were with me," Damos mumbled through his teeth.

"She's in this forest. We saw her," Kalea reported.

"You did?"

The slobbering, dog-faced vulture stalking closer cut their conversation short. Wikshen also approached fast on his powerful legs. Before the scouel reached them, he caught it, leaping onto its back to grasp its cheeks and steer its head away from the group.

Wikshen shot a feral stare at Damos and growled, "I told you not to touch my woman!"

The scouel bucked and tried to twist backward, but Wikshen held it firmly, riding it until he found the right moment to plant his hand atop its head and release another wraithlike blade that seared through its brain. Blood poured out under its jaw as the blade proceeded into the soft dirt below. The creature collapsed under Wikshen, and he stood atop it, giving Damos one more dark stare before continuing on to the next approaching threat.

Metta shuddered with a gleeful sound beside Kalea as Wikshen sprinted back across the field to lead the gathering scouels away from "his women."

Disregarding Wikshen's warning, Damos took Kalea's wrist. "We have to move," he said. He trekked cautiously around the field's perimeter, leading Kalea and Metta both.

As many huge, feathery bodies as littered the ground, the remaining scouels clogged the chasm's limited space. Their massive wings kept the wind churning as they circled around, and the seeds flew off the forlustweed branches to fill the air so thickly that they obscured the opposite wall behind their feathery veil.

Kalea jumped with a muffled, panicky shriek when one landed on her shoulder. She swiped it off frantically. Damos twisted to check on her, and she nudged him to continue. Along their way, she watched Wikshen move about, running this way and that, throwing blades and dodging scouels to keep their path clear. She worried for his lack of protection from the seeds entering his ears.

Ahead of them, one very agitated scouel with a missing ear and a trail of blood running through its fur landed to block their path. It opened its mouth and released a growled warning. Damos halted and threw both his arms out to the sides.

Several yards away, Wikshen paused in his concentration to send a blade spinning to stop the threat. The creature's head rolled a few turns from its body as blood poured out of its neck to muddy the ground in their path.

That heroic effort cost Wikshen a second too many. A low-passing scouel grabbed him by the shoulders and carried him off, high into the air full of gnashing fangs and parasitic seeds. From the ground, Kalea yelled at what she was helpless to stop.

Wikshen writhed in its talons. Other beasts swooped by to nip at him like a piece of bread in a seagull's beak, to be stolen away by its flock mates. He twisted his back and fought, but couldn't seem to point his palm in a good direction to kill the creature. Instead, he managed to hit a nearby antagonist, sending it freefalling to the ground, wings limp, feathers flying.

The scouel carrying him pumped its wings hard, working its way up higher in a definite direction. Kalea finally noticed where it was headed and why the scouels held such an interest in him. It carried him to a certain landing in a crevasse in the rock wall, which appeared to have been carved over yet another wooden door on a sculpted balcony. A pale woman stood on the landing, waiting for Wikshen to be delivered.

Kalea could only watch, along with Metta, as the scouel dropped Wikshen before the woman. He turned on his heel, ran, and vaulted over the rail to the open air. He fell a long distance and landed by chance on a passing scouel's back. It shrieked and spun, dropping him again. He fell the rest of the way on his own.

Time stood still.

Kalea froze in disbelief, unable to take her eyes off the spectacle. Her heart fluttered after a shocked, stabbing sensation. Wikshen fell. Dorhen...fell. He fell, back first, without any chance to grab anything to stop his speeding progression. He met an abrupt stop on the ground and lay flat.

Ignoring her pain, Kalea bolted after him. Apparently alive, he lay there, breathing—wheezing—as she drew near. He attempted to rise, weakly pulling himself to sit up, but paused to cry out in pain and hug himself around the rib cage.

Damos ran after Kalea, calling her name. Before she made it to Wikshen's side, another scouel swooped by and snatched him. He bellowed in pain. Kalea yelled for him. Damos caught her.

"Forget him! We have to go!"

Like before, the scouel worked to lift Wikshen all the way to the landing in the crevasse. The pale woman who patiently watched the action must be Grella. She didn't look like the leathery hag Kalea had caught Wikshen rubbing against down in the caves, but it was easy to assume she had ways of disguising herself to look more beautiful with her witchcraft.

She stepped back to let the beast drop Wikshen on the balcony again. This time, he couldn't jump off so quickly. In his pained state, men in black masks who'd been waiting with Grella overcame and dragged him into the cave.

Damos pulled Kalea to follow him through the doorway that Wikshen had opened up earlier.

"No!" Kalea barked. "What about Dorhen?" She reached her hand back, pointing high at the nook he'd gone into.

"I don't care!" Damos argued. He hauled her into the cave, away from the sunlight.

Chapter 33
One Hundred Demons

Lamrhath threw Talekas's cell door open. His Second squinted in the torchlight. That fool doctor's diagnosis had made Lamrhath so angry, he'd thrown them both into cells in the underground prison. Talekas got the ugly side of Lamrhath's rage because he'd recommended her in the first place.

"You are forgiven," Lamrhath said, and Talekas's expression of dread lifted.

With his best friend by his side once again, Lamrhath went as far as to open Falli's cell. Orinleah's recent tenderness made him feel extra generous lately. "Go to your apartment and wait for further orders," he told her.

"What about my dau—"

Lamrhath's attending guard whipped her. Gnashing her teeth, she let the guard lead her away, walking stiffly.

Lamrhath turned to Talekas, and the man's face showed the signature blankness which usually meant he didn't know what to expect and didn't like it. "Come," he ordered Talekas. "We've some work to do."

He told Talekas about Orinleah's requested gifts, particularly so he could send men out far and wide to collect such items. The chalk was easy, of course. As her second gift, she had asked for a golden statue of a frog, to which Lamrhath twisted an eyebrow. Busy work, that's what all this was.

A few days combing Lamrhath's massive treasure vault yielded a hefty, solid gold frog, looking grumpy in its meditative squat. He expected a little sensual interaction when he proudly delivered it on a platter with a velvet cover for unveiling, maybe a long kiss at least, but didn't get anything in return but a smile.

"I am pleased," she said formally. All he needed to hear, but it didn't cure his pain. Relief could only be found between Silva's legs, or a concubine's in a pinch. Nonetheless… Orinleah's approval…

Orinleah's approval. Those words helped him find a lovely, though vague, sense of peace. He let them repeat in his head over and over again while he slammed his pelvis hard against Silva's easy, wet cunt. Her pleasure screams drowned out everything else in the universe except those two words. He didn't linger in her room any longer than it took him to catch his breath, saying a silent prayer to Naerezek from the edge of her bed.

Straight to his office he went after dressing, to listen to whisper stones and ask the scouts in Norr if they'd yet found a white ox roaming the forest. Their search went on. He didn't worry about it yet—and he didn't know how many items Orinleah would request before that final elusive testament to their union. For the first time in several months, maybe years, he felt powerful.

Vivene found only two other ex-novices in their designated meeting closet: Millie and Sabina. "Where is everyone?"

"Honestly, Vivene, why do we even have these meetings anymore?" Millie asked.

Vivene stammered for an answer. "I want to make sure everything is all right."

"And what will you do when one of us isn't all right?"

While Vivene worked her jaw for a comeback, Sabina blurted, "Vera's dead, all right? There. That's our news."

Vivene shot her hands to her mouth.

"And I envy her," Sabina followed up.

"Don't say that. D-did Vera have the plague?" Vivene asked.

Millie's bored appearance disturbed Vivene even more than Sabina's coldness to Vera's death. The girl shrugged. "I don't care. She's gone. Sooner or later, another of us will be next."

"Shit, Millie," Sabina sneered, "don't be so cheerful. I can't take all this cheer."

"Look," Millie said, "both of you, I'm living my life while I can."

Vivene narrowed her eyes at her. "So, what are you doing?"

"Shining," she said, and flipped her blonde hair. It seemed glossier and more well-combed than ever before. "I'm doing what I can to impress. I'm climbing the ranks. I even served at the kingsorcerer's party last night."

Vivene blinked, her shock at that statement melding with the illness of hearing about poor Vera.

Millie spread her hands. "If we're going to live here, we might as well do our very best to thrive."

Vivene shook her head. "Millie, don't you think…"

Brushing past her, Millie clicked her tongue. "If you're not living, you're dying, Viv."

She exited the room with Sabina on her heels.

Vivene's knees and arms ached as she worked hard scrubbing the marble floor of one of the Chimera Tower's most beautiful sections later that afternoon.

If you're not living, you're dying, Viv. She drowned out the echoes of her friends' harsh words under her hummed rendition of Orinleah's lullaby. The elven woman had taken up singing again after Vivene's praise.

When voices and hard footsteps echoed down the corridor toward her, she stopped herself and crawled out of the way to wait by the wall on hands and knees for the troop of sorcerers to pass. She bowed her head as protocol dictated, but peeked as her own cheeky curiosity demanded.

Talekas, the kingsorcerer's "Second," led the charge of about six sorcerers marching with purpose. At their center, they hauled a person; Vivene couldn't stop her neck from stretching and bending to see who. A servant...

"Rose," Vivene whispered. Rose had gotten herself in trouble again! Dropping her gaze back to the floor until the area cleared, Vivene huffed. It was bound to happen.

The group turned the corner, leaving the wide, echoing space empty. She'd witnessed maids getting disciplined before, Rose included, but not quite like this. Vivene stood, abandoned her bucket but retained the scrub brush, and sprinted after them. Her idiotic curiosity again. If someone noticed her following, she'd probably get the same treatment, but she had to find out where they were taking Rose.

The stern, grumbling sorcerers toting Rose led Vivene all the way down to the bowels of Ilbith. To the Grave. She'd almost forgotten how bad it smelled since her long time away from it. The sorcerers and Rose disappeared into carved tunnels which Vivene had never seen before. Apparently, there were several.

Holding the damp scrub brush, Vivene crouched in a dark nook to wait for the busy area to clear. A chatty bunch of people crowded around down here in the soft glow of torches. Silence usually shrouded the cavern, save for the wind whistling through holes and the occasional whimpering from people at the bottom of the Grave who hadn't quite died yet.

The sorcerers planned something today, she gathered from all the talk. When the way cleared, she slunk along the wall of a downward-sloping path winding around the enormous chasm. The smell of torch smoke accompanied the usual stench of death and rot.

Vivene made her way out of the higher traffic area where sorcerers scurried about, coming and going as they prepared for one of their rituals. It couldn't be the usual sort of ritual, though. She'd seen this kind of bustle from them before, and sometimes heard their chants echoing long through the tower's stone corridors, but never from this pit. The Grave was just a garbage dump. She forgot she retained her scrub brush and squeezed her palm around it absentmindedly as she tiptoed toward the pit's edge.

Vivene cringed as she peered down from her perch on the winding path. Below her, other tunnels gaped along the chasm's wall, giving the sorcerers easy access to descend—and here she'd always assumed the Grave was merely a hole in the ground. She held her breath to scan the scene, not wanting to see all the filth their torches would illuminate. All the cluttered death and refuse sat pushed to the corners of the space to make way for a huge clearing at the chasm floor's center. A wide ring of many torches stood in the clearing around a drawn pentagram.

"They brought Rose...down here?" Vivene hardly realized she'd said it out loud. She crept along the downward slope, closer to the bottom of the pit, never minding the cloud of smoke and the rotten stench. She fell to a crouch and ducked her head when a set of young, laughing sorcerers burst from a tunnel below her perch and sprinted down the path toward the bottom.

The bustle at the chasm's center proved much to take in. Vivene scanned all the people to see where Rose had wound up. A stack of cages stood off to the side, containing chickens and rabbits and who-knew-what-else. The general flow of sorcerers to this hub curbed, and everyone slowed their steps and shifted into uniform sections around the pentagram. Their echoing voices lowered to murmurs, similar to the sounds in a large Sanctuary chapel.

Vivene sat on the edge of her path, putting her legs down first, and let herself drop to the lower level. She fell hard on her feet and collapsed her knees on impact. After her initial cringe of pain, she rushed forward, stepping lightly, to get a closer look. If she could find Rose, she might be able to whisk her away. Where she'd hide the girl after, she'd think about later.

Sneaking became easy when the sorcerers all faced inward, toward the pentagram's center. Talekas's shout hushed all the murmuring, and the groups shifted to allow a path leading from one of the tunnels, through which the kingsorcerer walked.

Lamrhath strode with a cocky confidence and hard step unlike anything she'd seen before, a stark contrast to the day she encountered him in the Chimera Tower. At a table set up by the outer edge of the pentagram, he opened a book and flipped a few pages, saying something to Talekas and others standing around him, Bargo included. Vivene couldn't hear their conversations from her distance.

He extended his arm and pointed at a group to the back, too far away for Vivene to make out what unfolded, and those men shifted about, doing something with objects. The kingsorcerer continued talking to his closest companions and found the page in the book he sought. From the faint echoes, it sounded like he relayed what he read. With more hand gestures, he gave some quiet order, and to the outer groups standing by, he raised his voice.

"And we'll begin at the tenth tap," he followed up.

Immediately afterward, a bystander began tapping a staff on the stone floor, and all around the cleared area, the sorcerers settled in. Standing at the book, Lamrhath dropped his head as if in meditation. The counting gave them all enough time to prepare, linking hands and warming up their voices.

After the tenth tap, all of the sorcerers hummed in nearly the same rhythm as a prayer her convent residents used to recite, except these sorcerers weren't worshipping the One Creator. A chill stabbed up Vivene's spine throughout the sound.

She tiptoed a little closer, taking advantage of everyone's distraction. Her path curved, bumpy and uneven. She drew closer to the bottom, where the floor lay the distance of a man's height below her. She stopped when she reached the stack of cages holding animals. Chickens clucked and lambs bleated under the louder rumble of men's voices in prayer. Many times, the name of Ingnet was invoked, one of the names often spoken by the sorcerers, although she'd come to know Naerezek as the more common Ilbith god.

At a certain point in the chanting, Lamrhath's voice became audible over all the others. He recited foreign words in a powerful tone. Vivene shuddered. Being subjected to it brought an ill feeling.

She moved on, scanning the area for any sign of Rose. A few dirty servants stood by the cages, all linked together with chains. They must've been pulled from the dungeon. Why they were brought to this ritual, Vivene couldn't guess. Past the chained people stood a girl in better spirits.

"Rose," Vivene whispered.

At first, Rose didn't hear her. She stood twiddling her thumbs, back straight, birdbrained as usual. She wore no chains.

"Rose!" Vivene hissed again. She feared that if she climbed down the ledge to meet the girl on the ground floor, she might not be able to climb back up. Perhaps she could try to pull Rose up so they could dash away into a tunnel.

Rose still didn't turn. Half of her outer smock hung from one shoulder, but she stood oblivious to all her imperfections. Vivene picked up the nearest pebble and tossed it at Rose's back.

She twisted around and smiled when she noticed her. "Vivene!"

Vivene threw her finger to her lips and gave Rose the most urgent expression she could. She waved her hand to draw Rose closer.

The kingsorcerer's voice stopped in its string of rolling syllables. "And now we offer Ingnet the life force he needs to open the portal."

When he started for the stack of cages, Vivene rolled back to the wall behind her to huddle as low as she could. A peek revealed Rose gawking up at her and the kingsorcerer approaching the cages to peruse the livestock within. He pointed to one, and his attending sorcerer opened it and pulled out a frightened lamb.

Returning to the pentagram's edge, Lamrhath waited by the book as the sorcerer proceeded to the center of the pentagram and tied the lamb to a post at its center. He jogged back to the crowd when finished.

Lamrhath began his chant, and a few words in, a marksman with a bow let loose his arrow. The lamb thumped over to the side and bled out on the floor. A massive dark cloud spiraled up around the slain animal.

Forgetting to stay hidden, Vivene edged to the ledge again and stared. The cloud spiraled and stretched high, growing thinner the farther it twisted until it dissipated, leaving in its place what Vivene could only make out as a black shadow. It moved over the lamb's blood pool.

Vivene's fingers gripped the rock ledge beneath her until they grew numb. The black shape rose, stretching to a tall height she couldn't gauge from her distance. It started…drifting—not walking—toward the edge of the pentagram to face Lamrhath, who stood tall and at attention.

Lamrhath spun and raised his arm to signal all the bystanders. The sorcerers dipped their heads, all wearing hoods. He turned to receive the newcomer, also bowing his head, and they stood in silence…

Vivene waited.

The sound of men's breathing filled the space. In this quiet, she expected to pick up whatever words Lamrhath would share with the person. The newcomer's black robes whipped as if a strong wind stirred them, from which tentacles slithered up to the person's head and secured a hood down over his face.

Not a person, this was a creature.

Lamrhath raised his face and looked at the being now. He gave a slight bow of diplomacy, and the creature drifted on to wait at the far side of the space.

Lamrhath turned to the crowd, and his voice broke the silence. "Let's try for another!"

When the chanting started up, Vivene took it as her cue to call Rose again. She waved her arm to regain the girl's attention. "Come here, now!" she hissed.

Rose stepped closer with curiosity in her eyes. None of the happenings around them bothered her. She was so oblivious—all the time.

Lying on her stomach, Vivene lowered both arms over the ledge. "Grab my hands." She didn't actually think she could pull the girl up onto her ledge, but she'd try anyway. Once it was proven she couldn't, she'd go from there.

"Vivene, aren't you supposed to be up there cleaning windows right now?"

Vivene threw her finger to her lips and shushed her again. "Be quiet, stupid! Come here, I said."

Their whispering drew attention, and Vivene rolled away from the ledge once again, praying the lighting was dim enough in this section to hide her.

"Who you talking to, girl?" one of the nearby sorcerers asked.

"Vivene," Rose said, and Vivene bristled in panic. She crawled along the shadow.

"You're as dumb as a log, aren't you?" The sorcerer returned to his business of checking the inventory of animals and prisoners as the rest finished their chant.

Vivene crawled back to her spot above Rose again. Lamrhath began his usual lines. A glance showed him wiping his sweat on his long glove, his voice slightly weaker than the last round. He grew tired already. Vivene couldn't imagine how his task could be taxing. At the predictable end of his speech, he once again turned to the stock of animals and prisoners.

"I wonder..." Drawing closer to the cages than before, his eyes drifted from them to the shivering, waiting prisoners. His gaze slid to Rose, and Vivene recoiled to avoid his golden stare.

Rose. She couldn't say it aloud to call the girl to safety, but the name passed through her head repeatedly.

Lamrhath lifted his arm. He pointed. To Rose. "Let's try something different."

The scenario moved slowly through Vivene's perception until he snapped his arm back toward the pentagram. From then, the scene sped up beyond what it should've. Lying flat on the stony path, Vivene tensed up beyond movement. She could only watch now, staring. Helpless.

Rose walked with the sorcerer, perfectly obedient, as he guided her by the arm. He held her firmly, but Vivene knew she wouldn't try to bolt. Rose was different from a normal person. Rose lacked independence. Rose was…innocent. He didn't even tie her to the post. He pointed at her face with a stiff finger, and even from the long distance, her oblivious smile could be made out, bunching up her sunny, round face.

Bile churned in Vivene's stomach and bubbled in her throat. She opened her mouth and cried out. Only a croak squeezed through. There was nothing she could do.

Lamrhath resumed his chant.

The marksman released.

The arrow arched…and landed hard in Rose's chest.

Rose stepped back to keep her footing, not crying out as Vivene would expect. She looked to Vivene across the great distance. She smiled.

She fell.

The black cloud lifted from the earthen floor around her. It grew bigger. Bigger.

It roared! *Hrooooooooaaahhhhhh!*

The cavern quaked.

Air whistled through the holes in the rocky spaces louder than ever.

Vivene screamed, clinging to the ground, half in anguish and half in pain under the pressure.

The black tornado flashed at its edges in a brief show of whirring flames. It pulled the air so strongly, rotten garbage flew from the mounds. Sorcerers had to duck and cover.

And then it died.

The garbage fell, some pieces raining down from high distances. A skull landed with a *clurk!* on the path beside Vivene. As the tornado completed its dissipation, a wave of movement spilled out as if from thin air—more visitors like the one the lamb's blood summoned, except many more.

A circular wave of the creatures drifted around Rose's body. They roved in and fell back as others rushed past them. Vivene couldn't count them. Creatures. Demons from Kullixaxuss invited by the sorcerers into the living realm. She didn't need or want to gain a closer look. She knew what went on over there. They took turns feeding on Rose's flesh offering. Dozens of them.

Listening to the many sanguinesents spill from the black tornado portal sped Lamrhath's heart. Avoiding their stares, his mind raced to beat it. How many were there? Why had the ugly girl's sacrifice gained so many? They had wanted to summon only six.

A tall shadow moved over him. Before he could bolt, two snake-like appendages whipped out and ensnared his head. The dry yet tacky skin made it impossible to wrench away.

Kingsorcerer. A booming voice spoke inside his head.

A short panic passed over him, too quickly to consider reacting yet.

Fear not, but listen, the voice continued. *Why have you called us from our station?*

He spoke back in his head, taking care to enunciate in this new medium of communication. *I seek your aid. My associate summoned one of you before, using himself as a sacrifice.*

Yes, the sanguinesent confirmed. *Our brother has since returned to Kullixaxuss. What does the kingsorcerer need, that he would summon us in such a great number using a divinely innocent sacrifice?*

Divinely innocent? Her innocence was what had bought so many summoned creatures?

Wikshen, Lamrhath answered. *Wikshen is out in the Darklands, and we need to obtain him. There's a Luschian out there too. I don't know her location or Wikshen's at the moment. Otherwise, I need to find the sword called Hathrohjilh, and my brother, Daghahen.*

A low, rolling trill emerged from the sanguinesent's physical throat. *You may meet my eyes,* it said. *Elves are immune to sanguinesent domination.*

Cautiously raising his chin with the tentacles still in his ears, Lamrhath's gaze swept up the layers of black robes to the skull-like head of the creature, which sat awkwardly atop the whole thing as if it had been placed there rather than attached. The thick ruff of black feathers around its neck looked like a cushion. Its long teeth stood neatly together, dry and free of any lips to inhibit them. The eyes sat in the huge eye sockets, glittering as nothing but clusters of diamonds. They didn't ensnare Lamrhath, but he could easily sympathize with any human they did ensnare.

The sanguinesent continued, *Since you have summoned us, we will perform one task each, or proceed as groups on shared tasks. So allocate us well.*

I need Wikshen here, Lamrhath said, staring at the bizarre sight. He was well aware of the many other sanguinesents behind him, not by their presences but by their psychic murmuring to each other, always in analytical tones. Lamrhath took a long, deep breath through his nose. *I desire the Luschian.*

The sanguinesent drew its tentacles out of Lamrhath's ears, dragging them slowly. They'd gone deeper than expected and could thin themselves to fit better. Their normal width matched a dainty woman's wrist.

The sanguinesent stood fixed on him with its staring clusters. *Your sacrifice of choice has gained you one hundred of us,* it said. Apparently, it could speak to him psychically now without using its tentacles. *We can divide our number to comb the surface world in search of your four desires: Wikshen, Luschian, Daghahen, and sword.*

"M-my lord?" Talekas approached with his eyes covered. "What is going on?"

All around him, the sorcerers took great pains not to look at the sanguinesents. The chained prisoners were already enthralled, trying to walk against their bonds to serve whichever creature had captured their brains.

"Talekas," Lamrhath said, "prepare the portal rods. The sanguinesents and I have reached an agreement."

Chapter 34
A Kiss Bites

Daghahen clapped Brother Elfric on the shoulder with a big smile. He'd done the same to the other mercymen who stood in a line with their hoods down. Elfric's lip quivered.

Daghahen's hood also lay on his shoulders. They'd discovered his elven heritage a while back when it fell by accident. The others had hardly offered a second look, only a faint comment of surprise from one, but somehow it had brought them all closer together. He shared stories of his youth—the magic button story he liked to dispense, as well as old tales from his Norrian culture—and they loved every one of them. Their large group of men, young and old, laughed and bantered and goofed off all night most nights, like carefree children. They were men with somber pasts who aimed to keep the present as joyful as possible. On more than one occasion, they'd created that same peace for Daghahen.

"N-n-now you be careful up there in those unholy mountains, Brother Ibex," Elfric said with a tear in his eye.

Daghahen let his grin widen as far as it would go. He loved this little man's name almost as much as the man himself. "No need to worry for me. It's you I worry about—all of you. Watch yerselves out there in this cruel land." His trip through the Darklands had been nothing short of surreal, to be honest. After leaving it the last time with Wik's holding sphere in hand, he'd made a vow never to return again. Fate never cared for his promises.

Brother Egan bowed his head and kissed his own index finger. "What happens to us is of no consequence. We will wander this earth until the One Creator decides we've wandered long enough. All we can do until then is help those who need us. You're always welcome back to our little rabble of lost men, Brother Ibex."

Daghahen's throat closed up, and he hid the emotion by dipping his head and turning to leave. "If I find myself back down here in the near future, I'll look for ya."

He and the group moved in two separate directions, none lingering to stare at each other. A sigh of relief washed over him as he trekked through the tall grass, alone again. Every one of those old men, and the young ones too, had survived all this way. They were a hardy bunch.

He did take one more glance over his shoulder at them to keep their image forever. Seeing them go, he caught himself absently touching the hood covering his head, their moral support being replaced with it instead. Although they'd survived all this way, and they'd hopefully survive long afterward, Daghahen couldn't say the same for himself.

Curled on the floor, Wikshen wheezed shallow breaths. Each attempt to fill his lungs stabbed him through the torso. A rib on his left side had broken when he hit the ground. The pain blurred his vision with hot mist. Now he really felt alive. Worse injuries than this returned to his memory: the past lives of Wikshen.

Gritting his teeth through the pain, he smiled. Mere hours ago, he was basking in the voice of that lovely brunette squealing in his ear when he tweaked her nipple. Which sensation was more exhilarating? His private laughter ended when another jab of pain pierced his side.

All around him, those feathery black dogs—scouels—sniffed and growled as if to keep him under control. He swiped an arm at the nearest one, unafraid of the monstrous creature. He opened his palm to send out a morkblade, but decided against it. Best to conserve his store of minerals and energy. He'd finally gotten the battleshift back, but he would need at least one good night to restore himself to full majesty.

The scouels parted, and a pair of dainty white feet appeared in his lowered view. He trailed his gaze up the smooth legs to a naked body. Grella had restored her youthful appearance, no doubt through some alternative sorcerous practice. She wore her black cloak at least, and her pale hair spread across her covered shoulders like white-hot, upside-down flames.

"Well," Wikshen said with a smirk, despite his continued wheezing and nauseating pain, "even though I have my battleshift now, your failure to stir my cock goes on. Perhaps try a different glamour next time."

His words didn't affect her stern expression. "Wikshen," she said, as if merely to recite his name. She took the opportunity to look at him a few seconds longer.

He wrapped his opposite arm around his broken rib. It was taking too long to fuse back together. The rib lay underneath the brand on his side for a noticeable, combined irritation.

"I'm not sure if you can be helped, Mastaren," Grella said.

He worked his way to his knees in effort not to look so pathetic.

"If your battleshift hasn't restored your libido, I'm afraid I have no use for you."

He hissed a short bout of laughter and cut it off after another stab to his side. "No use for *me*?" he echoed. "I think you have it backward, little tart."

Her eyebrows lifted and a smirk quirked her face. "Do I?" She took a slow step forward. "Mastaren, do you remember me?"

He huffed and shot her a glare. "In recent hours, yes. You betrayed me."

She shook her head. "I didn't betray you, you betrayed me."

He squinted.

"I've been alive for centuries," she continued. "Along my life journey"—she strolled closer to him, curving around the invisible ring of his own space—"through centuries of getting to know you and observing your ways and the rhythm of your existence, I've gained a valuable understanding."

He hardly listened to her as he worked his way to his feet. His damned rib still hung loose and sent pulses of pain across him! She stepped closer, and he met her with his tallest, squarest stance, looming over her head. She held her shoulders back and her voluptuous breasts forward with all the confidence he remembered of her.

"I understand now that I own you," she declared.

His mouth slackened. "You...own me?"

Her lips curled up at the sides. "Yes, Mastaren." She released the eye contact and resumed her circular walk around him. The scouels prowled outside of her ringed path, panting and staring at him, their eyes glowing. Wikshen let her perform her little walk of intimidation, standing at his full stature, ignoring the pain. He refused to demonstrate any weakness by spinning in place to keep her in his sight.

"Though you are exceptionally pretty in this form, I'm afraid you've taken a faulty host," she said.

Wikshen regarded himself.

"What kind of Wikshen can't perform his most treasured and enjoyable ability?"

He twisted around despite the pain. "No, no, no, what did you say about owning me?" Keeping his feet planted in place, he let his spine return to its normal position when she stepped back in front of him.

"It's a fact I've learned after serving six previous incarnations of you, Mastaren." Her lips parted around her teeth, sharp and luminous like a hungry succubus. "I control you. Don't you remember? You've killed certain people...because I put you up to it. Regardless of being First Sister, I've made you solely mine by blocking the other concubines' access to you. At times, you'd service no one except me." She stepped into his personal space, teasing her breasts an inch away from his chest.

He kept his breath steady, steaming through his nose, but he found it hard to hide his anger and offense. Her words rang in his ears, sparking echoes of the past and hazy images.

"And when I didn't need you anymore…" She burned her stare against his, complementing her steaming voice. "I disbanded you. Freed the pixie from its host."

Wikshen's fists clenched. "You're not getting me any closer to arousal."

She smiled. "Your divine arousal may not be necessary any longer, now that I see how flawed you are. It was never my intention for you to take such a random host."

His face twisted; he wanted to impose with questions upon questions, but patience would help more now. Such virtues were never a strong point for him.

"I kept to a good plan," she said. "I trapped Wik in a holding sphere to hoard for years, waiting to find the best possible candidate."

"You were going to choose my host?"

She nodded, ever shining her smug grin at him. "I canceled you with plans to recreate you."

"So, what happened? How did I wind up with this 'flawed' host you so disapprove of?"

"A bit over a year ago, I found a weary traveler in Hathrohskog by sheer coincidence." She spread her hands. "As you can tell, I require help to advance and operate this place, so with my plan in mind, I led him down here. He too had a plan, I quickly learned. He chatted me up with all manner of charm and frivolous words, not to mention his show of feigned foibles that made me laugh like a fresh young girl in spring. It didn't help that I'd drunk of one's life force right before.

"The traveler got his way in the end, and when he had me at my most vulnerable, he took the advantage and swiped the holding sphere from under my nose. Whether he knew it or not, he put an end to my grand scheme to create the perfect Wikshen. Now here you are."

She perused her eyes along his body. "A beautiful creature. Sculpted with the grace of an elf, the strength of a lion, and"—she reached up and brazenly touched his hair lying over his shoulder—"the rarest hair color in the world." A feminine pout replaced the grin on her soft, round face, adorable but fake. "But alas, your host is the worst I've ever seen. Your energy is running low, and you're feeling an excessive amount of pain. Even worse, you can't activate your holy phallus to bless your women."

She'd said enough. Wikshen snapped his hand out and seized her throat. His harnessed, steady mood withered in place of a rage that felt nothing short of right. He squeezed, relishing in the knowledge that her neck might snap in his grasp, and yet she watched him with a smirk on her annoying face.

"Who are you to tell me I'm flawed?" he growled.

His action rallied the scouels to defend their mistress. He raised his arm, slowly lifting her little bare toes from the floor, and still she smiled. The scouels moved in on them, trapping him inside their group.

"Who are you to tell me who to penetrate or when, or to decide it only happens to you?"

A little tingle of pleasure spread over his scalp as he squeezed her throat tighter, relishing her face's color change from white to red to purple. "Who are you to decide whom I possess or when? Or to trap me in a holding sphere?"

He exhaled hot breath through his nose. His body temperature climbed, particularly in his hands. The minerals moved through him with delightful vigor. "Or to burn me to death? A self-appointed judge, deeming herself worthy of separating the pixie from its host."

The minerals traveled up his arm in a winding dance of hot and cold, in preparation to emerge from his palm as a morkblade right through her neck. He squeezed tighter. The scouels intensified their growling and snarling, baring their teeth like wild dogs and spreading their wings high. The shredding pain in Wikshen's rib fell out of mind, replaced by the anger. The morkblade materials traveled closer to his hand in his bloodstream. He grinned at what would happen next, savoring Grella's puffy, purple face.

The scouels sprang.

The morkblade made its exit. The loud pinging of the blade hitting the wall and ricocheting echoed behind all the snarling, snorting muzzles with long, moist teeth. The scouels knocked Wikshen to the ground by an error of his own. On his back, he swiped at the huge dog heads. Enormous, rough paws with filthy claws raked at him. Grella vanished from sight in all the chaos. No way to tell if his morkblade had severed her head or not.

Eeeeeeeeyaaaaaaaaaah!

Practically a whistle in its impossible pitch, the voice pierced Wikshen's ears. His bones rattled painfully, sending awful goosebumps across his skin. Grella lived on. Her voice created a rumble in the stony atmosphere. Massive cracks sounded, particularly below him. The floor's strength buckled under her shrill call. In one huge mass of powerful, flapping wings, sharp teeth, and dogs' breath, Wikshen fell.

Kalea allowed Metta and Damos to lead her urgently through the winding cave corridors. Without their guidance, Kalea would've stayed in the field at the bottom of the chasm and screamed stupidly up at the place where Wikshen had been taken. Maybe she would've attempted to climb the rocks after him, but she couldn't even if she wanted to. She needed their support as her poison caused a rising dizziness in her head, probably sped up by her panic. Metta seemed to agree with Damos's plan, so Kalea went along with both of them.

"How are my friends? Where are they?" Kalea asked Metta.

"I don't know, I'm sorry to say," she answered. "But it didn't look good. We were attacked by the masked men. I managed to stay out of the violence, and thankfully, Dyii got distracted by all of it. I saw at least one of your friends get caught."

"Oh, no," Kalea gasped, and had to stop to catch her breath. Increases of her heart rate and emotion seemed to exacerbate the poison's effects. "Now we have to find my friends *and* D-Wikshen." She didn't want to speak Dorhen's name in front of Metta. Knowing his name felt like some kind of trump she had over the concubines. They were named for him, but Kalea held his name for herself.

Damos asked, "Have you seen them since coming down here?"

"'Fraid not." Metta kept her eyes forward, walking with purpose. She'd brought a Kraft Fire chime bowl from Wikhaihli to light their way through the darker tunnels. "I waited for you in the crowd," she said to Kalea.

"Back at Wikhaihli?"

"Yes. Your friend was to take his punishment, but you never showed, and after a while, it became obvious we wouldn't see the punishment either. I searched for you, and by chance, I saw the Mastaren climb over the wall and leave Wikhaihli. I managed to slip out too, but he proved too fast for me. I went in the direction he ran; the moon lit my way. Eventually, I found a set of wagon tracks and followed them."

"Our wagon," Kalea said.

"Out in the wilderness, I encountered that traitor warlock. He tried to kill me."

Kalea cringed.

Metta asked her, "What are you doing out here anyway?"

Kalea blinked. "It's too long a story." She simply didn't care to explain it to her.

"Well, now I'm glad I followed those tracks," Metta said. "Hoping to find the Mastaren, I came down here and went on a merry chase in these caves. There were hostile masked people and monsters and a witch who took the Mastaren's battleshift!"

Kalea replayed the image of Wikshen removing his scrap of clothing to put the battleshift back on. Metta had somehow found and brought it to him.

"When I heard she'd taken the battleshift, I made it my duty to get it back for him."

"Where did you find it?"

"In a locked box under magnified light."

Kalea mouthed the words "magnified light," remembering how quickly Wikshen had passed out in the sunny field.

"Their silly wards couldn't stop me." Metta beamed her proud smile. "It took some doing, but I was able to extinguish the light and cut the special yarn wards with simple witchcraft I learned from my ma. Thanks to me, our Mastaren has a better chance of rescuing us."

"Wikshen wouldn't have been able to get into a box under some light with simple wards?"

"Not light that strong," Metta said. "It made the iron fixings on the box hot to the touch, and the light itself..." Metta shook her head. "He would've weakened as soon as he entered the room, especially without his battleshift. Grella didn't count on someone like me sneaking into her chambers."

Kalea hummed beside her. "And what were the 'yarn wards?'"

Metta chuckled. "Simple witchcraft," she said, "something most other Wikshonites may not know about. But I do. The yarn is made from a special blend and requires a special pair of scissors to cut it. This yarn was wrapped around the chest again and again. I first had to steal the scissors, and then cut the yarn. What an ordeal."

Kalea might've asked further questions, but Damos piped up from his place in the lead. "Kalea."

She had almost forgotten about him. He'd heard all of their conversation, and it struck her how he knew nothing yet about Kalea's activities since their separation, particularly how she had gone to Wikhaihli and adopted their customs.

He asked, "After we get out of here...do you think...do you think we can talk privately for a short time?"

Kalea let out the breath she'd held. "Sure," she said. "Yes...I'm sure we can."

Kalea uttered a *Dear Creator* under her breath. Since Damos was alive, he would want to be filled in on everything he'd missed. He'd especially want to know where the two of them stood as of now. She'd almost made love to him, for the Creator's sake! If Wikshen had disrupted their moment any later, she and Damos would've become one. She owed Damos an explanation. She'd have to tell him about her ecstasies and how she didn't really desire to be with him.

Her face heated up in the following tense moment. He watched her, probably waiting for her to say more, but she didn't. She withered under his stare until he turned forward again.

"I wonder how my friends are faring," Kalea said in attempt to relieve the tension. "I fell into a hole and left them all up there. I hope at least one of them escaped those drones."

"That's another concern I have," Damos replied. "Before we leave, there's one more place I want to show you."

A rumble in the stone shut him up. The three of them took wide stances to ride it out as the rumble increased to raucous tremors. A voice echoed with it, a deep, guttural roar.

Metta's eyes popped. "The Mastaren!" She took off.

"Wait!" Kalea followed her, and Damos took up the rear.

"We shouldn't go this way!" Damos warned.

Neither Kalea nor Metta responded. By the time they found the chamber full of dust and a huge mound of rocks, the noises were reduced to a few falling pebbles.

"Mastaren!" Metta's voice echoed.

"Metta," Damos said, "you probably shouldn't shout considering the cave-in."

A masculine groan resonated back, and Metta scrambled up the pile of fallen rocks within a thick cloud of choking dust. Throwing aside the rocks she could lift, she called her Mastaren again in a softer volume than before. Kalea followed her lead, and Damos remained on the floor, watching them silently.

Kalea searched with her. She still didn't want to call for "Dorhen," but she didn't want to call him "Mastaren" either, for it would be too strange. An odd hunch made her wonder if calling him by the Wikshonite title would egg on the demon inside him.

Metta removed stones one by one, and Kalea raced her. Wikshen's dazed and dusty face appeared under one Metta lifted. Blood trails ran down from his nose and scalp. "I found him!"

Kalea gasped at his rough state. Balancing on the rocks, she waited to hear the report of whatever brutal injuries he'd taken on. Instead, she heard him say, "I'm gonna kill that bitch." At least he spoke easily enough.

Metta cooed and removed a few more stones, and he tried to sit up. He might not be as broken as Kalea had guessed. Metta tossed aside several more rocks, and he wiggled, using a great feat of strength to raise his arm out of the pile. Focusing his eyes, he put them on Metta.

"You're the one," he said. "You brought my battleshift to me." He grinned despite all the day's horrid events. He'd showered that grin on Kalea several times today. With his free hand, he took Metta by the back of her head and pulled her in.

He kissed her.

Kalea's stomach dropped. Her head lightened. She staggered in place.

"Kalea?" Damos said. "Are you all right?"

"Um…" Kalea attempted to step to a lower rock to get off the dangerous mound, but she no longer had her balance.

Damos darted up to catch her fall. Her vision faded. Regardless of how frantically Damos said her name and shook her to stay awake, all she could hear through it was the hideous, moist sound of Metta's and Wikshen's lips smacking as they parted.

It's over. Kalea's hand moved up and grazed the scabbed scratch line running across her clavicle. *Time for the poison to kill me.*

Chapter 35
Bitter Tea

Just one crate of Root McCrow?" the young man asked Lehomis in the back alley behind the brewer's house in Theddir.

"Just one," he confirmed with his lips around his pipe stem.

The gangly lad scrunched his nose after jotting down his order. "If ya don't mind my askin', sir, what's an elf gonna do with a bunch of bottles of alcohol?"

Lehomis took a long drag, smiled, and shrugged. "Throw a party for humans, I suppose."

He blinked and nodded. "So long as ya know what you're doing. My family won't be held responsible for anything that happens to you. I can bring that crate around tomorrow. What inn room are ya in?"

"Second floor, fifth room."

"Got it."

The lad walked away a bit uncertainly, still blinking. Lehomis knew why: elves couldn't drink alcohol; it was like poison to them, and the lad knew enough about elves to have such a concern. Lehomis had seen a few clueless *saehgahn* drop dead on pub floors in the Darklands before. Some idiots on their *caunsaehgahn* fell victim to it out of ignorance— ignorance and a handful of rowdy human friends jovially passing out the glasses. In fact, it was the very thing that had led to Lehomis finding out for sure that he'd become immortal. If he wasn't, he wouldn't be standing here ordering a round for himself.

After his business with the brewery lad, Lehomis stepped into what was probably the greatest oddity in the Lightlands: a teahouse run by elves in Theddir. By his standards, The Obsidian Fawn was a new addition to this mostly human-populated town, established about fifty years ago.

A little bell on the door announced his entry, and a young human woman dressed crisply in an elven *hanbohik* scurried around the corner to meet him in the foyer. She gave him a warm yet stilted welcome in Norrian. "*Kowhahere yuten.*"

"*Harranhennhi*, lass," Lehomis answered. "How's yer ma?"

The girl's eyes widened. "Excuse me, sir. You know my mother?"

Lehomis gave her his warmest smile. "I guess you don't remember me. You were but a wee little thing toddling around here when I last visited. To answer your question, I do know her, but it's yer stepfather I'm good friends with. I helped him build this place."

"Oh." She touched her own face and shrugged with a little nervous giggle. "I guess I'll never get used to dealing with your people. You all have such long memories." Her stepfather was an elf who'd married her human mother when she was pregnant with this girl.

"Sorry, I don't mean to embarrass you." He waved a hand at her. "I'm impressed with myself for recognizing you after all these years."

He sat down on the little wooden bench and allowed her to unlace and remove his boots as they did here. This teahouse mimicked Norrian culture to a high level of flash and flair for the amusement of its guests.

"This way, *saehgahn*."

Though he knew where to go, Lehomis followed her barefooted. "Just as I remember it," he mused aloud. It was structured like a traditional elven house, with a big, cozy *wyrrem* at its center where the guests took their tea and side rooms where the owners lived. It served to give traveling elves comfort, but the owner knew this business would collect its major income from the greater flow of human patrons—people hoping to be immersed in the exotic for an hour or so. Lehomis strained his eyes to view the *wyrrem* ahead, where he'd sit and be served his tea.

"Will you be needing a room for the night?" the girl asked. "My father says to ask all *saehgahn* who enter."

"Nah, but thank you, lass," he said. "I got a room at The Riverwalker."

When the girl's expression twisted, he only offered her a smile and a nod. The Riverwalker was a full-sized inn a few buildings down, the regular kind of place frequented by lots of rowdy humans, and owned by humans. Elven travelers typically didn't choose that place over this one… unless, of course, they required temporary female company.

"Which flavor of tea are you in the mood for today, *saehgahn*?"

"My name's Lehomis," he said, showing her a proud smile.

She threw a peek at him over her shoulder. Everyone in Theddir who knew anything about elves had heard of Lehomis.

"I'll take whatever's most convenient for you, lass," he went on. "But what I'm really looking for is to talk to some journeyman *saehgahn*. Are there any in today?"

"Um…" She put her arm out in invitation to descend into the lower level that made the *wyrrem*.

At this time of day, the house accommodated less than half its capacity; no elves sat among the patrons. No *faerhain* either. The employed help consisted of other women dressed in *hanbohiks*, drifting around the room to refill teacups and deliver little dishes of biscuits and puddings. *Faerhain* were locked up tight in Norr, so only male elves could be seen wandering around Theddir.

Nonetheless, he stepped down with a hum and took one of the tables near the center of the large, circular space. A little fire burned low in the sculpted fireplace at the north side of the *wyrrem*, another standard feature of Norrian architecture.

The girl bowed in the intensely formal manner usually reserved for the Desteer back at home. "I will alert my father of your coming and bring you some tea."

"Thanks, lass."

After she went on her way, Lehomis waited awkwardly upon his floor cushion. The human patrons around him wore lovelier textiles than he'd expect from the run-of-the-mill lower class. Middle class people—husbands aiming to entertain their wives or mistresses—visited this novelty establishment. More than one of the women, patron or server, shot stealthy glances at him.

No sooner had Lehomis put his elbow on the table to partially cover his face than the owner came trodding proudly along the circular gallery toward his table.

"The great Lehomis," he said.

"Cirinhen," Lehomis acknowledged him back.

Cirinhen gathered the ends of his long robes, the dress of a married *saehgahn*, and planted himself adjacent to Lehomis at the little round table. He also collected his long hair and laid it over his arm. "To what do I owe this rare visit from a dearest friend?" He glanced over his shoulder, and then leaned forward to whisper in Norrian, "And if you don't mind, let's use our native language. Paying customers enjoy listening to Norrian."

Lehomis returned his elbow to the table so he could rest his face upon his hand. "Dear Bright One, Cir," he groaned in Norrian as requested. "Where do I start?"

Cirinhen's warm smile melted.

"I came here to meet any young *saehgahn* who might be in the house."

Cirinhen leaned back and perused the current patrons, all humans. "Well, there's one, at least." He motioned to the general section of the house behind him. "A young one on *caunsaehgahn*. He's been helping me with the laborious chores, but will have to move on soon."

"Because of *caunsaehgahn*'s rhythm?" Lehomis guessed. *Caunsaehgahn* dictated that a journeyman couldn't remain in one place too long, especially in the early years of his journey.

"No, because I've strong suspicion he's been after my stepdaughter."

Cirinhen shrugged. "I'm not sure how to react yet, so I've left the matter up to my wife to deal with." He finished with a shake of his head. "Your air does not feel easy today, my friend. Is everything all right?"

"I need some help hauling a big load of supplies back to Lockheirhen. We've hit a few hard bumps…"

Keeping an open and concerned expression, Cirinhen waited for more.

Lehomis sucked in a breath and then went through all of it, from the raid on his village to Gaije tearing off after a band of dangerous sorcerers, and then the Tinharri campaign and his clan's loss of six *faerhain*. Lehomis ended with a shake of his head and an increase of acid in his stomach. What was taking that tea so long? "We're low on horses, we're low on *faerhain*…"

Cirinhen smiled and laid a hand on the side of Lehomis's arm. "Well, you know I owe you many, many return favors. Say what you need, and it's yours. I can buy some of your old treasures if you'd like. If you've got any more of those fine *hanbohiks* of the luminous Kristhanhea…"

"Nah," he replied, "I've sold about every piece already and have an inn room bursting with stacked crates and sacks. Maybe just the use of your young lad will do."

"Say no more." Cirinhen rose to his feet in one smooth, spirited motion—both males and females practiced a certain manner of grace when indoors, while outdoors was for bursts of energetic *saehgahn* foolery—and he disappeared into a back room.

He reemerged with a sleepy young thing with stringy limbs and hair barely scrubbing his shoulders. Cirinhen exchanged hushed Norrian words with him in a tone harsh and critical. "You'll speak to Lehomis," he said, raking his voice across the lad, Norrian sounds the eavesdropping guests should find exotic enough.

The lad shot more than one glance toward the door leading out to the kitchen as Cirinhen shoved him into the *wyrrem*.

"*Amonimori*," Lehomis said to the lad when he plopped down in the seat Cirinhen had occupied. All around them, the human patrons ogled the scene. Elves were a rarity in Sharr's domain, so this drama must make for great theater.

"*Amonimori*," the lad said with a slight bow of his head.

"This is Tey." Cirinhen slapped the lad hard on the shoulder. "Tey is strong, and he knows how to drive a cart. Take him out of my house, please."

Lehomis smiled in amusement. "Tey," he formally acknowledged.

Tey's face paled when he turned it ever so slightly to eye Cirinhen—

who didn't peer back at him. Instead, he crossed his arms and kept his gaze firmly on Lehomis, who nodded.

"I think Tey will do fine." He bowed his head and said to Cirinhen, "Thank you for your support."

Getting a *saehgahn* to help him haul his supplies back was vital. He hadn't brought one from home because he preferred them there to guard the place. He couldn't ask a sturdy human man to accompany him back because men were prohibited from entering Norr's deeper sections for many reasons. Lehomis had relied on knowing he'd most likely find a journeyman *saehgahn* right here in Theddir.

When the tea finally arrived, Lehomis didn't miss the quick glances between Tey and Cirinhen's stepdaughter.

"I hope the tea is to your liking," she said to Lehomis in Lightlandic, next placing a second cup for her stepfather. "*Pawbhen*," she said, calling him by the warm Norrian familial title, "will Tey be leaving soon?"

Lehomis pretended not to listen to their exchange as he took a casual sip from his cup. He wasn't sure what type of tea she'd brought him, but its bitter flavor curled his tongue. Shouldn't she know how to brew it properly if she'd been raised around so many elves?

Cirinhen beamed, crossing his arms again. "Brew him the tea of goodbye, *guenhihah*."

The young woman kept the rest of her body language cool but couldn't seem to leash her frantic eyes searching Tey for any form of communication. He stared down at the table, looking no happier than a stallion who'd suddenly found himself gelded.

Lehomis stood up after only a few sips of his tea. "Well, Cir, I thank you, old friend—"

Cirinhen snipped at him, "Say it in Norrian," and spread his hands to point out the paying customers all around.

Lehomis snorted and turned to Tey to tell him in the preferred language, "Lad, you can meet me at The Riverwalker tomorrow at dawn."

He reached out and took the lad's arm in a firm shake. Cirinhen shooed his young stepdaughter away after she spent an extended moment staring stiffly at the situation.

"*Harranhennhi*," Lehomis said to her before she left, and then, "*Hik-hik*." Sorry.

"Her name's Tilninhet," Lehomis told his other old friend, who'd taken the seat next to him in The Riverwalker later that evening. He felt a world more comfortable in this establishment—a regular, relaxed atmosphere without all the stiff gestures and pageantry of The Obsidian Fawn.

Sitting intimately close, Bevin gave him all of her attention like she'd done so many times before. Lines had formed around her soft eyes, once bright and kitten-like when he first met her, and now emptied of most of the love and innocence he used to admire when she was young. He'd found her exactly where he left her last time, working hard in this inn, wearing a colorful, expensive ensemble to display her prettiest parts, but now tired, aged, and no longer amused. She did drum up her warmer side for him, though, while he relayed another facet of his miserable story to her, a part he wouldn't dare share with anyone else.

He took a sip of water to loosen his throat. "I'll never see her again now. I'm glad…"

"You don't sound so glad, though," Bevin said.

"But I am. Really. It's the best thing to happen for her. Now she'll be taken care of by a real husband."

"You love her. If you didn't, you wouldn't be talking about her so much." The woman hovered her chin over his shoulder, close to his ear. They'd chatted like this for over an hour, like they'd done time and time again. "If you didn't, I might've seen you more often in the last fifteen years."

"But now I'm back, aren't I?"

Her crows' feet deepened and branched when she smiled. Soot from her eyelids was creeping into those wrinkles, but she still wore it well. "Yes, you are, my Leho."

"I've been married once, you know that," he said, and she nodded. "I've had my chance to enjoy that life."

"Awww, don't talk like that." She maneuvered her arm to stroke the back of his hair as they cuddled. "My sweet *saehgahn*, a person needs love—always. You deserve to have your love refilled."

"Too complicated. In my culture, I'm finished with love. Only females can marry more than once."

"Well, your Norr is such a cruel, cruel world, isn't it?" Her pout was as beautiful as ever. He knew her words were often genuine, but not always, and even when they weren't, they still worked to soothe wounds and lift the spirit. "Couldn't Tilninhet have refilled your love?"

"Tilly juggled her own issues. I hope more than anything that she's happy now. And I feel…" He took a breath. "Maybe you can understand… I wish to move on—from both of them. Kristhanhea and Tilninhet."

"I do understand."

"I need a clean slate, which, I guess, is also why I've sold so many of my wife's belongings."

Bevin clicked her tongue. "I know you, Lehomis, and I sense something deeper," she said. "Something has you bothered, greatly bothered."

"Well…" Lehomis quirked his mouth and reached for his cup to take another sip. He knew this prostitute also told fortunes for money. It was universally thought that *faerhain* were the only mortal creatures born with a sensitivity to the thoughts and feelings of others at a psychic level. In his long life, Lehomis had seen how close behind them human women could be.

"There's other worries too," he surrendered, and spilled the woes which he'd told Cirinhen earlier this afternoon. He could share some things with this woman that he couldn't share with a fellow *saehgahn*, however.

"God, I'm terrified," he said as if throwing it out into the room. "For Mhina. Gaije too."

She cooed sympathetically in the expected way. He allowed a smile to spread on his face despite his true mood, shook his head, and then laid it on the table. Bevin ran her fingers through his hair, and he closed his eyes at the soothing sensation. He hadn't even gotten that simple little touch from Tilninhet because her secret tea ceremony kept to some strict standards. His arm lay across the table beside his head, fingering the handle of his water cup. Every other person in the room drank ale.

"When I go back home," he said, "I'll have to hide all this from Tirnah and Anonhet. They have no idea of the dread inside me."

"Well, that's why I'm here, my Leho," Bevin said. "And I'll always be here."

"It's been so long. I'm beginning to think Gaije isn't coming back."

"Don't think such things."

"Can't help it." They sat in silence for a moment. He couldn't see the woman from this angle, but her fingers grazed his scalp.

"You have the silkiest hair I've ever touched, even counting other elves," she said.

"But it's Mhina that's the real tragedy," he went on. "She's just a little girl. I should've gone with Gaije. He begged me, and I didn't do it. If she's dead, it's my fault."

Bevin shushed him gently. She put her hands on his shoulders. "Why don't we stop talking and go up to your room?"

Lehomis sat up straight and met her eyes. He'd probably droned on long enough. A long evening like this was something he needed every once in a while. A little vacation away from Norr to be among humans and their carefree drunken nonsense. Singing their bawdy songs. Laughing. Cuddling with a soft, curvaceous body. Not that he'd accomplished very many of those activities today.

He smiled and shook his head. "Not tonight, lass. I don't think I can." He rifled through his pocket. "But thanks for listening to all my sorrows." He revealed the little hairpin he'd once tried to trade for fishing line, a lovely trinket made of bronze and encrusted with pearls and cloisonné. He placed it in her palm.

Chapter 36
A Fish Kisses

Back in the forest, Kalea rubbed her eyes and fluttered her lashes. A crisp morning wind wafted over her face. Pine trees. Towering pine trees swayed gently in the breeze, bowing over her. When she put her arms down, they landed on a fluffy quilt. The one she took from the convent. The one she told herself Joy must've made, which was very likely. Somewhere in her memory, she'd eventually dig out a little image of her best friend stitching together these very squares, some of them embroidered with the Creator's Flower and letters bearing religious significance.

"Good morning."

That voice! "Dorhen?" She sprang to sit upright.

He squatted naught but five paces away, stoking their morning fire. His hair hung in wet clumps, fresh from his morning constitution in the river.

He regarded her over his shoulder, wearing a little smile plastered to his sweet, youthful face. "Sorry I haven't fished yet," he said.

His hair was brown! Kalea stared at him hard. He wore all his old clothes: his brown mantle, his breezy white undershirt, his mismatched leggings. No battleshift. He was smaller too. Shorter legs, narrower shoulders. His infectious smile lived on as he turned back to his work.

"I got a late start," he continued. "Just didn't want to get out of bed." When he turned to look at her again, he was smiling to full capacity with his teeth gleaming in the morning light.

Checking downward, Kalea found herself fully dressed under all the blankets. She…always slept in her clothes because she hated the cold, and… Beneath her convent quilt, Dorhen's own blankets swathed around her legs. Last night she'd slept with him.

She stared up at him again and blinked her eyes to make sure some dream hadn't come to tease her. It was really him. Her breath sped up. "Dorhen," she said his name again, and he turned, beaming his handsome smile.

"Yes?"

She crawled out of bed, fighting their combined blankets, and launched across the short span of pine needles to throw her arms around him. She put her hands along his head and kissed the top of his hair. A tear or two leaked out of her eyes. He received her physical action with the support of his embrace. She kissed the side of his face, petting him, practically wrestling him, and he responded with several returned kisses.

"I can't tell you how much…" She sobbed and drew a hand back to cover her face.

"What's wrong?" he cooed and wiped her tears off her cheek with his hand. His large eyes glowed warmly, his expression shifting from deliriously happy to concerned.

"I had a nightmare." She dropped her face to his chest and cried into his shirt. The warm scent of his body soothed her.

He wrapped his arms around her, firm but comfortable, and breathed in her hair as she did his. "Well, I know about those a little too well."

They curled into a tight ball. He let her cry, stroking her hair and hugging his other arm around her. He made soft shushing sounds, and the act held so much power. This was all she needed. By the time her weeping slowed to a stop, he was cradling her like a babe, running his fingers through her hair. Her arm hooked up around his neck.

"Now look," he said suddenly, "the fire's out." He laughed despite it and hugged her tighter. He kissed her forehead.

A wisp of her voice creaked out. "Dorhen, don't leave me again."

"I'd never leave you." His deep voice hummed against her. "You were only dreaming."

A vague laugh puffed through her nose. "I know you wouldn't leave me. I believe you. I know we haven't known each other long, but I do. I really do."

After a few more minutes, they let each other go, and Kalea wiped her face and went to collect some extra twigs around their camp's perimeter while he clicked some flint to rekindle the fire. When she found no more, she settled down across the way to stare at him, hardly interested in doing anything else. She watched the way he moved, memorizing every shape, line, and color that was Dorhen. His hair…all his earthy tones made him a part of the forest. His turquoise eyes glowed brightly. He often looked up, and when their eyes met, they both exploded into uncontrollable smiles, his so beautiful.

"Kalea," he said.

"Hmm?"

He kept his eyes on his work while he spoke. "If—if you want…you can sleep in my bed again. You can sleep in it anytime you want."

"How about tonight?"

His smile refilled to its maximum width, and he kept his eyes on the little pile of firewood. "Yes."

"All right," she said, lacing a bossy tone into her voice for fun effect. "I'm going to sleep in your bed every night because I don't like the cold. How do you like that?"

His smile beamed on. "Sure."

"I might have to kick you out of it, though, so I can have more room to roll over."

That part made his smile fade. He stared at her differently now, searching for her reason.

Her laughter burgeoned until it burst out uncontrollably. Her mirth spread over to him, and he laughed with her. "I'm kidding, silly!"

His relief showed clear, and he returned to blowing at the small flames he'd created and adding in more kindling. He kept silent afterward, but looked at her again and again throughout his work.

Once the fire burned strong, he stood up and extended the stick he'd been using to poke at the logs. "Here," he said. "Don't let the fire go out. I'm going to find us some food."

Kalea's smile dropped. "Are you sure?"

"We have to eat."

"But you're..."

"I'm what?" He waited for her to spit out whatever she would say.

You're leaving me. We'll be apart. She couldn't bring herself to say it out loud. They *did* have to eat, and it would be berries and raw mushrooms if she didn't stay here and man the fire. "My bad dream ..." she said.

He gave her another warm smile and stepped toward her. "You've no idea how badly I want to stay here with you all day."

Kalea's cheeks heated up. She batted her eyes and dropped her gaze to her feet.

"But I told you I'd make sure you eat, and I'm not about to miss a day. No more starving."

"You mean fasting?"

He shrugged. "You're going to eat well as long as you're with me." He opened his arms, and she went into them in a few eager steps. He hugged her. Hard. She hugged back, nuzzling her face into his shoulder.

"Maybe while I'm gone, you can bathe in the creek."

She dropped her jaw and pulled away. He chuckled at her expression. He was right, though. She hadn't bathed since she left the convent. The fear of him possibly spying on her dominated all other reasoning. Then again, last night she had slept snugly in his arms, yet she still feared him seeing her naked? She'd seen him naked nearly every day so far.

Releasing him from her gaze, she huffed. "Promise me you won't double back to spy on me?"

He raised his hands and showed his palms. "I told you, I didn't know what I'd see in that window." He held his firm and sincere countenance for as long as she wanted to study it.

"Fine," she said. "I'll do some washing too."

Satisfied with the conversation's conclusion, he leaned forward with an awkward hesitance. She let him touch her hair and lay a kiss atop her head. Her affectionate attack of him this morning must've given him the permission he needed to extend such gestures; otherwise, he'd shown a clear and uncomfortable resistance to touching or sitting too close to her. She could feel in the air how badly he wanted to. Many, many years of strict convent education about sin and propriety lay between them for now. Even as she enjoyed his one last kiss before departing, those difficulties nagged at her. She reconsidered her promise to sleep in his bed tonight. Poor Dorhen.

He pulled away and beheld her with relaxed, tender eyes. "Remember to keep an eye on the fire. Kalea..."

"Yes?"

"Kalea.

"Kalea.

"Kalea! Wake up now!"

Dorhen's image and the scenery around them darkened. Each time he said her name, his voice deepened and hardened until it pounded her ears with ferocious authority.

Her eyes fluttered open to the image of Wikshen, his blue hair in long, stringy clumps along his grimy face. He shook her, and she finally noticed the sensation.

"Dorhen," she whined.

Damos and Metta were standing behind him, Damos's face all bandaged up and Metta's twisted at Kalea's utterance of the strange name. Wikshen was cradling her in his arms. He scooped up her legs and started walking over rocks and up and down slopes in the path.

"I'll lose her if I don't get Grella to revoke the spell," he said to the others. "That bitch scratched her with an enchanted thorn."

"Why didn't she say anything?" Damos asked in the background.

"Because it's none of your business," Wikshen said. He rushed forward, jostling Kalea all the way. She'd been poisoned before, so this wasn't entirely new, but the sensations did vary. This poison weakened her more than the venom from Chandran's claws. Without Wikshen to carry her, she'd die on the ground.

"Dorhen," she said, lying against him, "I'm glad I got to be with you in the end. I won't die begrudging Metta. All right?"

"What are you talking about?" His voice still ran hard. He walked forward with purpose, regardless of how dizzy it made her.

"I forgive her. And you."

"Forgive me for what?"

"Kissing her."

He snorted. "Why would you have to forgive me for kissing my future concubine?"

A wave of annoyance tweaked her heart and added more dizziness, stirring the poison as she'd observed. "This is what I'm talking about," she said. "I'm trying to forgive you before I die, and you're making it difficult."

He growled through his teeth, his hot breath steaming over her face. "You're *not* going to die."

Kalea could no longer handle this exhaustion. She closed her eyes.

"Wake up!" He shook her annoyingly.

She groaned. "Don't torture me anymore, please."

"I'll do as I like."

"Stop arguing with me."

"It's keeping you awake, isn't it?"

She huffed and let her eyes close again. He persisted in agitating her, but exhaustion dragged at her consciousness and her heart hurt.

The jostling and jiggling continued up a long, sloping path through the dark. Wikshen charged into dense shadows, and Damos and Metta bickered in their struggle to keep up. A little blue light reignited with a chime—Metta's Kraft Fire.

The howling of air passing through various holes in the caves helped to keep Kalea awake. Their upsloping path ended at a wide space where the wind howled loudest.

"This is where she broke up the floor with her voice and I fell through...for the second time," Wikshen said, mostly to the two more lucid than Kalea. The echo of his voice hinted at the size of the room. He started walking again. "Over here."

Metta's flame revealed the space they moved in; a big cavern opened up far beyond the glow, at the back of which loomed glowing, colored shapes, hazy behind the airborne dust and streamers of incense smoke. The crazy pillars of neon green and blue baffled Kalea's struggling mind.

"Am I dreaming?" she asked.

Heiyaaaaaaaaaah-ah!

Everyone froze at the shrill voice.

Wikshen's arms curled tighter under Kalea. "Grella."

When the long call ended, bigger Kraft flames burst to life—*whorf. Whorf, whorf-whorf!* The rest of the cavern came into view around the many big braziers holding blue flames. The colored things were giant mushrooms looming at the back of the room among a tangle of other plants.

Wikshen put Kalea on the floor and took a fight-ready stance, poising his hands and flexing his knuckles. The last ignited Kraft flame showed Grella sitting at the center of a load of fluffy pillows covered in maroon velvet. A thin curtain stood between her and them. At the back of the cave, more scouels waited in the mushrooms' glow. Their dog-like breaths added a humid stink to all the other odd, musty scents of the huge cavern.

Wikshen marched forward, and Damos and Metta ran to stand by Kalea. "Grella!" Wikshen barked so loud and sudden that Kalea jumped. His echo bounced off every wall.

Grella, for one, remained at ease. He stormed forward and ripped the curtain down. Inside the cozy little lounge, the witch maintained her pale, supple skin and explicit appearance.

"Antidote." Wikshen stood waiting at the entrance to her tent.

Grella stretched backward over a pile of cushions and yawned. "What antidote?"

He gestured behind him. "Reverse the illness you put on my girl before I cut your head off."

Grella regarded Kalea with a slight incline of her head to see around him. "Oh," she said. "Mastaren, I don't need to cure her. You have the divine means to do so already."

He balled his fists and tensed his muscular arms. "Bitch," he hissed, "I tried to bless you twice! You know I can't do it."

"Oh, dear." Grella's high voice sang like a delightful country maiden. "I only wanted to help you, my love. I figured if you desired this girl, your seed would cure her, and in return she'd remedy your impotence. I implore you"—she flourished her hand—"cure her."

Wikshen twisted around to check Kalea, who held herself up on her shaking arms. His eyes blazed inside a face declining to panic from its original rage.

"I'm already First Sister," Grella said, "so I'll be perfectly content to see you bless her before me. By all means, bless that other one after. I don't mind."

Grella stood up and sidestepped. Her supple breasts bounced and settled heavily on her rib cage. They looked about to burst. She waved a graceful arm, and her shining blonde hair spread behind it like a cloak. "Bring her in here and make her comfortable."

Grella paused and wiped her forehead. She dipped her head as if she, too, endured a dizzy spell. "Pardon me, Mastaren, I have to…" Panting, she threw a bunch of pillows aside to reveal a big trunk.

"Your color is fading," Wikshen said. Even in the bluish lighting, Kalea could tell her skin was shifting to an ill, greenish tint. Dark spots appeared quickly under her eyes.

She threw the trunk lid open, and inside waited a whimpering young woman, another of the half-dead girls from the wooden cages. The girl whined louder when Grella moved her hands into the tight space.

"What the hell are you doing?" Wikshen took a step forward, and as soon as he did, a massive wall of scouels lunged closer from the back, growling softly as if daring him to interfere. Apparently, there were more than Kalea first estimated.

Grella reached her hands into the trunk, and the girl's volume increased to shrieks and pleas and "no's." Her voice withered to gurgling, weak shouts of pain on contact. Wikshen took another curious step closer, and the scouels leaned in, their breaths steaming in the light, filling the room with a cloud of their sour, doggish steam. The girl's voice went faint by the time Grella took her hands away.

"How many girls have you kidnapped to keep yourself alive over the centuries?" Wikshen asked.

The ancient witch stood back up with her energy replenished, her skin soft and shining again. "Oh, I don't know," she sang. "I only get an hour or two of health and beauty out of each sip from their bodies, of which I only get about…" She counted silently on her fingers. "Three or four sips from each young body I collect."

"And it's been over six hundred and fifty years," Wikshen finished for her.

"Something like that." Grella beamed a proud smile. "Now, to be fair, my sweet Mastaren, I didn't need to do this until three hundred years ago. You can save all the girls I have in my store by giving me the blessing I need to continue living."

He grimaced in response to that. Before he could form an answer to her offer, a door closed off to the side and rapid footsteps pattered toward them.

"Kalea?" The sound of her name came with a twisted flare.

"Dyii," Grella said. "What are you doing here? You're not due to pick up the crates for a few days."

Damos echoed the word "crates" in a whisper beside Kalea.

When Dyii made it into the Kraft firelight, he searched until his eyes landed on Kalea. Wikshen stiffened, clearly wary of the triangle of people in which he stood. He edged over a little as if to try to shield Kalea from both Grella and Dyii.

"You know him?" Wikshen asked Grella.

"Don't worry, Mastaren, he's only a business associate. He runs trade between his faction and mine."

Wikshen's body tightened up even more. "'Faction?' As in *sorcery*?" He pointed an accusing finger at Dyii. "You pretended to be a warlock!"

Dyii put his hands up and gave a mischievous smile. "Truly, I'm not either warlock or sorcerer. Just a Thaccilian who listens to heartbeats." His eyes trailed to Kalea. Wikshen noticed this and bristled, his mouth turned deeper into its frown.

"What do you want, Dyii?" Grella asked.

Wikshen asked over her, "Which faction? Ilbith?"

"Ilbith," Kalea repeated the word in a whisper, her chest throbbing and aching. The poison was overcoming her. Her arms weakened and her head sank lower to the floor. Soon, she'd be lying on her cheek.

"Yes," Dyii answered, "Ilbith." He took a sidelong step closer to Wikshen and Grella. "Is good faction. Very powerful... You see...it took me in—as young man." He inched several more wary steps closer. "They have much control over Darklandic territories. Gives charity and protection."

"You must have one of those seedlings in your brain," Wikshen grumbled.

"Nah, nah," Dyii replied. He spread his hands as in casual conversation, and then put one into his robe's pocket. He took another small step forward, more toward Grella than Wikshen. "My lady here, she makes good trade with them. She can do many good things for Wikshonite cult, being this...how do you say...axel between them. She can make them stronger—"

Before he finished speaking, he whipped his hand out of his pocket, then raised and threw it down, releasing two shiny marbles that hit the floor with little shattering sounds. A fast plume of grey cloud expanded from one and an ear-shredding crash of thunder boomed from the other, releasing dancing wires of lightning to spiral and branch and ensnare whoever stood close by.

Dyii sprinted away as soon as the glass balls left his hand. The lightning bolts jumped to Grella, the closest conductor, and she screamed. Less than half of the other branches ensnared Wikshen.

The scouels flew into a frenzy of flapping wings and ear-shattering barking. Wikshen roared along with Grella, fell to the floor, and writhed around for as long as the spell lasted. Burning flesh dominated all other smells in the air.

Kalea's heart stopped for an instant. Her vision darkened and she screamed his name. "Dorheeeeeeen!"

The effort killed the last of her energy. She dropped her head to the floor. The sounds of chaos continued in the background: humming lightning, male and female screams, and beastly snarling. She reached up and weakly grabbed Damos's ragged tabard.

"I'm dying," she whispered.

There was too much noise, but he at least noticed her withering strength. Damos gasped and scooped her up. He didn't possess a fraction of Wikshen's strength, but he managed to stagger with her toward a darker side of the big space, muttering prayers to the One Creator to save her.

"No!" Dyii shouted over all the noise. He ran up behind Damos. If she could, Kalea would've warned Damos not to trust Dyii. "Not that way!" He'd lost his cool conversational attitude in favor of panic. "Oh, shit! I can barely hear it anymore!"

"Hear what?" Damos asked, and continued walking.

Dyii grabbed Damos's sleeve, but too late. Damos's foot slipped, and they fell through the hidden gap in the floor. The noise shifted to high above them, echoing indirectly now. They plummeted a long distance into a new cavern.

Wikshen endured the hot, popping energy of lightning swirling around his body, helpless to shake it off. It scorched his flesh deeply, hitting bone, grazing his heart, stopping it for a second or two. He found himself lying on the floor, sprawled randomly.

"Urgh…" he groaned. "Kah…"

He lifted his head weakly to check on her. She wasn't there! Instead, Metta danced in place, watching him but antsy to run for safety. He opened his mouth to tell her to do that, but a scouel swooped by and snatched her into its jaws. Wikshen roared in anger.

Although she'd received most of the lightning, Grella was already standing again. Wikshen roared her name, eager to get vengeance for her foul beast eating Metta up, but the scouel arrived by its mistress's side and dropped his girl, still alive, beside Grella's canopy.

"Well done, my love," Grella said to the scouel, and it proceeded to stand guard beside them.

Wikshen stood up, favoring his aching broken rib but already feeling the healing sensation in his burns. Vibrations under his feet hinted at a space below this level. Kalea must've fallen through one of the holes dotting the floor. But what about Metta? He stalled for a second.

Grella sang again, and her voice prompted the movement of vines at the back wall, which snaked forward to snag Metta.

Wikshen turned. *Kalea.* He knew which one he wanted. He clicked his throat to make the vibration which summoned Kraft Fire, and the blue flame ignited in the air to float and follow him. He darted backward to the openings in the floor.

Splash!

Kalea drifted from Damos's contact. She sank low, under a dense, black pool of cool water. She could find no more strength left to swim with. Time slowed enough to wonder if she'd drown first or fall to the poison. She'd become light, flying on the gently moving current of smooth, icy water filling her mouth, her ears, and probably her lungs.

Muffled sounds happened nearby. Splashing. Shouting. So far away. She sank lower, ceasing to care about anything. The sounds diminished to nothing. She drifted in peace.

A little nibble at her chest. Another. Tickling sensations. Fish were nipping at her poisoned scratch mark. It didn't hurt. Numerous fish joined in. They were eating her body, and she hadn't yet died. She couldn't count how many swam and nibbled at her collarbone.

The water around her warmed. Her limbs floated limply. She flew weightlessly. She'd reached a warm place of complete silence.

What will I do with you?

The humming voice brought her mind back to its thought processes. *What?*

If you don't stop getting yourself in such trouble, I'll be no more. The voice spoke loud and clear in her head. Concentrating on it, she forgot about the nipping fishes for the moment.

Who are you?

You still don't know? I've been with you all along, my girl, but you should be more careful. Here.

The water swirled and spun around her head, stirring her hair in its spiral pattern. Her lips parted, but water did not rush between them. Air did. The air filled her lungs. The fish continued to work at her scratch.

When her lungs were restored to normal comfort, a bubble settled around her mouth and nose. She began to move upward. The water itself carried her higher.

Am I dying?

A faint laugh with an inhuman echo responded. *Here,* the strange voice said. *Give this back to your friend.* She swore a hand brushed hers, but it was only the gentle force of the water. It pushed an object into her palm, and she gripped it tightly.

Her head broke the water. She coughed. The fish scattered.

"Kalea!"

A strong hand grabbed her clothing. Another swimmer. He pulled her through the water as she floated on her back, keeping the small object from the lake in her fist. She breathed in defiance of death yet again. No water in her lungs like she'd assumed.

"Boy! You there?" She knew that voice and its accent. Dyii?

"Where's Kalea? Did you find her?" Damos's voice.

Dyii switched to wading and dragged her closer to the bank until her rear end hit the rocky bottom. He lifted her by her armpits, and she found her footing. She walked from there. She could walk again. She trailed her fingers across her collarbone and found the scratch gone, only smooth, wet skin. Her energy returned by the second.

Stepping out of the water, Dyii took her by the shoulders. "You all right?"

She opened her fist and found a glinting ring with a big blue stone set in it. She turned to Damos. "Did you lose this in the lake?"

Damos's mouth dropped open at what she showed him. "Yes. How did you—"

"Don't ask," she replied, but cut her speech short to listen. No more echoing lightning. "Dorhen?" she said.

Dyii looked at Damos in confusion, and the younger man shrugged as he placed his ring back on his index finger.

The last she saw of Dorhen, he was thrashing on the floor with Dyii's lightning spell swirling over him. Remembering all of Dyii's treachery, she pushed away from him. "What happened?" she demanded.

"We got to leave this place," Dyii said.

Damos put his hand on Kalea's shoulder. "Let's go."

She jerked away from them both. "Not without Dorhen!"

A powerful male voice roared distantly through the cavern. A light plummeted down through the same gap where Kalea and Damos had fallen.

Kalea gasped. "It's him! He's alive!"

Wikshen dropped through the air with purpose, his battleshift flying up behind him, his hair too. He brought a Kraft flame with him. A horde of angry scouels followed, holding their great wings back for the dive.

Damos and Dyii each took one of her arms, squeezing tight. "Let's go!" they said in unison. They pulled her in two separate directions, realized what they were doing, and quickly agreed on one direction.

Kalea resisted. "Wait!"

"Wait for what?" Damos asked. "For all those monsters to eat us?"

"Wait for Dorhen."

In disagreement, they both reacted by pulling her anyway.

Wikshen stepped out of the subterranean lake and marched toward them. He'd taken mere seconds to swim through the water and meet them on the bank. His hair draped heavy and wet, slicked down to show more of his pointed ears than usual. The blue Kraft flame hovered over his shoulder as if it had a mind to follow him. It cast a wide, bright radius of light, revealing the damage of the lightning on his flesh. Hideous, black burn marks marbled all over him.

"Where are you going?" His voice hissed with menace. He might very well kill Dyii for releasing the lightning spell.

The scouels spilling through the ceiling rushed forward, splashing the water high. One last winged beast dropped through the hole and swooped into a glide before hitting the water. A luminous, naked woman rode on its back, contrasted against its black fur.

Wikshen lunged for Dyii and ripped Kalea from his hold. "You electrocuted me! You know how annoying that feeling is?"

Dyii froze in his hold. Kalea put her hands on Wikshen's arm.

"Dorhen, let's talk about it later!" She attempted to point to the glowing witch riding on the largest scouel, which padded toward them with a frothing mouth and bristling fur-feather combination.

Dyii landed on his backside when Wikshen shoved him away. Wikshen put himself between Kalea and the witch's beast and took his signature combat stance. With a powerful thrust at the air with his palm, the biggest blade she'd seen yet ripped out and shot between the scouel's eyes.

Its face split open, releasing steaming blood to mingle with the slobber from its mouth. Grella rode the beast's fall until it lay flat on the cave floor, dead. Behind them, a black wall of all the remaining scouels formed from the water. They waited for their mistress's order.

Feeling trapped, Kalea wrapped her arms around Wikshen's bicep, and he shook her off. "Don't crowd me."

Grella calmly stood up on the dead mountain of fur and feathers. "I'm disappointed."

"Yeah?" Wikshen replied. "In whom?"

"All of you. Dyii. Mastaren."

Wikshen shot a sidelong glance at the Thaccilian, who received it and distanced himself from the group a pace or two. Wikshen looked back at Grella. "I don't think you have the right to be disappointed in anyone.

Step down, Grella. You've overreached a hair too far."

Grella lowered her chin and sent him a demented glare.

"Look what you've done to yourself," he went on. "This isn't Wikshonism."

"I call it 'New Wikshonism,'" she said. "Imagine an empire of loyal followers"—she spread her arm to present the masked drones who waited on the sidelines—"with a figurehead, the First Sister, who speaks to God for all of the faithful." She pointed to Wikshen at the mention of a god.

Kalea's nausea reared up again to think of Dorhen in that role, a pettygod and a tool to be used by this…witch! And Kalea herself was as bad as any of them. She had drunk from Wikshen's fountain shrines, recited his prayers, and performed his Kraft Positions faithfully every morning.

Wikshen snorted, turned slightly, and worked his neck muscles. His eyes moved briefly across Kalea's. "New Wikshonism," he parroted, and coughed a laugh. "I don't see how—ha!"

Faster than anyone could anticipate, he flourished his arms and whipped his palm forward, throwing a morkblade out to surprise Grella. It shot out in the blink of an eye, spinning with many hooks and sharp edges. It passed through her.

She didn't fall. She kept still and solemn with her gaze trained on Wikshen, who now stood dumbfounded with his hands and feet in their ready positions.

"What just happened?" he asked.

Grella's lips curled and her eyes narrowed. One eyebrow crooked. "You can't cut me in this form, Mastaren."

Wikshen hissed out a breath. "Sorcery…"

The scouels edged in closer. Their humid air enveloped them, assaulting Kalea's nose and lungs. Grella walked forward along her dead scouel's back to its cleanly sliced head.

Wikshen whipped his hand out again, quicker and with less flourish. A smaller morkblade flew from his hand and passed through Grella, who was present only as an illusion.

"You're wasting your minerals, Mastaren." She raised her chin. "I suggest you accompany me back upstairs. My body is up there, clinging to life. You can still bless it."

Wikshen threw his hands around Kalea's waist, lifted her, and bolted. He shoved past Damos and Dyii, leaving them to the swarm of scouels. The blue light he'd brought died, leaving Kalea helpless to see any more of the goings-on or where Wikshen carried her. Only the sounds remained: growls and barks; heavy, clawed feet stomping the ground; and huge, leathery wings snapping.

Voices, muffled behind metal masks, yelled, and Wikshen growled back at them as if more animal than elf. Their adamant calls turned to gasps and whimpers when Wikshen lashed out with his free arm. Banging sounds. Pained grunting from Wikshen and screaming from other men.

Wikshen moved forward, up an inclined path. The space narrowed around them. By the shorter echoes, Kalea could tell they'd entered an upward-sloping tunnel she associated with a stairwell. Masked voices echoed behind and above them. Kalea hung helplessly, draped over his shoulder as Wikshen thrashed with his other arm, fighting off anyone who got too close.

He suddenly stopped with a jolt and roar, and put her down. Kalea balanced herself, bracing her arms against either side of the tunnel. "What's wrong?" she asked.

Wikshen's large form in the small space blocked their pursuers from harming her. "Run up!" he ordered. "Go!"

"I can't see a thing!" she countered, and he grunted back. Through all his work, he never became winded, but dispensed frequent sounds of pain. She couldn't tell if he was injured or if his burn marks still hurt.

One of Grella's drones came, carrying a light that revealed the space with each step he took toward them. Though it helped Kalea get her bearings, the lantern he brought made Wikshen wince and recoil. His grunts of annoyance intensified as he pummeled the men back with his fists. The dazed drones up front helped to bar the unhurt ones behind them.

"Get ready to run," Wikshen warned her.

He braced both arms on the walls as she did, but added an army of strength to his hold. The effort made him scream in pain, piercing her ears in the tight space, but he persisted anyway, reared a foot, and slammed it into the next fresh victim standing behind a knocked-out one. Kalea shuddered away from his violence as several more meaty kicks followed before he was satisfied and snatched her up again.

"Gyahhh!" Kalea bellowed, unaware he'd do that.

He carried her farther up the tunnel, leaving the lantern light behind, but it wasn't a long distance before the small space opened up at the top of the slope, revealing more blue and green light. They'd returned to the big mushroom cavern where she had fallen through the hole in the floor.

Kalea checked the tunnel behind her, praying Damos fared well down there against the specter-witch and her scouels. Silhouetted by the lighting, enormous winged beasts paced.

"Mastaren!"

"Metta!" Metta was the only person who hadn't plummeted into the lake.

Wikshen put Kalea back on her feet. "Hide," he ordered, and then charged forward to brave the scouels and rescue Metta.

Instead, Kalea picked up the nearest Kraft flame lantern and paced about the outer stretches of the cavern toward the tent-lounge. The scouels in here dwarfed the ones which had dived into the lake; their features were more mature, with bigger feathers and manes around their necks and red horns sprouting from some of their heads like majestic—albeit infernal—lions from Kullixaxuss. Kalea tensed up, her teeth chattering to have to gawk at the scene of Wikshen engaging these monsters. He strutted as if he were bigger and mightier than they.

Kalea tore her eyes away from the spectacle and used her lantern to scan the floor for more pitfalls. Several holes gaped in the shadowy areas on either side of the lit central pathway, sometimes looking like knotwork art. No longer dealing with the dizziness of the poison, Kalea picked her way tediously along the narrow trails. The good thing about this area was that the scouels avoided it like any sane being would.

At the grand center of this hall, Metta stood tied to a stone column supporting the tent of sheer, black silk. Kalea could make out the girl's shape and pale face behind the fabric.

"Metta!" Kalea's call snapped her attention from Wikshen's vigorous fight.

Once she cleared the network of pitfalls, Kalea ran forward. Metta was bound so tight, she couldn't move at all. Grella wanted to use her as bait to lure Wikshen back to this lounge.

Behind them, Wikshen's angry yells of struggle drew their stares. Arm over arm, he climbed up the fur of the biggest monster, which sported the grandest horns, and put a fist through its eye.

The thing roared and thrashed, shaking him off. Wikshen flew through the air and rolled across the stone floor to land precariously with his rear end dipped into one of the side pitfalls; his legs and one arm kept him from falling back into the underground lake.

As he worked to get his second arm aboveground, Damos's voice called shrilly from below, "*Keelinga!*" and a crash of lightning ripped through the air, shaking the earth with little wires of lightning that branched up through the holes to light up the entire floor at their level. He could now cast the spell thanks to Kalea returning his mage's ring.

The lightning helped Wikshen find all the motivation he needed to scramble out of his entrapment and roll away from the blazing wires, which chased him for several feet. He roared and rubbed the new swirling burn marks on his arm. His original ones were already fading due to his preternatural healing process.

He couldn't take a break to nurse his injuries, though. The scouels moved in, several at once, snapping their massive jaws at him. As big as he was in this transformed state, they could easily snap him up like a biscuit.

Kalea turned back to Metta and tapped her hips and belt. "I need a knife to cut your…"

On second glance, Metta was held against the pole by the newer ends of vines, which trailed back to a huge tangle from the wall. From here, the mushrooms looked as wide and tall as castle towers, and their colored light cast a beautiful glow on the curtain fabrics and Metta's face.

Metta worked her wrists against the plants. "It's a mere plant, though a magic one. Maybe I can…"

Kalea darted her attention around at all the happenings. Wikshen continued to work furiously at keeping the scouels away from their position, sprinting and rolling, leaping and climbing. He hadn't killed any with a morkblade since reentering this place—maybe he couldn't for some reason. Kalea recalled him placing his hands in the blood pools. He must not have enough minerals to perform the spell again.

She turned back to Metta to see if she could untangle her wrists, and something else pulled her gaze away. At the center of the veiled space, beside a tray of sweets she knew must be more of the aphrodisiacs Wikshen had eaten earlier, sat a mummy. White hair trailed down the dry, burnt-looking skin, framing a meditative expression. Supported by more of those clingy vines, it sat cross-legged with eyes closed, mouth wide open.

Kalea's hand pointed of its own will, and she stuttered, "Wh-what's that?"

Metta briefly checked what she meant and returned to fidgeting against the wicked flora. "That's Grella," she said.

"But Grella was…" She paused and pictured what they'd left on the lower level, the ghost-like woman standing proudly on a dead scouel, Wikshen's blade flying through her without effect.

"That lightning spell did her in pretty bad, so as a last resort, she projected an image of herself to go and entice Wikshen," Metta said as Kalea's mind skirted around a similar theory. "She wants Wikshen to produce a sampling of his blessing and drop it into her mouth. She's not quite dead yet, despite how she looks."

Layered waves of sharp hot and cold chills ran all over Kalea.

"Grella doesn't care who helps him to ejaculate: me or you," Metta continued. "She's desperate to keep alive at this point." Metta perused all the scouels flapping and leaping about as Wikshen ran, fighting and dodging them while masked drones arrived to join the struggle. "If we let it happen, things will be very bad."

Kalea leaped to helping Metta get free. "I wish I had a knife," she muttered. Her heart raced.

She checked behind her to see Wikshen falling off another scouel's fur. He landed on his back for the second time today and lay there wheezing. The scouels swarmed around him. Kalea gasped and lurched back toward the tent's exit.

"No-no-no-no!" Metta said. "Get me out of here! Grella won't let him be destroyed! Hurry!"

Kalea minded her. After a few frantic seconds of trying to make her violently trembling hands function and peel vines off Metta's wrists, a bigger hand landed on her shoulder. Kalea screamed and thrashed.

"Whoa, sorry! Calm, please!" Dyii threw his hands up and stood back.

"What do you want?" Kalea cried in fright, but she couldn't dwell on Dyii's threat with three scouels galloping toward them. "Do you have a knife?" she asked him. "Oh wait, of course you do! I saw you try to kill Metta!"

She stepped in front of her friend, but Dyii bypassed her and went straight for Grella's mummified body. Among the scouels, the wraith-form of the witch approached.

"Noooooooo!" Its screamed word felt like a stab to Kalea's ears. Throughout the sound, it shapeshifted into a pale beast-like form, perhaps the white version of a scouel.

Not even thinking, Kalea left Metta and leaped to the front of the tent. Dyii seemed to know what he was doing, so she'd make sure he wasn't distracted. Instead, she'd distract Grella, who was just a wraith. Or was she?

The white, winged, dog-like creature, smaller and sleeker than the other scouels, put its four legs on the floor and its razor-sharp toenails clicked against the stone. It was solid, and Kalea had made her choice. No time to recoil!

The feminine scouel opened her jaws and poised to snap Kalea's head off on first contact. Kalea winced and closed her eyes. Metta shrieked in dread. Dyii paused with a gasp.

A freezing vapor enveloped Kalea. She opened her eyes to see a wintery white mist split and drift in two different directions—no more scouel. Wikshen stood several yards behind it with his arm extended, palm pointed at her. One side of the tent fell down because he'd thrown a morkblade that had narrowly missed her but managed to dissipate Grella's scouel form.

They weren't safe yet, though. The two waves of mist re-formed into twenty or so child-like wisps, shrieking and running toward Dyii, who shut it all out again and grabbed Grella's browned corpse. He drew his knife; the motion caused him to drop a small drawstring bag by accident.

Paying no mind, Dyii carved the mummy's chest open between the two hanging flaps of skin that were once her breasts. Inside the leathery case, he pried open her brittle ribs to find a red, moist, beating heart. He cut it out, pulling it away from its severed arteries, stretching and snapping other little fastenings with his free hand. Its beating continued in his hand, but Kalea couldn't tell how long it lasted because Dyii fit his mouth around half the thing and bit down. He turned away from her and worked on consuming it completely.

Grella's crowd of wraith children exploded into a puff of shimmery vapor, but not before letting out one more eerie choir wail. When her amazement at the ghostly illusions wore off, Kalea remembered the pouch Dyii had dropped and picked it up for him.

The scouels all stopped moving, including the one who sniffed around the tent. As one, they shriveled and shrank smaller and smaller, until each one was naught but a man in a black metal mask. One or two fell over in exhaustion, clanking their headgear on the floor. Others fell bleeding with a limb or two missing—Wikshen had been using his morkblades after all.

Now he lay sprawled among them, his rib cage rising and falling heavily, finally winded after all he'd done. Leaving Dyii and Metta together, Kalea sprinted over and fell to her knees by Wikshen's side. He stared up at the ceiling, which was hidden beyond a long, dark distance.

"Dorhen," Kalea said softly. His eyes turned to her. Regardless of all his denial of his name, he still answered to it, maybe in capitulation.

"Little brunette witch," he said as a long groan. "I'm broken."

She couldn't help but smile. "You're not."

He sat up and paused to growl loudly. "It's my rib." He lay back down. "It broke the first time I fell. Hasn't fused back together." He closed his eyes and breathed. "I'll have to remember the Kraft spell for blocking pain…"

She put her hands on his arm. "Try to get up. The masked drones are beginning to rise." For now, they stumbled around incoherently, no longer with a queen to direct them.

One of the drones lying on the ground caught her attention. "Oh, my—! Dear Creator!" She left Wikshen on the ground to sprint to a man lying sprawled and gasping loudly under his metal mask. She dropped to her knees beside him. "Bowaen? How did you get here?"

Behind her, Wikshen managed to sit up, making pained sounds all the way. Bowaen failed to rise, instead grasping his left arm and lying back down, clammy all over.

"Kalea," he murmured through his mask, "my heart." Bowaen had not only been recruited as a drone, he'd also been transformed into a scouel!

"He's not well!" Kalea shouted, turning around to find Wikshen standing over her. Bowaen's eyes widened at him. She grabbed his battleshift. "Help him! Please!"

Wikshen crossed his arms, showing the same coldness he'd shown for Damos.

"He's dying!"

Meanwhile, Bowaen was trying to murmur something behind his mask, only making breathy ocean sounds.

"Bowaen?" she said again. "Dear Creator, I can't believe this happened to you!"

"I can't breathe in this," he managed to say. Surveying the scene of all the dizzy masked men, some lying dead in pools of blood, she realized Bowaen might not be better off than the others who had transformed into scouels and fought Wikshen. By sheer luck, he hadn't gotten any appendages cut off by a morkblade.

"What happened?" she asked Bowaen. "How did you get like this?"

Bowaen tried to talk, slurring in the country dialect Kalea struggled to decipher, until Wikshen reached down to put his hand over Bowaen's face.

"Take that stupid mask off!" he said, and just as fast, the metal disintegrated at his touch.

Bowaen relaxed back to the ground, finally free to suck in air unhindered but still grasping his arm. "We all got caught," Bowaen tried to explain between long breaths.

"Where's Gaije and Del?"

"Somewhere not far..." He panted some more.

In sympathy and sheer concern, Kalea reached for his forehead, but Wikshen snatched her hand away and retained her wrist. She thrashed him off and stood up in time to find Damos running toward them with a torch.

At the sight of fire, Wikshen closed the gap Kalea had made between them. Damos approached with a vengeance and waved the torch at him furiously.

"You got a death wish?" Wikshen roared with a nimble prance

backward.

"Damos!" Kalea said. She put her hand on his shoulder to halt his torch waving. "Bowaen isn't good right now. I think he's having a heart attack!" She'd been trying to keep calm all this time, but now her voice came out shaky and shrill.

"A heart attack?" He handed her the torch and knelt beside Bowaen. Just as fast, Wikshen was beside Kalea, prying the torch out of her hold and throwing it far across the cavern to fall through one of the pitfalls.

"Why'd you do that?" she scolded him, but he didn't answer. They still had enough light from the remaining Kraft flames to see by.

"Bowaen," Damos said, "hold up your finger like this." He demonstrated with his index finger.

Letting his left arm go, Bowaen mimicked him, and Damos touched his fingertip to Bowaen's. He took a deep breath, and then murmured a foreign word, similar to "keelinga" but shorter, and a quick snap of light lit them both up. Damos pulled his finger away fast enough to create an arched wire between them before it expired. The shock startled Wikshen enough to step back with a grimace.

After his understandable jump at being shocked, Bowaen relaxed and rubbed both hands down his face before attempting to sit up. Kalea chewed her thumbnail.

"How's your arm now?" Damos asked.

Bowaen sat up easily and flexed it. "Fine," he said with a note of surprise. "You fixed me. How'd you do it?"

Damos smiled. "Just a trick we have at Wistara. How do you think all those mages get so old? If it's minor enough, they found that they can cure each other's heart attacks with the right shock spell—using just enough electricity."

Bowaen made one more move to wipe his temple along his sleeve and finally stood up, cautiously at first. "You mages are smart people. It's good to have a mage with us, isn't it?"

Damos crossed his arms under his smile. He turned his head to share it with Kalea, but with Wikshen looming behind her, his lightheartedness died instantly and he started walking away. "We'd better get back to the surface," he said.

Against Wikshen's agitation, Kalea helped Bowaen to rise. "Are you all right?"

"Fine now, I think," he said. "Wouldn't be the first time my heart's acted funny."

"What?" she shrieked. "Why didn't you tell us?"

"Forget about it." He nodded toward the cavern's wall with all its tunnel openings. "Del and Gaije got masks on too. They shouldn't be far. They didn't…" He shuddered. "I don't think they changed like me. That witch…" He didn't look Kalea and Wikshen squarely in the face. He crossed his arms to rub his biceps. "She took control over our bodies like… I don't know how to say it."

"And she wanted the same manner of control over mine," Wikshen said.

Dyii and Metta approached from the tent, and Wikshen snatched Dyii by his shirt and spat in his face. "And now you can die for electrocuting me!"

Kalea wrapped her arms around Wikshen's waist. "No, Dorhen! Listen. Dyii killed Grella." She chose not to tell him about seeing Dyii try to kill Metta.

Giving the Thaccilian a hot glare, Wikshen smirked. "The heart-eater saved the day, huh? How did her heart taste?" He pointed to the bloody ring around Dyii's mouth.

Dyii took his threat in stride, flashing his own smile back up at the intimidating enigma. "Rotten. And Dyii couldn't have done such if Mastaren hadn't held back vicious beast-creatures."

"Don't bullshit me, Ilbith rat." He released Dyii, and the Thaccilian straightened his clothing rather than run away.

"I kill Grella, I save two girls—*your* girls."

"So I'll let you live for today," Wikshen replied, "but I never want to see you again. Anywhere." Wikshen crooked his fingers and snapped every joint in them independently.

Bowaen stretched his neck and pointed. "There they are."

Gaije and Del came running to join the group. None of the masked drones offered any more threat. They mostly kept their distance from Wikshen, and Gaije and Del acted no different. Kalea waved her hand to encourage their approach.

"Dorhen, take their masks off too."

"I got better things to do than pamper all these smelly men," he said. Nonetheless, he performed Kalea's request. Afterward, when he noticed Dyii lingering, he barked, "Leave!" and the Thaccilian turned.

"Dyii, wait," Kalea said. She held out the little drawstring bag he'd dropped. "This fell off your belt."

He smiled at her, took the bag, and sprinted into the shadows.

Wikshen took Kalea's arm and pressed his hard fingers in deep. "Let's go."

Dyii didn't leave the cave immediately. Long after everyone else cleared from the area, he returned to the tent in the light of the dying Kraft Fire where he'd eaten Grella's heart. The dead mummy husk lay where he'd left it, dried into its sitting pose but toppled over, chest cavity agape and void of the heart that had struggled to keep the witch alive until he put an end to it. He rubbed his stomach. It really wasn't the best meal he'd eaten, but it did offer him the energy he needed to carry on.

He took the rough sack from his belt, which he'd gone to the lower levels to find. Groaning and heaving, he did his best to shove the sack over the mummy. If the circumstances were any different, he would not have eaten her foul heart. He would've taken the little black-haired girl's heart, or any of those belonging to the drone men who ran about the corridors, frantically looking for a way out.

He tied the bag closed, glad to cover the thing up, wiped his face on his sleeve, and loosened the little drawstring bag Kalea had been nice enough to find for him. From it, he removed the whisper stone granted to him by the kingsorcerer.

"Is Dyii," he whispered over the stone. "I saw Wikshen in Hathrohskog. The witch is no more, so best to come get the rest of the forlustweed. Also, I got something you might find interesting."

Chapter 37
Painful Confession

Weeping into the carved hole in Orinleah's door, Vivene expressed every detail of the sorcerers' ritual and the sacrifice of Rose. Somehow, she'd made it back up to the Chimera Tower and resumed her duties, most importantly delivering Orinleah's meal. The warm-voiced elf-woman was the only person she could turn to—the only person to whom she wanted to express her woes since the other novices were so busy in their own harsh existences. Orinleah had all day in there to listen.

"A large black cloud?" Orinleah said after Vivene had spilled her words through the food slot.

Vivene nodded even though they didn't hold any eye contact. "It shook the whole cavern!" she reported. "I don't understand why you didn't feel it. But Rose..."

"I am sorry for your friend," Orinleah murmured.

"She didn't deserve such a wicked fate," Vivene said with a sniffle. "I mean, she was dumb, sure, but..."

"No one deserves such a fate," Orinleah replied.

"That kingsorcerer..." Vivene went on. "There's something very wrong about him..."

Orinleah kept silent in Vivene's pause for such a long moment that she bobbed her head to check if she was still there. Orinleah's shoulder was in the frame as she sat on the floor at the other side of the door. The silence chilled Vivene's bones for some reason.

The elf finally spoke. "Yes." The movement of her long ribbons of brown hair over her shoulder suggested she dipped her head. "He has committed crimes beyond those my people could ponder. He is an abomination of what we would consider *saehgahn*."

Sniffling and wiping her nose on her apron, Vivene leaned over to try to get a rare view of Orinleah's face—unsuccessfully. "You know what's awful?" Vivene said. Orinleah obviously waited for her to continue, but Vivene couldn't hasten her words. She didn't have to continue—she knew that, but she couldn't resist unloading her thoughts. "I..." She swallowed. "I think the Ilbith life is getting to me."

Orinleah kept silent. Vivene guessed she might ask what she meant or maybe shun her, but nothing came. Her shoulder and hair stayed motionless to complement her silence.

"I've been growing apart from the Sanctity of Creation."

"Is that your faith?" Orinleah asked.

"Yeah. I did more than lose interest in the institution, I drifted away from it, even when I lived there. Now… Now I feel estranged from the God we worshipped back at the convent."

Orinleah hummed, which wasn't enough to clue Vivene in on whether she understood or not.

"Seeing Rose get shot," Vivene said. "What a horrifying thing. It'll haunt me forever, I think. But there's more to it. Now, with her gone… It's like I can see how far I, too, have gone. I might be going in a direction like the kingsorcerer. Maybe such sights won't bother me soon."

Silence.

Vivene spoke again. "I've been enjoying what the sorcerers do to me. Certain ones, particularly. Others are too rough or mean." She tightened her fists, waiting again for a response. "I haven't confessed my sins since I arrived here." With a cringe, she added, "I've given my body to other servants as well. I seek out this form of sinful contact because it's better than the beatings and harsh words." In her tension, nausea churned her stomach. "The problem is, it's all meaningless, yet I desire it."

Uncomfortable in the following silence, Vivene peeked through the slot again, disappointed at what little reaction the other woman gave. She'd come up here to tell her all these things to get comfort, and she expected a bit more than this. Vivene's neck tensed up tighter than before. She didn't expect advice from Orinleah; maybe sympathy would've been enough. Perhaps a hum in reply to indicate she listened.

"Vivene."

"Yes?"

Barely audibly, Orinleah released a long breath. "Remember when I asked you to bring me a piece of chalk, and you brought it?"

"Yeah."

"There's another thing I need you to bring me…"

"What is it this time?" Mhina asked Lamrhath as he stood beaming over a basket with a huge red bow for her.

"Open it and find out."

"What if I don't want any more presents?"

"That's fine. You can throw it down the jakes if you don't like it— which will make me very sad, and I'll have to order a beating for your friend Bairhen."

Pursing her lips, she lifted the woven lid and found a little white kitten with a pink nose within. It mewed at her as soon as it saw her. Her mouth and eyes rounded, and she lifted the little creature out. Lamrhath waited, so far satisfied but watching her for further impression.

She didn't offer a "thank you," but he didn't mind at this time. Their relationship was still new and difficult.

"What are you staring at?" she asked, cradling the kitten in her arms like a babe.

"Just waiting to find out the fate of this innocent animal."

She scoffed. "I won't throw her down the jakes."

He smiled and raised his hands. "Just making sure. I'll leave you, then. You're welcome." She offered no response on his way out.

Back in Lamrhath's office, Talekas smiled and raised one of the whisper stones from its place in the padded, compartmented box. "We have a new lead. Wikshen's in Hathrohskog now. Word came in from our very own Dyii. He says the monster is headed back toward Alkeer."

"Send a message to Kilka about it."

"Already done, my lord."

Lamrhath gave him a smirk, the friendliest gesture he tended to offer his associates. "You've not missed a beat since getting out of the hole."

He smirked back and shrugged. "No hard feelings here, my lord. I'm too busy anyway." Talekas gestured with a rolled paper before resting it on his shoulder like a club. "Dyii is sending us something interesting, although I don't know what yet."

"Any word from the sanguinesents?"

"None yet. We're sending them out in shifts so as not to put the whole of the Darklands into a stir. And we don't want the other factions to see them yet. The next location will be Alkeer since we know Wikshen will soon be there."

Chapter 38
A Window Gapes

"Dorhen," Kalea whispered as she tiptoed along the rocky terrain with the acidic mud between each stepping stone. His presence radiated all around. No matter how far they trekked through Hathrohskog, he stayed with them, even though she hadn't seen much of him after exiting the caves. Metta sensed him too. He kept to the darkest shadows, watching over them.

He didn't answer her call.

"Kalea," Metta called softly.

Despite Wikshen's reassuring presence, Kalea dared not venture too far away from the group. She gave up on him—again—and retreated back to the campfire, where Bowaen held everyone's attention. "And then there was this serene nothingness. I guess I slept through it. When I woke up, I was definitely human again."

"Sounds like the witch was switching your presence on this plane with that of a scouel in another world." Damos shook his bandaged head. "It takes an enormous amount of power to accomplish a spell so grand and with so many beings, much grander than what happens with Azrielle. Makes me shiver to try to comprehend the dire situation we escaped." Damos's eerie feeling seemed to spread to everyone else.

"Damos," Bowaen said in a new tone. "Come here, let's see your damage."

Damos edged closer on their log seat and Bowaen carefully unwrapped the bandages from around his head. Damos winced every few seconds, and Bowaen mirrored him in empathy.

"You said you knew all about washing," Metta said to Kalea when she settled down on a rock to watch Bowaen and Damos. Kalea nodded her confirmation. "Well, Damos is going to need his bandages cleaned."

Kalea looked around her. "Um…" They didn't have enough water in their supply, and even if she found a lake, she couldn't promise her prayer could purify its water again. "I don't think there's much I can do. We'll be better off when we get to Alkeer," she said.

Del unwound the old bandage from around his wrist, his pipe putting off smoke beside him, and worked his wrist. It appeared to have healed well so far.

"Del," Kalea said, and he looked up to shoot her an impatient stare. "Did you know about Bowaen's weak heart?"

"Tch, no," he said, and then turned to make himself busy, rummaging through his and Bowaen's travel bags.

Gaije paced at the far side of the camp, chewing his thumb. They had retrieved his "blue-haired sorcerer," but still lacked any vital information needed to locate Mhina, plus they'd lost more time underground.

That was yet another reason why Kalea sought a moment alone with Wikshen: she'd ask *him*, since Dorhen couldn't provide an answer. Even as she sat there, wincing along with Damos's pain, she felt Wikshen's presence. Behind her. Beside her. Anywhere near a dense shadow.

Across the way, closer to the fire than her seat, Bowaen peeled the last damp cloth away from Damos's sticky, raw skin. He must've lain submerged below Hathrohskog's soil for a long time. Maybe Wikshen's distance did her party good. She and Metta were the only two in the group who didn't despise him. Her eyes trailed over to Metta, who sat in attendance to Damos's care. Metta's gaze roved over the shadowy forest more than once.

Now free of the bandages, Damos kept his face turned away from Kalea. Bowaen inspected him closely. "Gotta say, I expected worse," he said. "No infection. We should get back to town as fast as we can anyway. We'll get some salve, or at least some brandy to clean you up with. You'll be good as new, my boy."

Damos said nothing, only shrugged and crossed his arms. His feathery platinum hair helped to obscure Kalea's view of his wounds.

Bowaen stood up and waved his arm wide. "For now, we'll let your face have a night o' fresh air. Let's all get some sleep." He shot his own wary glare over their dark surroundings. "Best we make up our beds close together."

Kalea sniffed at his statement. The spell of terror Wikshen held over them had expired for her. If anything, she wanted him to rejoin them for the night.

Kalea awoke from her shallow sleep to someone nudging her arm. "Dorhen?" she groaned. She could only hope it was him. Her next guess was Damos. Maybe he wanted to try to reestablish their union, and she'd have to turn him down gently.

"It's me," Metta whispered.

Kalea rubbed her eyes and half-sat up. Everyone else slept soundly, and their fire had died down to embers. "What is it?" Kalea asked.

"C'mon." Metta put both hands around Kalea's upper arm and pulled.

"Time for midnight devotion."

Midnight devotion. Kalea played those words on her lips. Now, how could she excuse herself from this one? Of course…participation might mean seeing Dorhen, and she'd take any opportunity to do that. Also, it had been a little while since her routine at Wikhaihli was broken, and those meditative practices were nice, she had to admit. Would it be so bad if she did a little pose or two tonight?

"The maids practice devotion, right?" Metta asked.

"In a way," Kalea whispered. "We visit the fountain shrine and pray at the bell chimes, and…" She swallowed. "Knilma taught me some Kraft Positions."

"Good," Metta whispered.

When they'd moved a good distance away from everyone else, Kalea raised her voice closer to normal volume. "It's dark out here. Aren't you worried Dyii is lurking around? I mean, he tried to kill you."

"Of course, I'm not worried. Not with the Mastaren around."

Kalea swallowed. "Will the…Mastaren be at the devotion?" By slow progress, calling him by that title felt more natural.

"If he wishes." Metta used a mysterious tone similar to how the shamans spoke about Wikshen, and a chill ran over Kalea's arms and legs. It was easy to assume Metta experienced the same feelings.

"Metta…" Kalea said again. "We haven't really talked lately."

Metta remained silent, at least for now.

"I don't understand why it happened to me."

"Why what happened to you?"

"I think you know," Kalea said. "The ecstasies. I didn't tell anyone about it because the whole thing felt frightening…and embarrassing."

Metta stopped walking, and Kalea only knew that because she bumped into her shoulder. As dark as it was, Metta seemed to know where they were headed, and even how to avoid the denser patches of acidic mud.

"Don't ever be embarrassed about such a miracle." A sternness, or rather a seriousness, rang in her voice: sincerity. Metta's hand found her shoulder and squeezed. "It's a beautiful blessing. Almost as good as *the* blessing."

Metta slid her hand down to Kalea's hand, took it, and guided her forward. They walked hand in hand for the rest of the journey. "I must confess, I got jealous on an occasion or two, but there's no reason to be."

"Why not?"

She stopped again. "Because I experienced it too."

"Y-you…you did?" Kalea swallowed.

"Yes." The other young woman's voice hissed out quickly. "It was… I can't describe it… It was delirious and wonderful and wicked all in one or two seconds, but it left me with a deep longing."

Kalea's chill turned to a nauseous shudder at her words.

"The only other girl to get one was Brielle. Brielle's was more intense than mine, and yours was more intense than Brielle's." She squeezed Kalea's hand. "If you get to be the First…that would be much better."

"Why Brielle?" Kalea didn't realize she'd muttered it aloud.

"We've no right to question the Mastaren's delight." Another sickening choice of words that resonated until they stopped walking. "This is a good place."

Kalea might've questioned why this location, but the soft blanket of moss under her shoes rather than the usual squishy mud answered her first. "What are we doing?" she asked.

"Take off your clothes," Metta whispered, though she didn't have to.

"All of them?"

Metta hummed. "Probably leave your braies on. Are you wearing the tied kind?"

She meant the Wikhaihli standard braies. "Yes."

"Take them off, leave 'em on—it's up to you, really."

Kalea began undressing, all the while listening to Metta's rustling sounds. She tried to gauge what Metta did with her undergarments. Once she'd gotten all the way down to them, Kalea tossed them aside and made herself totally naked. It would be better if she could go a point further than her present competition.

"Now what?"

"Now we take the starting pose," Metta said. "Do you know it?"

"Of course." Kalea planted her feet upon the soft mattress of moss beneath her and spread her arms. The many tiny moss leaves settled between her toes, cool and soft. She could tell Metta took the same pose when their fingertips touched for a brief instant.

"Keep this pose for a while."

They did, and some amount of time passed. Kalea was pleased to find that her old leg wound went unnoticed throughout. Her damaged muscle must've gotten used to working again thanks to the gradual training in Kraft Positions. Her fatigue didn't come too soon either. She let her mind go blank, like a new form of restfulness outside of sleep. Her breathing steadied and slowed, and she relaxed. Her limbs held strong.

"And now rest," Metta said through a breath, and the two of them dropped to the cool ground. "Normally, we'd be doing this to a drum beat or a bell chime," Metta said.

Her voice rang from the dense darkness before Kalea's face. The forest seemed darker than before. Kalea laid her head upon the moss and stared upward at nothing.

"Is *he* nearby?"

Metta didn't ask who. "Of course he is. He never left us." She had fallen the opposite way, and their heads aligned on the ground.

Kalea closed her eyes and breathed. She reached her arms up high and held them there. She smiled. A little sliver of air slid up her arms and down her body. If he lurked around, could he see her?

"Did Knilma teach you any dances?"

"Dances?"

"Stay lying on the ground and arch your back like an ocean wave. Use your stomach muscles."

Kalea tried it. "She did teach me something similar, except while standing or kneeling."

"Imagine a ball rolling beneath you, from your shoulders to your pelvis," Metta said. "It's hard, but keep doing it." She made a little laugh. "In the morning, your whole front will be burning. It'll tone you up good." Her voice became breathy with her own motions.

Kalea focused on the exercise, lifting up on her neck and rolling her body as Metta described, raising her bottom last before setting it down. It *was* difficult, but she applied the same meditative mindset and quickly fell into a trance. Her breathing became as steady as her motion. She rolled her bare stomach high. Metta's breath became as loud and steady as hers. Kalea fell into the long rhythms of worship and hardly noticed.

"Kalea."

The call came watery and vague. She dismissed it as a mere dream. A delirious glee met her in the morning light. She smiled and stretched.

"Kalea!" Someone called her name.

She yawned. A small distance away, Metta slept tucked under her cloak.

A deep voice resonated beside her. "I heard a naughty little maid was playing in the forest last night."

She turned over to find Wikshen sitting cross-legged beside her. "Dorhen," she said, and smiled. "You're here."

She propped herself up on an elbow, and a glance down revealed her bare body. Wikshen smiled warmly as he watched her tuck her cloak around herself. The scorch marks all over his face and body from yesterday had vanished. "What happened last night?"

His smile stretched beyond his canine teeth. "You're asking me? I can't speak for you or her, but I've been resting for my strength." He leaned closer, practically hovering over her. "But I think I had a religious experience."

"Kah-lea!" The call of her name echoed again, and Wikshen perused their surroundings.

"You'd better get back before they think I did something to you."

Kalea sat up straighter, keenly aware of her naked back exposed to the cold air and anyone who might see it. The dampness all over her didn't mix well with the chilly morning breeze.

"Are you coming too, Dorhen?"

A blankness in his eyes overlapped his amused smile. She'd continue to call him "Dorhen" whether he liked it or not. "I'm coming," he said. "I'll see you in Alkeer."

"What do you mean?"

He shrugged and worked his way to his knees, where he reached over and grabbed the other garments she'd shed last night. "Not a good idea for me to walk into Alkeer right through the gate. I'll take the underground catacombs."

"So when and where will I see you?"

"I'll send for you."

Holding her cloak tight around herself, she dragged her voice out. "I don't like going anywhere without you."

Bowaen's voice barked her name again, ever closer.

Wikshen raised his chin and kept silent throughout the resonance. "You don't seem to mind the difficulty your friends have with me."

"*You're* the reason I'm here. In the Darklands."

He snorted. "Your fanatic Wikshonism flatters me, my dear."

Kalea wrinkled her nose. "My...fanatic Wikshonism?"

He spread his smile again, over his many big white teeth and into his handsome sculpted cheeks. "If you insist on worshipping me, then go to Alkeer, little maid. Take the concubine with you. We'll see what you can do for me."

Kalea stood up to face and argue with him before he could vanish again, but Bowaen's voice sounded louder. She'd have to dress quickly before he saw her, yet for some reason an odd presence of modesty stopped her from dropping her covering in front of Wikshen this morning. "Why are we going to Alkeer? Why are *you* going?"

He stood smiling at her, patient enough to let her get her question out. "I thought your friends wanted to find some sorcerers."

"Don't you know where Ilbith is?"

He spread his hands. "I wouldn't care if I did. I have an issue I need resolved, so I'm going to Alkeer."

She opened her mouth to ask another question, but he cut her off with a finger pointing to where Bowaen would walk through and find her in the next few seconds. Then he sprinted the opposite way.

"Kalea?" Bowaen entered her little mossy glade and halted with a short step backward to gawk. Down at her side, Metta finally stirred, offering a groggy sigh. "What the hell are you doin'?"

Kalea regarded herself and Metta, both naked beneath their cloaks.

"Um," Kalea began, "Metta and I... We just came out here...last night..."

Bowaen's mouth gaped below a set of eyes that lacked the luster they should normally have. "It's Wikshen," he answered for her. His arms hung limp at his sides after he'd held them ready to unsheathe Hathrohjilh. "You've been out here worshipping him...like a damn witch."

Kalea winced, not because of the words, but because of his disappointed tone. She stuttered for a better explanation than his, but couldn't find one. She *had* been worshipping Wikshen.

He spread his hands. "It's not my place to care what you do with your life. I thought you were different. A religious woman. I'm surprised, is all."

Holding her cloak firmly around her bosom, she stepped forward. "I *love* the Creator."

Bowaen stepped back again. "I get it if you don't want to continue with us to Ilbith," he said in disregard of her proclamation. His gaze trailed down to Metta and back up.

"Of course I'm coming. Wikshen is going to Alkeer."

"And are you going there to search for sorcerers with us, or are you going to be with him?"

Kalea shut her mouth. She desperately wanted to help her sisters and Mhina, and though Wikshen held no apparent intention to help their cause, the fact that he was going to Alkeer made everything convenient.

Bowaen shook his head at her. "Ever since Wikshen told you he was Dorhen..." He shook his head again. "That's all he needed to say to make you a Wikshonite?"

With a cringe, Kalea checked her side to see Metta sitting on the ground, listening to their exchange. She might've argued further, but didn't want Metta present for it.

Before she could speak again, Bowaen said, "Get dressed. You can travel with us to the city. Damos is also out searching for you. I'll make sure he doesn't stumble upon"—he waved his hand—"this."

And then he left Kalea and Metta alone to compose themselves, a difficult task when she'd never felt so exposed and ashamed in her life. She *did* want to continue with Bowaen's group, but how could she explain to her friends what was going on with her and "Wikshen"? She couldn't even sort it out for herself.

She turned her head slightly to view Metta. "I talked to Wikshen this morning," she reported. "He's going to Alkeer."

"Azrielle!" Damos cried when he heard her familiar parrot's call amid the trees. He followed up with a shrill whistle. Down the bird glided out from the mist, cutting through the crisp air and snatching Damos's raised forearm with a sharp and eager stop. Damos laughed as the bird flapped and righted itself on his offered perch.

"Good girl," the bird recited in mimicry of Damos's voice, a few octaves higher than his own. Bringing her to the level of his chest, he petted her with his free hand, and she nuzzled his palm. Azrielle rode on his shoulder from then on.

Kalea smiled to watch the reunion. Now Damos really lived again, although his face wore hideous blotches and raw patches as proof of his run-in with Wikshen. Kalea would pray for them to vanish quickly and not leave behind haunting scars.

Kalea kept her distance from Damos in hopes of avoiding an awkward conversation about all that had happened in the caves. So far, Damos seemed to evade her too, particularly to keep his damaged face averted from her view. Nonetheless, she smiled and acted as if Bowaen's confrontation never happened. He could think what he liked. Kalea was still very much a part of this group.

Practically staggering from their aches and pains, Kalea's party made their way across the Longwalk, a grassland commonly traversed between several locations on the east side of the Darklands. Empty camp sites stamped this region, used and reused, as well as the markings of nomadic communities come and gone, and fine roads carved by foot traffic through the tall grass.

Once behind Alkeer's gate, Kalea wondered if Dorhen had arrived yet, and when and where she would see him again. She almost asked the others how far they thought they were from Wikshen's temple on the pier. She didn't. She resisted asking Metta about him too, just because her friends walked in close earshot.

After dodging the patrolling Clanless members who sneered at Metta and Kalea's black garments, Metta led them to her mother's house for a nice long rest. Did they tolerate Wikshonites here, or only females who dressed the part?

Metta's old mother got straight to work at the sight of her daughter with a load of travelers on the doorstep, baking bread and serving them home-brewed ale—which Gaije declined, of course. Kalea didn't miss Metta rolling her eyes at the poor elf.

After gobbling up a good meal, the men, with Gaije among them, sat on the floor around the hearth, drinking and chuckling in a needed respite from the harsh conditions they'd recently endured. Kalea and Metta retreated to another room to mend the men's clothing. Metta's arm worked up and down in rhythm with a little bone needle as Kalea struggled to make her stitches straight.

She grunted. "I can't sew as well as Joy could." She dropped her project into her lap and took a moment to breathe.

"You'll get it," Metta said in her kindly chime. Her patience almost made Kalea feel like she was sitting with Joy again, like old times, except Metta's bosom squished together between the lapels of her fresh wrapped dress, mocking Kalea with their perky fullness. Even though she wore a similar garment, Kalea could show nothing by comparison. Not only that, but Metta's hair was so black and hung so neat, in smooth, straight strands. Kalea's hair strands liked to fly separate. Also, the dark soot Metta wore around her eyes...

Since they'd sat down together in here, all Kalea could think about was Wikshen kissing the other girl. No wonder Metta had so easily achieved concubine candidacy.

Damos's shirt lay over Kalea's lap. She couldn't keep him out of her thoughts either. She'd avoided him, slipping and twisting away from him at every meeting since entering this house. She avoided his eye contact and kept herself as busy as possible—and his body language did hint at his desire to talk. What would she say to the poor boy? That she didn't love him, but wanted the creature who had harmed him instead? What an awful hurt she'd caused him the night they kissed and touched! And now she dodged and ignored him.

Kalea picked the shirt back up and stuck the needle into its fibers. Metta sewed miles ahead of her, by two garments at least. Kalea attempted a few more stitches, which turned out worse than the previous set. Her mother used to do fine needlework too, but needles had never liked Kalea. They were prickly and difficult to maneuver, like angry little people who hated her. Now here she sat, feeling inadequate before a girl the same age as her…a girl who'd shared Dorhen's lips less than twenty-four hours ago. Kalea growled and dropped the garment with angry force.

"Are you okay, Kalea? You don't have to do that, you know. Take a break, and later I'll teach you some techniques. It'll be fun."

Metta's warm smile only stoked Kalea's anger. The emotion blended with a dash of guilt. Metta was a nice person who really didn't deserve any grief. For some reason of her own, she'd chosen the Wikshonite religion long ago. By a random and far-fetched coincidence, her Mastaren happened to be an elf who'd picked Kalea out of a whole region full of eligible women and worked his way into her heart before such tragedy befell him.

Wikshen and Dorhen didn't share the same consciousness, hence him telling her right after kissing Metta, *Why would you have to forgive me for kissing my future concubine?* Both Wikshen and Metta thought their kiss was the most innocent and normal thing in the world. Back in the Lightlands, the custom was to choose only one mate and marry them. Now Kalea endured a whole different world and didn't like it.

"I'm fine," Kalea told her. She tried a few more awful-looking stitches. "Metta, are you going to see Togha again soon?"

"Perhaps." Metta's arm swooped up and down merrily. "He'll probably escort me back to Wikhaihli if the Mastaren is busy."

Kalea's teeth clamped together. "Togha's really handsome—and mysterious," she said. "On first sight, I knew you were the one Togha talked so kindly about. You two would be so lovely together. He's such a good *saehgahn*."

"A *saehgahn*?" Metta erupted into laughter, trying to pronounce the word. "Like those stiff-walking Clanless? Like your Gaije—?"

She cut herself off and cleared her throat, but then snorted another laugh. "Togha's more like a penniless vagabond walking through a haze, handsome as he is. I suppose… I suppose that's why he stood out for me. I confess, for a few minutes I wanted an elf, but those *saehgahn* are awful, aren't they?"

Kalea's teeth now ground for a different reason. The Norrians were admirable and worthy of lots of praise. And love.

"Togha is outside of that institution. He's a wanderer. A wild spirit." Metta smiled fondly. "I like the free spirits."

"You like the wandering outsiders?" *Wandering outsiders like Dorhen?* Kalea's insides twisted.

Metta stood. "Can I get you more tea?" She leaned forward to lift Kalea's cup, and when she did, her cleavage deepened.

Kalea shot to her feet and snatched the cup before Metta could. "No thank you. I would actually prefer some fresh air before the sun goes down."

"Goats, man, did you note some of those strumpets out there?" Del said to the other men by the fire as Kalea entered from the curved hallway. "There's something about this town I like. We ought to visit a good tavern before we leave here, Bow… No offense to your sister, Gaije."

Gaije sat with his arms crossed, staring into the little flames. "You have no obligation to follow me."

Bowaen laughed. "Don't listen to him, Gaije." He tucked his head low and shared a naughty grin with the rest of them. "How 'bout that Metta?" he whispered. "Need I say more?"

He, Del, and Damos laughed together. Damos hadn't said much so far, but he smiled under his fresh, new bandages, which covered less of his face than before. He'd tipped his big cup of ale more than a few times since Kalea stepped into the space. He leaned heavily against Bowaen's shoulder, drunk—much more so than the others. His sleepy eyes rested on Kalea soon after her arrival.

Bowaen noticed Kalea standing in the doorway too. Choosing not to speak, she went straight to the front door of the old, creaky house. "What's wrong with her?" Bowaen murmured behind her.

Kalea threw the door open to the sudden sight of a visitor on the doorstep. She started backward and touched her heart. "Togha?"

He stood on the porch with his tar-black hair covering half his face, and the visible side…really was attractive. Staggeringly so. It hadn't been so easy to notice when she first met him after Gaije had punched him a few times.

Holding his fist poised to knock on the door, he froze at her abrupt appearance. Kalea stared back at him, tongue-tied at his gorgeous face, and managed to spit out, "Metta's inside. We brought her back like you asked. Please go talk to her. She misses you like a blossom misses the sun." Kalea's face heated up like the symbol in her simile.

Togha's slanted eyes widened, and he leaned in as if to peek inside the door. "This is Metta's house?"

"Yes." She began to rush forward and push her way past him before something else stupid and nervous spilled from her mouth, but he blocked her. "What do you need, sir?" she asked.

Though he made a visible effort to focus on Kalea, his eyes often wandered to the dark foyer behind her. "I'm here for you."

Kalea's face twisted. "Pardon?"

"The Mastaren. He calls for you." Togha's face held bland, matching the unenthusiastic attitude toward Wikshen that her friends displayed. "Please follow me."

Kalea nodded cautiously. "Is he at The Sword Swish again?"

"No," Togha said. "He didn't want to go there, so he's chosen a new inn."

A woman wailed and gnawed her apron in the corner. Dishes clanked loudly in the hands of various other barmaids. A lake of pungent spilled ale, apparently from one of the large kegs, spread across the wooden floor at one side. Broken glass littered the floor from one of the larger windows. Folk ran back and forth, and a young man worked hard to mop up a huge, dark puddle of blood before it stained the wooden floor forever. The noise rocked Kalea's head. Togha held silent as usual, but his eyes widened at the escalation of whatever situation he had returned to.

The innkeeper approached them. "Great Sea, what calamity! Damn you, you Wikshonite, get out of here!" He slapped Togha on the chest, but the elf didn't budge.

"Has Wikshen left?" Togha asked.

"Left? Left! I could not be so lucky, you little pointy-eared prick! No, he's upstairs, having his way! Look what he's done to my livelihood! My inn, The Spare Shield. It's ruined, and it will only get worse. I'd be a fool not to flee now. My livelihood—I inherited it from my father—and his father—and his!" Tears were running down the innkeeper's face, and he performed a similar gnawing motion on his thumb.

Kalea gawked, knowing he wasn't wrong. The Sword Swish must've also been a fine inn not long ago. Now it stood a mess of shadows and hysteric worship. "I'm sorry," she said, and the man paused to eyeball her.

"Well, you must leave, dame! *I'm* sorry, but I cannot serve another soul tonight. I suggest you run while you can, before *he* finds you. Find another inn. Go!"

Kalea reached out a hand, not that it would calm the man. "I'll talk to him. I'll ask him to leave, and you can have your inn back before any more damage happens."

The man squinted at her. "Do you know who we're talking about?"

She gave him a deep and sincere nod. "Yes, I do."

"If you could make him leave, dame, I'd feed you here as a guest for life!" He walked away, back to wringing his hands and contemplating the decision to stay or flee.

Togha turned to her. "He must be upstairs."

Togha didn't escort her to the upper floor, and she needed no direction as to which room Wikshen had claimed. The anxious whispering and flighty women led her right to it. The corridor was as dark as expected with its wall sconces doused, but every so often a lonely flame or two reminded her she still traversed the world of the sane and not the dark playground of sensual euphoria that Wikshen made wherever he went. Not yet.

A surprisingly calm chambermaid strolled past her from the opposite direction and bumped her shoulder. Kalea started to offer an apology, but noted the level of unspoken aggression about the woman's air—she wouldn't have bothered to step aside for Kalea, much less exchange any polite courtesies.

Before Kalea could brush the interaction off and continue on her way, the chambermaid flashed a set of beastly yellow eyes at her. Kalea jumped to the side, putting her back against the wall. The chambermaid paid her no more mind, but walked on through the darkness. Kalea watched for a few more seconds, catching her breath, to make sure the creature in the chambermaid's costume didn't decide to return. Then she dashed onward.

Farther down the hall, a line of people stood before a certain door—women. Another glowing lamp illuminated the group. They chatted softly, primping and shifting from foot to foot. Each one glared at her.

"No cuts, girl!" the woman at the front of the line said in a husky voice. She raised a hand, but held her swing.

"Is…Wikshen in there?" Kalea asked, and the line of women fluttered their hands and huffed.

"'Course, what do you think, ya dumb tart? But you have to go to the back of the line. And might I suggest some rouge? You look like a corpse."

"Oh, dear Creator, he's not…" Kalea said, and rapidly tapped on the door. When no one responded, she slapped the door with a flat palm and manhandled the knob, to the anger of the waiting women. Her breath stopped for now, and she fought with the door until it finally gave way and she stumbled inside.

She exhaled. No women in here. Wikshen reclined against the wall upon a messy floor mattress—alone, and flicking small morkblades quietly at the opposite wall. Steaming plates of food from the kitchen kept him company instead. The shutter lay torn off the window and a water basin stood upside-down over a wet stain on the floorboards.

"Welcome," he said softly—calm, as if empty of whatever burst of energy had caused such a mess. "Close the door."

Kalea's breath shook, though she knew she could relax now. She did as he asked.

"It's remarkable," he continued. "It only takes a thought, but one that I *mean*. Has to have a bit of negative emotion behind it, all-out rage for the bigger ones. They don't just come out willy-nilly. It's the perfect spell. The perfect way to kill."

Hundreds of nicks riddled the wall from previous pin-sized morkblades. Several dead flies lay on the floor where he'd expertly targeted them. Kalea stiffened except for a cold shiver.

She swallowed, put aside what he'd just said, and tried, "Dorhen, who are those women out there?"

"Idiots." He wore his battleshift as usual and appeared to have bathed all his grime off after Hathrohskog.

Kalea crossed her arms and shifted to one foot in an attempt to show her displeasure. "So is this why you wanted to come to Alkeer? To destroy an inn and contemplate killing? And why are all those women out there?" His nonchalant shrug helped to make her attitude real. "Is this how it is now? Are you planning to sleep with them?"

He paused in his morkblade flicking to look at her with a smirk, and then went back to his game. "I told you I was impotent. Do you know what that means?"

Kalea threw out her hands. "No. Do you think I'm the same, Dorhen? A common hussy like them? Did you call me here to stand in that line with them?" He paused again to watch her, holding his smile. "You think you can call me anytime it's convenient for you, but leave me all alone whenever you want?" He rested his arm on his knee. "I guess I gauged you wrong," she went on. "I appreciated your concern for me when I was poisoned, but I won't put up with your violence, and I certainly won't share my man with other women! You're going to have to decide—"

He leaped up, extended a long and hideous morkblade, and slashed it at the side of her neck, stopping suddenly before impact. He held it there until it expired and burst into a dusty plume. She winced, but managed not to lurch or shriek. She erupted in violent quaking, though, but held her stance and hoped he didn't notice.

"G-go ahead," she said. "When I left the convent, I decided to let my love for you guide me, but I've retained enough pride that I can let you go and die with dignity—not as a whore in a gutter, waiting for you to open your door to me one night and perhaps another."

She stared him down, and he stared back with an unreadable look on his face. "Women don't come to me because they love me," he replied. "They come to me because they want power." He focused hard on her, and his lips spread in his usual sly smile. "You didn't scream at my threat."

"Thank you for noticing."

"I wanted you to scream."

"Why?"

"I have a problem." He relaxed, stepped backward a few paces, and plopped back down on the bed. "Would you like to sit on my lap?"

She gestured a firm arm at the door. "Are you dense? I told you a minute ago…" She shook her head. "Maybe you really are Dorhen."

"There's that name again," he said. "You know what, you can call me whatever you like, but I want you to shout it"—he pointed to his ear—"right here."

"Why? I don't understand any of this."

"In the caves, your shouting made my cock rise. It won't rise otherwise—I can't make it work! And if I can't make it work…!" He rested his face on his hand in his first show of frustration since she'd entered.

She gave a shrug. "You just want to have sex? And apparently it doesn't matter with whom." She gestured to the door again.

His processing of her concerns about the women outside the door showed clear on his face. "If that worries you, say the word and I'll cut their heads off."

She grimaced and took a small step back. "Why would you say such a thing? No!" She took a deep breath. "You don't understand. I don't want you to kill anyone—ever again! But can you promise…? Promise me not to sleep with any women."

A short stream of laughter burst out after his initial snort. "Of course not. Don't you know how Wikshonism works?"

Kalea's expression melted, and her arms dropped to her sides. "Then I'm done here."

When she turned around, he sprang from the bed and grabbed her arm after one long-legged lunge that carried him halfway across the room. She knew she'd burst into tears on the other side of the door, but curiosity paused her emotion for now. She turned to regard him.

"Yes!" he hissed. "I promise. Are you happy now?"

He slowly released her arm, and she faced him again. Happiness couldn't be found anywhere within her, but she at least managed to swallow her welling despair. An essence of urgency flashed in his stare. He waved his hand. "Come to the bed."

"I don't want to, Dorhen." She huffed. "I'm getting tired of all this. I think I… I wish I could go home."

He stood straight to a level so high her head only reached his chest. "Now you're turning me down? Do you have any idea what I promised you? The great weight of what you asked and I agreed to?"

Kalea resisted looking up at the angry face he must be making. Just like that, he'd shifted back into the creepy, dark entity she first met at the Alkeer temple.

She chanced a small step backward. "Thank you." Her voice shook. "You know I'm staying at Metta's house," she said, forcing the words out. "Let's talk again tomorrow, perhaps in the morning light."

"Where do you think you're going?"

When she took another step, he snatched her hair, and she squealed in shock. He yanked her deeper into the room and manhandled her to the bed. She screamed freely, fighting back, but her struggle only egged him on. She fell hard onto the rumpled blankets and flattened straw mattress, and his weight followed, pinning her down. She gasped for air and found little in her panic. His long hair covered her face, and he breathed hard against her neck, crushing her leg beneath him. He twisted her hair tighter and tighter until the blossoming pain made her cry out.

"Again!" He jerked her hair, and her head went with it. She yelped in pain. If only she could keep quiet, maybe he'd calm down. Or should she scream voluntarily to make him happy?

He began panting, and it became obvious that he was touching himself again with his other hand. He leaned down and nipped her breast through her clothing when she failed to make any noise.

"Stop it!" she said. "Please, Dorhen, calm down!"

"Don't call me that!" He twisted her hair harder and listened to her whine as he played his other arm rapidly. She couldn't quite see his action, especially with the orange sunset through the broken shuttered window dying for the new dominion of night.

"I just spent an hour with an exquisite presence," he said through his heavy breathing. "A female troll. We performed a sacred ritual...but even her grandiose ability couldn't coax a blessing out of me."

"You mean she—" Kalea tried to pry, but his heavy weight squeezed off her voice. She had his hair in her fist too, she finally realized. She pulled. "Dorhe—! I can't brea—!"

Her attempts to fill her lungs came too short. Her vision darkened, and she couldn't tell if it was from loss of air or her eyes closing. She used the last of her gathered energy to yank the blue hair in her fist with all the might she could send to her arm.

He slowed his arm, panting. "Shit," he hissed. He shifted off of her enough to let her take a good breath, but kept focused on rapidly agitating his penis.

"Dorhen, wake up! I know you're in there!" She shouted it at his face.

"Dorhen, wake up! Wake up!"

He paused all his movements. From under his battleshift, he brought his hand up and covered his mouth. He crawled away, far enough to lean against the wall. He heaved, and a long splatter slapped against the floor. He reared backward and fell against the bed at her feet. She drew her knees up out of his way. Staring, frozen in shock, she pondered darting out the door, but she didn't because... Had her pleading worked?

His ribs pumped up and down as he caught his breath, and his penis stood straight up, tall and thick, from the slit in his battleshift. He turned his head slightly. A trail of moisture glistened from his eye. His lids fluttered.

"K-Kalea?"

Kalea nodded her head with her mouth agape. "Yes?"

He sniffled the loose mucus in his sinuses and turned over, never minding his exposure or the heavy coating of vomit on his chin. He pushed himself up with one arm weakly, and his hair fell over his face.

"Kalea," he said through his whimpering, "you can't be here right now. It's not safe."

"Dorhen?" She sat forward. She'd been roughed up harder than she'd realized; blossoming spots of pain were beginning to register all over. "Is it *you*?"

He answered with a sob, keeping his face shrouded behind his hair.

"Dorhen!" she said, and pitched forward to put her hands on his huge shoulders. She slid one comforting hand over his hair. "I'm going to help you."

"You don't understand, there's no..." He let out another sob. He took hold of her face. "You can't... You just can't... You have to..."

"Dorhen, please tell me what you're going through. I'm going to do everything in my ability—"

"You have to leave. And stay away from me. Ka..." He stared at her with the strangest, most intense urgency she'd ever seen. Kalea sat helpless. He retained hold of her face, just staring at her. He moved in and pressed his mouth against hers.

Kalea sat in shock for the first few seconds, but couldn't stay idle for long. The sour taste of bile spread over her tongue from his. She gagged against the awful flavor. The mess from his chin transferred to hers. He lapped his tongue against hers and grazed it along her teeth and the roof of her mouth—anywhere he could get it. She endured without the ability to ask him to wipe his mouth.

His hand found her breast, but he didn't pinch it. He handled her gently now, so it must be Dorhen himself. Insistent but careful. Kalea relaxed backward and he poured over her on the bed, straddling his long legs on either side of her.

Kalea let her head fall back against the padding, and he closed in whatever space she made. As everything registered better, she decided to kiss back. He was "Dorhen" again…wasn't he? She reached up to caress the side of his face with her fingers. His hair clung to his temples with the clammy sweat. He kissed her with a desperation she didn't know how to comprehend. His erection, poking her, grew harder by the second.

He might—she struggled to find the words even in her head—*bless me.* Was this wrong? Or would it soothe him…help him calm down? At least he was doing it with her…for now. He held and groped her so tightly, she wondered how easily she might get out of his hold. What if he hadn't really switched back to Dorhen's persona, and Wikshen was toying with her? Did this mean he'd finally resolved his "impotence"?

It's Dorhen's body, she thought. *This is what I want.*

If Wikshen indeed played a game right now, she'd feel like a fool, but it would always be Dorhen's body, and for her own sake, her desire to keep him near her and perhaps soothe his tension, she could agree. She let him continue his kissing and pawing to see how far he went.

He pulled his mouth away, but did not seem anywhere near finished. He lingered with his nose to her neck, breathing deeply. He put a gentle kiss on her cheek. A loving kiss. "It's sad, though," he said.

"What's sad?"

"I'm not sure if we should…"

"Are you talking about sex?"

He nodded.

One moment he was warning her to stay away from him, and now he was thinking about making love to her. At least she wasn't the only one confused here. "Are you worried about the demon?"

In his continued panting, his eyes spaced. A shaking began in his limbs, and he pushed his erection harder against her, grinding a bruise against her hip. The darkness thickened around them. He must be getting into that deep state of arousal like at Wikhaihli, his version of an ecstasy. Maybe her own would be along soon.

She would remain receptive for as long as her lucidity would last. She needed to hear anything he could tell her about his condition if she were to try to cure him. With a light touch to his face, she pressed, "What are you worried about?"

He shook his head despite his eager pawing and poking. "I want you, Kalea," he whispered. "But if we—"

A knock at the door cut off his words. Dorhen flew off of her and rose to his knees, fully alert, his eyes wide and bright in the dim twilight. Kalea finally wiped the stinging vomit off her chin.

A muffled voice beat at the door. "Mastaren? Are you in there?"

"Who's that?" Dorhen asked in a panicky whisper, ever in his peculiar confusion.

"It's Metta," Kalea said. "Did she follow me?" She turned back to Dorhen and put her arm around his neck. "Let's be quiet. Maybe she'll go away." She attempted to pull him back into the embrace, but he didn't take the invitation, fixated on the door. "I suppose I can get rid of her."

Kalea rose cautiously and approached the door, her legs wobbling all the way. She opened it by a crack. "Yes?"

"Kalea? You're with the Mastaren?"

Kalea nodded. "He called me."

A smile spread across Metta's face. "Please let me in. I have to ask him something." Metta pushed at the door and Kalea gently resisted. In his state of being, she didn't need or want anyone bothering him, especially Metta. But in her lack of confidence, she gave in and let the girl pass.

Metta stopped at the center of the room and rang her little metal bowl. A Kraft flame flared up with a bright blue flash. "Where is he?"

At Metta's question, Kalea spun around to find him gone, leaving behind Wikshen's careless mess: a pool of vomit; discarded dirty dishes, some heaped with untouched food; damaged wall panels; and the broken shutter that left the window open to the dark, wet night.

Kalea stood dumbfounded and shaky after their raucous episode. Sore places radiated all over her from Wikshen's roughness. "He...went out the window?" Kalea guessed.

Metta rushed to look out of it. "It's starting to rain." She took Kalea by the arm. "Let's go. Maybe we can catch him."

Kalea couldn't disagree. It might be better to stay indoors and not wander around the big, dark city, but Dorhen had gone out there, and she couldn't let him go.

Chapter 39
A Creature Emerges

Arm in arm, Kalea and Metta dashed through Alkeer's soggy streets. No walking clouds roamed, but the heavy sky threatened a downpour. They chose turns and alleys they could only guess Wikshen might've gone down.

"To the temple!" Metta said through her panting.

"No," Kalea responded, but couldn't give Metta a reason for her disagreement. It simply didn't seem right for Dorhen, in his own persona, to go back there.

"It's foolish for us to run about like this after dark," Metta said.

"Did you tell my friends where I—and you—went?"

"No," Metta said. "I saw you through the window, leaving with Togha. I knew it must have something to do with Wikshen, which is why I slipped out after you."

Kalea frowned. Metta wasn't about to let her find a moment alone with Wikshen, was she? Their feelings for him were similar enough, she supposed.

The rain picked up and soaked their clothing. Kalea didn't care if she caught a cold. Why did Dorhen always run away from her? Why wouldn't he let her help him?

When a tall, dark figure faded around a corner in the misty lamplight, Kalea made a sharp turn for that alley, and her shoulder hit an unlit lamp pole. She cried out and grabbed at the pain.

Metta's hands landed on her back. "Are you all right?"

If the pole had stood a smidge to the left, she would have knocked herself out. She took off again, giving Metta no choice but to follow. Around the corner appeared a well-lit inn packed full of people. The overflow of nocturnal merrymakers had crammed in under the jettied buildings to escape the rain. Kalea swung near the crowd.

"Did you see him?" Kalea asked the first drunken lout standing by.

"Who, my love?" he asked back.

"Wikshen! Did Wikshen come by here?"

"Dear Great Sea, I hope not." He and the others around him flashed a hand gesture, extending four fingers with the two middle held together, like some superstitious protection symbol. She ignored them and took off again. She reached a lonely, dark alley and stopped to catch her breath. Metta arrived seconds later, dragging her feet.

"Where have you brought us?" Metta asked. "I don't recognize this street." The nervous sound in her voice accompanied her gesture at a knife she'd fastened to her belt—probably a resolution she'd made after her incident with Dyii.

"Sorry, but I thought I saw—"

"I haven't seen a trace of the Mastaren since you started running into oblivion." Metta paused. "Something feels odd."

A brief hum arose in the air, followed by a flash of light blasting from around the nearby corner. Long overhanging roofs shielded any moonlight which might break through the rain clouds, making this alley the darkest spot they'd found.

Kalea jumped and gasped at the sudden, blinding light that lit every stone in the mildewed walls for an instant. She knew that flash well as the sign of a sorcery portal opening up.

Metta grasped her arm. "What's that?"

"Something…familiar." Kalea's teeth chattered. She lowered her voice to a whisper. "Let's backtrack."

They took literal backward steps: one…two…three. Another sound resonated in the darkness, something blending a cat's purr with a bird's chirp. They both froze in place. Metta let her arm go, and Kalea searched until she found the girl's shoulders and held on.

Ding! Instead of unsheathing the knife, Metta ignited the blue Kraft flame in the little bowl. It filled the alley with its glow, passing over the tall form and odd shape of a sanguinesent that drifted toward them, eyes glittering in the light.

"Come on!" Kalea shouted, and yanked Metta's arm roughly, pulling her into a sprint toward the alley's exit.

Clank! Metta's chime bowl hit the ground, and the flame winked out. Rain poured over their heads. They sprinted far, stumbling, panting, tripping, and relaunching.

"What was that?" Metta shouted, allowing Kalea to jerk her by the arm through the streets wherever she pleased.

Kalea didn't answer right away. "Just don't turn around or look at anything," she offered. "Where's your house from here? Or the temple?"

"I don't know," Metta said. "You'd have to let me stop so I can get my bearings… Kalea?"

Kalea couldn't stop, not until she knew for certain they were safe. Running blindly, she slammed into something, not a wooden light post, but something wearing fabric and as wet as she.

"Hold on now." A male voice. A strong hand to match the voice grabbed her wrist, and Kalea acted on her first instinct, thrashing and yelling in panic. "Stop it! Calm down, or you'll hurt yourself!"

Metta's hands joined the first set. "It's all right, Kalea, we're fine. This is a Clanless."

Kalea slowed her fighting to a stop. "Clanless? You mean an—an elf?" She blinked between raindrops, but could hardly tell who stood before her. His hooded shape showed clearly, though.

His voice carried a comforting tone of calm. "Why are you running?" he asked. "Are you in trouble?"

Kalea stuttered for an answer. His voice sounded a bit…Norrian. "Yes. I mean… I don't know."

"Sounds like you should come inside to get out of the rain, at least."

After a good trek farther through the rain on the hem of the dark stranger's cloak, a sliver of light cracked open on the wall they approached. The elf held the door open and eyeballed them both as they proceeded in.

"You're not Wikshonites, are you?"

Kalea halted on the old stones of the foyer. They'd entered a guard tower along some section of the city wall. All she could get out was, "Um," until Metta took over.

"No, of course not."

Kalea raised a speechless eyebrow at her. The Sanctity of Creation considered it a sin to deny one's faith. Though Kalea wouldn't mind denying Wikshonism, she was shocked to hear Metta do it.

"Sorry," the elf said as he stepped in and closed the door behind them. "I noticed you are both wearing nothing but black." His eyes landed on Kalea as he took off his hood. He wore a necklace strung with orange beads, as expected. "This tower is safe, and you can stay until morning."

"That's so kind of you," Kalea replied, and he smirked as he walked on.

Leading them toward a staircase in a little alcove to the side, he took a candle out of a box and lit it from the glowing hearth. "It's our duty. This way to the guest chamber."

Despite the narrow staircase, the rounded floors of the guard tower were spacious. "Good thing I found you," the elf continued as they climbed the stairs one awkward step after the other. Kalea couldn't keep her shoulder from brushing the wall. At least it was smoothed from centuries of traffic. "We spotted Wikshen in the city earlier today."

"You don't say," Metta said. She traversed the stairwell between the elf and Kalea.

"We're on high alert," he went on. "He even trashed an inn an hour or two ago."

Kalea chose not to reply and instead put out a huff. Poor Dorhen. Wikshen had done those violent and lewd things, not him.

"In olden times, the citizens of Alkeer had some sort of pact with Wikshen, and they supported his campaign even though they didn't conform to his cult," the elf said. "In return, he wouldn't ransack the city, but my clan is now working to reclaim the rest of the city from the gangs, and we don't need his interference—or his potential urge to take the city for himself. Our customs don't align with Wikshen's enslavement of women. Not at all."

"So you"—Kalea swallowed—"the Clanless are going to wage war on Wikshen?"

It took a few seconds for the elf to respond. "Not quite yet. But make sure you stay indoors at night. Keep far away from the Wikshonites."

An awkward silence accompanied them up the remaining few steps. On the next floor up, the elf opened the guest chamber for them, a tiny stone room with wooden rafters supporting a light-streaked upper floor where footsteps tapped around and the merry voices of other elven males echoed. Their laughter carried a certain foreign ring Kalea had come to know. At first, she frowned at the accommodations, but told herself it was the best they could do. Only a mound of straw and a tattered orange blanket awaited them on the cold floor. At least they had a clay chamber pot in the corner.

The elf didn't say much more before he placed the candle in the room's only wall sconce and turned on his heel, leaving them to try to find a way to be comfortable. Metta got straight to fluffing the straw and shaking out the blanket. Kalea lowered into a squat, watching her, and took her first quiet moment in hours to think.

"More like a prison cell than a guest room," Metta grumbled.

Her statement shook Kalea back to attention. "Hm?"

"What do you think that thing was in the alley?"

Kalea blinked her eyes slowly, holding them closed for a short moment. "It was a sanguinesent."

Metta stopped working and cocked her head.

At her confusion, Kalea explained, "It's a demon, a thing of infernal lore. Apparently, a real thing."

Metta squinted at her. "You don't seem very shocked to have seen one tonight."

"I am shocked."

Metta shivered. "Those stuffy elves probably can't protect us from such a thing. I don't want to stay here. I'd rather find the Mastaren, or at least the temple."

Kalea shrugged, and Metta went on to remove her wet clothing. "I don't mind sleeping naked, but how can we dry our dresses in this dark place?"

Her comment made Kalea shiver. She didn't feel like getting naked in the dark tonight. That last conversation with Bowaen, when he'd found them in Hathrohskog... She couldn't sort it out. She couldn't sort out much these days.

A rapid, three-beat tap at the door startled her out of her thoughts. Metta was halfway through undressing and backed into the corner. Kalea cracked the door open to find no one standing there. With a frown, she widened the door. At her feet waited a stack of folded cloth: linen gowns and extra blankets. She lifted them up.

"Thank you!" she called out, hearing only the echo of her voice in return. She closed the door. "I think we'll be able to dry our clothes now, Metta."

"Shy bunch, aren't they?"

"They are." Kalea handed Metta one of the gowns, and they both stripped off their soaking-wet garments. They'd dripped a good pool of water off their clothing, which seeped through the floorboards and probably dripped on the head of anyone who occupied the lower level. The muffled sound of cheerful elven voices chatted on above them, spouting combinations of both Norrian and the common tongue with its Darklandic accent.

In her average linen shift, Metta looked like any normal woman. Not "normal"—she was a radiant woman with her starkly contrasting features, black hair, and supple skin. If she'd only wear a green dress to suit her hazel eyes instead of black, she'd be dazzling. Kalea's study of Metta melted into a vision of Wikshen kissing her. His predicament hadn't mattered more than his desire to show affection because she'd returned his treasured battleshift prior to the event.

It wasn't Dorhen, Kalea repeated to herself. *Dorhen is not Wikshen. Dorhen is not Wikshen.* Maybe she'd been wrong to perform all those worship rituals... Of course, she had! If the One Creator hadn't turned His back on her for her recent behavior yet, He would very soon. Even as she considered that dire guilt, the lingering image of Wikshen dispensing his affection on her or Metta or *anyone* still lit a spark between her legs.

Chapter 40
Faithful Followers

It happened again. He really only meant to vault through the window, maybe squat on the roof outside to wait for Metta to leave, but shadow travel happened too easily for him, and Dorhen found himself back in the disturbing space between dimensions where shadows danced and otherworldly spirits roamed, looking for a door to some better place.

An eerie roar reverberated around him. Or was it behind him? Nonetheless, he launched into an aimless run in search of a way out.

"Wik!" he said, once again in need of the pixie's help. They'd made a pretty good team last time he had to shadow travel to get back to Wikhaihli. Maybe the spirit would help him return to Kalea again.

You disappointing little snot, what'll I do with you? Oh, wait, I know! The cruel voice laughed as always. *You have a hilariously weak grip on your shadow traveling technique.*

"Will you help me get out or what? Which doors lead to Alkeer?"

Are you sure you want to go to Alkeer? There are many other fun places we can visit before returning to Wikhaihli for a pleasurable respite.

"Pleasurable respite" was a good word for it. At Wikhaihli, the shamans provided him with everything one needed to relax: baths, feasts, fluffy bedding… He hadn't partaken of the women yet, but the shamans' insistence had, on more than one occasion, made him wonder if his worry about turning them into monsters was just silliness. At least he had Kalea there. But now he'd been separated from her again and had left her in that awful city. He so hated cities.

As a rude reminder, the ground beneath his feet dropped in its usual unpredictable way and rolled like the ocean. He stumbled and fell, hitting the ground hard, and it dissolved into some sort of goo that he sank into. He went deeper; kicking his legs and swimming with his arms did no good. This chaotic realm seemed impossible to traverse and navigate. Yet a way always existed, according to Wik. This space could be used to travel fast across the Darklands, cutting days from the journey. For now, he'd have to take whatever exit he found first.

After a few more minutes, the gooey substance he'd fallen into dropped him back into open air. He collapsed to a new level of ground below the one he'd fallen through. Nothing made sense. He could barely see, much less tell one object from another or what was a floor or wall. All hazy blues and blacks and occasional whites crackled and waved like a thunderstorm around him. Angry, drifting demons moaned and growled in the background.

An exit appeared sooner than expected. *There!* Wik saw it too. He didn't have to race for it, though: it stayed open long enough for his next step, and through he went, back to the world of the living.

A dark space enveloped him, highlighted by his supernatural vision. The momentum he'd built carried him well into this new place. His foot found open air, and he went down, falling off a ledge he couldn't have predicted.

A woman screamed. Actually two women, shrill and exhilarating. The ripping sound in his ear raised his cock and pushed it to the edge of climax. He gasped at the pleasure, despite falling and crashing against two bodies.

"Ow!" That voice sounded elderly. A younger voice to his other side expressed fright, one he liked more.

The hard hit of someone's elbow, his knee banging the floor, and a fingernail scraping along his forehead couldn't dull the strange, sudden urge to find release. The incense registered to his nose. Pennyroyal.

He and the other two bodies settled. The females groaned. He took the moment to curl up, bite his lip, and fight back the good feelings in his loins.

"Be quiet!" he ordered, and the two finally shut up.

"Mastaren?" The elderly voice again. Somehow, he had been lucky enough to fall on two Wikshonites. "Have you come?"

If only, Dorhen thought, but he knew what she actually meant. "Yes," he said.

The old one gasped, and the younger one kept strangely silent. His supernatural night vision sharpened, and he saw the two women. After taking a short moment, he managed to divert his mind and his erection slackened. He sat up and cupped his own face; a slick cake of blood covered half of it, probably from the fingernails.

"I'm bleeding," he said without much forethought.

The women moved away from him to opposite sides and bowed their foreheads to the floor in prayer. The younger one held her eyes on him, a blank stare because she couldn't see him in the dark as well as he could see her.

The elder's murmured prayer comforted him with its familiarity. At the tail end of it, she shouted with glee, "Praise Wikshen! He answered our prayer! Primora, bow your head!"

She followed up with a ring of her chime bowl to make a Kraft flame and crawled closer to see him in the light. "Mastaren, we have tried many times to call you, and you've finally answered."

"I have?" More like he'd accidentally shadow traveled again and wound up here by chance. He noted the cold, bare ground beneath him. The still air hung moist and dank. They were underground.

She paid no mind to his confusion. "Yes, Mastaren. My daughter Primora and I have been dragged through nothing short of the thorns of misery these past few days."

Would he ever get used to acting like a deity? It was the life he had been thrust into, and since finally regaining control of his body, he hadn't been able to figure out what to do with it besides play along. It was hard not to do so when his appearance elicited such strong reactions in people. "What do you want from me?" he asked.

The old woman raised her head from her crouch to look at the younger on his other side. "Get up those steps, girl, and get some cloth and water. Can't you see our Mastaren is bleeding?"

The young one leaped into action, crawling up a ladder and opening a hatch on the ceiling through which the night sky shone.

The old woman drew his attention back. "Mastaren, we are devoted Wikshonites. My daughter, sister, and niece are good and loyal. How humbling it is that your great majesty would answer our call—"

"What do you want?" He didn't mean to sound so hard, but these religious people had a special talent for drawing out a speech too long. They were full of wind and not enough facts. He admitted to himself, though, that he would've spared patience for anyone who was nice to him before he became a deity. It must be the "Wikshen" side of him who lacked patience for nice people.

She bowed her forehead to the floor again. "Forgive me, Mastaren. To put it flatly, the sorcerers who control this village have taken my sister and her daughter away from us. They are also looking for me and Primora. They invaded our house and chased us out, and today we've taken great pains to sneak back into the basement and set up this shrine.

"We've been praying and preparing offerings ever since, hoping to win your favor and to summon you—which happened by the sheer miracle that is you! We need your help. We've been in an ongoing argument about whether to stay here and witness your destruction of the sorcerers or—"

Dorhen's face went cold at the mention of sorcerers and how they might be right outside. "I'm in no position to deal with sorcerers."

The old woman blinked. "Of—of course, Mastaren, of course. We just…" She croaked and wiped her face, her voice raspy after her earlier screaming. "I couldn't guess what else to do and was in need of your wisdom." Dorhen sat there, watching her weep. "At the very least, sweet Mastaren, I thought perhaps you could bless Primora." Dorhen's eyebrows shot up at the turn of her words. "I dedicated her to you at birth. With Primora as a dreadwitch, she could fend off the sorcerers, or at least be well fit to make a pilgrimage to Wikhaihli. It's all we have to hope for."

Crouching low, she shook her head and shrugged. "Consider it your pleasure and my last revenge. I'm not expecting to ever see my family members again. Primora… She's the most beautiful girl in the village, more so than I've ever seen, and she's well-educated in the sexual arts. Surely she can inspire you."

He sucked in a breath through his nose and released it through his rounded mouth. A little bit of the erection caused by Primora's screaming still nagged him, and the conversation's new direction spurred it on with a sickening yet delightful mischief. He couldn't agree to the woman's request, though. If she wasn't Kalea, he wouldn't. He couldn't find the heart to say "no" right now, though.

At his silence, the old woman clicked her tongue. "Don't answer yet, Mastaren. Let us treat you to a feast of our absolute best ability. Rest yourself."

She reached a hand out and patted his knee, reminding him that she was yet another kindly old woman, much like Knilma. A large number of the Wikshonites were, in fact, old women who could cook and coo and make him comfortable. He'd never known such luxury in his old life. Arius Medallus had never given a wink about his discomfort out in the cold, muddy nights. Now he'd found this nice lady. She and her young daughter were alone here, and in distress.

The old woman rose to her knees. "My name's Kiamora. Remain here, Mastaren. We'll prepare a great meal for you, and later a worship to boost your energy."

Half of Dorhen wanted to close his eyes and enjoy the caress of the cool, damp cloth Primora lightly grazed along his face, and the other half wanted only to stare back at her. He managed to do a little of both. She displayed a quiet and thoughtful demeanor, which he didn't know what to do with. Most of the old women he'd met would chatter or pray at him, or at least keep a smile and warm disposition in his presence. Kalea was of the chatty type.

Primora rinsed the blood off the rag and went back to dabbing it on his face with little circular motions. The cold water refreshed his clammy skin. Sticky sweat covered him from the neck down. When he opened his mouth to ask for a bath, nothing came out, and he played as if he only needed to take a deep breath. The awkward silence prevailed.

The edge of her cheekbone glowed in the dim blue light. This setting must be dark for her eyes, but for him the blue flame added a radiant flare to her comely angles in an atmosphere of muted colors. She wore a few painted lines on her face, framed by her heavy dark hair, which hung straight and long. The mere shape of her silhouette… It added a level of comfort to everything else she did for him. Her gentle, quiet air… It was *right* somehow.

He opened his mouth again, but held back his words for the next swipe of her soothing cloth. "You're not dressed like any witch I've seen," he finally got out.

She hadn't dressed in much of anything today, just an open vest, basically, which was held down over her breasts by a belt around her waist. The typical kind of amulets with feathers and bones known to Wikshonism dangled between them. Under that, a pair of little black braies, the habit of all the prettiest girls in Wikhaihli, teased the eye. One thin little scrap of fabric protected her…

She held her silence a little longer at his comment. Her doe-like eyes studied him. Her mouth kept straight, lacking the sense of amusement any other flirtatious witch might display. "That's because I'm not one."

At her flat tone, his next instinct urged him to shrink back, though he resisted because of his station. He lowered his eyes to his crossed legs. His battleshift pooled around him, hiding the cushion they'd brought for him to sit on.

Primora continued her work, and he couldn't find the courage to inquire further. Most Wikshonites were witches. What was her position if she wasn't one? Where did she come from? What amused her? What was her favorite food? How had she come to be a Wikshonite?

She pulled her cloth away, stained dark with his blood by now, and burned a perplexed stare into him.

"What?"

"You have no wound." She considered her long, manicured fingernails, one broken off from striking him. "I've wiped all this blood away to find nothing beneath."

He shrugged and crossed his arms in a petty effort to act aloof. "Heals fast."

She replaced her serious expression with one of wonder as she rotated her bewilderment between his now-clean face, her broken nail, and the dirty rag.

"Wikshen heals fast," he reiterated. He dropped his arms and waited. Why she acted so confused was anyone's guess. He thought all Wikshonites knew about his powers.

She met his gaze and stared openly, without the usual reserve Wikshonites tended to show him upon first meeting. The deep shadows danced around the room to avoid the little flickering Kraft flame. She couldn't see him as well as he saw her, he reminded himself. How did he look to her? He felt more foolish sitting here before her than any other person in the religion. Yes, Wikshen healed fast. What else did she want from him?

"I..." she began. She blinked her eyes, fanning her dark lids with a pout. She slicked her slender fingers along her silken hair, putting a smooth lock behind her ear. "I'll go see if my mother needs help."

After she scurried up the ladder, Dorhen finally noticed the pounding of his heart. It occurred to him that he'd found his chance to dash into the shadow realm and get back to Kalea. He stood and paced around. He needed the densest shadow available...

Where do you think you're going? Wik grated in his head.

A twinge of nausea crept into his stomach. He clamped his hand over his mouth. Not a good time. The need to vomit usually indicated a shift back to Wikshen's persona, something he needed to prevent or he'd run amok and do goddess-knew-what. The pixie didn't like it when he didn't play along, and that's when the struggle usually reignited.

He lunged to the wall and patted it. Solid. Wik had guided him through the process before. He could walk straight into a shadow, even flat against a wall, and pass right through. A certain breathing rhythm helped make it happen, so Dorhen tried to work up to the necessary state of mind and body. The nausea caused panic, though. Casting Morkblades also required a certain type of breathing. This Kraft stuff was all about breathing, meditation, body movements, and gathering energy from minerals and vibrations. It shouldn't be so hard.

Dorhen stepped back several paces and drew air deep into his lungs. The mere thought of either woman coming back down the ladder pathetically stirred his heart to panic. He held his breath and released it slowly. He had to try it or he wouldn't get anywhere, so he ran headlong at the wall...and bounced off of it.

With a grunt, he slammed backward, hitting his head on the compact dirt floor. Pain flared up at both the front and the back of his head. He had a little too much faith in the spell working, but not enough practice behind him. Wik laughed hysterically in his mind. Lying on the floor, Dorhen groaned, half at the pain and half at his stupidity.

Voices above. The ladder squealed under the weight of footsteps! He sat up and did his best to collect himself. He took the end of his battleshift and wiped his face. Blood trickled from his nose.

Wik, Dorhen said inside his head, *why don't you help me?*

I am *helping you.*

Cursing the spirit silently, Dorhen crawled back to the cushion and cradled his aching forehead in his hand. Who knew how much more blood Primora would have to clean off his face now? Mortified, he waited for whatever they planned next.

Food. Thank the goddess. He'd eat and see about escaping to the shadow realm later. While he ate the bread and mushroom soup they had brought, they crouched at his feet, praying and humming. Kiamora did all that. Primora kept characteristically silent. Her full breasts mashed against her thighs as she huddled over, as if expecting the ceiling to cave in.

Dorhen tried not to look at either of them as he put small, slow bites into his mouth. It would be gone too soon, and then he'd have to sit awkwardly, waiting for them to finish their worship session. Every time Kiamora rang her little bell between prayer verses, a shocking burst to Dorhen's energy rose up and waved back down to calmness. A little ignited flame lit the pennyroyal incense...

He knew exactly how this would go. It happened in every worship ritual he'd participated in. All their chanting and instruments would work together with the smells of smoky incense and the sweet flavors he ate to raise his cock yet again, and he'd have to wait it out until they finally left him alone to sleep it off—or jerk it off, depending on his current level of self-discipline.

Being their deity in the flesh, he didn't know how he could possibly say, *Don't worship me tonight.* He could, he supposed, but it felt too strange a request to try. A while back, he'd realized what a game they all played. Although he didn't want to have sex with a girl he didn't know, the Wikshonites disagreed and would do anything and everything they could think of to tempt him because they knew they had a fair chance of getting their way.

This game was the soul of Wikshonism. He owned something they wanted, and in all reality, he stood as nothing but a tool to them. They wanted his magic semen for their own gain, or if not, they wanted him to kill this person or take that treasure or conquer some city for the benefit of the cult. Easily, one could get lost in an argument with one's self as to who played the real lackey in this institution.

This particular worship ritual went like most he'd seen so far: a well-planned effort to coax out a sample of his semen. Primora, the predetermined focus for his entertainment, did her part throughout the session, bending backward and forward, displaying her nearly naked body, and it worked. It *almost* worked. Dorhen shook all over, feeling the supernatural fervor they wanted him to feel, but he played his competitive part of the game well. They'd have to get Kalea involved if their side of it were to triumph.

Primora made love to the air on her knees, moving her spine like a snake and working her pelvis, sometimes even bending all the way back to make a half circle. Her breasts rolled out on more than one occasion as she danced on without shame, only to roll back under their covering when she shifted the other way. He couldn't deny his interest in that mesmerizing treat.

All the while, her face held the same bland expression. He still couldn't fathom what she might be thinking or feeling about all this. He couldn't shake his suspicion that she didn't like it, which made the prospect of giving in to her temptation so much more bizarre.

He closed his eyes, but it didn't help. All the scent and sound elements of the worship proved as tantalizing as Primora's dance with the darkness.

A long while later, as Primora panted on the ground among the swirling plumes of heavy smoke, her rib cage hoisting her plump breasts up and down, Dorhen held up no better. He'd become a weak, shaky ball of nerves. If one of them touched so much as his hand, he might dispense their desired token.

"Good Mastaren," Kiamora's croaky old voice sounded from some shadow across the room. They'd made him exactly as they wanted him to be, lying there with a throbbing cock swollen to some enormous girth and of a mind for only one thing. He fought it and tried not to think of Kalea; thoughts of her could send him over the edge without a touch needed. Instead, he thought of fire, the bright, raging monster that had taken his mother away from him and destroyed his life at the age of six.

A hand touched his face and slid back into his hair. A comforting hand.

He exhaled. "Mahhh…"

A feminine hum answered back. She'd come to watch over him. Her hair draped heavily along her face and over her shoulders.

He let his eyes fall slowly closed again, and all he knew for the moment was his foggy mind and needful body.

"Raise your head, Mastaren."

When he did, someone placed a pillow beneath it, and then a fur pelt covered him.

Silence.

He slept.

Dreamless darkness.

"So, you're Wikshen?"

At the voice, he twitched near waking. He hummed in response. It couldn't have been too long since he fell asleep. His erection held up, quite ready to burst. He reminded himself of the importance of resisting the urge. He couldn't let himself turn that pretty girl into a monster.

The voice beside him huffed. "I'm so confused… My mother doesn't even know how badly I disgrace her."

Dorhen listened to the deep female voice. A little smile quirked his lips.

"Can you at least help us?"

That's right. Her name was Primora. She and her mother needed help. He fought to wake up. A groan escaped his throat, and the girl gasped and edged backward.

"You," he managed to say. Primora occupied the basement alone with him now. He tried to sit up, but dropped his head again. His cock hurt after standing so long with no effort to relieve it. "Why'd you do this to me?"

The girl stuttered for her answer. "I… My mother ordered it. I can only go along with what she wants. Besides, it's worship. Aren't we supposed to do it that way?"

He hissed through his teeth, resisting the urge to touch himself to stop the pain. "Where's she now?" he asked.

Primora pointed her finger upward. "She left me down here to attend you. She's hoping you will…bless me."

He spat out the reply, "I can't."

Primora cocked her head, staring at him like she'd been doing since he got here. He lied. Of course he could, but he didn't know her. Despite how sultry and wild he'd found her dancing earlier, he wasn't yet convinced she wanted it herself.

"Why can't you?"

An awkward silence followed her question.

He threw the pelt blanket off. "Maybe you should come get it if you actually want it." He went as far as to expose his standing cock to the open air, then leaned back and waited for her to make a move. He clenched his teeth on the end of that bold invitation, though. Certainly, if he couldn't get out of this situation, his penis would start doing the talking for him—as if it, too, were an evil pixie. Even as he lay there, vulnerable and welcoming, she didn't make a move. He knew her eyes grazed its shape in the dim lighting.

"I have to go to sleep," he said when she failed to react, and then placed his battleshift back over it. Fresh air should help too. Maybe he'd go sleep in the forest. The more he considered it, the better it sounded. Fresh, cold air was all he needed. And aloneness. He forced himself to sit up and pushed to his feet.

Primora grabbed his arm and thrust her bosom against it. "Wait!" she said, showing him the first bit of emotion he'd seen from her all night. "What about us?"

He pinched his nose bridge, trying not to think of her firm, round breasts pressing against him. He had no idea how to help her and her mother, and she'd already rejected his cock.

"How fit is she?" he asked.

"My mother?"

He sighed. "Yes. She mentioned going to Wikhaihli. Can you make the journey?"

Primora put out a huff. "She wants to go, but I've argued with her about it. It's too far away."

Dorhen didn't know how far since he'd made it here by shadow travel. "I suppose it is," he replied. "Which direction is Wikhaihli from here?"

"East," she said. "Maybe northeast." Releasing his arm, she slid her fingertips across his chest, and he shivered. His erection leaped with a new tightness. "Won't you wait?" she said, and her resonant whisper made it all the worse. "My mother wants you to bless me. Will you do it?"

Is she kidding? He gazed into her lovely eyes, as empty as ever. She clearly didn't want what she asked for, or they'd probably already be finished by now. Her *mother* wanted him to bless her, not Primora herself. He couldn't deny that he wanted her more than she did him! In her hesitance to make a move, yet her persistent asking, it was as if she really did need him to make the decision for her. In his slipping self-control, she might just get it—if she could only show him a smidge more willingness.

She ventured her touch farther, up his neck to his hair. He snatched her hand and nudged her away. He scanned the room and lifted the knife off the platter of dishes from which he'd eaten.

Primora stiffened up, standing by the ladder where he'd left her. Dorhen used the knife to cut a lock of his blue hair off. He reached for her wrist and pulled off a little black ribbon tied loosely around it. He used the ribbon to secure the hair.

"Here." He extended the lock to her, and she slowly held out her hands. "Go to Wikhaihli as your mother bids," he said. "This token will not only get you in, it will get you a high place in the tower. You'll both be safe there."

"You're not going to—"

"No," he said. "And I can't stay here any longer." He pushed past her to step onto the ladder. Before launching up its first rung, he said over his shoulder, "Sorry I can't escort you there. I have important stuff to do."

He made quick work of climbing up into the night air, leaving the girl gawking below. A paleness seeping into the sky suggested dawn's approach. He didn't have the luxury to steal a moment to alleviate his tension. He dashed into the forest to look for a shadow dark enough to travel through.

Running between the trees, Dorhen couldn't shake the feeling that he'd just abandoned those two women. A lock of his hair? That was the best he could do to solve their problem? He couldn't have at least killed the sorcerers in their village one by one using his Kraft stealth? What a coward! However, he didn't know what the sorcerers had planned for him. The village could be riddled with all manner of spelled traps designed for him. At least on the road to Wikhaihli, Primora held some chance at survival. He shouldn't have to turn her into a dreadwitch. If she died along the way, it would be a better fate than that which his "blessing" offered. He didn't like either option, but he'd chosen one for her sake.

His next attempt to shadow travel back to Alkeer proved more fruitful than before, despite Wik's protests. A long, hard run through the negative space between dimensions followed, tossing and rolling him along the nonsensical terrain. Wik only insulted him for denying himself Primora's offered pleasure, so he managed on his own. There were vibrations to listen for and directional pulls to follow. He apparently possessed Wikshen-senses he should be able to tap into, although he couldn't yet.

The directional pulls... Primora had said Wikhaihli lay to the east or northeast of his position. If he could concentrate, he should *feel* which way was east... He made his choice and kept running in that direction no matter what he encountered. Eventually, he found a glowing door, the biggest one yet, so he took the chance and leaped through.

On the other side of the door, the sun burned down. Immediately, his knees gave way. He had run a long distance through the negative space, apparently long enough for the sun to gain height in the sky, bright enough to leech his energy away like a fish out of water.

He stumbled over a lazy, snoring animal, and could barely catch himself before face-planting into the soft, loose soil. Pigs, many of them, occupied the muddy pit. He couldn't have anticipated where he'd emerge—under the awning of a pigpen against a huge stone wall. The shadow was too shallow to recede back into, so he stumbled into exposure, weak and sluggish in stark contrast to how he had felt an instant earlier. Too many people moved around the vast field. Dorhen fought to his feet against his waning energy. It looked as if he'd found Alkeer—the big wall must be the city's—so now he had to get inside and relocate Kalea.

The subject has emerged from the between-realm, as calculated. Alert the kingsorcerer.

What was that strange voice in his head? Other rumbling voices answered it.

Too late to ask questions. Glittering eyes stared at him from the side. A second and third sanguinesent floated out of hiding from behind several stacked crates and the thick wooden post holding up the pigs' awning.

As much as Dorhen craved to take off, hurdle over the fence, and beat them mercilessly one by one, the sunlight gelded his virile Wikshen abilities. Fatigue quickly overcame him, even before the creatures did.

Giving it his all, Dorhen lurched for the nearest menacing, skull-like face with diamond eyes—all he had to do was dislodge them, but they had him surrounded. Three of them formed a triangle to box him in. Before he could reach his target, the long sticky tentacles of another slithered across him, pinning his arms down.

Chapter 41
A Deity Vanishes

Daghahen raised his head from the seventh bow of chanting and breathing to make the spell work, arching his back to touch his forehead to the smooth stone of the mountain on each round. He'd been at it for four hours and still had a lot to do. Lots of preparation preceded his mission into Ilbith. He'd only breached the Black Mountain region by a few miles, and had finally found the right place to set up his exit portal. This was where he and Orinleah would wind up when they fell through the simple portal he planned to cast.

The wind whistled around him, howling from the tall, distant slopes where the mountain crags became most treacherous. He'd collected a lot of energy and resources to make this portal big enough, powerful enough, to get two adult bodies through. Coming out here, they'd be well ahead of the sorcerers' pursuit—and he'd manage it all without using any gold. The Ilbith sorcerers used gold all the time for their sorcerous tasks, but one didn't need it if they had enough know-how, patience, and energy to see a spell through. Time and patience was all Daghahen had.

Another point done. He completed each point by setting tarnished silver coins gingerly in place. The object didn't matter, since he only needed them to stay in place, not draw attention, and possibly not be stirred by any animals. These old coins were blackened enough not to dazzle any thieving ravens. By the end of the day, his circle would have ten points, possessing only enough energy to last a limited amount of time, so he would have to use this portal fast.

Before moving on to the next tedious portal point, he flexed his creaky old back and stretched his arms. A gentle rumble under his feet put a new dread inside him. He knew he'd encounter *them*. They had started waking up last year from a century-long slumber, and must still be in that slow process. That was another reason he had opted to put his exit portal here, so close to the mountain range's entrance: their earth-shaking song could rattle his coins out of place and botch his spell. This was a safe distance away, but still close enough to feel the ominous trollsong. Pretty soon he would be underground, navigating the caves among them.

Without a window to alert her to the hour, Kalea awoke to the sound of Metta snoring beside her. Her head ached and her eyes didn't want to open. She forced them.

"Metta." She leaned over and shook the girl. "Get up. It must be morning." As groggy as she felt, she preferred to believe it was time to wake up. The events of last night rushed back to her. Regardless of whether or not morning had arrived yet, she needed to rise and get back out there to find Dorhen.

Metta reluctantly joined her in the waking world. "Running around made my legs so stiff," she whined sleepily.

"Let's go downstairs and see if our clothes are dry," Kalea said. Her own leg muscles screamed, but she ignored that.

Wearing the old chemises they were given last night, Kalea and Metta descended the stairwell together. Through the little doorway at the bottom, the floor gleamed a soft blue. Daylight. Kalea crossed her arms before venturing out, in case a bunch of Clanless *saehgahn* met them in the main hall.

Naught but a dirty beggar occupied the space. He didn't pay them any mind when Kalea stepped through the little archway with Metta on her heels. He busied himself turning a crank on a box which made a clicking sound, the only sound in the room besides the crackling fire. The many voices of a busy Alkeer babbled outside.

She and Metta went to their kirtles and undergarments hanging by the hearth, but she couldn't stop eyeing the beggar, another elf—a dirty one, and old too. Or maybe just dirty—she couldn't tell if any wrinkles lay beneath all the grime. His hair shone a pale blond, quite pretty where certain locks remained unsoiled.

Absentmindedly pulling her garments off the hanging poles suspended from the ceiling, much like she'd seen in the Desteer Hall back in Norr, she watched the elf's hands to puzzle out what he was doing. His other hand fingered a set of buttons attached to the box, and all the while his right hand kept the crank turning. Strange.

Klock. Klock. Klock. Something wooden within the box knocked as the crank turned. It must be a musical instrument…a broken one.

"Filthy Clanless," Metta murmured beside her.

Kalea shushed her, and the elf paid no mind. He kept turning his instrument with a faint smile always on his lips. Kalea finally shook her stare away, and she and Metta went back upstairs to change. When they returned again, the elf was still there, turning the crank in some meditative state. She finally noticed the little wooden bowl beside him with a little copper coin in it.

"He must be out of his mind, the poor thing," she mumbled to Metta. They turned toward the front door, but before leaving, Kalea fished through her coin purse and found a few small copper chips still hanging around. She dropped one in his bowl, and Metta sniffed.

"Why are you paying *him* anything? His instrument doesn't even work."

Kalea shushed her again, but the elf perked up at Metta's words.

"It's true," the elf said in a lovely voice with some sort of genteel Norrian accent. "I apologize, this hurdy-gurdy has been missing its wheel for years. Thanks for your generosity, though." He raised his voice to speak but looked toward the corner of the room rather than at either of them.

"Of course," Kalea said. She squinted and leaned over to try to see his eyes better, and then noticed how blankly they stared, cloudy and dull. He was blind. "Oh, dear," she said, and plunged her hand back into her coin purse for more money. At the sound of the additional coin ringing in the bowl, he perked up straighter and smiled widely.

"Sweet lady, there's no need for that." A little laugh squeezed up his throat. "But I will take it and give it to the next unfortunate soul I see." Kalea couldn't tell if he joked or not. He smiled, but his sincerity rang clear. He raised a finger. "In fact…"

He leaned forward and made a little effort to get to his feet. Once standing, he held his hurdy-gurdy down by his side from its tattered, woven strap and turned his unseeing eyes to Kalea. She knew there was no way he saw her, but he did appear to sense her somehow. His smile brightened and slackened.

"What is it?" Kalea asked.

"You're a kind soul," he said.

Metta's hands snaked around Kalea's arm in a silent message to leave. Kalea didn't budge yet. The elf actually appeared young and handsome when she imagined him without the soot smudging his skin.

"Why don't you let me pay you back?" he said. "Would you like some tea? And maybe a plate of breakfast?"

"Um…"

He talked on despite her sounds of hesitation. "I can cook like the best of them. Just point me to the hearth, and I can do it."

The hearth lay a few paces away, and he should probably already know how to find it. Didn't blind people have a good sense of directional orientation in places they knew? Kalea regarded Metta and found an expression torn between an urgency to leave and an admission of hunger. Kalea's own stomach growled audibly. She raised her hands, unsure what to do.

The pleasant smile beamed on the elf's face as he waited. "I'm not very good at being blind," he said as if to answer Kalea's unspoken confusion.

Metta snorted. "How long have you been like this?"

"A long time, but that doesn't mean I've gotten used to it. I'm passionate about my music, and often let it distract me. In my dreams I can see, only to wake up blind again."

Kalea and Metta exchanged more looks.

The elf snickered. "I know what you're thinking." He pointed his smile down at his hurdy-gurdy. "Nonetheless, I still hear melodies when I play this. Its whining songs are so sad, especially at night."

"All right," Kalea said. She placed her hands on the elf's narrow shoulders and turned him toward the hearth. He stood no taller than she. "There's a few canisters, I see," she informed him. "But I can do the cooking—"

"Nonsense," the elf said with a spirited snap. "You two will be my guests. Have a seat." He paused before proceeding and twisted around to point his blank, white eyes at them. "There *are* only two of you, right?"

"Right," Kalea said breathily with a nod she knew he'd miss.

The elf nodded, turned back to the hearth, and proceeded forward, feeling with his hand. Half of the suede sole under his right shoe hung off; he wore an old-fashioned pair of bicolored leggings with the feet sewn shut. His tattered robe dragged behind him. With his outstretched hand, he found the stones holding a mound of ash and little flames eating at a stack of twigs. He placed his hurdy-gurdy on the floor, propped against the hearth base.

"He's gonna burn his hands off," Metta muttered.

"Hush," Kalea whispered.

"There's already hot water for tea," the elf informed them. "Who's having some? Raise your hand." His smile spread wide.

"You have a healthy sense of humor about your blindness," Kalea said. "We'll both have one, I think."

He shrugged. "You have to, or else they win."

"Who wins?"

"The gods of suffering."

"I've never heard of them."

"I made them up." He burst out a laugh and bent over to hug himself. "I joke." At their silence, he shut up. "I'm not actually good at joking either. And the gods of suffering might as well exist—that's what I think."

He reached out to the shelf with the little porcelain teacups, which were chipped, mismatched, and probably salvaged from every corner of the city. "Comfort is a hard-earned luxury, but the perfect weapon against suffering, isn't it?" he went on.

In his indirect aim, the back of his hand knocked one off to shatter on the stone floor. "Oh, drat!" he said. "If I keep doing that, the Clanless will not let me back in here to rest again."

"He really isn't good at being blind," Metta said as they sat down on the available stools at a long, narrow table near the hearth.

Kalea leaped up a moment after sitting down. "Please, let me help you."

He put his hand out to stop her. "Nope, nope, and nope. I have to learn, don't I?"

"Then I'll pick up the pieces while you work."

"Don't let me step on your hands."

Keeping her seat, Metta grumbled, "He'll pour the boiling water on your head if you don't get out of his way."

"Metta!" Kalea snapped.

"Well, she's not wrong," the elf responded with a chuckle. He set two cups out, and then stood poised with the kettle. "Can you point me to the cups?"

Kalea huffed and turned his shoulders so he stood square with them.

"Thanks, my dear."

Kalea held her breath and watched him fill the first cup. Oddly, he didn't miss it, overfill it, or run the pour off track of it. The second one, he filled with the same precision.

"There we are." He turned back to the fire and rehung the kettle, also without incident. After picking up all the cup pieces, Kalea remained standing, poised to help him again should he make a mistake. He paused, turned his face to her, and waved. "Sit down, sit down, darling."

"O-okay." She did.

He placed a whole tea leaf in each cup. "So, what brings you two to this guard tower?"

"An elf brought us in from the rain last night. A Clanless," Kalea told him.

"Good thing too," the elf said as he reached up high to take down an old iron skillet. "This city is not a good place for two lovely young women to be alone outside at night. All manner of dreadful creatures lurk out there. When I say 'creatures,' I actually mean people."

"Yeah, we guessed as much," Metta said in an impatient tone.

Kalea crossed her arms on the table and rested her chin. "You're not wrong about 'creatures' either."

Metta hummed beside her. "I'm still curious about how you knew what was going on last night. You scared even me when you pulled me along."

Kalea clamped her lips, watching the elf take one long step to the side to fetch a basket off its hook, and then repeat the step back to his place before the fire. He fanned the flames to heat the skillet. Kalea didn't want to talk about it in depth, especially in front of a stranger, though it might be good to alert him. "I had seen an evil thing like that before."

"Right," Metta said. "So you said last night."

Kalea shuddered. "I don't know why it's here." She lowered her voice. "Maybe it's looking for me." She didn't need to look up to know Metta stared at her. The girl's unvoiced question entered her mind. Kalea shook her head rather than jumping into all the details, although she did whisper, "Wikshen killed one of them to protect me. They must be after me."

The elf cracked open two brown eggs from the basket, keeping strangely quiet. He'd most likely heard her whisper over the sizzle. A long, blond braid hung behind him; it would've trailed on the floor if it wasn't drawn up and tucked into a pocket on his robe. He must be old by elf standards after all; Kalea recalled Gaije talking about hair length being a sign of age.

At her mention of Wikshen, Metta's stare burned hotter. Kalea shook her head ever so slowly, as if the elf might see her do it. She reminded herself of his blindness. He took up a long knife and uncovered a loaf of bread from its linen shroud, placed it on the table, and cut two flat slices. Holding the slices with tongs, he toasted them over the hot coals. How he knew when any of this food finished cooking was anyone's guess.

"What do you mean, the Mastaren killed one? When?"

Kalea shushed her softly. She leaned over to whisper in her ear. "Several nights ago. The sorcerers summon these evil things."

Metta reared back. "Sorcerers," she hissed, and Kalea reminded her to be quiet. She checked the elf to find him smiling as he worked. He flipped the eggs with a spatula, covering their yellow centers with the crispy white cooked sides.

"I'll tell you later," Kalea followed up.

The elf carefully lifted each egg off the skillet and laid them on the bread before serving them to Kalea and Metta. Kalea lifted her piece and dug her teeth into the warm creation. The egg's yoke broke and seeped into the bread as well as her mouth. She didn't notice how fast she finished it. The elf took a seat across the table and rested his elbows, smiling as if he could watch them enjoy his cooking.

"So, tell me more about this 'evil thing' you met last night," he said, and Kalea coughed over her last bite. The elf frowned and reared back.

"Oh, dear. Metta, pat Kalea on the back. I'll get some water." He rose from his seat.

Kalea shook her head and reached for her teacup, now cool enough for her to take bigger sips. After soothing her throat, she paused. "Hold on." The elf halted at her word. Kalea took a second to calculate with her finger in the air. "I said Metta's name, but Metta never said mine. How do you know my name?"

The elf let his hands fall to his sides with a smile. "You'll have to forgive my rudeness. Here I've cooked you breakfast, and we haven't been properly introduced." He stepped back over to the table and extended his hand. "I mostly go by Ray."

Kalea blinked and stared at his hand. She trailed her eyes up his arm to his grimy face, a pretty face with delicate features and silky blond hair that, though dirty, trailed down his shoulders into the long braid at his back. "Ray," she repeated. "As in…"

"It's short for Adrayeth," he said, "but I haven't really gone by that name in ages." He waited for a response, but Kalea could only sit frozen in silent panic. He made another mirthful smile. "Are you still there?" He gave a short laugh. "I'm not talking to myself, am I? Happens all the time. The Clanless will give me a piece of bread with a pat on the shoulder and call me 'Elder,' but it doesn't mean they'll stick around to pay any more mind. No, no one wants to listen to the likes of me, especially now with my beloved broken…" He huffed and motioned to the hurdy-gurdy he'd set by the hearth. "You see, I came from N—"

Kalea sprang and dashed for the door as he continued talking.

"Kalea?" Metta called after her. Kalea threw the door open and leaped over the threshold to join the flowing crowds outside.

"Hey, watch it!" a man shouted as she clipped him. She worked her legs over long stretches of patchy earth and sparse old stones from a road built long ago. She ran on despite Metta's calls, eager to get as far away from the guard tower as possible. Let Metta catch up or not—she didn't care. However, she *did* care that Dorhen was somewhere in the area, and she wouldn't let Remenaxice's brother stop her from taking her place at his side.

What in the Creator's world? she thought. *What are the chances I'd find Adrayeth by sheer random luck? My rotten luck.*

She aimed for a little staircase running up the side of the city's great wall. It seemed like a good idea to hide up high on the catwalk to watch and wait until the road below was safe. Ascending to the top, she gave a snort between her huffs and puffs. Adrayeth was blind! She laughed out loud. How could he hope to follow her through the city when he couldn't see a thing?

Shaking her head, she braced her elbows in a crenel between the old merlons meant for protection against enemy fire. She took in the scene of the vast Darklandic landscape. It was a lovely, sunny morning in this land for once. Only a small group of people moved about in the fields down below, trekking away from the city to an intersection in the dirt path.

Kalea squinted. The people's shapes didn't look right. About five dark figures waved their arms...

She gasped. They weren't arms—they were tentacles! Sanguinesents! At their center, they dragged a person.

"D-Dorhen?" She shook her head. "Surely not."

The group of sanguinesents floated along to meet a set of people who began tapping golden rods on the ground. Sorcerers. Kalea's heart pounded. She gaped at the scene, gripping the stone, watching and knowing what would happen as a bolt of lightning sprang from one pole to the other to create a doorway in the air.

Dorhen fought them, blue hair waving in the morning breeze. But the sun was too bright, so he couldn't be very strong right now. He gave them a fuss, nonetheless. Kalea considered darting back down the stairs to help him, but couldn't peel her eyes off the scene. How could she help him all by herself? And she wasn't naïve enough to assume the Clanless elves patrolling around town could ever be convinced to help Wikshen.

Nonetheless, she didn't even have the luxury of time to get down there. The sanguinesents worked together, binding Dorhen in their combined tentacles until he was wrapped up like a spider's victim. The sanguinesents took him to the group of men with the open portal and loosened their formation. He must've lost his last ounce of energy under the sun and rode limp, head hanging.

Kalea watched helplessly from her high vantage. The sanguinesents carried him through the portal. A few of the men stepped through as well, but not all. She studied the ones who remained. If she could recognize them down in the streets, she might follow them to find out where the sorcerers were hiding out or to get information, or...something!

One of the men turned back toward the city, and she focused on him. The closer he drew, the more disbelieving she became. She'd definitely seen him before.

It was Dyii.

Chapter 42
A Lip Slips

Kalea's mouth dropped open, and it took a few short seconds for a weak moan to tremble out. The stone froze her clawing fingers. She watched the group in the field below: no more sanguinesents—they had taken Dorhen away from her to the-Creator-knew-where, leaving a small group of men standing on the path. After exchanging nods and words, they drifted in different directions. Dyii started back toward the city gate.

"Miss, you shouldn't be up here," someone at her left said, a Clanless elf patrolling this catwalk. "Are you all right?"

She ignored him, staggered back, and turned for the stairs. Metta stood on the street, gaping and twisting her neck to the left and right until Kalea waved and called her name.

"What's the matter with you? Even I thought it rude the way you ran off while the blind elf was talking."

"Wikshen's gone!" Kalea reported. Metta frowned. Kalea nodded her head and repeated the statement. "Metta! I don't know where he…"

"How do you know he's gone? Where?"

Kalea pointed at the gate, and Metta took a step toward it. Kalea grabbed her with both arms. "He didn't just stroll, through. They took him! Sorcerers!"

The image replayed in her mind of the sanguinesents carrying him horizontally through the portal with their many tentacles binding him up. His blue hair hung to the ground and obscured his face. He might be the reason they had come here—if not to collect her. Who knew what the sorcerers wanted with either of them? The fact of her Luschianity occurred to her as well. She'd told "the Dreamer" all about it.

Metta shook her head, showing her confusion clearly. She took both of Kalea's hands. "Let's go back to the temple. We'll alert the shamans."

"Go ahead of me," Kalea said. "I have to find my friends. I don't know if they're at your house anymore."

Metta gave another nod, and before she could take off, Kalea snatched the little knife from its sheath on her belt. At Metta's look of further confusion, Kalea said, "I have to borrow this."

Before Metta could react, Kalea sprinted to the shadowy alcove of the portcullis, pressed her back to the wall, and waited.

Dyii's purposeful steps tapped through the enclosed stone space. Kalea sprang with the knife poised and caught Dyii's smirk right before he snatched her arm, twirled her into an embrace, and took control of her knife hand.

"I thought you knew I can hear beating hearts," Dyii grated in her ear.

Dreadful images of him attacking both her and Metta flashed before Kalea's eyes. How could she be so stupid? Kalea made sounds of distress so the Clanless guards would hear her, but hushed herself. She wanted to talk to Dyii, not get him arrested and taken away.

"Damn you," she hissed, and he chuckled. He loosened his grip, and she wiggled free and whipped her arm to get the knife pointed at him. "Where did they take Wikshen?"

He didn't appear to fear her threat in the least, but his smile slackened. "You did really embrace that silly religion."

"It's none of your business!" She tightened her grip around the knife's handle and pushed the blade closer to his chest. Dyii still didn't express any fear. "I guess it's clear you were never a Wikshonite to begin with—because you're a sorcerer!" She got the impression he only raised his hands and kept respectful to humor her. Nonetheless, she kept the knife up.

"I'm not a sorcerer," he said with a sigh. "And I'm not a Wikshonite either. I'm just a Thaccilian. The sorcerers use my ability for their meddling. I am bound to them." His red eyes had rounded, framed between his shaggy blond bangs, which hung in oily clumps.

"What do they want with Wikshen?"

He shrugged. "I don't care." He dipped his eyes down her form and up again. "You should run. You're free. Free from them and free from him."

Kalea's knife arm lowered beyond her notice at his change of mood. When he moved to continue past the portcullis, she pushed him against the wall and held the knife to him again. Dyii made a long huff, the light dead in his red eyes.

"Where'd they take him?" Kalea demanded again.

Dyii's lips peeled back to show his clenched teeth. "You don't know what you do to me! Go home while you can!"

Kalea frowned. "Why?"

He shook his head and raised a hand to grip his shirt below his chin as if to tear it in the next instant. He held it instead. "Ilbith is looking for you too!"

"Well, I knew as much." Nonetheless, Kalea shuddered to hear that.

"Then you are stupid!" His words shot spittle across her face. "Because anyone who knows anything about Ilbith does not speak about them, much less seek them."

"It doesn't matter," she replied. "I have to find Dor—Wikshen! I have to find Wikshen."

Dyii eyed her under his lowered brow. The slight pout on his lips emphasized his narrow, sculpted cheeks. His lips had always appeared pouty by default anyway.

Kalea swallowed. "Tell me where they took him. Did they take him to their lair?"

"They took him to the kingsorcerer."

Kalea nodded rapidly. "And where is he?"

Dyii shook his head with an ill expression. "Don't go there." His eyes bored into her. Hot. His gaze trailed again to her body, her bosom. He found her attractive, she knew. Maybe he didn't know why.

She stepped closer to him, backing him into the corner. "Dyii," she said his name for sensual effect. "Tell me where the kingsorcerer lives. Please."

She didn't point the knife at him anymore. Holding it off to the side, she pressed her bosom against him instead. His breath picked up in weight. Her heart pounded at what she did, and he gave its rhythm his keen concentration.

"The kingsorcerer lives in a tower called Ilbith. It's in the Black Mountains, somewhere in the north. I hear of a path through the mountains, if you can find it." He relinquished the answer faster than she had anticipated.

"Black Mountains, to the north," she repeated for herself.

"Listen," he said, dropping half of his allured state of mind. "The Black Mountains are as dangerous as Ilbith itself. Don't go."

"Do you know what they're going to do with Wikshen?"

He threw his hands out to the sides. "I'm more afraid of what they'll do to you!"

"Did they ask you to find me?"

"Of course!" He huffed again and averted his gaze, working his throat apple with a smidge of difficulty. "I don't know how they know you, but you look like the description they gave me—and I don't wish to give you over. I can't do it!"

"Why?"

"Because I love you!"

Kalea's heart sped.

"I don't know why either," he continued. "Your heart grazes me with its rhythm. You *can't* go to Ilbith."

Kalea stepped back away from him. Dyii loved her? She shook off her surprise. He didn't love her, he was only drawn to her because they both were of rare compatible species: a Luschian and a Thaccilian. At least she wasn't affected by that same instinctive pull which made all Thaccilian men mad for her. Compatible species or not, it was no business of his where she went and what she did. She knew where to find Dorhen now.

She stepped farther back from Dyii as he stood like an obelisk about to crumble. She left him there.

The sound of an old woman humming long preceded Damos's eyes opening. He listened for a while, hardly registering the idea that it might be morning. In fact, the old woman—Metta's mother—gave him a nudge before he bothered to move.

"You want something to eat, boy?" Her croaky voice rang louder than he could handle.

Damos groaned. The sounds and movement stirred his head into a throbbing ache unlike anything he'd dealt with before.

"I knew it," the old woman continued. "You finished half my barrel of ale last night. You drank more than both Bowaen and his young friend."

Damos dragged himself to a sitting position at the mention of Bowaen's name. He used his best mind-over-matter technique to ignore the pain in his head and the churning in his stomach. He'd gotten himself drunk plenty since running away from home, but not like this. The sorceress he'd fallen in love with couldn't hold a candle to the grief Kalea had caused him.

"Where's Kalea?" he asked at the first thought of her, and Metta's mother answered quickly with a sigh.

"You missed her by about twelve hours. She ran outside with a warlock yesterday, while you sang and caroused. Metta went too. They're still not back."

The woman shook her head and wrung her hands, turning back to the hearth to grab a wooden cup from the cupboard. "I don't like those Wikshonites," she said. "They're the worst bunch I've seen around here, and their numbers have only increased over the years." She ladled whatever she'd been brewing over the fire into the cup. "Now she tells me Wikshen himself has arisen." She trilled a breath through her lips. "I don't quite know what that means, but it sounds like I've lost my daughter. Drink this."

She extended the cup to Damos, who received it with slow, shaky hands. He couldn't tell yet if the shaking was due to his hangover or what the woman talked about.

"You said Kalea ran out with a warlock?" Damos asked.

"I did." Metta's mother stirred the pot over the fire. "I'm pretty sure they left to go find *him*."

He raised the cup to his lips to brave whatever foul hangover medicine she'd created, but paused when he saw an extra, shiny bauble on his hand. "What in the Creator's kingdom?"

He turned his hand over to study the gold ring on his third finger, which was studded with bright green stones. The blue-stoned one on his index finger belonged to him; Kalea had somehow found it in the lake below Hathrohskog and returned it to him. But the green-stoned one was new.

Metta's mother observed his curiosity about it. "Bowaen put that on you while you slept this morning."

Damos wrinkled his nose.

"He didn't want to wake you, but he also didn't want to leave you here without a word. He and his two friends had somewhere to go, though, so he left you with that. He told me to tell you thanks for saving his life."

"Oh." The odd ring looked expensive. The green tone of the stones along the band reminded him of the livery colors of Carridax. "That's… nice of him," Damos responded in a murmur. He pulled the ring off— actually, he attempted to pull it off, but it wouldn't budge. He tried harder, and oddly, the more he tried, the tighter it felt around his knuckle, shrinking only to relax again when he stopped. It wouldn't come off, and he easily knew why. It was enchanted.

Damos stepped out of the house, dressed and wearing the ring. Metta had returned, but it appeared some warlock was preventing her from getting off the doorstep.

"Are Kalea's friends here, Togha?" she asked in their strained conversation.

The warlock, an elf with black hair, held her wrist as she gingerly tried to twist it away without making a scene. She saw Damos emerge, but paid no mind.

"Forget about them," Togha replied. "Now that we've finally met in Alkeer, we have a lot to discuss."

"We have nothing to discuss," she fired back.

He dropped her hand in defeat. She didn't run.

Damos piped up. "Kalea's friends have gone. Where is she, anyway?"

"I don't know. She ran off," Metta said, becoming a little panicky. "I'm not sure where." She turned back to Togha. "I need you to escort me to the temple."

Togha grimaced. "No, Metta, please…"

She shoved him, and he caught himself on the waist-high garden wall. "Are you a warlock or not? Take me to the temple!"

"Why so urgent?"

"Wikshen was taken!"

Togha and Damos both echoed, "Taken?"

Metta tried to hide her frown behind her hand. "My poor Mastaren. I don't yet know who exactly did it or where they took him, but we have to tell the shamans."

Togha's eyes shifted to view Damos, displaying a look of relief perhaps. Damos certainly felt relief at that news.

"Take me to the temple, or I'll go alone," Metta pressed.

"Fine," Togha said, dropping his arms so that they disappeared under his black poncho. "C'mon then."

"And what of Kalea?" Damos asked.

Metta twisted around, her lips pursed. "I don't know. If she doesn't come back to Wikhaihli, all the better."

They left Damos on the doorstep. *What of Kalea?* he had to ask himself. She'd done nothing but brush him off since their reunion. She loved that monster with a sickening obviousness. But she was somewhere around here, in Alkeer, maybe soon to leave.

He whistled, and found Azrielle not far. She glided over and alighted on the lamppost above him. If Wikshen had been taken by sorcerers, then things might get better. Maybe they'd destroy that blue-haired bastard—a good reason to find Kalea. Damos might still have a chance.

Chapter 43
Spilled Punch

Lamrhath threw the door open after a long, hurried journey across the tower and up several flights of stairs. A waft of bright heat hit him on the other side—torches, several of them. On the floor, Wikshen knelt at the center of a ring of sorcerers, slumped forward. A clutch of sanguinesents stood facing the walls to avoid accidental ensnarement of their allies. They must've helped retrieve the rascal.

"To what do I owe this triumph?" he asked the sorcerers who held Wikshen firmly within their uncomfortable fire ring. It hadn't been long enough for a briefing on these unfolding events. A runner bearing the sentence, "We got Wikshen," had found Lamrhath and led him straight to the portal chamber.

"Naerezek blessed us with a sunny day when we ran into this creature in Alkeer, my lord," the nearest sorcerer said with a beaming smile.

"Rewards for all of you." Lamrhath strode toward Wikshen. "Where've you been? You look like shit."

Wikshen breathed slowly and laboriously as much as his thick rope bindings allowed, but Lamrhath wouldn't dream of ordering them to back the torches up yet. For him, the heat merely caused perspiration under his layers, which would escalate to a hard sweat in time, but Wikshen looked as if he'd fall over at the slightest nudge. His body glistened with its own moisture; his hair hung in clumps. Lamrhath took a fistful of it to raise his head and inspect his vacant face. The sight made Lamrhath smile.

"You were doing so well," he said to the creature. "Why did you kill my men and flee?"

When Wikshen raised his eyes to meet Lamrhath's, they glowed that bright turquoise color which clashed with his blue hair. The color of *Dorhen's* eyes. Wikshen tensed up and trembled, gnashing his teeth.

"I must say," Lamrhath continued, "I don't really know what to do with you. Mhina tells me *you're* the one who snatched her up."

Wikshen showed no impression at his statement.

"Did you indeed take her as a gift for me?"

He didn't answer.

Lamrhath released his hair, and Wikshen supported his own head from then on, keeping a wary watch on Lamrhath. "Everything you do contradicts everything you've done."

He stepped back to take the creature in again. That same long, black drape was wrapped around Wikshen's hips. Lamrhath shook his head and exhaled through his nose. "There will be plenty of time to puzzle you out, though." He gave a nod to the sorcerers. "We've prepared a place for you until then."

At his signal, the sorcerers pulled Wikshen's ropes taut and half-dragged him out of the room. They had recently rigged up an attic in one of the towers with windows and various glass lenses where they would secure the creature like they had at the outpost, except here they were better equipped to research magic for making stronger light to shine on him. Wikshen wouldn't escape this place.

With Wikshen and most of the crowd gone, Lamrhath approached the head sanguinesent, which stood central to the rest. The otherworldly being turned fluidly around to face him, knowing psychically that he approached.

"You've done well," Lamrhath offered.

The sanguinesent's face, hard and devoid of any ability to show emotion, stared at him as emptily as any inanimate object. Its diamond eyes sparkled magnificently.

We need not your words of affirmation, mortal. The person Wikshen has been properly sorted according to your regard, and we've no fuel to continue.

"Fuel? So would eating more flesh keep you here longer?"

A rolling chatter reverberated in the sanguinesent's throat, and those around it who still kept their backs turned echoed that sound.

"Could I," Lamrhath tried, "contact you again, should I need you?"

Logic determines so, it said. *But one such as you should exercise caution.*

A slight chill ran up Lamrhath's spine. "Why?"

You sorcerers haplessly play, dabbling with interdimensional beings and magics you couldn't begin to understand. This is an example of what your world would call foolishness. Take caution.

It and its companions, about twenty or so, all vanished in a grainy puff of smoke. With one fifth of the sanguinesents gone, having done their assigned duty, Lamrhath could only assume the rest of the hundred were still out there, looking for his sword and his Luschian.

Leaving his men to worry about Wikshen, Lamrhath hurried back over to the Chimera Tower where another event awaited him. He entered the cozy little room to find Mhina standing with her nanny. Lamrhath regarded the woman and nodded, prompting her to turn to the table holding various implements for haircutting and styling. He'd warned the nanny not to talk about what they were going to do.

While the woman scraped the shears along the whetstone in the background, Lamrhath knelt before the little *farhah,* took her attention with his firm gaze, and blocked her from turning around with his hand outstretched.

"Don't be frightened," he assured her. He knew she wouldn't like this. *Farhah* in Norr never wore short haircuts like the boys did. After they had acquired Mhina, he asked Orinleah about it. Norrian *farhah* spent their days practicing grace and loveliness, besides the usual household duties. Getting her hair cut would most likely upset her, but Lamrhath desperately needed her hair for a better use than loveliness.

"What are you going to do? What's that sound?" she asked.

He blocked her face and turned it back toward him when she attempted to look again. "It's a pair of shears," he said in his softest voice. He wasn't quite used to speaking to children yet. "I know it sounds ludicrous, but we're going to trim your hair—only a bit."

Her face twisted into a heartbreaking display of innocent fear and confusion. She put her hands on her head, and he took her wrists and held them down.

"I told you not to be frightened." He checked his volume and cleared his throat. He realized how tightly he held her wrists and shifted to holding her hands instead. So tiny. Both of them at once couldn't fill his one hand. They were cold, so he cupped his hands around them and looked into her big, lavender eyes. He forgot about the nanny sharpening a loud metal instrument in the background.

Mhina stared back at him. His lips curled into a real smile—not a forced one. She illuminated the room, more so than the soft light through the window or the little flame in the fireplace. For that brief moment, Lamrhath could breathe easy. His aches and pains receded. He would stay in this room all day if he didn't have so much to do.

Mhina didn't smile back, but Lamrhath understood how difficult it must be to get comfortable in this new place. How might he make it better for her? What toys would she like? What color of dresses would boost her honey hair and purple eyes to a greater radiance?

Footsteps tapped toward them. Lamrhath's smile dropped. Who in the world dared to interrupt this holy moment? The nanny approached with the shears: a dingy woman in a threadbare headscarf with wisps of blonde-grey hair streaming out. Her apron pockets bulged ungracefully, stuffed with useful bits and bobs. Her posture wasn't quite straight, her face wan and cold. Her eyes showed empty and defeated. She didn't belong in here. Her tired presence sucked the life right out of the room Mhina otherwise filled with warmth and joy.

"Get out." Lamrhath let Mhina's hands go and stood to face the older woman.

The woman stepped back. "M-my lord?"

He stormed one step toward her and yanked the tool from her hand. "Leave. I don't want you anywhere near my girl."

The woman stuttered and wrung her hands until he gave her a helpful shove toward the door. "Tell Talekas Mhina needs a new nanny," he ordered her. "A younger, brighter, better one."

So far, he'd been kind, and the nanny knew it. She bolted out the door and closed it as fast as she could without slamming it. Now that he was alone with his treasure, Mhina's eyes darted between him and the shears in his hand. He held them unthreateningly down by his side.

"This is better," he told her. He motioned to the other table holding an array of treats with a pitcher of fruity red punch. "Go and have something. This doesn't need to be so scary." When she didn't move, he asked, "What do you like?"

"Nothing," she said, an answer which didn't surprise him. She'd been less talkative than ever since her separation from the elf-boy from her village.

Lamrhath kept his patience, placed the shears down, and moved to the food table himself. "I like these." He picked up a random item, a biscuit with dried berries on top. He actually didn't care much for food. He only ate exquisite recipes because he could afford to as the kingsorcerer. How would it look to his subjects if he ate mushy porridge and stale bread every day like the lower class? Just because he ate the best of the best didn't mean he paid any extra mind to it. He ate out of necessity and did it fast so he could get back to his bed and whatever woman waited in it.

Today, he put the biscuit in his mouth, bit off half, and actually *noticed* the sugary flavor running over his tongue. He smiled again as the delightful little creature at his side watched him with curiosity.

"It's good," he said honestly. "You must try one."

He held another one out for her. After a few cautious steps, she took it from him. He gave her a bigger smile and popped the rest of the treat into his mouth. He enjoyed it. Such a strange happening.

She appeared to puzzle over him as she chewed. He allowed it and made an effort to keep his warm demeanor.

"Which one is your favorite, Mhina?"

She shrugged as she worked on her biscuit. It took her more bites to finish it than it did him.

He dabbed the corner of his mouth with an available napkin. "Mhina," he said, "If there's anything you want, you can ask me directly." In that moment, he secretly decided Mhina could not only ask questions, but ask for things. He'd alert all who dealt with the little girl that she was not to be punished for asking questions.

When she swallowed the last of the treat, he followed up, "Did you like it?"

She shrugged.

"Is it different from what you used to eat at home?"

She nodded.

"It's better, isn't it?"

She had no response to that.

He stepped aside so she could access the table. "What else might you like?"

Stalling on the room's round carpet, she twiddled her fingers and lowered her eyes.

"Aren't you hungry?"

Another shrug.

"Here." He lifted the pitcher and poured the sweet, fruity drink into the crystal glass. The glass filled fast and brimmed before he was ready. "Oh, dear." He lifted it to his lips and sipped it down to a level she might handle better, and then extended the offering to her. "Try it."

She took it with both hands and drank after him.

"Is it unlike what you drank at home?"

She nodded.

He nudged her toward a little padded stool, short enough for her little legs. "Have a seat. This won't hurt."

Holding the chalice under her chin, she kept her wary eyes on him as he moved around her seat, back to the table of haircutting implements.

"Don't be afraid of this," he reassured her. "You might actually like having your hair cut. It's soothing to have someone work on your hair—which you probably know already." He took up the shears from their place beside a basket and a pile of strings, and inspected the shiny blades. "A shorter, more manageable hairstyle suits a young one such as you," he went on. "You'll be able to run and yell in the garden, and not worry whether you're collecting tangles. If you do, it'll comb out in a stroke. You'll see."

He took a seat in the taller chair behind her. Something in his gut fluttered when he started moving his hands toward her shimmering golden strands. He hadn't really touched her hair before. He'd mostly kept his distance so as not to frighten her. Gaining a child's trust required patience, calm, and kindness. And treats, of course.

His hand moved closer, closer. His breath trembled in anticipation of the silky texture against his fingertips. He forgot the shears he'd placed on the floor beside him for the moment. He ran his fingers through once. Twice. Thrice.

He grabbed the comb and proceeded to straighten her hair, running the little bone prongs all the way down her hair's long length. The task calmed him. Hypnotized him. Mhina sipped her punch as he worked. He was in no rush to finish this part. He combed her hair. He combed it some more, savoring the soft sensation on his hands.

Shaking out of his trance, he reset his mind to the task he actually needed to do. He needed the hair more than she did. Her particular specimen held so much beauty over the other elven ponytails they'd collected that he decided he'd keep the product made from Mhina's hair for himself. Surely it would provide power beyond the others, not to mention style.

He picked up the shears and put down the comb. Now his hands shook with dread. The first clip would be the hardest. He paused, remembering the importance of tying sections off with string first. With relief at his work's delay, he got to work tying off about eight different ponytails which would be hacked off with the shears. It hurt his stomach to pick the shears back up.

Scraaayyy... He squeezed the shears together, applying pressure to the curved metal section and making the two blades at the ends come together, passing the sharpened sides along each other. It was only a practice squeeze to make sure the blades were well sharpened and in working order. The sound hurt enough. He admitted to himself that there was something wrong about cutting her hair.

At the sound of his practice squeeze, however, Mhina tensed up and dropped her brimming chalice. It crashed before her, shattering, spreading red liquid and sharp shards in all directions.

"Shit!" came Lamrhath's raw reaction. He leaped to his feet, one lock of her hair in his hand, and somehow in his impulsive flail, the shears flew out of his grip. He lurched to catch them and fumbled.

At the end of the confusion, when his nerves had settled and his brain assessed what happened, he found a long, red line carved into his forearm. He dropped Mhina's hair.

She turned around to inspect, standing in a pool of punch with glass all around her feet. Her little white gown showed a stained splash of red. Only her thin pair of silk slippers protected her from the broken glass.

The blood ran out of Lamrhath's arm like a long, thin curtain, showing its coppery glitter in the firelight—a trait elven blood possessed. It dripped down to mingle with the punch on the floor.

Lamrhath opened his mouth to call for whoever might be waiting outside the door right as Mhina lifted a foot to take a step. "Don't move!" he said instead, and reached to stop her.

She threw up her hands in surprise at his barking voice, and one of them touched his bloody gash when he threw his arm around her torso. A cool sensation entered his body and traveled in all directions. A rush of delightful tingles followed and, for an instant, his vision dimmed, replaced by a blissful nothingness. The pain in his arm disappeared and the constant pain in his groin lifted away farther than ever.

In a blink, his sight returned. He fluttered his eyes open, almost reluctant to do so. He found his mouth open, gasping. Mhina still stood there before him. She quickly whipped her hands off him and leaned away.

Dazed and relieved, he looked around. The punch puddle spread wider among the little shimmering shards of glass. He rubbed his eyes and quickly checked the wound on his arm. He checked his other arm in confusion, then back to the arm he knew should have a big bloody gash on it. Blood remained. He wiped it with his hand and searched for the cut. He found none. Where exactly had he been cut?

In utter disorientation, he checked his shoulder and bicep. The cut no longer existed. He crunched across the broken glass in his hard-soled boots to get the napkin and wipe the blood off his forearm. No more wound.

He lowered his eyebrows and shot Mhina a quizzical look. "What just happened?"

She shrugged.

"Stop doing that—answer my question!"

She pointed to his arm. "You got hurt."

"Yes, I know." He inspected his arm again. A big, long cut used to be there, and now it was gone. It had left blood on his arm to remind him, but the skin had fused back together perfectly. "It was you," he said to her.

She clasped her wrist before her and nodded her head.

"You…healed me."

Her face twisted as if she'd cry.

He lunged and lifted her under the arms to place her in a glass-free zone. "How did you do it?" He bent over to put his face at her level, close enough to share breath.

"I don't know."

"How did you do it?"

Tears ran down her soft, round cheeks. She raised her hands and waited. Taking the cue, he put his arm out. She mimicked the event by putting her palms on his arm and then launching them off, fingers spread in the air.

"You simply touched me."

She nodded.

"You can heal." He huffed at a new flood of thoughts and feelings, too much to process at once. "You're an *elven healer*."

He knew of a legend about elven healers. In ancient history, Norr had boasted about having an elite sect of "healers" who could close wounds with a single touch—exactly as Mhina had done! They showed their greatest worth in battle as a military division, when they would restore their comrades who lay on the battlefield near death. As females and males could both be born with the ability, this was the only case in which females could be sent into battle. The legend of elven healers, in his experience, was treated as a mere fairy tale.

"Holy Naerezek's cock," he hissed, unable to tear his eyes away from the phenomenon standing before him. What did this mean? For him? For Ilbith? What did it mean that Wikshen had apparently collected her for Lamrhath? Did he know what he had taken?

Lamrhath took a breath. "Mhina," he said, "I've decided not to cut your hair. You have done well."

Mhina gave no reaction to his announcement.

"You are a very good child, and you please me."

He opened the door and found a few attendants waiting, their faces long and questioning since they had, no doubt, heard the earlier commotion. "There's been a minor accident with a glass of punch," he said. "Take Mhina back to her room. Clean up the mess. Don't proceed with the haircutting, and do not punish her for any reason."

Lamrhath set out back to his own chamber to clean himself up and ponder what he'd just experienced.

Chapter 44
Forceful Desteer

Tirnah's vibrato rang proudly at today's Faerhain Devotion. She might've lost her husband, but she truly had much to be thankful for. Anonhet stood beside her, sharing the song among numerous other *faerhain* and *farhah*.

There were only three *farhah* in the whole clan. All the other children in the village were *saeghar*, running and tumbling in the practice yard, learning how to shoot and hunt and fight with their fists. Even the newborn infants were boys. Those three *farhah* in the grove this morning had opened Tirnah's eyes. There would be four with Mhina present.

She couldn't bear to think about Mhina. Under her cloak, she wrapped her arms around herself. She had the future and Anonhet as a best friend, and Lehomis, who, in his great generosity, had taken them both into his care. With Trisdahen dead and her two children absent, Tirnah felt every bit the orphan Anonhet was; and now, strangely, she was back on Anonhet's level. Her age might as well have reversed too. Before long, Tirnah knew she'd be giggling with the younger *faerhain* behind the bush at the bathing creek, sizing up the *saehgahn* as the younger females liked to do.

She finished her note and let her voice rest. A hush fell over the deep, green grove. Only the sultry air moved amid the bowing trees and interwoven branches. Lanterns hung motionless on long ropes from the canopy. Soft lights flickered behind the colored glass.

At the head of the *faerhain*'s large group, the Desteer maidens stood in prayer with their wide sleeves unfurled to the ground, their bodices wrapped crisply around them. They wore all white, with their faces doused in a pearlescent powder and a purple stripe drawn across their eyes. Only their different hair colors set them apart from each other. Alhannah's hair showed the darkest, most ancient bloodline in Norr—much like Lehomis's. Her voice pierced when she prayed aloud.

"Bright One, see us!" She turned her stare to the crowd. "His golden eyes miss nothing!"

Reciting the phrases in Norrian brought a cascade of frolicking rhymes and rhythms. Every sermon rolled out as poetry. Alhannah motioned to the deeper section of the grove, where huge woven baskets waited, nestled into the forest vegetation. "Now you will file into lines and enter to tell the Bright One of all your worries and concerns."

Tirnah understood the Desteer maidens spent countless hours inside those baskets in meditation. On one day of each week, Faerhain Devotion, the clan's females entered the baskets and asked for His blessing.

After nearly an hour of waiting in line, Tirnah ducked her head under the little doorway to enter the tiny space in the large basket. It was barely large enough for two people. Every time she entered one, she thanked the Bright One secretly that she had chosen the hall at her *gaulaerhainha*. How miserable must it be to sit in the musty thing for so many hours per week?

"Tirnah," the maiden sitting inside said her name with a certain level of sternness. Alhannah remained outside, muttering garbled prayers in her fanatic, untiring way. "At last, you've come to speak with us. How many visits have you skipped in the past weeks?"

Tirnah shrugged. "I've been busy, and full of worries."

"Exactly the reason you are supposed to speak with us."

"Well, I'm here today. I have a concern. My daughter was taken from me, and my son is going after her—and that's not to mention my husband's death." She cleared her throat. "Can you comfort me in these days?"

"I thought you were receiving enough comfort from the elder," the maiden said. Typical Desteer games. It wasn't out of place to feel as though these meetings weren't merely to counsel *faerhain* as much as to talk them into a trap.

Tirnah narrowed her eyes and wrinkled her nose. "And what are you getting at, *Ameiha*?"

The maiden's mouth widened into a shrewd smile. "I don't need the Bright One to inform me how close you've drawn to him."

"He's my grandfather."

"No, he's not." The maiden spread her hands, displaying the dots of light shining through the wicker holes on her palms.

"He's my husband's grandfather, and so that makes him mine." Tirnah waved her hand and poised to lay it over the maiden's face. She stopped herself because such a rude action could get her a beating. She dropped her hand back to her lap. "I'm in mourning. Let me have my grandfather's support until I'm ready to remarry."

"We've seen the way your 'grandfather' looks at you."

Tirnah snorted.

"And did you not notice how savagely he attacked your Tinharri suitor?"

"He wasn't my suitor!" Tirnah corrected. "Lehomis is an honorable *saehgahn* and would never do anything to overstep himself." Tirnah took a breath. Desteer hardly counseled; they delved, judged, and accused. "Now, if we're finished here—"

The maiden caught her arm and squeezed it as Tirnah turned for the little wicker door. "I suggest you consider the shearing ritual for your particular condition."

Tirnah chose not to respond, even to ask for her definition of "particular condition." She took her arm back as gently as she could manage and ducked through the basket's opening. On the other side, the *faerhain* were lining up for that very ritual. Each week, the Desteer managed to convince a few more *faerhain* to cut their hair.

Tirnah found Anonhet and grabbed her arm as firmly as the maiden had taken hers. "Let's slip away silently," she whispered into the younger *faerhain*'s ear.

A hand landed on her own shoulder then, creating a chain consisting of Tirnah, Anonhet, and the newly come maiden. Tirnah put a challenging stare on her face. Without a word, the maiden reached into her lapel to unsheathe a pair of shears. Tirnah whipped around to view the haircutting line.

"The Bright One orders our hair severed," the maiden said with the usual blank expression. "This is a good spot to begin a second line."

The illness of dread returned to Tirnah's stomach. She moved her mouth, but couldn't find any words right away. She pulled her arm, but the maiden held it fast.

Tirnah lurched back. "Call for Tihen," she hissed to the younger one. Immediately, she knew what a terrible idea it was. House guardians were pledged to serve and die for the house *faerhain* as devotedly as any actual male family member. Getting their house guardian involved in any struggle with the Desteer could cause the first ripple in a horrible ordeal of *saehgahn* versus Desteer. It would not have a pleasant outcome.

Thankfully, Anonhet hesitated before tearing off to alert the lad. Tirnah pushed forward to hopefully shove the maiden off her feet. The maiden teetered but stayed erect.

"What's going on over there?" Alhannah inquired.

The maiden with the shears steadied herself and stepped forward with her free hand extended to grab at Tirnah. That's when Tirnah flailed and yelled. Their interaction escalated into a mess of hands, hers slapping chaotically while the maiden grabbed for her hair.

"Sister!" the maiden called to Alhannah. Tirnah's vision darkened as her anger peaked.

"Wait!" Anonhet squealed. "Stop!"

Tirnah reached into her bodice and unsheathed one of her late husband's old daggers to hold off the maidens before her head could get any lighter. "You think you're the only one who knows how to hide a blade in a *hanbohik*?" she challenged the maiden who brandished the shears. Nonetheless, she staggered to keep her own footing and found herself propped on both the maiden's and Anonhet's shoulders. The dagger left her hand and fell to the ground somewhere along the way.

"You need to stop this!" Anonhet said. "Don't you know what she's going through?"

Tirnah's knees gave way.

"Stand down, sister!" Alhannah ordered. "Give her some air!"

A brief dark patch preceded the moment when Tirnah's vision returned, staring up through the tree canopy with all manner of hands patting her face and squeezing her hand. She slid her other hand to her belly under her cloak.

Alhannah waved a fragrant herb under her nose. "Put the shears away, sister."

Thank the Bright One, Tirnah thought. *If they don't leave me alone, there will be a war.*

"*Maineha!*" a male shouted as one of the *saehgahn* approached. Anonhet must've called for Tihen after all.

Oh no, don't let him fight the Desteer! Tirnah prayed.

He didn't. He scooped her up in his strong arms. She preferred being in his care one hundredfold more than any Desteer maiden. "*Maineha*," he said again, addressing her in the formal way of house guardians and guests.

"Bring her into the hall," Alhannah ordered Tihen. Anonhet whimpered frantically at his side. "She'll be fine," the head maiden continued. "From now on, we'll be easy with this one. She may have to lie in until it's time—Anonhet, calm yourself! Here, breathe this scent." She held a little sack of herbs under Tirnah's nose.

Tirnah tried to breathe slow and deep. Finally safe in a *saehgahn*'s arms, she let herself drift off.

Lehomis paced back and forth in his inn room. "Damn stupid lad!" he said. "Don't make me have to pay for another day here."

He didn't mean Tey, the lad he'd found at the tea house. Tey waited outside with the borrowed cart loaded with all the sacks and crates of food and grains Lehomis had bought here—which wasn't too big of a haul because a great famine was sweeping through the human lands. As of now, he cursed one more crate yet to be delivered. He'd already added yesterday's additional inn fee to his bill; he didn't want to dish out any more. For all he knew, he'd have to return and spend more money if his clan's bad luck continued.

The hundredth stamp of his antsy foot on the floorboards masked the tap at the door, but he heard it nonetheless. He flew to yank the door open. A pimply young human lad stood in the hallway, hoisting one more crate.

"'Bout time!" He waved the lad in and pressed a coin into his palm, and then sent him out as fast as he'd come.

Lehomis wiped his sweaty brow across his wrist, observing the chest-width crate with little pieces of straw poking through the crevices. Although it was never too late to change his mind, he shook his head and avoided all thought about it.

Outside, he carried that last crate toward the cart.

"Lehomis! One more word!"

He froze at the voice of Cirinhen, the teahouse owner. One glance down at his crate ensured its label was hidden against his chest. Cirinhen strode toward him with a woman at his elbow. Lehomis squinted in recognition.

"Leho, my friend," Cirinhen announced with a huge grin, "you remember this fine woman, don't you?"

Lehomis's mouth dropped open. "Yes, I do." Forgetting its label, Lehomis gently put the crate on the ground. The woman beside his friend glowed, a smile on her plump face. She was middle-aged, with streaks of grey winding through her neatly twisted braids.

Lehomis held out his hand, and she blushed brightly to make contact. "Irina," Lehomis recited, "the beauty who made Cirinhen *truly* rich."

The woman burst into a girlish giggle despite her age and said, "Oh, come here, you silly old elf!"

She threw her arms around him and lifted his feet off the ground in a hard embrace. Lehomis knew Cirinhen's human wife from long ago, when the couple were newly married and her daughter just an infant. Though she stood taller than Lehomis, Irina was a graceful flower of a woman who complemented Cirinhen as nicely as any *faerhain*. Now, she was aged in her natural human years, and jolly too. Her young daughter already claimed her place as the shining flower of the teahouse. Cirinhen himself looked as young as ever. He couldn't have been too much older than Trisdahen.

Lehomis managed to subdue his stare during their catching up, but his thoughts ran wild. The lives of humans were so short, he was reminded. Poor Cirinhen. The age of the teahouse surpassed this woman by a few years, but she already sported crows' feet at her eyes. Soon, Cirinhen would be a widower too. Lehomis swallowed hard and hoped none of these thoughts showed on his face.

The couple excused themselves courteously, making note of Lehomis's waiting cart, and he turned to put his last crate onto it. Tey watched with a raised eyebrow. Yesterday, the young lad had loaded the bulk of Lehomis's purchases onto the cart. When that final crate hadn't shown up, Lehomis had Tey tie a tarp over the load and guard the cart all night, sleeping underneath it.

"Mornin', Tey," Lehomis said in the common tongue to the lad. "Boff any shop owners' daughters last night?"

Tey lowered his eyebrow. "No, Elder, of course not!"

Lehomis waved his hand. "I joke. Don't be so uptight, we're in Theddir."

Tey pointed to Lehomis's last crate. "Why does this crate bear the mark of Root McCrow?"

Lehomis threw his extra tarp over the crate and shot Tey a bland smirk. "I found the crate in an alley and used it to pack some bottles of syrup. My *faerhain* will love it on their biscuits."

Tey asked no more questions after that. Lehomis put his foot on the mounting step and paused. He'd forgotten his pipe in the inn room. With a brief gesture for Tey to wait, he hurried back through the inn's front door, passed the coal-filled brazier in the main hall, and lunged up the side stairs to the wing lined with small private rooms.

He bumped into a light body, and it flew backward with a feminine yelp. She'd emerged too quickly from one of the doors. Lehomis started. "Oh, dear. So sorry, madam…"

He would've lunged to lend her an arm, but instead stared at her as she collected herself. Something about her form…her hair. As she straightened up, her shawl fell off of her head and exposed her ears and delicate features.

"Oh, dear Bright One, you're an elf," he said aloud. Lehomis leaned down to take her arm, and she smacked him away.

"How dare you!"

Lehomis squinted and grabbed her arm anyway. "What are you doing here? Females should never leave Norr…unless there's good reason."

"I do have a good reason, and it's none of your business." Her sleek purple eyes with dark lashes crossed Lehomis's face. She hesitated before continuing to gather her shawl as Lehomis pulled her to standing.

He hardened his scrutiny of her. "You're..." He took her chin and forced her to show him her face. "I know you..."

"No, you don't."

He snorted. "Yer unpracticed lying will give you away anywhere, lass." She tightened her frowning lips.

"I *do* know you," he insisted. "It's hard to tell without your face paint, but not impossible. Why did you run away from your duties as a Desteer maiden, *Kennaha*?"

This was the same maiden he'd spoken to as she was leaving with the funeral team. Kennaha lowered her chin. She sported mesmerizing purple eyes, spaced slightly in opposite directions, deepening her mystery for all who gazed into them. Her enigmatic stare tended to make her appear older; she was actually one of the newer maidens in the gaggle.

"My lying improves each time I come here."

Lehomis's jaw dropped. "'Each time?' What in hell are you doing here?"

Those alluring eyes shifted before she decided to grab Lehomis's lapel and pull him into her room. She closed the door. "I'm going to tell you this once and I'll hear no protest. If you don't immediately leave me after I speak, my husband may return and kill you if he finds you in our sacred space."

Lehomis blinked at her detailed statement. "Husband!"

"Shhh!"

"What the hell happened with you?" Lehomis forgot all about Tey and his cart full of all-important foodstuffs. "What about the Bright One?"

"I'm hoping the Bright One will understand."

Lehomis laughed, but couldn't figure out why. His hands flew about of their own accord. He'd never seen anything like this. He buried his face in his palms by the end of his laughter. "Oh, dear Lord!" The exclamation came with some sort of dreaded boiling in his gut, not mirth.

"If you don't lower your foolish voice, Elder..." She gave him the signature Desteer sternness. It was odd to see a Desteer's face without its paint. In reality, she really was a person in the flesh, not a cold, thought-raiding phantom.

"You have to tell me how this happened!" he said.

"No, I don't."

He blocked her from storming out the door. "Oh, no, you can't say something so outrageous and then leave me here hangin'. You gotta talk, lass! You gotta!"

"Only if you shut up."

He crossed his arms and waited.

She blinked her eyes and turned sideways. "Well… Elder. You know how sometimes we Desteer travel to other clans to lend our talents if needed, or to help if other sects are short-handed."

"Yeah."

"Well…" Her voice grew breathy, and Lehomis sensed secret mischief. She'd probably never articulated her deed—or crime—before. "One year ago, Alhannah sent me to…another clan, and I…" She took a moment to pant a bit. "I helped them tend wounded *saehgahn* after the eradication of a pack of vicious wolves. This pack had been terrorizing the clan and their livestock for many seasons.

"That's how and when my hands first touched the bloody body of the one who is now my husband. He'd been bitten. It was a dire wound that almost killed him, a deep bite on his thigh. I personally worked to save him for hours, which became days. I became familiar with the feel of him. The curves of him. When he regained consciousness, we talked a lot as I tended him day to day. I felt… I can't explain it." Her eyelids fluttered through her stammering.

"You fell in love," Lehomis said for her, "as the humans would put it."

She breathed a heavy sigh. "Thank you, Elder. I can't bear to invoke the forbidden word; it feels so wrong. But yes." She dipped her chin, now standing squarely with Lehomis. He glued his eyes to her, eager for more of this juicy, irresistible secret.

"How did you manage to marry?" he pressed when she didn't speak soon enough.

She spread her hands to indicate the room. "This room is our residence. We came here together. I went along cluelessly—he had it all figured out. He took a shiny round thing out of his belt pouch."

"Money," Lehomis said. She wouldn't know what a coin was because they didn't use such things in Norr. They traded goods and skills back at home.

She nodded. "Yes, I know that now. On that particular night, my husband also explained to me the purpose of an inn as we hurried up the stairs. He locked the door and assured me of our security." Security was important in a marriage ritual. Usually, the groom-to-be would create a cozy space in the forest so the bride could feel safe. "And then we performed our marriage ritual in here," she said.

Lehomis's chin hovered over his crossed arms, his head pushed forward as he fixated on her story. There were few things in life he loved more than a good story.

"This room is ours," she said. "It's our marriage home. My husband goes back to his clan and I go back to mine, to the Desteer hall, while he keeps the rent on this sacred space paid so we may return whenever we can both get away. We return here to practice our marriage rituals."

"Dear Bright One," Lehomis said again. "You can't keep this a secret forever! The other maidens will find out."

"The maidens rarely conduct *milhanrajea* on each other," she corrected.

"Doesn't matter," he replied. "What will happen when you get pregnant?"

She raised an eyebrow. "You think a maiden is incapable of hiding a pregnancy?"

He narrowed his eyes. What a loaded statement! He had just learned more about the Desteer in the last few minutes than in two or three elven lifetimes.

He began in jest, "Well, when you do, make sure the child is raised in Lockheirhen." The more his sentence advanced, the less it felt like a joke. "In fact, I'll raise it if need be."

Her eyes rounded and focused on him more sharply than he'd ever seen from her. "You would do that, Elder?"

Yes, he would raise it. He'd rejoice to add a new child, even one from such an unlikely parent, to the clan. "Why do you think I wouldn't? Your secret is safe with me."

She made a slight curtsy, a gesture the Desteer didn't normally do. She'd left her maiden-self back in Norr; today she was *faerhain*. "I'm in your debt."

"I'll leave you now," he said, turning, then paused. "One question."

She waited for it.

"Why did you choose the hall?" He showed his helpless, empty palms again in his thirst for hard answers. "If you were destined to fall for a *saehgahn*, and ultimately ruin your vow of celibacy and standing as a maiden—to walk such a dangerous wire—why did you not foresee this on the day of your *gaulaerhainha*?"

She closed her eyes. "Goodbye, Elder." She herded him closer to the door and then shoved him out.

"Why?" he urged when out in the hall.

"I made a mistake." She closed the door with a sharp thump that echoed through the building.

Chapter 45
A Dream Weaves

Kalea, Bowaen, Gaije, and Del all sat around a campfire just like old times. No Damos. Bowaen had briefed her on it when she met back up with them in Alkeer. Apparently, Bowaen had bolted out of Metta's house with Del and Gaije when they learned Kalea had been out all night. Her friends had left Damos behind in Alkeer, and good for him. Kalea hated for Damos to have to share space with Wikshen after all he'd been through. The problem was Dorhen's absence. She'd lost him yet again.

Bowaen broke the awkward silence. "So... You and Metta are both all right? Did Wikshen bother you?"

Kalea tightened her arms around her knees. "No. We ran into that Clanless elf really quick. He took care of us. I'm just worried about Dorhen."

Bowaen kept his lips clamped. Otherwise, she knew he wanted to spew a lot about Wikshen not being Dorhen.

"This all might be for the best," Bowaen offered. "If the sorcerers have him... I mean... From the way you talk about how he fought down in those caves, maybe he'll stir the sorcerers' lair up good for our arrival."

Kalea made a weak laugh. "Bowaen..." She checked to see if the other two were listening. Gaije appeared to be sleeping, and Del sat a ways off, smoking. "I'm sorry about the way I've acted. Wikhaihli was..."

He put a hand up. "You don't have to say it. I was there too."

She shrugged. "I do have to say it. It drove me mad. They really made me a Wikshonite. I was praying to Wikshen and...doing rituals. But I felt I had to."

He tightened his lips. "We were just out there digging up clams and sometimes mucking out the stable. I was so anxious to get my freedom back..." He huffed. "I never stopped to think what they were putting you through."

Merely thinking about her devotion to Wikshen put those longing feelings back into her. Once again, the urge to go into the darkness and do a Kraft pose nagged at her every hair strand and fingertip. Those Wikshonites really had changed her. She'd fight it, though.

"I'm going to try to do better," she told Bowaen. "I don't want to be a

Wikshonite. But I do want Dorhen back. I'm going to save him."

Averting his eyes, Bowaen drew his mouth tight again, his prickly cheeks bunching. Whatever he might be thinking didn't matter. He could deny Wikshen's true identity all he wanted. Kalea knew what she had to do.

She sat up in the middle of the night, wringing her hands as her companions slept soundly. Dreamwalking. She could use it to contact Dorhen to see if he was all right. Dreamwalking was still a frightening, uncertain thing for her to try doing, but she had found success in it before. It had even saved her life.

She took a deep breath and let it out slowly. Dorhen was worth the risk. She *had* to find him. It might help her locate him.

"Dorhen," she whispered, and choked up on the name. She still loved him. She loved him so much, regardless of how unpredictable he'd become. He needed her help. Somehow, they would need to find a way to cure him. First, she needed to find him.

Trying her best to remember the technique, she lay down and closed her eyes.

Dorhen.

Kalea pulled another piece of warm, soft meat off the fish Dorhen had cooked for her and put it in her mouth. She looked around. Her smile dropped. She blinked at Dorhen beside her. Nothing amiss…right? Of course not.

Her momentary spell of confusion flipped back to contentment, and she ate another bite. Neither of them had spoken since supper began, but she smiled and hummed in delight at the meal. He ate his own fish and watched her constantly, beaming at her enjoyment of it.

Eleven or twelve days had passed since she left the convent and placed her trust in Dorhen. She'd made a great leap with her trust. Every day, he went off—to the-Creator-knew-where—and returned with a fish or two, or a bag full of foraged goods. Every evening he came back to her, somehow knowing where he'd left her, and they'd sleep under the stars, with no walls to block the wind or hide them from dangerous animals… or people.

"You really know how to cook a fish over a fire," she said.

Dorhen gave a bashful smile, his face glowing orange in their only light source. A dark forest with the pale remains of sunset hung behind him. He returned his attention to his meal, picking the fish apart with his fingers as Kalea did.

Tomorrow, they'd pack up their camp and walk. To where, she didn't know. They'd take whatever direction Dorhen pointed. He apparently wandered wherever Arius Medallus bid each day. He preached Arius Medallus's invaluable survival practices, especially when she argued with him, but he hadn't spoken to the spirit lately.

Putting the remains of her fish aside, Kalea loosened her bodice strings, widened her collar, and fanned her perspiring neck. She sighed. "I won't need a quilt tonight. Shame that I need it to protect me from the ground and insects. A house would be the perfect thing."

She turned to find Dorhen staring at her action. He quickly turned back to the fire and continued his chewing. "There, you've said it again," he pointed out.

"You mean 'house'? Yes, I said it. We need a house. I can take the hot summer nights, it's winter I'm not looking forward to."

"You're tough enough, I think," he said, keeping his eyes on his food. She smiled to think that such a simple motion, fanning her sweaty neck, would make him so uncomfortable. Knowing she could rattle him so easily brought an odd pleasure. His statement, however, added a twinge of annoyance.

"You only say I'm tough because you don't want your precious lifestyle interrupted." She caught his eyes before he whipped them away. He focused a little too hard on chewing his food. "Your lifestyle is already topsy-turvy," she continued. "With me, you have a lot to worry about, don't you think? You used to only have to look out for yourself."

He frowned around his chewing. "Topsy... Top?"

"Topsy-*turvy*," she corrected.

"Sometimes I think you like making me confused."

She shrugged and turned her gaze to the fire. "It's not my fault you don't know certain phrases. After all, you didn't grow up in a building with a library."

A hiss of a sigh escaped him. He lost interest in the rest of the meat on the fish bones and dropped all the remains. In past days, he'd shown that he could clean the bones better than she.

Kalea dipped her chin. "Although...I didn't grow up in the forest, learning how to fish and which plants are edible and which aren't. All very good skills."

A little tension between them during conversation had become normal since they'd been living together. Before they ever set out, she couldn't have guessed that parts of their interaction would be so difficult. His body language made it obvious he shared the feeling, except he might be harboring more frustration than she. She couldn't decide yet if she was glad for making this decision. If he had left her to her peaceful life in the convent, his life would also still be easy. She wouldn't be dragging him down or adding any level of difficulty to his evenings.

Dorhen rose and collected their dinner scraps. Every night, he dug a hole and buried their waste. He'd explained how burying it eliminated the smell which might attract bears and wolves to their camp. If she'd run away from the convent alone, the Creator knew she probably would have already been eaten by a bear.

As he did his part, Kalea gathered up their few cooking tools and bagged them for traveling in the morning, and then she spread out Dorhen's bed roll, leaving her quilt folded and out of the way. When Dorhen returned, he regarded their single bedding setup and held secret whatever he was thinking about the arrangement. She guessed he'd feared all day that she would change her mind about sleeping together.

She offered the explanation, "It's too hot tonight," and proceeded to unlace her bodice and pull it off her shoulders, exposing her chemise to him. Her heart sped up with the feeling of his eyes on her. Ignoring him and her own humiliation, she took out her comb and ran it through her hair.

One stroke. Two strokes. She made it to eight strokes before she decided to look at him…as he stared at her. "Well?" she said. "Are you getting in bed?"

He finally moved, pulled off his shoes, followed by his shirt, and slipped into his own bedding. She continued her combing, holding a firm understanding that it wasn't too late to unfurl her own quilt and sleep alone. This hot night should make his little bedroll an oven with the two of them in it. A tinge of confusion hit when she realized that yesterday's air had frozen her. It was only early spring…or was it summertime?

Kalea shook it off and stood up. In her chemise. Heart pounding. Lying flat under his blanket, Dorhen's face glowed in the embers. He was watching her, most likely wondering as much as she was whether she'd cross the leaves and slip in with him or spread out her own bedding. It didn't get past her how he kept to one side of his narrow bedroll, leaving room for one more body.

She knelt down to pray as she did every night. *Dear Creator…* She murmured her words slowly to draw out the time. She did this every night and knew how Dorhen watched her throughout. In the back of her mind, she hoped he'd fall asleep before she finished this part of her routine. No such luck. She had altered her prayers a bit since her change of lifestyle. She now prayed to not be killed out here in the wilderness, by a bear or an illness. She prayed for Dorhen's life too, for if he died, she'd be lost and alone, and would follow him soon after.

Amen.

A few soft steps across the camp brought her to Dorhen's bedside. He lifted half up. No smile could be seen on his face now, only two big, watchful eyes nailed to her, trying hard to predict her intention. He made a quick motion to lift his blanket up for her and stopped abruptly, so unsure of the unfolding event.

She forced a smile for his reassurance and knelt down to join him. His throat apple rose and fell deeply in the corner of her view. Despite the summer heat, she buried herself into the blanket up to her bosom and tightened it down around herself, pinning it under her arms. The forest sounds around them disappeared behind the thunderous pulses of her heart in her ears. He must be experiencing something similar.

Once she went still, he motioned to lean over, but stopped and lay down flat beside her. Did he want to kiss her good night? He must've lost the confidence she'd given him in the kisses all over his face this morning. At least now he shouldn't have any nightmares. She'd seen how they plagued his sleep, especially on days when they argued.

With that in mind, she leaned up on an elbow and gave him a warm smile. "Good night," she said. "Don't have any nightmares."

The smile he returned showed weak. She pecked a quick kiss on his forehead, and then quickly lay back down to close her eyes and feign comfort. His presence beside her felt less relaxed than before. Her gesture might've made things worse. As slowly and nonchalantly as she could, she turned away from him and cradled her head on her crooked arm. His body radiated heat against her backside. He let a long breath out behind her.

Minutes passed. A lot of them…or just a few long ones? Kalea's heart continued its stomping sprint. She'd never get to sleep this way!

"Dorhen," she said after a long while.

His presence tensed up—of course he wasn't asleep. "Yes?"

"Haven't you ever caught a pheasant? Or a quail?"

He relaxed again with another sigh. She detected a small level of disappointment. "No."

She didn't bother to turn and face him. She meant this as conversation to break any tension. Maybe she'd fall asleep after a few easy words. "Why?"

"Arius Medallus never told me to."

Kalea let her posture relax, her head lying heavier on her arm. How she missed her regular bed at the convent. Her old floor mattress full of straw was a luxury compared to this. "I wish I could eat a game bird again," she said along the same gloomy thought about the straw mattress. Dorhen didn't respond. "And a piece of bread. Fine white bread. Oh, how I'd love that." With a longing sigh, she turned partially to her back, where she could faintly see Dorhen in her peripheral vision. "With salt on the bird and cranberry sauce to dip each bite—mmmmm."

She smiled, and turned to share it with him. He watched her as usual, most likely calculating her words and body language. "Dorhen," she peeped, "won't you catch a hen for me? I know how to cook it. Won't you?"

"I don't know."

She wiggled a little closer to him, smiling brightly. It wasn't only heat shared between them; now they touched. While she relaxed in her fantasy of delicious foods, foods she'd eaten in better days before the famine, he lay more tensely than before. She wiggled against him and tucked her face into his bare chest. "Please?"

"Yes," he said. "For you, I'll do it."

She giggled and threw her arm around him. "Thank you!" She reared up to lay a kiss on his cheek. He tensed up to the point of trembling. So cautiously, he put his arm around her in return, but she quickly ended the embrace and went back to her side of the bed roll. "Get some sleep now, you'll need it. Those pheasants are quick."

A heavy sigh from him with a tremble on his breath followed her statement. He turned back to staring up at the stars as she flipped to her side again. His breathing never relaxed before she fell asleep; it sounded a little too controlled. The next day couldn't arrive soon enough for her. For once, she'd eat something other than fish for dinner.

When she opened her eyes again, no sunshine illuminated the forest. Night still reigned. And heat. Her eyes adjusted to the scenery of moonlit trees. The fire's embers glowed under a black mound of ash.

A tickling sensation registered on her thigh. An insect? She didn't want to panic and throw the blanket off and wake up Dorhen, but she didn't want a cricket or spider crawling on her either. Her senses restored a bit more, and Dorhen's breathing was no more rhythmic than earlier.

It was his hand. On her thigh. Grazing lightly up her contours to her hip. He lay closer than she remembered, against her back, his nose in her hair, adding steam to her already sweaty neck.

His touch made a fire rush through her belly. After gathering all the pieces of what was transpiring, her thoughts scrambled. She arched back, trembling as he did, and pushed herself against him. He applied more pressure to her leg and dragged his hand up to her belly, where he squeezed.

She sighed, letting a little moan out too, and the sound drove him further. He trailed his hand over her breasts to her chin. He directed her mouth to his and pressed his lips, soft at first and then firmer, wetter.

Kalea's body—both of their bodies—shook and burned. She turned over flat, and Dorhen rose to half-cover her, kissing with a burgeoning intensity, feverish and delirious. She wrapped her arms around his neck and pulled him down tight; she relished his scent. He drew back long enough to catch his breath, letting out an elated moan of his own.

Kalea's legs flared to shaking beyond her control. What was happening? Dorhen's hair enveloped her face as he bowed again for more kissing, leaving wet trails as he explored to her neck and back again.

He pressed his lower body firmly against hers, and a very hard thing poked her leg, like he had a dagger on his belt or something. She knew he didn't sleep with his knife buckled on—this was his...

She leaned away as her thoughts realigned, realizing what he tried to initiate. The pictures in Vivene's favorite book, with those twists and tangles the characters' bodies were in. She remembered a pinched look on the female character's face. Such uncomfortable, sinful drawings.

Dorhen moved his kisses to her neck and down to her shoulder where her sleeve fell low. Every touch of his lips spread tingles like ripples on water. She leaned away farther, and he covered the distance, not yet receiving her signal.

"No..." she finally said, breathy from all her bodily sensations. She'd never felt so strange in her life, except for maybe when she'd met him in her dreams a while back. Right now, those dreams were being realized. "No," she said a little louder. A little firmer.

"Hmm?" He hugged her tight, despite her sudden disconnect. "Kalea," he breathed her name, and the agony in his voice tugged at her heartstrings and sent a new thrill through her abdomen, but this went against everything she'd been brought up to believe. She hardly knew him. They weren't married. He was an elf...

"I said stop," she whined, and crawled away, away from the heat pocket they'd created and into the cold grass.

"Kalea?" This time he said her name with a trace of confusion.

She crawled a few paces farther and hugged her knees. Left alone in the bedroll, Dorhen panted and sat braced on his muscly arms.

"Where are you going?" he asked. "Come back to bed."

She hugged herself tighter against the chill of the night air. "No."

"Why?" His annoyance climbed.

"I don't want to do that."

Silence.

Dorhen grunted and dropped his head to hang between his arms. "Why not?"

"I shouldn't have to explain why."

Keeping his face hidden behind his hair, Dorhen stormed to his feet. Kalea winced. He didn't approach her, though. He went into the forest.

She shouted after him, "Where are you going?" He'd disappeared from sight by the end of her question. "Dorhen!" Her voice echoed far. "Dorhen!" Her second call squealed.

Perhaps he needed to cool down some anger. Settling back into his bedroll, she decided to wait and try to get some rest. He didn't return before she fell asleep.

When Kalea opened her eyes again, the light beat down on them. Birds filled the atmosphere with their songs. She sat up, rubbed her eyes, and looked around frantically, remembering that Dorhen had left her last night. She had no idea what was happening anymore, or what the point of this whole thing was. Maybe she should go back to the convent.

It didn't take her long to find him, curled up between the roots of a big tree in a miserable-looking ball. His head crooked to the side, his knees bent to his chest.

"Dorhen."

When she said his name, he jerked his head up, groggy and pained. He rubbed his face and avoided looking at her. Each morning, she usually asked him how he had slept. Today, it was obvious.

She considered saying the next words that popped into her head: *I'm sorry*, but why should she be sorry if she'd never agreed to…do that thing with him in the first place? Maybe it was rude of him to touch her while she slept and then maul her without asking.

The memory of it sparked her gut again. With a swallow, she pushed it out of her mind. People shouldn't just go about lusting and tumbling with each other under such circumstances. A good structure of protocol should precede it, but first she needed to figure out whether she wanted to do it with him at all. If she did, it would have to be in a real bed, not on the dirty forest floor.

Her own quilt still sat folded neatly. She held in her next urge to sigh; she didn't want to make a sound he could hear and read. Tonight, her quilt would go into use; she'd sleep alone.

Dorhen must not have gotten much sleep, and the day matured fast. He had slept in, hadn't bathed, and hadn't caught their morning fish yet. Now awake, he said not a word, but stood and walked into the forest, leaving Kalea to mope on his rumpled bedroll with all of her turbulent thoughts and feelings.

A little communication probably wouldn't hurt their situation, considering this new lifestyle they shared and all its complications. She ignored the idea of getting dressed and hurried in the direction he went, calling his name softly.

Her path led to a lake. Dorhen always paused their travels near a body of water, where he persistently bathed every day and caught fish. The water's surface rippled under the wind's force.

"Dorhen?" She frowned and scanned around. When she turned to try another direction, a splash stopped her.

Dorhen gasped for air and shook the water from his hair, quickly noticing her arrival. He didn't speak or smile. He turned his back. When standing, the water barely covered up to his hips. The rising sun outlined his muscly curves. Just looking at him renewed the tingles in Kalea's core.

"Dorhen," she said. He refused to turn and acknowledge her. "We need to do some things…before we can do *that*."

Now he did twist around to eye her.

She raised her index finger. "I want to eat different kinds of food." She added her middle finger. "I want to live in a house." She put in her ring finger. "We have to have a wedding ceremony."

At each of her points, he turned until he faced her fully. The water barely hid his genitals under its surface, and he showed no shame for it. When she didn't produce a fourth condition in the next few seconds, he asked, "And when I do those things for you, you'll let me touch you?"

She pulled her lips tight and considered. "Maybe."

He grunted and dipped into the water again with a splash. He ran his fingers through his hair to get the knots out, working fast and furiously.

"I'm thinking about it, but those three goals should make a sturdy starting point," she said.

He stepped a little closer to her in the water, and she cringed at the worry that he'd expose his private parts again. "You want food, a house, and a wedding."

"Yes."

He nodded his head in consideration. "A house, and food. What exactly is a wedding ceremony?"

"It's the most important part," she said, and stepped into the water to speak to him closer. "We stand before the Creator and pray—"

He hawked and spat in an arch that hit the water audibly. "I'm not confessing anymore!" In a sharp motion, he dipped his head under again.

"Dor-hen!" She stomped her foot to make her own splash. When he rose back up, she kicked a splash at him. "I didn't say you would!"

Closing his mouth, he watched her and waited, his heavy, wet hair plastered down to his face.

"Why do you have a problem with confession? Have you been thinking unclean thoughts again?"

He threw his arms out to the sides. "You don't leave me much choice!"

She stepped back, her stomach burning in dismay. A short staring contest ensued. With the way he held her eye contact, he didn't appear ashamed of his unclean thoughts anymore.

"Is that what you…" she began. "What exactly were you doing in the woods last night?"

He pointed a strong finger at her, and she shrank farther. He'd never thrown such anger and intimidation at her before. It confused her system by mingling another wave of arousal with her present disgust. She found herself breathing deeply to keep up with such feelings, her bosom pumping up and down under her thin chemise, her nipples pointing. She crossed her arms over them.

"Listen," he barked, and took a breath before continuing. "I'm going to get you your food and your house and your wedding ceremony."

Her posture melted. "Dorhen, I'm sor—"

"Don't be sorry." He deflated a bit too. "I suppose I had no right. I won't touch you if you don't want me to. I thought it would be okay since you've been acting so happy and friendly lately. I didn't know. I don't know what I'm allowed to do."

"You really want to do *that*…"

"I love you," he said. "I will protect you and do anything you wish. So why don't you make this easy for me and tell me what to do?"

Kalea's lip quivered. What had she done? She shook her head. Her thoughts and feelings whirled. Her body seemed to like the sight of him naked in the water, but her stomach churned, her brain spun with anger, and her heart burned. She tromped deeper into the water to meet him without a care for her clothing. They probably wouldn't start walking today anyway; she'd hang her chemise up to dry, and Dorhen would need to catch up on sleep as it was. He watched her with a miserable frown dragging on his face.

She wrapped her arms around his naked torso and laid her head on his wet chest. "I forgive you for whatever you did last night. And for trying to couple with me."

He didn't respond, so she took his face and kissed his lips. She knew the feel of them well already, yet the newness of their pleasure overwhelmed her. Pulling away proved hard, despite the difficulty of their conversations.

"A house, food, and a wedding ceremony," she said. "I'll hold you to it."

She answered both of their yearnings with another press of her lips. He didn't move his much, and she sympathized with him. Under the water, however, his "dagger handle" poked her once again. She gasped; its pale shape waved faintly in the water's refraction, sticking straight out from him.

"There's not much I can do about that if you're going to keep kissing me," he said. His low voice rattled with his somber mood. She couldn't help but notice he didn't turn it away from her. "It basically has a mind of its own."

A little breathy laugh escaped her, and she burst into a giggle. He didn't join her in laughter. She hugged him again, letting it poke her if it wanted to do so. He didn't hug back, and she couldn't blame him for his confusion. Eventually, they'd figure everything out.

Kalea left Dorhen alone to finish his bath and tidied their campsite, changed her chemise, and stoked the fire's embers back to life with a feed of new twigs. When Dorhen returned from the lake, he smiled. They didn't speak much, but the air was serene.

She took her turn at bathing when she got the chance, and still wondered if he would use his magic hood to spy on her while she bathed, a worry which had pestered her yesterday when she'd taken the leap to finally go through with the process. Today, she decided not to care. She had chosen Dorhen. Someday, they would be intimate together.

"A house, food, and a wedding ceremony," she recited in song, and it made her grin. Those three foundation blocks for their relationship would bind them. Now they had a goal, and with those three things in hand, she'd not feel guilty about going against her religion and societal upbringing. She'd marry Dorhen with the One Creator's approval. Maybe the three goals would make Dorhen happy too, now that he had an aim and an end to his suffering in sight.

Near the end of the daylight, Dorhen returned from his excursion, beaming. Kalea returned his infectious smile. "What's so funny?" she asked.

He extended his fist to show two beautiful pheasants hanging by their necks. "I got you your food!" His bright smile showed all of his front teeth.

Kalea leaped up with a squeal. "I don't believe it! You're amazing, Dorhen—amazing! How did you catch them?"

He placed the two dead birds down on the nearest rock and took a stance. "With a few hard-thrown stones." He mimed the way he had thrown them, showing a strong and capable form with one arm forward and one back.

Kalea squealed again and seized him for another kiss. "You've earned this." She kissed him a second time on his mouth, and then a third. He kissed back on the final round. She patted both sides of his face and shared her warm approval a few moments longer. "You're amazing," she said again.

She took his hand and led him to the fire. "Come here. I'll show you how to prepare them."

A few hours later, two juicy hens steamed on a spit, ready for devouring. She pulled off a piece of one bird carefully, stuffed it into her mouth, and closed her eyes. "Mmmmm." She opened her eyes to find him enjoying watching her eat. She pointed to the second bird. "Eat with me."

He smirked and shrugged. "I shouldn't. Arius Medallus told me not to bother with food other than fish, plants, and insects."

"But it's so warm and smoky. Taste it. You'll love it."

He frowned. "I don't know..."

She pulled off another piece with crispy, tanned skin and steaming white meat, and extended it toward his face. He reluctantly opened his mouth, and she placed it on his tongue. He closed his lips over her fingertips, and a carnal thrill rushed through her. She swallowed, dropping her smile while the feeling persisted. He retained the eye contact the whole time he chewed.

"H-how is it?" she asked.

"It's good."

She waved her hand over the roasted hens. "So eat some more."

He did. For the moment, she couldn't stop watching him as he put another pull of meat into his mouth. The way his throat apple moved when he swallowed... She couldn't tell if he tried to seduce her with these subtle gestures or not. He was only eating. She continued her meal too, a delicious meal that Dorhen caught for her. The naughty boy had determination in him. How long would it take now for him to stack enough stones to build the house she'd requested? He'd probably start tomorrow, if she knew him. Looking around, it didn't seem like a bad place to settle down. They had a lake, plenty of forest foraging, and temperate weather. They hadn't left the convent's region, from what she could guess.

"Dorhen," she said around a wad of pheasant in her cheek, "I really am sorry I've been so difficult." He continued picking at his hen as she spoke, consuming fastidious bites. "It's a little too fast for me. Too much too soon."

"I understand," he said in his usual monotone way.

"Well, I'm trying to understand myself. I'm just scared, that's all."

"I don't want you to be."

"Thank you." She let a little laugh out. "All I know about intimacy is what I saw in some stupid book one of my friends showed me. Its illustrations were hard to fathom."

He stopped chewing and looked at her. He swallowed. "So you don't know…"

"Do *you* know?"

He ripped off a larger piece of pheasant and stuffed it into his mouth, shrugging as he chewed it.

"What *do* you know about this business?"

He shrugged again. "I just have very strong feelings. It's like they're telling me what to do."

"You mean you have instincts. Interesting. I wonder if all men have more instincts about this than women."

She took another bite, trying to appear as nonchalant as possible. In truth, she was as terrified to talk about it as she was to try it out. Learning something about it would help first, though, especially if she were to finally take that big step after Dorhen built her a house and exchanged vows with her.

Dorhen swallowed his bite. "And I mean… It's not all about feelings."

She leaned in a little closer to him. "Then what is it? How do you know how to…?"

He turned his gaze away from her. "Sometimes, when you're walking around with a magic hood on, you…stumble upon things…"

"Like what?" She leaned even closer. "Animals?"

"No. Like…people…naked people. People who run into the woods for some privacy."

Kalea covered her gasp with both hands. "You've watched people?"

He huffed and buried his face in his hand, braced on his knee. They sat side by side on a log. "Please don't ask me to confess about this."

"So you've watched them?"

He spread his hands. "Wouldn't you?"

She clutched her bodice tightly together under her throat. "No."

Despite his embarrassment, he hissed a laugh. "Well, I guess you wouldn't learn anything about how it's done." He shared his smile at the awkward situation, his face red as a tart's filling.

"I guess not." She forced a laugh. They both took a few more bites, their hens diminishing to the bare bones. She edged a smidge closer on the log on which they perched. "So, then…how's it done?" She hardly heard her own voice under her pounding heart.

He shot a quick glance at her from the corner of his eye and swallowed despite the absence of food in his mouth. "It's like a dance," he said.

"Oh." She examined her hands, all greased up from handling the cooked meat. "That sounds nice."

"But not a pretty dance."

Silence.

He continued, "Not when you're the one looking on. Actually, the sounds are… I don't know how to say it."

"Sounds?"

He nodded, keeping his eyes forward; his interest in his meal had withered at this point. "You'd think the woman was in distress. At first, I thought she was and almost revealed myself to stop them. But actually… I think they enjoy it more than the men."

Kalea stuttered for a response of some kind.

"The men don't make sounds…usually."

"What do you mean, *usually*?" Kalea blurted. "Are you telling me you've watched people make love more than once? Didn't seeing it the first time fill you in enough?"

He shrugged. "Well, I—uh. You don't… I mean…" He huffed and slicked his hand over his hair. "I can't explain it. Sometimes I sneak into people's barns to escape the rain, and there they are. Apparently, barns are used for more than housing animals."

Kalea dropped her jaw to show her disgust. "I don't know what to say to that!"

Dorhen continued avoiding her gaze. "Say nothing."

"So, what about *you*? Have you ever…*danced* in a barn?"

He gave her a serious stare now. "No. I've never done it before. You're the first woman I've ever even talked to."

The crackling fire did the only speaking for a minute or two. "How many times have you seen this of thing?"

He shrugged. "A few."

"And you indulge in the sight every time?"

He gave another shrug. "It's not my fault. I'm just the invisible elf passing through or trying to stay dry. It's nothing I feel I should confess."

Kalea pursed her lips. Her hen waited half-eaten, but she'd lost her appetite. "You said…" She sucked in a deep breath. "You said it seems the woman enjoys it more than the man?"

Dorhen nodded. A smile quirked on his lips. "I used to assume that from what I've witnessed, but now I don't know... The way you've made me feel already makes me think the man enjoys it very much." His bright blush lived on.

"How did you feel?" That question was a probe, she admitted to herself.

"Similar to how watching others made me feel, but much, much more so." He stole a peek at her and returned to staring into the forest.

"Both people enjoyed it? Were they doing any back-breaking, twisty poses, getting knotted together?"

He burst into laughter, louder than what he'd been doing, and turned his head away for it. "From what I've seen, they did a simple arrangement, with both people interested in seeing it through."

"Neither were...in pain?"

He gave her a warm smile as he shook his head. "No."

In the following calm moment, he reached over and took her hand. He didn't try to make eye contact, he simply held her hand. Knowing how brightly she must be blushing, she let him hold it, and gave back a squeeze.

Dorhen flew out of the bedroll in the middle of the night, throwing his side of the blanket over her. She'd opted to sleep with him again after their established agreement.

"What's wrong?" she asked.

He dashed to the woods, but didn't make it far. He fell against a tree with a moan and spilled the contents of his stomach.

The pheasant, Kalea thought with a groan of her own. She'd made poor Dorhen sick by tempting him to eat it. Arius Medallus must have told him to eat only fish and forest vegetation for good reason.

Kalea rushed to his side—or rather, behind him—and rubbed his back, which arched when he heaved again, throwing out everything he had eaten. She gathered up his hair and held it away from his face.

"You poor thing! I'm so, so sorry!"

Dorhen wasn't finished yet.

"I didn't know," she went on. "I'm going to take care of you now, don't you worry."

Dorhen responded with a weak moan. "Am I going to die?"

She wanted to giggle at that, but he didn't need her laughter right now. "No," she said. He shook beneath her caressing hand. "We just have to get all the bad stuff out of you."

As if to illustrate her point, he vomited again.

Kalea murmured while she listened to his sick sounds, "I suppose I'll be foraging now for things to brew to settle your stomach." He needed liquids the most. "Dorhen, are you finished? Go lie down."

Though he'd stopped heaving and making sounds, he didn't respond. "Dorhen?"

Silence.

She tapped him on the back. "Dorhen?"

He turned slowly around to face her. His hair hung long over his shoulders. Longer. It had turned…blue.

Over a chin covered in pale vomit, he grinned eerily. His eyes took on a dark, empty stare. Kalea gasped and stepped backward.

"Would you like to sit on my lap?" Wikshen asked her.

Dorhen woke up. "Kah…" he said in a gasp. He couldn't feel his limp body. Opening his fluttery eyelids proved difficult. It hurt to try.

He persisted until a sharp line of fire burned his sockets, flaring into his skull. "Ahh!" All he could do was loll and pant weakly. When he tried again, objects formed in the intense light. Trying to orient himself only increased his dizziness.

Magnified flames. He moaned at their dancing, hot presence. Sharp rays of light pierced him. He must be in Kullixaxuss again. Although… He attempted to force his eyes open at the risk of them burning away. They'd burn away soon anyway. Maybe it should've happened already.

A big, thick lens with an oil-fed flame behind it stared him in the face. A heavy, wooden chair cradled him with… He attempted to lift his head, but his weak neck dropped it back. Ropes secured his arms. He wasn't in Kullixaxuss, he was…

Windows lined the walls. Stones warmed by the many flames supported his feet. The Ilbith sorcerers had imprisoned him. They'd done this same thing to him before. The magnified flames shouldn't have such an effect on him, but being Wikshen made him vulnerable to light and heat.

How could such a rotten thing have happened to him again? He couldn't remember, only piece together memories of shadow traveling and Kalea's face and…some other woman's face.

He let his head fall and hang again. He whimpered, unable to free himself, yet also unable to sleep. After a while, the intense pain of the burning would make him pass out, the usual cycle when in this situation.

Hhhummm-mmm-mmm. A soft sound perked his ears with rising and falling notes. Someone was…singing? *Oooh-laaah-taaa-hummm-mmm*, it continued behind the roaring headache the light caused.

Yes! He couldn't make out the muffled words, though. The sound comforted him. Otherwise, a slight hiss put off by the aggressive oil flames eating away at big, braided wicks filled the silence and drove him near madness. Without the distracting, distant noise, he felt like those hissing flames were baking his flesh.

That voice…Dorhen listened hard. Who was it? His stomach dropped at the thought. A new alertness put the starch back in his neck. He raised his head and widened his eyes despite the white-hot rays bouncing all over the circular space.

"Kalea," he rasped. The sorcerers must have her too! "No," he groaned. She needed help.

He fought against his bonds, several lengths of crisp, new rope. His void of energy didn't matter. He'd make energy. He wiggled and fought, trying to kick, but his ankles were tied to the chair legs. "Kalea!"

Apparently, she didn't hear him. She continued singing for some reason. None of the details made sense, but he couldn't stall to puzzle them out. He had to get her out of here.

"Kaaaleaaahhh!" He found the strength to roar it. His ropes creaked against his strength. He shouted her name again. The song continued, and he fought to exhaustion.

Chapter 46
Sharp Blade

"What? You mad at me?" Bargo asked Vivene as she dressed after today's session.

"No, sir." Throughout his handling, she hadn't been able to shake the image of him standing in attendance at Rose's sacrifice.

He chuckled. "I know you're lying. Lots o' women have been in this room since it was granted to me, women who've come and gone." He never stopped staring at her while she dressed. His eyes carved her up like a slab of steak he wanted for his dinner table. "Some got a plague—past plagues," he continued. "Others got old. A few got murdered by their competition, or by angry sorcerers. It's all the same to me. Maybe you'll die too, pretty soon. It won't matter. None of this matters. Understand? I'll find someone else. Another dumpling with big, juicy thighs."

At this point, Vivene waited, shaking in anger. Frustration. Despair. She wanted to leave. She couldn't just walk out while Bargo was talking. Servants had to be excused, but he just kept talking.

He dragged from a pipe he'd left glowing on the side table while he had boffed her, still naked in his filthy bed. "When you come into this tower"—he shook his head—"it's an end. Even for us." He shrugged. "What are ya gonna do, though?" He studied her, waiting patiently. "Don't you have to take a meal to the whore upstairs?"

"She's not a whore."

Bargo raised his eyebrows, pipe in mouth. He chuckled again. "She's not, huh?"

Vivene shook. "I do have to do my duty."

He waved his hand. "Then do it."

Vivene hurried out of Bargo's room and couldn't get away from it fast enough.

Down in the kitchen, she couldn't keep from trembling as she prowled for one specific thing: a knife. Orinleah wanted her to bring a knife. After her request, Vivene had finally realized that knives never went in with Orinleah's dishes. She got a little two-pronged fork, but otherwise, none of the food she ate actually required a knife.

What did she want with one? To slit her own wrists? It was bad enough that Vivene had lost Rose to the sorcerers; if Orinleah committed suicide—she wouldn't blame the poor elf-woman, but Vivene couldn't bear the thought! The only other thing Orinleah might be planning to do with the knife…Vivene didn't want to think of that disastrous outcome either.

But Orinleah had asked for a knife. How could Vivene not deliver one? The problem was getting one. Only authorized Ilbith residents could use them. Apparently, suicide was a popular out in this harsh society. Getting her hands on one would be as hard as obtaining a piece of gold.

This morning, she could spot only one knife in sight, the one the cook attentively used to prepare the sorcerers' breakfasts. How Vivene might get it from him was anyone's guess. Afterward, she'd have to hide it somewhere on Orinleah's tray of dishes and pass it through the food slot.

Luckily for her, in walked Sabina, another novice. Vivene whispered her name, and Sabina gave her the frightened deer eyes. Vivene smiled and waved her over.

"You better not get me in trouble," Sabina warned.

Vivene gave her the most sincere expression she could while also pretending to be casual in this public space. "I would never do such a thing."

"You were a rotten apple at the convent, and I can't imagine you're any better here. Remember when you put that tack in my shoe? I still know what that pain was like. I limped for two days."

Vivene shushed her, trying to keep the sound soothing rather than urgent. "I just have a question since you work in the kitchen."

Sabina moved to the counter to knead some dough she'd left waiting. "Get me a knife."

The girl paused. "You gonna kill yerself? The Creator won't like that."

She shushed her again. "It's not for me, it's for a friend."

Sabina sniffed and pounded the dough harder. "I'm not giving you one. Getting something like that is under tight protocol. If I do that, they'll know where it came from."

"How do I get one?"

Sabina gestured to the cook, who lifted the spoon from the big pot and carefully tasted its contents. "See those wooden tokens on his belt? They're passed out by the sorcerer who oversees the kitchen each morning. Having a token gets you whatever tool it indicates from the locked closet, and permission to use it for the day. If you're found with a knife but without a token, they'll use it to cut yer throat."

"So I need to get a token."

"Yeah, and good luck with it." After forming the dough into a round shape, Sabina sliced three lines on top and placed it on the tray next to twenty others. Vivene might've asked more questions, but the cook came too close, and she knew Sabina would answer no more. She might not get the knife today; she needed a plan.

Lamrhath fingered the little gold lantern which would be his next gift for Orinleah, running his index pad along its sculpted arcs and grooves. The idle act soothed him. He never would've found this object to be so pleasing and special in the past. It probably would've been melted down and made into a teleportation pole if Orinleah hadn't requested a lantern as her next gift.

She didn't need any additional lighting in her room. It was easy to assume this was a common courting gift of tradition: a typical lantern a *faerhain* might hang outside the door to her new household. Maybe it served to help her husband find his way home through the forest. The elves most likely thought of this tradition as another symbol of their god, the Bright One. Of course, traditionally, it probably didn't have to be made of gold. Lamrhath chose this exquisite piece because this was a courting gift for his own future wife.

He placed the cloth cover back over the lantern when his door clicked open and Talekas walked in. He asked before the man finished walking across the carpet, "Did you find it yet?"

Talekas paused. "My lord?" He blinked. "Oh, you mean the pelt. I'm sorry, but we've no white ox pelt to present to your wife yet."

Lamrhath exhaled through his nose. "Then why are you here?"

Talekas held his hands behind his back. He shifted his feet. "To speak with you about the young elf-girl."

Lamrhath bristled but couldn't fathom why.

"Are you sure we shouldn't cut her hair, my lord? Even with the incoming donation, I'm afraid we'll wind up short." He produced a rolled leaf of paper from his belt and unfurled it. "If you look at the plans here—"

"You're dismissed," Lamrhath said, waving his hand and turning away.

"My lord?"

"You won't touch her!"

Talekas blinked again rapidly. "What, are you...?" He replaced the paper back in his belt. "Are you just"—he appeared to be on a careful search for his words—"keeping her?"

Lamrhath harrumphed and moved to the wardrobe full of his tabards and robes. He chose one of the shorter coats, with sleeves laced all the way up their lengths and a collar of long grey fur.

"I'm on my way to visit her," he said. "I'm going to learn more about her ability." He pushed past Talekas toward the door. Though his chamber was a wide space, Lamrhath stepped around no one. "For all we know, cutting her hair might ruin it."

"Good point," Talekas said in the old familiar way they used to speak. Lamrhath paused before exiting. "Talekas."

"Yes?"

"What is Wikshen doing today?"

Talekas shrugged. "He's the same. Slumped over in his bonds. At least the light keeps him subdued."

"Have you thought of cutting off *his* hair?"

Talekas's face muscles slackened. Lamrhath hadn't thought of it until right this moment either.

"He's an elf," Lamrhath pointed out, "and he's a pixtagen." He left his Second with that thought.

"Mhina," Lamrhath said her name, more for himself than her as he stepped into the cozy little chamber.

The lovely *farhah* sat neatly by the window. Clouds rushed by at this elevation. She took her eyes off of them when he entered. He smiled once again to look at her, the most radiant gift he'd ever received. Since her arrival and the revelation of her great power, he'd thought much about what her place would be here. Should he introduce her to Orinleah? No. His answer to that question came quickly. Mhina had to live separate.

She still didn't offer a greeting. Holding the pose her nanny, no doubt, had set her in, Mhina just stared at him with her huge, lavender eyes. Her hair shimmered in the daylight. She wore a fine dress, made from the most expensive silk he could acquire. Her fair-faced new nanny, Audrielle, had also enhanced her eyes with a thin line of charcoal to make the color pop.

Lamrhath stood with his back to the door, wondering if he should allow Talekas to follow him in for this session or shut him out. He left the door unlocked and stepped forward. "Mhina," he said again. He motioned to the buffet of treats he'd ordered this morning. "Have you enjoyed my gifts?"

She didn't answer.

He stretched his neck to look across the way. "The tarts are particularly sweet today." She hadn't touched anything yet. He stifled his annoyance and cleared his throat. "I want to see your amazing ability again."

At her silence, he forced another smile and moved to sit in the larger chair beside her. Her little, round face held blank, more pouty than pleased. "Tell me, when did you realize you could heal people?"

"I don't know."

He'd come to expect that answer. "How many did you heal before you healed me?"

She let her eyes roam around the room as she played with her fingers. "A little cat," she finally said. "I didn't want to tell anyone."

"Why?"

She shrugged.

"Is that all? You healed a cat. Anything else?"

"A *saeghar*."

"A boy from your village?"

She nodded.

"How did he react to it?"

"He ran."

"Did healing the cat or *saeghar* make you feel tired at all?"

She nodded. "The *saeghar* made me feel funny, but…"

"But what?"

"I heard Dorhen afterward."

Lamrhath reared his head back. "It happened the night you heard Dorhen's voice in your head?"

"Yes."

"And then what happened?"

"Gaije called too."

"Who is Gaije?"

"My *sarenkin*."

Lamrhath clenched his eyes shut to try to piece together what that meant. He knew only a little bit of Norrian. His mother used to speak it to him and Daghahen so long ago, but they had never lived in Norr, and once they went to the Darklands there wasn't much use for Norrian at all.

"*Sarenkin*," he parroted, tasting its familiarity. "He's your brother."

She nodded.

"So Gaije was there, and Dorhen too. Did Dorhen pick you up at that point?"

She nodded.

"And you've healed no one else since—besides me accidentally."

She wrung her hands, watching him unsheathe his dagger. "I want you to do it again. I will ask you questions. You must answer them as best as you can." Mhina's frown withered to dread. "Don't be afraid," he assured her.

He let his coat slide off his arms and pool in the chair behind him. Underneath, he wore a thin shirt with cap sleeves. Swiftly, he turned his arm over and drew the knife across his soft skin, similar to the original cut. A few beads of crimson popped up in the slit before the whole length filled with red and ran down the curve of his arm. He didn't bother to worry about the amount of blood that dripped onto the rug.

Mhina stood there in horror, and he reminded her not to fear. He thrust his gushing forearm at her. "Heal it."

A little whimper worked up her throat; she tried to hold it in, but her lips buckled. She reached for his arm, and as soon as her touch connected, a rush of tingling, roaring euphoria spread across him—all over, farther than his arm. His vision faded as before, his head went light, and serenity washed through him. Cleansed him! Like before, the pain in his groin vanished, his unending sexual need left him, and a sense of calm and comfort he hadn't experienced in forever replaced it. Maybe he had never experienced it.

When all of his senses returned, he found himself with his head thrown back, mouth agape. Mhina watched him with an expression of quiet fear—rounded eyes, pouting mouth. She'd already taken her hands away.

He dropped his head forward and caught it with his other hand before rubbing his forehead with a groan. When he attempted to think scientifically again, he couldn't say exactly how long the healing process had taken to complete.

He composed himself and opened his lips to continue with the interrogation, but his voice failed. Too soon, however, did the pain of his ailment return, and with it his wits. "Mhina," he tried again. "H—" He swallowed. "How long did it take for the healing to be done?"

"A few seconds maybe."

He nodded. He'd probably relished the feeling longer than the healing process had taken. "How do you feel now?"

"Fine."

"All right." He took the knife back up. "Here."

He dragged the blade across his skin, an inch higher than the first cut, which had left behind no trace besides the stain of blood stamped with her little hand prints. The cut hurt as much as the first one; he noted the feeling of his flesh parting in addition to the usual pain that would grab anyone's attention.

He quirked his lips into a sort of smirk in his observant concentration. He noted the details of the pain too, which sent pulses of energetic sensation in all directions. With one touch from the little goddess standing before him, his pain would snuff out. The skin would fuse back together. He held his eyes wide, intent on watching the entire process from beginning to end, to see the skin snap together in contrast to how it parted.

The blood ran over his arm in a bigger torrent than before. He pushed the wound forward. Mhina stood a step farther away this time. Her face showed wan.

"Do it," he ordered.

She breathed heavily and stepped forward to throw her hands out as if to get it over with. Her fingers grazed him, and a rush of pleasant nothingness overtook him again. He couldn't hope to keep his eyes open and his attention on the happenings. A wail of pleasure emerged from him. He couldn't stop it. He couldn't control himself, force himself to sit forward.

He found himself collapsed backward in his chair, draped over it like a shroud. The tingles traveled, and he made note of each one buzzing and flitting across his scalp, his limbs, his fingers and toes. He undeniably enjoyed it, but reminded himself of his quest for knowledge to unlock the secret of this rare creature's powers.

"Mhina." He dragged himself forward with an amazing looseness in his normally stiff muscles. His voice grated. "Do it again."

He searched for the knife, which had fallen on the floor, and lifted it to his bicep this time. "Mhina, come here!" He didn't mean to demand, but each new second brought his pain back a smidge closer. Mhina had retreated a few paces, as if she'd rather hide in the corner.

The blood from the new gash raced down Lamrhath's arm to drip off at his elbow. He used the damaged arm to beckon her. He attempted to sound more child-friendly. "Come here."

Mhina stepped slowly back over. She shook, but he hardly paid any mind to her state. As long as he could bask in the delirious and delightful sensation again, followed by a few seconds free of pain…

"Mhina," he whispered now.

She reached up for his arm. He dropped from his seat to kneel before her so she could reach him better. She did it again.

"Uhhhh." Lamrhath breathed and enjoyed. He couldn't possibly keep himself collected enough to watch the magical occurrence.

After the soaring, buzzing butterflies of delirium cleared, he found himself leaning back against the chair, his elbow hooked around the wooden arm support.

Fluttering his eyes open, he found Mhina swaying on her feet. It finally occurred to him to ask about her status. "How do you feel now?"

She shook her head, looking ill and drained. She staggered, her hands soiled in blood that matched her red dress.

Lamrhath untangled himself from the chair and crawled forward in search of the knife he hadn't held onto. "Listen," he said in his wavering voice. "Listen…" He spoke slowly to collect his thoughts. "Mhina," he began again. Sitting upon his bent knees, he used the knife to cut his shirt and wrench it open with his fists. He put the blade to his breast. "I want you to heal me here next."

She never bothered to offer a word. Her body language stated her unwillingness, but he needed this. He waved her closer. Teetering on her feet, she made her way back and reached her hands forward. He took one of her wrists and placed her hand where he wanted it, retaining contact to see if he could feel anything beyond his own perception as a recipient of her healing.

He felt nothing more than the same euphoric intoxication and emptiness where there should've been the usual ripping pain in his abdomen. He enjoyed every breath, every wisp of an instant, and every gust of air that grazed his cheek in the brief seconds it took for Mhina's loving presence to move through and soothe his every discomfort. He smiled.

When he opened his eyes again, she was half-lying on the floor, off the rug. She'd tried to crawl away. "Mhina," he called. The name put a sweet, ethereal flavor on his tongue. "Come here." He worked back up to his knees and leaned over to retrieve the knife. "Come," he repeated.

Mhina made a difficult effort to collect herself. She let out a soft sob. "Please," she whimpered.

"One more, my love. Come here." He placed the knife's tip on his stomach, barely below his navel.

She shook her head.

"Come." The little tickle of the blade on his skin sent a new thrill across his limbs. Touching the blade to his skin let him know a sharp pain would happen right before the greatest sensation of his life—and maybe the end of his ailment. "Come," he ordered a little more firmly.

He began to press the blade in.

"No!" Mhina cried.

A tap at the door made Lamrhath pause. He'd created a nick instead of a slice. "What?" he roared.

"My lord?" Talekas said at the other side of the door.

"Not now!"

Talekas knocked again. "My lord, I have news. You'll want to know this."

Lamrhath growled in frustration as Talekas pushed the door open and entered to find him kneeling on a rug stained with spots and strings of blood. He paused in surprise, and his gaze trailed to Mhina as she lolled on the floor.

Lamrhath himself couldn't keep from staring at his little treasure. "What do you want?" he demanded.

"My lord," Talekas said, "I didn't think you'd want this piece of news delayed. I got a whisper stone message."

"And?"

"And they've found and killed a white ox. They're proceeding with the skinning and tanning."

Chapter 47
A Mountain Moans

Kalea awoke with a shudder to find herself once again cold and alone. No, not alone: her friends slept nearby. That had been such a realistic dream, and it was sad that it had turned out to be one. She couldn't even tell if she'd successfully dreamwalked. There was still so much she didn't know about this inborn ability she possessed.

Without the luxury to mope and lament about failed dreamwalks or Dorhen's loss, she rose up, the first one in the early rays of dawn, to pack her bedding and contemplate a quick breakfast. She had even beat Gaije to rise early. Yesterday, he had charged into the grassy fields at Kalea's recital of Dyii's instructions to walk north into the Black Mountains and search for a path to Ilbith.

The sultry morning mist swirled around her as it drifted along the ground. It wasn't a walking cloud, just a normal sort of mist. It would be a frost if they were a few months later. Kalea didn't want to think about having to rough the Darklands in winter. She couldn't collect Dorhen and return to the Lightlands soon enough. Although the horizon wasn't obscured, there was no way to tell how far they'd trekked yesterday. For now, only the grey Darklandic sky hovered over an endless sea of rolling, grassy hills. No wonder they called this region the Longwalk.

As she stuffed her quilt into the shoulder basket in which she used to carry convent laundry, she replayed that dream in her head. The dream's content indicated it probably hadn't been the magical practice. Dreamwalking ventures were usually about the here and now, not about the past or alternate destinies—she'd at least learned that much through her own experiences.

It was interesting to ponder, though, how it might have been if she and Dorhen had successfully run away together without the bother of sorcerers and convent raids. She liked to think she wouldn't have been so harsh with him if they had united in the forest as planned. With the way Dorhen made her feel now, she also liked to think she wouldn't have been so uptight.

Leaning over to lace up his boots, Bowaen grumbled in his scratchy morning voice, "Shoulda tied that red-eyed freak up and made him lead us to Ilbith."

Kalea huffed. "I couldn't have strong-armed him into being my captive. Maybe if you'd been there…"

Gaije interjected, "This is fine." He stood looking to the north, ready to take off in search of the mountains.

Bowaen shook his head. He looked older than ever this morning as he sat idly with his arm resting across his knee after finishing his boots. "Dyii knows we're going there, and he's runnin' loose. He'll tell the sorcerers all about us."

Gaije paced back to the center of their group, grabbed Del's travel bag, and tossed it to him. Del jolted to catch it before it could hit him in the face. "I don't care," Gaije said about Bowaen's concern. "Let's go."

Kalea leaped to her feet after finishing with her shoes. She took her place beside Gaije, more than ready to find Dorhen, who was probably in the same place they'd find Mhina. Before them stretched the unknown, something that could not be seen over the long field beyond the constant veil of fog.

For two days, they walked through mist and tall grass, stumbling over hidden rocks and sinkholes. Kalea often noted how Gaije squinted forward, including after they stopped, in search of the mountains Dyii had told her about, as if he might spot them before everyone else, or maybe miss them in the blink of an eye. On the quiet nights when they stopped to eat and sleep, she didn't try to call him away from his constant stare forward. They'd gained tremendously on their goal by now. They had a name for their destination and a rough idea of where to find it: Ilbith, the sorcerers' hive.

In the morning, it wasn't the light that roused Kalea from her uncomfortable slumber amid the damp grass so much as the tremor. A faint vibration, but one she could detect. Gaije held both of his hands to the ground, and the pose gave her a flashback of Wikshen with his palms planted in a puddle of blood.

"You feel it too, huh?" she said with a shudder. "What is it?"

"I don't know." He took his hands off the ground. "I felt it yesterday too."

"You did?"

"It's stronger today, I suppose because we've come farther since then."

Kalea hummed and rose to do her morning routine in preparation to walk another long distance. "No way we can guess what's making the earth shake," she said.

"There's also an odd smell in the air." Gaije sniffed to demonstrate.

Kalea tried too, sucking in a long pull. "I can barely notice anything," she said. "But of course, my nose is stuffy in this damp air."

Gaije walked over to rouse Bowaen and Del each with a nudge of his foot. Kalea felt sorry for them as they grumbled and dragged themselves to upright positions. Gaije probably awoke earlier with each passing day. She couldn't blame any of them for whatever negativities they felt.

The farther they walked, the darker the sky grew, which had nothing to do with the sun's position. They did stop in confusion when it became apparent that the sun was setting earlier today than ever before.

"Let's catch our breath and have a bite," Bowaen suggested.

"I smell smoke," Gaije said.

Bowaen shrugged and rummaged for the dried rations gifted by Metta's mother beside Del, who was quick to settle down and light his pipe.

"I smell it too, Gaije." Kalea flexed her stiff muscles and let her knees collapse under her weight as she joined the men in their snacking. Her time at Wikhaihli had spoiled her, even with all the hard work. At least it gave her a roof under which to sleep and brief rests throughout the day with fresh, cooked food every night. Of course, without Wikhaihli's worship routine, fountain water, and Wikshen around, she could think clearer. No more ecstasies.

"It's what I've smelled all along," Gaije said as he reluctantly dropped to sitting beside Kalea. "Something is burning in the distance, and it's big."

"Wikshen's violence again?" Del suggested.

"Of course not," Kalea snapped at him. "Dorhen was kidnapped by the sorcerers."

Del snorted over his pipe. "You must be the only person here who doesn't see Wikshen and Dorhen as two different people."

Kalea opened her mouth but wound up saying nothing. They *were* different people...but they also weren't. She decided to ignore him.

The smell of smoke strengthened with the darkening of the sky. They took to debating what could be causing such strong pollution. After the initial guess about Wikshen destroying another village, suggestions of charcoal being made were passed around, among a few wilder ideas. A large refinery or smelter possibly functioned up ahead.

What stumped the lot of them was how the sky grew blacker and blacker the farther they ventured. They awoke to a dark sky the next morning, the sun blotted out behind a massive noxious haze. The air thinned so much that Bowaen batted Del's pipe down when he attempted to light it.

"You dumb, boy? Breathe real air while you can get it." Del didn't argue with him.

The grass beneath their feet thinned until it vanished in place of dust and rocks. Any tree that had once grown strong and leafy now stood as a hollow, dead chunk of wood over a mound of dried leaves which scattered in the breeze.

Bowaen shook his head at the scenery with a grunt. "This ain't a charcoal kiln or smelter. Whatever's going on is making charcoal out of the standing trees."

Instead of grass, rocks sprang up around them in the dense, smoky air. It made one miss the walking clouds which used to hinder their travel. The rocks were…

"Strange," Kalea said as she ran her hand along one flat, wall-like stone. Along the base, it bore rounded holes, giving the impression of man-made shaping. Through the holes, hot hair hit her feet, the next strange aspect about this area. Something smoldered underground.

After a while, Gaije shed his shirt and led the way with his bow in hand and his quiver and travel bag strung across his bare back. The other two men acted similarly, Del twisting his hair up into a topknot and Bowaen tying a cloth around his forehead.

The rocks around them became taller and more numerous. More round holes, some perfectly circular and some oblong, appeared along the bottom of the wider and higher walls. They had entered a canyon-like place in the rocks, devoid of any way to see the sky or what lay ahead. The rocks shifted into a chaotic maze that could easily turn them around and send them into a dead end, where they might starve to death if not suffocate in the smoke first.

"Aw, shit!" Bowaen said after the overwhelming complexity of the setting became apparent. "Should we turn back?"

"No!" Gaije barked in reply. "Going back will only prolong our journey!"

Kalea couldn't help but side with Gaije, but she couldn't deny Bowaen's point either. Getting lost in this place would be unquestionably deadly. Nonetheless, at Gaije's steadfast insistence, the group continued into the complex of tall rocks. The sky only grew darker as they went.

In a shallow cave nook, they found fresh airflow from deep within the earth, cool and accompanied by the smell of water they all recognized. They stopped to set up camp there. At least they wouldn't die from lack of air.

Kalea opened her eyes to the bright morning. Yesterday's black sky had cleared. The cold, damp air made her groan and wish for a drink of the underground spring below. Her sound woke the others.

"Everybody alive?" Bowaen asked.

Del climbed to his feet and took several pained steps toward a drop in the rocky ground, untying his pants for the usual morning constitution. He paused before the step down. "Damn… Gaije?"

"What?" Gaije called back to him with irritation crisp on his tone. Gaije had good reason to be stressed these days.

"I think I found your 'Black Mountains.'"

Gaije scrunched his face after rubbing it with both hands. "Oh, yeah?"

"Yeah." Del pointed forward, prompting Gaije to lunge to his side to see what he meant. Kalea did the same.

Gaije yelped and halted, throwing his arm out to stop Kalea before she could go too far. The little ledge Del planned to urinate off of was actually the mile-long drop of a cliff, with sharp rocks jutting below and a peek at the grander Darklandic landscape through a narrow opening in the adjacent rock walls. Down there, a walking cloud covered half of the visible ground. Kalea sucked in a breath. They'd been walking along ledges in the dense smoke for days and could've fallen off any one of them!

"We're on the mountain," Del said, holding his pants closed with one hand.

Kalea looked the opposite way at the taller rocks behind them. They'd climbed up the gentle mountain slope without realizing it, and there were higher paths to tread later.

"This is good," she said. "Now we only have to find a good path to follow." She turned back to the nook to gather her things up for today's walking. "We're going to find them, Gaije," she said for his confidence. "And how lucky are we for the smoke to have stopped? We can see where we're going now." The sky showed blue above them, if not slightly obscured by the residual puffs of smoke from yesterday. "We'll easily find the path, so let's hurry," she continued.

Again, she longed for a drink of the cold water under the mountain on which they'd slept. She leaned her hand against the mossy wall to pick up her shoes, favoring her sore back. The tickling of eight legs crawled across her hand, and she shrieked in surprise, pulling her hand back to shake it off.

"You all right, Kalea?" Bowaen called.

"Yeah, it's fine!" she confirmed. She let the spider crawl away on the ground, replacing her hand on the moss-covered wall. It crumbled beneath her weight. Actually, the rocks jumped forward—to grab her!

A loud, crumbling ruckus roared around her. She fell into a ball to protect her head from the falling rocks. An envelopment of them formed around her and pulled her in. The air shifted from the outside sunny warmth to an interior chill. The light was snuffed out in favor of darkness.

Chapter 48
Silent Chamber

Grandfather?" a familiar voice echoed through the trees as Lehomis rolled into Lockheirhen village. He had let Tey drive the cart all the way from Theddir as he sat wordlessly beside him, mostly puffing his pipe in deep contemplation.

At the sound of his proud title, he stood up in the wagon seat. "*Ah!*" he blasted his voice between his cupped hands to answer Anonhet. The young *faerhain* ran toward him with Tirnah floating along behind her. "What's wrong?" Lehomis leaped down from his perch before the wagon came to a complete stop.

"Nothing, Grandfather," Tirnah said, walking to catch up with Anonhet. The younger female threw her arms around him and clung for a long moment.

"Have you heard anything of Gaije? Or Mhina?"

Tirnah's expression showed no cheer, only a ghostly blankness. She shook her head.

Lehomis patted Anonhet on the head, and she finally pulled away. "How'd Tihen do? Was he good? Did he do his chores well?"

"Yes, Grandfather," Tirnah said. "He's strong...and capable."

Lehomis studied her and Anonhet. Anonhet shot a quick look over her shoulder, and Lehomis didn't miss the flare in Tirnah's eyes at the younger one. What were they hiding?

Tirnah forced a smile at Lehomis. "You got many goods, I see."

"Yes," he confirmed. "A bunch of crates will go to our house. The rest will get dispersed through the village." He whistled to Tey, who waited with the reins. "Just up the path there to the left, around the thicket of hydrangea."

"*Ah,*" Tey said, and rolled the cart forward.

With him gone, Lehomis narrowed his eyes at his two household females. "Are you sure everything is all right?"

Tirnah stepped forward, broadening her smile, and took his arm. "Of course, Grandfather. You are tired; let's get you inside. I'll order Tihen to help the lad unload."

Lehomis didn't argue. He entered his cave home to find it aired out, freshened up with washed linens and added herbs, and with a pantry full of foraged goods, some ready for use and others in their drying process. A decent load of fish had been caught while he was out, most of which waited packed in salt while a few fresh ones were ready for the skillet, caught this morning in anticipation of Lehomis's return.

He couldn't rest yet. He sectioned off stacks of boxes and piles of sacks and instructed Tihen where they went and who in the village they should be distributed to. He let the younger *saehgahn* take care of it from there, and then put his own lone crate casually beside his household's pile and waited until the females busied themselves in the kitchen before whisking it off to his room and locking the door on his way out.

At dinner, he avoided mentioning Gaije. He longed to ask again if Tirnah had received a letter or some other hint, but she'd talk about it if she had. He knew she kept up her pleasant disposition throughout dinner not only for his sake, but also for the other *saehgahn*. Tihen was sharing their meal one last time before he returned to his mother's household, and of course Tey had earned a good meal for his help. Something bothered her, and it was most likely the same thing which bothered him. His grandchildren. Dear Bright One, she must be aching inside. It hurt him sharply enough, but those were her children!

He kept his mouth shut throughout the meal, except to eat, of course. If only he could share a funny story from Theddir, but it hadn't been a good trip this year. He'd gone there in attempt to keep his clan fed, and had run into that devious Desteer maiden, and...

He sighed to think of it. As pleasant as his reunion with the teashop owner's wife had been—a lovely and loving woman—he'd come away from it with a heavy heart. She wouldn't live nearly as long as Cirinhen. She'd leave him alone and longing, just like Kristhanhea had left Lehomis. At least Kristhanhea had lived many long elven years. Cirinhen wouldn't have quite as long as Lehomis to enjoy the love of his life.

"Grandfather," Tirnah said, "that's the fourth sigh you've breathed since we've sat down. What's the matter?"

The fourth one? "Nothin'," he responded. "I'm tired, is all." He curled forward to give Tirnah a bow. "Thank you for the meal, *faerhain*."

"Why are you talking so formally?"

Lehomis stood up. "I'm going to retire early."

"Grandfather," Tirnah whispered, though everyone clearly heard. She continued in a mumble, "You've never retired to your room so early before."

Anonhet, Tihen, and Tey kept stone-silent. The two visiting males would depart after dinner.

Lehomis left his plate mostly full behind him. He couldn't remember how much he'd eaten. Solitude in his bedroom awaited.

Another week passed. Every day, Lehomis watched Tirnah run out to meet the courier at the sound of his braying donkey. Togha had yet to return in that position. Even the donkey was different from the one he had ridden—the weird lad used to dote all over the beast. Nonetheless, Tirnah trudged back to the house each day empty-handed. Still no sign of Gaije or Mhina. How long should they wait before arranging a sort of memorial for the two? Lehomis couldn't bear to consider it yet. He wouldn't speak of it. He'd let Tirnah lead the way if she desired some form of service to help her to move on.

Today, as she walked back past the kitchen pavilion to the house, Lehomis stuck his pipe between his clenched teeth and squeezed his eyes shut, hoping he wouldn't have to make eye contact on another one of these occasions. He hated having to offer a smile of encouragement anymore, especially after the way she'd spring out the door and dash up the path to the road where the courier would pass.

Lehomis waited for the sound of the door to close before opening his eyes again… Nothing.

A tingle on his scalp turned to a shiver over his spine. He jumped and twisted to find Tirnah sitting beside him, sticking her fingers into his hair. She smiled wanly, as if making an effort to comfort *him*. The feeling made his heart race. He scooted forward to gently break the contact.

"Grandfather?" her voice peeped behind him.

He didn't turn to face her. "What?"

"You've been dragging your loose hair around for days. Why don't you let me braid it?"

Mhina used to braid my hair. He didn't share his reason, of course. He offered a simple shrug. None of his answers to the question were cheerful.

A few seconds of hard silence preceded her next line. "I don't want you to worry about Mhina and Gaije."

Clenching his eyes, he pulled his lips in tight. "I don't want my hair braided right now." He rose and scooped up the long end of it.

"Don't you have work to do?"

He started toward the house to lock himself in his room again. "I'm going to retire now."

"But it's so early."

The sun still hovered high in the sky, in fact. He didn't listen. Carrying his long mane of hair, he went straight to his place of solitude, fumbling for the key in his pocket.

✳✳✳

Tirnah watched Grandfather go once again, back into the house where he'd inevitably spend the rest of the day locked away without so much as a word of good night. He'd crack the door so Anonhet could deliver a plate of food to him, and that would be the end of it. In the morning, Anonhet always collected last night's dishes after he finally emerged.

In such bright afternoon light, Tirnah marched straight to where the girl busily cleaned out the big cauldron and tapped her on the shoulder. Anonhet met her with a kerchief tying her hair back and a big smudge of soot on her face. Tirnah asked, "What is Grandfather doing in his room every night?"

Anonhet shrugged and went back to her scrubbing. "Resting."

"He's in a dark mood. You've lived with him for ten years; does he always do this?"

"Off and on. You've lived with him a long time too." Anonhet's knees rose high in her squat as she reached her whole upper body into the large pot.

Tirnah dropped her mouth open. "Even before Gaije and Mhina left?" She hadn't noticed his odd patterns because she'd spent several periods with her husband. Her family life had kept her happily distracted, fussing over Gaije as he grew up and came out of the practice yard with this injury one day and that injury another day; and then Mhina, the one who would carry on Tirnah's proud *faerhain* spirit when she took her place as house matron. Mhina had had much to learn, so Tirnah had fussed over her the most.

"Sometimes." Anonhet's voice echoed in the enclosed metal chamber. She leaned out to meet Tirnah's gaze again. "You have to remember he *is* a widower."

Tirnah sucked in a breath through her nose. All good answers, but Lehomis *couldn't* sulk around in depression these days. "Well, if he keeps doing this, I'll have to fetch Tihen back to serve in his place." Tirnah's spine stiffened as she drew closer to a resolution; her neck stiffened too, and her lips. "I'm going to knock on his door."

Anonhet scrambled out of the cauldron and reached to catch her hand before Tirnah could walk away. "Please don't!"

Tirnah twisted her face at the young *faerhain*.

"It's one of his sternest rules not to bother him when he's in his room. Please."

Tirnah watched her for a moment.

"Give him tonight. He'll be better tomorrow, I guarantee it."

For the first time ever, Tirnah gave Anonhet a motherly glare. "Tonight," she complied. "If he acts like this again tomorrow, I'm going to bring Tihen back into the house."

Anonhet gave a deep nod.

Throughout the rest of the day, whenever Tirnah past by Lehomis's chamber door, she couldn't help stopping and studying it. As quiet as she kept on the outside, absolutely no sound came from within.

Chapter 49
A Vestal Falls

Bowaen, Gaije, and Del all leaped to attention at the sound of falling rocks.

"Avalanche!" Del yelled.

But it wasn't. A hole opened up in the rock wall where Kalea had been standing.

"Kalea!" Bowaen called. All three of them rushed to the site.

"She fell in?" Gaije said, putting his foot on the ledge over the cold, open hole in the mountain.

Bowaen pulled him back. "Don't be rash, or you'll fall in too!"

"Well, we have to—"

Bowaen halted Gaije's words with a raised hand. "Something's odd." The two younger men stood and stared. "This was a solid wall a minute ago, right?"

They both nodded.

Bowaen grabbed both their sleeves and hauled them backward. "Look at this."

They all took another backstep. Another. Bowaen extended his hand. "This rock. It's strange, ain't it?"

He referred to the inside of the mountain wall, exposed by the cave-in. The damage revealed an imprint on the wall in the curved shape of a ram's horn. It was a perfect cast, and huge. Too huge. Under the horn shape was the impression of an ear, similar to Gaije's but with two extra points along the side.

In awe, the three of them stepped closer to touch the cast. They yelled for Kalea and got no answer, only echoes. The horn impression wasn't the only odd formation either. Four big grooves had somehow been made on the side of the wall opposite the horn. Like fingers.

"It's like…" Bowaen began. He dabbed his forehead with his cloak and swallowed. "It's like there was a monster embedded in the rock."

The echoing rocks rumbled all around Kalea.

This is it, she thought. *I'll die now. Goodbye, Bowaen and Gaije and Del… Dorhen.*

Air whistled through slits hitting her with a strong chilly force—horizontally.

Thud! Thud! Thud! The rocks ground together, and she crouched, trapped in some tiny pocket they'd created around her. A roar blasted above, complete with some form of sulfurous, hot air to challenge the cold.

"AHHH." Now the rocks sighed with a deep rumble. Kalea finally realized she wasn't falling in an avalanche after all, which made no sense. The rocks had loosened from the wall, so shouldn't she be tumbling with them, deep into the cave?

She huddled and shivered in sheer panic. The rocks must be burying her in her final grave! How long would it take to starve to death in this little encasement? The rumbling noises settled down, yet the surface upon which she sat moved, and she braced herself on the surrounding rocks.

Rocks? Hold on…

She patted the platform beneath her rear end. Leathery, but also rough, like rock and leather combined.

A sudden growl erupted above her again with another smelly plume of hot air. "HMMM."

The rocks loosened around her, and she jumped at the unnatural movement. They pulled away by a few inches, allowing more cold air to blow past. Little could be seen beyond a dark shape hovering overhead. A new sound like a moist popping happened next, and two soft crescent-shapes lit up above. Eyes?

She opened her mouth and sucked air into her lungs. She began to shout, "Bow—"

Too quickly to comprehend, a ceiling pressed down on her. It didn't crush her; it covered her gently.

Thud! Thud! Thud! An up-and-down pressure suggested she was moving in a walking motion.

It took great effort to turn her thinking to the last possible theory she cared to entertain: that this moving, rocky wall was actually a living creature. A whimper escaped her throat. She curled over in the palm of what must've been a massive hand cupping her as if she were no bigger than a beetle, and rode along the thing's course to whatever her fate might be.

Through many caves and tunnels of various heights, colors, and echoing sounds, the giant carried Kalea, each chamber darker than the last. Low-hanging stalactites whipped by, too close and too fast. She kept low to the leathery skin of the creature's palm for a measly sense of security.

The giant put out little grunts now and again as it strode with purpose through the twists and turns, ducking under and stepping over the obstacles. Its stinking, hot breath steamed like a geyser over her head in sparse, inhuman patterns.

Rumbling voices jabbered back and forth ahead. She pressed herself lower to the huge palm, as if she could hide from the dangers toward which she rode. Enormous creatures like the one who carried her populated the widening chamber they entered, along with…bleating goats?

Big yellow lights—more eyes—popped open in the surrounding shadows to glare at her. They hovered like swaying stars in the dark circumference of the room, where a little herd of goats hoofed around in a pen made from stacked rocks in the center. Dim, filtered light from the ceiling illuminated the goats' little circle.

The booming rumbles of the space altered to different tones as the creatures conversed, probably about Kalea. The one who carried her boomed back to them, making throaty syllables with a rolling tongue, each beat vibrating her head with a blast. Kalea could not begin to understand them; the whole thing sounded like an articulated thunderstorm, swiftly ushering in a headache.

They calmed down a little, sharing only a few solitary syllables before erupting into a great roar of laughter that rang shrilly against the walls and shook the ground under her monster's feet. Kalea cupped her ears and wailed at the pain.

At the tail end of the laughter, one of the rocks along the dark wall moved forward, half under the light. The shapes of these beings finally came forth from the shadow for her to see. A massive, silhouetted horn curled out from the side of the creature's head. Only one glowing yellow eye with a horizontal pupil glared at her. The other eye had been lost sometime long in the past; scarred flesh now covered the socket. A set of boar-like tusks sprouted from the creature's bottom jaw, and thick, twisting beard hairs like roots hung off its chin. The rest of it appeared as a hulking, thick mass of tattered shrouds that streamed to the ground with its long grey hair. A mirthless, almost angry, yet wise look held fast to its face—no, more like its face was petrified in the unamused expression.

By comparison, her giant exhibited pale and supple skin, with greenish fuzz like moss growing on the sides of its face. These creatures' heights didn't seem so great in relation to their girth. They walked on short legs, making them all look squatty and thick. Their arms hung long and could almost be used to walk like quadrupeds. Instead, they walked with their own version of sophistication, decorated with jewelry made from goat pelts and bones, or gnarled vines twisted into necklaces or bracelets.

All feeling fled her body as Kalea sat and stared at the approaching monstrosity in what would probably be her last moment alive. At the sharp, foreign words of the one-eyed creature, Kalea's captor bent to place her inside the goat pen. From her new vantage, she could finally see how young the creature who had found her must be, at least compared to the one-eyed elder. He—she was sure it must be a "he"—looked fresher, less petrified, but no less ugly.

It spoke with the other giants as they argued and pointed at his find. One of the older-looking ones became impatient with the younger one and reached out to grab her. Kalea scampered away, wary of the dozen horned goats in the space. When she found herself running circles around the pen like another piece of livestock, the laughter rose again. Other giants tried to poke at her with sharps sticks, and some threw big rocks. Kalea narrowly escaped one, and it proceeded to smash a goat, killing it instantly in a bloody mess.

The one-eyed elder lifted a hand at the younger one who'd made the mistake. The veins in his arm leading to his fist brightened to a blue glow. Instead of hitting the other one as Kalea expected, he shouted a bark powerful enough to knock the young one down with sheer wind pressure, and it hit Kalea's eardrums sharper than any sound she'd ever heard. It left her with a ringing. In the cave-wide vibration, all the other creatures staggered back.

Despite the possible damage to her ears, Kalea's adrenaline kept her moving after the vibration knocked her down, but how long would it last? She tried not to scream, but whimpered as she sprinted and tumbled, dodging and jumping over goats and kids. She managed one hopeless scream as a giant hand cornered her, and just as its large, clawed fingers began to wrap around her, they all stopped at the sound of the more familiar voice of a smaller creature. A human voice.

"Errrahtahhh!" it roared in the giants' own language, mimicking the rough-edged tone.

Kalea paused along with the giants, gasping in terror more than exhaustion. A much smaller figure appeared, draped heavily in linens and scrappy leather, leaning against the outside of the pen and spouting off more odd words to the much larger creatures.

The huge creature dropped Kalea, and she scampered back to the center of the pen. The newcomer leaped over the fence and sprinted to stand over her, his robes brushing her. She resisted clinging to his leg in absolute fear.

The person stepped forward, making shoving motions with both hands. "Rrrroash, rrrroash!" He was telling them to back off.

Surprisingly, the giants did. In obvious confusion, the great, horned monsters leaned in to each other to exchange hushed, rumbly words. This gave the newcomer time to twist and check on Kalea. Though his hood obscured his face, one thing stuck out as quite odd: he wore a mercyman's hood.

Kalea squinted to see more, confused that she would find such a thing down here. She opened her mouth, but her nerves ran too high to think or act properly.

The mercyman threw his hood back to reveal a weathered face and wispy hair—and the ears of an elf. He scooped her up by her armpits and steadied her on her feet. "Better stay standin', madam. The trolls respect a show of strength."

Kalea panted, steeped in panic and staring into his blue eyes. "Trolls?"

"Stand tall now, lass, shoulders square, and stare." He put his face uncomfortably close to hers. His breath smelled no better than the troll who'd carried her. "Stare right at them, right into their souls—if ya can."

Kalea nodded and did so, but which one to stare at? Many sets of ominous glowing eyes hovered along the outskirts of the oasis of light.

The elf threw out a string of more rough, deep, booming words. He followed his own advice, trying to mimic the way the trolls talked and glaring hard at them as he spoke. He waved his arm at Kalea, clearly talking about her, hopefully in her defense, and then he hooked her arm and held her close.

"They've recently come out of hibernation," he explained. "They're hungry, as you can understand. And that one…" He pointed to the original troll who'd carried Kalea in here. "He's a young one. Didn't know what kind of creature you were. Otherwise, he might've gobbled you up on the spot."

Kalea swallowed and continued to ogle the trolls as she listened to those dreadful words. Her gaze worked more as a reaction of fear than an intimidation tactic, though. "What are they going to do with me?" she managed to get out through her chattering teeth.

"Nothin', so long as I'm here." He shot her a brief smile of reassurance. "I have some experience with them, you see. Long ago, I traveled through here and had a run-in with them. Long story short, I'm still alive because I've convinced them I'm a troll too… You, though…" He looked her up and down. "They've never seen a woman before, but I'm telling them you belong to Wikshen."

A chill ran up Kalea's spine at that. How right he was, in fact. It crossed her mind to tell him Wikshen really had chosen her.

The elf spoke again with the trolls, spittle flying in his effort to make their sounds. Kalea recognized it now when he hawked the name "Wik-shhhhen!"

The trolls dropped their arms and took a step back in a shared reaction of awe.

"They worship Wikshen, you see," the elf explained quickly. "I'm recommending they keep you intact and return you to his care so he may... Well, it doesn't matter. This'll get you out of here, lass. Also, the trolls don't even know what I'm really talking about since they don't do the thing mortals do to reproduce."

"You mean sex?" Kalea managed to gain a smidge of starch in her stance at the unfolding events. It helped a lot that the trolls all dropped to their knees and hummed long notes that shifted in pitch every few minutes. A prayer...to Wikshen? It was almost beautiful. The mystery of the strange rumble in the mountains was now solved. Trolls lived underground, real live ones unlike those from the children's stories she'd never taken seriously.

"Yes, that's what I mean," he confirmed. "This is workin' out. Look at them."

As the prayer progressed, their volume rose to an uncomfortable height, and Kalea and the elf both covered their ears. "You get used to this!" he shouted over the noise. "They sing several times a day!"

Kalea gnashed her teeth and took back her thoughts about the prayer being beautiful. How on earth could anyone get used to this? She eyed the elf as he endured. No doubt he suffered some form of madness, but he'd saved her life. Until the prayer ended, he studied her too. His eyes lit up and his mouth quirked, but he could tell her nothing of his amusement at the moment.

"What?" Kalea asked when the earth-shaking hum died down.

The elf still couldn't answer because the one-eyed elder troll rose back to his feet, gaining little height in the act, and shuffled to approach them. The elf squeezed his hand around her arm protectively.

The troll opened his mouth with noticeable labor; rocks cracked and chipped with his jaw's movement. "YOU... ARE... A... TREAT... OF... THE... MASTAREN'S..."

Kalea dipped her chin in an unsettled nod.

The troll continued, "THEREFORE... WE... WILL... PLACE... YOU... AT... HIS... ALTAR... TO... HIS... DELIGHT... WHEN... HE... COMES... TO... US..."

The elf grimaced and shot her a look—of panic or fear or simple uncertainty, she couldn't tell. Nonetheless, he roared back an answer to the trolls in their own language that sounded like agreement. The elf squeezed her arm tighter.

"That hurts," she whispered, but he didn't loosen his grip; maybe he feared being separated from her.

The elder troll pointed his long, knobby finger. "FOLLOW."

Another troll on the opposite side of the space started down a sculpted corridor in the rock.

"Don't be afraid," the elf whispered as he led her that way. "I won't leave you."

"What do you mean?"

"They're going to keep you on an altar like an offering and wait for Wikshen."

Kalea's heart fluttered. That was good news as far as she was concerned, though the elf's tone sounded grave. "When will he come?"

"I don't know, hopefully never...but there's no way to tell. He may very well neglect to visit these followers during his short lifetime."

Kalea's hope withered. She knew firsthand that the sorcerers had taken him. Dorhen couldn't rescue her. She had to depend on herself to escape this cave, and then she would rescue *him*.

The elf hissed through his teeth as they walked behind the heels of their troll guide.

"What's the matter?" she asked him.

"You're not out of danger yet, I can't lie."

"Why?"

"They...might kill you. I'm not sure. I'm trying to make sense of what they've told me in their language."

"But they said I was for Wikshen's 'delight.'"

"That's just it..." He paused to swallow. "Like I said earlier, the trolls don't understand what sex is, though I can tell you it's what Wikshen delights in... But..."

"Just tell me!" Kalea demanded. "There's no time to stall if I'm going to die!" Her shouting went unnoticed by the trolls who walked before and behind them. She couldn't hope to shout quite as loud as they talked.

"Well, the trolls..." He dabbed his forehead with a cloth from his robe pocket. "Wikshen also delights in food, and the trolls delight in eating... creatures of all manner. So there's a...slim chance they're planning to kill and prepare you as a sort of dinner for Wikshen's arrival."

Kalea lost all feeling in her legs again. Her body went cold and clammy. She stared at the elf as they walked arm in arm.

"But don't worry," he said. "I'm going to reason with them. I'll try to tell them what Wikshen likes best." He cleared his throat in discomfort and repeated, "I won't leave you."

"Thank you." Her voice shook beyond her ability to control it. "W-w-why are you being so kind?"

She assumed it was because she was closer to his species and he was taking compassion on her down in this dark and scary place, but asked anyway. His answer shocked her to the core.

"I told you I'd remember you, didn't I?"

"What?"

The openings in the ceiling combined with the glow of many trollish eyes to create an indirect lighting that kept him visible to her. He smiled. "A few months ago. At the hospital in Tintilly."

Kalea squinted and frowned.

"I was a tired and hungry mercyman. You showed me mercy back then. Now, I will give you mercy in return."

"That was you?"

His smile brightened to show his teeth. "It was me. My name is Daghahen."

Chapter 50
Graceful Fingers

Lamrhath stood with his arms crossed as he watched his men snip the hair off Wikshen's head lock by lock, leaving uneven fringes behind among little bleeding cuts which fused back together in seconds.

Talekas stood with his ledger open on the table in the hot, bright room, making notes about everything he witnessed. "My lord," he said to Lamrhath, "even in this light-enhanced chamber, his healing ability is strong."

Lamrhath hummed in reply. It was good to have Wikshen back in their care and be able to perform these experiments on him, but Lamrhath could hardly find excitement in this particular development anymore. His thoughts drifted back to Mhina, and often to Orinleah. How close he inched to winning her love. Mhina's love might have a while to go, but he'd have it soon enough. Children were so much malleable than adults.

Wikshen's head lolled from side to side, depending which one the sorcerers worked on. An assisting sorcerer followed the cutter with a basket to catch the blue hair locks.

Talekas took a moment away from his writing to lift one out and hold it up to the light. "Remarkable," he said. "How it shimmers." He turned his amazed expression to Lamrhath, who could see Wikshen as nothing better than a stupid oaf who used to be a stupid elf.

"Wikshen!" Lamrhath barked.

In the bright light, he could act no more in response than a slight twitch. At this point, only a rat's tail of hair remained at the back of his head.

"How do you feel about getting your hair cut?" Lamrhath asked.

At his question, Talekas scurried back to his ledger and poised to jot down the answer, but it never came.

"Wikshen!" Lamrhath snapped his name and scoffed a second longer before leaving the sorcerers to finish up in here.

"Um…my lord?"

Lamrhath paused halfway to the door. "What?"

"It's… Look at this, please."

Anxious to get on with the rest of his daily rounds, Lamrhath approached the big chair with the oaf strapped down to it.

"It's growing back, my lord. It's…" Talekas swallowed and presented the spectacle with flared hands. "It's growing back already." Indeed, the bared scalp over Wikshen's skull was filling in with more and more blue fuzz that would soon become long lapis strands.

"What'd you expect?" Lamrhath asked, despite his own wonderment. "I guess if his wounds close up fast, his hair will return the same way. This is good for us."

The sorcerer with the shears turned a greasy grin toward him. "He's like a damned sheep! We'll shear him for hair and do it again the next hour. We'll never run out of hair."

Lamrhath returned his excitement with a smirk. "Keep an eye on him," he said. "We'll have to study his hair before we can use it for any purpose. It might have wildly different attributes, for all we know."

The sorcerer nodded. "Right."

Lamrhath turned to the door again, but stopped when a different voice rang.

"Are you really my uncle?"

Lamrhath turned back around to find Wikshen eyeing him, his rapidly growing hair now reaching his ears and moving on to jaw-length. "Yes," he answered, "I am."

The oaf must be speaking as Dorhen right now. How long would it take for Dorhen to depart the body's consciousness forever and be replaced by the fiend called "Wikshen"? The fact that he spoke at all was miraculous. Ever since the first day after he had been reborn, Wikshen had acted like a sleepy, stupid beast with blue hair. He had exchanged only that one conversation with Lamrhath back at the outpost, in which he'd sounded more like Wikshen should, demanding a bargain of freedom.

Lamrhath awaited more from him as Wikshen panted miserably in the room's heat. The sweat poured off of him. The sorcerers, too, dabbed their foreheads now and again. Out of sheer curiosity, Lamrhath leaned to blow out one candle, taking the room's glow down a tad. The slight difference allowed Wikshen to lift his head and open his eyes.

Lamrhath pulled up a stool to face him squarely. "So, are you Dorhen right now?"

Wikshen nodded in his miserable, moping way.

"What is it like to be Wikshen?"

"Trapped," he relinquished. He could only seem to speak in faint hisses.

"Trapped," Lamrhath repeated in study of the subject. Wikshen's blue hair now brushed his shoulders. "Have you been to Wikhaihli?"

Wikshen—*Dorhen*—nodded.

"And what did you do there? Have you made any dreadwitches?"

He shook his head.

"How many followers do you have?"

"I don't know." He spoke faintly and breathily, but Lamrhath dared not snuff any more candles. His eyes rolled up in their sockets, only to pull them back down in his struggle to stay awake. Or alive. When he managed to keep them forward, his eyes shone bright. "I want to know why."

Lamrhath considered his question silently for a moment. Should he tell him why? "Your father did this to you."

"But why? Why did you take me away from h—from the convent?"

"Why were you in the convent?" Lamrhath countered. "To be fair, your fate was your own fault."

"I was…" A little smirk crooked Dorhen's lips. "I was 'boffing' all the girls."

A smile—a real one—twisted Lamrhath's own mouth as he studied his nephew, or rather what used to be his nephew. "Yes, you were. You're really no different from any of us."

Dorhen dropped his head again as he appeared to run out of strength. "Can you blow out another candle?"

After a little consideration, Lamrhath nodded to a sorcerer, who snuffed one more. Dorhen lifted his head again, instantly stronger as a result.

Lamrhath went on to ask more questions while Dorhen's lucidity lasted. "So, why didn't you make any dreadwitches? Do you not have any gorgeous women at Wikhaihli?"

Dorhen nodded. "I can't do it."

"Why?"

"I saw the dreadwitches in a book… I didn't like those pictures. I don't want to hurt anyone."

"But doesn't being Wikshen compel you to…" Lamrhath searched for his words. The sound of Talekas's quill scratched furiously behind him. "Don't you have certain urges?"

"Yes," he breathed, drained despite the second cold candle. "Awful… powerful urges. I'm trapped."

"So, then…" Lamrhath squinted. "You live with urges to act in certain ways. Violent ways?"

Dorhen nodded.

"Doesn't it feel good to act on your urges?" Lamrhath pressed.

"Yeah. I actually… Sometimes when I let it all go, I don't feel trapped."

"So why don't you let go?"

Dorhen pulled his lips in and released them in a huffed breath.

"Help me get the picture," Lamrhath said. "If you don't think about being trapped, if you act out—fight, fuck... If you do whatever you feel in the moment, the feeling of being trapped goes away?"

"Yes, exactly."

Lamrhath smirked again and spread his arms out. "So do it. Free yourself. If I could solve my discomforts so easily, I would"—he snapped his fingers—"in a heartbeat."

Dorhen shook his head, leaning it back against the chair. "I'm scared I'll hurt people. I've already done it before. Can't let it happen again. But as always..."

Lamrhath waited, holding his breath.

"Wik talks in my head."

"Does he?"

Dorhen did his best to nod; he moved like a marionette with slack strings. "Wik desires to do as he wishes, and I resist."

"Does he ever take over?"

"Yeah..." Dorhen's voice grew faint again, and Lamrhath snapped to have another candle killed. "I go to a dark place when he does, and from there, I can..."

Lamrhath waited, but his impatience prevailed. "You can what?"

"I can stop him from using his—I mean *my* cock. I have kept him from doing it so far."

"Fascinating." Lamrhath relaxed in his seat and marveled at the creature before him. "You're saying you have a certain mental power over your body when Wik controls it?"

Dorhen rested his head back. His hair now crawled down his chest. "But it traps me." He blinked drowsily.

"How exactly do these candles make you feel? Describe the sensation."

"Uncle?"

"What?"

"Please tell me..."

Lamrhath waited. "Tell you what?"

"I have to know before I die..."

"You think you're about to die?"

"Tell me about my mother."

Lamrhath's amusement dropped.

"Tell me what she was like. How did you know her?"

How did he "know" her? He *knew* her in the best way possible. Lamrhath didn't give him that fact, though. He couldn't be sure what to tell him just yet. Should he allow him the knowledge of her status? Would a reunion help either of them? This little game piece was something he'd have to sit on and ponder a bit.

"She was a very kind *faerhain*," he told him, "like a flower with hundreds of soft and gentle petals, shining above the rest. She loved me. Your father is evil, and she hated him. She was never meant for him."

At the end of his statement, he found Dorhen glaring from under a tense brow, maybe quizzically.

"You saw your father's treachery for yourself. He made you this way. I only wanted you to live with me and be my heir."

"I can't say the same for you or my father," Dorhen said, "but she loved *me*."

Lamrhath crossed his arms. "I wouldn't go that far. You were the bastard product of an illegitimate union. She only put up with you out of obligation."

Dorhen's sleepy countenance turned to ashy anger. Tension began at the tops of his hands and traveled through his neck and down to his bare feet. "Shut up." His breathy hiss turned to a growl.

Lamrhath had hit a nerve there. Maybe Wik tempted him to hand over control as they spoke—visibly. Lamrhath decided to test the theory a little. How close did anger carry Dorhen to shifting back into Wikshen's persona? If emotional enough, would Dorhen freely give him control?

"Is that why you spent your nights fucking young girls in a convent?" he asked his nephew. "Because you were subconsciously looking for the love your mother never gave you? Did you slip yourself into only the little brunettes, or did you also like the blondes and the redheads? Were you hoping any of them would replace your mother?"

The leather straps around Dorhen's arms creaked. His eyes flared to a brightness that combatted the many candles, and his hair reached its normal length, hanging down his chest.

"My lord?" Talekas said behind him. At the back of the room, an oily haze gathered along the lower walls as if Wikshen's miasma crept in from the cracks between the stones. Wikshen's essence wanted to challenge the light.

Lamrhath stood up and nodded, giving his men permission to relight the candles they'd snuffed. Doing so dissipated the swirling black mist. Another man turned a few mirrors to catch the sun and flash an overwhelming beam on Dorhen's face. He winced away from it and withered back to the usual enervated state.

"Not too much, lads," Lamrhath reminded. "We don't want him to die yet."

Orinleah ran her fingers through the thick, soft fibers of the last item needed to secure their marriage. The white ox pelt's long locks slid over her ivory skin.

"So?" Lamrhath said. "Are we married now?"

She remained fixated on the item. He'd ordered it hastily delivered via portal. It still put off the strong, bitter smell of tannin as well as its natural flesh. Lamrhath waited for her answer. He'd finally delivered the last item he needed, and Orinleah would approve and give herself to him once and for all.

She nodded her head faintly, and he stopped the motion by taking her chin in his hand, forcing her to look at him. He struggled to read her feelings past her blank stare.

"It's up to you now," he urged in the deep, rugged voice from which he couldn't sweep out all the lust and longing built up over the last several days. He'd fornicated as little as he could manage while delivering all the trinkets she demanded and waiting for this pelt's arrival.

"I am pleased," she said at last. No smile. No warmth.

He snorted and released her chin. "So that's it?" He was already standing close, but when he took a half-step closer, she winced ever so slightly. He grazed his fingers along her cheek, bringing her eye contact back to him.

"In my culture," she said, "the bride needs a period of self-preparation before the final night. Let us mark a date to consummate our marriage. I told you it would be a ritual. I'll need a night or two to meditate. To speak to the Bright One. To prepare myself internally."

He made a great effort to give her a smile. Was she actually trying to stall him longer? He ached so badly. Tonight would probably be another one of those nights in which he gave in to his pain, thinking of Orinleah during the process.

"Whatever you need," he submitted.

She reached out two graceful hands. "Bow your head, Lambelhen."

A slight hesitation preceded his acquiescence. Lamrhath bowed his head to no one. She had called him *Lambelhen*, though… Maybe Lambelhen could bow his head to the *faerhain* of his literal dreams.

So he did, and when they could reach, her lips stamped his forehead. A tingle ran from the spot to the rest of his body. He straightened from his bow in shock to find Orinleah smiling warmly, such a rare sight.

"Better yet," Lamrhath said, "I have another gift for you. This one is a gift of my choosing."

She rewarded him again with the warm smile of approval he craved.

Chapter 51
Locked Door

Sorry it took me so long to get here, lass," Lehomis said as he took his seat on the freshly washed and fluffed cushions in the *wyrrem*. Besides the little hearth fire embers, he didn't have much light to see by in the deep cave home.

"It's no trouble," Tirnah said softly. She took her seat after placing his teacup on the short-legged table and then lifted her own to her lips. "I am sorry to take you away from your work, Grandfather."

He waved a hand, poised with his cup as he waited for the tea to cool. "It's good to get a break from all the horse manure." He followed up with a one-beat laugh and pondered their dark settings again. Despite the fact that he'd chiseled his house out of a cave, it really shouldn't be so dark in here. He squinted through the arched doorway to the side and found she'd covered the window in the dining nook.

He lowered his brow and returned his eyes forward, to Tirnah's blank expression. "Did you want to talk or somethin'?"

She dipped her chin, slow and deep, to give the gesture of solemnity elves tended to express in certain moods. She'd already been drinking from her cup, and Lehomis took his first sip, nerves beginning to dance. The steaming water burned his lip.

"We just…" Tirnah shrugged. "I feel like we don't talk anymore. Ever since we returned from *Laugaulentrei*."

Lehomis began some kind of unplanned reply, only to make a stutter. "Do you have tension, Grandfather?"

He took another scalding sip. "Well, of course." He shook his head, staring down at the cup in the dim, dim light. "It's not easy being the elder. There's a lot of business to look after. Lots o' worries and hand-wringin'."

"Of course. How could I not understand? I've lived in your home off and on for years, practically ever since I got married. Now I'm a permanent resident, and no longer married."

He raised an eyebrow. "Until you remarry, of course."

She batted her eyes and took another sip. "I'm not concerned with such things right now. Probably not for a long while."

"Yeah," Lehomis sighed. "I don't approve of rushing it…"

"You don't?"

A spark of embarrassment made Lehomis's neck hair stand on end. "Um—yeah—you know. I hate that Trisdahen died. I loved that lad! He was my great-great-great grandson."

"He was a fine *saehgahn*, wasn't he?"

"More than even you know, lass. Yes." Lehomis took three consecutive sips.

"Grandfather, you seem so tense…"

With a mouth full of sloshing tea, Lehomis shook his head and showed her his palm. "I'm fine," he said after gulping it down. He looked around again.

Surely not! he thought. *She wouldn't do this! Not Tirnah…with me!* He couldn't deny how dark she'd made the house for this meeting. She had been acting strange lately, like something bothered her mind. And she'd hugged him before he left for Theddir, and then…touched his hair the other day.

"Where's Anonhet?" he asked when he finally noted how quiet it was too.

"She's helping Tihen's mother today. I sent her to go and do some chores in her house as a sort of return favor for the week Tihen spent with us."

"Ah," Lehomis said, and he took another sip. So Tirnah had conveniently gotten rid of Anonhet for the day. Everything added up and pointed to… "Do you know when she'll be back?"

"Not for several hours."

Lehomis's heart pounded now. This couldn't be happening. This was wrong! This was…! Lehomis sipped his cup repeatedly. Hopefully, the darkness kept Tirnah from seeing how much his hands shook.

"Grandfather, what's wrong?"

"The tea's really good, lass!" He tipped it up again, only to find the cup empty. He'd already swallowed the bitter grounds at the bottom and hardly noticed. Nonetheless, he retained the cup in his hand.

Tirnah took a deep breath and placed her cup on the table.

No, lass, pick it up! Pick it up, girl!

Now he could barely hear anything over his heart pounding in his ears. What in the world made her think they needed to incite a *karra kar shirinhen* ritual? And so soon! He couldn't have guessed the lass would be so lusty! Usually, widowed elves lived alone for a hundred years before resorting to that sort of desperate contact. Tirnah, such a young and upstanding *faerhain*, shouldn't engage in this taboo! She could get in so much trouble if the Desteer found out! Although… Tilninhet hadn't been very old or widowed long before she initiated the ritual with him. But Tilninhet was different!

Inciting the ritual with none other than him was the rashest thing Tirnah could do these days. Didn't she realize it would change their relationship forever, regardless of how they were supposed to pretend, even to themselves, that it didn't happen? And if he knew anything, one could get dependent on the ritual. It was too dangerous to test out that first little foolish, curious incitement. Too dangerous!

Lehomis managed a desperate peek at her cup as a feigned nonchalant stretch. Sure enough, her cup still held liquid. In the "tea between widows" ceremony, the participants put their cups down without finishing it. Just because he had already finished his didn't necessarily mean he'd declined the offer.

He kept his cup in hand and kept talking to put across the message of his intention. If nothing else, it would imply his ignorance of the tabooed arrangement, but what if she didn't care? What if she proceeded with it, having the same shameless determination Tilninhet had exhibited? Should he let her? Or should he excuse himself and hurry outside? His body made its own decision as of now; the ambience she'd set up let it know instinctively what was about to happen. His mind proved a stronger entity, though.

"Boy, the tea sure was good!" he said in his most loud and cheerful voice. He stood up. "I almost want a refill, but you know what? The stables are heaping with horse shit, and I can't let those little fillies and mares and cute little colts return to a dirty house. No way. I gotta go. Nice chat. Yer a good granddaughter-in-law. The best! And I'll see you tonight at dinner."

And the next thing he knew, he was outside in the hot sun, closing the door behind him, teacup still in hand.

"I tried to tell him, but he started acting stranger than ever," Tirnah whispered to Anonhet as they washed the dishes after dinner.

Anonhet dunked the next clay cup in the clean water bucket to rinse it before setting it on the shelf to dry. "Stranger how?"

"He got nervous for some reason and started talking too fast for me to get a word in. I didn't know how to react. He ran out the door before I could say the two simple words 'I'm pregnant.'" She huffed as she scrubbed the cookpot they'd used earlier to boil the turnips. "I'm trying to understand what's bothering him. It wracks my nerves to think of having an honest conversation, let alone share my news."

Anonhet patted Tirnah's back after drying one hand on her apron.

By the time they went back inside, carrying the cleaned dishes, Lehomis had disappeared into his bedroom—already!

"I guess you're too late for tonight," Anonhet said as they both took in the empty *wyrrem*. After placing the heavy stack of dishes down, she fanned herself with her hand.

Tirnah scoffed down the hallway where Lehomis had surely gone. "He retreats back to his room earlier and earlier every day. He didn't bother to say goodnight yesterday. Looks like it's the same today."

Anonhet shushed her. "Grandfather likes his privacy."

Tirnah threw up her hands. "I don't care. I'm tired of all this. I'm going to pound on his door and get some issues out in the open."

"Wait!"

Tirnah marched into the corridor when Anonhet hissed after her. Her footsteps pattered behind. Tirnah didn't stop. Anonhet grabbed her arm, and Tirnah pushed on. "Let me go!"

"Tirnah, please! Grandfather doesn't like to be bothered when he's in there. I've lived with him longer than you."

"So what is he doing in there, then?"

"I don't know, but it doesn't matter. Please come away! He needs his privacy."

"And who in the world ever said *saehgahn* could have privacy? Hmm?"

Anonhet pouted. She resorted to wringing her hands and watching helplessly as Tirnah went to the larder where she knew Anonhet hid a spare key to his room in an empty canister.

"Please, Tirnah, please!"

Tirnah marched with purpose, and Anonhet followed, taking many extra steps in her panic. She brought herself to tears as *faerhain* often did to get their way with *saehgahn*. Such a tactic would never work on Tirnah. Anonhet could cry and beg all night if she wanted to.

She jammed the key into the slot, turned it to make the loudest click possible—to send Lehomis a message—and when she swung the door open, Anonhet fell silent, turning off her weeping as quickly as she'd started.

"Lehomis?" Tirnah said in her hardest voice as she stepped into the room. A single oil lamp struggled to light the large bedroom. He appeared to be in bed asleep on the left side of the generous space.

She clicked her tongue in annoyance and twisted back to regard Anonhet, who huddled in fear in the doorframe. "Can you believe him? Falling asleep while this oil goes to waste. *Cha*! Wake up!"

She traversed the step where the main part of the room was raised up. He'd thrown the heavy curtain closed on the back wall. One big window served to light the space during the daytime. A vanity and wardrobe stood at the right side of the higher floor. Tirnah eyed the femininely carved comb placed neatly on the desk beside an old perfume bottle. The rest of the room was decorated in masculine artifacts from ages past, like splintered old shields and spears on the walls—and, of course, a few old bows on display.

On her way to the bed, Tirnah stumbled on something on the floor. Liquid on the floor seeped through her slipper. She hopped aside and swished her dress hem out of the way.

"What a mess." She picked up a fallen bottle and shot Anonhet a quizzical look. The younger *faerhain* kept blank for the most part. "What's this?" Tirnah asked.

Anonhet shook her head.

Tirnah put her nose to the bottle's opening and winced. It smelled bitter. Poisonous. "What is this liquid?" she demanded, and Anonhet shrugged.

"Lehomis!" Tirnah stepped over the puddle and approached the bed where he slept. "Wake up!" He didn't, and she tried again. "Wake up, I said!"

She shook his bare arm and got no reaction. The harder she shook him, the more his silky black hair fell over his face. Tirnah stopped and listened.

"Tirnah, let's—"

"Shh! You hear anything?" They both listened.

"I hear nothing," Anonhet said.

"Neither do I." Tirnah's hackles rose in fear. "Lehomis?" She bent over him and stroked the hair away to reveal his pale face. She whispered his name.

"Oh, dear," she said, and shot Anonhet a stare full of dread. "He's... not breathing. Bring the lamp." The new nearness of the light made the scene all the worse. Lehomis was lying there with his eyes half-open. His pupils didn't react to the bright light. "Oh, dear Bright One. NO!"

"What's the matter?"

"Grandfather—Lehomis!" Tirnah's voice shook, and she shouted beyond her ability to control it. "He's dead!"

Chapter 52
Withering Keys

Vivene eyed the wooden tag hanging off the cook's belt. Whoever held the one with the symbol of a knife painted on it could use one, but where to get a ticket? She hadn't seen Sabina yet, and didn't think the girl would relinquish any more information to her. She suddenly regretted all the pranks she'd played on her when they were children: ink in her hair, a frog in her bed. It was obvious that even in Ilbith, the girl hadn't forgotten. Sabina had received the worst of Vivene's jokes.

She kept her head low as she swept the floor. A kitchen assistant stood at the hearth with iron tongs, flipping the four slabs of meaty ribs and spicing their undersides with a big hog-hair brush dipped into sauce. Vivene's mouth watered to see and smell those lovely hunks of lamb. Never did the servants get to eat any; they ate only gruel and sloppy leftovers. The best foods were only for the privileged pricks in red.

Vivene sighed. She peeked over her shoulder again to view the cook, who hacked at a stack of leeks with the only knife in the kitchen. How to get one of those knife tokens…or maybe the knife he was using?

"Vivene!" a new voice in the kitchen shouted.

She jumped and threw her broomstick to the opposite hand. "Yes?"

The newcomer, a young sorcerer, grinned. "Bargo's askin' about you."

Urgh, what does he want? She would've asked for Bargo's location if questions weren't illegal to servants, so she curtsied and waited for more information.

"Get to the shitstalls. That's where he is, stupid! Go on."

Vivene marched for the door, more annoyed at having to abandon her mission from Orinleah.

The "shitstalls" was a long corridor, low in the tower, where the sorcerers went to relieve themselves. Higher-up members of the faction had garderobes in their bedrooms. The rest of them—and the servants—came down to this smelly, old, tunnel-like corridor with little stalls of seats with holes in them.

This section was a bit too close to the Grave for her comfort. The closer she drew, the sharper the images of Rose's face in her last moment before a sorcerer's arrow sank into her chest materialized. The memory didn't keep to inside her mind either; it flashed in front of, beside her, farther down the hall, and especially in dark corners.

Shivering, Vivene scurried through the rank corridor, surveying empty stalls, some occupied with a man or woman sitting and doing their business, while others had men standing to piss into the stall's hole. So far, no Bargo. She turned the corner and noticed too late a man standing there.

Slap! Stars swirled in Vivene's vision. He'd struck her.

"You little bitch, are you trying to get my head cut off?"

"Bargo?" she said in her instant daze. Of course, it was him. He took her shoulders and forced her into the nearest toilet stall, his wide form blocking her in.

"What the hell are you doing?" he demanded. "Don't you know they watch you? You've been dallying far too long in the kingsorcerer's wife's foyer! Are you speaking to her?"

"No, sir!" Vivene pleaded. "I swear! I would never do anything to endanger you."

He slapped her again. Her skull collided with the wall, and she squealed.

"Shut up! And don't lie. I did you a favor when I got you that job. Why have you been spending so much time in there? You're supposed to slide the tray through the food slot and leave. What's so hard about that?"

Vivene stuttered for an explanation. She didn't have one. "Nothing is going on," she said. "Please don't hit me. I do love my new position. I'm doing the best I can. Please!"

"So how are you going to reassure them I wasn't wrong to recommend you?"

Vivene would have to stop talking to Orinleah, but she sure as hell would pass the knife as requested. "I'll do better, I promise! The only reason I have stalled is because I struggled with the key and getting the shutter open. Sometimes it gets jammed, and I'm not strong enough to fix it. I'm getting the hang of it, though. Please, give me another chance."

"Another chance isn't in my power."

As soon as she noticed Bargo's voice calm, she ever-so-slightly pressed her pelvis against him. He noticed. "Let's be calm about this," she whispered. When he didn't react at first, she pressed a little firmer. His expression softened. "Bargo," she breathed his name. "I haven't enjoyed your treats in a few days. What's the matter?"

"I've been busy." His voice ran hard, but his body language gave her hope for her tactic's success.

"I sure am hungry," she said, and untied her chemise top to let her plump bosom out in the stale air. She sat up on the jakes behind her and hiked her skirt over her knees. "Feed me a sausage?"

He untied his codpiece and let out his long, meaty member. She moaned as he put it to use, enduring a little pain because they'd skipped their usual ritual of foreplay. Her line about sausage was his favorite euphemism. After she'd eat a heaping tray of cakes and pies, he'd say, "Now you have to eat the sausage," and it led into the rest of their routine. Maybe that line saved her today: her life, her position in the tower, who knew? If she could hold onto her duty of serving Orinleah's dinner for one more day, this was more than worth it. As usual, she denied her other feelings about it. The throbbing pain in her face and skull would disappear along her journey to climax.

"Bargo," she squeezed out as he thrust in and out of her, "I gotta tell you something."

He grabbed her hair and used it as leverage for his work, cocking her head to the side. "Oh, you bold little slut. What do you want now?"

"I love to cook! Oh God, I love it!" Her breathy statements strangely aligned with her panting pleasure. It was a lie, of course. Back in the convent, she'd taken every chance she could get to be lazy. She only enjoyed eating the food. "Food, food, food, don't you love it?"

"Shut up," he moaned back at her.

"Bargo," she said, and boldly followed up, "what does it take to become a kitchen attendant? One who can actually prepare food? Cook it all day?"

He chuckled, keeping his steady rhythm. "You think because you got yourself around my cock, I'll let you ask me a question?"

"Oh, come on, Bargo." She giggled. "You know I'm good. I'll eat your cakes and scream your name and stay nice and fat just for you, just how you like it. We're good friends, don't you realize?"

"To me, you're just a little warm muffin who likes to eat my sausage with your lower mouth."

At that, she pushed against him.

"Hmm?" He sounded annoyed, but he did budge back at her prod. She pushed him until he pulled all the way out of her. She dropped to her knees before him.

"Oh, you little tart!" He leaned back against the toilet bench.

"Not only my lower mouth, my lord."

"You get a kitchen duty by talking to Argey and"—he grunted in pleasure—"gaining an audience with the man in a higher seat than he: Manchawn."

Vivene made a mental note of those names as she slid her mouth back and forth along his shaft. Every pass hurt her throat; this was usually easier when she sat on top of him. She kept up her work, though, eager to *suck* all the information out of him she could.

"Aw, shit, girl!" In his frenzied delight, he took her by the head and worked it on himself like a masturbation tool, thrusting at the speed he wanted until a great spasm rattled along the length of his meat.

He pulled it out, leaving a trail of semen along her tongue and dribbling down her lips. "Now look what you've done," he said. His voice lost its warm, sensuous tone and now carried something dark and unsettling.

Vivene stood up to face him, unsure if he'd punish her for asking him a question outside of his inebriation. He pinched her face in one huge hand and engulfed her mouth with his, sucking his own essence off her lips.

"You didn't manage to have your little pleasure fit. What a shame. Guess you'll have to help yourself, because I got no time for this nonsense now."

He left her in the stall, legs shaking. She'd gotten her answer but not her soothing sensation, and she'd never felt so filthy in her life.

Find Manchawn: Vivene's new task. She also had her normal duties to begin, but for Orinleah's sake, she'd get as close to finding a knife as she could today. This might be her last day delivering her dinner.

She drew close to the Chimera Tower, a few corridors away; not all sorcerers with societal power lived there, since a manager of Ilbith's lower branches could be stationed anywhere. Someone who allocated the kitchen duties could very well hold his office in a region close to it. She listened hard for that name, hiding around corners or under tattered red window drapes whenever two sorcerers exchanged words in the halls.

"Manchawn says to bring up more candles from the storeroom."

Ha! Vivene sucked in her breath as she pressed her back flat against the wall. He must work somewhere in this quarter, but how in the world could she approach him to ask for kitchen duty? Could she tell him the cook had requested an extra set of carving tools? Could she steal a knife ticket from wherever he kept them?

"More candles?" The sound of rustling paper accompanied the responding voice. "This isn't good. Candles aren't cheap; we'll have to scour the towns and villages for their supplies. The kingsorcerer has *got* to find a different way to restrain the Wikshen. Perhaps by magic."

Vivene went cold. *Wikshen?* She couldn't help stretching to peek around the stones to view the two men as they flipped through their papers and fretted about supplies and finances.

"I'll talk to the kingsorcerer. There must be a better solution out there. For now, go and count the candles already burning."

The two sorcerers split, and Vivene followed the one who took the order. Wikshen was here? He still owed her a favor, though she couldn't expect to get out of Ilbith now. Her chances had been much better down in the misty Darklandic hills when, unfortunately, Wikshen was not lucid enough to complete his part of the bargain.

Tailing the sorcerer wasn't the easiest task. He took her on a winding route through the corridors to places she'd not yet seen and didn't know if servants were allowed to go. The worst paths crept up tight little staircases behind doors. She let the man go up a few steps before ascending behind him. If she let him get too far ahead, she could lose him at the top when she finally emerged.

Tap, tap, tap. She followed the sound of his footsteps and tried to memorize the rhythm. She had never gained a good view of his face while he conversed, so recognizing him in whatever busy atmosphere might be waiting above was out, and he wore the same old red robe every other sorcerer donned. He didn't walk with a distinctive gait, so his step rhythm could easily be lost.

As the stairs climbed higher, the sound of a door clacked shut above. Had he exited the stairwell? A new exchange of voices confirmed otherwise: someone else descended the stairs. Vivene shook into a panic and pressed against the wall. A small hole in the wall at the left side of every coiled turn shone daylight into the stairwell; otherwise, she'd be in total darkness. A choice faced her: she could dart backward and scamper back out, or brave it forward and bypass the oncoming sorcerer. Either way, she could face trouble for being away from her duties.

No time to make a decision. The sorcerer tapped around the bend.

"Are you joking?" he asked, and she winced. "Tell me you're joking. Are you stuck in here?"

A cold sweat beaded on her temples and ran down her back to add to her regular sweat. She shook her head. "No, sir."

He scoffed. "You're in my way. Make room. Move!"

Vivene pressed harder against the wall to let him pass. Instead, she found herself in an awkward jam with him. The space was too narrow, and she was too fat for two people to pass each other. He wasn't very lean either. He cursed and squeezed and elbowed her when he got angry enough.

"I'm so sorry. Sorry—oof!" This happened in a section where no light shone into the damp stone space.

"Damn you!"

In their struggle, she got her hand on a jingling ring of keys on his belt, but the confusion kept her too distracted to wonder if she could steal them. She wouldn't know what key went to where if she did. He took to straining and grunting to push himself past her. It would have been much easier if she backed down the stairs to let him exit before continuing. At this point, she might've lost her target sorcerer.

Without much of a plan, she squeezed the keyring, knowing they typically hung on a circular mechanism with a hinge for a quick release off the belt.

Click! The keyring came off, and she retained it in her hand. He didn't notice in his fluster and determination to get through their entanglement.

She put the keyring around her wrist. "Allow me, sir." She pushed him to her left, in the direction of descent. Her cold sweat turned to ice in her knowledge of what she'd just nicked off of him.

"You stupid bitch!" he protested, yet budged himself with her push. "Why are you using these stairs at all?"

She didn't answer and hoped she didn't have to. She apologized as profusely as before.

"When I get out of this jam—ya!" He broke free and took a few seconds to catch his breath. Vivene squeezed the keys in her hand by her side to prevent any sound. "Get out of my sight," he said, "I'm too busy for you, but go and tell your superiors what you've done to me here."

"Yes, sir." Vivene scurried upward. The sorcerers really did expect the servants to come clean about what they'd done because they usually followed the order out of fear. One learned quickly here that it was better to get it over with rather than rack up worse punishments in a string of deception.

At the top of the stairs, Vivene peeked through the door. Not much went on in this quiet space. She tiptoed out and followed the curved path. Here, multiple corridors crisscrossed each other, making an interesting maze out of the little vaulted spaces. At the center of this neighborhood of many doors, one stood out on a rounded wall. It hung open less than halfway, enough to show another set of stairs going up a much brighter stairwell than the one she'd ascended. An empty chair waited beside the door, abandoned by some guard. Could that be where the sorcerer had gone?

Vivene stared at the door. Faint footsteps shuffled around in adjoining corridors, but no one occupied this area. She squeezed the keys she'd haphazardly decided to steal, hiding them under her apron, unsure what in Kullixaxuss she'd do with them. Maybe she could ditch them in a corner and walk away...if she couldn't find whatever cabinet the knife tokens were locked inside.

A long shadow slithered down the stairs along with the familiar sound of tapping footsteps. Vivene lunged to the side and flattened herself into the closest and darkest shadow, but leaned over to see who was coming down the stairs. It appeared to be her sorcerer. This hub in the midst of the crisscrossing pathways turned a degree darker when he closed the door behind him and proceeded to lock it. He took a moment to frown at the empty chair and shouted the name "Jobar" for the missing guard.

Vivene focused on the door when he wandered away in his search. That must be where they kept Wikshen. Her feet moved before she bothered to think about it. What were they doing with the strange creature? Could he be useful to her?

She tried the knob and found the door locked—of course. She sifted through her keys and tried one in the lock. Nope. No. Not that one. Maybe not all sorcerers bore the key to Wikshen's room. She should really get out of here before someone caught her. Jobar, the guard, couldn't be far away. For the sake of curiosity, she stuck one more into the lock.

Click.

Her heart pattered. She swung the door open and, before she could consider the logical idea to abandon her course, she jogged up the stairs.

The bright, hot space at the top gave her pause. It did nothing for her already-sweaty body. She had entered an oven, so bright the stones of the room beamed white. The orange glow from the sinking sun through the windows made it worse. She staggered back to let her eyes adjust. Many tall iron candleholders littered the space, along with wooden structures holding up huge, polished lenses and reflective silver trays to bounce the sun- and candlelight onto the central figure—*him!*

"Wikshen?" She whispered it, but the silence of the room carried her voice far. The worst sound in the room, after the many hissing candlewicks, was his shallow breathing. He sat tied to the chair, exactly as she'd seen him before, except this time he drooped like a thirsty blue flower. His wet, blue hair stuck to him. His lips bore no color, but his cheeks showed the rosy red of a person too hot.

Vivene swallowed and stepped forward. Whatever danger the sorcerers thought Wikshen posed, he lacked such ability now. She had underestimated his size at first glance. Seeing him like this made her forget how angry he'd made her. He really was a pathetic lump. Why did he make the sorcerers so nervous? And why all the candles?

She moved around to the side of him where his head hung, and found him staring blankly like a dead body. His eyes shone a bright color. At their last meeting he'd been blindfolded, so this was her first glimpse of them. She waved her hand and snapped her fingers in his face, only to get a slight hesitation in his breathing rhythm. He might soon die of thirst.

She turned around to blow out a candle, and he twitched. She snuffed another one, and his eyelids began to flutter. Obviously, anyone would be uncomfortable in this room of powerful reflected light, but somehow it kept Wikshen totally incapacitated.

"Hey," she tried, venturing to poke his cheek with her finger. He twitched, and finally his eyes shifted to focus on her. "Remember me? I'm back."

He closed his mouth and worked his throat. "No." His voice came understandably dry.

"You were supposed to help me escape, and now look. They brought me to this tower, and I'll never get out." Her words brought her anger about it back.

He closed his eyes and sighed, working again to moisten his throat. His chest rose and fell heavily with the ropes bound tightly around it. They creaked under his strength. He rolled his head against the back of the tall chair to the front in a visible effort to come more fully aware. Vivene went about blowing out more and more candles. Each candle to go out added a slight bit of extra starch to his neck.

"I don't think you can help me this time, though," Vivene said, stepping back over to him. Now, he could regard her with a more normal amount of attention. "What have you to say for yourself?" She didn't really know the point of this taunting; it came from her anger at him, she supposed.

"I don't know...what you're talking about," he rasped.

She clicked her tongue and grumbled, "Bastard." She sucked in a breath. The thought of hitting him over the head with a candleholder crossed her mind more than once, but that sort of foolery wouldn't help her in the long run.

His mouth twisted into a show of anguish and his brow tensed. "I don't know what they did or where she is."

"Who?"

"I shouldn't have left her in that inn."

Now Vivene twisted her expression.

"Everyone's right." His anguish turned to something near weeping. "I *am* stupid."

"Who are you talking about?"

He sobbed his answer. "Kalea."

Vivene threw her hands over her mouth, her key ring jingling as it slid down her arm to her elbow. "Dear sweet Creator... You *are* the elf she was seeing."

His turquoise eyes popped open and glared at her. "Are you one of the novices? Like her?"

"Yeah," she said, "I knew Kalea. Where is she? What's going on?"

His face twisted up again as his emotions threatened to take over. "I think they have her."

"What?" Vivene rushed to close the small amount of space between them. "Where? How?"

He shook his head. "You have to find her and tell me if she's all right."

"I haven't seen or heard of her here—you have to be more specific! Oh my God, this changes everything! Rose said she was coming—she must've been right. She must've been clairvoyant or something—oh, dear Creator!"

Wikshen shushed her. "They'll hear you." He huffed, and his chest pushed hard against his ropes in his blossoming energy. "I haven't seen her here, but I swear I've heard her voice."

Vivene blinked. "Really?"

"In this room...in the air."

Vivene frowned. "What, like a ghost?"

He grimaced, and Vivene waved her hand. "I didn't mean to suggest she died or anything. No sense in you getting upset for no reason. If I find out she's dead, I'll tell you. In the meantime, I need your help... Um." She perused his pathetic, restrained state. "What can you do? Back at the camp, you told me you can see in the dark even with a blindfold on. What can you do here?"

"I need the darkness," he said. "Wik's trying to tell me something." He closed his eyes and mouth and concentrated. "He's faint in all this light."

Vivene moved to untie his bonds. "I'll let you out. Can you fight them?"

"Stop!" he barked. "You'll only get yourself killed. I don't know if I can fight them yet."

"Well, when can you? Last time, you told me to be patient, but you never got around to helping me, and here I am—!"

"I said, shut up!"

Vivene snapped her lips together at his roar. They were being dangerously loud. Wikshen calmed himself and opened his eyes to point them at her. She shook like gelatin under his breathtaking stare.

"I need a knife," Vivene said, "for an important purpose."

"A knife." His wide mouth tightened and quirked downward. "I'm completely...empty."

"Empty?"

"It's a sensation I've known sometimes since I've been Wikshen."

She mouthed the words, *Since you've been Wikshen*, unsure how to process the statement.

"Give me something metal," he said.

Considering his words, she perused the many options the room offered and put her hands on the thin pole of a candleholder.

"Not that," he said quickly. "They'll notice it gone. They come in here often, sometimes bringing more of those, and then count and replace the candles. What do you have on you?"

She fingered the ring of keys on her wrist.

"Yeah." He nodded to them.

At a loss for what was going on, she held them out to him, though he didn't have the ability to take them with his hands tied down.

"Put them on the floor, under my foot."

Another bizarre request from Wikshen. She did as he asked, and he put his bare foot right on top of them. He sucked in a breath and waited. Vivene watched his foot intently as the little tip of one key in view shriveled smaller and smaller, until it disappeared under his heel.

He sucked air through his teeth with his eyes closed, a sight similar to when the sorcerers found their moment of climax with her. "Listen," he said, "it won't last long. It'll be solid for a while because you had those keys to offer, but it won't last forever."

"What won't last?"

"A morkblade only lasts a second without metal."

"A what?"

He didn't take the time to remedy her confusion. Without the ability to raise his arm, he spread his fingers to show his palm. Vivene leaned over to see what he tried to show her.

"Get out of the way, or it'll carve through your head like a turnip."

Vivene lurched backward right as a black thing shot out from his palm, leaving a red, open gash in his flesh. She yelped, and a sound rang behind her. *Ting-tap-tap!*

"There," he said.

She whirled around and chased the course of the thing he'd produced through his hand.

"Don't cut yourself, though," he added.

She squatted to inspect the sleek, black thing on the floor: a little blade with a wavy body and several sharp angles.

His voice deepened behind her again. "Like I said, use it quickly because it'll expire."

She attempted to lift it between two fingers. "How long do I have?"

"I don't know."

She tore a strip off her threadbare skirt and did her best to wrap it around one side of the blade to make a handle.

"In return, I want you to find Kalea in here and tell me if she's alive and unhurt. If she's not…" The emotion returned to his already-miserable face. "I won't live much longer either."

Vivene resisted asking him why. She now had a knife from a bizarre and unlikely source. She wrapped her hand around the makeshift cloth handle and swiped her arm in practice—not that it was hers to use. This, she'd give to Orinleah tonight.

"Better get away from here," Wikshen warned.

Chapter 53
A Mercyman Performs

Kalea's new elf-friend, Daghahen, stared forward with an air of naked uncertainty as they passed under the crevice lighting in the dark caverns. All ten of his long fingers dug into her arm. He'd told her the trolls *might* kill her, which meant he could be wrong. His expression did nothing for her confidence.

"Do you have a plan?" she whispered.

The thinness of his fingers and wrists suggested the rest of him might be nothing but a tall, crane-like figure under all those layers. His hair hung in thin locks, waving easily on the slight breeze of his movement, and the light revealed the edges of his bony, old face at every other turn. His eyes shifted to her often. Why did he care so much for her well-being? She decided not to analyze such good fortune too much yet.

He didn't answer her question, so she began a new one in her need to break the tension. So far, it seemed the trolls didn't mind them talking. "So…um, did you ever find your son?"

She waited. When he didn't answer, she reminded him, "Back when we first met, you said you were looking for your son and that he would die. Has he died?"

"Yes."

She waited for more, but he didn't offer anything else. His fingers dug harder, and she wiggled her arm for relief. "That really hurts."

He let her arm go. "Sorry," he said, and wiped a hand over his face. He had talked so much back in the goat pen, so why the silence now?

"There's a strange coincidence going on," she said with a smirk, intent on trying to make herself feel more relaxed. "I'm actually looking for Wikshen."

He missed a step and responded quickly this time. "Why?"

"I wish he could actually come here and get us."

"You don't look like a Wikshonite."

She considered her black dress, the one she got in Wikhaihli. "Really?"

"No." He let out a heavy breath through his nose and returned to staring forward. "Why did you think you'd find him down here?"

"I'm looking for a place called Ilbith."

He stopped walking, and she got a few paces ahead. "What's the matter?"

He took a few long steps to catch up, and then he grabbed her shoulder to stop her progression. The trolls ahead gained a considerable distance on them, and the ones who trudged behind drew closer. Daghahen opened his mouth and acted as if he'd speak. Instead, he looked her over with great scrutiny. The trolls approached behind them, too close, and he pulled her on by her hand, walking with purpose now instead of his earlier display of hesitation.

"What's the matter now?" she hissed.

"Just let me think!"

"What did I say?"

As usual, he didn't answer.

The cavern of their destination was the grandest yet, with a cascade of tiered stones carved into the center. Upon each tier sat various items of religious sentiment, things all too familiar to Kalea lately: aromatic incense, food, herbs, and other things the witches preached about Wikshen's fondness for.

"This must be the chapel," Daghahen offered as they drew near the grand sculpture of rock.

When the trolls stopped walking, they turned and roared long, slow sentences in their language to Daghahen. As he stared up at them, Kalea watched his face drain of color with every new second. The trolls went straight to tending the altar, moving things around and clearing off a tier. One emerged from the shadows with a large roll of leather to place before Daghahen. He stared down at the roll with a frown.

"What's going on?" Kalea demanded, and he only gave her a hollow glare. One of the smaller trolls grabbed the roll and snapped it open to reveal a set of massive rusty blades.

"They're convinced Wikshen will want to eat you," Daghahen said.

"BURRHHH-GHA-TA-RRRRRHAAA-MAST-ARRRREN-TAH-NOKH," one of the bigger, older-looking trolls said to Daghahen, and pointed to the hideous instruments.

The elf stared down at them with his arms hanging by his sides, reluctant to touch any of the tools. "They want me to do the butchering, because I'm smaller and can carve you into finer slices…" He met her eye contact. "For 'the Mastaren's delight,' of course."

Feeling numb once again, Kalea shook her head. "You won't do it, though, right?"

He blew a breath through his cheeks, and the trolls led his attention to a particular flat rock with matter-of-fact Trollish words. "They make the sacrifices here," he translated. "Usually goats and such, but they're happy today to offer him a…'graceful human.'"

"But you won't do it!" Kalea repeated. "You won't. Right?"

The trolls broke into another hum in prayer. Daghahen stormed toward her and grabbed her arm again. She shrieked and winced, but was too slow to dodge him.

"You're going to have to trust me," he told her as he roughly yanked her toward the sacrificial rock. She had nowhere to run. If she tried, one of the trolls would catch her, as they all stood in a circle around the two. "Stand here," he said, and then retrieved the roll of tools, dragging it across the smooth cave floor. Some of the blades were more like swords in size.

At this point, Kalea shivered, soaked in sweat and frozen to the bone. If the elf didn't plan to kill her, how in the world would he get her out of this?

He took a few long blades out of the kit and laid them on the ground to examine them. He stood up and flourished his arms to the trolls with another speech in their language. To Kalea's horror, they seemed to nod in approval. The ones who hummed escalated their tones to an uncomfortable level.

Daghahen stepped away from the tools and, from his pocket, dropped something that bounced once and settled on the floor. An acorn? Kalea squinted at it as he said a few more words to the trolls. He raised one arm and said something about Wikshen, raising a howl of excitement from the giants. During their distraction, he dropped another object: a handkerchief or something.

He rushed over to Kalea and pulled her close, holding the trolls' attention with his waving arm. Behind her, he dropped a smoking pipe from his pocket. She twisted around to puzzle over it, but he pulled her to stand somewhere else. He paced a few more steps away and dropped what looked like a melted-down candle stub. How well could the trolls see in the dark? Should they be suspicious of Daghahen's actions?

He raised his hands and spun on his heel, causing his tattered robes to wave gracefully. He bent down in the same motion to pick up one of the smaller blades. He turned to her, as if dancing with the rhythm of the trolls' song, and lunged toward her.

Kalea jumped and yelped, but he caught her. It passed through her mind that she should've darted away, but… He had been nice to her, so why would he murder her now? He'd recounted the story of when they met in the hospital and reassured her that he'd repay his mercy debt to her down here.

With his hand under her throat, he nudged her backward, toward the sacrificial rock. As she backed up, she searched his face for some hint of his intent and found it eerily unreadable. He wouldn't really do it, would he?

She mouthed his name under the great noise of the troll song. He didn't react, but nudged her all the way down to lie on the freezing stone. He brandished the knife in his other hand, crossed it over himself to his other shoulder, and then arched it high above his head in a circular motion.

Kalea's breathing flew out of control, sucking in short, quick pants as she lay flat on the stone under this stranger holding a knife. He placed it by her head, and she strained her neck to watch him walk away. He threw down another item—she couldn't tell what.

He suddenly erupted in savage laughter. "Hahahahhh!" The beastly sound mimicked the way one of those trolls would laugh, and he followed up with more of their speech. Every muscle in Kalea's body tensed up in her vulnerable recline. She peeked again to see him drop something else. What all did he have in his pockets? His wide, flowing robes hid a lot of things, she supposed.

He returned to where she lay and grasped her throat lightly. He pulled, prompting her to sit up. Everything he'd done since this ritual started, he performed with a dance-like show.

"Stand," he whispered, but she couldn't hear it over the noise; she could only read his lips. He picked up the knife and showed it to the trolls with his hand on her throat.

Kalea tried to swallow, but found her pipes unresponsive in her fear.

He slid his hand around the back of her neck under her hair, and leaned in close. "Hold on."

She couldn't fathom what he meant, and didn't have time to ask or ponder it. He dropped the knife, reached into his pocket again, and threw down something that shattered against the rock floor. He locked his arm firmly around her waist and sprinted forward. Kalea found herself hanging off him. She gripped his robes to keep from falling.

"Jump!"

She wouldn't call it a jump, but she lifted her feet off the ground as he leaped forward, carrying her weight. When they came down, they traveled farther than expected. Kalea's ears clogged. A wave of cold water, or something similar, grazed over her.

Down.

They fell.

Farther.

Kalea's faint acquaintanceship with this person didn't matter—she clung to him with her every limb, screaming, both their hair and clothing waving wildly.

Their fall slowed to a stop in midair. They changed directions and fell the opposite way. Physics no longer made sense.

"Oof!"

She collided with him as they met a sudden stop from a shorter distance than anticipated. They lay on the ground. When Kalea opened her eyes, a bright light bombarded them. A cool breeze laced with the scent of the mountain smoke wafted around them.

"We're outside!" She rolled off of him and swayed on her hands and knees for a moment, head spinning. "How did we get out here?"

The elf climbed to his feet faster and easier than she could. He knelt beside her, took her by the shoulders, and said, "Tell me what you know about Wikshen and Ilbith!"

Kalea blinked at him for a few seconds. She preferred to let her dizziness pass first, rather than rush to spill her personal business. Only out of sheer nerves had she spilled some of her secrets to this stranger down in the caves.

"First, you have to tell me what's going on. How did we get here? Where are we? And where are the trolls?"

The elf's face shifted from tense back to blank. He dropped his hands from her shoulders, rose, and paced around to pick up tarnished coins from the ground Kalea hadn't noticed before. "The trolls can't hurt you now. They're a good distance across the mountain, and we're in broad daylight. If they're stupid enough to chase us out here, they'll petrify themselves to the core.

"I cast a minor portal. Takes a lot of casting to make everyday items into portal pillars. That's energy I can't get back, so because of you, I just used up the spell which was supposed to get me back out here from my actual destination." He returned to face her once he'd collected them all.

Kalea squinted. "Portal pillars," she repeated. "Like the golden rods the sorcerers use?"

He narrowed his brow at her. "You really gotta tell me what you're up to, miss. Why are you lookin' for Ilbith?"

"I'm going there to rescue some people. Do you know the way?"

"All too well."

Kalea's hands tensed. "Then you must take me!"

He crossed his arms and scrunched his nose. "I can't take you until my question gets an answer."

Kalea made a fast decision that getting to Dorhen trumped all other concerns regarding sharing her story with a stranger. "The sorcerers took Wikshen to Ilbith," she relinquished. "I saw it happen; they carried him through a pair of those golden 'portal pillars.'"

He shook his head and stood up.

"Do you not believe me? We have to go and free him! He needs help! He needs *me*. It's hard to explain, but…he's not really Wikshen. He's actually a very sweet elf named Dorhen."

When Daghahen turned back around, his eyes were reddened. He huffed, and his show of emotion made Kalea step backward.

"What's wrong?"

He shook his head and said through gritted teeth, "Doesn't matter, as long as he's killed the kingsorcerer."

She spread her hands. "As far as I know, the kingsorcerer is alive."

Daghahen dropped to his knees and grasped his own hair, releasing a far-echoing yell. At a loss, Kalea stood back, blinking at his antic.

When the cold mountain breeze carried the last echo of his anguish away, a different voice answered back, "Hellooooooooh!"

Kalea ran to check over the edge of a rock, where a grander view of the scenery spread out. Three figures stood on another landing below. She shouted, "Bowaen! Gaije! Del!"

They waved and responded. Kalea flew back and shook Daghahen. "My friends are down there! You've brought me right to them. Come! You must show us the way to Ilbith!"

Daghahen collected himself from the ground. "That's it, then," he mumbled. "That's why I had to use up my escape portal. Because nothing is random."

Letting those cryptic words stand, he led Kalea along a narrow, winding ledge around big rocks and through shallow tunnels until they merged paths with her friends, whom she excitedly embraced and told her story to, using flashy, descriptive words, possibly with some slight exaggeration. She gave all the credit to Daghahen, and once she let on that he knew the way to Ilbith, Gaije and the others refused to let him out of the errand of guiding their way.

The strange old elf knew the mountains better than she could've guessed. The deeper into the region they ventured, descending into caves as dark as the one the trolls inhabited, the more nervous she became about how they'd find their way out again.

"You won't abandon us, will you?" she asked him when they stopped to rest and eat rare edible mushrooms they foraged from among the armies of poisonous ones in shady corners.

He said over his crossed arms, "If I wanted to abandon you, I would've done it a long time ago—easily." He met her gaze on the tail end of his statement, an empty stare. Since their conversation on the high mountain perch, he'd developed a certain look in his eye about her, one she couldn't place. Bowaen appeared to study him in scrutiny of that stare.

Kalea would've asked after Daghahen's thoughts, but couldn't find a good way to go about it, and he'd refused to answer any questions about why he was going to Ilbith anyway. In all, Daghahen had said little after joining her companions, and he retained his somber mood after hearing about the kingsorcerer.

"How much farther, Daghahen?" she peeped in the silence as they delved deeper into the mountains, under veils of colored light reflected by underground ponds.

"One moment," he said as if he needed to think. More than once, he'd answered in that way without relinquishing any actual explanations.

He chose a path darker than any they'd ventured down yet. Around the bend, an illuminated chamber dazzled her eyes. Daghahen moseyed to the back wall, where some strange breed of lichen caused the soft green glow. He took a glass vial from his pocket and perused the little glowing buds, picking the brighter ones off to bottle up. With several pieces of plant taking up half the space in the bottle, he filled the rest of it with water from his flask. He replaced its cork and held the makeshift lantern up by its little strand of twine. The water magnified the floating buds' light in the little bottle.

"There," he said. "That's how we see the way to Ilbith. As long as they don't touch any sunlight, these little pretties can last for days after being plucked." With the wondrous new light source in its little glass vessel dangling off his wrist, he led them back to the main path.

Eerily, the trolls weren't far off. If the original group of them weren't storming through the tunnels in search of their escaped sacrifice, it might be a different clan in some nearby cavern, humming and making more smoke to pollute the air. Daghahen suggested it was the latter.

"Why do you think they call it the Black Mountains?" he countered when the subject of the smoke came up. They walked a long, wide trail around a circular underground lake through the chill it added to the air. "The trolls are up to all manner of activity down here. They cook. They cast spells…"

"Spells?" Kalea said.

The old elf nodded under his hood, which hid his eyes. Only his big, crooked nose stuck out from it between his long locks of wispy, blond hair. "They're intelligent," he said. "Frighteningly so, complete with a language and a religion, lore, recipes… They've passed all their knowledge down to the young ones for eons."

"Their religion is Wikshonism?" Kalea said.

"A version of it, yes. They were the originals. After Wikshens of the past made all those dreadwitches"—Kalea caught Daghahen shudder during his pause—"they and other witches shaped the version of the religion which plagues the Darklands today."

Bowaen, Gaije, and Del kept mostly silent as they trekked through the darker caves, ever wary about hidden trolls. Kalea considered her run-in with them a blessing now that the adventure was far behind her. If she hadn't fallen into that horrifying situation, she never would've met Daghahen. They would have been lost in the mountains for some indefinite amount of time.

Kalea shrugged. "I much prefer the Wikshonites to those sorcerers any day."

"So do I," Daghahen said with a sigh, "although this is only the beginning. The Wikshonites have been a horrible lot in the past. Wikshen…is someone we shouldn't tangle with."

Kalea kept her mouth shut; nonetheless, she felt Daghahen's eyes on her.

He hummed beside her and missed a step. "Look at this," he said. "I know this arch." He referred to a formation in the walls and ceiling that looked amazingly like a cathedral archway.

"Oh, my," Kalea said. "How could it look like that—like it was done on purpose?"

"'Cause it *was* done on purpose," he said. The whole group took a moment to gawk at their surroundings. Indirect light illuminated the amazing shapes the cave took on in this section. "It looked much better two thousand years ago, I presume."

"What is it?" Bowaen asked.

"It's the entrance…"

They all waited. The question poised on Kalea's tongue until she could take the suspense no longer. "We're…close to Ilbith?"

"We're there, my dear." He put his arm around her shoulders and pointed forward, into the far side of the cavern. "The remnants of the old city are one hundred times bigger than the sorcerers' tower itself. Welcome to Ilbith."

Chapter 54
Salty Kiss

Y ou're allowing me out again?" Orinleah asked Lamrhath, taking a cautious step to the door he held open for her.

Holding his hand out, he replied, "Maybe once we're married, you'll go out more often to stroll in the gardens with me."

"Where are we going?"

He squinted at her. "What's the matter?"

She blinked her eyes and averted them, and he found her bashful display shockingly comely and arousing. "Nothing," she said.

He stepped forward with his hand still offered. "Trust me, you'll like this surprise. Come." When she finally gave him her dainty hand, he snapped at his attending servant, who handed him her cloak. Lamrhath put it around her shoulders himself and raised the hood over her head. "Can't have anyone out there seeing too much of you."

He took her on a hasty trip through the halls to a wing where she'd never been before. Her eyes bugged as she took in the new environment. Sorcerers strolled about this area through a mess of crossing, looping corridors. Many little rooms behind closed doors cluttered the wing, where the sorcerers spent their daily hours copying spells and experimenting with herbs and salts. He led her to a central door in the main hub, among a number of openings branching in all directions. Beside this door sat a guard on a chair. Lamrhath nodded to him, and the man jumped to unlock the door for them.

Before going in, Lamrhath said to Orinleah, "I must warn you, it's hot up there." He untied the cord under her chin to release her cloak, which he handed to the guard. He took a deep breath. He didn't know what else he could tell her before showing her what he kept in there. "Um…" he began, searching for his words. "This may be a shock. There's not much I can explain about it."

By the look on her face, he could tell he wasn't helping her comfort level. He opened the door to reveal a staircase leading up. Every step glowed under the bright light from above, a great contrast to the dark atmosphere in which they stood. The heat became immediately apparent. He ascended first, retaining her hand behind his back. Her wary closeness to him delivered a sense of pleasure: that she'd cling to *him* for security.

He guided her slowly. Would she love him after this? He didn't want to consider whether she'd hate him. What would he have to do to redeem himself if she did? What sort of comfort could he give her when she found out…?

He ascended to the landing at the top and stepped aside so she could see.

Orinleah's hands shot to her mouth. Among all the many candles and sunbeams shooting through the room, intensified by the glass lenses, Dorhen—her son—sat at the center of the room. Tied down. They'd covered his face with a cloth, thinking the sight of his miserable, unconscious expression would only upset her.

She stepped forward again and again. Did she know?

She ran the rest of the way to him and let out a sob.

Lamrhath quickened his step to keep up. "Do you know who this is?"

She put both of her shaking hands on Dorhen's limp one, which was draped off the end of the chair arm. She wept on his hand, laying her cheek upon it. Lamrhath's mouth dropped open. How could she recognize him?

Orinleah reached up and pulled the cloth off Dorhen's face. "Ohhh!" She howled it amid her torrent of noises and tears, an ill sound, as if she'd vomit. Void of consciousness, his eyelids hung halfway open and his eyes had rolled up in their sockets. She practically climbed on his lap to reach his head and tenderly stroked his hair away from his face to kiss his temple. Long strings of sorrowful Norrian words streamed from her mouth, of which Lamrhath recognized only a few.

"He was made into a being called Wikshen," Lamrhath told her when her wailing calmed a bit. She used the sleeve of her fine gown to dab the sweat off Dorhen's face.

Orinleah half-turned to hear his explanation, but kept her attention on her son.

"We have to keep him restrained up here because he's dangerous. We must find a way to cure his plight." He lied, of course. No cure for Wikshen's condition existed. The sorcerers actually planned to use Wikshen for whatever profitable whim they could think of.

Orinleah turned her head and nodded. "H-how did this happen?" she asked through her weeping.

He wished he could tell her the truth of how Daghahen had done this horrible thing to their son, but Lamrhath already had her believing Daghahen was dead, so he lied again. "By no one's fault but his own. The boy was wandering in the wilderness. He stumbled through the tangled forest called Hathrohskog and fell victim to the pixie who haunted it.

Luckily, my men had entered the forest around the same time." He resisted asking her how in Kullixaxuss she recognized him as Dorhen.

She fell into a rhythm of stroking his blue hair. Lamrhath paced, unsure how much time was appropriate for this situation. Now that she'd seen him, he'd probably have to bring her up here every day to keep her happy. They'd certainly make sure to sedate Dorhen for it, either by using light or potions or magic.

When Orinleah began to sing her Norrian lullaby, Lamrhath decided to end the reunion. He took her hand and Orinleah stopped her song to shoot a look at him, with a subtle cue of offense, maybe a warning.

"We do the best we can to keep him comfortable and the pixie restrained," he explained. "Let's go back now."

Orinleah bit her lip, shot a glance back at Dorhen, and then regarded Lamrhath. She reached up and took Lamrhath's face to pull him into a bow and kiss his lips. The salty flavor of Dorhen's sweat transferred from her lips to Lamrhath's tongue, and he didn't even mind in his elation about her awarded affection.

"Lambelhen," she whispered his true name against his mouth, "it's time."

Chapter 55
Cold Shiver

Tirnah and Anonhet stood in Lehomis's silent room embracing each other in their initial shock. "This doesn't make sense," Tirnah whined. "He can't be dead—he's immortal!"

"What will we do?" Anonhet asked one beat before letting out a sob over Tirnah's shoulder.

She forgot all about her soggy slipper, soaked in the noxious liquid Lehomis had drunk. "We must employ a house guardian. Or one of us will have to get married."

A gasp made the two jump—a sound from Lehomis!

"He's not dead!" Tirnah hissed.

Lehomis groaned as if waking up from the deepest sleep of his life. Tirnah tugged Anonhet's sleeve, and the two of them shot out of the room and closed the door as quietly as possible.

Tirnah leaned against the door, blinking. "What in the Bright One's radiant eye…?" She turned to regard Anonhet and held her stare in demand of an answer.

Anonhet shook visibly. "I don't know, I really don't!"

"You've never seen him sleep like that?"

The younger *faerhain* shook her head rapidly.

Tirnah took her sleeve again and pulled her down the hall. "Let's hope he doesn't realize we were in there. Don't speak of this."

"I wouldn't dream of it," Anonhet said. "I told you he didn't like people in his room." Her face muscles contorted, mouth rounding. "We didn't lock it again—he'll know indeed what we've done!"

Tirnah clicked her tongue and pulled her onward. "Maybe he owes *us* an explanation and not the other way 'round."

"I prefer that we not speak of it."

"Fine," Tirnah agreed. "We must've misunderstood the situation. Still, I can't deny how quickly he fell into such a deep…death-like sleep." Tirnah shuddered. The image of her poor Trisdahen lying dead on their marriage bed hung fresh in her memory. Lehomis hadn't looked too different in there.

The two *faerhain* split off to their rooms and went to bed. In her shock, Tirnah skipped a few steps of her nighttime routine, like washing her face and laying out tomorrow's *hanbohik*. She lay wide awake in bed, shaken. Even if she wanted to confront Lehomis about his odd behavior and the puddle of sour drink on his floor, she wouldn't know how to approach it.

So, when Tirnah woke up the next morning, she considered it a new day, dismissing the past. Lehomis trudged into the tea room where they sometimes broke their fasts, looking no better than last night. His hair dragged on the floor, covering half his face like a thick onyx curtain.

Tirnah clamped her lips shut. A "good morning" never got past them—her voice refused to sound. She'd gotten through the process of fixing his bowl of oats and berries while ignoring the notion that maybe he hadn't survived the night. A seed of doubt had lingered for his life, but here he stood, upright on his own feet. She decided never to bring it up. Writing it off as her imagination running wild in her current state was the only thing she could do to carry on.

Lehomis dropped into his seat at the little round table across from Tirnah. He opened his mouth to bid her good morning, but acted too late. She sprang up and scurried out of the room. He groaned and cupped his face. In the long break from it, he'd forgotten how much of a headache that nasty drink, Root McCrow, gave him. He let Tirnah go with a plan to exchange his pleasantries with her later.

"G'mornin', lass," he said to her when he finally emerged into the outside world, ready to face another day of being the elder of a failing clan. Another day devoid of practice in the yard with Gaije, or the delight of Mhina's little face at lunchtime when he would surprise her with a sugary treat.

Tirnah glanced at Lehomis and hastily turned her back, balancing a laundry basket on her hip. "Good morning, Grandfather!" Her cheerful tone sounded off somehow. Forced. "I'm off to the river. See you later."

Lehomis blinked in her dust as she ran down the path like an adolescent *farhah*. How urgent could that laundry be? She'd been acting strange ever since he returned from his trip, and the reason was anyone's guess. Anonhet, too, kept her exchanges of words brief any time they passed.

At one point, in the foyer of the house, he caught her arm. "Did something happen to Tirnah while I was gone?"

Anonhet's eyes spaced like a deer's. "She's fine, Grandfather."

Lehomis narrowed his gaze, searching her for any indication of withheld information. Elves were forbidden by law to lie, but they certainly got away with holding information back. The Desteer excelled at it. "I'm going to the Desteer hall for the mid-month conference. Should I ask them about Tirnah while I'm there?"

Anonhet's empty stare proved unceasing. "No, Grandfather. Tirnah will carry on with strength and grace in this time of mourning."

Lehomis sniffed and let her arm go. "You probably would've fit in well with the Desteer, lass."

Anonhet half-turned away to grab the broom from the corner by the door. She kept her gaze averted suspiciously. "But I can't stand the Desteer, Grandfather."

"Who can?" He turned on his heel and strode out the door, destined for their very hall.

"I hear you went to the human lands," Alhannah said smoothly as she sat in her prominent place in the Desteer hall with all of her sisters in balanced numbers on either side of her. They sat in the same formation that geese flew, with her at their head. There sat Kennaha at the end, freshly arrived from her "duty in a neighboring clan." Lehomis tried very hard not to linger his eyes on her.

"Had to," he said, crossing his arms in his seat before them, one against fifteen. "After all we've been through, we're low on grains, horses, females, and even *saehgahn*."

"Have you been getting into trouble there, Lehomis Lockheirhen?" Her eyes narrowed at him and a sleazy smirk stretched her lips.

He gave her his own dark scowl over crossed arms, back straight in his proper sitting position. "Is this the mid-month conference or my trial? Now listen to me: things don't feel right around here anymore, and I no longer feel it's because of the raid and loss of two children. There's something else in the air. Care to fill me in on whatever information you're garnering?"

"Garnering from what, Elder?"

"The clan. The country. The outside world!"

"Keep your volume in check, Elder."

"Stop treating me like a *saeghar*!" He pointed at the lot of them. "You bunch are the ones trespassing into all the *faerhain*'s minds, telling them what to do, making them cut their hair short, and going as far as driving wedges between married couples. Why don't you talk to me so I can help the clan too?"

Alhannah and the other maidens sat motionless on their floor cushions, staring at him. Their ghostly, white faces glowed in the soft lighting.

"I'm the elder," he reminded with a growl. "I'm supposed to be the clan's leader, and no one tells me anything anymore!" At their continued silence, Lehomis relaxed his spine. "You all are supposed to have psychic abilities. Haven't any of you received a signal from my granddaughter yet? Or Bairhen? He has parents here withering away in grief at his loss. Bright One willing, the two children are together wherever they are. Can't you help to ease their parents' pain? Or have you been pressuring Tirnah and Bairhen's poor mother to cut their hair instead?"

Of course, the Desteer couldn't produce a response. For an instant, a dark thought sped across Lehomis's mind: why did the clan need a Desteer cult at all? From what he could tell, they only made things worse with their secrets and their pressure and their punishments.

Alhannah finally reacted with a breath released carefully through her lips. Would she finally relinquish an answer, or give him another matronly pat on his head and a speech about how he shouldn't concern himself with their more important business? Lehomis didn't hold his breath.

"Elder," she said, "I'm going to tell you a secret." In the next beat, her sisters turned their heads to her with a slight widening of their painted eyelids. Now he did slow his breathing to a stop in anticipation. "For a long while now, I have been in direct contact with the Bright One."

The other maidens gasped and bowed their heads to the floor, some of them huffing and puffing, others whimpering in the onset of hysterical awe. Alhannah kept calm.

Lehomis's head went numb. He stuttered. "You—you've been… talking…to…?"

"Yes," Alhannah confirmed with a deep bow of her head. "He appears to me in great displays of fire on certain nights and in different places in the forest. He is a magnificent…" Alhannah gasped, unable to carry on her description. "I'm unworthy to utter how wonderful, how warm…"

She bit her lip. Shaking all over, she took a moment to bow down low like the others, her black hair pooling on the floor around her. She cupped her face and murmured prayers to which Lehomis couldn't catch all the words.

"However," she said breathily as she rose again, "He has not told me of Mhina or Bairhen. What He has done is told me how the clan females must conduct themselves. He requests their hair, long strands of it. He tells me it pleases Him to be gifted with such an intimate and cherished object; and the more hair we gift Him, the happier He feels."

So why have you not cut your own hair? Lehomis held his tongue as the question ran circles in his mind. None of the Desteer maidens wore their hair short yet.

Alhannah waved at the maiden beside her, who rose smoothly and glided out of the room to return with a large bag made of red velvet, which she handed to Alhannah.

"The Bright One gave me this in return." She stood up and held the bag out to Lehomis. "Thank you for selflessly selling your treasures in the human lands to help us, but take this now. It will be more than enough to get us through the winter."

Lehomis strode over to take the bag. Its weight sank his arm, causing him to add muscle to his effort. He peeked inside to find many large silver coins. "Silver?" Although an impressive amount of wealth, the fact that it was silver didn't feel right.

"Of course, silver," Alhannah said. "What's the matter, Elder?"

Lehomis shrugged, staring into the bag. "I thought the Bright One had golden eyes and a sun-like shine."

Alhannah smiled and her eyes rolled up into her eyelids. "Oh, He does. He's an elf just like us, but so much more as well."

"Well, silver's not as good as gold. It shines, but soon it turns black. It's more moon-like than sun-like."

Alhannah's expression of ecstasy dropped to a frown. "Do you spurn the Bright One's gift?"

Lehomis stepped back and put his hands up. "No—it's just that…"

She stormed toward him, and he retreated farther. "Do you blaspheme against Him?" She pointed both hands at his head, as if to perform *milhanrajea* for his mental evaluation.

He dodged her clawing hands. "No, you don't understand…!"

"Come here, Lehomis Lockheirhen."

He could not let her perform the spell on him. He'd managed to not get evaluated for so long, and in that time, he'd collected so many secrets. Tilninhet, Togha—his latest son—his recent purchase of alcohol. *Karra kar shirinhen!* He'd been a naughty lad lately.

A cold sweat across his skin formed in a blink. Though he did back away slowly, he couldn't run because it would make him seem even guiltier. "I got a lot of work to do today, *Ameiha*." He hadn't addressed her by the formal Desteer title in ages. He bent over properly for a bow. "Thank you for this money for the clan. I will use it well."

She pursued him, hands reaching. "Hold still, Elder, this will only take a second." Behind her, her sisters crowded in but kept back a few respectful paces, Kennaha included.

Lehomis clenched his eyes shut and tried to employ the mind-clearing discipline *saehgahn* secretly shared to block most of *milhanrajea*'s reach, but he hadn't practiced it in ages.

Kennaha glided forward to stand beside Lehomis and Alhannah. Her gaze met Lehomis's in a tense split-second. He had promised to keep her dangerous secret, and she knew it.

"What do you want, Kennaha?" Alhannah asked, keeping her piercing eyes on Lehomis.

Kennaha smiled at both of them. "There's no need for this negative energy, sister." Her statement made Alhannah pause and Lehomis raise an eyebrow. "You haven't known the elder as long as I have," she continued before slapping her hands along his face, quick as a snake. "One must know how to handle him."

He couldn't pull away fast enough before a great hot light engulfed his vision with a cold chill that ran over his scalp from Kennaha's fingers to the back of his neck. The sensation left him with his vision darkened for a few seconds after, accompanied by the ill dread of what it meant. She'd done it. She'd seen inside his mind. For the first time in generations, Lehomis had undergone *milhanrajea*. Their eyes met again for a panicked instant—his panic—because she knew it all now. All of his dirty secrets. But he also had hers.

Kennaha smiled at Alhannah. "He's absolutely clean, my sisters."

Lehomis gawked, stunned at every unfolding second. She *lied!* She lied to all the Desteer!

"Honestly, I don't know why you would doubt our noble elder." Before taking her hands off his head, she patted him on the cheek.

Alhannah stuttered before coming out with, "That doesn't make sense! He all but convicted himself!"

Kennaha reclaimed her place on the floor. "Lehomis is often not really as smooth as his legends tend to claim. Rest assured, I found no unclean thoughts inside him."

Alhannah blinked. "Well, Elder." Alhannah motioned to the bag of silver in his hand. "Please spend that wisely. Our clan depends on you. You are dismissed."

Chapter 56
Red Ox

Lamrhath couldn't keep his hand from shaking when he put the golden key into the slot in the door. Orinleah's door. The moment finally approached.

He'd spent the entire day preparing himself for this moment. A grooming ritual had preceded this evening after a long afternoon of sweaty romps with Silva and his hardiest concubine to get him up to the normal level of comfort where he needed to be for his ritual with Orinleah. After tonight, he might have to dismiss all his concubines because he'd no longer need them.

Absolute elation accompanied him into the foyer, where he stood alone in the dark space for one more moment before his life changed forever. He blew a breath out and proceeded with the second locked door. His heart pounded as if this would be their first engagement in the coming activity. Nothing would be the same after tonight.

He swung the door open to a scene prepared for his visit. All of her candles flickered with life, red roses from the balcony garden hung all about, and the white ox pelt—the symbol of Norrian marriage—covered her bed, so large it draped down the sides.

Something else new had been added too: she'd drawn on the walls with the chalk he gave her. They were excellent sketches of a young elf boy, most likely Dorhen at the age he was when he disappeared into the wilderness, to the life of running wild and scavenging for food. In these drawings, he looked happy, well-mannered, and groomed. He held a frog in one scene, and in another, he was laughing with his arms raised high, running or skipping as any child would.

Lamrhath decided to ignore the drawings and focus on his miraculous evening. Why would Orinleah not draw her son, whom she missed, especially since reuniting with him after sixteen years?

Lamrhath forgot all of his thoughts when *she* stepped out from the corner shadow beside her large wardrobe.

"Orinleah," he breathed.

She wore the robe she'd requested as one of her marriage gifts, as well as the beautiful ruby necklace he always loved to see around her graceful neck. He had ordered the robe made special because she wanted a particular kind with twelve ties for some reason. It clung neatly to her upper body and flowed around her legs, a midnight-blue color as per her request.

She approached him slowly. He wasn't entirely sure how she wanted this night to play out, so he waited, eager to do it properly. He needed every bit of her approval he could get. It would cure his ailment.

"Welcome," she said softly.

That word. It was exactly what he wanted to hear. The most soothing word in the world! He shook all over and fought to swallow through his dry throat. The beginnings of arousal stirred in his loins.

"Thank you," he whispered despite some difficulty with his pipes.

She knelt before him and took his hand. She slowly pressed her lips to the back of it, where they stuck in the slight bit of moisture from her mouth. His cock stood for that slight sensation. Excitement washed over him a little too quickly, but he fought it. He needed to do this her way, for himself as much for her. Otherwise, he would've thrown her on the bed and forced his way in—as *Lamrhath* would've done.

"Lambelhen," she whispered after disconnecting her lips from his skin. His old name helped to remind him not to act on Lamrhath's desire. He should be *Lambelhen* for now, and give in to Orinleah's seduction as it unfolded at the delightfully tantalizing pace she bid.

She looked up at him from under her brow, head level with his erection. She asked, "Are you ready? To enter into a sacred union ordained by the Bright One?"

"Yes." The dryness in his throat had increased since he last tried to speak.

She drew back to her feet to face him squarely, tall for a *faerhain*. She leaned in close and took his head in her two soft hands. She teased her lips along his. He wanted to take over from there and shove his tongue into her mouth to get this ceremony started, but he abstained. Could this be a test? She didn't kiss his mouth, but guided his head down to press her lips to his forehead, a kiss to seal their arrangement. Tingles ran from his head to the rest of his body, and especially down to his penis, which stood engorged. It must be purple at this point. He went lightheaded, trembling all over.

"Will you be my *daghen-saehgahn*?"

"Yes."

"Will you protect and love me?"

"Yes." Sweat beaded at his sides.

She continued her teasing with her mouth close to his, and grinned. Her white teeth glistened in the candlelight. "Then an arrangement is in order." She led him to the bed and motioned for him to stand at its foot. She lay down before him. "The ritual proceeds with you untying each of these knots."

Lamrhath wasted no thought before tearing open the first one, located over her knee.

"Try to stay calm," she said. "Don't be rough with me."

Now he knew the reason why she wanted the robe. Untying the knots before having sex must be part of the ritual. To him, it felt more like opening the greatest birthday present in the world. Thank Naerezek she hadn't tied them firmly. Each satin cord knot parted with ease. Going about it slowly drew out this wonderful moment, despite the strain it put on his patience. Each knot that slid apart revealed a little bit more of her flesh and added a new throb to his cock. It grew so hard and close to climax that he paused the ritual.

"Forgive me," he rasped, and undid his codpiece to let it out. He could easily get it into her from the halfway point in the knots, which exposed her up to her bellybutton, but he'd rather die than ruin this ceremony.

With his salivating member in hand, one little pinch of his fingers around its head was all it took to release a thick load of ejaculate to shoot out and slap against the floor. He panted rapidly throughout the shock of orgasm for the next few seconds. Orinleah raised her head to puzzle over his deed, losing half of her seductive countenance.

"Lie down," he told her, and she obeyed. Now he could continue his work, and maybe he'd gained a few more minutes of lovemaking with her before the next discharge.

Without bothering to put his everlasting erection back into his pants, he untied the next knot, and then the next. After finishing the topmost knot waiting against her throat, he slowly peeled the sides of her robe open, revealing her pale, supple body underneath, ripe and waiting for him. He took the next second to marvel at it. His eyes watered, and he wasn't sure why. A tornado of emotions surged through him.

"Lambelhen," she whispered.

He barely heard her over his pounding heart. One of his eyes spilled a tear down his cheek.

"You may begin."

Panting and groaning as if they were already in the throes of passion, he fell on her breast and took the whole thing into his mouth, tasting it and telling himself it was the first time. He believed it. All of this was a first as far as he was concerned. He sucked it hard, drawing the nipple to the back of his throat.

He trailed his other hand below her navel, where she spread her legs.

He found moisture, actual female moisture—for him. Definitely a first in their relationship. Releasing her breast, he leaned down to that part of her, and she stopped him with a hand on his shoulder.

"Wait."

He waited with his mouth agape, excess saliva trailing out of the corner of his mouth. He burned to know what her moisture tasted like.

She gave him a smile. "I think you forgot to undress."

She opened his shirt, and he let her; every little thing she did this evening drove him to madness. His cock stood ready to burst again. It did when she moved her hand down to unlace his leggings so he could remove them. The white glob shot out and splatted her knee this time. Ever smiling, she traced her fingers through the mess and drew a line with it up her thigh and into her feminine crevice as if to add more moisture to herself, an act which, in itself, brought him back to readiness.

Barely able to stand it anymore, he moved in to pin her down, and she put up her hands to stop him. Desire turned to frustration and frustration skirted around anger in her teasing slowness to let him have his moment with her.

"I believe you made a special request when we agreed to this."

Lamrhath tried to remember what he'd asked for, but thinking proved difficult right now.

"Lie down, my love."

He gasped. That's right, he'd asked her to be on top. Now that they were both completely naked, he moved up the bed and laid his head on her pillow, under the wooly white pelt so important to this ritual. It was softer than anything he'd ever tried. He tended to decorate his bed with enormous wolf pelts, but they couldn't hold a candle to this.

Lying flat, he let his penis stand straight up for her to do with as she pleased, and hopefully soon because his testicles ached at this point. Ejaculating by mere touch with his hand never soothed his pain or even settled the erection down.

Orinleah bowed over his head and kissed him on the mouth. He slipped his tongue in and licked against hers. All of this play brought his penis to a painful bulge that leaked precum down the shaft. She wrapped her hand around it, and it shot off again. He didn't see where it landed. Rather than relief, he received a new level of dread.

"Orinleah," he whined. "You have to..." He groaned as another orgasm spasmed up his cock and released yet another glob into the air. She slicked her hand up and down it, masturbating him and watching as the orgasms continued with interest. It only increased the pain.

He grabbed her hair. "Do you see?" he said, fighting the urge to throw himself on top of her and be done with this agony. "This is my curse. You must heal me!"

"Ahh!" she shrieked when he gave her hair a firm tug. "Please don't be rough, I said."

Releasing her hair, he let a sob out and lay flat on her bed in a mindset caught between pleasure, delirium, sadness, and suffering. His penis stood tall through it all, needing a certain kind of attention.

"Don't be in distress, my lord." She caressed her hands down his chest. "I will heal you now."

She put her naked leg over to his other side and had to raise up high to mount the tip of his throbbing cock, and then she slid down upon it, swallowing it into herself. Her inner body formed a tight, fleshy sheath around it. Comforting.

Lamrhath's tears stopped. He breathed through his mouth, staring up at the ceiling, feverishly waiting. She settled all the way down to his pelvis, and then they were one. He opened his eyes and found her smiling down at him, raising slowly up and down again, delivering tender care to his most hurt body part. It needed her care.

He breathed with her slow rhythm, and it helped to ease his pain back to pleasure. He could look at her beautiful body as she danced on top of him, curving her spine, breasts toward his face, and pulling back, waving gracefully and limberly like a snake. Even his most talented concubine couldn't dance like this. He reached with both arms and let his fingers graze along her movement. Sometimes she arched back so far, he could watch her pelvis lift off of his and catch a peek at his joyful member in its true home.

Her breathing picked up and her speed increased. The dance carried him beyond his body to a splendorous spirituality of euphoric elation. She swayed and bucked and began to race, pushing down on his cock and pulling back on it with a tight suck again and again. The caress numbed in this rapid movement, and all his lower sensory feelings became one glorious, pulsing sensation.

He put his hands on her hips and pushed to help her. At one point, they collided with a hard force against each other, up to the moment when her secret muscles tightened and spasmed in orgasm. She bit her lip but made no sound to cheer what he'd helped her accomplish.

"Why are you so quiet?" he asked through his own steadfast effort to find his sacred moment. She'd never made a sound in the past before her willingness to do this, so he'd assumed tonight would be different.

"Don't you know?" she countered, as soon as she could find her voice again. "*Faerhain* can't make sounds during this process. Never."

"Why? The sounds a woman makes are nice."

She shook her head. Her body glistened beautifully in her own sweat. "My mother told me so. Her mother told her, and so on. It's tradition." Throughout her speech, she kept up her snake-like dance, stroking his cock inside of her.

As much as Lamrhath didn't prefer that tradition, he couldn't be too disappointed. It meant she hadn't kept quiet out of hatred for him—just tradition. He motioned to sit up and turn her over. Women were usually too relaxed to remain in control after their orgasms.

"No," she said, and planted her hands on his chest to hold him down beneath her. "Let me heal you."

It was all Lamrhath needed to hear. He let himself relax and concentrate on his most important moment ever: the moment his ailment would vanish with the help of Orinleah's love and care. He closed his eyes, took hold of her hips again, and found his rhythm. He thrust from his horizontal position to complement Orinleah's goddess-like dance. After she healed him tonight, he'd make her into one. He'd commission statues and paintings of her in this motion, and proclaim it their new religion. The woman with the power to heal with her body.

His breathing steadied, and he drew near his coveted moment. This time, his semen wouldn't fly off and land somewhere random; it would go where it belonged. He lost himself in the frenzy until she leaned over him to dangle her sacred breasts. He licked them. He sucked them. He wrapped his arms around her and held her down, pushing his cock into her as deeply as he could, and rubbed his large hands down her small, sweaty back.

The big moment approached. He put his hands back up behind her shoulders and worked her body against his, thrusting again and again. His special little spasm hung on the edge.

Orinleah lifted up, and his slippery hands lost her. She raised her arm and forced it down.

Something had gone very wrong.

A punch to his throat delayed his orgasm. He yelped and lurched, putting his hand to his neck, and she hit him with her fist again. His hand came away red. He was bleeding! She'd stabbed him! If she wasn't arching back for another strike, he'd stare and puzzle about it. He caught her wrist and found she'd somehow obtained a knife—a strange one— black and hooked, sparkling with little green and purple specks.

He wrestled her, and in the slippery confusion, she got the blade into him again. "Haaaaaarh!" he roared in her face, and used every bit of his strength and precision to flip her over and mount her.

He slipped his penis into her again and maintained control of her wrist. His other hand pinned down her throat. He thrust at the same time as attempting to survey the damage she'd made. Already, he could see the bright, pink glow of Naerezek's protection power, keeping most of his blood in—keeping him from dying as the deity had promised him long ago. It wasn't easy to assassinate Kingsorcerer Lamrhath, and Orinleah had now found that out. Her eyes bugged as she watched the glow of Naerezek's power ignite.

Lamrhath went back to his concentration. His misery would persist if he didn't complete the session. The blade in Orinleah's hand dissipated into a featherlight black dust. Her eyelids drooped as he held her throat tightly. Grasping an old rag used as a handle for the strange knife, she didn't realize the blade was no longer there.

He pushed into her, hard, giving his cock the massage it needed. With this turn of events, he wouldn't be cured now. He slapped her face. "Stay awake!" he ordered. "I want you to see what you've done!" His orders turning to moans, he pushed and pushed until it finally happened.

Orinleah passed out on the ox pelt in naked shame. Lamrhath had dropped a lot of blood on it. She had stained their beautiful marriage bed with her treachery.

Chapter 57
A Prophet Speaks

The farther Kalea's party ventured through the caves of Ilbith, the more elaborate those old carvings and arches became. They emerged into a blaze of sunlight in the narrow streets between high rises of rock walls. The mountain had been carved into a city, like Daghahen had described. Window and door arches of houses abandoned over the centuries appeared, now empty shells. No wooden doors remained to cover the entryways; only scraps of bent iron hinges made it obvious doors used to be there. Lizards and spiders and bats made their homes in this once-magnificent city of stone.

"This is Ilbith's city?" Kalea asked as she marveled at it all.

Daghahen dropped his hand from the grasp he'd held on his hood as if it might fly away, although there was no strong wind. "Used to be," he said. "Now it's a piece of rocky cheese—full o' holes. The better part of Ilbith is a horrible tower surrounded by water. A long-dead emperor used to call it his home. Now the sorcerers claim it, and it's where they get their name."

Bowaen whistled, also fascinated by what they'd discovered. "Sure is out of the way, isn't it?"

"Very," Daghahen said. "The sorcerers like it for its secrecy. We're about to enter the most dangerous spot in the Darklands, even more dangerous than Hathrohskog."

His statement made Kalea clammy. "How will we get out of there when we need to?"

Daghahen shrugged his bony shoulders. "We'll think of somethin', I usually do." He pointed ahead. "The city is about to recess underground, where I've got a little place made up for myself. Haven't seen it in years, though, so my stash of comforts may not be good anymore."

As Daghahen predicted, the city became an underground one. Ages ago, it might've operated on two levels, with the poorer class living below the richer. They spent yet another day trudging through the dark without much to reassure them that the little sounds here and there weren't dangerous animals.

"Just bats," is all Daghahen would tell them, no matter the sound. His repetitive answer achieved the opposite effect for Kalea than he intended.

"Ah, here we are," Daghahen said after several more hours, at a point when Kalea prepared to cry out in grief for how long they'd spent in the smothering dark. Daghahen shone his light made from glowing fungus over the wood grain of a door. "The only door left in this underground city, and it's mine. If ever you could say I own a home, this is it."

"Well, let's get in there before my feet fall off," Del said.

Daghahen pushed the door wide open, and the hinges' whine echoed far through the tunnel. "Welcome. Get comfortable, and we'll attempt to enter the sorcerers' lair tomorrow. The lady can sleep on the bed—if it hasn't rotted away—and we'll sleep on the floor."

Kalea braced herself to enter the dark, musty space. She huddled in close to Bowaen so as not to be the first person to walk into any unseen spider webs. Daghahen went straight to igniting magical lights that hovered over pedestals made from different materials or objects, like a tin vase and a clay cup.

"You can cast light like the elves of Norr," Gaije said to him, referring to the glowing night orbs they'd seen along the trails in his home country.

"Not exactly," Daghahen said, "though this is similar. I developed my own version of it."

Gaije narrowed his eyes at him. "Elves may only use the magical talents they are born with."

"Oh, I was born with some," Daghahen replied. "But throughout my long, miserable life, I've found the need for more tricks in my repertoire."

Gaije bristled more and more as they exchanged these comments. "So, that means you're…you're…!"

Daghahen put his hands out. "Spit it out, lad."

"A sorcerer."

Daghahen dropped one hand and lifted one finger on his other. "No. Sorcerers borrow their power from demonic deities and pixies. I practice concentration feats using my own energy. That makes me a mage."

"Like Damos," Kalea put in.

"Like those in the Lightlands," Daghahen confirmed, nodding his head heartily. "But I *used* to be a sorcerer—and that's what's going to work in our favor. I know how to get into the Ilbith tower, and I know my way around inside. So be glad and stop trying to accuse me of something your country considers a crime. I'm hardly Norrian anyway."

Daghahen left Gaije gawking and continued his work sprucing up the cave home he'd left idle for so long. He checked his collection of big clay jars full of pickled foods and crates of salted goods. He announced a few of the food jars "gone bad" after unsealing them and releasing their horrible smells into the small space. He worked with the other men to move the jars outside, and then went to the musty bed to shake out the blanket, releasing a large plume of dust. Kalea coughed and wondered if she should sleep on the floor alongside everyone else.

Daghahen brought attention to the fire pit carved into the room's center, charred black from years of use. He gathered up two buckets and employed Del to go out to the nearest water source to fill them, leaving Kalea with Bowaen and Gaije.

She shook the blanket out again and tidied up the bed's area. The wooden frame wobbled and the old straw smelled worse than the blanket. She put the blanket over the straw, deciding to sleep under her cloak and use one of her spare garments as a pillow. She wished to go to that water source Daghahen had mentioned and wash her clothes—everyone's clothes. There was no time to do such a comforting, leisurely thing before the terrifying next step of entering the Ilbith tower. She longed for the quiet contemplation. Instead, she sat down on Daghahen's bed, shivering internally.

Dorhen. She mouthed the word as it rolled through her head. Was he hurt? How badly were the sorcerers treating him? Her nerves played tug-o-war worrying about him besides her own safety and that of her friends. By the sound of Bowaen and Gaije's bickering, they suffered a confusion of many worries too: whether to trust Daghahen, whether one of them should keep awake all night to watch him, how they'd get into Ilbith, and what to expect once they did. They could only trust the mysterious old elf.

Naught but two hours later, Kalea retreated to the bed, leaving the four males to remain around the little fire, murmuring in the same wary manner, dreading the future. As usual, Gaije remained hell-bent on finding his sister once and for all. This task belonged to him and Kalea both. Daghahen also needed to go to the Ilbith Tower, although Kalea couldn't guess why.

"Kalea."

One of them approached her bed as her eyes were finally about to close. He stood over her, casting a shadow between her and the warm fire.

"Hmm?" She twisted around, knowing it couldn't be Bowaen's or Gaije's voice, or Del's either. "What is it, Daghahen?"

He dropped to his knees beside the bed, and his hair followed an instant later. "I just wanna know..." He swallowed. Kalea leaned up on her elbow. "I mean, I wanted to ask... It's not actually a concern of mine, or my business. But you said something the other day, and..." He took a seat and leaned his back against the bedframe.

"What's the matter?" she asked. "You can ask, I don't mind."

He turned his head to look at her with one eye and rested his forehead on his hand with his elbow propped on his knee, shielding the sight of his face from the other men. Bowaen eyed them discreetly as he nibbled some dried mushrooms found in Daghahen's store.

Daghahen whispered. "You said the name 'Dorhen.'" Kalea raised her eyebrows. "How do you know Dorhen?"

She countered, "Do *you* know Dorhen?"

A great pain fell over Daghahen's face. He nodded.

Kalea released a breath through her nose and spread her lips, not quite a smile. "I met a lovely elf named Dorhen in Tintilly when he got in trouble. At first, I didn't realize how lovely he was. It's a long and confusing story..." She huffed. "I'd never formally met an elf before. I didn't want to trust him, but...it's like he chose me. After a lot of worry and guilt, I decided to let him have me."

Quickly, Kalea realized she'd spilled some intimate thoughts to this stranger. She could've simply said, *Dorhen is a friend of mine*, but so much more had emerged. Daghahen stared off into the dark corner as he absorbed what she said. Should she stop talking? She didn't. If she died tomorrow trying to save Dorhen, maybe Daghahen could carry her message to him or whoever needed to hear it.

"I never got the chance to be with him," she continued, "as if it was never meant to be despite all his persistence."

"He showed you persistence?" Daghahen asked. A little smile cracked on his thin lips and a glint of moisture showed on the edge of his cheek. Was he crying? Kalea couldn't see it well enough from her vantage to know for sure.

"He was sweet, caring, doting. He wanted to take care of me."

"But you were a vestal," he put in.

"Yes. I lived in a convent. I wasn't supposed to talk to Dorhen, much less fall in love with him."

"Was he strong?"

Kalea reared her head back. Why did Daghahen want to know that? "I can't fathom how strong. He fought people on more than one occasion. For me. To protect me."

Daghahen closed his eyes. "Was he bad?"

"Only if you consider his sneaking around, trying to get close to a vestal. For me, though, he was nothing but good."

Daghahen laughed one beat through his nose. He crossed his arms over his knees as if to ponder everything Kalea told him. "I see." He huffed out a slightly louder laugh. "Heh, I suppose all young elves will be rascally when left to their own devices." Daghahen's teeth glistened in his smile. He kept quiet for the next few moments. "You were going to marry him?"

Kalea hesitated to answer. "Yes, I guess that's what I meant when I said I'd 'let him have me.'" She leaned over to try to view Daghahen's face better. "Daghahen…" He didn't meet her eyes. "Are you his father?"

Daghahen rolled to his feet and walked away in one smooth motion. His robes hung heavily off his shoulders.

What did I say wrong? She'd asked an honest question. Daghahen's particular inquiries about Dorhen had led her to that very conclusion. Looking at Daghahen's profile during their conversation, his contours nearly matched Dorhen's, though his nose had been broken sometime in the past—he had the same strong nose bridge and high cheekbones. The hairline too, although Daghahen's hair was thinner in his age.

Daghahen passed the other men and settled into the corner on the far side of the stone house, pulling his mercy hood over his eyes. Kalea lay her head back down and tucked her chin. What kind of secrets bothered him so? A new feeling introduced itself and mingled with all the other uncomfortable ones she harbored: sadness for Daghahen.

Kalea woke up the next morning to the sound of the door creaking open. It woke everyone else up too. Giving her no time to orient herself, a figure strode right into the cave dwelling with a long, red robe flowing around its feet.

"It's one of them!" Bowaen sprang from his blanket, and the other males stood to face the intruder. He unsheathed Hathrohjilh with the loud ringing sound of the blade scraping against its scabbard.

The red-robed figure hopped backward and threw the hood off his head to reveal wispy blond hair and a familiar wrinkly face with large blue eyes.

"It's Daghahen!" Kalea shouted, already halfway across the space to throw her arms around Bowaen's waist. He froze with his sword poised overhead. Gaije held an arrow drawn and trained on Daghahen's head.

"It's me!" Daghahen confirmed with a defensive hand outstretched. His other hand held a sack over his shoulder.

Bowaen lowered his sword. Gaije let his bowstring slacken. "Why the hell're you dressed like that?" Bowaen shouted. His voice rang against every stony wall of their enclosure. "You know how on edge we are about going into those slimy sorcerers' lair? Now you're gonna walk right in here dressed as one?"

Daghahen held out the bulging sack he'd brought. "I put on my old robe to get in there!"

Bowaen's face twisted. "You've been in there already?"

Daghahen nodded and dropped the sack. "Only to the lowest level. I snatched some clothes from the laundry cave for you all to disguise yourselves. I got another red robe for one of you. Kalea can't go prancing around in there looking like a Wikshonite. Ilbith has three kinds of citizens: sorcerers, servants, and whores. Though you two men already look like you fit in with the servants, I figured a standard apron or familiar tabard can't hurt for your camouflage."

He bent to pull out each garment he'd stuffed into the sack. One of the outfits consisted of a jute sack with a rope belt; he handed it to Kalea. "And I didn't forget milady." A little pair of sandals went with her ensemble. Kalea pursed her lips at the horrid thing. It would scratch her skin with a vengeance.

Daghahen tossed out the only other red robe he'd managed to acquire. "I suggest the redhead wear this one, as it's the only garment with a hood. I don't know how many elves have joined their faction since I've been in there, but I'm guessing the number is small. Lambelhen and I were the only elves back then."

Gaije repeated the name "Lambelhen" as if to test each meaningful Norrian syllable.

"My brother," Daghahen said. His stance stiffened and his mouth turned to a hard frown. He turned half away. "Make sure you cover your features under the hood. And leave your bow here. Sorcerers don't carry bows."

"I refuse," Gaije said with a warning in his tone.

Daghahen ignored him and eyed Bowaen next, who'd sheathed his sword since drawing it on Daghahen. "And suddenly the scruffy man seems familiar to me." He dropped his eyes to the sword as Bowaen finished wrapping the belt around his waist. "Is that Hathrohjilh?"

Bowaen squinted at him. "Yeah." He continued his strained survey of Daghahen. "Shit," he said. "My eyes have gone bad, otherwise I woulda recognized you sooner. You're Ibex, the old man who lost it to me in a bet!"

Daghahen smirked and tossed the last dull garment from his sack to Del. "I should've also known, lad. The law of synchronicity dictates all of this, especially after learning that my son's fiancée is standing in my house right now. Why would Hathrohjilh's new owner not also be here?" Daghahen followed up with an apathetic shrug and moved to a locked chest in the corner where he fell into a squat, bright-red robes pooling around him.

Kalea stiffened up as everyone turned to gawk at her. "What's the law of synchronicity?" she asked Daghahen.

He replied without looking up from his rummaging. "A complicated philosophy about reading messages in randomness. It's a reminder that nothing is actually random, and that the world moves in rhythm." He tossed his hair over his shoulder. "Seeing its clues has always been a skill of mine. I guess I was born with it, but it took growing up and recognizing those patterns to actually be able to use them."

He shot a smile at Kalea over his shoulder, and the light beaming down on him from a sliver in the old stone ceiling obscured his wrinkles for an instant and made him appear young and handsome in the radiance. "Reading star patterns is a good way to find tips. It's surprising how much they can tell me about this and that." He turned back to his rummaging, and the spell of his youthful aura passed away. The other men were staring at Kalea.

"'Son's fiancée?' You mean he's related to Dorhen?" Bowaen asked, pointing a finger at the back of Daghahen's head.

Kalea shrugged. "Synchronicity," she murmured faintly.

"Well, I suppose we're all set," Daghahen said, turning from the chest. He paused to eyeball Hathrohjilh again, now secured to Bowaen's waist. "I didn't count on Hathrohjilh drawing so close to Lambelhen."

"Is there something you're not tellin' us, old man?" Bowaen asked in reply.

Daghahen stared at him with blank eyes and a limp mouth. "I haven't caught any signals about this turn of events." He took a breath and exhaled through his nose. "Maybe it's coming together now, though. When you see him, you must give the sword to Dorhen."

Bowaen lurched back and shot his hand to the sword's hilt as if to guard it from Daghahen. "Yer crazy!" He pointed to Kalea speechlessly, turning his head from her to Daghahen a few times.

Daghahen continued, "Hathrohjilh is the only weapon that can kill Lambelhen. I know this from a direct message the stars once showed me, and later learned my son would do it, which was why I—which was why *he* became Wikshen. He's stronger as Wikshen."

Bowaen blinked, checked Kalea again, and asked Daghahen, "You mean... Yer sayin' Wikshen really is Dorhen?"

Daghahen gave a silent nod.

"Well, I'm not giving this thing to no slimy Wikshen! I don't care how you're related to him," Bowaen spat.

Daghahen showed no care for Bowaen's choice of words. "Fate dictated that he would become the monster, don't you see?" He pointed to Kalea. "Lambelhen must die, but this young lady has already told me that the kingsorcerer still lives, so Dorhen hasn't accomplished his destiny yet. I'm betting that at this point, he must use the sword to do it."

Kalea's mouth hung open as she listened. "He…he…" She breathed heavily. "His duty? Kill the kingsorcerer? Become…Wikshen?"

Daghahen nodded to her. "And he won't survive the task either, I'm sorry to say. It's why I'm so surprised to hear you…to hear about you." His shoulders slumped by the end of his statement.

Kalea's stomach burned at his words. She already knew that no one survived being possessed by a pixie, although she was determined to find a way to save Dorhen nonetheless. Now, Daghahen had a projection of how it would all happen on this venture?

"So let's get this straight," Bowaen said. "We're going in there to locate Mhina." He pointed to Gaije, who nodded with a firm indication of his will to see that detail completed. "Then after that, we'll free Wikshen so I can give him the sword he'll use to kill the kingsorcerer?" Daghahen bowed his head deeply. "To put it simply, yes, but it won't be so simple. We'll have to make our way up through the tunnels into Ilbith, and up from there. There will be locked doors to stop our progress." He nodded to Del, knowing by conversation of his skill in picking locks. He pointed to Bowaen. "You must keep the sword hidden. If the sorcerers manage to take it from you, it's all over." He drew a finger across his throat, a gesture which made a shiver run up Kalea's spine. "We'll return from there with the little girl and Lambelhen dead, once and for all."

Kalea frowned. He'd failed to mention that they'd also leave Ilbith with Dorhen. Did he really believe Dorhen would die today in his effort to kill the kingsorcerer?

She shook her head and said, "Hey," to get all of their strained attention, "don't forget about the novices. We must also rescue them." She regarded Bowaen and gave him a hard look. "If something should happen to me, make sure you save them."

"Nothin's gonna happen to you," he said, and held the stare for a long second afterward, until Kalea turned away. Whatever happened to Dorhen…just might happen to her too.

Chapter 58
Faraway Screams

Naerezek's protection spell held Lamrhath's arteries together long enough for him to stagger over to Mhina's room to make use of her healing power. For only a brief minute, his anger fled away with the pain. The damage Orinleah had caused fused back together neatly, leaving nothing behind but a memory. A memory which held the power to summon back the anger.

He left Mhina alone and retreated to his own room, drifting blankly without the pain, but maintaining the same overwhelming feeling of... so many negative emotions. Loss might've been the most painful. For the last week, he'd enjoyed a thing he rarely got to experience: hope. The hope he'd enjoyed, Orinleah had replaced with loss. Why? What in this world could ever make a *faerhain* do something so evil? Maybe she'd been evil from the start. How she'd appeared in his dream originally and seduced him, how coldly she'd treated him over the years, how cruelly she'd lied to him about enacting a marriage ritual before she...

Lamrhath sat on his bed, looking into the nearest mirror. All the wounds were indeed gone, but he couldn't wipe the deeper wound from his expression. He exchanged the inner pain with numbness by the grace of Naerezek and, using the mirror as an aid, he formed his mien into something hard. His eyes glowed under the hood of his brow. After donning a fresh, casual robe, he went back out the door.

Outside, he found Talekas and a few others waiting nervously. He'd only taken a brief moment to tell Talekas what had happened along his way from Orinleah to Mhina. "My lord, we...haven't made a move to punish her..."

Lamrhath raised a hand to silence him. "Shears." After giving his order, he continued walking. The sorcerers scrambled behind him, and between the lot of them, they produced a pair to deliver once he reached Orinleah's doors. He'd left both of them standing open.

Inside, he found her sitting up on the bloodied ox pelt which covered her bed, a tangible symbol of the marriage she'd ruined. She swayed on her seat as if she'd awoken in the last few minutes, naked, her hair a mess, and her body stained with his blood.

Alertness lit her eyes when he entered. She worked her mouth, but couldn't seem to find her voice. Lamrhath tightened his grip around the shears behind his back. Maybe she deserved the same treatment she'd given him. Which method would teach her best?

When he took a step forward, she shrank back. Another step, and she leaned away. He sprang and threw out an arm to catch her long hair.

She screamed and weaved into it the plea, "Noooo!"

Lamrhath's forehead had gone cold. His vision blurred, and his body kept moving regardless of how passive his mind became.

A distant rush of sound at the fringes of his consciousness winked into being. Dorhen flinched. In this barrage of white-hot light, he yearned to drift away again, to not see, hear, or be, but the foreign sound pierced on, unending, reminding him a world existed around him. Even Wik couldn't soothe him in the dark place with this inferno, which sucked away his air—his life. This must be the slowest death anyone could ever curse him with. He'd be more than happy to give in and let it be over, but that sound…

He opened his mouth and tried to put words out with his shallow breath. No more sweat to dispense existed in him, and the blisters took over.

"Aaaaaahhhhhhhh!" The shriek sounded so faint, but this one came through as a human scream. A woman.

"Kah…" he managed to get out. He closed his lips and tried to swallow, tried to sit up straighter in the chair they'd bound him to. The sound of the scream never really ended; it merged into new screams. His body began to shake with the realization they were hurting her! Kalea!

His anger peaked, despite his exhaustion. Forcing his mind to focus and be alert, he called the darkness. *Wik! Come to me! Now!*

His call was rewarded with the return of the miasma wisps spilling down the wall from some of the darker stone crevices.

"Come!" he demanded, using every ounce of energy and every fingerhold he had around his Kraft skill. "Kah—!" He tried her name again and fell short. She needed him, and he'd do anything and everything it took to save her!

The miasma crept closer across the floor. If it prevailed, if he could gather enough of it, it could smother the candlelight.

"Come!" he demanded again. He remembered his breathing. Kraft needed total focus and bodily energy. A honed mind could master the body, and together, the two could master Kraft. With full use of Kraft, he'd be unstoppable.

Closer, the miasma crawled, eager to obey, to serve the deity who ruled the darkness. The darkness craved to spread itself.

But the candlelight. And his lack of energy. He hadn't eaten or drunk a drop in days.

Dorhen was empty, and the miasma too thin.

His head flopped over again to hang limp as always. In the bright beams, the miasma vanished, evaporating like a raindrop in a bonfire. All Dorhen could do was listen in his daze until the screams stopped. He could only hope and beg Wik and the goddess for the sorcerers not to kill his Kalea.

Chapter 59
Beautiful Secret

The Desteer maiden gained a long distance of ground before him. Lehomis held back with a slow pace to lessen the inevitable sounds of his feet crunching down on leaves and twigs as he tailed her without her knowledge. This maiden had set out in late afternoon into the forest without a proper *saehgahn* escort to protect her. Lehomis had gone after her on mere seconds of notice when Kennaha passed him in the bustle of the clan's common area.

"Follow Inahet," she'd murmured to him, and then smoothly drifted off with the crowd, leaving him no chance to ask questions. Luckily, he crossed paths with Anonhet on his way to the Desteer hall and told her in a similar brief manner that he'd be going out for a while and couldn't predict when he'd be back. Like the good lass she was, Anonhet didn't ask questions.

Inahet emerged from the Desteer hall with none other than Alhannah. Lehomis ducked his head and watched from behind one of the living, woven tree-walls that separated the hall's grounds from the rest of the village. Alhannah tied a small, wicker crate to Inahet's back using the supportive sash of a discarded *hanbohik* section, and Inahet wasted no time in trotting into the darkening woods without a soul to accompany her. Her aloneness justified Lehomis's pursuit because females couldn't leave the village without protection, Desteer maidens included.

So Lehomis kept a dutiful eye on her beyond her notice, and she led him into a deep section of the forest on the outskirts of the village. Not a trail or muddy patch existed to mark the way for a casual traveler in this overgrown, wild area. It would be a section that more commonly received couples out to perform the marriage ritual without the worry of being accidentally discovered. Lehomis cringed at the idea of stumbling upon such a rendezvous. First-time mating sessions usually put male elves into a savage state of aggression. Violence would naturally follow the already awkward meeting of a third-party male.

The sun was poised to disappear from the red sky by the time Inahet's trek wound to a stop. She paused at a cliff face where two tall rocks stood like pillars, a random formation caused by the troll attacks of centuries past. Inahet untied her silken sash to release the crate and placed it at the base of the two standing rocks. She bowed down on her knees and kissed the ground, immediately going into a string of prayers to the Bright One.

The Desteer had made a shrine out of this rock formation? Lehomis squatted down comfortably behind a nearby hedge and watched. She continued her prayers for at least twenty minutes before rising and backing away slowly, hands folded before her. Spinning back around, she ran in the direction she had come from, before Lehomis was ready to resume the chase. She probably intended to get back before night took over. The elves of Norr feared the dark and didn't want to be out in it, and she knew very well she wasn't supposed to be alone out here.

He sprang to his feet and considered running after her, but his eyes trailed back to her offering, the wicker crate she'd abandoned on the ground. He chose to stay and open the crate. The moment he began to step over the bushy patch in his path, however, a flare of light startled him, and he dropped down behind the bushes as before.

A…seam opened up in the space between the two standing rocks. Lehomis gawked, trying to make sense of the sight. The seam glowed like lightning, but hung in the air for much longer, and it arched high. A scene—another place—appeared in the light's arch. Waiting with bated breath, Lehomis didn't notice how hard he clutched fistfuls of leaves on the hedge.

A dark figure appeared in the arch—a man, not an elf. He hesitated before leaning through to the outside world. Lehomis checked to make sure he really wasn't visible. Reassured he was alone, the man stepped one foot through the arch, leaned down, and took Inahet's box. In a snap, Lehomis lost his chance to peek inside.

The stranger twisted around quickly to place the box down on his side of the arch, reached behind him to somewhere Lehomis couldn't see, and then dropped something in the crate's place: a bag. He retreated back into the arch, and the whole thing vanished, snuffed like a candle, leaving nothing but a wisp of smoke behind.

Lehomis kept his squat, frozen in shock for the following few seconds. He couldn't help but think he'd imagined it, yet proof of the occurrence had been left behind. He leaped over the hedge and bounded toward the Desteer's secret makeshift altar to see what had replaced the crate. It was a red bag like the one Alhannah had given him. He lifted it. Heavy. It jingled too. Inside, he found silver.

Lehomis's heart pounded. Alhannah's possession of silver was odd enough in the first place. Norrians didn't use such a currency; they traded for everything they needed. Now he knew where the silver came from. He left the bag alone for Inahet, or one of her Desteer sisters, to collect in the morning.

He inspected the standing stones next and took a new shock of surprise. It was well-hidden and wouldn't be spotted easily by any casual passerby, but he managed to see it before the light left the sky completely: gold. A thin line of gold was embedded in the sides of the standing stones, like a doorway. Someone was trespassing into Norr by way of magic, and it wasn't the Bright One. Whoever the culprit was, they had successfully beguiled the Desteer.

A long, numb journey took Lehomis home to his outdoor kitchen. He bypassed it, unconsciously deciding not to smoke any tobacco as he usually did. He went straight through the door and ignored Tirnah and Anonhet as they stared from the center of the *wyrrem*.

"I'll see you tomorrow," he said absently to both of them without slowing down to worry about good nights or other small talk. At the mouth of the hallway, he paused and slowly twisted around to note their stances. Tirnah stood solemn, her mouth in a frown, her eyes bland. Anonhet wrung her hands in visible fear.

"Is everything all right?" he asked, finally paying them the attention they deserved. More than a day had gone by since he'd interacted with either of them. He shifted his eyes between them. "Why are you looking at me like that?"

Now knowing something bothered them, he turned all the way around to face them squarely. Perhaps they needed his reassurance—his *saehgahn* protective comfort. Inviting a second *saehgahn* to live with them for an added bit of security and liveliness could be in order in the near future. It had become eerily quiet in the house lately. He'd hoped Gaije would return home with Mhina sooner. Gaije's presence in the house would increase his chances of Anonhet choosing him for marriage over someone else, but Gaije had left long ago and it hurt Lehomis sharply in the gut to think about. He might not come home at all.

"Everything…is fine, Grandfather." Tirnah said, though she didn't look at all like she believed her own words.

Lehomis took a step closer to them. "May I have a cup of tea?" he asked. The two females exchanged a quick look, and Anonhet shot to the hearth.

"Grandfather," Tirnah said a little too stiffly and formally, "would you like to take your tea outside on the kitchen rug—with me by your side?"

With me by your side. She wanted to be alone with him again? She really was up to some mischief and aimed to drag him into it. He cocked his head at first, and then nodded. "Sure." How long could he resist her mischief? He didn't feel much headstrong confidence in himself right now, that was certain.

He put up one finger, signaling her to wait, and then rushed to his room for his pipe. Before her face left his sight, her expression tightened, mirroring Anonhet's tension.

On his way back out, Anonhet said, "The tea will be ready in only a few minutes."

"That's fine," he replied, unsure what was so special about it. He'd only requested it to try to break the tension.

He found Tirnah outside, standing beside the kitchen pavilion's corner post. She had lit the lanterns hanging from the ceiling; otherwise, the soft embers from the oven's earlier use glowed in the dark night, casting an orange light across the fur he used to love to sit on each morning and evening. He acknowledged her with his pipe raised, and her frown increased.

"I wish you wouldn't smoke anymore," she said as he approached. "It makes you smell."

He took a seat and grabbed a ready rush candle to light his pipe. He did have to pause at her statement, though. During their last interaction, she'd tried to enact the "tea between widows" ritual, and now she wanted him to smell better? His stomach boiled at the thought.

Sitting on the rug, his shoulders stiffened as she sat across from him, a little too formally for comfort. The ambient little flames flickering behind the lavender glass in the lanterns set off her blonde hair in playful colors. He tried not to look at her. She was… No. He couldn't acknowledge the dishonorable thought.

"Grandfather, why don't you look at me?"

Damn it, now he had to! "What's on your mind, granddaughter-in-law?" He made sure to emphasize his relation to her.

"There's something I must speak with you about."

He struggled to swallow the thick lump in his throat, heart throbbing. His head began to throb too, replaying their interaction in his darkened house, teacup in hand, hers abandoned and unfinished, the…feelings she had caused him. He swiped his sleeve across his temple and waited. What could she possibly find so attractive about him, and why did she see no shame in it? Was she about to confess her attraction? Was she hiding a marriage token in her sleeve? He couldn't accept it! He'd get his head cut off by the bloodthirsty Desteer.

Tirnah extended her hands, but snatched them away before he could receive them. "Grandfather… There's going to be another added to our house."

Lehomis relaxed at her words, relieved she hadn't said what he'd expected. He started a second later. "Wait, what? Are you getting married?" Half of his relief came after hearing it wouldn't be him.

She blew out a breath. "No." The way she scrunched her face hinted at the quirky mirth she would show on a normal day in the long-ago past. "If I were getting married, don't you think I'd be leaving your house instead of saying 'another added to your house?'"

Lehomis shrugged. "I have no idea what's going on anymore," he said honestly.

She reached out and put her hand on his knee. He'd forgotten the pipe in his hand, letting off a ribbon of smoke into the night air. "It's actually quite wonderful, Grandfather," she said. "You see, before Trisdahen left us, he left one more gift for his clan." Erratically, she burst into tears at the end of the statement.

Lehomis's mouth dropped open. He took a moment to puzzle through what she was telling him. He dropped the pipe onto the fur, and it lit up a few hairs, prompting him to slap the pelt to put the little flame out. He rose to his knees. "You're pregnant?"

She cupped her mouth behind both hands and nodded deeply.

A weight lifted off of him. She didn't want to have an affair with him—she was pregnant with Trisdahen's last child! He should've known! He'd already gone through the process of wringing his hands over the idea, but had dismissed it when she didn't tell him sooner.

Finding himself right back in the role of "grandfather," he cooed and threw his arms around her, squeezing her tight until she gave in and lay against him. He shushed her tenderly. "It *is* wonderful," he whispered over her hair. "It's the best..." He had to snip off the sob building in his throat.

She wept through her effort to say, "I-I-I was afraid to tell you. Didn't want to—to worry you unnecessarily."

He cooed some more. "Now, now, now." He smiled, hoping she'd hear it in his voice. "Worrying over you with your news is the most necessary type of worryin'."

He nudged her to look at him. He met her moist, reddened eyes. "Tirnah," he said, "you got nothin' at all to fear. I got lots of money and know-how to make sure you have a pleasant, warm, and bountiful winter. Everything is and will be fine. You can count on me."

She grabbed his braid tight. "Do you mean it, Lehomis?"

He sucked in through his nose. She rarely called him by his name. "Sure as my name is Lehomis Lockheirhen." He squeezed her shoulders as tightly as she clutched his braid. "Tirnah, yer my hero because of this.

You're a hero to this clan. From now on, my life is yours."

Chapter 60
A Mountain Rots

Wearing the makeshift sack dress, Kalea itched the whole way during their hurried trek through the winding tunnels toward the sound of rushing water.

"Things get a little slippery from here on," Daghahen warned. He appeared as a hooded red form from behind, with another just like him, Gaije, and then Bowaen and Del, who could easily be recognized in their altered costumes.

At his words, everyone turned to share their concerned expressions with Kalea, who wore a new, pathetic pair of sandals to complement her beggar-like outfit.

"Don't worry about me," she said.

Bowaen offered, "You can grab my arm if you need—"

"I'm fine." She waved them on and continued picking her way across the dark floor she couldn't see. Any kind of slithering creature or sharp rock or old shard of glass could be littering her path, and she wouldn't see it until too late. Walking in the cold, open air numbed her toes, and the sandal strap pinched across the smaller ones.

Daghahen's claim about the terrain becoming slipperier turned out worse than she imagined. A bright, grey light beamed at the end of their tunnel, as did an echoing roar. White water flowed around in a looped formation before hurrying on beyond a rock crevice, and at the loop's rounded center stood a huge stone formation. After all their days underground, the Darklands' filtered sun seared Kalea's eyes when she tried to look up at the marvel.

"This is it," Daghahen said beside her as they stood at the mouth of the cave. "Ilbith." The stone wall rose far beyond a veil of mist kicked up by the river. He pointed out, "This river curves around the whole thing, not to mention the mountainous wildlands we're in. Going through all those caves is the only way to walk to Ilbith. The sorcerers get in and out using portals."

Everyone took a minute to gawk at the tower. Many windows gaped along the curved walls, some fitted with glass or covered by wooden shutters, while others were drafty, open holes.

Kalea considered her clammy toes at the edge of the rock. "This doesn't seem right," she said. "There's nowhere else to step. Are we going to swim?"

Daghahen snorted. "No, lass." His red sleeve waved like a flag when he extended his arm. He pointed to their right, at a narrow shelf with algae at its edge and water lapping constantly over it along the outside of the cave wall.

Del cursed under his breath at the sight. Kalea's stomach twisted.

Scoffing with the rest of them, Bowaen asked, "But where does it go?"

"Down," Daghahen answered. "In fact, here." He dropped to the ground, picked up the nearest stick, and drew some lines in the soggy dirt under the sunlight. "There's a complex of caves under the tower. I'm sure they haven't altered the layout too much since I've been in there. We're going up through this way. See?" He traced his finger up the shaft he drew below the line that represented the ground floor. "In this cave, they do a lot of menial chores—it's right above the dumping cave they call the Grave. Are you following this?"

"Not really," Del said. They were all blinking down at his drawing.

"Bah!" Daghahen replied. "Bear with me. I advise we split up and meet right down here where we come in."

"How shall we split?" Bowaen asked.

"Since the redhead and I are dressed as sorcerers, we'll go to the upper levels where we're most likely to find his sister. You three humans can keep to the lower levels. Keep your heads low and just lurk around. Act busy. You'll probably find your friends in those levels."

Kalea nodded. "That sounds easy. But what about Dorhen?"

Daghahen huffed. "I've no idea what they would do with him, lass. Whether he's up high or down low…" He looked at Gaije. "Both our groups will keep our eyes and ears peeled. Once we've gotten everyone together, we'll smuggle the lasses down to the lower levels, get everyone assembled, and trek back the way we came. Any questions?"

None spoke. Kalea's heart pounded. She'd already gone into Wikhaihli and acted like a maid, so this really sounded like something she could do.

Daghahen clapped his hands. "Now are we going, or are we going to let the sorcerers continue their depraved designs?"

Kalea pushed past the others, practically shoving Del back into the cave. "I'm getting Dorhen out of there." She planned to do everything in her ability to keep him from dying as Daghahen had predicted. Sacrifice of one's own life for the greater good sounded wonderful in stories, but it made her want to vomit whenever she thought of Dorhen in that role— her sweet, brown-haired elf with his innocent turquoise eyes and loving smile.

"Lass, you should let me go first," Daghahen said, but she ignored him. With her hands on the wall, she shimmied along the ledge as the freezing water rushed up and down, sometimes as high as her ankles. A short session of bickering sounded behind her, and at the end of it, Gaije shimmied in beside her.

"If Daghahen were smarter," Gaije murmured to her, "he would've brought a rope to tie us all together."

Kalea didn't reply, but continued her steady forward shuffle. Ahead of her, she couldn't tell where the ledge would take them. Far ahead, it disappeared from view as the canyon wall became riddled with vines and leafless bushes emerging from every crevice. Daghahen's cursing ensued behind Gaije as they went on, with comments about how he should've gone first.

Kalea's confidence didn't rise the farther she moved. As she listened, finally willing to admit he was right, her foot slipped right off the slimy rock as a particularly big whitewater wave crashed against them. She screamed, expecting to be swept away.

The water crashed down, beating against her as if it wanted to snatch her. She hung on until it passed. Gaije grunted behind the sound of the roaring water, holding her arm with his other hand—his fingers—grasping a narrow rock crevice. Daghahen also grasped her sack dress in a measly effort to keep her from falling.

"Ya see there?" he nagged. "I told you! I had it all planned out: the lass goes between the men, I go first! But does anyone listen to me? No! No one ever listens to Dag!"

While he bickered with himself, Gaije pulled Kalea back onto the ledge and made sure she regained her footing. Bowaen and Del grumbled amongst themselves about the incident, but there was nothing anyone could do besides push on.

"Stop!" Daghahen shouted when she arrived at a certain point. She wouldn't have continued much farther anyway, as she could clearly see the ledge soften and disappear into the brush ahead.

"Now where to, old elf?" Del demanded from the back of the line.

Daghahen pressed Gaije against the rock wall and awkwardly stepped around him. "You gotta let me closer." He edged in behind Kalea rather than attempt to put her behind him as well. "The water's high today," he noted as he peered over her shoulder at the raucous river flowing by them. "Otherwise, there's a…"

Kalea waited. She saw nothing but a dead end and a lot of water crashing precariously close by. The worry of someone in the tower seeing them through one of those many windows set in. The two who wore bright-red robes should easily be spotted against their earthy setting.

"A what?" Kalea demanded during his long pause.

In their close quarters, Daghahen's eyes slid to hers. "You'll have to reach it. Earlier this morning, the river flow wasn't so bad, and I could go farther. It's different at this hour."

Kalea blew a breath through her cheeks. "Tell me what to do."

Daghahen smoothed his finger and thumb along each side of his hairless chin as he squinted past her at the rock formation. "Hard to recognize now, but below you, up ahead maybe, there's a grate with a latch. I suppose the path dips down into the water, but it does flatten out and the grate rests on top. You may get your ankle broken if you blindly walk forward too far."

Kalea frowned. "You need me to unlatch the grate?"

"Yes, but be careful. It's obviously underwater now, and it's deadly slippery, even at sunrise today when it stood above water."

"I'm going to get my disguise wetter than it already is," she said. "And when wet, it itches beyond—"

Daghahen waved his hand. "Not a concern. I'll find you a new one when we get up there." He pointed to the tower and checked the others behind him. "Your elf-friend was right. I should've thought to bring a rope. I can't have my daughter-in-law-to-be swept down a Black Mountain river."

He put his hands on her shoulders and pointed her forward. "I'll hold you, and the redhead can hold me. Scruffy man, you hold the redhead, and the snot-nosed smoker can hold you." He changed to holding Kalea by her belt. "Walk gingerly forward and look for a step down in the rocks. It's treacherous, so take care. After two or three steps down, feel around for the grate."

Kalea took another deep, unconfident breath. *Does he expect us to immerse into a watery hole and swim underwater? We'll drown! Creator, why?*

Shaking her head, she stepped forward slowly, probably slower than Daghahen intended. Her thoughts continued in her heightened nerves. *Dear Creator, if I make it through this... just let me and Dorhen live happily ever after.*

At the tail syllable of her prayer, a large wave bypassed cleanly without wetting her down. A formation of fish showed within it during that quick instant. Right afterward, a solitary splash in the shape of a human figure hit the rocks ahead of her. It was gone as fast as any splash.

At the sight of it, Kalea shouted, "Arius Medallus! What do you want?" As soon as the words left her mouth, self-consciousness hit. She'd never told her friends about Arius Medallus. From behind, the others all stared at her. Daghahen released her belt. Disregarding them, she decided to try something. "If you want me to save Dorhen, then help me out!"

She jumped when the water made another big flourish of movement. Against the laws of physics, it twisted in its flow and veered unnaturally around a space below the water.

"That's it!" Daghahen shouted, pointing over her shoulder. He took Kalea by the belt again. "Hurry."

She stepped along the slimy green stones as quickly as she could. The stone steps showed clearly before her with the water out of the way, leading to the old, rusty grate Daghahen had described.

Now that there was enough room to do so, Daghahen put himself before her and took care of the stubborn latch. At her back, a wall of water waited, with a school of silvery fish watching her as if through a glass window. Had Arius Medallus also possessed the fish, or just the water itself? She shot her hand to her chest as she thought about it. In the subterranean lake under Hathrohskog, a small group of fish had healed her poisoned wound...

Gaije helped Daghahen throw the grate open, its hinges groaning all the way. "Got it!" Daghahen said. "Get in there! Hurry, before whatever spell this is wears off!"

He descended first, on steps apparently built into the ground. Gaije went next, but not before shooting a glance at her. Bowaen also openly stared at her when he approached the grate. "Kalea the mermaid," he said before waving her to enter before him.

The fish in the wall of water scattered when she took a step down into the slimy underground shaft. Echoing drips sang in the atmosphere. She didn't voice her concern about drowning once the "spell" did wear off. Instead, she mumbled under her breath, only loud enough for herself, "It's *Luschian*, not mermaid."

"We'll drown when that water decides to drop," Del said in her stead when he tapped down the steps behind her.

"Nonsense." Daghahen's hushed voice echoed loudly from the dark ahead. His bottle of glowing fungus flared to life when released from his pocket and illuminated a cave much like the ones they'd seen all week, except slimier. Freshwater mollusks clung to the walls in the lower corners. "See how the path slopes upward? There's an air pocket that makes this place passable. Normally, I'd pass through here on a dry day, when the river flows lazy and low. Hurry, this way."

The group squeezed in a tight line through the following corridors, which were sometimes unbearably cramped. "Don't be afraid of this,"

Daghahen assured them as they worked through one of the narrowest spaces. "We'll make it. 'Tis the last place you want to think of being claustrophobic."

Del huffed behind Kalea in response to many of the things Daghahen said. "You're the most comforting madman I think we'll ever meet, elf."

"Hmm?" Daghahen said, "Did someone say something? I was referring to Kalea and myself."

"Ha ha," Del mocked.

Kalea gave out a little giggle as she pushed past the close walls; her companions' jests helped her nerves. She took Daghahen's advice and ignored her discomforts. She couldn't deny Daghahen's gruff voice carried a warm resonance, which brought a lot of comfort. Dorhen didn't sound so rugged, but the resemblance in their voices could be heard clearly.

"Not far now," Daghahen reported. "We've traveled *under* the river. Above us, the tower climbs to the sky, so up we'll go from now on."

He led them straight to a certain fork in an open space. The glowing lichen bottle dangling on his wrist created the only light to see by, and it didn't help in preventing a stubbed toe or bruised shin. Stalagmites grew from the floor, many of them broken off. The way Daghahen flitted around in his antsy search for the path helped no one.

"Kalea," he called. "Where are you? Did you survive the tunnels?"

"I did." She was in no mood to hurry back into another squeezed position, but couldn't stay in this dark little hole.

"From here, things will get dangerous," Daghahen warned. "Keep your mouths shut—especially you, redhead." Gaije said nothing in reply. "Follow my lead," he continued. "Redhead, walk next to me. Act like you own the place. In a way, you do. The rest of you keep your heads down and act obedient to us—to anyone you see wearing red or purple. There are white-robed sorcerers too, which are low-level students. They also command respect. Are we ready?"

This time Gaije did speak. "Yes." He approached the mouth of the upsloping tunnel beside which Daghahen stood.

"Then come."

After another difficult squeeze up a carved, spiraling shaft, Kalea found her next chance to take a breather in a space as wide as the trolls' section of the Black Mountain caves. She regretted it immediately when her lungs filled with a noxious smell that scratched her throat and soured her stomach. Her hands shot to her mouth to stifle the effect, though too late. Distant torches lit the far corners of the place from high ledges, carried by people traversing up and down the spiraling walkways.

Daghahen pulled them into a huddle. He didn't gag and try to hold his breath as everyone else did. "This is the lowest level of Ilbith. They call it the Grave. It's where they throw their garbage."

"It smells like the dead," Bowaen pointed out.

"Of course." Daghahen didn't elaborate on that. He pointed to a group of men with tattered clothing making their way down to the Grave's floor with a large barrel on wheels. "We have to get out of here because it looks like it's incineration day. They'll douse oil on the mountain of decay over there and light it on fire."

His words brought attention to the source of the stench. A silhouetted mound, heaped as big as a barn, showed before the torchlight. Kalea found herself walking the opposite way, eager to put more distance between herself and the filth of Ilbith.

"Not that way!" Daghahen lunged to catch her arm. "You don't want to run into anyone yet, not down here. Too suspicious."

On closer inspection, the path of the men with the barrel wound right around toward the sloped path Kalea would've chosen. Bowaen considered Daghahen for the moment. "You've been down here before."

Pulling Kalea by the hand in the direction of his choice, Daghahen said, "Several times. The Grave made the best place to look for an alternative route out of this place." He twisted around to show Bowaen his toothy, sly grin despite the noxious air. "And I found one, didn't I?"

Gaije trotted to catch up to him. "Where will I find Mhina?"

"Probably in the upper levels, like I've told you," Daghahen said. "Makes the most sense that Lambelhen would treasure a female elf if ever he caught one." Daghahen's mood suddenly sank. "He's found at least one other."

"Who?" Kalea asked, genuinely interested in the answer.

Daghahen turned his eyes to her lifelessly. "No, wait, he's calling himself Lamrhath these days. Now, everyone shut up and follow me."

Keeping to the shadows cast heavily under the lip of each tiered path, they moved up the spiral formation, dodging whatever sooty worker they encountered.

On one occasion, Daghahen was caught out in the light after pushing the others into the first available hiding place. When the two workers noticed him, they paused to grovel at his feet. In response, he swiped his hand across each of their heads.

"Hurry, you fools!" he barked at them. "No dallying!" The men jumped and went on their way at a faster pace. He turned back to Kalea's party with a firm jaw.

"Do you think you could've been more phony, old elf?" Del asked.

Daghahen shrugged. "I wasn't exactly in the habit of yelling at the servants when I lived here, but it's what the sorcerers do."

At the top of the steep path, the floor leveled off to a busier hub. "You all think the Grave smells bad now," Daghahen said, "wait until they light it on fi— " Stopping his statement mid-syllable, he hissed and pushed Gaije's chest to make him wait before climbing higher.

"What is it now?" Kalea whispered from the back of the line.

Daghahen waved his hand for them to creep up a little closer and showed his palm to stop them. They peered over the floor above at the goings-on.

"Beware of them," Daghahen said. He didn't have to point at what he referred to: a monstrous set of creatures that stood guard by the largest doorway. "I suppose they've come down to oversee the pyre. Those are called naerscouels." They were men with heads like dogs—fur, ears, and all. The glowing yellow eyes made for the creepiest parts of their presentation besides their big muscular bodies and narrow muzzles.

Kalea stifled her gasp behind her hands. They were...familiar. "I've seen them." Everyone turned their quizzical stares on her. "What are they?" she asked instead of trying to explain her dreamwalking to them.

"Lamrhath worships a pixie called Naerezek, who performs most of the impressive feats which benefit this place," Daghahen said, his tone strangely bland for what he reported. "This includes a spell to transform disappointing sorcerers into more useful, but stupider, creatures: naerscouels, as the name suggests. Don't make eye contact with them. Act like good, respectful slaves, and this should go fine."

His words failed to comfort Kalea this time. Reality hit all too hard that she'd wound up in the place of her first, accidental dreamwalk: the Dreamer's home, where he really did have dog-headed men as guards.

With Daghahen leading the way and Gaije close at his shoulder, the group bypassed the dog-headed guards and went toward a side portal carved into the rock wall. Kalea walked with her eyes practically squeezed shut to avoid rousing the naerscouels' attention. They smelled like dogs too, one detail she didn't remember from her dream.

They left the mingling smells of dog and decay behind when they passed under the next archway. The sound of the river babbled in the next area after several looped corridors. In this cavern, a wall gaped open to the outside and the river flowed swiftly through, under a sort of awning made by the cave. Many baskets stood around, and dingily clothed women worked hard at scrubbing fabric. When one of them looked up, Daghahen pointed a stern finger, and the woman dropped her head to make a show of hard work. At least these people posed little threat to blowing their cover.

Daghahen didn't bother speaking, but instead motioned with a finger toward a side space where a large basket of dirty clothes waited. "This is where I found your costumes," he whispered. His voice could easily be missed under the echoing rush of water through these open chambers. He pulled out garments one by one and tossed them to everyone. "Better to walk around dry in here. Replace what you need to."

He considered Kalea, fidgeting in her itchy sack, and plunged his arms into the smelly fabrics. Truly, this basket of clothes belonged on the garbage heap soon to go up in flames. He pulled out a little thing, shiny and purple with gold-colored trim. "Guess who gets to wear this."

He tossed it to Kalea. It landed at her feet followed by another piece or two, and she pouted at the pool of shiny fabrics before deciding to pick them up. It was even skimpier than the thing Chandran had made her dance in.

"At least it shouldn't irritate your skin. Hurry and change before someone sees us," Daghahen warned, and everyone turned their backs for Kalea's sake.

The skirt hung off a little beaded string from her hips in thin panels. The top didn't bother to cover much either. A measly front and back panel provided a generous view of the sides of her breasts with another string of beads to hold the panels together. Kalea crossed her arms over her chest when the men faced her again.

"Don't be embarrassed," Daghahen told her. "There will be many women dressed similarly above." He frowned and looked at the ceiling as if he could see through it. "And if Lambelhen is kingsorcerer now, there's probably many more than when I lived here. Let's go."

Kalea started to tie her washing bat back to her belt, but Daghahen snatched it away.

"Not a good idea to carry this, lass."

"Why?"

"You're a fancy girl now. Fancy girls don't wash clothes, you get it?" As she openly frowned at him, defenseless without her bat, he secured it under his robes where he stowed a bazaar of other items in his bulging pockets. "Stick close to me," he said. "You'll get this back if dire trouble happens."

The only damp things Kalea had left were the sandals Daghahen had originally brought her. She didn't see any other shoes to borrow. Without a towel to dry off more thoroughly, she walked cold and clammy through the drafty halls. Her hair clung to her nearly naked back where her top dipped low. She suspected her costume clung too close to her damp breasts, especially after she caught Del's lingering eyes at one point. She sneered at him and raised her hand. Daghahen hissed at them both and harshly gestured for her to lower her hand. She was supposed to act meek and submissive in this place.

When they went up a few more stairwells, they began to see more and more people, many of them ragged servants, but some of them red-robed sorcerers.

"You!" One such red-robe pointed to their group. Daghahen stiffened and Gaije gawked beside him. "What are you doing all the way down here?"

The whole group parted to leave Kalea feeling miles away from any of them, and at the center of attention. The accusing sorcerer stormed forward. "Shouldn't you be in rehearsal?"

At a loss for words, Kalea pointed to herself.

"Yes!" Daghahen said, scrambling to join her side. "I found her in the level below. She'd lost her costume in the laundry, and now I'm taking her to where she needs to be." He stood at her side with no room between their arms. He towered over her at his full height. Between the two red-robed people, Kalea felt small and more alone than ever. Her throat dried. Thank the Creator that Daghahen was here to speak for her.

The accusing sorcerer narrowed his eyes at Daghahen. "Do I know you?"

"Don't think so," Daghahen said quickly and loudly. He cleared his throat.

The sorcerer quirked his mouth and crossed his arms. Behind him, one of those naerscouel guards crossed the room, sniffing the air as if it drew him toward the strangers. Daghahen stiffened more than before.

"If you'll excuse me now—" he attempted.

"I *should* know you," the sorcerer said, stepping closer, "because I take roll at each ritual. What's your name, sir?"

Daghahen grabbed Kalea's wrist, hidden by his long sleeve. He pushed against her with his body. Kalea sidestepped to stay balanced, unsure what he wanted her to do. "The name's Ibex," he said quickly. "And you don't recognize me because I've been away, out doing the kingsorcerer's work in Carridax. I can't talk now."

A deep, rumbling growl started in the naerscouel's throat, and the sorcerer moved closer into their tight space. "None of your claims sound right to me."

"Do they have to?" Daghahen countered. "I'm a busy man, can't you understand?"

"You look oddly familiar," the man said.

The naerscouel's yellow eyes brightened. Its furry lips drew up to show a big set of wolfish teeth sprouting from moist, pink gums. Traces of meat from its last meal were lodged between the teeth.

Kalea couldn't tell what her friends were doing on the other side of Daghahen and the two Ilbith residents. Daghahen pushed against her again, and she took a step to accommodate. Maybe he planned to take off?

As the sorcerer opened his mouth to speak again, the naerscouel made a loud, dog-like yelp of pain. It turned around and revealed an arrow sticking out from its thick, hairy neck. Gaije stood with his bow in hand.

Daghahen growled and put a fist in the air. "I told you to leave the bow behind!"

Disregarding his scolding, Bowaen unsheathed Hathrohjilh, which he'd smuggled under his tabard and apron, and swiped it across the sorcerer—too high to sever his head, but not too high to chop off a section of his skull.

The man went down, but the naerscouel wasn't so easy to kill. It dodged Bowaen's next strike and twirled its staff to gain space. Del lunged to get out of its way. Gaije struggled to pull his next arrow from its hiding place down his cowl's neck hole.

Other men's voices began to sound in the adjoining corridors. "What's all that noise?"

Daghahen didn't give Kalea a moment to watch and see if her friends defeated the monster; he pulled her through some door. She assumed he didn't know where it would lead. He slammed the door behind them.

Chapter 61
Solemn Prayer

The light beaming down warmed Vivene. It had invited her from her trudge through the halls toward the kitchen. Her hands clasped together desperately. She didn't want to get caught, but nothing in this world could make her want to drop this pose.

"I'm so sorry," she whispered with a sob approaching. "I didn't want this to happen. None of it. I don't want to be here. I shouldn't be here. None of us should." She bowed her head, weeping under the light, feeling every bit the fool she reprimanded herself for being. "If You could just… help me. Somehow. Help me, please."

She paused to unleash a new flood of sobs. She was filthy, and felt every bit so. She wasn't worthy to even do this, to speak to…Him, but she continued anyway. "If You can do something for them, save the rest of my sisters, I'll gladly die. I'll do what I can at any cost…even if it kills me." She bowed over again. "I can't do this anymore. If I can't carry on, how can they?"

Footsteps tapped toward her, echoing sharply. She sucked in her breath with her next few words. She extended her index finger and kissed it, an old sign the novices used to do in the Hallowill convent. "Bless us all, amen," she hissed and quickly stood, wiping her tears and arranging her greasy hair to obscure her emotion.

She hurried down the hall and curtsied to the sorcerer whose footsteps had brought her prayer to an end. Outside of that beam of sunlight in the shadowy halls, the chill crept back over her.

She shook her head, wanting to believe the Creator could get her out of here, but…how? Her prayer had ended too soon. She wanted to ask Him to save Orinleah. She hadn't heard the elf woman's voice through the pipes since their last talk, and couldn't deny the illness that churned her stomach for her friend.

"Vivene!" the cook shouted when she entered the kitchen. "Where've you been? What'd you do to mess up yer high duty with the kingsorcerer's wife?" He snickered as he returned to binding up a big wad of mutton with string. The kitchen attendants around her hid their snorts and comments.

Vivene took a bold step forward. "Who's delivering her dinners now?"

Were they kind to Orinleah? The poor woman lived alone up there and needed a friend's caring words to break up her day, someone besides Lamrhath.

"None of your business. And there's nothing you can do about it if you do find out," the cook replied without raising his eyes from his work.

Vivene frowned, helpless. That strange blade Wikshen had given her… She never should've handed it to Orinleah. Vivene turned on her heel and marched toward the corridor leading to the lower levels. She'd been assigned cleaning duties in the bowels of Ilbith again since they'd caught her spending too much time in Orinleah's foyer. Way down here, she wouldn't hear her lullaby anymore, but they'd let her live. They hadn't even delivered a beating for her mischief. Vivene broke into a cold sweat whenever she thought about that. It had only been two days; just because they hadn't punished her yet didn't mean they wouldn't.

Kalea stumbled into a dark room where a sliver of light seeped through another door ahead. Daghahen's voice growled behind her, saying foreign words: a spell of some sort.

She jumped, but held in her scream when he unexpectedly snatched her hand. "That'll only hold for a few minutes," he said.

"What will?"

"I put a seal on the door to lock us in."

She worked her jaw and flailed her hands. The one he held came free. "What about my friends? They're out there!"

He shushed her and whispered, "I think they'll be fine."

"But we have to—"

"No!" His gruff voice didn't sound so warm and comforting anymore, especially in this dark space. "They brought Hathrohjilh and the other weapons I told them not to bring."

He wasn't wrong. From the sound of a slashing sword, Bowaen fought well.

Daghahen went quiet, listening too. "We'll stick to our plan," he said. "They're keeping low, and we'll work our way up. We'll find Wiksh—I mean Dorhen—Mhina, and my wife."

"Your what?" He shushed her again as a reminder and turned toward the door across the room. Kalea grabbed his red robe from behind. "You said your wife. Is Dorhen's mother alive?"

He whirled around. Kalea could see him by his silhouette. "I don't actually know if she… I'm here to find out for myself."

Kalea's mouth dropped open and she blinked. She hadn't known previously that Dorhen's father lived, and now they might also find his *mother*? Poor Dorhen thought his father had murdered his mother. What would he think by the end of this when he saw them both alive and together?

A new hope propped up Kalea's posture. So much was unfolding during this adventure. Good things, perhaps. Daghahen's prediction that Dorhen would die while trying to kill Lamrhath stayed fresh on her mind, but that was where Kalea would do whatever she could to change fate. What an amazing day it would be if they all walked out of here together: she with Dorhen, Dorhen's parents, her friends, her sisters, and Mhina!

In the next beat, Daghahen planted his ear against the door. The thin line of light highlighted the edge of his nose. "I think we're near the kitchen," he whispered. "Probably not a good idea to walk through it. We need to take side routes. Apparently, you're a dancer, so we should take sensible paths leading to places dancers typically go."

"And where would that be?"

"I've no idea. It's been a human lifetime since I lived here. They've remodeled the place, even down in these servant levels." He held his hand out to her. "No choice but to get out there and wing it until we find our loved ones."

She smiled and took his hand. He squeezed it, but let her go right after. "Remember, stay close behind me. Act meek."

When he opened the door, she tucked her chin. He walked out with a similar hidden visage. Her nerves rose the more people they encountered in the corridors, but not until they reached one particular hub flooded with other red-robed men did Kalea take on a new panic at a problem she had never anticipated: the back of Daghahen's robe matched everyone else's! Up until now, she'd focused on his tall, red form in front of her. No matter who or what they encountered, whether servants carrying heavy sacks and boxes or naerscouels sniffing at the air and patrolling around with big, ugly spears, she kept her eyes on his back. With his hair hidden under his hood, he had been just a tall, red wall to shield her from danger. Now a confusion of red-robes moved about, some mumbling softly to one another, others striding swiftly every way. Many red fish were swimming around in this bucket, and she concentrated hard on not losing a certain one.

"What have we here?" A big hand snatched her shoulder and jerked her off the path. Daghahen's particular red robe disappeared in the throng. Kalea yelped beyond her will to stay calm.

"Please!" she whined. Hopefully, Daghahen would hear her sounds and know she'd been sidetracked.

The sorcerer who'd taken interest in her pushed her against the wall and leaned into her. "Don't you have somewhere to be in an hour? What are you doing all the way down here?"

Kalea stuttered for an answer, wishing to reuse the excuse Daghahen had given earlier about tracking down her costume in the laundry room. She couldn't act as smoothly as he. Before she could offer a story, the man slipped his hand into the side of her top to squeeze her naked breast.

"She does have somewhere to be!" Daghahen's voice raked beside them. His weathered face appeared with it, his wispy blond hair hanging out of his hood in strings. "The lord sent me after her, so if you don't mind…"

The sorcerer squinted at him, as suspicious as the last one who had stopped them in their tracks. This time, they didn't have Bowaen to cut his head off.

Paying no attention to his suspicion, Daghahen yanked Kalea away as hard as any other sorcerer would have, and she gave a yelp. He kept her hand and marched away before any new conversation could spark. He didn't look back at her or bother to speak, but only huffed hard breaths out.

He chose the next empty corridor he could find, a back way that was narrower and more likely to be trod by servants. "Listen," Daghahen whispered harshly without stopping to talk. "It's not a friendly place in here. You might…see or hear things, and you might…" He huffed. "Whatever happens, remain calm. I'll do what I can to get you out of situations. If I can't…you'll survive. Got it?"

Kalea stared at his back. She guessed at what he tried to say, but didn't want to continue that thought. She preferred to dwell on the positive outcome they worked toward.

When doors began to appear along their route, Daghahen stopped to listen at them. The first two, he rejected. "Just a storeroom," he said, and peeked into the next one, only to declare that they didn't need to enter the servants' living quarters. In this quieter atmosphere, he didn't relax, but shook his head and took a few breaths more.

She reached out to touch his sleeve. "What's the matter?"

He paused to lean against the wall and cupped his face in his hands. "I haven't been here in a long while," he said on a drawn-out moan, "but I feel like I never left."

"Daghahen," she said, "you *did* leave. It will be over soon." She tugged his sleeve. "Keep going. We'll find them."

He nodded and stood tall again. "I recognize a lot of these rooms and corners." He pointed. "In that spot, there was a…" He closed his eyes, and his pronounced throat apple jumped. "I couldn't. I just couldn't live here anymore."

"It's good that your memory is so sharp," she offered. "You'll use it to our advantage, won't you?"

He didn't answer, but continued on until he found a door to another, well-lit hallway. "This one," he said. "No one's out there, and I know it leads to a main artery going straight up through the tower. The higher the better, I assume." Kalea nodded. He continued, "But I won't always keep to empty spaces. There will be more sorcerers—"

"I know, and it'll be okay." Kalea waved her hands at him. "Let's hurry."

He opened the door, and out they went into the-Creator-knew-where. All she could do was trust Daghahen's decisions. In the new hall, they walked past a woman with a bucket who scrubbed the marble floor, making lonely swishing sounds.

The scene transported Kalea back to Wikhaihli, where she had done the same chore, hoping the shamans wouldn't find Del's lock picking tools in her apron. The woman crouched over, her full figure made into a ball. Her long, dark hair hung over her face. Kalea watched in pity for as long as the scene lasted.

Daghahen went around the bend. In the last instant, before Kalea whipped her face forward again to follow him, the scrubbing woman swiped a hand across her sweaty forehead.

Kalea paused. The woman paused. Their eyes met.

Kalea cocked her head and studied her harder. "Viv—" was all she could utter.

The woman gasped, straightened her back, and then worked to her feet. "Kah-leah," she breathed the word. "Is that you?" Shock lit her face. She trailed her eyes down Kalea's scantily-clad form and back to her face.

"Vivene?" Kalea threw her arms out. "Vivene!"

Vivene's mouth hung wide open. She obviously wanted to shout Kalea's name back, but she kept herself in check. They ran into an embrace and squeezed each other until neither could breathe. Kalea found herself weeping when they pulled away, and Vivene's face glowed red and wet.

"Kalea, did they get you too? I told myself over and over they didn't." She observed her dancer's costume again.

Kalea cupped Vivene's face as if to physically hold her attention and make her understand what she'd tell her. "Vivene, no. I'm here to get you out of this place with everyone else. I've brought my friends. Understand?

You must show us where everyone is."

Vivene gasped, eyes springing to something over Kalea's shoulder. She lurched backward and bowed. Checking behind her, Kalea saw that it was only Daghahen backtracking to retrieve her.

Kalea threw her hands to Vivene's shoulders. "He's not a sorcerer!" she said. "This is Daghahen. He's helping us. He lost someone here too. You can trust him."

Vivene's shock persisted. She shifted her eyes from Kalea to Daghahen and back, and then over Kalea's outfit again.

"I found these clothes in the laundry. It's only a disguise. We have a plan."

Vivene shook physically. Her soft body jiggled.

"Don't be afraid." Kalea stepped forward to hug her again. This time, Vivene melted into her for comfort's sake, desperate for it. She smelled strongly of… It was hard to tell. She smelled like a lot of things beyond her own body odor. Servants in Ilbith didn't bathe often, Kalea realized.

"Kalea," Daghahen hissed behind her.

She pulled away. "We really have to carry on. Come with us, Vivene. We have a lot of people to rescue. There's three more of us. Bowaen is scruffy and has a big sword, Gaije is an elf with red hair, and Del is a young man with a pipe hanging off his shoulder. He's good with opening locks. He wears a headband around his brow."

Daghahen took Kalea's shoulder to urge her to move. Regardless, Vivene might be too much in shock to get her to act just yet.

When Vivene finally did open her mouth to speak, other voices rang down the hall—the confident voices of sorcerers. As if in reflex, Daghahen pulled Kalea by the hand to continue the pompous sorcerer act and make her follow. Vivene dropped back to her knees by the bucket and scrub brush.

"Wench!" one of the approaching sorcerers said, pointing his accusatory stare at Kalea. "Don't you know where you're supposed to be? Kingsorcerer Lamrhath's party starts in less than an hour."

Daghahen stiffened again. Kalea waited for his smooth excuses to flow, but only a breathy, stuttered echo of "Kingsorcerer Lamrhath" crept up his throat. She blinked up at him, and then said when he failed to deliver an answer, "I…I'm sorry."

The sorcerer eyed her up and down. "A little skinny, but you've got some luminous skin, I see. Better get up there, 'cause the kingsorcerer will notice *you* missing."

Kalea made an awkward attempt at a curtsy. "I will."

The sorcerer turned his head and made a shrill whistle with two fingers in his mouth. A set of naerscouels came stomping to meet them. Kalea shrank at Daghahen's side in the next few long seconds, and found him too frozen to do or say anything on her behalf.

"Don't let his little dancer miss her performance," the sorcerer said to the naerscouels.

Daghahen stood and watched as the towering men with big dog heads and tall, upright ears took her by each arm and marched her down the hallway. Kalea managed one more glance at Daghahen, who kept his place where he'd originally frozen, face drenched in sweat. His wide eyes stared in panic.

In the clutches of the evil beasts, Kalea moved forward alone.

Chapter 62
A Dancer Falters

When Kalea and Daghahen slipped through the door across the corridor, Bowaen poised himself with Hathrohjilh. The naerscouel who stood between them and the door shouldn't last long with an arrow lodged in its neck.

"Del! Gaije!" Bowaen barked. "Get that door open!"

The naerscouel snorted and charged, spinning its halberd at him. Bowaen had to drop his ready stance and dodge.

"Gaije! A hand?" he yelled as he collected himself. Now trapped between the creature's whooshing weapon and the stone wall, Bowaen had to choose between bolting through an unknown door to his left and hurtling over a barrel placed to his right.

Gaije struck the beast with another arrow, causing it to arch backward with a howl. Its sounds of distress would be sure to draw more enemies to their position. Bowaen took the fast chance to stab it in the gut while it was distracted.

"It won't open!" Del yelled with a curse.

"What won't?"

"The door they went through—Kalea and Dag! They locked it!"

"Bloody great!" Bowaen spat. Before he could order Del to try unlocking it, another door opened, and in rushed a stream of red-robed men.

"What's going on in—"

Bowaen sliced the man's throat before he could finish. No acting all servant-like now. The rest of them launched into a frenzy, some drawing their daggers while others began chanting spells. Gaije buried another of his arrows into one's throat to cancel the spell.

"Call for reinforcements," one sorcerer ordered a younger one in a white robe, who split down an adjoining hallway.

"Del," Bowaen called, since he stood closest to that man's route, "get him! Don't let him get away!"

Armed with his heavy fighting pipe, Del obeyed, leaving Bowaen and Gaije to take on the group.

The words rattled up Kalea's throat. "Where are you taking me?"

Asking the dog-headed men proved useless; they couldn't speak through their beastly, whiskered lips. They didn't even offer her a growl. Supporting her mostly by her armpits, they dragged her through the tower, leaving Daghahen and Vivene behind. Now on her own, she could only stare numbly as things progressed beyond her control or consent.

The naerscouels' bodies, pressed snugly to each of her sides, smelled hotly like a predictable medley of man and dog, perhaps like men with dogs' breath. Her feet mostly dangled as they took her along, sometimes dragging awkwardly. Beneath their roomy sleeves, their arms felt huge and solid, offering no chance of escape.

Many different halls, rooms, and people passed her along the way, none of them familiar. Plenty more red-robed sorcerers strolled around or contemplated by windows in any given area. None of them paid much attention to her, thankfully.

She searched for more novices and found none. She'd had barely a second to consider that she'd amazingly made contact with Vivene before they tore her away. This was happening because Daghahen had chosen a dancer's costume for her disguise. Whether it was a good or bad choice was yet to be seen.

Without a sound more significant than a sniff, the naerscouels stopped at one particular humble door and tapped on it. A weathered woman with dark, baggy eyes opened it up with an air of caution and surveyed the scene they presented. The creatures pushed Kalea through the door, practically into the woman's arms.

"Who's this now?" she asked, but the naerscouels couldn't answer her. They marched away, leaving Kalea to try to figure out what to do with this new person.

They weren't alone in the room, she realized. A load of identically dressed dancers stood in formation, each quietly practicing a handful of different motions.

The woman blinked at Kalea. "I don't know you," she said.

Kalea shrugged. "Here I am, though."

"Did they pull you from your normal chores? Can you dance at all?"

"Yes," Kalea said to the first question. "And…yes. Sort of."

The woman scoffed. "'Sort of.' You better dance well, because it'll be my head if you don't."

"They were very persistent," Kalea said, using her best act.

The woman studied her. "It's your looks they like." She raised her hand and snapped her fingers, prompting the other girls to drop their gestures. "Make room. We got one more."

When Kalea stepped into the line, the woman observed her with a look of dread. "Follow along as best you can."

For Kalea, the next few minutes were nothing but a mess of gawking, stumbling, and watching the girl next to her too closely to see how the dance went. It turned out to be similar enough to the dance Chandran had taught her, with waving arms and jiggling hips rattling up her whole form and sending her breasts bouncing every which way due to the lack of a bodice to hold them down. The other dancers wore the exact same thing, so nothing about the jiggling turned out to be wrong.

Kalea chose not to worry about this turn of events. She kept her focus on Dorhen, Vivene, and Mhina—and getting back together with her companions. Until then, she'd do whatever it took to see more of this place. There were plenty of other girls here much better at the dance than she. Maybe she'd go unnoticed.

For the next half-hour, the older woman drilled her through the specific moves. "Lean back!" the woman barked, pushing Kalea with the power of her voice into a terribly painful backbend, deeper and deeper the more she ordered. "Show them your bellybutton. Now snap your skinny little fanny muscles! Harder!"

Kalea couldn't begin to guess what she looked like in this awkward twist, which was more disgusting than Chandran's choreography—and it got worse. The next move required her to join hands with the girl at her right and perform intertwined twists with their bodies, like slithering lizards getting into a tangled dance of limbs and tails.

A knock at the door halted the practice run before Kalea had to press against the other woman's body even more.

Oh, Creator, please let it be Daghahen here to get me!

"They're ready," a man's voice—not Daghahen's—grunted from outside the door.

The older woman peeked out of it, keeping him from seeing the dancers. "We may need more time," she said.

"Don't care. Just bring 'em in. The feast has begun."

Kalea's stomach dropped at those words. *It's not over yet,* she thought. *Daghahen might intercept our course.* She told herself similar things all the way through the tower, up several staircases, and through bigger, brighter halls with sculpted arches and windows. They must be entering an elite area of Ilbith.

The next door led into a recessed area with no windows; only a few candles and colored magical flames danced in braziers to illuminate this nested lounge. A long, cushioned couch stretched along the wall, packed with men in red and purple robes. Other women, dressed similarly to the dancers, moved about, pouring wine and serving dainty dishes of food. Some men were already drunk and slouching in their seats. Others kept a business-like mien, straight-faced as they murmured to each other in short, to-the-point sentences. Their soft conversations over the pleasant melody of a single harp kept the atmosphere comfortable.

From the center of the line of dancers, Kalea stretched her neck to take in all she could in the few short moments before her performance began. At the back of the room, a grand canopy on a dais rose above everything else. The presentation reminded her of Wikshen's throne, but slightly lesser. This cozy space couldn't allow a throne such as his.

She checked the servant women who moved about in their skimpy, beaded brassieres and skirts. One of them struck her as familiar. She squinted until their eyes met. The other woman brightened into a surprised stare, but it quickly withered to dread.

"I know you…" Kalea said. "Millie?"

"Kalea," Millie whispered back.

Kalea openly stared at her until Millie turned around and hurried away to refill someone else's cup. Kalea studied her turned back. Her bare legs showed long and sleek—sinewy. Throughout the pouring of wine from her pitcher to the man's cup, he reached out to run his hand up the back of one leg and beyond, under her short skirt. The girl didn't flinch at his touch as Kalea would have. Millie had been shaped into a voluptuous new beauty a world different from Kalea's convent memories. After only a few months since the raid, the poor girl looked ten years older. She was only seventeen, younger than Kalea! What had they done to her sisters?

Kalea could hardly continue her thought before the harp playing shifted to a new song and the other dancers took position. Kalea moved a beat later than everyone else. A dizziness of nerves and dread washed over her. What were those moves again?

The dance started simply enough for her not to stumble: they all joined hands and walked, facing outward, in a circle around the room. When Kalea did her pass by the grand seat at the back, she could better see who sat there. She squinted in the dim ambient light. It was a blond man dressed slightly different from the rest, without the usual red robe. This one lounged in greater relaxation too, leaning against a beautiful woman. Another woman was bowing over his lap—she couldn't tell why, but his eyes were glazed and he paid no attention to the dancers. He leaned his head over and touched the beautiful woman's chin with his two fingers, prompting her to kiss him deeply, without a care for all the other people in the room who could see them. The indecent public behavior was enough to light Kalea's stomach in a strange way.

The dance progressed to the more intricate arrangement she dreaded. As before, she held her eyes constantly on the girl next to her to keep up with the moves. Jiggle the hips. Lean back. Far back. At least she'd done this recently enough to remember the dance mistress's barked orders.

But Kalea found herself falling! She gasped. Stumbled. A dancer caught her under the arms from behind. "You little bitch," she hissed. "Keep your feet!"

"Sorry." Kalea did her best to get back into the rhythm. If only Daghahen would come in and find her somehow.

The sorcerers who saw her mistake chuckled and gulped their drinks. They turned out to be quite aggressive, regardless of the dancers' need to concentrate. The dancers moved again in a circle to the right; Kalea made the first step long after everyone else. She knew she performed this dance like a mule in a bank of swans.

The sorcerers ogled and groped and laughed and tossed their alcohol all the way back as Kalea made the round. When she shimmied back around to the grand canopied seat and the blond man with his female companions, he was gasping with his eyes closed, half-lying on the beautiful woman's lap. The other woman who leaned over him reared her head back to slide her mouth off of some tall thing, as if regurgitating what Kalea finally noticed was his penis!

She shut her eyes to avoid seeing more of that ugly sight, and soon her circle's rotation pushed her onward to a view of more sorcerers, one now kissing and groping Millie as she sat on his lap, holding her pitcher with an air of helplessness. Their eyes met for another instant.

The part of the dance came for one of those intertwined poses with another dancer, which meant hoisting her leg high and wrapping it around the girl's waist while her partner did some twists and flourishes of her own. Grossly unprepared despite her practice, Kalea wobbled and swayed on one foot. Instead of embracing her partner, she clung to her to keep from falling, earning a growl from the other girl.

"Sorry," Kalea mumbled again, but the laughter drew her attention to the wall of men who mocked and pointed—at her.

"Dear Naerezek, she's terrible!" one said, and slapped his knee, spilling half his drink on Millie.

"Is she even a dancer?"

"I've never seen that one before."

"Well, I would've remembered her—and stuck her a few times with my cock if I'd seen her before."

"She is a nice-looking one, isn't she?"

"Shut up!"

The whole room fell silent at the strong voice. The blond man now stood at the edge of the dais, fastening his pants. He was a tall, bright figure who drew the eyes and commanded respect.

Kalea cocked her head and squinted at him. A bizarre familiarity struck her. "Daghahen…" The whisper slid through her lips before she could think to keep them sealed.

"What did you say?" The blond man descended, causing everyone to bend backward like grass in a strong wind as he moved through the room, dancers included. But not Kalea. Her head emptied of what to do now.

"What did you call me?" His approach revealed he wasn't a man, but an elf instead, with yellow-blond hair shining along its waves in the light. Golden eyes, glowing within his sockets like a cat's at night, brightened as they settled on her. Kalea stood frozen under his looming form.

"Nothing," she said in answer to his question. This wasn't Daghahen. Daghahen always expressed a hint of warmth in his eyes and radiating off his being. This person emanated only coldness. He also boasted fuller hair, smoother skin, and command of all these people.

The other dancers edged away, leaving her with the intimidating elf in their own wide space. He took Kalea by the chin, his hand strong, his fingernails long. "You look familiar. From where do I know you?"

Kalea pulled in her lips, and he pressed his fingers deeper into her cheeks until it hurt and her lips popped back out. Rather than waiting another moment for her answer, he moved his hand into her hair and grasped it to tilt her head.

"You look so…fresh." He studied her closer in the next instant, now breathing through his mouth. "How do you do it?"

"Do what?" she countered. At her question, all the people around them winced.

"Keep yourself looking so radiant?" He closed his teeth, but kept his lips parted as he took it upon himself to run his thumb across her mouth. The act felt vaguely familiar. His lips tightened into something closer to a smile.

"Wait." A short breath, almost a laugh, burst out of him. "You came." A new flood of personality lit his face, eyes focused, lips tight, teeth glistening. "You've arrived. Did the sanguinesents bring you?"

Kalea sucked in a breath. It hit her too. "Are you…the Dreamer?"

He eyed her up and down. Indeed, he was the frightening elf in her dream who had cast a spell to help her escape Valltalhiss. Somehow, fate had brought her to him. Her mouth dropped open in astonishment. All of it pieced together: Dorhen was here, Dorhen's father had brought her here, and Dorhen's father resembled this person to an extreme—they must be twins. All of the coincidences settled in as related facts. But how?

Daghahen's voice rang in her memory, *Hathrohjilh is the only weapon that can kill Lambelhen. ... I later learned my son would do it, which was why he became Wikshen.*

Daghahen had spoken of a thing called the law of synchronicity, and that nothing was random. The world moved in rhythm. Staring into the animalistic glow of this elf's eyes, she no longer feared for Dorhen's fate.

"I'm here," she whispered. She nodded her head as a reassurance to herself. She was here because Arius Medallus had sent her.

"Yes, you are."

She had come here to help Dorhen. He would supposedly kill this person, the kingsorcerer, and the fact that she had gotten caught up in all this "synchronicity" was proof that her support would keep him alive. She alone had come to save Dorhen. Kalea smiled.

Left out of her thought process, "Lambelhen" smiled to match her. "I'm pleased too," he said. He took her by the arm and led her over to one of the red-robed sorcerers. "Take her to the north wall conference chamber and make sure she can't leave it."

"Yes, my lord." The sorcerer bowed to the blond elf, took Kalea's arm, and forced her to walk with him toward the door.

"We'll talk in a few minutes," the kingsorcerer's voice echoed behind her before the door closed.

He had lost Kalea. Daghahen dabbed the nervous sweat off his brow. They had taken her to... They had taken her... He couldn't even think about it. Maybe she would be fine. She would survive, as he'd told her.

In a shady corner, he took down his hood, gathered his messy hair up tight, and tucked it down into his collar. He replaced the hood. If *he* saw it—Lamrhath—he'd recognize him. Daghahen couldn't have that. He couldn't take any chances. That's why he'd chosen to go up without her. He just needed to find Orinleah fast and go from there.

His nervous sweating didn't let up, especially when he found the Chimera Tower. It had changed the most, from the full-blown structure remodeling to the shiny new marble floor tiles. This wing was bright and immaculate...and somehow more uncomfortable than ever before.

He slipped into a servants' closet and took off his red robe. Beneath, he wore his old tan hides. He balled up his sorcerer's robe and stuffed it into his bag. Concealing all color was vital to casting Gariott's Blend. The invisibility it granted was vital to doing his next set of tasks.

Under the security of his low-grade invisibility spell, Daghahen approached the first door that looked important. Anyone's guess was as good as his when it came to locating clues to Orinleah's whereabouts. He took out a valuable trinket he'd held onto all these years: the tower's skeleton key. He inserted it into the slot and tried to turn it.

A tiny hum gave him a warning, and he knew to throw himself away from the door, landing on his backside. The little shock still managed to snap his hand, but he might've died if he'd kept contact with the key.

"I should've known," he whispered. The key fit. Understandably, the sorcerers had reused many of the tower's old locks in the restoration, but had added the security of a deadly ward. This tower's residents would each have a special key to bypass the wards. Thankfully, Daghahen knew enough sorcery to dispel them.

He placed his hands on the wood surrounding the lock. Touching the metal would be a mistake. He worked up the nerve to whisper some of Ingnet's favorite words, since Ingnet was one of Ilbith's five patron pettygods and most likely the one who owned these wards. Good thing Daghahen had gained that pixie's ear long ago when he had obsessively studied to catch up to his brother's vast ability. Naerezek had always refused to hear him out, for he'd always hated Daghahen and loved Lambelhen.

Success. The ward's hum faded away. Daghahen fell backward and groaned. Sorcery, a terrible magical practice. It sucked his energy away— as if Ingnet drank his blood in return for performing the spell for him. Daghahen owed the pixie for it.

All the sorcerers owed their pettygods for the spells they cast, so they took it from the innocent and gave more and more to the powerful pixies. This was what had withered Daghahen's face into its current elderly state. Other sorcerers stacked spells upon spells upon practice upon offerings upon rituals to keep their lives in motion: to stay young, energetic, rested, healthy—all on top of performing their extraordinary, ambitious spells. To be a sorcerer, one had to love oneself first, foremost, and forever.

Daghahen dragged himself up and turned the key, which was now free of electricity. An office. He made quick work of rifling through it. Nothing. He'd be using much more sorcery to get into many more doors throughout today. If he could help it, once he got out of here with his wife, he'd never use that soul-eating magic again.

Chapter 63
Rattled Tower

Vivene was left staring after Kalea's departure next to the tall sorcerer with whom Kalea had associated herself. As confused as she'd ever been on a day in Ilbith, Vivene inched away before he decided to turn and notice her. Kalea might've labeled him a friend, but he had still stood idly and let her be hauled away.

As soon as Vivene reached the corner at the end of the hall, she bolted. The farther she ran, the more she disbelieved she'd seen Kalea at all. She'd inhaled the stench of the Grave to the point of poisoning her brain. If only it were real. However, Wikshen had told her...

Her panic certainly was real, though. She couldn't guess where to run. If that tall sorcerer believed she'd broken some rule, she would feel a big hurt later when they found her. *Oh Creator, don't let them suspect me of anything! I didn't do anything!* She must have hallucinated in that moment, which couldn't be a crime.

She ran straight down to the kitchen. She'd take up her chores and act like nothing had happened. When she burst through its door, she bent over to catch her breath. To her side, under a long, wooden table along the wall, a young man hid. She grimaced down at this person she'd never seen before.

"What are you up to?" she whispered.

He put his finger to his lips, eyes desperately wide, and shook his head.

Across the way, a set of double doors flung open and banged the walls on either side. Two naerscouels stormed in, necks arched with hair standing up in hostility. They growled with bared teeth. Vivene found herself falling shortly to the side to lean her hip against the table and hide the young man beneath it. The naerscouels gave the cook a fright; he yelped and knocked over a bowl of flour.

"Damn ye, mutts!" He flung his hat at one of their canine faces defiantly.

The creature snapped its jaws at him in return before resuming its search. They both sniffed the air and soon found themselves sneezing uncontrollably in the cloud of airborne flour. The two angry creatures pushed on, circling the room, sniffing in every corner and making big sneezes.

Vivene kept her ass against the edge of the table, allowing her skirt to cover the hiding man. When the naerscouels made their way to her side of the wide kitchen, she took a page from the cook and pretended to accidentally knock over an open jar of pepper, flinging a handful in the air and dusting her hands. This made the naerscouels blast more roaring sneezes through their snouts uncontrollably and hurry to exit through the door she'd entered.

"What in Kullixaxuss are they riled up about?" the cook yelled. "Get over here and sweep this up, woman!"

Before hopping to obey, Vivene gave the hiding man a look with a pointed finger, signaling for him to wait. She took her apron off and threw it over his section of the table. After she cleaned up the cook's floury mess, she made eye contact with the stranger again and waited until the cook turned his back. She opened the door, waved for the man to go out, and followed behind him.

"No, no, this way! Come here," she told the man before he ran down a hallway that would lead him to the lower-level sorcerers' dining hall. He obviously didn't know his way around.

She tugged his sleeve, and he followed her into an alcove outside the kitchen door where they stored extra aprons and hats on hooks. "I've never seen you before. What's going on?"

He leaned against the wall in the shadow, panting as if he needed to process what he'd been through. "Can't talk…"

She crossed her arms and widened her stance to make sure he wouldn't dart away. "Well, you'd better talk. You don't just get those naerscouels chasing you all around for no reas…" She trailed off as she observed his headband. Kalea—if she really had seen Kalea—had described a person with a headband. He also carried a large metal smoking pipe like she'd described. "You're not actually a servant here, are you?"

The young man responded with a panicked look on his face.

"Do you know Kalea?" Vivene asked bluntly.

He jumped away from the wall to face her squarely. "You do?"

"What's your name?"

"Del."

A chill rushed through Vivene's being. It sounded like the name Kalea had quoted! "Oh, dear Creator, I didn't imagine it! You're here with Kalea?"

"Yeah. Where is she? And Daghahen?"

That name also sounded familiar. Vivene's heart fluttered. It wasn't an illusion! Kalea had come here with some people to rescue her!

Vivene cupped her hands over her mouth. She didn't know whether to yell with glee or vomit. She couldn't yell—too dangerous. In fact, having an intruder here could be a deadly situation, but she couldn't give him away. This might be her chance to...! She couldn't even think what might happen! But she could try.

She reached over and pulled the headband off his head to let his greasy hair down around his eyes. He lurched in panic at her action and dropped something that clattered against the stone floor: long metal tools of silver and bronze. He watched her in shock as she picked one up.

"A lock picking tool?"

He didn't make any indication if she'd guessed right, but he didn't have to. He probably didn't know if he could trust her, but she couldn't dally long enough to make his acquaintance for comfort's sake. With his headband off, she grabbed one of the spare wool hats off the wall and shoved it over his head. Falling into a squat, she wiped her hands on the floor to pick up its thick dusting of soot and grime. She smudged his face all up with it to make him blend in better with the soiled, run-of-the-mill Ilbith servants.

"That's better," she said, stepping back to observe her work. "Follow my lead. Get your things hidden." He scrambled to collect all his thieving implements and rolled them up in their knitting needle pouch. "We've got a lot of people to free."

The "north wall conference room" was something close enough to what Kalea imagined: a moderately sized space with a rounded outer wall. One big window allowed indirect sunshine to seep in and reflect off the pale stones, bathing the whole room in soft, cool light. They were quite high up in the tower; outside, clouds drifted by *under* the window, if not at the window's level. "Interrogation room" would be a better name for it. A set of curved benches placed at three different levels focused on one chair at the back of the room, which had leather straps hanging off it. Would Kalea be facing a room full of sorcerers today?

"Sit," the sorcerer ordered her, and then he pushed her down into it. Kalea couldn't find precise enough thinking to struggle. Now alone, she hadn't a clue where she should go or what she should do to find Dorhen and help her friends, let alone escape her own captor. The sorcerer tightened the belts over her wrists on the chair's arms, and she didn't even offer to struggle in her fear.

The door swung open behind him as he finished securing her second wrist. He didn't bother with the ankle or torso straps, thankfully. The kingsorcerer hadn't wasted much time in following after he sent her here.

"My lord," his subordinate said with a half bow, "I'll go and alert—"

"Don't bother," the blond elf said. He pushed the sorcerer aside with a firm hand to his chest. "I want to be alone. Fetch whoever you want, but make them wait outside."

"Yes, my lord."

The kingsorcerer hurried up the long rug behind the sorcerer to lock the door after him. Kalea swallowed, watching these events. Now alone with him, her numb confusion melted into nervous fear. When he turned from the door, he slowed all his gestures, taking a long moment to look at her before striding back down the tiered floor to her central interrogation chair.

"What are you going to do with me?" Kalea peeped.

His lips curled into a grin as he stopped to view her closer. "Many things." His shining hair cascaded over his shoulders like a heavy hood, extending into the triangular shape made by his cloak. He kept his hand tucked into one pocket of his cloak while the other ignored the armhole, hidden from view. Under that, he wore a dark-maroon shirt with long sleeves bound with crisscrossing gold chains around the forearms, and a tight pair of leggings with leather sections sewn around the thighs and calves. Pointed gold claws tipped his black leather boots.

"We have much to talk about," he said, ending Kalea's study of his rich adornments. He pulled up an extra chair from the corner and turned it around to sit and cross his arms over its back. "So, you're the little starling I've been dreaming about," he began, staring hard at her.

She blinked her eyes, suddenly feeling vulnerable in her helpless position and loose, open outfit. Her nerves set off faster knowing he had caught her speaking Daghahen's name in the lounge. She'd probably blown his cover. If this elf knew she'd come here with him, he'd have the whole tower turned upside-down and all of her friends would be caught.

"Where do we start?" he said, still grinning.

Kalea waited. It was amazing how much like Daghahen he really appeared. Daghahen's baggy skin and blue eyes easily set them apart, but otherwise they could be the same person—discounting personality, of course.

"So, you escaped from the heart-eaters' hive, I see."

Kalea nodded her head rapidly. "I did, thanks to you."

He spread his hands from their interlaced pose. "And you escaped… untouched?"

"Yes," she said, pasting a false pleasant expression on her face. "I am glad."

He smirked. "So am I. I'd hoped to get you here in your purest form."

"May I ask why, sir?"

"I'm the kingsorcerer, and my name is Lamrhath, but you will call me 'my lord.'"

"May I ask why, my lord?"

"No." He chuckled. "Only the elite are allowed to ask questions in Ilbith."

Kalea burst out a loud, nervous laugh. She couldn't stop it and couldn't figure out why she was having so much trouble keeping calm and reserved. That first sorcerer had been a little lamb compared to this person and his ill-feeling presence.

"Actually," he continued, "perhaps I'll let you ask a few questions... but after I'm finished with you."

"Finished with me?" Once again, her voice burst out shrill and shaky—and she'd asked a question, she realized.

Lamrhath closed his lips and gave her a simpler smile, as if waiting for her to shut up. "So, the sanguinesents *did* bring you?"

"Yes, my lord, he did." She said it a little too quickly.

"'He,'" Lamrhath repeated. "As in that single one I sent to Valltalhiss to retrieve you?"

"Yes sir,"

"Hmm." He played his fingers along the rough wood grain of his simple chair. "That's odd."

"Why, my lord?"

"You keep asking questions," he pointed out.

Kalea clamped her mouth shut.

He continued, "It's odd because I happen to know that that particular sanguinesent has passed back into Kullixaxuss. Apparently, someone dislodged its eyes." Kalea sucked in a breath and held it. "Did you defeat it?"

She shook her head, knowing she wouldn't be able to keep up any lie about fighting a sanguinesent.

"Don't be afraid," he said. "Answer my questions honestly. I want to know all about you. Who defeated the sanguinesent?"

"Wikshen did."

Lamrhath nodded. His smile faded into something straddling blankness and the warmth he'd been trying to uphold. "Wikshen did," he repeated. "Makes sense enough. The fact that you know this must mean you were there when it happened. You're friends with Wikshen, aren't you?"

Kalea nodded, unsure if she should say anything about this matter. "Has he touched you?"

His question reeled Kalea's jitters back in full. She shook her head to answer an honest "no," but not before her memory played back her writhing in ecstasy and Dorhen fighting himself to keep from giving in to her pleas. Kalea closed her eyes and savored the memory. When she opened them again, she found her knees spread wide and Lamrhath observing her pose. She snapped them back together.

"What are you doing now?"

Her heart pounded. "Nothing. I haven't been touched—you wanted to know. I haven't."

He kept his eyes on her as he rose from his seat and turned to the door. "You're a little high-strung," he said on his way back up the sloped floor. He turned the key in the door and stuck his head out to whisper to whoever waited outside, and then resumed his seat as before. "Tell me about your Luschianism."

Kalea shook her head and shrugged. "I know nothing about it. It allows me to dreamwalk, and that's where I met you." He eyed her, waiting for more. "That's all I know," she reiterated.

"How could you not know?"

"Why should I know? The way it happened was I got poisoned, passed out from the illness, and accidentally found your dream. Before that, I was oblivious. Maybe *you* should tell me what it means to be a Luschian!"

He narrowed his eyes at her, and his attempt at being warm and pleasant washed away. "All I know is what folktales have told," he said. "It's believed that a pixie named Lusche picked out babies in their cribs and endowed them with special powers."

She repeated the words in a whisper, "Picked out babies in their cribs... So I *am* human, then?"

His grin returned. "You thought you weren't human? If the crib myth is correct, I think it means you haven't lost your humanity, only gained a magnificent ability."

A tap at the door stopped his progression. He hurried and opened it only a crack, slid his hand through, and brought in a bottle from whoever had tapped. He closed and locked the door up tight. This time, he pocketed the key rather than leaving it in the lock.

"Do I really need to be strapped down like this?" Kalea asked nervously as he returned bearing the bottle of mystery drink.

"Yes." Instead of reclaiming his seat, he hovered over her and pulled the cork out of the bottle with his teeth. He tilted her head up. "Drink this."

"What is it?"

"Just rum. Drink it."

"Why?" She dodged his hand so he couldn't grab her chin, which only made him frown. His displeasure proved much scarier than his blankness.

"It'll relax you! Maybe if you drink, I *will* undo your buckles."

Instead, she squirmed in her seat and squealed until he held her so tight it probably bruised her cheeks. He put the bottle between her lips and tipped it straight up. The strong liquid poured down her neck, chest, and beyond, and much of it flooded her mouth. Enough of it got down her throat and burned like fire.

"If you don't shut up and drink some like a good girl, I'll have them bring the hookah and get you flying through fairyland!"

When she didn't stop squirming or squealing, he reared his hand back and slapped her face. Kalea wailed.

Dorhen perked up at the odd sounds scraping at the outer bounds of his consciousness. The burning roved over him. Closing his eyes didn't spare them from the bright light. Opening them made it so much worse, though.

"Aaaiiiiii!" A sound so shrill and sharp echoed as if in a metal container. Similar sounds had nagged him for days, but now it echoed louder.

He made a new effort to move. He'd been bound to the big chair so long he'd forgotten his arms and legs. The thin leather strips cut into them, so they probably didn't receive blood anymore.

"No, please! I don't want to!"

He gasped at the female voice. He didn't like it. It... It... It had to stop. She was suffering, and he couldn't let the abomination go on! He opened his mouth and tried to speak. Only dry air emerged at first. He tried to moisten his throat, and it helped little. He rounded his lips. "W..."

He growled when another feminine scream echoed through the metal space. "Wik," he managed to say. He could only finish in his head, *Where are you, bastard?* Wik couldn't communicate thanks to all the damned candles and hot sunshine through the windows, but he lurked somewhere deep inside.

Dorhen relaxed against the chair, weak, exhausted, and... Something happened in his body. With the next whimper that rattled up the metal pipe, it spiked in his abdomen. His cock stirred. The feminine scream gave him a certain amount of…excitement.

Roughed up, drenched with alcohol, and growing tired, Kalea gave up, took the bottle between her lips and gulped down a good amount of the awful-tasting brew.

Lamrhath was seething by now. He took the bottle away with only a little left in it and threw it against the wall with a loud shatter. He squeezed her face. "Now, was that hard?" he demanded, took a breath, and dropped into the chair for a moment's respite.

Kalea panted with her eyes closed, no longer wanting to see him. If they would throw her into a cold cell, she'd like it better. The rum boiled in her stomach. It made her feel more sick than relaxed. She wasn't used to drinking so much concentrated alcohol. The convent's wine was watered down for propriety, and she never partook very much of the ale served at the inns she visited with her friends. She moaned out her grief. She did it again. And again.

"Now what's the matter?"

When she opened her eyes, the room seemed shadier, as if a cloud was passing right over the window, but she couldn't twist around enough to see for sure. Lamrhath watched her with interest.

"I feel different," she said, and leaned her head back. She let her knees fall open wide.

"It's the rum," he told her, and she shook her head in disagreement.

Dorhen panted for a new reason. His energy built enough for him to sit up and open his eyes. His cock stood up straight and tall, making a tent-like formation under his battleshift.

Aggression. He wanted to break something—maybe someone's face. His voice returned. The candles dimmed under a growing haze of greasy darkness, the one with a life of its own that tended to follow him around. It shaded him from the uncomfortable heat. It restored him

He pushed against his bonds, making them creak and groan. The first of many snapped.

"What's wrong with you?" Lamrhath demanded, leaning forward in his chair. "Describe what you're feeling."

Kalea panted, her chest rising and falling deeply. Her thin top clung to her wet breasts. She could hardly care how exposed she was, not when she felt so…naughty. Another ecstasy had hit, but she couldn't tell him. She didn't want him to know, but she could hardly help her behavior when her intimate area throbbed—it ached! Her thighs trembled. She needed…

She opened her lips to utter the word, "Please."

"Please what?" Lamrhath rose halfway from his seat. He darted his eyes up and down her form, often slowing over her breasts. "What do you need?"

He must've received his answer when she let out a long moan and widened her knees as far as the chair allowed. He reached out to push aside her slit skirt. He fell off his chair to his knees before her. He smelled the air.

"You're…" He unsheathed a small knife from under his cloak to cut open her undergarment and expose her private area. "Flush," he finished, and breathed heavily.

He lurched backward and crawled away on his elbows. "No," he said. "I can't!" He curled over and covered his face like a scared child.

His behavior almost distracted Kalea from her turbulent arousal, but her ecstasy trumped her brainpower at the moment. Every time she opened her mouth to speak, she screamed in need instead. Her voice rang off the walls, but she hardly cared.

"Please," she heard herself say. She stretched out her fingers toward Lamrhath. "Come here."

He moved his hand to peek at her, his face wan and sweaty. He reared up on an elbow and shook his head. "I shouldn't. You're too valuable as you are, don't you see? No." He worked up to his knees and onto his feet, and then limped up the carpet between the benches to the door. "I have to get out of here."

He stopped and turned to look at her again. Apparently, his self-control wasn't much to boast about. His eyes glowed, wild and vacant. He came back limping, bent forward as if to guard his genitals.

Sweat rolled down the side of Kalea's face. She held his eye contact and her legs wide as if to pull him by a mental lasso, and back he ventured.

"When I do this, you'll lose it all," he said. Yet still he approached. "I have to keep you pure so you can perform great feats for Ilbith." He drew closer. "I should go back to my room instead, to soothe my ailment."

Nothing he said mattered. He dropped down before her, his face level with her crotch, and he breathed her into his lungs as if to gladly replace oxygen with her feminine essence. "It hurts so much," he said.

Kalea caught a tear rolling down his face, but couldn't take a lick of interest in anything outside of her body—except perhaps a kind soul who could fill her emptiness. "Please," she whimpered, "I need…"

He considered her face for the moment. "So do I." Beyond her line of sight, he reached down and worked at something she knew must be his clothing. He was releasing *it* from its entrapment. Kalea could feel her own moisture building between her legs in anticipation.

"You're practically dripping," he reported from his direct view. For once, the expression on his face seemed honest. He was allowing her a glimpse of himself as a real person, the side of him who had feelings and fears and needs.

"When I do this," he said, "I hope you will heal me. For good. Maybe your power is strong enough to…end my suffering." He panted out every word. Before proceeding, he tore off his cloak and spread it on the floor. He threw his shaking hands to one of her wrist restraints and unbuckled it.

Kalea could stand the waiting no longer. She put her leg up around his head and drew it into her. For one quick second, his lips kissed hers— her *other* lips. Both of them cried out with desire. He licked his lips greedily, but otherwise resisted her distraction and unfastened her other buckle.

She slid off the chair, and he caught her. To the floor, they rolled together and couldn't even make it to the cloak bed he'd created. He struggled again with his codpiece to throw it off and have it out of the way.

In that agonizing wait, the door crashed open, splitting into several large, jagged pieces, and a heavy black smoke spilled in and crawled along the walls on either side. From inside the black miasma, a figure leaped through the air and put a foot down on the first bench, blue hair tumbling down its shoulders after the abrupt stop.

"Dorhen!" Kalea said from under Lamrhath's shaking body, too weak to do more.

Dorhen lunged across each tier of bench to the bottom level, where he ripped Lamrhath off of her and threw him against the wall. The blond elf roared and crumpled to the floor.

"Snap out of it!" Dorhen ordered as he pulled Kalea upright. She flopped in his arms like a doll and rested her head against his chest.

"Please," she whimpered weakly, and reached up to touch his chin.

A soft glow enveloped Lamrhath's body. It propped him up so he could stand. His lips moved and his breath put out syllables. The word "Naerezek" was the most audible.

"You gotta stand on your own," Dorhen growled to her. He patted her face. His prodding helped, even though his own essence fed her state of mind. The miasma kept to the walls for now, dimming the light from the window, which helped Wikshen stay energized.

Trying to take his advice, Kalea shifted to stand on her own. Wikshen's bare feet absorbing minerals from the flagstones made them crumble and crack, and to make things worse, Kalea's legs shook like a newborn deer when she tried to stand.

"Ah, yes," Lamrhath rasped as Kalea began to make her attempt to wobble away from the impending violence. "I almost forgot. You're his woman, aren't you?" He made a menacing grin at them both. "'Dorhen and Kalea.' Has a nice ring to it. How could I possibly think to step between a *saehgahn* and his deified bonded female?"

Kalea looked over at Dorhen, who kept his attention trained on Lamrhath. His toes tightened and loosened on the stone floor as the little cracks under his feet grew and branched. He let Lamrhath talk to bide his time. Morkblades would be flying soon.

Lamrhath shook his head at his own words and extended his index finger. "Hold on, not a *saehgahn* at all. You're Wikshen!" He pointed to Kalea. "And I guess that makes you his dreadwitch!"

Something about his statement stung. Kalea's ecstatic state let up a little more. Her mind began the slow process of clearing away the hazy cloud of drifting, erotic thoughts, particularly the one where she thought Lamrhath would be a good candidate for her relief.

"Wha…?" she replied.

"Don't listen to him!" Dorhen barked while holding his attention on Lamrhath's every movement. He burst into action, shouting, "Get back, Kalea!" Spreading his stance, he waved his arms in that fluid dance she'd seen him perform in the caves under Hathrohskog.

Lamrhath acted before he could muster the first morkblade. He shot forward with an inhuman, wolf-like howl erupting from his throat. Within the pink glow surrounding him, his hands reached forward beyond their normal shape and became claws that raked down Dorhen's bare chest.

Unable to clear the claws' reach completely, Dorhen dropped to his back and let Lamrhath's momentum rush over him. He grabbed his uncle's ankles while he lay on the floor and yanked them up to make Lamrhath topple forward. His big, wolf-like arms crossed before his face on impact.

In the same beat, the rest of his body shifted in the blink of an eye to some sleek animal form and then back to humanoid, causing Dorhen to lose his grip on Lamrhath's ankles when his animal feet slipped out of his boots. Dorhen threw each one at his opponent's head as a distraction while taking the moment to remind Kalea to vacate the room.

She hurried up the steps and stopped at the wrecked door—the second door Dorhen had broken to fight sorcerers for her. From there, she watched the fight, battling her own mind to ignore the ecstasy and think of a way to help him. He continued absorbing minerals from the floor stones, and they crumbled under each step he took.

Kalea gasped and stared as the floor opened up in a thunderous crash and a huge plume of dust. She trotted back down the steps, using what limited strength her ecstatic state afforded, but the huge cloud of rocky dust obscured her view. Sounds of the two males struggling on the floor below echoed up. Dorhen yelled in anger, and Lamrhath yelled back with a beastly echo behind his voice.

The slow-moving dust cloud persisted, leaving Kalea with the decision to wait and see if she could jump down and be with Dorhen, or take her chances in finding her way down to him.

Bowaen stood with Gaije in a room of fast-flowing blood. Combining their skills with Hathrohjilh and Leho's Bow, they'd cleared the space of every sorcerer before the first quick spell had been cast, and Del hadn't even returned yet. Bowaen couldn't help but meet Gaije's attention with a smirk.

Gaije didn't share his amusement. "The elder elf said Mhina might be on a higher floor," he said, turning to consider the nearest corridor. "Look for stairs."

"Hold on, wait a minute now!" Bowaen barked. "What about Del?"

The last he'd seen of his long-time friend and apprentice, the boy was launching off to stop a sorcerer from getting help. Bowaen shifted on his heel and pointed in the opposite direction from the one Gaije favored. "He went through this corridor, I think." He had gotten too disoriented during fighting to remember well.

Gaije threw up his hands. "I don't care. Just find me some stairs going up."

Bowaen shook his head in doubt as to which corridor Del had actually used; there were three corridor mouths and five doors.

"Hurry!" Gaije said, and Bowaen picked one.

"Anyone's guess is as good as mine," he said. "Either way, we can't be found in all this carnage." He tucked his tabard tightly over his sheathed sword to make sure no one would spot it. "C'mon."

"Where the hell're you taking me?" Del asked as Vivene led him through the hallways up the tall, curved tower. "I'm supposed to stick to the lower floors to look for novices."

"You've found me. The other novices will be fine for a few minutes. How good are you with those thieving tools?"

Del snorted in reply. "Look, dame, I don't want to get caught doing your petty mischief."

"Then make quick work of it." She cast a glance over her shoulder to see his unreadable face. "How do you know Kalea?"

Del huffed behind her. "She made friends with my master. She's a loon we met on the road."

"On the road?"

"Of course, she ambushed him in a tavern. Now we're in the Darklands." Del's tone lost all its life while talking about Kalea.

"She came here to save us, her sisters."

"You're one of those novices, huh?" he asked.

"Yes… Well, not anymore, actually."

"I gotta tell you something about that girl, though," Del added.

"You mean Kalea?"

"Yeah." Del cleared his throat. "I don't know how much it is you and your friends who brought her here…or Wikshen."

Vivene froze in her step. She turned around to face him. "Wikshen?"

Del held his unamused countenance. "She's bewitched by him. Downright enthralled, actually."

Vivene blinked. "The fact is, she's here and she brought along allies." She turned back around to continue walking but hesitated. "It's not surprising," she said. "I've suspected that he—Wikshen—used to be the elf who broke into our convent."

"You too, then?" In two quick steps, Del caught up beside her. "None of us—Bowaen, Gaije, or me—none of us believed it. Dag says otherwise. He—Wikshen—in fact, made her into a Wikshonite. He cast a hard spell on her."

"I think," Vivene replied, "he cast it long before all this mess. He *is* the elf from the convent. Maybe the formula I'm seeing with all these events is just what we need to get out of here."

"Now you're talking like that senile old elf," he grumbled, and shut up when footsteps shuffling toward them made Vivene spring to throw her hand over his mouth.

She pushed him into a sculpted nook in the wall, and they waited a few seconds. It didn't sound like the clawed feet of a naerscouel; if it was, they'd be found in a sniff. Maybe she should've smeared scrap cheese on him to prevent whatever smells of the outside he wore from alerting the creatures' keen noses. Too late now.

The person who passed their nook turned out to be a servant. "Millie?" Vivene hissed. "What are you doing here at this time?"

Millie shifted her head to make sure they were alone before hopping into the space to join them. "The kingsorcerer's orgy ended early. Vivene, it's a miracle: Kalea is here!"

"I know!" They clasped hands like they would've done as innocent students in the convent. Vivene put her hand on Del's shoulder. "This is Del. He's here to help. We're getting out of here, Millie."

For the next long moment, Millie stared at her. Vivene spread her hands and shared her excited smile. "The Creator sent her. I believe it."

Millie's eyes glossed over, and Vivene understood why. She still found it a little unbelievable. Kalea's presence didn't yet mean they would successfully escape. Millie huffed out a breath and asked Del, "Is there anything I can do to help?"

Del shifted his gaze between the two. "I don't know. I..." He shrugged.

Vivene shot her arm out to grab Millie's before the other girl could lose any confidence or hope. "I'll tell you what to do. Go and round up all of the other novices, as many as you can spot."

Millie's eyes took on a new brightness. "I think Opal is beating rugs on the lower patio right now, and I might find Maggy tidying the apprentices' dormitory."

"Good!" Vivene said. "Del, from which side of the tower did you enter?"

He pointed to his right, but then crossed his wrists to point left as well. "From below. I don't know..." He slicked his hand through his hair. "We visited the laundry room..."

"Okay," Vivene said to Millie. "Get the novices to the lower caves."

Millie nodded sharply and hurried on. It wouldn't take long for someone to catch them conversing here anyway. Vivene pulled Del along by his hand.

Kalea didn't have to make the decision to climb down into the cave-in or sprint out the door. A hand appeared on the floor, palm slapping the stone. She gave a sigh of relief at the black gloves that announced who the hands belonged to.

She hopped forward, feeling more balanced than a few minutes ago. "Did you kill him?"

Dorhen gave a grunt as he lifted himself by his strong arms alone. Instead of answering her question, he sprang forward as soon as he had a foot in place and grabbed her. Kalea's feet lost the floor, and she found herself hanging from his arm. He dashed out the door with her, leaping over the broken wood he'd made of it.

A howl chased them through the echoing halls. "Is that Lamrhath?" Kalea asked, clinging to Dorhen's torso in an effort to keep steady.

"We're leaving," he said, and pumped his legs harder. Their speed increased to something beyond that of any normal human. The muscles in his thighs bulged as his knees drew up with each step. His battleshift whipped, loud and raucous, behind them.

"Not yet," Kalea urged. "We have to find Mhina and get everyone together—"

Several yards behind in their tracks, a glittery, pink smoke filled the hall as if another explosion had occurred in the room with the broken floor. Kalea could only watch as it pursued, gaining on them by the step. "Dor—!" Kalea tried to warn him, but couldn't push any more through her tight lips. She shivered and clung tighter.

The pinkish cloud rushed past them, making a galloping motion in the shape of an animal on four legs. As fast as Dorhen could run in his Wikshen-form, the cloud proved faster. Kalea went suddenly upside-down when it met them. Dorhen's speed allowed him to leap up on the wall and take several sideways lunges.

Now behind the cloud, he leaped back to the floor with an ungraceful tumble. He meant to stop. Too fast for Kalea to fathom what happened, she found herself rolling along the floor, elbows and knees hitting hard stone.

Several paces away, Dorhen landed on his heels until he too rolled to a stop. He'd been running much too swiftly. At the end of his roll, he bounced back to his feet like a circus tumbler, and reversed his direction to collect Kalea from her sprawl on the floor.

Ahead of them, the pink cloud filled the room, and from it the form of Lamrhath materialized, as neat and grand as always, except far less amused than when he and Kalea had shared those few awkward moments alone.

Dorhen abandoned his plan to pick her up and run the other way. Instead, he placed her on her feet, wobbly and senseless with adrenaline.

He took his stance between Kalea and Lamrhath, toes curling on the cracking and chipping stones beneath him.

Kalea cringed. *Oh no, he'll break the floor again!* At least the last cave-in hadn't devastated him, though. If the crash had fazed Lamrhath, it hadn't lasted long.

Dorhen didn't spend as long soaking up minerals this time; he threw two sets of morkblades at Lamrhath from his palms. The kingsorcerer leaned way over to the right. The pink smoke billowed around him, similar to Wikshen's miasma. Lamrhath's eyes glowed a brighter gold than before. His teeth glinted in the light coming through the window as he dodged each jagged morkblade. His silken hair draped elegantly over his shoulders and waved gracefully whenever he dipped his head under the projectiles. In their face-off, they were like fire and water with the contrasting colors of their hair and clothing, two opposite souls who'd never get along in any given situation.

Lamrhath struck back at Dorhen with his partial transformation, making his hands claws and his teeth big and sharp like a wolf's. Dorhen showed no concern for his threats. Streaks of blood still decorated his chest and stomach from Lamrhath's initial strike.

Suddenly, Dorhen made a vicious leap forward, hands clawing savagely, and seized Lamrhath's throat. Kalea stiffened in place, frozen to gawk at what happened next. The kingsorcerer fought back by scratching at Dorhen's face with humanoid hands and nails longer and sharper than what they should be.

Dorhen reared backward for every swipe he made, tasked with keeping his face, particularly his eyes, away from those claws as he worked to strangle Lamrhath. By the look of the thinning pink smoke and the kingsorcerer's lack of urgent transformations, Dorhen had successfully distracted him, but the thinning veil of Naerezek's essence only revealed more danger: a group of red-robed sorcerers swarming through the hall to assess the noise.

Lamrhath called to them in a weak yelp as Dorhen squeezed his throat ever tighter. From her vantage, Kalea spotted a glimpse of Dorhen's fierce eyes burning down on him. His lips curled up past his gritted teeth as he worked to choke off his opponent's oxygen.

The sorcerers hurried forward, shouting at each other as well as at others down the hall.

"Wikshen!"

"He's out!"

Kalea couldn't decide whether to run or wait and see how Dorhen handled the new challenge. "We have to go!" she shouted. His grin deepened; his turquoise eyes brightened in their bloodthirsty delight. Her fists clenched in anticipation, held protectively before her. "Dorhen!" He paid no attention.

"Ha!" He breathed a sharp hiss as he managed to make two morkblades emerge while he gripped Lamrhath's throat.

Blood poured. The sorcerers stopped in their tracks, gasping. Lamrhath sighed as his face quickly relaxed. His eyes rolled back.

Dorhen let him slump to the floor. Suddenly cold, Kalea stayed back as Dorhen slowly rose to his feet. From behind, he appeared taller in that moment, his shoulders wide and square and thick-looking after the effort they'd exerted. His long hair hung to his waist, a heavy blue curtain.

He turned slowly around to face her. Kalea couldn't stop herself from taking a wary step backward. Lamrhath lay dead behind him, and he showed no concern for the group of remaining sorcerers. Like Kalea, they all gawked at the spectacle.

She worked her throat to speak, hopefully to find out that he was still *Dorhen* and that he wouldn't turn his aggression on her. What if he'd shifted personalities back to *Wikshen* during that brutal act? Lamrhath's death was such good news. Together, Kalea and Dorhen could rescue all the innocent people from this tower, unless *Wikshen* had different plans. Kalea dreaded to think of it.

A resonant groan shot through the air in the next minute. The sorcerers cheered and pointed to Lamrhath. Their kingsorcerer stirred on the floor, alive. Kalea didn't have to alert Dorhen due to the uproar of laughter from the sorcerers. Lamrhath's cut throat laced back together with a bright pink glow similar to the smoky aura of his pixie guardian.

"He must be—" Kalea tried. "He must be…possessed also?"

Dorhen sprang into action. This time, he lunged for Kalea. The sorcerers reacted to his movement. Half their group rushed to attend the recovering kingsorcerer, and the rest spat out ideas for what to do with Wikshen.

"Hurry, get a blinding mask! It's the only way!"

"But we've barely practiced with them!"

"I don't care. Go!"

Dorhen jerked her by the arm to follow him. "Ow!" Kalea cried, but he offered no apology. He picked a nearby door and broke the old lock with one powerful kick. The office inside showed empty. He stormed in, picked up the ornately-carved chair behind the desk, and threw it through the elaborate composition of window panes.

"How strong are your arms?" he asked Kalea.

She shrugged and flexed her bicep. "Laundress strong. Why?"

He knelt down, facing away from her. "Climb up."

Kalea considered the window he'd opened and his back as he moved his hair out of the way. "No."

"Do it!" he barked.

She jumped at his volume and mounted his back, wrapping her arms over his shoulders and her legs around his waist. "I hope you know what you're doing."

"I never know what I'm doing," he said, but he didn't hesitate to step onto the windowsill outside of the glass shards.

Kalea's throat dried when she glanced over her shoulder at the long drop below them. Miles of breezy air separated them from the ravine below. On this side of the tower wall, no ledges or sculpting offered a stable surface on which to climb, only the odd jagged stone, broken and with a crack here and there. Dorhen's movement made her feel unstable and looking backward at the elevation made her feel like she'd throw off their balance, so she tucked her face into the back of his neck and squeezed her limbs around him. A shaky wail squeezed up her throat, but she was too frozen in terror to notice.

What are you going to do? She meant to ask it, but the words couldn't flow. The question turned out to be unnecessary anyway because he didn't spare any breathing room before he crouched down to take the ledge with his hands and let his feet drop down the wall.

"Ha!" Kalea half-yelled, half-exhaled at the short fall and sudden stop. She shook now, and was fairly certain she'd strangle him to death if she squeezed any tighter. "I'm going to fall," she whined.

"No, you're not." Dorhen's hard back muscles worked against her body as they began a slow progression down the wall of rugged, ancient stones. The rocks flaked and crumbled as his hands absorbed minerals out of them—which could easily cause them to give way if he remained in one place too long!

"This is crazy," she said in a huffy panic. "Couldn't you think of a better way to get down to the lower levels?"

"Nope." He panted while he talked, which gave Kalea no confidence in his dangerous task. "We wouldn't have fared well making our way through all those sorcerers."

"Why did Lamrhath return to life?"

"I don't know," Dorhen said. "He must have a deep level of protection from a pixie similar to Wik. I really thought I'd killed him for a minute, though." A cocky note sang in his voice. Throughout the conversation, Kalea kept her eyes clamped shut. "At least the sun isn't too bright today," he added as he worked his way down.

Kalea hadn't considered that factor before letting herself into this situation. The sun weakened him because of his strange condition. He wouldn't have been able to do this climb without an overcast sky. Yet another worry to add to her list throughout their slow and deadly descent.

Instead of thinking about how high up they were, or how he relied on the grip of his fingers and toes to hold them to the wall, she thought about *him* instead. His hot body to which she clung. All those firm, toned muscles moving and grinding against her. The smell of his hair right under her nose, and the light perspiration on him.

"I'm glad I found you."

He didn't reply, only breathed and concentrated on his chore.

"I guess you found me, actually." She gave a little giggle. "How did you know where I was?"

He snorted. "How do you think?"

"You can sense me when I have an ecstasy?"

"I like to think I followed my cock."

She gave a shrill laugh, but remembered their position. "You're so bad since you became Wikshen."

"Am I?" Now his deep voice hummed darkly. "I'm the same person as always, just a little less afraid to speak my mind now. For some reason."

She hummed in consideration of his words, holding her face against his neck as he kept his head tucked to look down for the next foothold. His body movement had taken on a lizard-like winding motion to keep them on the move. "Of all the side effects of your condition, you mention your boldness with words," she said.

"Yeah."

"Well, why were you so afraid to speak your mind before?"

"I said as much as I could, but I was terrified of making you hate me."

"And you're not worried about that now?"

"No," he said flatly. "There's a lot I don't worry about anymore. I have a whole world's worth of new worries, though."

"Do those new worries involve me?"

He waited a minute before answering. "I haven't lost all of my old worries about you."

"What are the new worries?"

"This is a strange discussion for where we are and what we're doing."

Kalea opened her eyes and immediately snapped them shut. "You reminded me again!" She blew out a breath to calm herself, and he froze in his current place. He shivered.

"Don't breathe on the back of my neck."

"Sorry," she whispered, and smiled despite everything. "Did you like it?"

"Are you still in that intoxicated mood?"

She giggled again. "I drank a lot of rum, is that what you mean? Or are you referring to my *other* mood?" Although she joked, he huffed as if in some particular form of frustration.

"When we get out of here," he said, "We're going to have a long…"

She waited for his next word. Talk? Or was he planning something else? With his statement, he also stopped moving, and she opened her eyes to find they'd scaled to a window. He leaned over to peer inside. It was dark at first, but a warm light quickly filled it as sorcerers ran to the window with a torch!

Dorhen sucked in a breath, and every muscle he owned tensed up. He assessed the distance below them. Too far! He looked up. Too late.

Angry male voices bickered in the chamber behind the window. Out came the torch. In his panic at the waving flame, Dorhen flinched and attempted to shimmy to the side. Instead, they fell.

"Don't let go!" he shouted.

She wouldn't dream of it. She'd hold him tightly until they reached their deaths below.

Chapter 64
Shiny Picks

For the sake of his health, Daghahen prayed he wouldn't have to undo very many wards today. The first one he'd done pulverized his energy, taking from him at least half a day. He tried at least one more, whispering those hellish words he hardly knew the meaning to, invoking Ingnet once again to eat away the energy from the lock as well as from him. This lock was made of gold, which meant it could conduct an immense amount of energy, certainly enough to kill him on the spot if he ventured to stick the skeleton key into it.

He felt himself sway on his knees, eye level with the lock as his spell worked. Ingnet had come through again. Now to find out if the skeleton key worked like it had on the older lock he'd tried down the hall…

Footsteps shuffling along gave him pause. Throwing up his hood and chanting Gariott's Blend, he ran, practically diving behind a column to hide. In his fright, he dared not try to peek around at who it was or where they went. It sounded like two people whispering to each other. They didn't come past his hiding place, thank the Creator.

A door closed eventually, and with it their sounds stopped. Time to move. Yet he paused again at the door beside which he crouched. A fancier door than the others. Maybe Orinleah was kept in there, if Lamrhath thought highly of her. It also had a golden keyhole plate.

Daghahen placed his hands on either side of it as usual, said the chants, and then endured the consequent wave of exhaustion. By now, he had to fight to right himself again, stand back up, and insert the skeleton key.

It turned. He cracked the door open. A flamboyant room of frescoes, tapestries, and mirrors waited inside. Standing in the doorframe, he squinted.

"I've seen this room before." It had changed, but sure enough, he had. The kingsorcerer's room. He flinched backward. "Oh, God."

Back when Daghahen had been in his prime, this room had belonged to an older man, fat, cruel, and ambitious to the point of being unbearable. He'd grown lazy in his station after a while. He stayed in his bed most of the time, eating and listening to his concubines play instruments all day. He'd also grown strangely sickly. Daghahen and Lambelhen had once been summoned to this room to be given some order. However odd it had been to walk in on that scene back then, this time...

Daghahen shook his head. He wandered forward. There stood a harp to the left, on a rug with cushions. At the center loomed a grand canopy bed, so much grander than back then. Their old kingsorcerer had had simpler tastes, choosing linen drapes and sheets, a fabric much cooler in the summer. Now, it was swathed in bright-red and gold silks. A white wolf pelt spread the length of the enormous mattress.

Daghahen ran his hand along a divider with a painted scene. Hideous demons with bodies more animal than human raped frightened women, some ripping their clothes, others pulling up their skirts and sliding forked tongues between their cheeks. More women were being carried high off into the distant sky, wailing. It was only oily paint, but Daghahen could hear the sounds. It put a new cold sweat on the back of his neck.

The horrendous scene wasn't confined to the divider. The walls carried it all around the room in an unfolding story that told of a newly throned god by the end. The god who sat on the great throne atop a mountain made of bodies in orgy was his brother. Lambelhen.

Daghahen stared at it, numb for the moment. What should he think? What *could* he think? For now, he could drum up nothing. He wasn't even sure if he was surprised. His brother really was kingsorcerer. This was what Lambelhen thought of himself. His dear brother. That young lad in Theddir, behind the inn. Running. Playing. Laughing with Daghahen. This was what he'd become.

"How high up are we going?"

Del didn't have to speak for Vivene to guess how nervous he was becoming. His grip tightened the farther they ventured, and a slight tremble entered the contact.

"There's one certain person we have to rescue," she told him.

"Is it the little elf-girl?"

Vivene paused to eye him. "*Little* elf-girl?"

Del nodded. "Yeah," he whispered. "Gaije's little sister. She's eight years old. Blonde, I understand."

Vivene shook her head. "Dear Creator..."

"What's the matter?"

She huffed, turned forward, and led him onward. Any time a sorcerer appeared around the bend, Vivene dropped his hand and shot off generic words about how the floors should be swept and how to clean the tapestries in the Chimera Tower, as if Del had recently been assigned new duties. So far, none of the sorcerers had stopped them.

Vivene's nerves climbed as well the closer they drew to a certain door. *Oh please, Creator, let her still be alive!*

"Are you all right?" Del asked. "Where are we?"

"You gotta keep quiet here. This is the area where the kingsorcerer lives."

"Shit," he hissed, and ogled his surroundings.

"Don't be afraid." Dancing in place, Vivene checked down the hall and back behind them. "I don't hear anyone coming. How about you?"

"No."

She pulled on the handle of the door with the golden keyhole, and it didn't budge, hopefully a good sign that things were well on the inside. If Orinleah were dead, they wouldn't have locked it…would they?

Vivene patted the wood grains softly with her palm. "This door. Open it."

Del raised his eyebrows. "Open it?"

"Yes, I brought you up here to do it. Get your tools out."

He shifted his head to the left and right before acting. "You better not get me killed." Before sticking any of his thin, metal bars into the keyhole, he closed one eye to look into it. "It's dark in there," he noted.

"It's a foyer before another room. Hurry."

He perused his many different lock picks, some thicker than others and varying in color and signs of age and wear.

"Where did you get all those?" Vivene asked.

"I made 'em." He slid a bronze-colored one out of its narrow pocket sewn into the rolled case. "When I was young, I learned how to use them when I fell in with some street thugs. Made some good eating money doing burglary."

"You stole from poor innocent people?"

"Yeah, but I never took anything of true value," he said. "A pretty vase here and there, short lengths of fabric, and maybe bronze items for scrapping."

"And you forged these picks?"

"Yeah. Bowaen taught me whitesmithing, which is the reason some are made from silver. I got my hands on a scrap of silver or two."

"You didn't spend the silver pieces you got?"

"I found it more profitable to make new picking tools from the silver so I could burgle more. It's like investing."

Vivene snorted as she watched him insert a second tool, a silver one, into the lock with the first one he'd been stirring around in it.

"Very gently," he hummed as if to himself. "It's a delicate—"

The sound of footsteps made Vivene jump and put her hands on his shoulder. "Hurry!" she hissed.

"Ah," he said after the click happened within the lock.

No time to breathe. As soon as the door swung open, she pushed him and they fell into a jumble. She scrambled to lean out and pull the door closed behind them, shutting them up inside.

"What if they're coming to this room?" Del asked.

She shushed him and threw her hand over his mouth. They waited, huddled together in the quiet dark until the footsteps passed. Apparently, they were safe for now, but leaving this room would be another story.

"Now you have to unlock the second door," she told him in a whisper.

"How the hell am I supposed to do that?"

On her knees, Vivene groped around in the dark for the door to Orinleah's apartment. She tapped on it. "Orinleah? Are you all right? Are you in there?"

No answer.

She threw open the food slot, allowing a beam of soft sunlight into the foyer. With a sense of ill desperation, Vivene peered through the slot for any sign of her friend. "Orinleah?"

Still no answer.

A rancid stench wafted out. "Oh, dear God," Vivene moaned.

"Is she alive?"

Her voice cracked. "I don't know." A covered tray of food occupied the platform inside the door. Vivene slid it out. Maybe the food had gone bad—which wasn't a good sign. It would turn if Orinleah wasn't alive to eat it. "Smells like dead fish."

The revelation made her stomach churn. She lifted the lid off the tray anyway, using the sunbeam to see what had become of the food. A bunch of dead eyes stared back at her. Raw fish heads. Vivene dropped the lid and stared at the heaping plate of foul-smelling garbage that was today's dinner for poor Orinleah. By the look of them, it might've been dinner from yesterday or the day before. She dropped the tray, and the slimy heads went everywhere.

"Geez!" Del hissed and gagged, rolling back to keep the mess from touching his feet.

"Unlock it."

"I can't breathe."

"I don't care. Unlock it."

"It's too dark."

She shoved him toward the door. "Just do it. Now!"

Unable to shake his sick sounds, Del fumbled with his toolkit, straining to see the lock in question. "I'll try the ones that worked on the first door," he said, and cursed and jerked in the long time he struggled with the task and its conditions. Awful scraping sounds happened inside the lock, and at one point a *snap!* preceded a particularly nasty word Del dispensed.

A few more curse words followed. "Shit! Damn it all!"

"Keep your voice down," she reminded him.

"I broke one."

"Well, you know how to repair it when you get home, don't you?"

Del grunted as he worked.

"Orinleah, hold on," Vivene said through the food slot.

Click!

They both froze. The light lit half of Del's face. His mouth hung open.

"Open it," Vivene whispered.

He swung the door open slowly, and the sunlight flooded from Orinleah's window into the foyer. Vivene's heart pounded. She didn't know how she'd take it if she found her friend dead inside.

The red curtains along the window were torn down and lay on the floor in two heaps. They'd left torn threads dangling from the fixtures over the window. The whole scene was...messy. Messier than it should've been. Everything about Orinleah, from what Vivene had seen through her food slot, was neat and graceful. Smeared chalk drawings graffitied the walls, half-destroyed with dark water splashes that had seeped into the stone. At least one red stain littered the wall too: blood. And much more blood colored the balled-up fur pelt of otherwise beautiful white.

Her eyes next scanned over the bed, messy and rumpled. Someone sat at the far side! Vivene froze before rushing forward. The person didn't bother to turn and inspect who'd come in. She was bald and...wounded. Red nicks, some with dried blood drips, cluttered the unevenly-shorn scalp.

Vivene put her hands over her mouth and dared a step forward, followed by another. This slight, weak, bald person had pointed ears. Vivene didn't really notice Del stepping into the room behind her, but she subconsciously took strength from his warmth at her back. She ventured forward, one numb step after the other, until the person's profile turned into view.

The elegant, feminine features of the woman's face looked more like a teenaged boy in its scuffed-up state and without the long hair. Dried tears streaked through dirt all the way down her cheeks. Despite her lack of hair, Vivene couldn't find a scrap of it anywhere. She knew how long and full Orinleah's hair should be. It had been taken away instead of left in the wreckage of her room.

"Orinleah," Vivene tried again softer, as if any hard edges in her voice could place additional punctures and bruises on this poor creature.

Orinleah finally responded to her presence. Her lips trembled and a new stream of tears glazed her cheeks. Vivene moved around to face her squarely, leaving Del to wait a few paces back.

It got worse. The other side of Orinleah's face was one huge, lumpy, purple bruise from her temple to her chin. Her other eye was no longer there.

Chapter 65
A Secret Slips

Bowaen fell to the floor on his hands and knees. "S-s-sorry, sir!"

"You should be," Gaije said back sternly, a little too fake for comfort, not that Bowaen could act his part any better.

Bowaen grunted—for real—when Gaije's foot collided with his ass, pushing his face to the floor. This roleplay would quickly get old.

"What now?" a sorcerer asked.

The presence of sorcerers had launched them into this play. Apparently, the two, dressed as a sorcerer and a servant, were seen walking together too cozily. At the first sign of confrontation, Bowaen had immediately shouted for mercy and mumbled about how he'd "never do it again."

"What did he do?" the sorcerer asked Gaije, who couldn't offer an answer. The elves of his country weren't much for lies and phony acting. In fact, Bowaen recalled from their travels a debate on which story to tell for that night's entertainment. Gaije had mentioned elves only told true stories about the past. They never made up any fiction for late night campfire fun.

To cover for him, Bowaen sputtered out like a foolish older man, "I ate one measly roll I wasn't supposed to, boss. I'll never do it again. Can't you forgive an old man? I can't do the extra chores he's tellin' me to, boss, I just can't! Please have mercy on an ol' fool!"

Gaije held his shoulders square and his lips tight the whole time. He nodded firmly to the other sorcerer to confirm the story. "That was *my* roll," he said.

Ah, geez! Bowaen thought. It was, however, his own fault for coming up with such a stupid story.

The other sorcerer snorted and walked away. Bowaen worked to his feet, feeling every bit the tired old servant he portrayed, and nudged Gaije to walk on first. He feigned a crooked hobble behind him.

Kalea and Dorhen's fall stopped short, the jolt so fierce she nearly slipped off his back. Her arms clung around his torso after she managed to retain the contact. Above them, the sorcerers peered down from the window, at a loss for how to reach them.

The one with the torch purposely dropped it, with Dorhen's head as the target. Seeing the thing coming, Dorhen swung to the side to avoid it, and Kalea caught sight of what he'd done. His hands were slowly releasing metal wires instead of morkblades. Wikshen, in his evil ways, had once used the same spell to snag Del when they had fought him in Hathrohskog. Now, the wires caught firmly to the stones with sharp barbs along every few inches.

Kalea said, "Dorhen?"

He didn't answer. He concentrated hard, breathing steadily, sometimes grunting. The emerging wires caused open wounds in his palms, and blood ran freely down his arms. As Kalea and Dorhen left the sorcerers farther and farther above, their heads receded into the building, most likely to form a new plan on how to catch them. They'd probably rush down to lower floors to meet them at other windows.

"I don't have enough minerals to get us all the way down," Dorhen warned.

"What do we do?" she asked, and he kept silent.

They dropped a little farther on the growing wires. Dorhen walked his feet along the wall as they went. Not far below them, the wall yawned into a concave balcony. Pausing to lean over and assess the formation, Dorhen concentrated hard on one of his hands, which released its barbed wire to spring up and whip around before settling against the wall. He used his free hand to reach back and pull Kalea up higher so she could reattach to his shoulders and wrap her legs around his middle.

"Hold tight," was the only clue he gave her before he started jumping along the wall, releasing more and more wire from his one hand. They shot out a little farther each time, until the last leap, when they fell into the recess of the balcony. He let the wire leave his hand, and they landed inside with a rolling tumble.

"Unhh," Kalea groaned when they settled. He'd managed to land beneath her, but his effort didn't spare her a scraped elbow or two. "Your hands."

"They've closed up already," he said without losing his serious, urgent tone.

She took in his pale, clammy face. After a few seconds of continuing to look around them for danger, he settled on her eyes.

"What?" he asked.

She took his face in her hands and kissed his lips. Firmly. Although she expected him to push her away and scold her about their situation, he didn't. He kissed back and used his tongue. That sweet, honey flavor of his saliva returned to her mouth once again. Kalea's body shivered back to arousal from the adrenaline. If he wanted to take her right here in Ilbith, she wouldn't refuse. She moaned and leaned over to let him cradle her where they sat.

He pulled his mouth away. "You *are* in that intoxicated mood." He laughed. "Come on, get up." He helped her to stand.

"Sorry," she said, rubbing her face as if she needed to wake up from some unshakable dream. "I don't know what's wrong with me. This has been happening ever since..." Images of Damos responding to her arousal flooded her head. She'd been having ecstasies ever since her first trip through Hathrohskog. Ever since she'd caught Wikshen's attention. "I think *you're* doing it to me."

He was already tiptoeing deeper into the recess of the veranda. "I didn't do anything to you."

"Right," she said, "it's Wi—"

She stopped herself. His cockiness right now reminded her more of Wikshen than Dorhen. She preferred to believe Dorhen controlled the body, but how could she be sure? It probably didn't matter who he was when simply looking at him—his muscly back and his long hair—made her effect increase. She needed to stave it off long enough to escape from this place.

She walked briskly in effort to shake it off. "Let's go," she said as if taking charge. She paused before reaching the door to the inside. "Although I don't know if we should actually go up or down. We can't leave until we've rescued everybody."

He took her hand and put himself before her along their way. "*We're* going down, out of this shithole."

Kalea tightened her lips before the argument commenced. Whether "Wikshen" was to blame or Dorhen's *saehgahn* protective instincts, he would act out of selfishness, she supposed. She wouldn't be able to defeat his strength if it came to a physical struggle over leaving or staying, so she'd have to think of some way to get him to save everyone else. Maybe he could be persuaded or...manipulated if she used her feminine wiles. After all, she knew he wanted her just as badly as she wanted him.

She did, however, hesitate a little, and he apparently sensed the tension in her stance. He turned around. "I won't let them hurt you anymore," he said.

She batted her eyes and patted his hand, which held hers. "It's okay. Lamrhath didn't hurt me. You stopped him in time."

"No," he said, "they've been hurting you for days. I know this."

"What are you talking about?"

"There's air pipes running through the better parts of Ilbith," he explained. "I listened to your screaming and crying through one of them for far too long. So, we have to go."

"But I've only been here since today."

Dorhen cocked his head and squinted at her.

She stepped forward. "Look at me, Dorhen." She brushed her hair away from her face. "You can look at me all over. I have no marks on me. They haven't touched me, besides what you saw with Lamrhath."

"Doesn't make sense," he said. "I heard you."

"Must've been someone else."

"But it was you."

"Then look a little closer." She put his hands along her face. He did inspect her closer. He brushed her hair aside, and she shivered at his touch. "Look," she continued, and pulled her top down to show him her chest right above the breasts. He ran his hand along her skin. She pulled up the end of her top and showed him her belly. "Besides these new scrapes on my elbows, no one has bothered me. I've just arrived today—to save *you.*"

"I don't understand." He gave her the familiar, innocent stare of the Dorhen she used to know. "It sounded so real."

"It wasn't." She held his hand warmly and gave him a smile of reassurance.

His large hand tightened around hers. "We're still going straight out of here. I'll swim you across the ravine if I have to." He pulled her onward, through the door, giving her no choice to resist his pull.

In the time they'd spent on the outside wall, the inside of the tower had leaped into an alerted frenzy. Anyone with legs ran this way and that. Dorhen grabbed the back of Kalea's costume to prevent her from walking around the busy corner. He pulled her to stand against him, and a film passed over her face. Wikshen's dark essence: Dorhen was summoning it to hide them in the shadowy corner by the door to the veranda. If not for him, she would've collided with a servant man who ran by, yelling, "I checked the study hall—no Wikshen there!"

Apart from the servants, the sorcerers had taken on a face of total concentration, almost meditation, and roved through the halls as if conducting a deeper kind of search. Dorhen's arms squeezed tighter around Kalea when one such man wandered near their supernatural hiding place. She held her breath under the pressure.

The sorcerer extended his gloved hand—the same type of glove she'd grown to fear—and the jewel embedded in the leather palm flickered a yellow light. Kalea didn't feel so hidden anymore. The sorcerer gasped, rounded his lips in preparation of shouting a word beginning with W, and Dorhen sprang past her. The oily shadow of Wik's essence didn't shield her from the sight of his palm releasing a morkblade straight into the man's head right before her. The horror-phenomenon came with a disgustingly moist popping sound and the follow-through of metal scraping against broken bone.

The blood sprinkled her face like hot rain. Kalea's nerves took over for the instant, pushing and pulling loud, fast breaths in and out of her lungs. She couldn't blink, and it took long seconds for her to realize she wore some stranger's blood.

The incident blew their cover, and Dorhen knew it. Ignoring what he'd just done, he picked her up and started running fast, like before. Kalea hooked her arms around his neck and hung on through all the turbulence, wanting to close her eyes, but unable to. The eerie howling up ahead announced a load of naerscouels taking the formation of a solid wall-to-wall wedge in the corridor.

Dorhen skidded to such a hot stop, his feet left blood trails along the stones from the intense friction. Now idling in place, the cracking and flaking commenced beneath him to repair and refill his mineral store. Behind them, all the sorcerers they'd passed gathered to clog the path of retreat. Dorhen spun backward and forward, unsure which side to give his full attention. He could only turn sideways to try to face both groups at once. Putting Kalea down, he kept her tucked under his arm jealously.

Ahead of them, the naerscouels parted and tapped the ends of their spears and halberds on the floor to announce the arrival of another group: Lamrhath with an entourage of yet more sorcerer lackeys.

"What'll I do with you?" Lamrhath asked, strolling past the naerscouels with his robe replaced and his throat still glowing with the power of his pixie-god holding his flesh together. "With both of you?" He crossed his arms and considered them for a moment. Dorhen's arms held Kalea ever tighter to his side. "I was kind to you from the start and look how you've repaid me. And you…" He turned his eyes to Kalea. "Now I have you to puzzle out. Do I keep you separate and study your ability as a Luschian? Or should I put you two in a room together and see how long it takes him to finally make a dreadwitch?"

"You wouldn't like it if I did," Dorhen grumbled back.

Apparently, Kalea made a confused face, because Lamrhath smirked at her. "I don't think she quite understands how Wikshen works yet."

She did. Or actually… "I know he blesses women," she blurted out.

Lamrhath let out a short snicker, and Dorhen winced. "Is that what they preach at Wikhaihli?" He shook his head at them both. "Well…" He stepped forward. "It may not be exactly wrong. They can call it whatever they like. The fact is, they've made something romantic out of what is actually an instrument of war."

At their silence, Lamrhath spread his hands. "You don't know this? Haven't you seen what he can do?" Kalea worked her jaw, at a loss. "When well-honed, Wikshen can destroy an army with the swipe of his hand, so long as he's sharp enough and absorbed enough minerals. Even without the minerals to create lasting projectiles, those morkblades can cut through anything within short range. Wikshen is a weapon, my dear. A vile and angry being, long ago born from the combination of a dark pixie and a bloodthirsty warlord."

He paused and nodded to Dorhen. "I've done a fair bit of reading lately, and it gets better. Wikshen commands an army of his own—an army of demonic females, each as deadly with their own ability as he is with his morkblades. It looks to me like your Dorhen wants you to be his first little treat."

Kalea shrugged and shook her head. "I don't understand. Dorhen?" When she checked him, standing tall beside her, he looked stiffer than she'd ever seen him, every one of his jaw muscles popping.

"Should I spell it out for the laymen?" Lamrhath asked. "Having sex with him will turn you into a monster."

A shiver ran up her spine. *Wikshen's blessing is power.* Several Wikshonites had said those words, and up until now, Kalea had assumed they meant political or religious power. She thought it would at least get her the title "First Sister" and the best slice of dinner and a seat beside her Mastaren at the table.

"Is that true?" she asked him.

"Yes," Dorhen said, his voice like a hammer hitting a drum. He didn't look at her.

She turned her attention back to Lamrhath. Numb. Unable to form an opinion yet. She waited for what he'd say next.

"But here's where it gets interesting," Lamrhath said without missing a beat. "You're a Luschian. What do you think will happen when he splits you?"

"You make no sense," she countered. "Earlier, you tried to 'split' me."

Lamrhath shrugged. "That's the other side to this fascinating coin. I have an illness in need of attention. What would've happened if we weren't interrupted?"

She had no answer for that. She knew as much about Luschians as she did about dreadwitches: nothing.

Kalea tried to wiggle out of Dorhen's grasp, but he maintained a desperate hold on her arm. "All right, Lamrhath," she said in the strongest, loudest voice she could manage in her bewilderment. "What's more important to you? Having your 'weapon of war?'" She motioned to Dorhen. "Or getting your 'healing?'"

Lamrhath smirked and cocked his head at the turn of the conversation. "What do you propose?"

She didn't miss a beat. "I propose to have sex with you so my Luschian magic can heal you, and in return, you set Dorhen free. After we're done, you set me free too—whether the spell works or not."

Throughout her speech, she watched Lamrhath's face twist into grinning amusement. A strange fire erupted in his eyes.

"Not in this life!" Dorhen jerked Kalea back and shot a morkblade straight at Lamrhath. He couldn't dodge it fast enough, but that didn't matter because the gaping hole it made in his forehead quickly filled in with more of Naerezek's pink light. It remained there, shimmering, looking like a third eye.

It suddenly dawned on Kalea that the morkblades would never kill Lamrhath. He'd just been hit straight through the brain with one! But Daghahen knew what would kill him: Hathrohjilh. He'd told Bowaen to give the sword to Dorhen, but she had lost him!

The sorcerers and naerscouels erupted into action around them, leaving her no opening to tell Dorhen of her revelation. Reacting to the attack long before Kalea ever would've, Dorhen pushed her head down to make her crouch beside his legs, where she clung to his battleshift. The following confusion of sound was a clamor of chaotic choking. It rained inside the building as many red droplets hit the floor around her, and a mass of bodies followed. Some sorcerers fell dead as two pieces instead of one.

Dorhen performed the feat again, waving his arm in a wide, horizontal arc to release a shower of long morkblades that hacked through the people and naerscouels like weeds. Lamrhath remained standing without any new magically fused wounds because his men had protectively jumped in front of him. On the second round, he merely ducked as Kalea did. Now, streams of blood flowed past their feet.

The two mutilating swipes gained Dorhen enough room to sweep Kalea up and lunge over the dead bodies to a clear path down the hall.

"He won't get far," Lamrhath announced behind them, menacingly calm despite the decimation of his sorcerers. Around him, the sorcerers swarmed in panic.

Dorhen didn't give Kalea time to watch what the sorcerers would do; the next turn of a corner shrouded them in another protective shadow.

Chapter 66
Dark Scars

Vivene couldn't stop the shaky moan from creeping up her throat. "What has he done to you?" She covered her mouth to hold back the oncoming sob.

Del moved in beside her and knelt before Orinleah. He winced once to see the poor woman's empty eye socket, crusted over thickly with scabbed blood, but otherwise acted rationally by tearing a strip of cloth off his tabard.

"This should help," he said softly. "It'll keep the dusty air off at least." He wrapped the cloth around Orinleah's head diagonally, taking gentle care not to tie it too tight over her bruised cheekbone.

Vivene rubbed Orinleah's hand as he worked. The new tears continuously streamed down the better side of the elf's face. "We're getting out of here today," Vivene whispered.

Orinleah shook her head. She opened her mouth and moved her jaw side to side, possibly to see if it still worked. "I…I don't want my son to see me this way."

That made a rush of tears wet Vivene's cheeks. She reached up and dabbed Orinleah's away with her sleeve. "You're beautiful," she told her.

Orinleah's remaining eye closed, and she swallowed with visible difficulty. Vivene finally noticed the bruises on her neck. Hand-shaped bruises. She'd survived strangulation. Vivene couldn't help but run thoughts through her mind as to how long this poor woman's torment had gone on before he finally left her alone. How many times had he strangled her and then let up to allow her to breathe, probably to be strangled again? The "he" in her mind needed no name.

As soon as Del finished his work, he opened her wardrobe. "Got any cloaks in h…?" His voice trailed off when he saw its emptiness. A shredded undergarment or two littered the floor.

"Lambelhen took my best pieces," Orinleah said, managing to push the emotion out of her voice. "I don't care about them anyway."

At the moment, she wore a sleeveless chemise with a torn strap tied back down. Enough of her body showed beneath the thin fabric that Vivene decided to hand over her apron. Strangely, though, a ruby necklace decorated Orinleah's naked collarbones. It occurred to Vivene to tell her to take it off because it was too flashy, but she didn't. If they could keep it, it might buy them good food and lodging when they got out of here. Orinleah would need a comfortable place to heal—not to mention a doctor!

Del removed the wool cap Vivene had given him, leaving his shaggy, dark hair in a flattened shape. "You better wear this over your ears," he said, holding it out to her. "Daghahen said elves should keep their heads covered around here, so—"

Orinleah shot to her feet, holding the cap down by her side. "What did you say?"

"I said elves need to cover up," Del repeated with a shrug.

"No." Orinleah's voice returned to full volume, along with a new stiffness to her spine and squared shoulders. "That name you said."

"Daghahen?"

Orinleah reached out and pulled Del closer. Vivene reared back to watch the interaction. "You did say it. Is there someone named Daghahen here?"

"Yeah," Del said with his helpless hands hovering out to the sides. "A funny old elf. Strange accent. Blond hair."

She let Del go to cover her own gaping mouth. "He is alive! And he's here! I knew he'd come for me! Lambelhen's a liar, and I knew it all along!"

"Daghahen?" Vivene mimicked the name she knew she'd heard before. He had accompanied Kalea dressed as a sorcerer, if Vivene remembered correctly. "Who is he to you?"

Del showed the same level of interest in her answer.

"He's my *daghen-saehgahn*," Orinleah said. "My true husband."

Gingerly closing the door behind him, Daghahen left the kingsorcerer's room and backtracked down the great corridor to the door he'd left unchecked. Better to see the room before moving on, since he'd spent the energy to remove the ward.

Inside the door, he near fell flat on his face, slipping on a pile of nauseatingly putrid rotten fish. "Eech!" Another door gaped open in here, with daylight coming through. Odd set up. Beyond that he found a vacant room—vacant and wrecked. The bedsheets were on the floor. Torn nightgowns. A broken water basin. A bed with torn curtains…

And wall drawings in chalk. Drawings of a child he knew very well.

"Dorhen," he whispered. He thought he'd never see such a sight again, images of his poor son in blissful youth. Days long gone. Days he'd personally ruined.

A dark dread passed over Daghahen to survey this broken room. Orinleah was alive after all, but what had Lambelhen done to her? Where was she now? He wiped his tears on his sleeve. Maybe it was time to put the red robe back on. At least he knew she'd been here recently. Orinleah. He'd find her.

Through every empty hallway, Bowaen and Gaije dropped their act and sprinted. Bowaen kept his hand firmly on the sword hidden under his tabard to prevent it from waving around too much, and Gaije did a similar thing with his hidden bow. Hiding a short bow and quiver under a sorcerer's robe was a more complicated feat. Still, neither of them knew where they were going or if they drew any closer to Mhina, and they had already run up more than ten staircases. The higher they climbed, the nicer the tower started looking.

"Hold up!" Bowaen called between his heavy panting. "Gaije!"

Gaije slowed and threw an impatient glare over his shoulder.

Bowaen raised his hand. "Cool down. Listen. We got no idea where we're going."

"I know that," Gaije barked back.

Bowaen shook his head. "We're high up in the tower now. I think it's time to keep our eyes peeled for a clue. Otherwise, we could run into who-knows-what."

Gaije threw his hands out. "When you see one, let me know."

"Calm down, you hothead!"

Gaije paused in his progression again. Bowaen trotted to catch up to him, his thin leather soles scuffing along. "Have you noticed something about this higher level?" he asked, hushing his voice down.

Gaije waited, holding his impatient glare.

"There's more women walking around. Prettier ones than in the caves below."

"I haven't."

"What are you, a monk? Use your eyes," Bowaen said, thrusting two fingers at Gaije's face. "Maybe some smarts and cunning is in order now. Maybe say some things to get one of them to slip where any children are being kept. Huh?"

Gaije shifted his eyes like he did anytime someone made a good point.

Bowaen put his hands to his own chest. "But I got no authority to say anything of that nature up here. You do." A feeling of horrible dread shaded his mind as soon as he suggested it. Gaije was terrible at acting like a sorcerer. Bowaen cleared his throat. "Repeat after me: 'The kingsorcerer wants to know the status of the elf-girl.'"

Gaije did. His hard, flat-toned voice wasn't too bad for a sorcerer.

"Now I'll be one of the servant women." Bowaen shifted his voice high. "Yes, sir. She is well."

Gaije's hard mood flickered, and a faint smile appeared on his tight lips.

"Make fun of my lady voice later," Bowaen said. "Now ask where she is right now."

"Where do you keep her?"

"No, no, that's no good. Maybe we all know where she's kept, so they can't know that we don't know."

"What?"

"Ask this one: 'Has she been fed yet today?'"

He did, but Bowaen quickly realized that question would only earn a "yes" or "no." He assumed they'd get an unhelpful "yes" at this late hour in the afternoon.

"Okay, hold on," Bowaen said, chewing on his roughened thumb. "We gotta forge a conversation good enough to yield the clue we need."

"There you are!"

The two jumped at the sudden new voice.

"Dag," Bowaen hissed. The old elf glided toward them with his red robes waving. "Good thing you're here. We need you to act like a sorcerer. We're looking for— "

"Good thing I found *you*," Daghahen interrupted. He sucked in a breath; apparently he had run quite a distance. "My wife is somewhere around here, and some madness has erupted on a lower floor. I heard it through the vents. We *need* to get the sword to Dorhen."

He followed up by reaching for Bowaen's tabard, Hathrohjilh's hiding place, and Bowaen slapped his hand away. "What are you doin', old man?"

"Give it to me. Hurry!"

"No!"

The situation escalated to an all-out scuffle. Gaije gawked as they locked arms and started dancing in circles, sometimes attempting to fling the other away. Their shouting increased, and though Bowaen shouted back at the foolish elf, Gaije knew instinctively not to. Daghahen showed no signs he'd ever let up. His maniacal blue eyes flashed fiercely.

"If we don't deliver the sword, Lambelhen will keep on living. It's the only way to kill him!"

"Shut up!"

Gaije's shout rang loud and far, echoes bouncing off both stone walls all the way through the corridor. He'd drawn his bow and trained an arrow on Daghahen. His hood had fallen down, and his red hair feathered lightly in all directions with a static charge. Behind him stood a shocked servant woman with her rag and bucket in hand. Bowaen and Daghahen froze in their struggle.

Gaije noticed her a few seconds later and jumped. He turned his arrow on her. "Where's the elf-girl?"

Bowaen winced.

The woman's fright tightened to a teeth-grinding strain. "I-I-I…"

"Her name's Mhina. Where is she?"

The woman stuttered some more.

"Take me to her!"

The woman took one step, and Daghahen leaped backward, ripping the sword from Bowaen's hands. Bowaen gasped. Gaije and the woman went forward through the hall. Daghahen ran back with the sword.

Left by himself, defenseless, Bowaen faced a decision. A strong, nagging urgency to have the sword back suddenly screamed in his brain and sent him sprinting after Daghahen.

"My lord, I don't know what this is about," the woman said, fumbling her keys as Gaije's arrow poked the side of her head. "I'm not supposed to open this door for anyone but the kingsorcerer."

"Do it anyway." Gaije's wits scattered as far as this woman's, but for a different reason. Mhina had spent too long away from her family—her mother—and he wouldn't allow another second. He had no intention of shooting this woman, but she didn't need to know that. He just needed his sister. Now.

She'd brought him to a clean, pristine area of the tower with fresh white stones and the fragrance of new wood, particularly the door at which they stood. It smelled strongly of the lacquer which gave it a deep, glossy look. The woman opened it and hesitated until Gaije nudged her with his arrow.

"Go in first."

"I'm not going back there!" a shrill voice shouted from within as soon as the woman entered.

The sound set Gaije's nerves flying. He pushed into the room, shoving the woman aside. A small fire in a fireplace kept the space warm, and there were fancy drapes with a matching canopy for the bed. Only one soul inhabited this splendid chamber, a short little person he almost didn't recognize. Her long, blonde hair hung in fancy braids that twisted around each other and returned to lie neatly on her shoulders. The red velvet dress she wore was finer than anything he'd seen here yet. Her head reached higher than he remembered.

"What do you want?" she asked with a heavy drag of hesitation.

He threw his red hood off, and her face turned to shock, rounded mouth and eyes. He fell to his knees, and she ran forward. He even dropped Leho's Bow, never minding the servant woman who bolted out the door in his distraction.

"Gaije!" Mhina shouted in his ear. "You came. I knew it. I knew it!"

Relief washing over him, he leaned over from their hug to show her the bow. "Your grandfather sent me."

She cooed at the thing, running her tiny fingers across the sculpted horses on the bow shaft. "I knew it," she said again. "But I didn't think how long."

"I did the best I could," he said.

"I wasn't worried," she replied, meeting his eyes again. "Father told me you'd come, and I believed him."

Gaije raised his eyebrows. "What do you mean, Father told you? He's not with me."

"But he did tell me."

"Mhina…" Gaije dipped his chin. In fact, he dropped into a crouch of humility for what he needed to tell her next, putting his nose to the floor. "Mhina, Father is dead," he said. His throat tightened up to say it aloud, especially to this young one, although they couldn't mourn right now. A risky escape awaited them.

Her hands landed on the back of his head. "I know. That's how he could tell me."

She showed little worry when he regarded her questioningly, despite the place they were in. Putting her cryptic claim aside, he picked up the bow and stood. "We have to go now."

She nodded once and turned to start stuffing food from her tea table into a scarf, and then tied its ends together. At the new sound of mewling, she widened her eyes. "We can't leave Kikya behind."

"*Kikya*," Gaije repeated the Norrian word. "You have a cat?"

"She's a baby cat," Mhina said, running to pick up the little white ball of fluff from the bed. "Lamrhath gave her to me, so she needs rescuing too." Holding the kitten with one hand to her breast, Mhina threw open an ornate little chest in the corner and pulled out a silk hard-shell purse. She placed the cat inside it and tied the flap down.

"It better not make any noise," he warned, prompting Mhina to put her finger to her lips and shush the satchel. He waved his hand at her. "Do you have anything plainer to wear? Flashy clothing stands out too much out there."

Mhina huffed and considered her wardrobe and the adjacent chest. "I can find something, but it's all very fancy. Lamrhath only wants me to dress pretty."

She chose a dark-blue dress trimmed in gold, probably the least gaudy thing she owned in here. "Turn around," she demanded of him, and he jumped to do so. She must've grown up a little since he last saw her, before he left for the army.

Facing the open-standing door reminded Gaije of the danger. The servant woman had fled, probably to alert the sorcerers about him. When he turned back around, Mhina was making quick work of the bodice strings on the human-style finery.

"Hurry now," he urged, and she lunged for her food sack and the purse with the cat. He took one more second to sigh at the dilemma she posed. Anyone would recognize her in the halls, but they couldn't dawdle to think about it. "Stay close to me always. Keep your head low. Arrows are going to fly."

Chapter 67
A Brand Burns

The strange howls the naerscouels made sounded even more horrid as the creatures fell dead, their bodies and heads sliced cleanly through by morkblades. Dorhen stood over what must've been the twentieth group of those creatures, not counting all the sorcerers they'd met, looking sultry and stippled with blood spray. He didn't seem to mind at all.

When he turned back to Kalea, he grinned menacingly.

She frowned back despite his pride. The words *weapon of war* spiraled through her head, intertwined with, *He'll make you a monster*. The more he killed, the more beastly characteristics he took on. If she joined with him, she would apparently become something similar.

"Are you coming?" he asked, seeming not to take offense at her lack of enthusiasm for his feat.

"Yeah." She walked to keep up, tired, sore, and chilled from spending all day running around Ilbith. Even Daghahen's musty, rickety bed seemed inviting at this point. At least they drew close to the bottom of the tower. Warmth radiated from the kitchen. After Dorhen's performance, she no longer worried about whether they'd get through or who would be waiting behind the next door.

The change of scenery confirmed her guess because she recognized some of these halls. More servants than sorcerers milled about down in these lower levels. How many sorcerers were left after all the ones he'd killed? For all she knew, despite his failure to kill Lamrhath, Dorhen had liberated these people from their dominant counterparts. They obviously weren't aware of what had happened on the floors above, because some froze and others darted away when Kalea and Dorhen walked through. On second thought, the sight of Wikshen should normally make people fly into panic.

"Are you Wikshen?" a man called from behind, stopping them both.

"What do you think?" Dorhen countered cockily.

"My lord." The man bowed low. "I wish to thank you!"

And here Kalea had been pondering the major changes occurring in this tower.

Wikshen narrowed his eyes. "So then…what? Are you going to convert to Wikshonism?" He shot Kalea a smirk, but she couldn't find it funny. Not at all. These people didn't need to become Wikshonites, they needed true liberation. The One Creator's love would heal them of all their years of suffering and misery.

She paused in her thoughts. She hadn't thought much about the One Creator in a long time. She'd spent far too long in Wikhaihli pretending to worship Wikshen, and on some occasions actually worshipping him. Now she had him to herself, his crowd of adoring women left far behind. Though he'd been using his "Wikshen" skills to get them through the thick of the tower, she wished he could be "Dorhen" again.

The dusty servant man bowed several more times, stuttering excitedly while she was in her thoughts. Dorhen glared down at him over his folded, muscly arms. "It's right through this door, my lord. We have it all laid out. We were so thrilled to see what you did for us, and we got right to it. You must be starving, my lord. Come, you deserve it."

"I *am* hungry," Dorhen confirmed, looking at Kalea. "I'm always hungry..." He smiled at her. "For many things lately." He held his hand out, and she took it.

"What are we doing?" she asked.

"We're going to eat."

She canceled her next step. "Is that wise?"

"I don't see why a few bites would be unwise. Besides, I'm also dying of thirst. You know how hot it was in that tower?"

"But—but..." She stuttered. "We're not out of here yet..."

"Relax," he said. "You can sit on my lap if you like."

"Sit...on...your..." Those words resonated with familiarity. "Dorhen, I don't think..."

Her hesitance didn't seem to matter. "Safest place in the world, not to mention the most fun." He pulled her forward. The door swung open. Inside, no feast awaited them. Red filled the dining room—long rows of red-robes. Lamrhath stood to the side with his arms crossed.

At the center of the robed men waited a stranger one in tight, red leather. Instead of a robe, he wore a red skirt similar to Wikshen's battleshift. The leather upper section of his costume went all the way up his throat. He pulled a mask that punched out his eyes over his face. Blood trails ran down his cheeks, and he screamed at the pain but proceeded through his ritual in defiance of his bodily discomfort. Once the mask was in place, a yellow gem on the forehead lit up, along with two in his gloved palms.

Dorhen half-turned to backtrack, but couldn't dodge the effect of the masked man's spell. His Wikshen gloves and armbands vanished. In confusion, he threw his hand forward, but nothing came out. His morkblades were absent. Dorhen leaped backward out of the room, pulling Kalea with him.

"What happened?" she asked.

"Wik tells me they've blocked me!" He steadied himself and chose a direction to sprint. When he picked her up and started running, he breathed more heavily than before.

"What does that mean?" she said through all the bouncing turbulence of the ride.

"They've blocked my magic ability! I can't function anymore! And it makes me..." He panted, not needing to tell her the rest of the statement.

The sorcerers weren't about to let them get far, she realized when a bolt of hot, yellow lightning raced down the hall and caught them. Dorhen threw Kalea out of his arms and she rolled, gaining more scrapes to her knees and elbows as he screamed within the menacing lightning behind her. Kalea screamed in sympathy throughout the spell, unsure how to help him. She couldn't.

The lightning spell ended, and he came out of the bright chaos swaying on his feet, alive but smoldering and wearing those swirling burn patterns she'd seen him collect before. She took his arm, and they ran together, narrowly whipping around the corner before the next bolt bounced off the walls, missing them this time. Nonetheless, the sorcerers' laughter echoed after it. Naerscouels accompanied them, howling and yipping with excitement. Apparently, many of Ilbith's tyrants had survived, and they'd delivered a serious blow to Wikshen.

At the end of this corridor gaped a breezy window. Dorhen marched to it. "How strong do you feel now?"

"Oh, no," was all she could say. "No."

"Any better ideas?" He knelt down with his slimy back to her so she could climb on, his blue hair sticking to it. She brushed it out of the way and did as instructed.

The shouting and yipping grew louder. Dorhen lowered himself out onto the wall and down a few stones, with Kalea clinging to his back even less confidently than before. His arms shook as he worked them. He grunted, but kept his teeth clenched tightly by the sound of it. Kalea clamped her lips. She didn't want to talk and throw off his concentration. If they fell, he wouldn't be able to catch them on morkblade wires again.

Above them, three or four sorcerers stuck their heads out the window. To prevent any torches from falling on his head, Dorhen shimmied to the side and descended a little faster. Kalea wanted to remind him to be careful and not go too fast, but she abstained. He knew that anyway.

The sorcerer's heads all receded save for one, a man who hummed and focused his energy in one hand. "He's going to cast!" Kalea warned, and Dorhen tensed up.

Below them, the river crashed against rocks in its whitewater fury, closer than it had appeared when they last scaled the wall, but still too high and treacherous for comfort. If they fell, they fell. At least they would have made the best attempt at escaping this place.

With shaking limbs, Dorhen scaled a little lower and farther to the side. The lightning burst from the jewel in the man's red glove. It arced, dancing from side to side faster than a blink. It struck the wall—actually a metal rod jutting out from it, falling short of Kalea and Dorhen's position.

"Damn!" the sorcerer yelled, and spun around to retreat inside and regroup with his people.

A great tension left Dorhen's body through his mouth. He'd latched onto the stones, apparently hoping to ride the spell to the end without falling. It wouldn't have saved Kalea from the electrocution, though.

Dorhen moved again, frantic, bits of his voice squeezing out in his effort to keep them from falling. She chose not to complain about slipping lower in her cling. Her muscles trembled and her fingers numbed in their laced position around his neck. Her legs wouldn't be able to grip around his torso much longer.

Before she slipped, Dorhen did. Both of them released a desperate shout. The fall only lasted an instant as he found a new grip to catch them. He pulled himself up, shaking more violently, as if he could no longer stand the weight. Kalea's grip suffered worse. Dorhen threw his head back briefly to check the distance again.

No, don't drop into the water! Kalea gritted her teeth so tightly they squeaked. *It's too high!*

He didn't drop. "See the window right there?" he asked, referring to the next closest one coming around the curve of the tower wall. "How good are you at climbing?"

"Oh, no," Kalea repeated.

"Look." Dorhen pointed with his face at another iron rod like the one which had saved them from the lightning. "I'm going to get you to it. Grab it, and then climb to the window from there."

"What about you?"

"I'll be right behind you."

As much as she hated the idea, she knew she couldn't burden him with her weight any longer. They might move quicker when climbing separately. Once she got her hand on the rod, however, her life depended on herself. No more relying on Dorhen's stronger body—stronger than hers, even with his powers blocked.

"Get your feet into some crevices," Dorhen said. "There's one. Put your right foot into it."

I can't do it! She resisted saying that out loud. This was no time for whining, but her arms really were weak and shaky. She tried not to think about how she'd pull herself up onto the windowsill when she reached it.

"Hurry!"

Dorhen's voice set her off. She couldn't disappoint him, especially by falling to her death. She got both of her feet between some stones, and then brazenly shifted her hold from the iron bar to the higher cracks in the wall.

"It's working," she said. "I can do this."

"Of course you can," Dorhen said. He worked beside her, shuffling along at her pace, using mostly the same footholds she chose.

She made good time and finished strong, but not a moment too soon. She approached the window from below, her cold and sore fingers throbbing, and Dorhen warned, "Stay quiet as you get in there."

She moved up one stone—two stones. The smoother, carved stones around the window before her face announced that she'd made it. She put both hands on top. Now to pull herself up.

Two strong arms shot out, grabbed her, and hauled her up fast, before she could react. The room beyond the window was packed wall-to-wall with grinning, red-robed men. They passed Kalea along to the door at the other end, where Lamrhath waited in the hall.

"It's not so easy to escape Ilbith," Lamrhath said with a bland mien.

Kalea turned around and shouted, "Dorhen, don't come in here! They'll catch you!" The sorcerer who held her jostled her to shut up.

"Where is he?" Lamrhath asked the sorcerers by the window.

"He's not there, lord."

Kalea twisted her face. *He didn't fall, did he?*

"Well, that's all right," Lamrhath said, turning his attention back to Kalea. "At least I have you."

"My offer still stands," she said.

He smirked. "But your stud got away already. He left you with me." He waved his ringed hand. "This is actually much better. I'm glad things turned out as they did. If we had enjoyed a fuck together, I would've lost a valuable opportunity to learn all I can about you."

He reached out to touch her face, but she wiggled too much, and he gave up. He directed her attention to the sorcerer with the eye-gouging mask. Its forehead jewel still glowed, which Kalea took as a clue that he maintained the spell which blocked Dorhen's Wikshen abilities. "And with your stud left impotent as he is, his seductive effect shouldn't bother you again."

"So you'll let him go, then?"

"No," Lamrhath said flatly. "I intend to harness his ability for Ilbith."

He raised his hand high to signal another sorcerer who stood shoulder-to-shoulder with the rest of them. This one had a heavily tattooed face, over which he wore a circlet with chains running down to connect to a collar around his tattooed neck. At Lamrhath's signal, he closed his eyes and mumbled a low chant. He put his gloved hands together as the jewels in the palms ignited.

"We'll have Wikshen back with us soon, don't you worry another second, my dear." He raised his chin to say, "Let's go," to the others, and the sorcerers flooded out of the hall, all headed through a certain door. The humming sorcerer began walking without stopping his eerie tune and the masked one walked beside him, somehow uninhibited by his blindness.

Dorhen grabbed a root growing between the rocks to stop himself from being swept away by the strong current of the river. He hadn't meant to fall and leave Kalea to the sorcerers, but his anger would provide enough strength to get him back into that goddess-forsaken tower. Gasping for air, he crawled up on the rock and out of the torrent.

Before he had any chance to rest, his body went up in fiery pain. He screamed in response. The feeling radiated from the brand on his side. It burned as hot and infernal as it had when he got it, possibly more so. The effect left him weak and screaming. By chance alone, he didn't roll mindlessly in the wrong direction, back into the river, although he would've liked the relieving touch of water. Left helpless and miserable, with no ability or knowledge to stop it, the sensation took his thoughts back to her. The one he loved. His mysterious goddess. He'd see her again soon.

"There he is," a male voice said with a jovial ring to another.

In too much pain to care about what went on around him, Dorhen screamed on. His brand glowed bright-red, physically hot.

The two men laughed as they stepped onto his rock. "You get his feet."

To Dorhen's surprise, they didn't yank their hands back in pain when they touched him. His skin, though it felt like fire to him, didn't burn them. The fiery sensation roved over his whole being again and again, all the way back into the tower.

Chapter 68
A Link Melts

Do something! Kalea urged herself as she walked awkwardly next to Lamrhath amid the flowing sea of red-robes through the hall. His snake-like eyes slid to view her briefly, or rather her scantily-clad body. In this big crowd, she could go nowhere, but she couldn't give up! If only she could dart back to the window and jump out...

In all the murmuring of the sorcerers as they walked, a random cough caught her ear. To the side, a big, toothy grin glinted at her from under a red hood, curtained on each side by straggly, blond hair.

Daghahen. Kalea's team wasn't finished yet. Her friends still appeared to be sneaking around. A dingier person made his way beside Daghahen and bumped his shoulder hard enough to take his attention off Kalea. It was Bowaen!

Kalea's heart pounded. She didn't know what those two intended, but she couldn't let Lamrhath take her somewhere to lock her up.

"Aahh!" Kalea whined, raising her tone at the end of it. "Oh, no!" She absently reached out and grabbed Lamrhath's sleeve. He stopped to observe her sudden behavior. "It's happening again!"

She squeezed her legs together for an instant, put out her best ecstatic moan, and pretended to fall backward. Enough men were crowded around to break her fall and ease her to the floor. On the way down, she tore half her bodice to show Lamrhath one breast.

"It's Wikshen!" she cried. "He still has such a bad, bad effect on me! Unhhhh..."

Now lying on the ground, she reached for Lamrhath, who gawked down at her and, within the minute, flinched and put his hand to his stomach. He hissed through his teeth. She could plainly see the deep and solemn desire clouding his mind. She didn't know what condition tormented him, but it clearly plagued him with irresistible animal urges on the flipside of his intelligent, calculating mind.

He worked his lips as if to try to shout an order at his men—who also stalled to gawk at Kalea, though showing far less effect than Lamrhath. No voice emerged from his mouth, only a groan to match her fake ones, an honest communication of body triumphing over mind.

He fell to his knees beside her and ran his fingertips over her exposed nipple. He shook violently. Kalea had never really tried to seduce anyone, but this person must be the easiest in the world. Pain twisted his face in a bizarre blend with the desire.

"You little whore," he growled, trailing his hand down her navel. His other hand held poised on his legging strings. Was he tempted to have sex with her right here? In front of everyone?

She kept up her act no matter what. "You wanna taste me again?" She took his hand and brushed it over her skirt.

Lamrhath closed his eyes and shuddered. "I told you, I won't ruin you before I've studied your abilities." He took his hand away and snatched her face. "But you've got other holes that are just as fun," he said around gritted teeth. His fingers pressed hard, stabbing into her cheeks.

Thunk! Cling-chik-chik! Mere feet away, a head fell and rolled, spilling a huge pool of blood. The tattooed man with all the chains over his face—someone had cut his head off! His dead eyes stared at her from the floor, his golden headdress doused with blood.

Lamrhath lurched back, stunned along with everyone else. Under the cover of Kalea's distraction, Bowaen and Daghahen had unsheathed Hathrohjilh and snuffed out the important spell-caster. In the brief moment of confusion, they both held the sword.

Lamrhath pointed a finger at Daghahen. "You!" His voice roared far through the space.

Daghahen opened his hands from around the sword's handle, and Bowaen took it over. Kalea scrambled to her feet before anyone stepped on her. The next person to eliminate, besides Lamrhath, was the other spell-caster, the one with the red mask who maintained the block on Wikshen's magic ability.

"Get him! Don't let him escape!"

When the room erupted, Daghahen let himself disappear in the confusion of red, leaving Bowaen to swing the sword in a chaotic, uncalculated defense.

"And that's my sword! Get it from him!"

Kalea knew she should try to help Bowaen somehow, but she'd easily be trampled under all the frantic feet. If only she had her washing bat... Finding Dorhen was her other urgent task.

To cover more distance, Gaije carried Mhina through the halls, which were empty for the most part, to his relief. Maybe getting back down to the caves wouldn't be as hard a task as he'd dreaded.

"Wait, Gaije, stop," Mhina said, patting his arm. "Bairhen's here too. We have to find him. And there's other children with us."

Now he had to worry about a whole clutch of children? He huffed.

"Let me down," she said. He did so reluctantly, and she hurried into a specific corridor with bright windows. "In here. I used to live in this room."

She opened a certain door and revealed all of them. The children all froze, sitting on the floor, their mouths and eyes rounding at the intruders.

"Mhina?" one of the children said.

"Where's Bairhen?" Mhina asked.

Before anyone could answer, a woman who had been sitting in a chair behind the door leaned forward. Gaije snatched Mhina up protectively. It was only a young woman, but he couldn't take any chances.

"Wh-who are you?" she ventured to ask.

He hardened his brow. "Where's Bairhen?"

The woman squinted. "You're an elf too?"

He realized with a jolt of panic that he'd forgotten to put his hood up.

She clasped her hands over her bosom, which was raised and bulging up high by her tight bodice. "Have you come to rescue us?"

Mhina pulled away from Gaije's hand. "Yes," she told the group. "We're all going home. But we need Bairhen. Where is he?"

The woman lurched forward and grabbed Gaije's lapel. Her cheeks brightened and her eyes glistened. "Oh, please," she begged him. "Take me too. Please sir, take me. Take me with you. I can look after the children. But please, don't leave me here!"

Her fast action left Gaije with a brief choice to fight her off in case she might pose a threat, but he wound up doing nothing and found her clinging to him and weeping.

She pressed her lips to his throat. "I'll do anything for you, anything! Understand?"

Her kiss against his neck sent odd tingles shooting through him. Shivering, he peeled her hands off of him. He didn't know what was happening, but he couldn't have Mhina seeing whatever it was. "Where's Bairhen?" he pressed.

She nodded. Hope lit her pretty face, which was framed by hair the color of a fawn's coat. "I know where he is," she said. "My name is Cornelia. We can find him together. Come. And we should gather my sisters too."

"Sisters?" Gaije said. "As in novices?"

She smiled, holding his hand warmly to her cleavage. He hadn't even realized she'd retained it.

His hungry eyes often shifting back to Kalea, Lamrhath personally pulled her away from the violence as Bowaen fought off the room full of sorcerers.

"Where are we going?" she asked, and his lip curled in anger.

He reared and delivered a slap to her face that knocked her backward. On the rebound, he hunched over and hugged his stomach in pain. "Don't ask questions," he warned.

On the floor, she curled over and cupped her face. The shock of pain hung around, and she didn't bother to move until he snatched her, grabbing her face and squeezing it between his strong fingers. His eyes lingered on her pouting lips. He leaned down and licked them, taking off the blood his slap had caused.

Kalea shook beneath him, half-expecting him to do as she expected he intended to do—on the floor among all the sorcerers. Frozen in fear, she could only watch, trying to gauge the evil, enigmatic look on his face until behind him, a darker, angrier figure approached. Kalea's expression shifted from terror to surprise, and Lamrhath turned in time to receive Dorhen's vicious blow, knocking him off of her.

"Dorhen!" she cried involuntarily.

His hair hung in wet clumps. He must've fought off his captors when the tattooed man had died. Far across the room, the man maintaining the blocking spell kept his concentration, a half-moon formation of sorcerers standing to protect him. As long as he kept undistracted, Dorhen's magic abilities would remain stifled. Dorhen had already laid flat a number of sorcerers while Lamrhath was struggling with Kalea.

Lamrhath rolled to his hands and knees in a moment of disorientation. Half of the sorcerers in the room leaped to their kingsorcerer's defense, and Dorhen stood between them and Kalea to face them all without a flinch or wink of doubt. Without his superior Wikshen strength and morkblades, he wrestled one after another, punching and kicking and sometimes slamming them against the wall to add to his impressive body count.

Even without the supernatural side effect, Dorhen's reformed body performed well. His vigorous chore of keeping his feet and knocking away attackers got him quickly across the room from Kalea. For a minute, she debated whether to help Dorhen or Bowaen in their struggles, and then it occurred to her to find Daghahen because he had her washing bat.

Out of nowhere, Lamrhath's hand locked around her wrist. "Where do you think you're going?" he growled, standing bent in pain.

"No!" she yelled in his face, raised her knee, and kicked him in the groin as hard as she could.

She darted away as a gap opened up in the floor, leaving him crouched over, groaning in agony. She leaped over and around people, heading in Dorhen's direction, unaware of what burgeoned behind her.

Dorhen pushed his current attacker aside and pointed. The pink haze billowed around Lamrhath like before. He was calling his pixie again, except now Dorhen couldn't face its supernatural power with his own! This time, it didn't remain as mere smoke; a furious pink fire erupted, along with the ominous, echoing howl of an infernal beast.

Long arms with white fur reached out of the blaze, claws raking. The flame moved with them as if they were its body, shifting into a long, galloping torso that leaped across the floor, leaving behind brief, fiery footprints. It bounded for Kalea.

Dorhen swiped three men aside and hurdled over two others, pressing their heads down like a game of leapfrog. It all happened at once. Before she knew it, the galloping fire animal that was Lamrhath landed on the floor beside her. She leaned away from its intense heat. Dorhen reached her simultaneously and grabbed her arm. The old stone floor couldn't take the abuse. The flame creature's feet broke through upon landing.

They fell. It fell. Kalea found herself hanging, caught in Dorhen's grip. He lay on the floor spread-eagled, his other hand precariously holding the unreliable floor stones.

Below her, the stones tumbled down. A huge hiss and explosion of steam blasted up past her, into their story. A sorcerer took advantage of Dorhen's compromised position and drove a knife into his chest. With a roar, he let go of the stones, and both of them fell. Despite all the happenings, he held onto her.

They landed in water with a splash. Kalea's feet touched tile at the bottom. It wasn't deep water, but it still steamed and bubbled from when Lamrhath fell in. Wall sconces provided light to see in the steam-filled room. They had fallen into an indoor bath.

Alive and strong despite his new stab wound, Dorhen retained his hold on Kalea and rushed her out of the water. So far, there was no sign of Lamrhath.

She observed the bleeding hole in Dorhen's chest as he kept his attention urgently on all their surroundings. "Are you all right?"

"I'm still Wikshen," he reminded her, not bothering to check his own damage. He shook his head at the space when the mess settled. Shouting echoed shrilly above. Bowaen was up there swinging the sword.

"We must be close to the bowels of Ilbith," Kalea said. "The garbage dump." She looked up through the hole in the ceiling at the floor they'd left behind. "Bowaen!" she called up.

His head appeared over the hole. Maybe he'd thinned the enemy by now.

"We fell down here. We're fine!"

"I'll meet you down below!" Bowaen responded, and launched back into the fight.

Other voices echoed on their new floor. "That was a mighty boom," someone said, a voice Kalea recognized.

"This is the bath house, and through there is the privy cave." That voice too.

"Del? Vivene?" Kalea called.

The two sprinted around the corner, and their questioning looks shifted to relief at who they found. Vivene paused fast when she noticed Wikshen standing beside Kalea, who ran forward to throw her arms around her.

"Dorhen, this is my friend Vivene, and you know Del."

Vivene didn't return her hug. To Kalea's confusion, she turned and retraced her steps back into the shadowy corridor. "Come on now. It seems safe."

"Did someone say 'Dorhen?'"

A third person entered after Del and Vivene, a tall, slight, beaten woman wearing a wool cap. Bruises on her face had bloomed to such deep colors that Kalea winced in empathy. She would have to commend the two for rescuing such a poor soul.

On second thought, Kalea started at this new person's recital of Dorhen's name. The beaten woman held her hand extended cautiously on the side with a bandage across her eye. A simple torn gown under an apron covered her. She dropped her hands to stare openly with her one eye at those who stood before her.

"Dorhen," the woman said with her eye aimed right at him.

Kalea looked to Dorhen for answers, but he appeared blank. "Do you know her?"

The woman pulled her cap off, revealing a bald head and pointed ears—an elf! Her lips tried a smile, slow and tender, as if it hurt to do so. "Dorhen," she said again.

Kalea blinked in shock. She looked the beaten woman over again and again. Bald head. Bruises. One big, feminine eye gleaming in the dim light. She might've been beautiful in another time, but…

"Who is this, Dorhen?"

Dorhen stepped forward, holding Kalea's hand. His spellbound draw toward the other woman stung, but... Kalea remembered what Daghahen had told her at the start of their journey through the tower. *Could this be her?*

"It's me," the elf-woman said to him.

Dorhen tensed up beside Kalea and squeezed her hand. "Kalea, this is..." he whispered. "You're my mother."

Daghahen's assessment had been right! Dorhen had told her his mother was dead. He'd told her his father—Daghahen—had murdered her long ago in a house fire.

Dorhen's mother opened her arms as he approached, giving him a warm smile. "I finally found you," she said.

He dropped Kalea's hand.

Vivene looked at Kalea, amazed, and shrugged. "She told us she wanted to find her son," Vivene explained. "I didn't think she meant *this* person."

As the pool behind them continued to bubble and hiss, Kalea grabbed Dorhen's arm. They didn't actually have time to discuss who knew who.

Dorhen ignored Kalea's prodding. "How did you recognize me?" His shaky voice threatened an outburst of tears.

"I don't need anyone to point me to *my* son."

Del gasped and stepped back, pointing past Kalea. "Kah—!" he hissed, but couldn't seem to spit out any more.

Kalea whirled around to see Lamrhath rising from the fizzing water. He had returned to his natural elven form with his clothes intact and a new dark stare and creepy smirk to complement it. Dorhen spun and leaped to a defensive stance in front of them, pushing Kalea behind him.

To add to the strangeness of his presence, the water evaporated off of Lamrhath in big puffs of steam. His pink, glowing stab wounds remained despite his transformations. Kalea took it as an effect that would last until the wounds healed properly on their own. His pixie couldn't heal him instantly like Dorhen's could.

The noises no longer echoed above; they stood in the grave silence of Lamrhath's presence. Kalea stepped up beside Dorhen to face Lamrhath with him. "Lamrhath," she said, "what will it take for you to let us go? Do you want Hathrohjilh back?"

Lamrhath's lips spread past his white, bloodthirsty teeth. "Ha!" he mocked, with such spite that he lurched forward.

Dorhen pushed her behind him again. "You can't negotiate with him," Dorhen growled, never taking his eyes off the kingsorcerer.

"Dorhen," his mother said, keeping her snug place between Vivene and Del, "it was all him. If I die today, I want you to remember that he took me from you when you were a child. He was jealous of your father."

Lamrhath shot a pointed finger at her, and Dorhen tensed up more. If he didn't have a block on his magic, Kalea knew he wouldn't be standing still right now. Lamrhath countered, "This *whore* seduced me in my dreams!" He pointed his other hand at Kalea. "Just like this younger whore wishes to do!"

Dorhen bristled so sharply, Kalea's own flesh flared.

Lamrhath regarded Dorhen's mother again. "But this whore, whore number one... She really got inside me. She burrowed in..." He caressed the side of his own face. "Into my mind like a tick sucking away my soul and possessing my husk. This whore is special."

He took a breath and surveyed the lot of them, but settled again on Dorhen's mother. "Orinleah," he said her name as if tasting it on his lips. "Isn't it a dreadful crime in Norr to tease a *saehgahn*'s body and feeble mind like that? Did you do the same thing to Daghahen?"

Dorhen flinched. Kalea could tell he wanted to turn around and see his mother's impression of all this, but couldn't abandon his focus on the threat Lamrhath posed.

Lamrhath shook his head, appearing far more relaxed by now than Dorhen. "You were a bad whore, my Orinleah. My shining ornament. My pretty pet. My silky pussy. Like pink velvet, warm and wet and ready to embrace me."

He closed his eyes and smiled. He bowed his head. "But thank you," he said. "Thank you for remembering to wear your necklace today."

On the last word, he raised his hand, and the pink light erupted around it. Orinleah gasped and grasped her throat.

Vivene screamed.

Del lurched.

Dorhen dropped his guard.

In the sudden panic, Kalea couldn't tell what had happened. Orinleah lost her footing, and Vivene and Del caught and eased her to the floor. Dorhen launched in the opposite direction to pounce on Lamrhath. Shoving his uncle back into the tiled pool, he pushed his head under the water.

"Breathe deep!" Vivene said urgently to Orinleah. She dabbed her throat with her skirt, but each swipe stained it with more and more blood.

Del patted the better side of her face. "Stay awake! Stay awake!" he said.

All of it happened too fast. Kalea stood frozen in the moment. Helpless. Numb. Everything rushing around her.

"Hey! K'lea!" A shining blade caught her eye. Bowaen peered around the corner, holding Hathrohjilh. He'd found his way down to them. "C'mon! I think I found the way back to the big garbage grave."

Kalea snapped out of her trance and shouted Dorhen's name, and then ordered Vivene and Del, "Lift her up!" They cradled Orinleah's light body between them. "Follow Bowaen!"

Lamrhath wrenched himself out of Dorhen's angry hands and sprang out of the pool, this time dripping wet, and then threw down an exploding object from his belt pouch. A golden light flashed and settled into the shape of an archway. Lamrhath ducked under it and vanished through the magic portal. It closed immediately after him.

Kalea hissed. "Of course he has portals! He'll come back, I know it!" she warned Dorhen as he stepped out of the pool, also dripping, but so angry his body heat steamed the water off. His pixie had already healed his stab wound despite his magic block. Kalea ran to meet him. "We should run now. Hurry to the caves."

They weren't far from the huge, stinking garbage pit at all. The problem was, it raged with fire, so hot they felt it long before they entered its massive cavern. The intrusion of its bright light slowed Dorhen's steps, though he pushed on.

"Shit!" Bowaen stopped to gawk at the raging inferno with the rest of them. "How do we get out now? We came from the tunnels at the bottom of the pit!"

"Oh, Creator!" Vivene wailed as she and Del gingerly placed Orinleah on the pebbly ground.

Orinleah's stare grew vacant. Dorhen ran to kneel beside her, and Kalea followed. The ground here slanted toward the Grave's edge, steeper and steeper the farther they went, making it a challenge to stand and walk around at certain spots.

Kalea finally saw what had happened to Orinleah. Her ruby necklace had broken—or burst, leaving several open wounds in place of each jewel, wide and crusting over already. The burn marks on her skin resembled the necklace's original shape, as if it had melted into hot, liquid metal.

"Venom," Kalea whispered. "Her necklace was spelled." The wound reminded her all too well of the nasty poisons she herself had endured in recent history.

Orinleah moved her mouth fruitlessly.

"*Aahmei*," Dorhen uttered and curled over, weeping as he watched his mother edge closer to death. He looked to Kalea often, a question of some sort in his eyes, but Kalea had nothing to offer him.

Orinleah's eye glazed over, but she fought to keep alive, to move her hand, reaching it to his face. He leaned down to let her touch his cheek.

"Don't," she whispered weakly. Dorhen sobbed, but Kalea listened hard to try to catch her message and convey it to him later if need be. Orinleah, tried again, her eyes fluttering closed. "Dorhen... Don't...give uhhh…"

Her last breath hissed out. Her hand dropped. Dorhen cradled his mother's head; his weeping joined the cavern's many noises.

"Let me down. Let me down right now, Gaije!"

Behind Kalea, Gaije arrived with a little blonde girl who wiggled out of his arms and slid feet-first to the ground. In her daze, Kalea hardly registered that he'd finally found his sister. The little girl ran toward her, Dorhen, and Orinleah's body. Bowaen approached Gaije and put a hand on his shoulder in a gesture of camaraderie.

The little girl—Mhina—dropped down by Orinleah's head and put a hand to her forehead. She waited, lifted her hand, and put it back. A hurt look crumpled her little mouth and brow.

"I'm sorry," she said. Frowning, she crawled backward and dropped her head into a bow to the floor. "I am sorry," she said again. It must've been a Norrian show of respect.

Kalea stood over Dorhen and embraced his head to her bosom. She'd forgotten about her ripped top until now.

Mhina's shrill scream cut the moment short. A glowing pink lasso pinned her arms down, and Lamrhath stood at the other end of the tether.

All around the cavern's sides, the sorcerers appeared at openings to occupy every ledge and walkway in the complex. *Wrooph!* A wall of ethereal fire erupted between Gaije and his sister; the sorcerers all worked together to cast and maintain it. Bowaen, too, was trapped on Gaije's side of it. The wall wound around Lamrhath, Mhina, Kalea, and Dorhen, blocking their friends' help.

Dorhen placed Orinleah's head down and rose with a new anger—a new vigor that didn't need Wik to fuel it. The sorcerers on their side of the fire wall moved in with their red gloves charged. Kalea and Dorhen stood together, ready but without a clue how they could ever survive this day. On a nearby ledge, Dorhen's blocking sorcerer stood with his glowing jeweled mask. The blood from his eyes under the mask had dried and flaked. If she could somehow get to him and distract his concentration…

"Gaaaaaije!" Mhina called through her screaming as Lamrhath dragged her toward him, arm over arm by the magic lasso.

Gaije attempted to shoot an arrow at Lamrhath through the fire wall, but it burned up like a twig in the intense heat. Gaije only had a few arrows left. He stood planted next to Bowaen in their position inside a loop of fire, waiting for some chance to make a fruitful shot.

Dorhen widened his stance and gripped Kalea's wrist to the point of pain. The rows of sorcerers all pointed their jeweled palms right at them, as if to zap them with some spell if they moved wrong.

"My darling, where've you been? Let me hold you, my sweet dumpling," Lamrhath said when he had Mhina in range of grabbing her.

She screamed and thrashed, red-faced, as he lifted her up. He held one of her hands and waited for his stab wounds to close up, including the one on his forehead caused by Dorhen's morkblade. When all of them had been healed, Mhina swayed in sleepy lethargy.

"I think she just healed him," Kalea murmured to Dorhen. "She must've tried to heal your mother."

Mhina lay her head down on Lamrhath's shoulder as he swayed in the way one would lull a child to sleep. He cooed to her in a voice manufactured for the sweetest of infants, calling her "my pretty pet" and "my soft little kitty-cat," all of these terms a little too close to the disturbing nicknames he'd called Orinleah. He smiled easily with her in his custody. Smug, as if he'd settle in and watch the impending violence unfold from the sidelines.

"Well?" Lamrhath said to his men. "What are you waiting for?"

At that, they all released an earth-shattering lightning bolt from their gloves. Dorhen pushed Kalea away from him, and she tumbled to the ground. All of the bolts struck him, and none touched her. When they all cleared, she found him lying on the ground, as dead-looking as Orinleah.

Vivene and Del found themselves blocked off from everyone else behind a fiery partition. Del gripped his heavy smoking pipe, but had no one to strike with it. From their position, Vivene watched the lightning bolts swirl toward one central figure in the commotion: Wikshen, with Kalea dangerously close to him. She called Kalea's name in fright, and then a crack of the thunder put her on the floor with its startling boom.

"You all right?" Del asked, and helped her up.

She didn't answer right away. Their vantage showed how the fire wall wound and wove around several groups, trapping in Kalea and Wikshen, Lamrhath and the little girl, and everyone else in their own section. The sorcerers who hummed and concentrated all around the cave added to those divisions. A new wall whooshed to life and stretched across the way to add even more complication to the odd chessboard below.

Vivene grabbed Del's shirt and pulled him close. "We gotta distract them and mess up their casting."

"What do you propose?"

Vivene shook her head and looked around. Pebbly debris was abundant in their section, which must mean it got less foot traffic. Vivene picked one up, aimed, and chucked it at the nearest spell-caster on a ledge above them. He staggered and fell out of his murmuring. The fire thinned at one point.

"Are you crazy?" Del growled under the fiery roar. "Do that enough times for them to notice, and we'll be the next lightning rods!"

Vivene pointed to Wikshen's body lying singed and smoking on the ground below. "We'll probably be next anyway."

Kalea squealed to see Dorhen in such a state and ran to him. He sat up, still alive.

"Stay away from me," he warned. "They're going to cast spells until they've subdued me. All lightning spells will hit me because I'm the strongest conductor here."

The sorcerers murmured as one, causing a deep, echoing rumble through the cavern that mingled with the roaring flames of the refuse heap and the fire walls.

"Go!" With a hand to her rear end, he pushed her away, and she stumbled.

Dorhen leaped to his feet and ran at one such group to distract and stir them up, and to confuse any of their associates who cast a spell in his direction. Taking Dorhen's word, Kalea looked around for a way to be useful. She focused on his blocking sorcerer, perched tall and proud on his ledge.

Dorhen's antics proved useful. He held a man's wrist and refused to let go. "Cast it! Cast it, you bastards!" They all hesitated, knowing that if they hit him with lightning, their comrade would take the bolt with him.

Lamrhath rolled his eyes and stepped forward, supporting Mhina as if she were his own. "Cowards! Here, I'll do it!"

He raised his glove and let a bolt spring forward with ease. It arched across the long distance and hit Dorhen, traveling through his body and into the sorcerer's. By the end of the tense, loud lightshow, both of them had fallen. Kalea cringed for Dorhen, but he remained hard to kill regardless of his blocked powers. The fire caging them in was another story.

"Re-form, you idiots!" Lamrhath ordered, stepping back to resume his observation.

While Dorhen lay on the ground beside the charred corpse of the sorcerer, the others straightened up their lines and charged their gloves for another round. When Dorhen rose up and attempted to manhandle or pester them, they released horizontal pillars of flames from their jeweled palms instead of lightning. What had been a game of lightning conduction became a game of chasing Wikshen around with the element he hated most.

"Psst." Someone caught Kalea's attention as she stood near the blocking sorcerer's ledge, at a loss. "Kalea." The only sorcerer present without any red gloves stepped forward. "You forgot this."

"Daghahen?"

He handed her the washing bat he'd smuggled under his robe. Before she could say anything, he backed away and blended himself in with the sorcerers. She gripped the bat in her hand for about a second before knowing what to do with it. She climbed up the rocks skirting the masked sorcerer's ledge, reared the bat back...

"Hey, what are you doing, bitch?"

They'd already spotted her! No time to reconsider her plan. She hurled the bat at the sorcerer.

In his blindness, he never saw it coming. It hit the jewel in the forehead of his mask, causing a chaotic reaction of sizzling and flying sparks. He yelled and grasped at the mask. Even though her damage probably did the job fine, his threat ended for good when he toppled over the ledge and fell into the fire wall below.

Kalea looked back toward Dorhen's struggle in time to catch his black gloves and armbands reappearing. Toeless socks materialized on his feet. Wikshen's full capabilities had returned.

"Get her!"

But Kalea's bold action wouldn't go unpunished. A section of the fire wall vanished to make way for a clutch of hooded red-robes sprinting toward her, gloves poised, and she no longer had a bat to bash into their fragile, magic-conducting jewels.

Vivene gasped and pointed to Kalea's treacherous situation. "Del, can you hit them?"

He grunted. "Too far! I guess Kalea's on her own."

Vivene swallowed against her rising nausea. She had plenty of other sorcerers to throw rocks at, though. Maybe with some deductive reasoning, she could figure out which ones controlled certain sections of the fire wall...

"Get your pipe ready," she said, and launched a rock with all of her might at one of them. He went down, out cold, and hard enough to alert his companions. They dropped their concentration, and narrow holes in the fire wall opened at random places, including right in front of Vivene and Del.

"Now's your chance!" she shouted, and shoved Del through into the neighboring section.

"Hey!" he cried. The fire wall healed behind him, leaving them separated in their own hot compartments.

She pointed despite his upset. "Keep your eyes open as I throw more rocks. Get to Kalea!"

He scoffed. "I'd rather get to Bowaen and help lay flat some of these pricks."

Vivene picked up the next palm-sized rock. "They don't even have access to fight anyone." She chucked and missed. "Damn it!"

Kalea ran from her pursuers toward Dorhen. His movements weren't much quicker in the bright heat of this cavern, but at least his morkblades were back, which he threw in big, horizontal arcs, cutting down rows of sorcerers where they stood. Kalea gave a yelp and froze as one big, black blade, spinning end over end, rushed past her and sliced cleanly through one of the sorcerers.

Dorhen turned to that occurrence with horror on his face. "You wanna get cut in half?" he barked at her.

Before she could answer, the rest of the sorcerers ran up and snagged her. Cussing under his breath, he threw a heavy side kick into the head of one of his opponents, and shot to help her. Her captors scattered and chanted to charge their gloves for different spells, especially one that caused a shield to spring from their palms to protect them from the morkblades.

Outside their section of the fire wall, Kalea caught glimpses of Daghahen moving among the sorcerers, performing little tricks to throw off their concentration, tripping one and spitting words into others' ears which apparently foiled their chants. The damage to their formations and morale grew. More and more gaps appeared in the fire wall. Daghahen's efforts opened up a large gap, which allowed Gaije and Bowaen to move through and aid Kalea and Dorhen.

"Bowaen!" Daghahen called. He pointed to Dorhen, a signal for Bowaen to hand the sword over. Bowaen ignored him.

After stabbing a morkblade into the head of the last sorcerer in their vicinity, Dorhen sprang toward Lamrhath, who looked slightly less confident than before. He would soon make it his task to escape with

Mhina. Gaije charged in his direction too with an arrow drawn, but he didn't release it with his sister in the line of fire.

Reacting fast, Lamrhath blew on the jewel in his own glove and pushed his hand forward, creating a blast of wind to stop Dorhen and Gaije. Gaije fell flat to his front and waited for the spell to be over. Dorhen, however, tumbled backward down the slope and fell into the Grave.

Kalea rushed to him and found him clinging, one-handed, to the ledge. The flames below licked up at his feet. His eyelids drooped sleepily. "No! Dorhen! Keep strong!" She grabbed his arm to lend him support. "Hold on! You can't fall asleep!"

Like a raindrop evaporating in the sun, the intense fire sucked away his energy. If he couldn't pull himself up, he'd fall and be gone forever. Fire was the only thing that could kill a Wikshen.

Kalea held his arm. "Give me your other hand!" she shouted, but he didn't respond.

The heat blazed against her too. His skin heated up hotter than she could stand—metal moved through it, after all, minerals he'd worked to absorb from the stone floors. None of that would matter anymore if he fell. All the fighting they'd done, all that work. She wept in her struggle, but refused to give up. "Dorhen!"

Bowaen appeared beside them in his own struggle with two sorcerers. He ducked one's blade and attempted to strike the other, but the man's sorcerous shield held off Hathrohjilh as efficiently as the morkblades. The one with the dagger tripped him, causing him to drop Hathrohjilh, and it skidded off the edge and into the fire pit.

Back flat on the floor and teetering at the edge, Bowaen reacted fast and rolled at their feet. One sorcerer flew straight off, and the other tumbled over to hang as Dorhen did. Bowaen rose and stomped on his fingers until he, too, fell.

"Damn it!" he yelled. "My sword's gone!"

"Bow-a-eeeennnn!" Kalea called.

He joined her in grabbing at Dorhen to keep him from falling. "If the bastard would wear real clothes, we wouldn't have this problem." He gripped Dorhen's hair. "Wake up, you bastard! Pull yourself up! Don't be a sissy!" His agitation made Dorhen's eyelids flutter. "Come on, get up here, you stupid lech!"

Dorhen reached his other hand up, and Kalea and Bowaen both grabbed it. It took their combined strength to lift him up until Dorhen lay on the ground, safe but exhausted.

The fight raged behind them. Lamrhath used Mhina as a human

shield to keep Gaije from firing any arrows at him. Del ran about with his pipe in hand, and Vivene joined his side when she found a break in the fire, where she continued to throw rocks at sorcerers from the bunch she'd gathered in her skirt. She caused a few more to lose their concentration. Otherwise, fire flew every which way. A new group of sorcerers approached Lamrhath; apparently, he'd been waiting for them.

Kalea shook Dorhen as Bowaen ran to rejoin the fight. "Help us, Dorhen. Help me."

He dragged himself up. His mother's body lay motionless nearby, amidst the violence. Perhaps the sight of her set him off again, and soon he was running and throwing furious morkblades. He thinned the room of sorcerers until no more extra fires burned except that which roared down in the Grave.

Kalea approached Vivene to throw rocks with her. Vivene gasped and pointed. "Over there!"

A large group of women—with Cornelia in the lead—were coming down the winding path, each one carrying or holding a little child's hand. They were all novices! After Cornelia, Kalea recognized Millie, Opal, and the rest.

"Gaije!" Cornelia shouted. "We did as you said. We made it here!"

Gaije was too busy to get the message, but Kalea waved in excitement. When Gaije did notice, he threw his hand up, signaling them to stop on the path. It wasn't safe enough for them to descend yet. Lamrhath remained at the center of an army of dead sorcerers who'd tried to protect him before his last resort, another magical portal, crackled in the air. This one showed up larger and appeared between the golden rods wielded by two specialized sorcerers.

Lamrhath leaped through and Gaije sprang in after him, sparing not a moment or ounce of energy in doing so. The two sorcerers released their poles, and Daghahen jumped from the crowd of remaining red-robes to catch one of them. He growled, hands sizzling on the pole to keep the crackling portal open. His hair waved wildly in the magic energy. Dorhen killed the two sorcerers before they could fight back and ushered more people to duck through under Daghahen's arms: Bowaen, Del, and Vivene.

Kalea called to Cornelia's large group. "Hurry! This is our way out!"

Daghahen screamed through his gritted teeth. It must've hurt like the lightning Dorhen had endured. Dorhen ran toward the women and children. He took two youngsters under his arms and pushed them through the portal to whatever unknown place it led. The long line of women approached with the rest of them, and he herded them through.

He looked at Kalea next, but she was concerned with Daghahen.

"I can't hold it!" Daghahen warned. "Get through there, girl!"

"What about you?"

"Go!"

Kalea looked back once more to make sure no one else lingered, only poor Orinleah's cold body. Daghahen's wife. Dorhen took Kalea's arm, ready to shove her if she didn't move fast enough.

"Wait!" she urged him. Kalea leaned over and kissed Daghahen's clammy cheek. The supposed electricity of the portal didn't transfer from him to her on contact, but she did feel a cold force pushing against her lips from his face. "Thank you," she said, and then she too went through the portal with Dorhen after her.

Cold air. Kalea leaped into a cool evening atmosphere, a sharp contrast to the burning Grave. Many voices shouted, especially the men's. Dorhen lunged past her to join the action. Kalea didn't have to turn around to know that Daghahen hadn't, and couldn't, follow them through the portal. He had made himself into a portal pillar.

They had wound up in a grassy valley in the Black Mountains. The men cornered Lamrhath up ahead, hell-bent on getting Mhina away from him. He clung to the poor child jealously. Kalea needed only stand and watch with the other women.

When he gained an amount of space, Lamrhath checked his belt to find one more glass spell ball. He raised it above his head. In the instant before he let it fall, Gaije took a shot, using his greatest feat of marksmanship to hit Lamrhath's shoulder and miss his sister.

Lamrhath dropped her with a pitch and a stagger. The arrow stood out from his flesh. He reached for her, but his portal opened beside him and Dorhen was already swiping her up like a hawk, now fast and alert in the darkening fresh air.

Gaije pulled back another arrow, and Lamrhath had only a split second to fall through the portal before it dissipated. Gaije's arrow pierced the grass where he'd been.

Chapter 69
A Shadow Confesses

It wasn't too hard to find Daghahen's cave dwelling from where they'd emerged through Lamrhath's portal. The space lacked its owner's welcoming presence. Daghahen had stayed behind to use whatever sorcererous ability he retained to hold the portal open long enough for seven people, plus a load of refugees, to run through at the last minute. Knowing all of this made Kalea's heart burn as she reentered his home.

She counted her novice sisters along the way back. They'd lost so many, including Rose. Vivene told her the horrible story with tears in her eyes and hardly a voice to get through it.

They'd also lost Orinleah. So far, Dorhen hadn't mentioned her. He walked silently at the head of the group, leading the way through the caves because he could see in the dark best. Kalea didn't try to prompt him. In fact, she let him have space to walk alone, unable to gauge if he wanted company or not.

She didn't know how to act around him during these raw hours, so she kept to her novice sisters, finding comfort in their nostalgic presence, though they'd all changed since the convent. None of them acted like the same young, foolish girls they all used to be.

And they'd lost two priceless weapons, Hathrohjilh and her washing bat. Maybe they didn't need them anymore. She didn't regret losing her washing bat to the fire because it had won Dorhen his freedom to cast spells again, which had turned the tables in their favor. Spells supplied by a dark pixie. The pixie still owned half his mind. They might've defeated Lamrhath and rescued Mhina and the novices, but Wikshen remained another matter. At least she had gotten him out of Ilbith and reunited with him. That's what she wanted…right?

Daghahen's house wasn't big enough to shelter everyone, so Bowaen, Gaije, and Del got to work situating other spaces and old housing shells for the women and children to sleep in. Kalea stripped the blankets off Daghahen's bed and handed them off to keep the others warm. She could sleep on the bed's flattened straw. With the activity winding down and everyone settling in, she finally realized her own soreness and exhaustion.

Walking past the nook Gaije and Mhina had chosen to sleep in, she couldn't help but notice Cornelia hunkered down next to them. "Do you two know each other?"

Cornelia nodded enthusiastically. "We all have Gaije to thank for getting out of there. He found me and the children. He's a hero. He's my hero."

Gaije sat beside her stiffly, devoid of anything to say. Kalea blinked her eyes at both of them. Moving along, she patted Mhina on the head as the little girl snuggled into Gaije's side. Beside her sat a young boy-elf, also rescued from Ilbith, although the boy sat proudly on his own outside of Gaije's and Cornelia's parental comfort.

Kalea said to Mhina, "I'm so happy to meet you, Mhina. I've heard a lot about you."

"Like what?" Mhina asked, giving a wide grin with a hint of mischief. She showed a lot of spunk considering the day she'd endured.

Kalea laughed. "Like how pretty you are and how nice you are, and your brother was right about all of it." She leaned down and gave Gaije a kiss atop his head. His eyes changed from content to curious at her action. "Good night," was all she said.

She followed the carved path, bidding almost everyone good night in the same way. She hugged Vivene hard. When they pulled apart, Vivene cried quietly. She put out a laugh as if to cover her tears and shook her head. Kalea couldn't hold in her emotion very well at seeing her.

"It's still hard to believe," Vivene said. "I can't fathom looking at you right now." She sniffled.

"Don't be a soft-hearted-ninny on me," Kalea said, and they both shared another teary laugh. "Will you be all right tonight?"

"Yeah," Vivene said. "I made a friend in Il…up there." She nodded to Del, who stood talking to Bowaen a few paces away.

Kalea couldn't restrain her smirk. "Ooooooh, I see." She shook her finger. "You'd better behave yourselves."

"Ha!" Vivene shot back, and gave her a little push, much like she used to do back in the day.

"Hey, Del!" Kalea called, drawing his attention. "See? Not all vestals are bad."

Del smirked in return, and Kalea left them at that and retreated to Daghahen's little house behind "the only door in the city." She found the inside of it empty save for one lantern she'd left lit.

"Dorhen?" she called. He wasn't in here. She thought she'd seen him somewhere along the path as she made her rounds, but she had assumed he'd meet her back here.

He'd better not have run off again. She blew out a breath and leaned out the door to call to Bowaen. That's when Dorhen appeared.

"There you are," she said with a start. "Do you want to have a bite to eat with me before I go to sleep?"

He didn't reply. He bowed to enter the dwelling, causing her to step back.

"Are you all right?"

He stood tall over her. She couldn't read him, but he'd come into some kind of dark mood. Had he shifted back to Wikshen's personality after all of today's violent activity?

Kalea's heart sped to pounding. "Dorhen, listen—" He put his hands on her arms and pushed her deeper into the house, walking backward. "What are you doing? Hold on. Dorhen?" He squeezed her arms. "Wait, stop."

He didn't. Apparently, her volume increased, because Bowaen's face appeared in the doorway to check on her. She didn't know what to tell him. Dorhen pushed her toward the bed.

"No!" she squealed.

Del's face appeared, followed by Vivene's. Dorhen pushed her farther. "They're watching," she protested. "Not now, not here!"

"Kalea?" Bowaen barked and lunged over the threshold. Dorhen ignored him.

Kalea shook. He was really going to do it? Force her to the bed and…force *himself* on her? She didn't know how to feel about this. The suddenness wasn't appropriate for the time and place. She wanted to do this, but not in front of her friends! She assumed he would come to her for this eventually, though. Maybe he thought of this as some strange way to deal with his grief.

"Dorhen, please!" She at least wanted to reassure her friends she'd be okay and close the door like a decent human being.

When the backs of her legs hit the bed frame, Dorhen dropped before her, dragging his hands down her dress and wrenching the hem in his fists. He let out a sob. He was crying?

Bowaen stood behind him, frozen mid-step on his way to haul Dorhen outside. At his change of gesture, Bowaen dipped his chin and ushered the others away from the door. He did Kalea and Dorhen the courtesy of closing it.

Now alone with him, Kalea put her hands on his head and combed them through his hair. She sank down to sit on the bed, and he laid his head on her lap. She whispered, "I'm here." After a few minutes of letting him weep into her skirt, she pulled on his arm. "Come on. On the bed."

He obeyed, crawling up with her and curling his knees due to the bed's small size. Its wood creaked under his weight. They got into a coil together, his face nuzzled into her bosom as she tenderly and absently stroked the hair on his temple.

She hummed softly, and he listened, not yet ready to speak. They would probably sleep the whole night like this. Since arriving back here, she'd reclaimed her old clothes and changed into her chemise for the night. Its drawstring collar loosened, and she paid no mind to how slackly she lounged.

She leaned down and whispered into his smooth hair above his ear, "Dorhen..." She meant it as much as a comforting sound as a statement-opener. "I love you. I'm going to stay by your side. Okay?"

He shrugged his shoulder and sniffled. He kept his eyes closed and his face buried in her breasts. She caressed his cheek and jaw. In this private space, she could find the liberty to touch him in any way. She couldn't refuse right now if he wanted to...

She put that thought aside. "Listen," she whispered again, "I'm going to try..." She took a breath. "I'm going to help you. I'll do anything and everything in my power to cleanse you of this demon."

He sucked in a long breath and readjusted his comfortable position. "You don't understand," he said into her cleavage.

"Understand what?"

He sniffed. "You don't get it."

"What?"

He took his head back a bit and reached up to pull her chemise farther off her shoulder, exposing the line between her arm and her breast. He traced his finger along the curve of her naked shoulder.

"I don't want to be cleansed."

Epilogue

Dorhen, his only son, gave Daghahen no more than a sidelong glance before stepping through the portal after Kalea. Immediately, Daghahen dropped the golden portal rod and blew on his burnt hands. No time to think of Dorhen and his radiant fiancée, or worry over whatever injuries he'd taken in the heat of the moment. He was trapped between a tower full of sorcerers who'd happily kill him and an enormous, raging garbage fire blocking his exit route. And he no longer had his low-level portal setup; he'd already used it up to get Kalea out of the trolls' cave. That choice, he'd never regret. Ever.

Orinleah still lay dead on the ground. The battle had rotated and expired around her. She was the one he'd come here to save. His luminous lover wouldn't ever smile for him again. She'd smile for no one.

Against his churning, dread-filled stomach, he went toward her. What had that bastard done to her? She wore a ripped cloth over one eye. He removed it and winced. He retched, not for her appearance but for the horror. Poor *faerhain!*

He allowed his weeping to commence, running his fingers down her grimy, tear-stained cheek, colored in all manner of painful bruises. This was the consequence of being Daghahen's wife. This was what *he* was responsible for because he couldn't muster the bravery to stand up to his brother. Because he'd stalked her around her village and then one day ventured to befriend her. This was *his* fault.

Distant voices under the flames' roar startled him out of his grief. Would there ever be time to mourn? No. The sorcerers were coming with reinforcements. He could only hope his son—Orinleah's son—managed to avenge her murder in whatever place that portal had led to.

Hurrying against the sorcerers' pace, he scooped Orinleah up and carried her to the edge of the huge fire pit. The Grave. It would be both of their graves tonight. The place where they would lie together forever.

He took the moment to lean over and kiss her forehead. "Good night, my dream."

He extended one foot over the drop. The flames licked up straight below them.

Stop! Dag, what the hell are you doing?

"Huh?" Daghahen put his foot back on solid ground. "Ibex?" He hadn't heard Ibex in several weeks. The sorcerers drew closer and had already begun chanting for spells. "I have to drop Orinleah's body into the fire so the sorcerers can't get it. They'll use it for Creator-knows-what horrifying magic. Can't have them capturing her soul either. And I'm going with her."

Don't do it! Your son's out there, still alive, and so is Lamrhath!

He made a good point. Dorhen might need him if Lamrhath managed to escape all their efforts to snuff him out. Orinleah might be dead, but Dorhen wasn't. She'd want Daghahen to support their son, and he knew that with every fiber of his being.

"For Dorhen, my love." He kissed her forehead again and dropped her into the inferno, doing her the courtesy of a restful death that avoided what the sorcerers would have in store.

He didn't want to turn around, but he did. The sorcerers charged down the ramps. Daghahen raised his hands and dropped to his knees. He had nowhere to run. He had no choice but surrender.

Primora wailed, extending her voice over the long, rolling hills beyond her cliff perch. Her mother's body lay at her feet, defeated and cold. Dead. This was the sight she'd woken up to. She knew all along her mother could never make the journey to Wikhaihli. Primora wasn't so sure she could herself; she was only an altarpiece. She knew very little of navigating the wilderness. At least her mother had been a companion.

Escaping from the sorcerers' dominion to their holy land was all just an unrealistic daydream. Behind her lay sorcerers. Before her lay the same fate as her mother's, or if she made it… Who could be sure?

She dropped to her knees and curled over to caress her mother's dead, staring face. "I'm sorry, Mother!" she cried. The poor woman had no idea what a disgrace her daughter was, who'd lost her faith in the religion she was dedicated to and then gained it back in reluctant confusion. This was *his* fault.

"Wikshen," she hissed. The bastard who had refused to help them. He wouldn't bless her or kill the sorcerers. Instead, he sent them out here to die! And this had come after Primora had been arguing with her mother. While camping in the woods and using their altar and resources to try to summon Wikshen, she'd nearly convinced her mother to remain at home. It was her undoing when they finally succeeded in summoning him.

Lip quivering, Primora turned and crawled to their packs. She dug through her mother's bag for the sacred shroud they prayed to nightly.

The old woman had brought it along so devotedly, ecstatic from the visit and instructions she'd received from her beloved deity. The "hero." Yes, what a *hero* he was.

Primora spread the shroud over her mother's body. She hadn't the strength to bury her, even after a night's rest, much less the tools. Her body ached. She flattened the corners lovingly, and then searched around for rocks to weigh down the fabric. This would be her poor mother's grave.

Primora took a moment of silence, praying internally—to Wikshen as habit dictated. She looked over the vast landscape framed between the tall evergreen trees. Far in the distance, a haze rolled over a massive grassland after several more miles of forest. The sun's early position indicated that was her direction: east.

She faced the choice of moving on or staying put to follow her mother in death. Well aware that death might strike her down the road, she gathered up their belongings. She still had a good amount of food. No other choice than Wikhaihli. Wikshonism was all she knew. And she still wore the blue lock of hair in a little bag around her neck. The holy place would accept her.

Making her way down the path from her high cliff, she pondered the whole thing deeply.

Wikshen.

She recited his name over and over in hatred.

Wikshen.

She burned to punish him.

To be continued...

I hope you enjoyed "Flesh Embodied."

If so, please consider leaving a review at your favorite retailer. Leaving a review is the best thing you can do for your favorite books and authors! It not only helps other people to make the decision to buy, it causes the retailer to show the book sooner in search results and in those "just for you" suggestions.

Let me tell you, writing books is NOT easy! It has been my dream ever since 1998 when I was a lonely, unpopular thirteen-year-old girl hiding away in my bedroom, surrounded by my hundreds of colored pencil drawings and stacks of rock and roll cd's. This story is something I've planned and developed ever since then. It was the steepest mountain of my life. I can honestly say that these characters, particularly Dorhen and his ladylove Kalea have been every bit a part of me as my shy personality, my odd fashion sense, and my love for metal music. When I finally reached the finish line of publishing the book of my dreams, I found life to be harder than ever before—not easier. That's why I'd like to ask you for an honest review. I love hearing feedback from readers and I do remember what they say and consider their advice while writing future books. You don't have to say a whole lot in the review, just that you liked it, or that the book was at least adequate—hahahah!

For more information, news of future installments, art, and merchandise, please visit www.jchartcarver.com.

I now have a mailing list! Scan this QR to join:

Now turn the page for some art already!

Wikshen worries for Kalea's life.

Arius Medallus speaks to Kalea under the water.

Daghahen saves Kalea in the trolls' cave.

Lehomis misinterprets Tirnah's tea party.

Wikshen and Kalea scale the tower of Ilbith.

Gaije and Mhina

Glossary and Pronunciation

Characters (* main characters)

Adrayeth: (Ad-rā-th) Remenaxice's brother. Also known as Ray.

Alec: (Al-ek) A high-ranking servant in Ilbith.

Alhannah: (Ahl-hawn-ah) the head Desteer maiden in Clan Lockheirhen.

Anonhet: (Ah-non-het) A young elf woman who works in Lehomis's household. Gaije is in love with her.

Arius Medallus: (Air-ee-us Meh-dahl-us) A fairy who used to watch over Dorhen. He sent Kalea to find Dorhen, by following the sword called Hathrohjilh.

Argey: (Är-gā) A high-ranking sorcerer who manages the servants in Ilbith.

Bairhen: (B-er-hen) A young elf boy who was abducted from Clan Lockheirhen alongside Mhina.

Bargo: (Bar-go) A high-ranking sorcerer in the Ilbith faction who favors Vivene.

Baromond: (Bār-o-mond) A sorcerer in the Ilbith faction.

Bowaen: (Bō-ay-en) A rugged, middle-aged swordsman and runner for the Wistara White Guild. He was employed by Lord Dax to find and bring home Damos, the Grey Mage. Kalea travels with him because of the mysterious sword he carries.

Brielle: (Brī-el) A young woman whose wealthy father gave her to Wikshen as an offering.

Chandran: (Shan-der-an) A sorcerer from the Ilbith faction who had kidnapped Kalea in the past. He summoned the sanguinesent and also transformed into a monster, which Bowaen defeated.

Cirinhen: (SEEr-in-hen) Lehomis's old friend who owns a teahouse in Theddir. His wife is named Irina.

Cornelia: One of the kidnapped novices.

Cygnet: (Signet) A comely young Wikshonite. Falli's daughter and Primora's cousin.

Damos: (Day-mōs) a young Grey Mage born to a noble house in Sharr.

Del: (Dell) A skilled thief and lover of tobacco. Bowaen's apprentice.

Dyii: (Dī) A mysterious Thaccilian man who poses as a Wikshonite.

Glossary

Fallie, Aunt: (Fal-ē) A midwife, talented in the healing arts, and a devoted Wikshonite. Primora's aunt.

Gaije: (Gāj) A young elf, talented archer, and debut *saehgahn* from Clan Lockheirhen in Norr. Lehomis's grandson.

Grella: (Grel-uh) An ancient dreadwitch, once Wikshen's First Sister, and now his mortal enemy.

Haerdar: (hay-er-dar) A sorcerer in the Ilbith faction.

Hetael: (Het-tāl) A member of the Wikshonites.

Ibex: (Ī-beks) A voice inside Daghahen's head. Also an alternate name Daghahen uses sometimes.

Inahet: (EE-nah-het) A member of Clan Lockheirhen's Desteer chapter.

Kaskill: (Cas-kil) A young sorcerer in the Ilbith faction. Wikshen bit his finger off.

Kennaha: (Ken-aha) A member of Clan Lockheirhen's Desteer chapter.

Kerlin: (Kur-lin) The King of Valltalhiss who tried to marry Kalea.

Kiamora: (Ki-uh-môr-uh) A Wikshonite shaman. Primora's mother.

Kilka: (Kil-kah) A shaman and prominent member of the Wikshonite cult.

Knilma: (Nil-mah) A shaman and the oldest member of the Wikshonites.

Kristhanhea: (Kris-tHan-hā-ah) Lehomis's legendary wife who lived and died long ago.

Lamrhath: (Lam-wrath or Lam-er-hath) The current kingsorcerer and leader of the Ilbith sorcery faction.

Liam, Father: (Lee-ahm) A priest Kalea used to think of as a father.

Opal: One of the kidnapped novices.

Orinleah: (Or-in-lee-ah) Dorhen's mother, Daghahen's wife, and a member of the Linharri clan.

Primora: (Prim-ôr-uh) A Darklandic woman who was raised in the religion of Wikshonism.

Lehomis: (Lay-ah-miss) A legendary elf, master of archery, writer, and elder of Clan Lockheirhen. Gaije and Mhina's ancestor.

Maggy: One of the kidnapped novices.

Millie: One of the kidnapped novices.

McShivvy, Daghahen: (Mik-shy-vee, Dag-uh-hen) Dorhen's father and Lamrhath's twin brother.

McShivvy, Lambelhen: (Mik-shy-vee, Lam-bell-hen) Lamrhath's original name. The twin brother of Daghahen.

Metta: (Met-uh) A fetching young member of the Wikshonites.

Togha's sweetheart.

Mhina: (Mēn-ah) A seven-year-old elven girl who was kidnapped by Wikshen. Gaije's younger sister.

Millie: One of the kidnapped novices.

Mirral: (Mir-ôl) A member of the Wikshonites.

Myrtle: A young woman who pledged herself to Wikshen.

Nan: (Nän) A member of the Wikshonites.

Remenaxice: (Rem-en-ak-sis) A mysterious elf in Carridax. Also known as "Rem."

Rose: Kalea's friend and one of the kidnapped novices.

Sabina: (Sah-BEE-nah) One of the kidnapped novices.

Selka: (Sel-kah) A chamber mistress at Ilbith's Lightland outpost who gave Dorhen his first sexual experience.

Senna: (Sen-nah) A member of the Wikshonites.

Silva: (Sil-vah) Lamrhath's second wife. A woman from a Darklandic tribe of nomads.

*Sufferborn, Dorhen: (Suffer-born, Door-en or Door-hen) An elf who fell in love with Kalea. He was kidnapped by the Ilbith sorcerers during Kalea's convent raid. A mishap involving Daghahen and the sorcerers caused him to fall to the possession of the pixie, Wik.

Tamas: (Tam-us) A young woman of primitive Darklandic heritage who pledged herself to Wikshen.

Talekas: (Tal-ek-as) A sorcerer in the Ilbith Faction.

Tey: (Tä) A young journeyman *saehgahn* whom Lehomis hires for his help.

*Thridmill, Kalea: (Thrid-mill, Kah-LEE-ah) An ex-vestal from the Hallowill convent. She had planned to run away with Dorhen before he disappeared while trying to rescue her when the convent was raided. Now she's out looking for him and the kidnapped novices.

Tihen: (Tee-hen) An eligible *saehgahn* from Clan Lockheirhen. Lehomis calls him the "pride of Lockheirhen."

Tirnah: (TEER-nah) Gaije's mother.

Togha: (Tōg-uh) Gaije's distant cousin who ran away and wound up joining the Wikshonites.

Trisdahen: (Triz-dah-hen) Gaije's father. He was killed in a raid led by Wikshen.

Tumas: (Toom-as) A member of the Ilbith sorcery faction.

Vivene: (Viv-een) A friend of Kalea's, and one of the kidnapped novices.

*Wikshen: (Wik-shen) The flesh embodiment of the pixie, Wik. A living deity worshipped by the Wikshonites. Also known by the unofficial titles: "The King of Shadow," "King of the Darklands," "The Black Shadow God," and the Wikshonites call him "Mastaren."

Places & Things

Alkeer: (Al-kir) The largest known city in the Darklands.

Azrielle: (Az-ree-el) Damos's pet parrot.

Battle-shift: A sacred shroud, made by the trolls, woven with a special blend of fibers, and dyed black with a specific formula. Wikshen wears it around his hips like a kilt. It's usually the only garment he wears and comes with various magical abilities. The battleshift is also a physical representative of the pixie, Wik.

Beldamin: (Bel-dam-en) A city in Sharr.

Black Maids: An order of servants within Wikhaihli who rank higher than all the others and whose duties entail keeping up Wikshen's inner chambers. Black maids are characterized by their uniform black dresses (unlike the common maids who tend to wear leftover rags of undyed linen or wool).

Black Mountains: A large mountain range located at the north side of the Darklands, characterized by thin, smoky air and dead vegetation. The trolls clans are said to dwell beneath these mountains.

Blinding Mask: An invention of the Ilbith sorcery faction which aids a sorcerer's effort to block another person's magical ability.

Block (spell): Any of various spells used to obstruct another spell caster's magic ability.

Braies: (brā) Underwear usually made from linen. Also refers to a piece elves wear with their *sa-garhik*.

Bright One, The: See "Lin Yilbarhen" in the Elvish/Norrian language section.

Carridax: (Cair-i-daks) A city in the Lightlands established by two noble houses, the Carri's and the Dax's.

Chips: A motley assortment of valuable metal scraps used as currency in the Darklands. The Darklands have no official government and therefore no official mint. Chips can range anywhere from foreign coins or coins left over from old Darklandic civilization, to thin "chips" or nuggets, to broken jewelry.

Clanless, The: A ragtag clan of Norrian misfits who've gathered and organized in the Darklands. Each individual has opted not to return to Norr for his own reason.

Creator's Word: The official religious tome of the Sanctity of Creation.

Darklands, The: The northern side of the continent of Kaihals, consisting mostly of wild lands and territories, famous for being overrun with disreputable ruffians, warring tribal peoples, cults, and evil creatures.

Dendrea: (Den-dree-uh) the official Lightlandic currency.

Desteer, The: (Des-tīr) See "Desteer" in the Elvish/Norrian Words section.

Dream-walking: A magical practice in which the "dreamwalker" enters another person's dream to communicate with them.

Dunce: A slang term for a certain league of minion in service of the Ilbith sorcerers.

Elder: The male leader of any Norrian clan, whose position is complemented by the head Desteer.

Fairy: A bodiless spirit from another dimension, possessing the ability to store energy and evolve to higher levels.

Gaulice: (Gôl-iss) A city in the heart of the Lightlands.

Goblin Country: A large boggy region at the heart of the Darklands.

Grave, The: A huge cave under Ilbith where the sorcerers throw their refuse (including dead bodies).

Grey Mages: A faction of mages who train in Wistara and serve the Kingdom of Sharr.

Haxikhrah (spell): A mythical sword summoned from Kullixaxuss through sorcery. Its blade material could be similar to that of morkblades.

Head Desteer: The female leader of any Desteer chapter of the Norrian clans, whose position is complemented by the elder.

Hael: (Hāl) One of the five pixies favored by the Ilbith sorcery faction.

Hanhelin's Gate: (Han-hel-ins gāt) A huge fence, made of a metal that looks like iron, running across the entire continent. It was built to end a war with the Darklands and continues to protect the Lightlands today.

Hathrohjilh: (Hath-row-schil or Hath-row-jill) A mysterious sword Bowaen won from Daghahen in a game of dice.

Hathrohskog: (Hath-row-skog) An ominous Darklandic forest located between Alkeer and Wikhaihli.

Holding Sphere: A.K.A. "spell glass." A hollow, glass ball used to catch and hold pixies and similar spirits, as well as spells that can be used quickly by shattering the glass.

Ilbith: (Il-bith) The most powerful sorcery faction, known for their ability to cast portal spells and their appeasement of five powerful pixies. Also a tower located in the Darklands.

Ingnet: (EEn-yet) One of the five pixies favored by the Ilbith sorcery faction.

Jumaire: (Joo-mer) A city in the Lightlands where Kalea first met Damos.

Kaihals: (Kāls) The name of the continent.

King-sorcerer: (King-sorcerer) The leader of the reigning sorcery faction in the Darklands within a network of many warring factions.

Kraft: (Craft) The magical discipline practiced by Wikshen and the Wikshonites in which one's own bodily energy is channeled to accomplish various feats. Focuses on (but is not limited to) transitioning minerals and humors, and channeling vibrations.

Kraft Fire: An ethereal blue flame accessible through Kraft magic.

Kraft Positions: A series of poses the Wikshonites practice to hold for long periods of time as a way to worship Wikshen. These poses are largely meant to entice Wikshen.

Kraft Shout: A Kraft spell which uses vibrations of the voice to achieve various supernatural effects, most commonly in the earth.

Kullixaxuss: (Kul-iks-aks-us) The underworld where unearthly beings dwell and originate, also known as Hell.

Leho's Bow: (Le-hōs Bō) A legendary weapon wielded by the famous Lehomis, possessing magical capabilities.

Lightlandic: The most prevalent language in the Lightlands. The official language of the Kingdom of Sharr. Also considered the common tongue.

Lightlands, The: The southern side of the continent of Kaihals, shared by the Kingdom of Sharr and the Sovereign State of Norr.

Lockheirhen: (Läk-air-en) An elven clan in Norr, established by the legendary Lehomis Lockheirhen, whose primary function is raising and trading horses. Gaije's home clan.

Longwalk, The: A large area of grassland located at the lower eastern side of the Darklands. Darklanders call it as such because it takes a long time to walk across it to access any of the neighboring cities and settlements.

Lusche: (Loosh) A benevolent pixie of legend who was the enemy of Thaxyl.

Luschian: (Loosh-ē-an) A child who was "chosen" by the pixie, Lusche.

Mastaren: (Mas-tar-en) A variation of the word "master." The official form of address for Wikshen.

Miktik: (Mīck-tick) Lehomis's favorite horse back in ancient legend.

Morkblade: (Môrk-blade) Wikshen's signature Kraft spell, which only he can master.

Naerezek: (Nair-e-zek) One of the five pixies favored by the Ilbith sorcery faction. Lamrhath's patron pettygod.

Norr: (Nôr) The Sovereign State of Norr. A large forest in the northern Lightlands and also the country of the elves, consisting of a union of many clans.

Norr elves: (Nôr elvz) the most common term for the elves who originated from the region of Norr. Note: no other type of elf is known, but the Norr elves' own cultural worries point to there being others.

Norrian: (Nor-ē-an) Of the Sovereign State of Norr. The language of Norr.

Obsidian Fawn, The: A tea house in Theddir, established by an elf, Lehomis's old friend, which is meant as a tourist attraction and mimics elven culture.

Overseas Taint: A genetic corruption in the Norr elven bloodline said to have been brought from overseas and bred into the population via foreign elves.

Pettygod: (petty-god) Any of various stray spirits (ghosts, fairies, demons, etc.) to have inspired cult followers whose appeasement of such spirits can often evolve into actual religions of various sizes and popularities. Pettygod cults are often hostile and their practices are frowned upon or condemned by normal society.

Pixie: A high-level fairy with enough power to possess a mortal person.

Pixtagen: (piks-tah-gen) "Pixie-taken" A new being created as the result of a pixie taking possession of a human (or elf's) body. Wikshen is a pixtagen.

Portal: Any of various spells which can create magical doorways for long-distance travel.

Portal Pillars: What the sorcerers typically call the golden rods between which they open magic portals. Any object can be made into a portal pillar through intense magical technique, but golden rods are the most powerful and efficient.

Ravian: (ray-vee-an) Giant mythological birds of brilliant colors and benevolent demeanors, possessing faces and feathers like parrots and bodies like lions. They are said to have once existed in greater numbers long ago. A few are still accessible through magical practices.

Ravivill: (Rav-ee-vil) A village in the Darklands that has accepted Wikshonism. Knilma lived there for a long time.

Sacred Shroud: A black linen cloth, made in the likeness of Wikshen's battleshift, the Wikshonites use as a worship symbol.

Sanctity of Creation, The: The belief in a single master architect, known as the One Creator, who made the entire universe and rules over all he created. The official religion of the Lightlands.

Sanctuary: A building used for worship of the One Creator.

Sanguinesent: Sentinels from Kullixaxuss, whose main duty is to sort resident souls and keep things orderly.

Scouel: (scowl) A malicious birdlike creature with black feathered wings and bodies like that of a dog. Most come from Kullixaxuss and are accessible through magical practices.

Shadow Travel: A means of covering major distances by stepping into an "in between" dimension and then back out to the mortal plane. Wikshen can use this spell easily by stepping into any dense shadow.

Sharr: (Shär) A large island south of the Lightlands and also the name of the ruling kingdom of the Lightlands (excluding Norr).

Sharzian: (Shär-zē-an) Of the Kingdom of Sharr.

Sister Scupley's (or Vivene's) Love Manual: Actually titled, *An Exploration of Love in Three Forms: Poetic, Symbolic, and Carnal*, Sister Scupley, the Mistress of Novices in the Hallowill convent, owned this forbidden book. It detailed the mechanics of sexual intercourse. Vivene used to like to thumb through it when she was supposed to be tidying up.

Sorcery/Sorcerer(ess): Any of various magical practices which involves the appeasement of otherworldly spirits in exchange for magical tokens, spells, and favors.

Sprott: (Sprät) A minor type of fairy who can easily be captured and controlled (usually by sorcerers). Kalea and her companions fought a sprott at the inn of Jumaire.

Suffer-born: A constellation that appears every few decades and remains for a limited amount of time.

Swine, The: A supremely powerful demon, who resembles a pig and dwells in Kullixaxuss. Often used as a swear word ("holy Swine" etc.). He's also a pettygod and founder of the most common dark magic practice. Spell books with his face on the cover can commonly be found in all regions.

Sword Swish, The: A very old tavern in Alkeer the sixth Wikshen used to frequent.

Taulmoil: (Tôl-moy-l) A small town in the heart of the Lightlands where Kalea is from.

Thaccilians: (Thak-shee-lee-uns) A race of people, characterized by their red eyes and light-colored hair, spawned by the power of the pixie, Thaxyl.

Thaxyl: (Thak-sill) A once-great pixie and pettygod.

Theddir: (Thed-deer) A town built on stilts to tolerate frequent flooding located immediately to the south-east of Norr. The last town in the Lightlands where elves are welcome.

Tinharri: (Tin-ärē) The ruling clan in Norr.

Tintilly: (Tin-til-lee) A town located on the edge of Hallowill forest where Kalea met Dorhen.

Troll: An ancient race of beings who live underground. The trolls worship Wik and Wikshen, and have invented the original version of Kraft.

Valltalhiss: (Val-Tal-hiss) An ancient, decrepit city located at the center of a forest of poisonous trees.

Vandalyns, The: (Vand-uh-lins) A faction of sorcery in the Darklands and rival of Ilbith. Known for their use of curved blades which can channel magical lightning.

Vestal: A celibate woman whose life is devoted to worshipping the One Creator.

Warlock: A male who practices any of a variety of magics. The common male followers of Wikshonism, who don't practice magic, are also referred to as warlocks.

Wexwick: (Weks-wik) A rundown town on the west coast of the Lightlands, north of Ravian Cove, where bandits and thieves tend to hide out.

Whisper Stones: Magical stones the sorcerers use to communicate over long distances.

White Owl Guard: The personal guard of the reigning king or queen of Norr. Gaije's father served as a White Owl and Gaije had been drafted to train for the guard before he deserted.

Wik: (Wick) A powerful pixie and pettygod. One of the five pixies favored by the Ilbith sorcery faction.

Wikhaihli: (Wick-hay-lee) "Wik Haven." The main hub of the Wikshonite cult.

Wikshen Adornka: One of the Wikshonites' sacred rituals.

Wikshonism/Wikshonites: A religion centered around Wikshen, which focuses on waiting for his next return and then submitting to his violent will. Followers of Wikshen are called "Wikshonites."

Wistara: (Wist-ahra) A peninsula between the greater Lightlands and Sharr, serving as common passage between the two land masses.

Witch: A female who practices any of a variety of magics. The common female followers of Wikshonism are referred to as witches.

Elvish/Norrian Words

Aahmei: Informal "mama."

Glossary

Ah: "Yes."

Ameiha: Formal "mother." Often used to address Desteer maidens and queens.

Amonimori: "Good morning."

Awl: "I" or "me."

Caunsaehgahn: "Coming into service." A coming-of-age journey male elves must complete before they can graduate to full adulthood.

Cha!: A sound Norrians make in annoyance.

Daghen-saehgahn: "Guardian-servant" a husband.

Desteer: "Whisperer." The largest spiritual order in the Norrian religion. The Desteer members are always female and referred to as "maidens."

Fa: "She"

Faerhain: "Life carrier" adult female.

Farenkin: "Sister."

Farhah: "Soon to be life carrier" young female.

Gaulaerhainha: "Choosing her fate" a female's coming-of-age ceremony in which she chooses the "hall" or the "home."

Ghaish: "Hot." This tends to be an exclamation the elves shout out when they are burned by something hot.

Guenhighar: A pet name for a young boy.

Guenhihah: A pet name for a young girl.

Hanbohik: The traditional Norrian dress, worn by females, consisting of a long skirt that fastens over the breasts with a collection of thin underdresses, long sleeves, tied lapels, and small jacket or hip-length tunic worn over top.

Harranhennhi: "Thank you."

Hik-hik: Informal apology, used mostly by mischievous children. Spoken as two fast hisses with abrupt stops from the back of the throat.

Ing: "You."

Karra-kar-shirinhen: "tea between widows." A tabooed and illicit ritual in Norr.

Kowhahere yuten: "Welcome."

Kwrerr: Chalk. Based on how Norrian speakers interpret the sound of the chalk scraping against stone.

Laugaulentrei: "The lake of the dead tree," the final resting place for deceased elves.

Lin Yilbarhen: "The Bright One." God of the elves and the official religion of Norr. Seen as the "light" who leads his children through the wilderness.

Maineha: "Miss" or "mistress," a formal title a guest calls the matron/

hostess of a household.

Milhanrajea: "Mind Viewing." The practice in which a Desteer maiden uses her psychic ability to delve her sight into the mind of an elf to see their thoughts, intents, problems, and/or desires.

Pahkahen: Formal "father."

Pawbhen: Informal "papa."

Sa: "He"

Saeghar: "Too young to serve." A young male.

Saehgahn: "Servant." An adult male. Also an official, sacred order to which all male elves must join and adhere.

Sa-garhik: Traditional leggings, worn by males, consisting of two separate pieces for the legs fastened to the braies, a garment that covers the pelvic area. *Sa-garhik* is similar to human culture's leggings, except for their open design, often exposing the hipbone and the sides of the buttocks.

Sarakren: "He is forbidden." Sarakren is a status given to *saehgahn* who are forbidden to marry. This status comes with a brand on his left buttock (always visible between his braies and leg coverings) to warn *faerhain* away.

Sarenkin: "Brother."

Shi: "Old" or "elderly."

Shi-hehen: A retired and elderly *saehgahn* who no longer has to answer the call of *saehgahn* duty, except in dire village or family emergencies.

Shi-helah: An elderly *faerhain* who's household workload has decreased and been taken over by younger females.

Tok: "No."

Wyrrem: adjective: "Warm" or "Warmth." Noun: A *wyrrem* is the rounded central sitting area of a traditional Norrian house. This is where the family congregates, drinks tea, tells stories, and relaxes on a large collection of pillows and cushions.